PENGUI
FIRST LIGHT

Born in 1934 in Faridpur, now in Bangladesh, Sunil Gangopadhyay came as a refugee to Calcutta in 1947, following the partition of India. The family suffered extreme poverty initially and Sunil, though only in his teens, was forced to find employment. He still managed to continue his education, taking his Master's degree from Calcutta University.

Sunil Gangopadhyay began his literary career as a poet, starting the epoch-making magazine, *Krittibas,* in 1953. Storming into the field of the novel with the trendsetting *Atma Prakash* (1966)—a powerful portrayal of the frustration and ennui of the youth of Calcutta—he soon rose to become the leading and most popular novelist of Bengali. *Sei Samai* (1982), which won him the Sahitya Akademi Award, *Purba Paschim* (1989) and *Pratham Alo* (1996) are among his best novels.

*

Aruna Chakravarti took her Masters and Ph.D. degrees in English Literature from the University of Delhi. She has held the post of Reader in Janki Devi Memorial College, one of the affiliated colleges of the university, for many years and is, at present, its principal. She is also an author and translator of repute.

Her first translation, *Tagore: Songs Rendered into English* (1984), won the Vaitalik Award for excellence in literary translation. Her translation of Sarat Chandra Chattopadhyaya's immortal classic, *Srikanta,* is deemed her best work, having won the prestigious Sahitya Akademi Award for 1996. *Srikanta* was published by Penguin India in 1993. *Those Days*, a translation of Sunil Gangopadhyay's award-winning novel *Sei Samai*, also published by Penguin India, followed in 1997. Aruna Chakravarti has also authored a biography of Sarat Chandra entitled *Sarat Chandra: Rebel and Humanist* (1985) and a work of literary criticism entitled *Ruth Prawer Jhabvala: A Study in Empathy and Exile* (1998).

SUNIL GANGOPADHYAY

First Light

Translated from the Bengali
by Aruna Chakravarti

PENGUIN BOOKS

Penguin Books India (P) Ltd., 11 Community Centre, Panchsheel Park,
New Delhi 110017, India
Penguin Books Ltd., 80 Strand, London WC2R 0RL, UK
Penguin Putnam Inc., 375 Hudson Street, New York, NY 10014, USA
Penguin Books Australia Ltd., 250 Camberwell Road, Camberwell,
Victoria 3124, Australia
Penguin Books Canada Ltd., 10 Alcorn Avenue, Suite 300, Toronto,
Ontario M4V 3B2, Canada
Penguin Books (NZ) Ltd., Cnr Rosedale and Airborne Roads, Albany, Auckland,
New Zealand

First published in Bengali as *Pratham Alo* by Ananda Publishers Pvt. Ltd. 1996
First published in English by Penguin Books India 2001
Copyright © Sunil Gangopadhyay 1996, 2001
This translation copyright © Penguin Books India 2001

10 9 8 7 6 5 4 3

Typeset in Sabon by Mantra Virtual Services, New Delhi

Printed at Basu Mudran, Kolkata

For Poocham and Bhai—to grow up and read...

Introduction

In 1882 Rabindranath, the young scion of the Thakurs of Jorasanko, published a slim volume of poems entitled *Bhagna Hriday*. Though the poet was practically unknown, even in Bengali, the book found its way, somehow, into the royal palace of Tripura. The maharaja, who had recently lost his queen consort, read the poems and was so moved by them that he sent an emissary to Calcutta bearing gifts and a citation for the poet. This historical event is recorded in the opening chapters of Sunil Gangopadhyay's *Pratham Alo* (*First Light*).

In a critical way, this book is a sequel to the author's earlier novel *Those Days*—a transcreation in English of the award-winning *Sei Samai*. They are both mega-narratives designed on the same lines and the reading of one is enriched by the other. But the two novels are structured as discrete texts linked by some common themes and characters. The undeniable resemblance between the two gives rise, inevitably, to the speculation of whether or not *First Light* brings to a conclusion the story of *Those Days*. It also opens up questions regarding the extent of history and historical authenticity in the novel. It might be profitable,to open the introduction by attempting to answer some of these questions.

The events of *Those Days*, actual and imagined, took place between 1840 and 1870—a period which witnessed a unique movement in Bengal, the highlights of which were the germination and slow stirring into life of a social and religious consciousness and the emergence of a middle class that idealized British rule and used its support to usher in considerable change in Hindu society. This movement, which came to be known as the Bengal Renaissance, spread gradually to encompass the whole of India. Evoking time as protagonist and characters, historical and fictional, as bit players in the destiny of a nation, Sunil Gangopadhyay created a modern epic offering valuable insights into the era that saw this phenomenon.

In the present novel the same exercise is stretched further. *First Light* takes over from where *Those Days* left off. Spread over a vast canvas that stretches across three continents, the novel depicts the social, political and literary awakening of India during the years that followed—another thirty years, approximately between 1880 and 1910. Many of the historical characters are easily recognized for they occupy spaces inherited from their predecessors in *Those Days*. Rani Rasmoni is dead but her spirit lives on in the persona of Ramkrishna the priest of the temple she built in Dakshineswar and after him, in that of his spiritual successor Vivekananda. The Thakur family of Jorasanko is a strong presence in *First Light*, as it was in *Those Days*, but the focus has shifted from Dwarkanath and Debendranath to their progeny. Infact the title of the novel derives from the genius of the greatest of them all—Rabindranath the poet, playwright, painter, composer, educationist and nationalist. The dawn or 'first light' of Rabindranath's creative inspiration evolves, over the course of the novel, into a powerful symbol of awakening. The latter half of the book traces the first stirrings of resentment against foreign rule and the growth of a nationalist consciousness. It also documents the revolutionizing of life and values sparked off by the scientific discoveries of the West.

Other historical characters of the period, who are household names in Bengal and outside it, are also present here. Stoking cultural memory the author offers astonishingly lifelike delineations and penetrating analyses of lives and characters of the poet king of Tripura—Maharaja Birchandra Manikya; the eminent physician and fiery liberal Mahendralal Sarkar; the scientist Jagadish Bose; the poet and terrorist Aurobindo Ghosh; the notorious courtesan and brilliant actress Binodini; the freedom fighters Tilak and Gandhi. These and many more who follow in the wake of the historical characters of *Those Days* fill the pages of *First Light*. Is *First Light*, then, an inseparable part of *Those Days*? No. To use the novelist's own explanation—'*First Light* is not another volume of *Those Days*. It is a sequel in time.'

The greatest challenge before Sunil Gangopadhyay was to give these men and women a voice and dialogue with their counterparts, historical and fictional. The extent of his success can be gauged from the taut energy of the prose they speak and the vibrant authenticity of their thought and action. For, as in *Those Days*, the novel is wedded to facts but flirts with fiction. The magnificient personages listed above move in and out of the pages in free interaction with vividly imagined figures—the bastard prince Bharat; the bondmaid Bhumisuta; the 'sullied' beauty Basantamanjari and her protector—the expansive, ease loving, big hearted Dwarika Lahiri; the atheist turned Muslim fundamentalist Irfan. The strains of their unsung tales are skilfully woven into those of the lives of the great men and women they encounter. Bhumisuta acts with Girish Ghosh and Ardhendushekhar Mustafi; is a friend of Sarala Ghoshal's and cherishes a secret infatuation for Rabindranath. Bharat, an illegitimate prince of the dynasty of Tripura, meets Gandhi and Rabindranath and, caught in a struggle to deliver his motherland from bondage, develops close links with Aurobindo Ghosh, Khudiram and Hemchandra Kanungo. Dwarika is Bankimchandra's protege, has studied in Presidency College with Vivekananda and knows Mahendralal Sarkar.

History has never been presented in a more colourful package. But a novel such as this throws up other questions as well. What perspective or ideology colours the author's delineation of historical characters and events? How much of it is fact and how much fiction? To answer this I must fall back on the author's own comments. 'History is a record of palpable facts,' Sunil Gangopadhyay wrote in the epilogue to *Sei Samai*. 'Fiction is not. The fiction writer, even when depicting historical truth, has to invest it with the light of the imagination.' Consequently Sunil's historical characters think, act and feel as he sees them do in his mind's eye. Critics have had problems with some of his delineations—in what they perceive as distortions and trivialization of some of the most eminent men of the land. Mahendralal Sarkar is projected as an abusive bully who uses foul language. Ramkrishna is wimpish and fretful. Vivekananda's passion for tobacco and spicy food is at variance with his declared ideals of austerity and abstinence. Bankimchandra's arrogant self-confidence is a mask and his fear of gossip and slander swamps his fatherly love. And above all—Rabindranath. Rabindranath, who is used as a nodal reference in Sunil's multidirectional novel, is loaded with attributes some of which are distinctly unpalatable. For he is not only a self-centred artist who neglects his wife; he needs women, other than her, to liberate the poetry trapped in him—his sister-in-law, Kadambari, in the first flush of his youth, and his young niece Indira in his prime.

Sunil Gangopadhyay, however, is non-judgmental, and herein lies the strength of his novel. A judicious balance is maintained, on the whole, between fact and fiction and the large cast of characters is well controlled. The novelist, however, denies any attempt to control his created world. 'As the narrative flows on to an undefined end,' he writes in his epilogue to *Pratham Alo*, 'so do the characters. When I first brought the king's bastard Bharat into the narrative I didn't dream that he would come to dominate the entire novel in the way he has done. I had thought to make Rabindranath the hero . . .'

New Delhi   Aruna Chakravarti
December 2000

List of Characters

The Kingdom of Tripura

Maharaja Birchandra Manikya - King of Tripura
Bhanumati - his Queen Consort
Monomohini - Bhanumati's niece
Radhakishor - Birchandra's eldest son
Samarendra - another son
Bharat - Birchandra's illegitimate son
Radharaman Ghosh - the king's secretary
Shashibhushan Singha - tutor to the princes
Mahim Thakur - the king's bodyguard

The Singhas of Bhabanipur

Bimalbhushan Singha - Shashibhushan's eldest brother
Monibhushan Singha - Shashibhushan's second brother
Krishnabhamini - Bimalbhushan's wife
Suhasini - Monibhushan's wife
Bhumisuta - a bondmaid

The Thakurs of Jorasanko

Maharshi Debendranath Thakur - founder of the Adi
Brahmo Samaj
Dwijendranath - his eldest son
Satyendranath - his second son
Jyotirindranath - his fifth son
Rabindranath - his youngest son
Balendranath
Satyaprasad - his grandsons

Gaganendranath
Abanindranath - his grandnephews
Gyanadanandini - Satyendranath's wife
Kadambari - Jyotirindranath's wife
Mrinalini - Rabindranath's wife
Surendranath - Satyendranath's son
Indira nicknamed Bibi - his daughter
Pramatha Chowdhury - Bibi's husband
Madhurilata nicknamed Beli - Rabindranath's eldest daughter
Renuka - his second daughter
Meera - his youngest daughter
Rathindranath - his elder son
Shomi - his younger son
Swaranakumari - Debendranath's daughter
Janakinath Ghoshal - her husband
Sarala - their daughter
Akshay Chowdhury - Jyotirindranath's friend
Ashutosh Chowdhury - Pramatha's brother and
Rabindranath's friend

The Theatre

Girish Ghosh - an actor, director and playwright
Binodini - a famous actress
Amritalal nicknamed Bhuni
Ardhendushekhar - actors
Mustafi nicknamed Saheb
Amarendranath Datta nicknamed Kalu - an actor,
director and producer
Pratapchand Jahuri
Gurumukh Rai Mussadi - wealthy Marwari financiers
Gangamoni nicknamed Hadu - an actress

The Freedom Fighters

Aurobindo Ghosh - a scholar and a poet
Barin - his brother

Satyendranath - his uncle
Rajnarayan Bosu - his maternal grandfather
Hemchandra Kanungo - terrorists, along with Barin
Amitbikram   and Satyendranath
Jatin Bandopadhyay - leader of the group
Kuhelika - his sister
Balgangadhar Tilak - an eminent freedom fighter
Count Okakura - a Japanese scholar

The Hindu Revivalists

Sri Ramkrishna Paramhansadev - priest of the temple at
Dakshineswar
Naren Datta alias Swami Vivekananda
Brahmananda
Saradananda   - Ramkrishna's disciples
Balaram Bosu
Margaret Noble alias Sister Nivedita - Vivekananda's disciple
Joe Macleod
Ole Bull   - Vivekananda's friends

Others

Mahendralal Sarkar - an eminent physician
Jagadish Bose - a scientist
Abala Bose - his wife
Shibnath Shastri - a Brahmo, founder of the
Sadharan Brahmo Samaj
Dwarika
Jadugopal   - Bharat's friends
Irfan
Basantamanjari - Dwarika's mistress
Banibinod Bhattacharya - a priest

Satyendranath – his uncle
Rajnarayan Bose – his maternal grandfather
Hemchandra Kanungo – terrorists, along with
Aurobindo   and Satyendranath
Jatin Bandopadhyay – leader of the group
Kshetika – his sister
Balgangadhar Tilak – an eminent freedom fighter
Chuni Oshthar – a Japanese scholar

The Hindu Revivalists

Sri Ramkrishna Paramhansadev – priest of the temple at
            Dakshineswar
Naren Datta alias Swami Vivekananda
Brahmananda,
Saradananda   Ramkrishna's disciples
Balaram Bose
Margaret Noble alias Sister Nivedita – Vivekananda's disciple
            Joe Maclead
            Ole Bull   Vivekananda's friends

Others

Mahendralal Sarkar – an eminent physician
Jagadish Bose – a scientist
Abala Bose – his wife
Shibnath Shastri – a Brahmo, founder of the
            Sadharan Brahmo Samaj
            Dwarka
Jadugopal   Bharat's friends
Jiten
Basantmanjari – Dwarka's mistress
Ramprasad Bhattacharya – a priest

Book I

Book 1

Chapter I

It was a lovely day. The clouds had parted and the sun's beams fell, soft and silvery, on the mountain peaks that loomed against a sky of flawless blue. Trees, grass and creepers, glistening with last night's rain, tossed joyful heads in the balmy air. It was the day of the festival, and Nature was rejoicing with Man.

From early dawn throngs of tribals could be seen walking out of the forest, down the green slopes, their strong bodies naked in the morning sun. They were dressed, men and women alike, in colourful loincloths but the women had flowers in their hair and garlands of *koonch* berries, *gunja* buds and bone chips hung from their necks. Plumes waved gaily from the heads of a few chosen men. It was as though a river, rainbow hued, was gushing down in full spate. But in reality, they were streams—separate and distinct. Riyangs from Amarpur and Bilonia walked in quiet files behind their Rai whose small, compact body atop a mountain pony, was shaded by an immense umbrella held high above his head. The Rai's eyes were soft and drowsy with last night's liquor, yet a sharp even cruel glint came into them every time he looked around. He was a ruthless chief and would not tolerate the slightest indiscipline within the clan. His second in command, the Raikachak, a fine figure of a man, walked briskly behind him. Though far from young, his chest seemed carved out of black marble and the hand that held a long spear was strong and muscular. Whenever he stopped in his tracks two youths sprang forward and, kneeling on the ground at his feet, massaged his calves and ankles. A drummer and a flautist brought up the rear. Some of the men and women sang with the music—a merry ditty that made the others sway in mirth and laughter rang through the throng like tinkling bells.

From Kailasahar, Sabroom and Udaipur came the Chakmas. They were Buddhists—quiet and sedate. But confusion broke out in their ranks every time they passed a flowering bush or vine. Their women ran eagerly to it and, picking the blooms with quick

3

fingers, wove them into garlands as they walked. The Lusais and
Kukis came from Dharmanagar and Kamalpur. Though many of
them had embraced Christianity the Lusais found it hard to
understand or practise its doctrine of love. They were warriors
and head hunting had been the clan's custom for centuries. Now
the priests were telling them to love their neighbours. The Lusais
believed themselves to be superior to the naked Kukis. Their
women had learned to cover their breasts with *riyas* made out of
bits of wool they had knitted together and dyed a fierce coxcomb
red. Some of the younger men even wore pantaloons.

Others—Jamaliyas, Halams, Noyatiyas, Mugs, Bhils, Garos,
Khasiyas and Orangs—followed, stream after colourful stream.
And last of all came the Tripuris, thronging in large numbers
from all directions. Some of them were on horseback; others on
elephants. The elephants were gifts for his Royal Majesty, the
Maharaja of Tripura. The other tribes carried presents too—bags
of cotton, baskets of the wild, sweet oranges that grew on the
sunny slopes of Jompui, bunches of pineapples, sacks of newly
harvested *jum* and a fawn or two.

They had all been walking for days towards a common
destination. Today was the tenth day of the Durga festival and
they were bound for the king's palace where His Majesty had
arranged a great feast for his subjects.

Surrounded by his courtiers, Maharaja Birchandra Manikya
stood on the balcony of the royal palace of Tripura—the only
independent kingdom in a country governed by the British. It was
rumoured that he was descended from King Yayati, mentioned in
the Mahabharat. The dissolute king had ordered his sons to
surrender their youth in his favour enabling him, thus, to prolong
his life of vice and profligacy. The princes who had declined were
banished. One of them, Prince Druhuh, left his father's kingdom
of Aryavarta and proceeded to the north east of India where, after
vanquishing the king of Kirat in battle, he established the
kingdom of Tripura. Maharaja Birchandra was said to be the
hundred and seventy-fifth descendent from Druhuh in an
unbroken line.

All this may well have been hearsay. The kings of Tripura had
no resemblance whatever to their Aryan ancestors. In fact, their
features were as Mongoloid as those of the tribals they ruled and

4

the Manipuri princesses they wed. Birchandra Manikya was not tall but his body was hard and strong and his face keen and intelligent. The most noticeable thing about his physiognomy were the whiskers, thick and luxuriant except for a patch just under the nose that was carefully shaven. Though past middle age, his movements were quick and packed with energy. He had just returned from Udaipur after offering the mandatory worship at the temple of Tripura Sundari on the ninth day of the Durga festival.

Though a hard ride, it had to be undertaken for custom decreed that the king be present for the great feast, the mahabhoj, and sit down to a meal with his subjects. It proved that the king made no distinction between the tribes. They were his subjects, all together here under his roof and he was to all, equally, the gracious host.

On a courtyard facing the balcony was a structure thatched with straw. Here, on ten clay ovens, *payesh* and khichuri were being cooked in enormous pots. It was the king's command that his subjects be served as often and as much as they wanted. And they could eat prodigious amounts. There were many who sat down to the feast at sundown and rose only with the dawn. It seemed as though they were putting away enough to last them a year. Come morning and many were discovered fast asleep, curled up beside their leaves.

The king moved about among his subjects, his face concealed in a black shawl, taking pictures with his new camera. Birchandra hated the British and always endeavoured to keep them at arm's length. He preferred Bengali to English and had retained it as his state language long after other rajas had given up their native languages. He had no use for European merchandise either, except for one exception—the camera. He had an excellent collection of cameras, brought over from France and England. He had even built a dark room in the palace in which he developed negatives.

It was his passion to take photographs—of his queens, princes, friends and even of the hills, trees and streams of his realm. But, much as he wished, he could not capture his subjects on camera except by stealth. For he had had a bad experience once. Hunting in the forest he had come upon a Kuki youth with a

5

body so perfect—it seemed hewn out of a block of granite and a face flashing with spirit and intelligence. He had decided to immortalize the splendid specimen and, to that intent, had made the boy pose beneath a tree. But focussing takes time. The youth waited, the warnings of the king's attendants ringing incessantly in his ears 'Be still. Don't move.' Suddenly the magnificent body crumpled in a heap on the ground. The limbs thrashed about painfully. The eyes rolled and foam gathered at the corners of the boy's mouth. He was revived in a few minutes but the damage was done. Rumour, swift and silent, spread from clan to clan that the king had captured the youth's soul and imprisoned it in a little black box.

Keeping close to the king was a man in his prime, a handsome man with a fair complexion, long curling hair and chiselled features. In his dress he was quite a dandy. He wore a finely crinkled dhuti and a silk banian. A pair of gold-rimmed glasses sat on his high, aristocratic nose. His name was Shashibhushan Singha. He was a graduate and a Brahmo and had been a regular contributor to Deben Thakur's *Tatwabodhini Patrika* for many years. He was one of the men the Maharaja had sent for from Calcutta to facilitate his governance and gear it to progressive ideals. Shashibhushan was tutor to the young princes.

Standing by him and talking in a low voice was a famous singer from the Vishnupur gharana. Jadunath Bhatta was court musician; one of the nine gems that graced the royal palace of Tripura. The two were observing the guests through a pair of binoculars and trying to identify the different tribes. 'They all look the same to me,' Jadunath said. He was a simple man with no pretensions to any knowledge beyond his music. 'Look carefully,' Shashibhushan urged. 'Some have skins like polished ebony; others the colour and texture of charcoal. Yet others are dun coloured like earth. The *riyas* of the Orang women are shaped differently from those of the Lusais—'

At this moment a servant approached the king with the message that the Mahadevi awaited him in the palace. Every year, on this day, just before the mahabhoj, the Maharaja put aside his ceremonial robes and donned the apparel of a Vaishnav. And every year, these garments were draped on him—not by servants but by his chief and reigning queen.

This year Mahadevi Bhanumati had spent the whole day in preparation. She had strung the garlands with her own hands and kept the sandal paste, both white and crimson, in readiness. As she fitted the silk garments, one by one, on the royal person the Maharaja hummed a little tune. '*Jadi Gokulchandra braje na élo,*' he sang, a little smile flickering at the corners of his mouth. He was not only a connoisseur of music, he also had a fine singing voice.

Birchandra had so many wives and concubines that he had lost count of them. Many of his queens were princesses from the bordering states of Assam and Manipur. The kachhuas or concubines were mostly tribal women—gifts from his subjects. These women were kept in the palace awaiting the king's pleasure. Occasionally one would catch the royal fancy and be the recipient of his attentions but, in the absence of a marriage ceremony, she could never aspire to be a Mahadevi.

Birchandra and Bhanumati were of the same age and had been playmates before they were wed. They still shared the old camaraderie and, though Birchandra had younger and more beautiful queens and his nights were mostly spent in their company, he was in Bhanumati's rooms often during the day teasing and quarrelling with her. Unlike the other queens Bhanumati was not overly respectful of her husband and gave as good as she got. Her voice, raised in sharp reprimand, could often be heard by the maids who attended on the royal pair. Once they had even seen her running around the room weeping passionately while the king followed her, abject and humble, his hands folded in supplication.

Marking her husband's forehead carefully with sandal Bhanumati murmured, 'Take me with you tonight.'

'Where?' The king looked up startled.

'To the mahabhoj.' Bhanumati's voice was young though she was past middle age. Her body was still shapely and her long, slanting eyes glowed with spirit and vivacity.

'You're mad,' Birchandra smiled benignly at the smooth, brown face just above his own.

'Why? Can't the Maharaja have his consort by his side on a day of rejoicing?'

'You'll never grow up Bhanu,' the king chucked his wife

7

under the chin, 'Has a Mahadevi of the realm ever been seen by the common folk? Give me my nimcha. It's getting late.'

'Sit still.' The command came swift and sharp. 'I'm not finished yet.' Continuing her careful marking of her husband's forehead Bhanumati went on, 'The queen walks by her husband's side one day in her life, doesn't she? The king does not see her but thousands of her subjects do.' Dropping her voice to a whisper, she added. 'If you don't take me with you tonight I shall not burn with you when the time comes.'

'Bhanu,' Birchandra sighed. 'You talk of my death on a day such as this?'

'I only said I wouldn't burn with you. I'll kill myself first.'

'But why?' Birchandra lifted his brows in mild surprise. 'Don't you wish to enter the blessed state? A sati is worshipped like a goddess on earth. And eternal heaven is hers hereafter. You're my queen consort—the only one of my queens who will be given the privilege of dying with me.'

'I don't care for it. Let Rajeshwari—that ugly, flat nosed, low-born slut, that snake, that ghoul—burn with you. Burn to ashes. I'll look down from heaven with pleasure.'

Birchandra Manikya burst out laughing. It was natural for co-wives to be jealous of one another. Only, none of the other queens would dare to express such feelings in the king's presence. With Bhanumati it was different. She had been his playmate and he had no control over her.

'Low-born slut! Ghoul!' he exclaimed. 'What sort of language is this? People think we royals are very circumspect in our speech and manners. Really Bhanu! If one of the others had spoken like that I would have cut her head off with a swish of my sword.' Bhanumati walked swiftly to a corner of the room and picking up the king's Nimcha, brought it over to him. It was rumoured that this sword had been presented by Emperor Shah Jehan's son Sultan Shuja to Birchandra's ancestor Gobinda Manikya. Though the king dressed in the robes of a Vaishnav on the occasion of the mahabhoj, custom decreed that he carry this weapon.

Bhanumati pulled the sword out of its jewel-encrusted scabbard and said, 'Kill me, then, and put an end to my sufferings.' Pausing a moment, she added, 'You'll be declaring

8

Radhu as your crown prince and heir this evening, will you not?'
A shadow fell on Birchandra's face. His good humour vanished.
It was true that he would pronounce the name of his eldest son
Radhakishor as successor to the throne of Tripura in the evening
when all his subjects were gathered together. But only two
persons knew. Even Rajeshwari, the boy's mother, had not been
told. How had the news reached Bhanumati's ears? 'Your son
will be elevated too,' he said gravely. 'I'll be giving him the title of
Bara Thakur. I'm doing it for your sake though there's no
precedence —'

'You don't have to. I'll send Samar away from Tripura. I'll
send him to Calcutta.'

There was a rustle at the door and the two turned around as a
girl came into the room. She was a beautiful girl with an innocent
face and a golden body that swayed and rippled with the sap of
youth. Each movement was music. A yellow silk pachhara
encased her lower limbs and a riya, green as the tenderest leaves
of spring, stretched taut and smooth over her newly swelling
breasts. Birchandra gazed at her, amazed. 'Who is she?' he asked
his wife. She wasn't a maid—he was sure of that. No attendant
would dare walk into a room in which the king and queen were
alone together.

Bhanumati forced the tears back from her eyes. 'What is it
Khuman?' she asked with an indulgent smile. The girl's eyes were
fixed on the king, not in fear but in awe—the kind of awe with
which one looks upon a snow capped mountain peak. Turning to
the queen she said, 'Biloni and Phullen want me to go up to the
roof with them. But Mejo Ranima says I mustn't. What shall I
do?' Bhanumati cleared her throat and signalled with her eyes.
'Make your obeisance to the king first,' she commanded. The girl
obeyed instantly. Lying prostrate on the floor she touched her
hands and forehead to the king's feet. 'Who is this wench?'
Birchandra couldn't keep a note of impatience out of his voice
though he raised a hand in blessing. 'I'm Khuman Thorolaima,'
the girl answered. 'She's my sister's daughter,' Bhanumati
explained, 'You've seen her as an infant. Don't you remember?
She's been with me here at the palace for about a year now.'
Birchandra gazed in wonder at the girl's loveliness. She was
young, very young, but she had promise. There was no doubt

9

that, in a year or two, she would grow to be a woman of surpassing beauty. She would be the brightest jewel of the court and men would swarm around her like flies.

'I've given her a Bengali name,' Bhanumati went on, 'I call her Monomohini.'

'You've given her a Bengali name but you haven't taught her to wear a sari?'

'I will in a year or two. She's playful still and the sari keeps slipping from her shoulder.'

'Go to the roof and watch the scene,' the Maharaja smiled kindly at the girl. 'If anyone stops you, tell them you have my permission.'

'Go child,' Bhanumati urged as the girl hesitated. 'Being a woman you can't go out of the palace, so see whatever you can from the roof. After you're wed even that freedom will be taken from you.' Monomohini brought her palms together in reverence to her royal uncle and sped out of the room with the grace and swiftness of a doe.

'Why is she with you?' Birchandra asked his wife. 'Where is her mother?'

'You don't remember a thing. Didn't my sister burn to death two years ago?'

'Did she burn as a sati?'

'It's one and the same. Burning to death is burning to death.'

'The girl's ripe for marriage. It's time you found a husband for her.'

'I have found one already. Her future husband is the most eligible man in Tripura.'

'Really! Who is he?'

'Maharaja Birchandra Manikya.'

'What an outlandish idea!' The Maharaja tweaked his wife's nose affectionately. 'Do I have the time to get married?'

'You must find the time. Tell me truly, did you not like her? She's a lovely girl and good and sweet. I'll give her to you. Enjoy yourself with her. You needn't go to that sour faced bitch Rajeshwari ever again.'

Birchandra embraced his wife tenderly and said,'Leave all that for now Bhanu. You know I love you the best.' Bhanumati resisted an overwhelming urge to lay her head on her husband's breast. Instead she said sharply, 'That's a lie. I'm old and ugly and you don't love me anymore. If you do, take me to the mahabhoj.'

'How can I do that?'

'The subjects don't even know I'm the queen consort. Radhu is your heir and Rajeshwari will be queen mother. I'll be treated as her handmaid. They may even drive me away from the palace.'

'That's nonsense. Everyone knows that though there are dozens of queens in the palace there is only one Mahadevi. And her name is Bhanumati. Even the king is in her debt. By the way, the treasury is nearly empty. You'll have to lend me a lakh of rupees. I must go now. I'll come back to you tonight after the mahabhoj.'

'Will you really?' Bhanumati's voice softened and her eyes grew moist with love.

'Of course I will. We'll sleep together in your bed tonight and I'll sing my new song for you.'

Birchandra walked out of the queen's wing and, crossing the gallery with its floor of chequered marble, entered a room where servants waited with his shoes. His brow was furrowed in thought. Bhanumati was his first wife and the daughter of a powerful king. She was wealthy, too, in her own right having inherited the taluk of Agartala with its vast fort from her father. There were many in the palace who would take her side. What if they conspired to kill Radhakishor? But in a moment he rejected the idea. Bhanumati wouldn't do anything so drastic—not during his lifetime at least. They were held together in a bond, if not of love at least of friendship and affection. He shook his head sadly. Bhanumati had all the qualities required of the first lady of the realm. She was a princess of Manipur. She was beautiful and stately and commanded respect from all her subjects. However, the second queen Rajeshwari took precedence over her in one thing. It was she who had borne the king's sons. Bhanumati had lost face. For what was the worth of a woman who could not give her husband a son? How was she superior to the concubines the king kept for his pleasure? Eventually, of course, she had redeemed herself. A son had been born to her but only after Rajeshwari had presented the king with three princes.

Now that the time had come to choose an heir Birchandra found himself in a delicate situation. Should he nominate the son

of his queen consort or should the privilege go to his first born
son? Much as he cared for Bhanu's happiness, he knew it had to
be the latter. For even the British upheld the law of
primogeniture. He had dispensed with precedence in elevating
Samar to the position of Bara Thakur. By right it belonged to
Rajeshwari's second son, Debendra. But Bhanu was hard to
please. He sighed and, waving away the other shoes, let the
servants fit a pair of simple wooden *khadam* on his feet. Then,
rising, he walked down the gallery. Passing Rajeshwari's wing he
stopped for a moment. Should he meet her once before going
down to the mahabhoj? Then he thought better of it. He would
not go to Bhanumati that night either. He had made a solemn
promise, it was true, but promises to women meant nothing. He
was tired of Bhanu's nagging and tears. It would give him far
greater pleasure to hear the music that would come after the feast.
Nisar Hussain would play the veena and Kasem Ali Khan the
rubab. And the brilliant drummer Panchanan Mitra would tap
his pakhawaj to Jadu Bhatta's singing. He would avoid Bhanu for
the next three or four days then, comforting her with a few more
lies and get the one lakh of rupees out of her. There was nothing
wrong with lying to a woman. It was policy. Humming a little
tune the Maharaja walked down the stairs to the great hall where
his courtiers were waiting.

Chapter II

Maharaja Birchandra Manikya sat in state, nine courtiers standing behind him in a row. His hookah bearer waited on his left and on his right stood his chief counsellor and bodyguard Colonel Sukhdev Thakur. The handsome colonel in his impeccable uniform was the king's constant companion as was Radharaman Ghosh, his private secretary. Radharaman was a plain, middle-aged man of medium height. He was always very simply dressed and kept his feet bare. Looking at him no one would dream that he held such a high position in the realm. Birchandra took a few puffs from his hookah. 'Ghosh Moshai!' he said, 'Every year, on this occasion, I make some announcement pertaining to the welfare of my subjects. What is it to be this year?'

'I've given it considerable thought Maharaj. The announcement you will make will cover you with glory not only here in Tripura but throughout the country. I've discussed it with Colonel Thakur and he is in total agreement.'

'What is it?' Birchandra asked curiously.

'You will issue a decree against *satidaha*. The burning of widows is a savage custom and a blot on our old and venerated culture.' Birchandra sat silent, his eyes downcast as he listened. 'Your subjects hailed you as their deliverer when you abolished slavery,' Radharaman continued. 'Your fame reached —'

'No,' the king interrupted. 'The time is not yet ripe for issuing such a decree. *Satidaha* is an ancient practice rooted in the history and religion of our land. No woman of this realm has ever been forced to become a sati. Our women burn with their husbands voluntarily and joyfully and are rewarded with eternal bliss hereafter. I cannot and will not strike a blow against the faith of so many of my subjects.'

'Maharaj,' Radharaman replied,'You may not know it but Lord William Bentinck has put an end to this practice with an act of law and the rest of the country has accepted it. Shall Tripura

13

lag behind?'

'Don't forget,' Birchandra said gravely, 'that Tripura is not governed by the British. They are foreigners and do not understand our ancient traditions. I'm not obliged to obey their laws.'

'Maharaj,' Radharaman pleaded, 'The practice of *satidaha* is not an integral part of our Dharma. If anything, it's a perversion of the Hindu religion.'

'Let the argument rest for now,' Birchandra lifted a hand in command. 'It is an ancient rite—one that cannot be put aside upon a whim. I'll have to obtain the views of my subjects before I form an opinion. But have you not thought of anything else?'

'There is the matter of your successor. Kumar Radhakishor will be nominated by you today. That will be a welcome announcement.'

Birchandra's face, which had been flushed and ponderous with self esteem till now, crumpled like that of a child's. Signalling to the courtiers and his hookah bearer to withdraw, he leaned over to Radharaman and whispered,'I want to postpone the announcement. We can see about it next year.' Colonel Thakur almost recoiled with shock but Radharaman's face did not register even the mildest surprise. 'That will have disastrous consequences,' he said quietly. 'Why?' the Maharaja's voice had a pleading note in it. 'Why should one year's delay make a difference? I'm strong and healthy. I'm not likely to die in a —'

'May you live to be a hundred Maharaj. All your subjects hope and pray for it. But consider the kumar's age. He has left his youth far behind and is now a man, strong and sensible and mature enough to shoulder the responsibilities of state. If he is given charge of some of your affairs you could devote more time to your music, painting and photography.'

'Then give him some responsibility. Let him collect the rents. And open a few schools.'

'It is imperative that he gets his rightful title first. Are you reconsidering the matter Maharaj?'

'I didn't say that. I do not question his right or ability. I only wish to postpone the announcement.'

'That will come as a blow—not only to him but to many others.'

14

'You've been talking about it then!'

'I've only told one or two people. But these things can't be kept secret.'

'What is likely to happen if I withhold the announcement? Do you fear that the prince will revolt against me?'

'He won't. He is gentle and unassuming. And he respects you. But I cannot vouch for his followers. They may flare up. The prince is extremely popular.'

'But you must know that Mahadevi Bhanumati wields a lot of power in the palace. And she hasn't withdrawn her claim on behalf of her son. What if she incites the Manipuris against me?'

Colonel Sukhdev cleared his throat and said, 'We've considered that already Maharaj. Our spies are in their camp. According to reports received, Kumar Samarendra's followers, though disturbed and angry, are not yet ready for action. They are voicing the opinion that the queen consort's son should be king but that's all. They lack the power to revolt.'

'Kumar Radhakishor must be given control over the police force before his nomination,' Radharaman said, 'Then no one will dare oppose him.'

'Kumar Samarendra's ambition must be nipped in the bud,' Colonel Sukhdev Thakur added, 'Or else there'll be trouble —'

Suddenly the king flew into a temper. Grimacing horribly he glared at his bodyguard. 'How much money has Radhakishor bribed you with, you rogue,' he shouted, 'that you pimp for him so shamelessly? Am I dead already?' Then, rising, he rushed out of the room down the gallery and out of the lion gates. His chest heaved with indignation and helplessness at the situation in which he had been caught. But peace descended on his soul the moment he stepped out into the open. A soft breeze floated about him cooling his fevered brain and his eyes beheld the autumn sky, clear as glass and spangled over with tiny stars. A moon, lustrous with ten days of waxing, rained its beams on him, soft and white like the powdery pollen of flowers. It seemed to him that the moon was a woman, a beautiful woman, and that she was smiling at him.

Torches flared at his entry and a thousand voices rose in welcome. But he heard nothing; saw nothing. He walked towards the brilliantly lit dais as if in a trance and sat down to receive his

15

subjects. One by one, the tribal chiefs came up with their gifts. He spoke a courteous word to one; nodded affably to another but all could see that his mind was elsewhere. From time to time he glanced up at the sky. It seemed to him that the moon had left her place in the heavens and was coming down to him. Closer she came and closer, swaying a little as she moved. 'Ghosh Moshai,' he turned to Radharaman. 'Do you know who wrote the verse *O hé binod rai kotha jao hé?*

'It was Bharatchandra Maharaj.'

'I wonder why I thought of it just now. Do you remember the rest?' Radharaman nodded his head and recited softly

O hé binod rai kotha jao hé
Adharé madhur hashi banshité bajao hé
Naba jaladhara tanu shikipuchha shatrudhunu
Pita dharha bijulité mayuré nachao hé
Nayana chakor mor dekhiya hoyechhé bhor
Mukha sudhakar hashi sudhai bajao hé

'That's it,' Birchandra's face brightened in a flash. '*Mukha sudhakar*—a face like a moon. Look! Just look at the sky! *Shikhipuchha* is a peacock's feather, isn't it? What is a *chakor?*'

'It's a night bird. The gifts have been received Maharaj. It's time for your announcement.'

'I've told you I'm postponing it.'

'Your subjects are waiting in eager expectation. Even the Political Agent has expressed his wish —'

For the first time that evening Birchandra looked at the crowd in front of him. As he did so his eyes fell on his eldest son. Radhakishor stood a little apart from the rest, his two brothers by his side. A little knot of men from the powerful Thakur clan stood with him. Samarendra could be seen too, surrounded by the Manipuris. Taking a deep breath, just as if he was about to plunge himself into the icy waters of a mountain stream, he said, 'Very well Ghosh Moshai. You read it out.'

'It's a very important announcement Maharaj!' Radharaman exclaimed, 'Your subjects would like to hear it from your own lips.'

'They can hear it from yours. It's the same thing.'

'It isn't proper that I, your secretary, be given the onerous task. Shall I request the Honourable Dewan?'

'You do it—or leave it alone. I'm hungry. I'm going for my

16

meal.'

Left with no option, Radharaman cleared his throat and began ponderously:

'In accordance with the command of the Lord of Tripura Sri Sri Sri Sri Sri Birchandra Manikya Bahadur Maharaj of the Dynasty of Chandra . . .' Birchandra's heart beat fast. The news would reach the palace in a few minutes. It would devastate Bhanumati. She had taken it for granted that the king was still considering the matter and hadn't made up his mind. That was why she had wanted to be by his side this evening. Had he done right in nominating Radhakishor? It was true that Radhu was his eldest son. But age had nothing to do with the ability to govern. Had he not wrested the throne, himself, from his elder brothers Chakradhwaj and Nilkanta? What consolation could he offer Bhanumati? She would never trust him again and he needed her help and trust. However, the die was cast and there was nothing he could do now. He rose from the dais, his brows lowered in distaste, even as the exultant cries of his subjects tore at his ear drums.

'Ghosh Moshai!' he cried impulsively. 'I'm dying of hunger. How much longer do I have to wait?' Suddenly the air felt chill on his body and he shivered involuntarily. He felt himself standing on the brink of a newly created world, dark and cold and he was alone—utterly alone.

As he lowered his bulk to the ground before one of the leaves spread out in a ring he felt a sharp pain at his side. The butt of his Nimcha was pressing against his ribs. His face contorted with pain but he didn't utter a sound. Yet, when a servant placed an immense silver plate, the thala, before him he turned on him, eyes blazing with fury. 'What is this?' he shouted hoarsely, 'Take it away.' This was, in fact, part of a tradition. Each year a silver thala was placed before the king and each year he waved it away with feigned anger and ate from a leaf like the rest of the company. The scene was enacted with the purpose of impressing upon his subjects the extent of his simplicity and humility. But this time his anger was real and, in waving away the thala, he gave it such a hard shove that it went spinning off in the opposite direction.

His bad temper notwithstanding, Birchandra was the perfect host. He touched his leaf only after all the tribal chiefs had been

17

served. But after the first two or three mouthfuls he could not eat. He liked khichuri and this was hot and spicy. But it tasted like sawdust in his mouth and he felt his appetite gone. He was about to rise when he remembered that, if he did so, the others would have to rise too. Crooking a finger at his hookah bearer he ordered the hookah to be brought to him. Then, smoking, he called out from time to time, 'Eat well, my guests! Do justice to the food which is excellent!' And all the while he was thinking furiously, 'Where do I go now? To Bhanumati or Rajeshwari?' The thought of going to Bhanumati sent shivers down his spine. And he couldn't go to Rajeshwari either. Turning to Radharaman he said, 'I shall be spending the night in the Forbidden Wing. Send for Kasem Ali, Jadu Bhatta and Nisar Hussain. They shall play and sing all night. And see that no one else comes near me.'

Chapter III

Shashibhushan's *pathshala* had all the trappings of a real school. Tables, chairs, pens, paper and inkstands were laid out, every morning, with clockwork regularity and he, himself, was always in readiness. But the school rarely saw a pupil. In consequence, Shashibhushan spent his days in forced idleness in the charming house by the lake that had been allotted to him as tutor to the royal princes. The salary was a generous one for a bachelor who lived alone, and the position prestigious. The king's advisor Radharaman Ghosh had held the same position on first coming out to Tripura. Being a shrewd politician he had risen by degrees and was, now, the most eminent man in the realm. Shashibhushan had no political ambitions and, being a man of conscience, was often consumed with guilt at the thought of taking a salary without doing any work. He had often complained about the non attendance of the king's sons; had pleaded with him for intervention and even offered to resign. But Birchandra had laughed his scruples away.

Looking out from the window of his school room, one morning, Shashibhushan's attention was caught by the sight of a boy standing under a jackfruit tree reading aloud from a book that, even from that distance, appeared to be old and tattered. He had seen the lad once or twice before and presumed that he was the gardener's son. Agreeably surprised to see him with a book in his hand, Shashibhushan beckoned to him to come closer. As the boy approached him Shashibhushan saw that he had a slender, handsome figure and long dark eyes that seemed etched in kohl against a smooth nut brown skin. But his dhuti was coarse and barely covered his knees and his feet were naked and covered with dust.

'What's your name boy?' Shashibhushan asked, looking on him with interest.

'I'm Bharat, Master Moshai.'

'What is that you hold in your hand?'

19

The boy handed him a sheaf of printed pages that turned out to be old issue of *Bangadarshan*. Charmed and surprised Shashibhushan asked curiously, 'Can you read what is written here? Have you learned the alphabet?' The boy shut his eyes and recited in one breath: 'Their wealth is inexhaustible in this land of ours and their power unparalleled in this day and time. Is there one merchant in Bharatvarsha who can, at one word, throw down a crore of rupees in cash against a bill of exchange? When Mir Habib ransacked the city of Murshidabad he could but take away two crores of Arcot rupees from the house of Jagat Seth . . .'

Shashibhushan was amazed. The boy was reciting, word by word, from Bankimchandra's *Chandrashekhar*. It wasn't even poetry, which was easier to remember. He had obviously read this issue over and over again. Shashibhushan decided that he would write to Bankim Babu and apprise him of the fact that he had an ardent admirer even here in this mountain land so far away from Bengal.

'Who taught you to read?' he asked curiously.

'No one,' the boy said shyly looking down at his feet. 'I learned by myself. But I'm not very good. What is an Arcot rupee Master Moshai?'

Shashibhushan made up his mind to take the boy in hand. Not being a prince, he was debarred entry into the school room. But he could surely be taught outside, under the trees. After a few lessons Shashibhushan discovered that his new pupil was not only extremely intelligent but that his thirst for learning was insatiable. He had only two or three books which he had learned by rote but, basing his knowledge on these, he asked innumerable questions about lands and climes outside his known world of Agartala—their history, geography, races and cultures. After every lesson Shashibhushan was left wondering anew at the unpredictability of the human mind. From what hidden source did this orphan boy, living on the king's charity in the servant's wing, derive his scholarly bent of mind; his passionate zeal for the written word? Was it the dark, suffocating aridity of his life that had impelled him to seek light and freedom in the pages of a book? Yet, surely there were others like him—innocent children deprived of love and care and nurture? How many of them were driven to seek knowledge as an escape from sordid, mundane reality?

20

The lessons continued through the winter, spring and summer. Then the rains came lashing down accompanied by violent winds, thunder and lightning. Sitting out of doors was no longer possible and Shashibhushan was left with no alternative but to bring Bharat into the school room. He could, of course, have discontinued the lessons but he had no wish to do that. Bharat was making rapid progress. He had picked up the English alphabet already and had learned a good deal about the solar system.

One morning, when master and pupil sat poring over a lesson, Kumar Samarendra walked into the school room along with his cousin Sukhchandra. Glaring at Bharat the latter said roughly, '*Ei* Bharat! What are you doing here? Get out of this room this minute!' Bharat rose meekly from his seat but Shashibhushan stopped him with a gesture. Turning to the others he said, 'He isn't doing any harm. Surely you can all learn —' Before he could complete his sentence, Kumar Upendra burst into the room with his own gang of brothers and cousins. Knitting his brows he asked insolently, 'Who has allowed him to come in here? A kachhua's son! How dare he aspire to sit with princes?' Bharat picked up his books and sped out of the room before Shashibhushan could utter a word. The princes hurried out as unceremoniously as they had come leaving Shashibhushan sitting in the school room deep in thought. A kachhua's son! That meant Bharat was of royal birth. Though out of wedlock, it was the king's seed that his mother had carried in her womb.

He understood the hatred and rancour of the other princes. Bharat, though illegitimate, was a force to reckon with. He could, at any time, become a pawn in the hands of power brokers and be used against them. Shashibhushan suddenly thought of another Bharat—also a child of love. No rites or ceremonies had sanctified the union of Shakuntala and Dushyanta. Yet no one despised their son for being a bastard. This great land of Bharatvarsha was named after him.

Bharat avoided Shashibhushan for the next three or four days but the latter was on the lookout and caught him one evening. 'Go to the king,' he advised. 'Tell him who you are and ask him for a favour. Say you want nothing from him except permission to take lessons from me. If he gives it no one will dare stop you.'

21

One morning, when the sky was overcast with cloud and rain pelted down in torrents, the Maharaja came into the school room. He could have sent for Shashibhushan but he was an impulsive man and acted upon his whims. He had composed a lyric the night before and he wanted to show it to his resident tutor and seek his opinion on its quality. They conversed for a few minutes, then the king rose to depart. But no sooner had he reached the door than something came hurtling from outside and fell, with a thud, at his feet.

'Who . . . What's this?' Birchandra cried out, startled.

'I'm your worthless son, *Deota*!' Bharat raised pleading eyes to his father's face. 'My name is Bharat.'

Birchandra had never seen Bharat before but he took the announcement quite calmly. Smiling down at the handsome face at his feet he asked, 'What is your mother's name boy?' Bharat brought his palms together and touched them to his brow. 'My mother is in heaven, *Deota*! Her name was Kiron Bala.' Birchandra knitted his brows, thinking. Kiron Bala! She must have come from Assam. The Assamese call their fathers *Deota*. Yes, now that he thought of it, the name rang a bell. He wondered why. She wasn't even a queen. Kiron Bala! She had been a comely girl and had laughed a lot. He remembered her laughter. Yes, he recollected now, she had died after giving birth to a son. The king looked down at Bharat with affection in his eyes. He had a soft corner for his bastards. They were, after all, living proof of his virility.

'Get up boy,' he put out a hand and hauled Bharat to his feet. 'What do you want from me?'

'He is a very meritorious student Maharaj,' Shashibhushan answered for the boy. 'He has learned a lot already. He will go far if given the opportunity to study further.'

'Well! why not? If that is what he wants. Teach him a bit of English. If he learns enough to be able to converse with the Political Agent he can even earn a salary from me.'

Bharat's destiny changed from that day onwards. Not only was he allowed to take lessons without interference, he was moved out of the servants' quarters and given a room in the house of the king's secretary. Radharaman Ghosh ordered two sets of clothes befitting his status and arranged to pay him a stipend of ten rupees a month.

22

His lessons over, Bharat would spend the rest of the day wandering around the lake. Kamal Dighi was surrounded on all sides by lush greenery which formed an excellent cover for the shy youth who wanted to escape the eyes of the inmates of the palace. Hour after hour he lay among the tall grass and ferns, reading and thinking his own thoughts. Under Shashibhushan's tutelage he was not only gleaning a lot of information about the outside world, he felt his own inner world to be in a state of flux, changing contours and teeming with possibilities. All these years he had believed that heaven lay somewhere beyond the blue sky and that his unhappy mother had found a place in it. But Master Moshai said that heaven and earth did not exist except in the minds of men. 'Where is my mother then?' he had asked. 'And where do the gods dwell?' 'You are receiving an education,' Shashibhushan had answered grimly, 'Learn to think for yourself. There is one Supreme Being and one alone. It is He who created the universe and all things in it. He is without form and substance. He permeates everything you see from the sky above your head to the earth beneath your feet. Kali, Durga, Lakshmi, Saraswati and the entire range of gods and goddesses that we Hindus worship are only clay images made by the hands of men.' A little shiver ran down Bharat's spine. Even the thought of denying Kali was frightening. What if she was watching him and saw what went on in his mind? Would she not mete out a severe punishment?

A little patter of footsteps behind him made Bharat spin around in alarm. Was Ma Kali . . .? A girl was coming towards him—a girl of twelve or thirteen with gleaming eyes and smiling lips so full and sweet that they seemed drenched in honey dew. She wore a sari but it was wrapped so loosely and clumsily around her that it threatened to slip off any moment. Was she . . .? One could never be sure. Gods and goddesses often came down to the earth in human form.

'*Ei!*' the girl called out in a voice of command, 'Who are you?' Then, receiving no answer, she said 'I know. You're the servant boy turned kumar.' Giggling and putting out her tongue at him she added, 'If you're a prince why don't you comb your hair?'

'Who are you?' Bharat asked in a faint voice.

'Don't you know me? I'm Khuman. No, no I have another name. I am Monomohini.'

23

Bharat had never seen Monomohini but he knew that Queen
Bhanumati had a neice by that name. The princesses of Tripura
were kept in strict purdah but Monomohini came from Manipur
where women enjoyed many of the privileges of men and were
famous for their wit and repartee. She had romped and played
freely with her brothers and cousins in childhood. Here, under
her aunt's care, she felt as stifled and confused as a caged bird and
slipped out of the palace whenever she could. Pointing to a tree
that stood a little distance away she said, her eyes bright with
mocking laughter, 'Young prince, why don't you pluck some fruit
for me?' Bharat glanced in the direction of the pointing finger.
The tree was laden with clusters of star apples but the fruit was
hard and green and inedible. 'I can't climb trees,' he said shortly.
Her presence made him uncomfortable. Talking to a girl in the
middle of the day in a secluded spot like this was dangerous. If
anyone saw them there would be trouble.

'Come. I'll teach you,' Monomohini tucked her sari tightly at
her waist and proceeded to climb the rough trunk with
accustomed ease. The sari rose to her knees revealing her slim,
shapely legs. Her golden back was naked to the waist. 'Come,
hold my hand,' she called. Bharat broke out in a sweat. He felt the
world dissolve around him. This was not real. This wasn't
happening. It was a scene from a book; a romance by Bankim
Babu. Was the girl before him Shaibalini? But he was no Pratap.
He was Bharat—the king's bastard. He felt his heart thud
violently within him. His ears blazed. He turned and started
walking away in the opposite direction. '*Ei! Ei!*' Monomohini's
voice came out to him, clear and intrepid, 'Where are you going?
Come back quickly you dolt or I'll pull the dhuti off your middle.'

Bharat covered his ears with his hands and ran and hid himself
among the trees.

24

Chapter IV

The musicians had succumbed to the exhaustions of the day and had fallen asleep beside their instruments. But the listener was wide awake and eager for more. Birchandra's energy was phenomenal. He could keep awake for three nights in succession without feeling a trace of fatigue. He had wanted to hear the raga of the morning, his favourite raga, but there was no hope of it now.

Sighing with disappointment, he walked out of the audience hall and stood on the balcony. Dawn was breaking over the mountains and, before his entranced eyes, a huge hibiscus-coloured sun swam into view. He brought his palms together in reverence but did not utter any mantra. Instead, he started humming a song in the morning raga Bhairavi. Suddenly he stopped singing and a worried look came into his eyes. He had remembered Bhanumati. Leaning over the rail he called out to the guards, 'Lock the gates and don't open them for anyone. I wish to be alone.'

This set of rooms, situated at a little distance away from the main palace, was Birchandra's favourite haunt. It was called the Forbidden Wing because entry into it was forbidden to all except a few close associates of the king. Birchandra pursued his hobbies here—painting, music, developing photographs and reading poetry. When he was in retreat, as he was now, even the most pressing matters of state could not draw him out.

Birchandra stood gazing for a while at the beauty of the scene before him. Then, raising his arms above his head, he stretched luxuriously. 'Aaah!' he cried with deep satisfaction. 'Aaah!' came a voice, prompt as an echo. As Birchandra turned around in the direction of the sound a bundle of clothing gathered itself together from a corner and sat up. It was a man, very tall and thin with a nose like a rapier and long untidy locks tumbling about a pair of hollow cheeks. The Maharaja knew him. He was Panchananda, a notorious drunkard and drug-taker with a saucy insolent tongue. But Birchandra liked him and let him hang about the Forbidden Wing preferring his rough and ready manners to the oily flatteries of his courtiers.

Panchananda stifled a yawn and said. 'I almost dropped off in the middle of a song, Maharaj, so I slipped away fearing my snoring would disturb you. Aa haha! What a voice Jadu Bhatta Moshai has! *Phirayé dité élé shéshé shonpilé nijéré.* A brilliant composition! I'm not going home without hearing the rest of it.'

'Then you'll have to wait till sundown. Darbari Kannada cannot be sung in the glare of the day! You'd better get yourself home. Don't forget that a desolate heart is pining away for a glimpse of you.'

'It will do the desolate heart good. A woman likes to pine away for the man she loves, Maharaj. It enhances his value in her eyes. If she's denied the opportunity she gets bored and sulky. It's like eating a sauce without salt and spices.'

'Humph!' the king grunted. 'You're never at a loss for words. Well! I'm going for my bath Panchananda. If you decide to stay you must make yourself useful. Go to the studio and start mixing the paints. I mean to finish my picture this morning.'

Birchandra stepped into the studio an hour later to find Panchananda standing with a brush in his hand gazing thoughtfully at a painting propped up on an easel. It was a landscape—a view of the forest from the West Wing. Birchandra had started work on it a month ago then, losing interest, had abandoned it. Clearing his throat, he said with mock severity, '*Ohé*! Are you trying to improve upon my handiwork?' Panchananda bit his tongue in exaggerated humility. Wagging his head from side to side he exclaimed, 'Would I dare take such a liberty Maharaj? Would even one of my fourteen generations of ancestors dare? Can I play God? But, forgive me Maharaj, I was sorely tempted.'

'Tempted to do what?'

'Forget it. It's of no consequence.'

'What do you think of this picture?'

'Shall I express my opinion freely? Or shall I exercise caution?'

'I've never seen caution within a mile of you.'

'You ask me to be candid then?'

26

'I command you.'

'The picture is too crowded Maharaj. There are too many trees. This poor little doe in the middle has no room to breathe. A painting should have space.'

'Take a look at the forest from the West Wing. It looks exactly like this.'

'That may be true but the painter must see with the eyes of the mind . . . And here, look at this silk cotton tree. The flowers on it are too red, too bright. The onlooker's eyes are irresistibly drawn to this spot and the rest of the picture is lost. Don't you agree?'

'Hmm,' the Maharaja nodded, considering the point. 'You're right. But tell me, what were you tempted to do?'

'Wipe out the scarlet blooms.'

'Is that possible? Scarlet is too strong a colour to be wiped out.'

'One can lighten the red with a film of white and blur the effect. That's why I dipped my brush in white.'

Birchandra took the brush from Panchananda and worked on the painting for a while. But his mind was restless and disturbed and he could not concentrate. Standing back he surveyed his handiwork. 'No,' he shook his head with dissatisfaction. 'It's no good.' Flinging the brush away he said, 'I don't like this picture.'

'I don't like landscapes either,' Panchananda said. 'Why don't you paint portraits Maharaj? The human body is the most artistic of God's creations.'

Birchandra moved to another part of the room and stood before a piece of canvas which had the figure of a nude woman painted on it. 'Why is it so difficult to paint the female form Panchananda?' he asked fretfully. 'The face is easy but the limbs—I never seem to get the proper symmetry, particularly in the standing posture. European painters turn out nudes by the dozen.'

'They use models Maharaj.'

'They use—what?'

'Models are real living women. Or men as the case may be. They stand, sit or lie down for hours at a stretch at the painter's command. He studies their anatomy closely, observing every line and curve, and paints what he sees.'

'Nonsense,' Birchandra waved a hand in dismissal. 'What

27

woman would agree to strip herself naked for the sake of a picture? Europeans cannot be that dissolute! They couldn't have conquered half the world if they were.'

'They don't consider it immoral Maharaj. They call it Art. Women from good families will never agree to pose nude, of course. Models are generally prostitutes and are paid by the hour.'

'You mean they are hired. I've never heard of anything so bizarre.'

'I've lived in Chandannagar for some years Maharaj and I've heard Frenchmen boast about their heritage. There are schools in the city of Paris where young men take lessons in art from renowned masters. A whore or servant maid is hired for each class. The master makes her pose naked by the window or leaning against a wall and the young men observe her contours and paint what they see. There's nothing immoral about it.'

'Perhaps not. But that kind of thing would be impossible here.'

'Why?'

'Am I to go shopping for a whore or maid?'

'Why should you take the trouble? Are there not hundreds of servants waiting eagerly to do your bidding? Besides, there are pretty wenches by the score in the palace. I've seen one with breasts like newly swelling shaddocks—the bloom still clinging to them like a sprinkling of moon dust. Her hips hang like heavy gourds from an arched waist as slim and taut as that of a lioness. And she moves with the grace and majesty of an elephant. Her name is Shyama.'

'*Chup!*' Birchandra thundered. 'I'll have your head if you dare cast lecherous eyes on a palace maid. You have a chaste and beautiful wife. Yet you lust after another woman. You're disgusting!'

Panchananda trembled in pretended terror and brought his palms together. 'Maharaj!' he begged. 'Don't take my head. I wish to keep it on my shoulders for a little longer. If you command me I'll leave Tripura and never show my face here again. But consider my words Maharaj. The artist is no lecher. He sees his model first with the eyes, then with the mind. And what he creates on his canvas is physical reality filtered through the

28

light of the imagination. Besides,' he added with a grin. 'Which of
our scriptures enjoin us not to feast our eyes on other women even
if we have wives at home? And if there is such an injunction does
your Majesty follow it?'

Birchandra burst out laughing. 'You've got a tongue as long
as a snake,' he said, wagging his head from side to side. 'I'll have it
pulled out some day.' Then, lifting his voice, he commanded the
servants who stood on guard outside the door. '*Oré*! Go fetch the
queen's handmaid Shyama. I wish to see her at once.'

The servants didn't have to go far to look for Shyama. She was
right there at the gate giggling and flirting with the watchmen.
The moment the king's command reached their ears the two
worthies fell on her and dragged her, protesting, into the king's
presence. The door slammed shut . . .

Like her husband, Mahadevi Bhanumati had stayed awake all
night. She had been perturbed and angry when news of
Radhakishor's elevation was first brought to her. But her spirits
rose the moment she heard that the proclamation had been made
not by the king but by the Chief Secretary. Ghosh Moshai was her
sworn enemy. But his stratagems would avail him nothing. The
king could withdraw the proclamation any time he wished. And
he would do so. Radhakishor could have the estates of Kumilla.
She had no objection to that. But her son Samarendra would be
king. Her husband had promised to spend the night with her. He
hadn't kept his promise but that didn't disturb her either. He
would come in the morning. She was sure of it.

Bhanumati spent the night playing cards with her niece
Monomohini. But her mind was not on the game. Tense with
expectation, she waited eagerly for the reports that kept coming
to her, by the hour, from the three trusted maids she had posted in
different parts of the palace. She loved her husband and trusted
him. He wouldn't let her down. He hadn't come to her—it was
true. But he hadn't gone to any other woman, not even to
Rajeshwari who had dressed herself in her finest clothes and
jewels and had waited in her rooms, in vain. At this last bit of
news Bhanumati's heart was filled with triumph. 'Serves the low,
conspiring bitch right,' she thought spitefully. 'Let all her hopes
crumble to dust!' When news came that after the mahabhoj, the
king had proceeded straight to the Forbidden Wing, Bhanumati

29

heaved a sigh of relief. No woman was allowed in there.

Even though she had spent a sleepless night Bhanumati rose at dawn, bathed and dressed with special care. Her husband would come in any moment and he didn't care to see her sleepy and dishevelled. Wrapping a new sari about her, she commanded her maids to twine garlands of fresh flowers round her hair and neck and mark her brows with sandal. She was a strong, healthy woman and there was not a trace of fatigue on her face or in her manner. As soon as she was dressed a maid brought in her morning meal. 'Has the Maharaja eaten?' she asked, 'What has been sent to the Forbidden Wing?'

'He has had a pot of bel sherbet,' came the answer, 'And some tea. He has sent away everything else.'

The king's favourite breakfast was a bowl of rich halwa eaten with piping hot luchis fried in pure ghee. He hated English food and wouldn't touch bread or biscuits out of a misconception that they were made from flour mixed with mucus. On hearing that he had left his *luchi*-halwa uneaten, Bhanumati signalled to her maid to take everything away except the bel sherbet which she drank straight from the pot pouring it down her throat in a steady stream. Then, turning to Monomohini and the maids, she said, 'You must leave the room as soon as the Maharaja arrives. And you mustn't come back on any pretext. We wish to be alone together. If I need anything I'll come out and ask for it myself. Remember, you're not to come in even if he stays the whole day and the whole night.'

'The whole day and the whole night?' Monomohini echoed in a wondering voice.

'You don't know,' Bhanumati smiled at her niece, 'how much the Maharaja yearns for my company. We have so much to say to one another. Twenty-four hours is nothing.'

The morning passed. The sun rose high and crossed the zenith but there was no sign of Birchandra. News came that he was still in the Forbidden Wing and that he had had nothing to eat since his morning tea and sherbet. Twice his servants had taken food for him only to be sent away. On hearing this Bhanumati waved her noon meal away.

'I'm not hungry,' she announced.

'Rani Ma!' her maid Shyama exclaimed. 'You've been

30

starving since yesterday. Eat something or your limbs will start burning with bile.'

'I've had a pot of sherbet. That's enough for me Shyama. Can you find out what the Maharaja is doing? Is he listening to music? Or is he talking to someone?'

'Those rogues at the gate refuse to tell us anything Rani Ma. He wouldn't be listening to music. I could hear no sounds of sarangi or tabla when I was there a little while ago.'

'He's probably busy with some affairs of state.'

'Shall I go and call him Mashi?' Monomohini offered.

'Silly child! How can you leave the palace? Besides, women are not allowed to even peep into the Forbidden Wing. The Maharaja will cut off your head if he finds you there.'

Monomohini smiled mischieviously. She had seen the inside of the Forbidden Wing a number of times. In the afternoons, when the inmates of the palace were napping, she slipped away into the forest often meeting the bastard prince Bharat on her rambles. There was a tree just outside the Forbidden Wing from the top of which she could see the inside of one of the rooms. There were many pictures on the walls and a gun in one corner. 'The Maharaja hasn't forgotten you, has he, Mashi?' she asked suddenly.

'It's quite possible,' Bhanumati replied with dignity. 'He has so many things on his mind. Even we who have so few worries are so forgetful. Look at me! I forgot to feed my parrots only last evening.'

Bhanumati's wing was not very grand though it was the best in the palace. The large, carved mahogany bedstead on which she sat took up most of the room which was quite small and crammed with furniture and decorative objects. Bhanumati had a fascination for clocks and had a large collection, seven of which could be seen ticking away on the walls. One was a cuckoo clock; another had a blacksmith hammering the minutes on a tiny anvil. The room was poorly ventilated with little windows set high up close to the ceiling. But Mahadevi Bhanumati, herself, looked splendidly regal. The sari she wore was a bright yellow and matched the counterpane of gold and black striped silk. Heavy gold ornaments encircled her shapely arms and the rings on her fingers glittered with their burden of precious stones.

31

'Even if the Maharaja has forgotten his promise,' one of the women sitting on the floor around the bed, asked, 'Can he not be reminded of it?'

'No one is allowed into the Forbidden Wing,' the queen answered dejectedly. Then, her glance falling on her favourite maid Shyama, her spirits rose. Shyama was a very pretty girl with plenty of intelligence. Besides, she had very winsome ways. The guards at the gate wouldn't be too tough with her. Even if a message could be sent through one of them . . . 'Go to Chituram Shyama,' she commanded. 'Tell him to mention my name casually to the king when he takes in the next meal. My husband will be sure to remember his promise, then.' Shyama sped out of the room. In a little while news came that Shyama had managed to gain entrance into the Forbidden Wing and was upstairs in the presence of the king. The information was puzzling but welcome. He would be here any minute now.

But the afternoon wore on and Bhanumati's relief changed to anguish. What was Shyama doing? She had been instructed to remind the king of his promise and return to her mistress. Why hadn't she come back? Had any harm come to her? Surely the Maharaja hadn't taken her life! '*Oré!*' she called out to the other women. 'Go tell the guards that I'll have their houses burned down if they don't give us news. Why is Shyama taking so long? I demand to know the truth.'

When Bhanumati's message reached the guards their spines stiffened with alarm. They knew the queen's power. A couple of houses was nothing, a whole village could burn at her command. But the news they had was so shocking that they dared not disclose it. Shyama was in the king's studio, alive and unhurt. They could hear her gay voice and pert laughter wafting out of the open windows from time to time. But it wasn't only that. One of the guards had peeped through the key hole and seen her standing in front of the king, stark naked—one hand resting on the back of a chair.

After another hour of waiting Bhanumati could bear it no longer. 'Shyama! Harlot!' she shrieked, though Shyama was far out of the range of her call. 'I'll have your eyes plucked out for this you bitch. Just you wait!' But no one came. 'Shyama! Shyama!' Bhanumati kept calling, beside herself with impotent fury. Her maids went running to the Forbidden Wing but the guards, though trembling in fear of the Queen's wrath, dared not carry her message to the king.

The afternoon passed and dusk set in but Shyama did not return. Bhanumati tossed and turned on the bed as if in a delirium, tore at her ornaments and flung them against the walls. Panting like a tigress she screamed in a voice that was hoarse and broken, 'Bring the whore to me! Put a rope around her nostrils and drag her into my presence.' Suddenly she jumped off the bed and, pouncing on the maid nearest to her, closed her hands round her throat. 'I'll choke the life out of you, you lying bitch. You know where she is. You know. You know.'

'She's with the king,' the girl shrieked out in fear,'In the room in which he paints his pictures.'

'Then why don't you bring her to me?'

'The door is locked from within Rani Ma. The Maharaja lifted the latch himself.'

At these words Bhanumati's hands slipped from the girl's throat. Her body went limp and the fire died out of her eyes. She looked blankly around her for a few minutes. Then she said in a voice that had suddenly become flat and toneless, 'I want to sleep. Leave the room—all of you. Even you, Khuman.' Before bolting the door from within she said 'Don't call me. This door will not open again.'

Bad news travels fast, leaping over high walls and breaking out of locked doors. When the Maharaja came rushing out of the Forbidden Wing, late that night, he found Bhanumati's door had been broken down and the inmates of the palace were gathered around her bed. They had heard the queen's moans, heart broken and anguished, and had called out to her over and over again to open her door. But she had not answered. And then the moaning had ceased . . .

Maharaja Birchandra stood by the bed, his eyes glazed with shock. Bhanumati's hands were clasped over her breast. Her eyes were open. Her limbs were bare of their ornaments which lay scattered all over the floor. There was no sign of injury on the body nor was it discoloured with poison. Kneeling at the foot of the bed he commanded the assembled throng to leave the room. Then, placing a hand on her feet, he burst into tears.

Chapter V

A stunned silence had descended on the palace and the king was sunk in grief. It was not grief alone—a terrible rage swept over him against himself and against all those around him. His subjects had never seen him in such a state before and did not know what to make of it. Bhanumati had been his favourite queen. She had been strong, healthy and beautiful and her sudden death had come as a shock. They could understand that. But the Maharaja's behaviour was inexplicable. He raged violently at someone at one moment and then withdrew completely within himself at another. He had clung to the body for a whole day and night refusing to part with it. It was only when Radhakishor and Samarendra had begged him with tears in their eyes that he had let go of it. A corpse had to be cremated within twenty-four hours of death. If not, the burden of a grevious sin fell on the whole family.

The Maharaja did not accompany Bhanumati on her last journey. He locked himself, instead, in her room and did not leave it for even a minute. No one dared come near him. Memos and despatches awaiting his signature piled up in the secretary's office. Servants knocked timidly at the door with food and drink in their hands but were turned rudely away. His queens called out to him to come out of the room; to bathe and eat, but he turned a deaf ear to their pleas. The only person he dared not disobey was his mother. But she was in Udaipur and knew nothing of what had happened. Ghosh Moshai was at his wit's end. If the king carried on like this what would happen to the state? He gave the matter a great deal of thought and, gradually, a plan formed in his mind.

Three days later the king came out of Bhanumati's room and went straight to his studio in the Forbidden Wing. Taking up a brush, he commenced painting a portrait of the late queen. But his mind was in a whirl and his movements jerky and out of control. Standing before the easel he found he couldn't recall Bhanumati's face. How was that possible? He had seen her face for three whole nights—vibrant and glowing

34

in the dark. Why couldn't he see it now in the light of the day? Why did it seem blurred and unreal as if submerged in rippling water? Throwing his brush away in frustration Birchandra sat down and wondered what to do. He had taken several pictures of Bhanumati. Should he pick out one and paint from that? A strange lethargy seized him at the thought. What was the use of painting a portrait of a loved one who was lost even in the mind? Why was he losing Bhanumati?

At that moment the Maharaja heard a clear, penetrating voice, raised in recitation. The words were not in Sanskrit but in Bengali. He came to the window and saw Ghosh Moshai pacing up and down the veranda just outside. The voice was his and he was reciting the exquisite lines:

Lady! Little do you know with what invisible strings
You bind my heart as it walks its lonely path,
Holding it close, with power, if perchance it strays
Keeping the goal in sight . . .'

'What are you reciting, Ghosh Moshai?' The Maharaja leaned out of the window. They were the first words he had spoken in a normal voice since the tragedy. 'Whose poem is it?' Radharaman Ghosh approached the king with folded hands. 'Namaskar Maharaj!' he said. 'I read these verses in a book I borrowed from Shashibhushan and found the sentiments original and appealing. Our Vaishnav poets write volumes on the pain of parting with a loved one. But they always attribute it to the female. Radha's suffering! Radha's grief! Do men not feel grief and loss? This poet has written of it—'

'Who is he? Hembabu? Or Nabin Babu?'

'Neither, Maharaj. He's a young man who goes by the name of Robi Thakur.'

'Thakur? Is he one of the Thakurs of Tripura?'

'No Maharaj. There is no poet in Tripura—barring yourself of course. Robi Thakur lives in Calcutta.'

'The verse is beautiful! Exquisitely beautiful! Recite some more, Ghosh Moshai.'

Radharaman cleared his throat and recommenced his recitation:

'Else my heart falling like a star by night

35

Wrenched from its axis, would spin in vain
In the dark bosom of the eternal sky

'Aa ha ha!' Birchandra cried out with fervour, tears glittering in his eyes. 'This is just how I feel. Go on.'

'I don't remember the rest Maharaj,' Ghosh Moshai said with a shade of embarrassment. 'I've read the poem only twice. Shall I fetch the book from Shashibhushan?'

Shashibhushan was in his pathshala giving a page of English dictation to Bharat. 'Once upon a time,' he read out from the book in his hands, 'there lived a . . .' when, glancing out of the window, he saw the king walking rapidly towards them with Ghosh Moshai following close behind. Birchandra was unbathed and unshaved. He wore a soiled dhuti and clattering khadams on his feet. 'Where is the book you lent me?' Ghosh Moshai said, 'The one by Robi Thakur?' He was panting with the effort of keeping up with the king who, when he wanted something, could brook no delay. 'I gave it to Bharat,' Shashibhushan answered surprised, 'Where is it Bharat?'

Bharat had it in his satchel. Taking it out he handed it over, then stood with his back to the wall, trembling in awe and apprehension.

The Maharaja read a few more lines and cried out 'My sentiments! My sentiments to the letter! How does this young poet know my pain? Has he suffered a similar loss? Has his favourite wife left him for ever?'

'Maharaj,' Shashibhushan coughed delicately. 'Robi Thakur is very young. Barely twenty. He's not married.'

'Why not? Don't Calcutta babus marry at twenty?'

'Many do. But Robi Babu is a scion of a very high and esteemed family—the Thakurs of Jorasanko. He is Deben Thakur's youngest son. They are Brahmos and—'

'Ah! Dwarkanath's grandson! We're related to that family, I believe. A marriage was arranged, if I recall rightly, between . . . between . . . But it's of no consequence. I've heard of Dwarkanath and his son but I've never met them.'

'The Thakurs bring out a monthly journal from their family mansion in Jorasanko. It is called *Bharati*. You may not have seen it, Maharaj, but I subscribe to it regularly. Robi Babu writes extensively for *Bharati*. The name is not printed but I recognize the style. He's been writing from boyhood upwards in other journals as well and has even published a few books—at his own expense of course. His prose is even better than his poetry.'

'A mere boy of twenty!' the king wagged his head in awe and admiration. Turning the book over in his hands he caught sight of the title. *'Bhagna Hriday,'* he read aloud,'Composed by Sri Rabindranath Thakur. Calcutta. Printed by Balmiki Press. Price Re 1.' On the next page was a dedication to Srimati Hé.

'What does it mean?' he asked surprised. 'What kind of name is this?'

'Might be short for Hemangini,' Radharaman suggested. 'Or Hembala.'

'But you said he wasn't married.'

'She might be his mother. Or sister.'

'Don't be stupid,' the king snapped at him. 'Would anyone dedicate a book like this to his mother or sister?' The two men had no answer to this and fell silent. 'What other books has this youth written?' the Maharaja asked Shashibhushan.

'I've read a play called *Rudrachanda*. It isn't very good. Not like his prose pieces.'

Birchandra read a few more lines of *Bhagna Hriday*. Then, handing the book over to Radharaman Ghosh, he said 'You have a good voice. You read it out to me.'

The reading of poetry is not without its uses. For the first time since Bhanumati's death Birchandra felt the urge for a strong curl of tobacco smoke in his lungs. He hadn't smoked for days. In fact, he had forgotten all about it. Now a restlessness seized him for this luxury. And with this restlessness, the mist that had clouded his brain and heart for the last few days dissolved and disappeared. He stroked his moustache thoughtfully. Something was stirring in the pit of his stomach. Was it a pang of hunger? And, for the time, he remembered that he hadn't eaten for five whole days.

Returning to the palace he allowed the servants to give him a luxurious bath and massage, then sat down to a plentiful meal. Having eaten, he reclined on his bed with his hookah. But he had scarcely drawn the first two puffs when sleep overtook him. It was deep and restful and lasted four hours. His brow was unfurrowed as he slept and his lips were relaxed and smiling.

Birchandra took up his normal duties from the next day. The first task before him was the organizing of the funeral rites. He

had decided to perform the shraddha in Brindavan as well as in
Agartala. Both would be on a grand scale as befitted the status of
the deceased. Maharaja Birchandra would journey to Brindavan
accompanied by his queens and a large number of servants, maids
and sepoys. But the treasury was nearly empty. 'Ghosh Moshai,'
he asked his Secretary. 'Mahadevi Bhanumati's shraddha will
cost a lakh of rupees. Where is the money to come from?'

'This is the month of Kartik, Maharaj, and the harvest is a
long way off. This is not a good time to impose fresh taxes. If we
put too much pressure the peasants might revolt.'

'I know that. I do not wish to tax the peasants. Is there no
other way?'

Radharaman thought for a few minutes. 'You may sell some
gold,' he said at last. 'The price of a mohur has risen from
eighteen to nineteen rupees.' The king's brows knitted at this
suggestion. Shaking his head, he said 'I can't sell gold here. I'll
have to go to Calcutta. And once I'm there the newspapers are
bound to scent the truth. You saw how *Amrita Bazar Patrika*
hounded me over the matter of the Political Agent. When they
find out I'm selling my gold they'll inform the whole world that
I'm on my way out. As it is, people expect me to abdicate to the
British any day now.'

'Tripura will never go the way of Oudh,' Radharaman said
with conviction, 'But certain reforms will have to be carried out.
The Political Agent is putting a lot of pressure.'

'I'll take up the matter after the funeral,' Birchandra said
hastily. 'You haven't answered my question. Selling gold is out.
What else can I do?'

'Some months ago,' Radharaman said after a few minutes'
thought, 'an Englishman approached you with an offer to lease
the Balishira Hills. He was prepared to pay you one lakh, twenty-
five thousand rupees. But you didn't agree. Do you remember?'

'I do. It was a good offer but I didn't accept it because he was
an Englishman. I don't want sahebs in my country.'

'We can't stop them Maharaj. If they wish to come they will.
Let us be thankful that the man is not a government official. He's
a prospector mining the hills for metal. Our hills are lying idle.
We lack the means of mining them ourselves. Besides, the sum he
is prepared to pay is generous.'

Birchandra sat in silence pondering the question. The

proposal was not bad. But the man had been turned away. Who knew if he was still interested. Even if he was, it was going to be a difficult task to execute—calling for the utmost secrecy. 'Ghosh Moshai,' he said with a deep sigh. 'There was one who could have given me a lakh of rupees for the asking. She has left me forever. And it is for her that I beg from door to door. Is it not ironic?' Then, a practical note creeping into his voice, he continued 'Anyhow, you had better leave for Calcutta at once and track down the Englishman. Take the agreement with my signature on it. And send the money here as soon as you can. Remember that this affair has to be handled with the greatest discretion. My subjects must be convinced that I bring sahebs into the country for their own good. Prepare the proclamations accordingly.'

'That would be no lie Maharaj. When the sahebs start their mining they'll need a work force. Your subjects will find employment and a means of living.'

The Maharaja stood up and went to the door. Then, stopping suddenly, he turned back. 'I have another duty to perform,' he said twirling his moustache in embarrassment. 'After returning from Brindavan I wish to fulfil the queen's dearest wish. It was her last request to me and I cannot ignore it.' Ghosh Moshai trembled at these words but only in his heart. Outwardly he appeared calm and composed. But his mind was working fast. Radhakishor had been declared heir and had been accepted as such by the subjects. He was immensely popular. If the proclamation was withdrawn there was bound to be trouble. An uprising could not be ruled out. Birchandra read Radharaman's thoughts at a glance. 'Have no fears Ghosh Moshai,' he said gently. 'I don't want any disturbance in the realm just now. We'll discuss the matter after you return.'

He left the room but came back once again. Placing a hand on Radharaman's shoulder he said, 'You have another duty to perform while in Calcutta. Dwarkanath Thakur's grandson is a fine poet. His verses have given me much comfort. He deserves an award of distinction from the Lord of the Realm. But the English bastards will never acknowledge our great men. You must go to Jorasanko as my Viceroy and offer a purse of gold mohurs and a shawl to the young poet.'

Chapter VI

Bharat struggled out of deep sleep with a sense of impending doom. His chest felt tight and his lungs were fairly bursting for lack of air. As his eyes flew open he saw a man, large and dark as a demon, leaning over him and pressing a heavy hand over his nose and mouth. 'Quiet!' the man hissed in a grating whisper. 'Utter a sound and you die.'

Bharat's body lay still but his mind was working furiously. 'What's happening to me?' he thought. 'Is this a messenger from Yama, the God of Death? Am I dying?' The man tied Bharat's mouth tightly with a towel, then yanked him out of bed by the hair. 'Come on,' he said dragging him to the veranda where another demon stood waiting with a spear in his hand. His huge body was naked except for a flimsy bit of cloth covering his genitals. A stench of stale toddy wafted out, in sickening gusts, from his mouth. The men pushed and pummelled Bharat out of the house and into the open where two horses stood waiting. Bharat looked wildly about him. The palace loomed in the distance like a dark, shadowy mass. Torches flared at the gate but their light was shrouded by a thin mist that had rolled up from the lake. It was a cold night and the sky was heavy with cloud.

One of the men sprang on to a saddle pulling Bharat up after him. Then the two horses galloped rapidly out of the city into the woods. 'They could have killed me as I slept,' Bharat thought, 'Why didn't they? Where are they taking me? Could it be to the temple of Ma Kali? Are they going to hack me to pieces in her presence? Is this my punishment for doubting her?' Thoughts crowded into Bharat's head, like a host of moths chasing one another. 'How can they see where they are going? It is so dark. I can see nothing. Will it hurt terribly? Only the first blow and then—oblivion. But the first? It should be swift and sharp. Malu Karati could cut off a buffalo's head in one stroke. After every sacrifice he would hold the falchion high in triumph and look around with bloodshot eyes. 'An elephant,' he would cry hoarsely. 'Why does no one sacrifice an elephant? I can cut off the head in one stroke.' . . . 'How long have we been riding? To which temple are they taking me?'

Coming to a small clearing in the forest the men reined in their horses. Pushing Bharat off the horse his abductor sprang to the ground where Bharat lay and planted a large, ungainly foot on his chest. The other tied the horses to a tree and lit a bidi. 'Why are they torturing me before the sacrifice?' Bharat thought as he watched the two men smoking and chatting. 'Even a goat is fed and fattened—' The gamchha had come loose and he could have cried out. But he dared not. What if that great heavy foot on his chest was clamped on his mouth? He opened his eyes as wide as he could. The clouds had scattered and he could see the sky sprinkled over with stars. Those who led good and virtuous lives on earth were changed to stars after death. Was a star watching him? His mother? But his mother had been a kachhua. She had lived a life of sin. He was born in sin. But redemption was at hand. Soon he would be sacrificed to Ma Kali and his soul would be free.

The man who had tied the horses now took up a shovel and started digging. The other urged him to make haste. 'Hurry!' he cried, 'Do you want to stay here all night?' Taking his foot off Bharat's chest he went to inspect the depth of the pit. Quick as a flash, without a moment's thought, Bharat sprang to his feet and ran with the swiftness of a wild boar. His chest swelled with triumph. No one could catch him now. But the demons were quicker. A spear came hurtling through the air and caught him, with unerring aim, in the back of his thigh. He fell forward, face to the ground. The man strode up to him and laughed. A searing stab of pain tore through Bharat's body as the man pulled out the spear and said, 'You're dead, boy. How far can you run?' Bharat groaned, not so much with pain as at the thought that, scarred as he was now, he was unfit for sacrifice. His soul would not be released. He would be murdered by these men. The hole in the ground would be his grave. He knew that now. He would come back to earth in another body to be cursed and kicked in the next life as he had been in this. His beloved Master Moshai's face swam before his tortured eyes. 'Be a man Bharat,' he had said again and again. 'Don't cower before your fate. Be brave and overcome it.' He *had* been brave in trying to escape. He hadn't surrendered without a struggle.

The demon dragged Bharat by the hair to the spot where his companion was still digging. 'That's quite enough,' he said roughly. 'Let's pack him in.' Lifting him by the armpits the two men shoved Bharat, feet first, into the hole, then, grabbing his shoulders, pressed him deeper and deeper in the way a bolster is crammed into a tightly fitting cover. But, though Bharat's knees were bent double under the weight of the pressing hands, the hole wasn't deep enough to contain the whole of him. His head stuck out like a toadstool from the soft soil which the men packed about his body. Punishment of this type was not rare in Tripura and Bharat had heard of several cases like his own. When a man was banished from the realm the soldiers, whose duty it was to see that he never came back, took the precaution of burying him in this manner. They could then rest easy for he would either die of hunger or become food for wild animals. In either case, he wouldn't come back. And this way the sin of murder would not weigh heavy on their conscience.

As the men pressed the earth tightly around his neck with their feet Bharat's thoughts raced ahead of one another. What had he done to deserve such a punishment? Who had given the order? One of the kumars of course. But why? He had never offended them by word or deed. In fact, his servile humility before his brothers had angered Shashibhushan. 'Why don't you stand up to them?' he had asked time and again. 'Are you not the Maharaja's son?' A sob rose in his throat at the thought of Shashibhushan. '*Ogo!*' he let out a wail that cut through the dark silence like a knife. 'Why do you treat me so cruelly? What have I done? Don't leave me here to die. Have pity!' The men jumped at the sound of his voice. '*Ei!*' one of them shouted in a startled voice. 'How did this spawn of a bitch loosen the gag?' The other one dropped to the ground and delivered a series of stinging slaps on Bharat's cheeks. 'Open your mouth whoreson,' he roared, 'Or I'll smash your head to pulp.' Stuffing half the gamchha into Bharat's open mouth he secured the rest firmly around it. After this the men brought out a razor and commenced shaving Bharat's head. Bharat had a fine head of hair that rippled, dark and silky, to his shoulders. Their work completed, they rose to leave. 'Son of a pig!' one cursed as he moved towards his horse. 'Making love to a Laichhabi!' the other spat venomously on the ground, 'Who can save you now?' Then, mounting their horses, the two men rode away.

How long did it take to die? Not very long, surely. There were wild animals in the forest. Prince Niladhwaj, the king's brother, had shot a number of tigers and their skins now decorated the walls of the palace. The men had chosen a clearing in the forest to bury him so that his head would be easily visible to the prowling creatures that swarmed the jungle. Any moment now and one of them would find him. And even if they didn't he would die anyway—like Jesus whose hands and feet had been nailed to a cross. Shashibhushan had told him about Jesus. Crucified at sunrise. Dead by sundown. Would Bharat take longer to die because he was buried in the ground?

Though his body had disappeared Bharat could move his head. He turned it this way and that, his eyes straining to see something—anything. But the darkness surrounding him was impenetrable. Tilting his head upwards he saw the stars winking and glowing, pale gold against a purple sky. His body was inert but his brain ticked away:

Twinkle twinkle little star
How I wonder what you are
Up above the world so high
Like a diamond in the sky.

Was it *what you are* or *who you are?* How did one spell *diamond*. Was it D-I-M-O-N-D or was it D-I-A-M-O-N-D? Why couldn't he remember? 'What does it matter anyway?' he thought suddenly, 'I'm dying. I shall be dead in a few hours. I'll never take dictation again.' *Making love to a* Laichhabi! What did that mean? Manipuri maidens were called Laichhabi. Like that Monomohini. 'Don't fool about with a *Laichhabi*,' Ghosh Moshai's servant Tarakda, had warned him, 'They can be dangerous.' But Bharat had never fooled around with Monomohini. In fact, he had gone out of his way to avoid her. It was she who couldn't leave him alone. She followed him around, peeped in at his window, teased him and laughed at him. Oh, the things she said. They made him blush to the tips of his ears. He kept the door latched against her but the wood was old and

43

rotting and there was a gap between the panels. Once she had slipped a twig through the gap and managed to drop the latch. Terrified at the thought that she might force her way in, he had stood with his back to the door while she hammered on it with all her might. Then, her strength failing, she had poked the twig viciously into his back, over and over again, till it was raw and bleeding. And all the while she had laughed—peal after peal of mocking laughter.

Bharat knew that the game she was playing was dangerous for him. There were some in the palace who kept a close watch on them. And, when the time came, they would shower all the blame on him. She was a Manipuri royal and the queen's niece and he was a bastard and lived on charity. Bharat had communicated his fears to Shashibhushan but the latter had laughed them away. 'You've grown so handsome!' he had exclaimed. 'It's but natural that women will fall in love with you. Why do you not go to the queen and ask for her niece's hand in marriage?'

Only last evening it had seemed to Bharat that his troubles were over. Monomohini, as was her custom, had been standing outside his window laughing and calling out to him. She had thrust her arms through the bars and, standing on tiptoe, was trying to grab him by the hair. 'Tchu Tchu!' she made teasing noises with her tongue. 'Come out of the room, little suckling infant! Let me tweak your nose for you. Mother's baby would like some milk, wouldn't he? Come out and I'll give you some.' She had looked ravishingly beautiful in a pachhara, the colour of sunset, with kanchan and marigolds twined in her hair. Her breasts, tightly encased in a scarlet silk kanchuli, were pressed against the bars. At this moment the Maharaja had come striding in. He often came thus, unannounced, if he had something urgent to discuss with his secretary. He took in the scene at a glance and turned angry eyes on Monomohini. 'What are you doing here you worthless wench? Disturbing the boy when he's trying to study!' Then, lifting an admonishing finger, he warned 'Don't ever come here again. If I catch you once more I'll—' Monomohini flashed her eyes vivaciously at the king, then ran like a doe in the direction of the palace. Turning to him, the Maharaja had said kindly, 'Go back to your books, boy. Work hard and do well.' Overcome with gratitude, Bharat had knocked his head on the royal feet.

The Maharaja was not displeased with him. Bharat was sure of that. There had been kindness in his eyes. Who, then, had sent him to his death? And why? Why? Bharat's knees were buckling under the weight of his body. The spear wound throbbed with a fiery intensity. But his physical pain was as nothing to his tortured mind that ran round and round like a rat caught in a trap. Who were these men and why did they shave his head? That question plagued him more than the thought of imminent death. How much would they get for the job? He had seven rupees and two annas tucked away under his pillow. Who would get the money? Could it be Monomohini who had sent those men? The Manipuris were very powerful. And cruel. The Maharani's brother Birendra Singha could have a man tortured and killed upon a whim. Why was the forest so silent? Tigers prowled about at night, so he had heard, but not one had come near him. No, no—he didn't want it to be a tiger. An elephant was better. Tripura was full of elephants. Now, if an elephant came strolling by and placed a gentle foot on his head it would be squashed flat in an instant. Would that be less painful then being mauled by a tiger? Suddenly Bharat fell asleep and when he awoke it was broad daylight. The forest had come alive and was teeming with noise and movement. Birds chirped gaily from the tops of trees and three gambolling fawns streaked away, in a flash, before his burning eyes.

The morning passed and then the afternoon. Evening came and was followed by night and morning again. But nothing happened. Bharat felt no hunger; no pain. He slept and woke by turns. His thoughts, during his waking hours, were getting jumbled and disjointed. Faces came and went before his eyes. Monomohini's face—vibrant and insolent. No! No! He didn't want to think of her. He wouldn't. He would recite poetry. But the verses were getting mixed up and the lines blurred over in his mind. Why couldn't he remember anything?

Bharat stayed like that for three days and four nights. On the afternoon of the fourth day he heard human voices for the first time. They sounded faint as though they came from another world. He wondered if they were real. It could be that, yearning so passionately for the sound of a human voice, he was hearing it in his imagination. Sometimes it seemed to him that he could hear

45

a group of people singing; at others—a chorus of whispers. And then, an odour, delicious and familiar, came wafting in the air. Someone was cooking khichuri in the woods. This, too, he dismissed as imagined. People had such hallucinations when they were starving. He shut his eyes in weariness and utter defeat. But when he opened them again they beheld the most wonderful of sights. Two children stood close, very close to him. They were very young, may be five or six years old. They had healthy black bodies without a stitch of clothing on them. They were so beautiful they seemed to Bharat to be child gods just descended from heaven. He shook his head to dispel what he thought was a vision. But the children remained where they were. They smiled at Bharat flashing white teeth in shining black faces. Bharat tried to smile back but his mouth was tied. He couldn't smile; he couldn't talk. The only thing he could do to prove that he was alive was to bat his eyelids rapidly. The children, thinking this to be a game, burst out laughing. Then one said something to the other after which they ran hither and thither collecting sticks and stones in a pile.

These they proceeded to throw at Bharat laughing merrily all the while. Though Bharat tried to dodge the blows by turning his head his way and that, he got struck several times. The stones had sharp edges and they cut deep into his shaved head sending runnels of blood down his face and neck. The children played this game for a little while longer then, tiring of it, ran into the jungle. 'Oré! Why do you go?' Bharat's mind shouted in desperation, 'Hit me all you want but don't go. Don't go leaving me here alone.'

But all the answer he got was the rustle of leaves and the scampering of rabbits.

Bharat's heart sank and a terrible depression overtook him. He had come close to being saved. The children were not alone in the jungle. He was sure of that. There were adults nearby. But he had lost his chance. No one would come near him now. Sinking his head on the earth he burst out weeping. His sobs were inaudible but the tears, gushing out of his eyes and soaking the gamchha around his mouth were visible enough.

Chapter VII

Journeying from Agartala to Calcutta was no easy task. Thanks to the arbiters of India's destiny iron wagons with steam engines in them were carrying goods and passengers with amazing speed in many parts of the country. But Tripura lay outside British territory. The nearest rail station from Agartala was Kushthia on the border of Bengal. It took quite a few days to get there. Radharaman commenced his journey on an elephant with Shashibhushan as companion. Shashibhushan had welcomed the chance of travelling at state expense to Calcutta where certain property disputes pertaining to his family awaited his attention.

It was a cool bright day of early November when the two set off, sitting side by side on the howdah. There was a nip in the air and the yellowing leaves shuddered in the trees. The elephant swayed ponderously over the uneven forest track stopping, from time to time, to nuzzle the orchids that clung to the trunks and branches of trees. Every time the elephant stopped the mahut rapped his head with a stick and cried *Hee ré ré ré*. Walking behind were six coolies and two guards with guns. Shashibhushan had a gun too. He was as skilled with a gun as he was with a camera. He wore Western clothes with a sola hat on his head and kept his gun in readiness for any game that might cross his line of vision. Ghosh Moshai, in a plain dhuti and shawl, puffed pensively at his hookah.

All of a sudden Shashibhushan leaned forward and tapped the mahut's back with the palm of his hand. 'Stop! Stop!' he whispered, then turning to Radharaman he pointed a finger to his right. There, partly concealed by some bushes, was a patch of bright red. Radharaman wondered what creature it could be. But before he could utter a word a volley of shots rang out and five woodhens rose like a scarlet cloud into the brilliant blue sky. There was a sharp squawking and flapping of wings as two large birds tumbled down hitting the branches as they came. The coolies rushed forward with cries of delight. The flesh of the woodhen was juicy and tender and had a wonderful flavour. The eating of fowl was taboo among caste Hindus, the bird being considered unclean since it was eaten by Muslims. But Shashibhushan and Radharaman were modern men, educated in Western thought and culture. Besides, they had spent several years in Tripura where chicken and duck were eaten freely. Both were pleased at their luck and looked forward to the delicious fowl curry that would be an added bonus to the evening meal.

As the elephant lumbered along Radharaman said, 'I'd like to ask you a personal question Shashi. I hope you won't take offence.' Shashibhushan lit an expensive English cigar. Blowing a cloud of scented smoke he asked curiously, 'What is it?'

'What are you doing here in Tripura?'

'What am I doing?' Shashibhushan laughed lightly, 'I'm earning my living. I couldn't get a job in Calcutta.'

'That I can't believe. You have enough merit to secure a suitable employment even in Calcutta. Besides, I'm convinced you don't need to earn a living. You live far beyond the salary the Maharaja gives you. And your tastes are as expensive as his. Why do you not stay at home when you have the means to do so?'

'It is true that I've inherited some ancestral property. But before I answer your question you tell me what you're doing here. Your English is as good as the sahebs' and your grasp of the convolutions of the law is outstanding. Had you stayed in Bengal you could have easily secured the post of a Deputy.'

'But I didn't want to spend my life as a Deputy or a school master—the only two options open to me. Of course, my coming out to Tripura as tutor to the princes was upon an impulse. I had thought of spending a year or two in this beautiful country then going back where I belonged. Gradually I realized that if I stayed on I could rise very high—to a position I couldn't dream of in Calcutta. The Maharaja is whimsical and a poor administrator. If I made myself indispensable to him I could enjoy a great deal of power. And I have done so. The Maharaja depends on me for everything.' He stopped for a moment and added, 'I thought at first that you had the same idea Shashi. I have changed my mind because if it were so you would have hit out at me long ago. I've set spies on you and the reports are astonishing. It seems you are perfectly content to sit in your pathshala teaching one little boy. I find that very difficult to understand.'

'Have you ever considered that I may be a British spy?'

'There is one such person in the Maharaja's innermost circle. But it is not you. You see, I have gathered quite a bit of information about you. I know you lost your wife within a few months of marriage. And though that was many years ago you never remarried. You have two elder brothers who love you and are anxious for your return. Yet you stay on in Tripura. There must be a reason. A sentimental one, perhaps?'

'Not sentimental in the way you think. But, yes, there is a reason behind my coming to Tripura and staying on here. It's a long story and you'll have to be patient if you wish to hear it.' Taking another puff at his cigar Shashibhushan went on. 'My father had some property in Kandi in the district of Murshidabad. A house stood on it, a beautiful house with the river running on three sides and a forest stocked with game behind it. I was fond of hunting and enjoyed roaming in it, all by myself, with my father's gun. One day, as I was stalking a roe, I sensed the presence of others in the forest. They were trespassing but I didn't mind. The forest was swarming with rabbits, wild cats, boars, deer, even leopards. How much could anyone take away? Anyhow, after struggling for hours, I managed to shoot the roe. But when I reached the spot where she lay I was weary and wet and scratched all over by thorns—' Shashibhushan voice faltered and sank to a hoarse whisper. His face reddened and his limbs started trembling.

'Why? What is the matter Shashi?' Radharaman cried out in alarm. 'Come, come. You don't have to tell me any more.'

Shashibhushan glared at Radharaman. 'You must know,' he continued in the same unnatural whisper, 'That deer hunting is even more difficult than tiger hunting. At the very moment that I reached the roe two Englishmen came riding up with their orderlies. They took the roe away by force.'

'They took away your kill! The British don't usually stoop so low. They have a sense of fair play and—'

'You have no idea how low the British can stoop.' Shashibhushan's voice, suddenly regaining it's full strength, rang out like thunder.

'Perhaps the saheb also fired at the same animal. He may have

49

thought—'

'No. I heard no other shot. They came up to me and asked roughly, "From where did you steal the gun? You must be a dacoit." I was on my own land, Ghosh Moshai, in our own taluk. They were the trespassers. And they called me a dacoit!'

'The taluk may have been yours but the country belongs to the British. It is possible that they did not recognize you in your bedraggled state. Calm down Shashi. There's no need to get excited.'

'There's more to come,' Shashibhushan continued grimly. 'I spoke to the men in English. "The gun is my father's," I said. "It was bought from Smith and Anderson in Rani Mudini Lane. And this forest has been part of my family property for generations." The sahebs didn't even glance in my direction. Ignoring my words completely, they commanded their orderlies to take away my gun and pick up the kill. Then, turning their horses, they rode away. As they passed me, one of them—I learned, later, that he was Mr Hamilton, the Police Commissioner of Berhampore—kicked me full on the mouth. I fell to the ground—'

'The sins of our ancestors!' Radharaman's voice trembled with anger, 'Our Mir Jafars and Jagat Seths. We are paying the penalty.'

'No Ghosh Moshai. Let us not blame the past. I came back and reported the matter to my brothers and other important men of Calcutta. They clicked their tongues in sympathy and looked mournful but no one would help me avenge my humiliation. I lodged a case against Hamilton but the judge was British too and he dismissed the case. Hamilton simply said that he hadn't kicked anybody and his statement was accepted. I took the matter to the press but the newspapers reported nothing. And do you know what my brothers did? They were so fearful of offending Hamilton that they sold that beautiful property for a song. Can such a race of cowards ever hope to rise?'

'Is that why you came away to Tripura?'

'Yes. I decided I could not live in British territory any longer. Tripura is the only independent state in—'

'I'm sure you've realized by now just how independent Tripura is.'

'At least it doesn't pay tax to the British. Ghosh Moshai! I have a resolution burning within me and I'll bring it to pass some day. I'll kick an Englishman in the face the way Hamilton kicked me. I don't care how long I have to wait. I'll do it before I die.'

'What a terrible thought! Don't attempt such a thing my friend. We'll be the first to clamp you in jail.'

Chatting thus on various subjects the two men passed the long days of the journey to Calcutta. Every evening, just before sundown, a clearing was selected, a tent hoisted and a fire lit to keep wild animals away. Ghosh Moshai fell asleep immediately after the evening meal but Shashibhushan stayed awake for hours smoking his cigar and listening to the sounds of the forest. A sudden flapping of wings as a snake made its way into a bird's nest; the distant roar of a tiger or the shrieking laughter of a hyena—all these entered his ears but his eyes were elsewhere. Scenes from the past flashed before them flickering and disjointed.

On the afternoon of the fourth day they reached a small *ganja* by the river. Here they were to start the second phase of their journey. Standing on the ferry ghat, his eyes on the row of boats tossing about like the loose husks of a banana flower on the current of Meghna, Shashibhushan thought of his first voyage out to Tripura. He had sailed down the Meghna on just such a boat. It had been a wild stormy afternoon with the river in spate. He had trembled with fear when the boatmen had called out to Allah to save their flimsy craft from being dashed to pieces in the sucking, seething waters.

The boat that they were to sail in was ready with their luggage stowed away safely. It awaited Ghosh Moshai who was buying some provisions for the journey. The *ganja* was crammed with people—touts and pimps, beggars in rows on each side of the road; gamblers sitting on strips of matting with their cards and dice; travellers awaiting their turn on the huge jewel boats that ferried people across. There were three shops selling everything from pestles and mortars to safety pins and two hotels standing side by side—one Hindu, the other Muslim. Behind them was a brothel.

Shashibhushan moved from shop to shop looking for a box of cigars but the shops of the *ganja* catered to the tastes of simple folk, not an aristocrat like him. It was a hot oppressive afternoon

51

and, fatigued with the exertions of the day, Shashibhushan decided to sit in the coolness of the boat and wait for Ghosh Moshai. But as he stepped into the boat he was overwhelmed by a strange sensation. He felt he had left something behind him; something very valuable. An urgency rose within him. He had to go back and look for it. Turning on his heel he walked rapidly back to the *ganja*. Though he didn't know what he was looking for, he did not waver or hesitate. He walked straight to the rows of beggars and looked around with keen eyes. A little distance away a youth sat under a *jarul* tree. His shaved head was smudged with clotted blood and he was stark naked except for the dirty rag that hung from his loins. He was so pitifully thin that Shashibhushan could count every bone in his frail rib cage. He was obviously demented for he kept nodding his head and singing to himself. 'Bird! Bird! Bird!' he sang in a shrieking falsetto. Shashibhushan examined his face closely and cried 'Bharat!' The boy stopped his song for a moment but not a flicker of recognition came into his eyes. He recommenced nodding and singing with the rhythmic regularity of a clockwork doll. Shashibhushan took the boy by the shoulders and shook him. 'Bharat!' he cried again. 'What are you doing here?' But still Bharat went on nodding and singing. Stooping, Shashibhushan picked him up in his arms and walked rapidly in the direction of the river.

Reaching the boat, Shashibhushan washed the blood and grime from Bharat's wounds and wrapped a clean dhuti around his emaciated frame. Then, mixing a bowl of chiré, curds and treacle, he fed him as tenderly as he would a child. Radharaman looked on in silence, then, when the boat was ready to sail, he said quietly, 'Take Bharat back to the ghat Shashi. He cannot go with us.' Shashibhushan stared at his impassive countenance for a while, then said in a wondering voice, 'Take him back to the ghat! What are you saying, Ghosh Moshai?'

'We have no choice Shashi. Don't forget that I'm travelling on a secret mission. Kumar Upendra wanted to come along but the Maharaja wouldn't let him. Tuck ten rupees into Bharat's waistband and let him go.'

'Impossible!' Shashibhushan exclaimed.

'Listen Shashi. Bharat's links with Tripura are broken. When the news of his disappearance came the Maharaja was not agitated in the least. "Good riddance," he said indifferently, "Feed a dog ghee and he'll vomit all over your floor." In that moment I knew that Bharat's days in Tripura were over.'

'But why?' Shashibhushan asked in a bewildered voice. 'What has the poor boy done? He is gentle and well mannered and has never involved himself in anything that was not his business.'

'Perhaps not. But someone has involved herself with him. The Maharaja is about to marry again. Did you know that?'

'The idea is preposterous. Rani Bhanumati has been dead only a fortnight.'

'It may be preposterous for people like you and me but kings do not follow the rules of commoners. He wishes to marry Monomohini.'

'Monomohini! But she's only a little girl. And the Maharaja is not a day below fifty. Besides, she's his neice. He should look upon her as a daughter.'

'Our sense of the proprieties is different from theirs.'

'Are you implying that the Maharaja engineered Bharat's disappearance?'

'I can't say. It might be the work of the Manipuris, that is Monomohini's brothers and uncles. But they couldn't have done it without the Maharaja's permission. It is, naturally, quite inconceivable that a future Mahadevi's name is linked with that of another man. You don't understand politics Shashi. Mahadevi Bhanumati is dead. Her son Samarendra was not declared heir. The Manipuris are like dry tinder ready to burst into flame. The only way the Maharaja can appease them is by marrying Monomohini. It is a marriage of convenience.'

'I'm glad I don't understand such dirty politics.'

'Even so, you must understand that the Maharaja has driven Bharat out like a dog though he is his own son. We are servants of the state. How can we give him our protection? Leave him to his fate. He will find a way to live if it is so ordained.'

'I can't abandon the boy Ghosh Moshai! Such an action will go contrary to all my principles. If there is no room for him in your boat I shall take another.'

'So be it,' Radharaman smiled blandly. 'I respect your high ideals Shashi. But if you can't part ways with the boy I'm

53

constrained to part ways with you. Go then. Choose a good boat
and instuct the *majhis* to row carefully. I can't wait any longer.'

At a signal from Radharaman the *majhis* lifted the sleeping
Bharat and, carrying him out of the boat, laid him on the bank.
Then the boat sailed away. Shashibhushan watched it till it faded
from sight and became one with the great heaving body of water.

Chapter VIII

Shashibhushan and Bharat spent the night in a dirty little hotel of the *ganja*. Next morning they travelled by boat to Kushthia and from there by train to Calcutta. Alighting at Sealdah station, Shashibhushan hired a hackney coach to take him to his ancestral home in Bhabanipur.

The mansion in Bhabanipur was a large one. Here his two brothers lived with their families in amity and concord. They had sold their estates some years ago and started a business in jute. Jute was in great demand owing to heavy export and the business had flourished beyond expectation. In addition, the second brother Manibhushan had opened a factory for the manufacture of gunny bags in partnership with the Armenians. With so much money and goodwill in the family it was inconceivable to many why Shashibhushan preferred to live in self-imposed exile in Tripura.

Arriving at mid morning, travel stained and weary, Shashibhushan took a long, cool bath washing away the grime and fatigue of the journey. Then, after a lavish sixteen-course meal served lovingly to him by his sisters-in-law, he made preparations to go out. As he stood before the mirror combing his hair his eldest sister-in-law Krishnabhamini came into the room. She held a silver box in her hand with paan in it. Her mouth was full of paan too and its juices, trickling over her lips stained them a bright, fruity red. She had a plump comfortable body and a homely face with big dabs of sindoor on the brow and in the parting of her thinning hair. 'Thakurpo,' she said without preamble, 'Aren't you ever going to marry again? I have to hide my face in shame before our relatives and friends.'

'*Arré*!' Shashibhushan exclaimed in surprise. 'Why do *you* have to hide your face? I'm the one who isn't marrying.'

'O *Ma*! Just listen to the boy's prattle! Am I not responsible for you? And isn't it natural for people to wonder why a fine, rich, well educated young man like you doesn't have a wife? Unless, of course, you've kept a mistress in Tripura.'

'Boudimoni!' Shashibhushan shook his head at her. 'Do you really believe I would—'

'No I don't. I tell everybody that my Thakurpo is like a diamond without a flaw. But I've had enough of your nonsense. I've decided to marry you to my Pishi's daughter. She's a lovely girl as sweet and pretty as an image of Lakshmi. You only have to see her once and you'll like her.'

Shashibhushan smiled. Manibhushan's wife Suhasini had made an identical suggestion just before the noon meal. She had arranged a marriage for him with her Mashi's daughter—another girl as pretty as an image of Lakshmi. He wondered wryly how many Lakshmis there were in this country. But it also left him mildly worried. If his sisters-in-law continued to pester him so he would find it difficult to live under their roof. On the other hand, going back to Tripura was ruled out after to his quarrel with Radharaman. He might have to look for some other accommodation.

Next morning, to his utter surprise, Radharaman came to see him. He looked elegant and foppish with his silver-headed cane in one hand and the frill of his exquisitely pleated dhuti in the other. His face was as calm and composed as if there had never been any friction between them. 'Well, Shashi,' he said in a perfectly natural voice,'When did you get here? How's the boy? Has a doctor seen him yet? By the way, have you found out how he managed to reach the *ganja?*'

In answer Shashibhushan led him upstairs to where Bharat was sitting nodding and jabbering to himself. '*Ei* Bharat!' Radharaman called out sharply,'Look at me. Who took you away that night? And where did they take you? Who shaved off your hair? Do you remember anything?'

'Bird! Bird! Bird!' Bharat shook his head more vigorously with every question till Radharaman gave up in despair. 'His brain is still heated,' he said at last. 'Take him to Doctor Mahendralal Sarkar. People say he's a *dhanwantari*, He'll surely find a cure.' Placing a hand on Bharat's naked skull he said gently, 'Don't be afraid my boy. Shashi will look after you and all will be well. Won't you offer me paan and a smoke Shashi? After all I'm in your house for the first time.'

Over the hospitality that followed, Radharaman coolly inserted the question, 'Are you planning to go back to Tripura?' Then, in response to Shashibhushan's look of surprise, he added, 'It will, naturally, not be possible or expedient for you to take Bharat along. There is a boarding house in Shimle which takes in boys for a fee of eighteen rupees a month. From what I hear the boys are cared for and educated reasonably well. You could send Bharat there. As for the fee we could split it between us. What is your opinion?'

'It sounds a good idea. Let me think it over.'

'Do that. The decision rests with you. Remember that if you wish to remain an official of the state of Tripura, I will not stop you. By the way . . . The mission on which I came out here has been successfully concluded. Its success, in fact, has gone beyond my expectations. But I have another task before me. The Maharaja asked me to call on the poet Robi Thakur and offer him some gifts in person. I'm on my way to Jorasanko now. Would you care to come with me?'

'Why not?' Shashibhushan cried joyfully. 'I have been curious to see the young poet for a long time now.'

'Wonderful! Let's go then.'

It was Shashibhushan's first visit to Jorasanko. In comparison with Bhabanipur, which was the village of Rasa Pagla slowly aligning itself to the city, Jorasanko was packed with people and its roads congested with traffic. Handsome buggies and stately landaus rolled regally past streams of hackney cabs and bullock carts. Serpentining their way through the crowds and vehicles, pedlars with baskets on their heads hawked their wares in resonant voices.

Alighting at the *deuri* Radharaman and Shashibhushan gazed at the handsome, imposing mansion with admiring eyes. Superior in size and splendour even to the royal palace of Tripura, it was humming with activity. The space between the gate and the main building was full of people. Officials of the estate, servants and maids, hawkers and hangers-on came and went in endless streams. On one side were the stables where five horses were being rubbed down by energetic grooms. On the other were the servants' quarters. Behind them an ancient banyan tree reared its head to the sky. A little knot of women with *gharas* at their hips

57

walked slowly towards the tank beyond. No one deigned to cast a glance at the two strangers. Hesitating a little, they crossed the yard and entered the building.

Walking into the first room, they found two men sitting on a *chowki* spread with a white sheet busily writing in long ledgers bound with red cloth. Stacks of papers and official looking documents were ranged around the walls. 'Namaskar,' Shashibhushan greeted them politely, 'We have come all the way from Tripura to meet Rabindra Babu. We have a message for him from the Maharaja.'

One of the men looked up. Tripura, obviously, meant nothing to him. 'Rabindra Babu,' he repeated thoughtfully. 'Who is Rabindra Babu?'

'Debendranath Thakur's youngest son. He is the author of *Bhagna Hriday*.'

'Oh! You mean Rob Babu,' The man understood at last. 'Is he here? Wait a minute. I'll send for him.' Walking up to a door on the left he shouted into the adjoining room. 'Haricharan! Go up and see if Rob Babu has returned. Two men have come to see him.' A disembodied voice from the next room took up the job by shouting in a hoarse voice, 'Raské! *Ei* Raské! Run upstairs and tell Rob Babu Moshai . . .' The message was passed on to another and then another in succession, the voices getting fainter and fainter as they travelled towards the upper regions where, his visitors presumed, Robi Babu dwelt.

Radharaman and Shashibhushan felt very uncomfortable. There were no chairs in the room and, having politely declined to sit on the *chowki*, they had no option but to remain standing. Time passed and neither man nor message came from within. Suddenly, one of the clerks raised a face from his ledger and said inconsequentially, 'Jyoti Babu Moshai and Natun Bouthan are in Chandannagar.' Radharaman and Shashibhushan couldn't make head or tail of this communication. 'We have come to see Rabindra Babu,' they repeated politely. The clerk, still writing busily, had no answer to that. After a long time a servant poked his head into the room. 'Rob Babu's door is locked,' he said casually, 'He has gone out of Calcutta.' Shashibhushan and Radharaman exchanged glances. But before either could say a word, a young man came bustling in. He was slender and

58

handsome and had an open, innocent face. 'Bhujangadhar,' he addressed one of the clerks,'Give me twenty rupees from my monthly allowance. I have to buy food for the street dogs.'

'Pardon me,' the man he addressed as Bhujangadhar answered quietly,'You've already drawn your allowance.'

'So?' The young man said with a touch of asperity. 'Shall the dogs starve because I've drawn my allowance? You can adjust the amount next month.' Then, turning to Shashibhushan, he asked curiously,'Where are you coming from Moshai?'

'We come as ambassadors from the Maharaja of Tripura.'

'Tripura! It nestles among the hills and no one can see it. And the kings eat pearl dust and diamond dust. Is all this true? But Baba Moshai is in Almora. You can't see him now.'

'We have a letter for Rabindra Babu.'

'Robi! Robi is only a child. What can you want with him? He has run away from England and is hiding in Chandannagar. Didn't you know that?

'He has written a book of poetry which—'

'Yes, yes.' The young man cut Shashibhushan short. 'Robi writes poetry. Good poetry. We get his books printed but no one buys them. Do you know who I am? I'm Robi's brother—Som. Don't you believe me? *Ohé* Bhujangadhar! Am I not Robi's brother—Som?'

'Yes. You are Som Babu Moshai.'

'I write poetry too,' the young man smiled sweetly at Shashibhushan. 'Robi sings well but I can sing even better. Would you like to hear me?' Then, bursting into song, he raised his arms above his head and started twirling round and round, stamping his foot to the beat. Gradually the twirling and stamping turned into a wild dance. Putting out his hands he seized Shashibhushan by the waist. 'Come, dance with me,' he urged. 'It will put a smile on your glum face. Dancing improves the temper.'

At this moment another man entered the room. He was portly, fair and good looking with well-cut features. 'Why Som! What are you doing?' he cried clutching the dancing Som by the shoulders. 'Don't you see there are strangers present?'

'I'm not doing anything,' Som whirled around. 'I was singing . . . I sing better than Robi, don't I Gunodada? And I asked them to dance because dancing is good for the health.'

59

'No Som,' Gunendranath said, gravely. 'One should not dance in public. Come let's go into the house.' Putting an affectionate arm round Somendranath's shoulders, he guided him gently out of the room.

Chapter IX

'Moran's Garden' in Chandannagar was a stately mansion so close to the Ganga that it created the illusion of having risen from it. A flight of stone steps, ascending from the water, merged into a wide and beautiful veranda and beyond it to an elegantly appointed salon. The rooms of the house were situated on different levels and of varying shapes and sizes. The windows of the salon were of stained glass in rich, dim old colours. Each depicted a separate scene executed by skilled craftsmen. One of them stood out the most from the others in its beauty. On a swing, dangling from the bough of a leafy tree, a pair of lovers sat side by side their faces turned to one another in enrapt empathy. A large garden laid out with flowering vines and bushes surrounded the house on three sides. Beyond it was an orchard with some fine, old fruit trees. Here, duplicating the scene in the salon, a real swing hung from a branch of a spreading mango tree. In front of the house a *bajra* swayed gracefully in the wavelets of the rushing Ganga. This was a private ghat and no other boat could cast anchor in these waters. The indigo trade having fallen on evil days, Moran Saheb was constrained to rent out the villa from time to time. Jyotirindranath Thakur and his wife Kadambari were its present occupants.

It was evening. The Ganga, rippling and shimmering like a sheet of silk, reflected a sky flushed with sunset. Boats, big and small, darted about on the waters, their sails catching the iridescent hues, like thousands of winged moths. On the steps of the ghat a young man with a tall, powerful frame, high nose, large dark eyes and wavy hair stood watching the scene and sipping tea from a porcelain cup with a silver handle. He was Jyotirindranath, sixth in line among Debendranath Thakur's fourteen children. Of all the latter's offspring Jyoti's personality was the brightest and most multifaceted. A keen sportsman, horseman and hunter, he was also an able administrator. In his father's absence it was he who was entrusted with the running of the estates. With all this he was also a fine litterateur and musician. He could play the violin and piano, write songs and set them to music. He was also a good playwright and his plays were often performed in professional theatres. Famed throughout Bengal he was the pride of the Thakur family and everyone had great hopes of him.

'Where is Robi? Why hasn't he come down?' Jyotirindranath turned to his wife who sat in one of the chairs scattered about in the garden. Kadambari Devi was a tall striking woman with handsome dark eyes, heavy brows and long lashes. There was something about the planes of her face and the proportions of her body that reminded one of a Greek goddess. In consequence her intimates in the Thakur household had devised the nickname Hecate for her. She had another name and that was Natun Bouthan. Athough many brothers and sisters had followed him, Jyotirindranath was addressed as Natun Babu or Natunda. Hence, his wife was Natun Bouthan. Kadambari Devi's hair was framed around her face in elaborate scallops after the fashion of the times. She wore a white silk sari over a blue velvet jacket with puffed sleeves. She, too, had a teacup in her hand. A book rested on her knees. 'Robi doesn't drink tea,' she answered in reply to her husband's query.

Robi's favourite haunt was a round room with glass windows that opened out on all sides. It was right on top of the house. Here he stole away whenever he could and wrote his verses. He heard his Jyotidada call out to him now and hastened to put away his papers. Then, skipping nimbly down the stairs, he came to the garden where his brother and sister-in-law awaited him. He was a shy lad of twenty. He wore a pleated dhuti and kurta embroidered in fine silk and vamped slippers on his feet. His hair was parted in the middle and combed neatly down on both sides. He had an open, innocent face with the faintest suggestion of down clinging to his cheeks and chin.

Robi had, recently, abandoned ship on his way to England leaving it even before it entered the territorial waters. Of all Debendranath's children the only one who had succeeded in making a living for himself was his second son Satyendranath. The others used their time and energy in spending their father's money. His sons-in-law were no exception. Unlike other families the Thakurs did not send their married daughters away. They kept them along with their husbands in the house. Debendranath spent most of his time away from Calcutta in the hills or in boats on the rivers that meandered all over rural Bengal. But with all his travelling he kept himself informed about everyone and everything in Jorasanko, through letters and messengers.

As of now, Robi was the youngest of Debendranath's children. A son, named Budh, had been born after him but had died in infancy. Two of Robi's elder brothers were insane and the others were whimsical and capricious. Disappointed in his older sons, Debendranath had pinned all his hopes on his youngest. He was convinced that, with his exceptional intelligence and robust health, Robi would do well in life. He could qualify as a barrister or pass the ICS examination like his brother Satyendra. That is why Debendranath sent Robi out to England at the age of sixteen, for the first time, sanctioning Rs 150 a month for his expenses. This was later raised to Rs 240—a princely sum even for England.

Robi spent a good part of his first year with Satyendranath's wife Gyanadanandini Devi who was in England at the time with her children Bibi and Suren. Then, after her return to India, he was left to his own devices. Taking up accommodation as a paying guest with an English lady, he enrolled himself in London University College. He was terribly homesick at first and found it hard to adapt to the country and climate. But, little by little he overcame these negative feelings and began concentrating on his studies. But, just as he started picking up the language and adjusting to his new life his father ordered him to return. The reason for the peremptory recall was that rumours had reached Deben Thakur's ears that Robi was getting too friendly with his landlady's daughters; that they sang and danced together, went on picnics and held planchette sessions in darkened rooms. Debendranath was also disturbed by the articles Robi sent regularly for a column entitled 'Letters from a Bengali youth in England' in *Bharati*. These articles, in Debendranath's opinion, were inflammatory and arrogant and struck at the roots of Bengali society and culture. One letter, in particular, titled 'Slaves in the Family' incensed Debendranath for in it Robi had lashed out at the insensitivity with which the older members treated their younger counterparts in Indian families.

63

In consequence Robi had to return. He had spent nearly two years in England, wasted a great deal of money and come back without a degree. But was it his fault? Yet everyone looked askance at him and asked pointed questions. Robi had made up his mind then that he would go out to England once again and study at the Bar. No matter how hard the struggle he would return with a degree, he had promised himself. He applied to his father for permission and it was granted. But this time Debendranath took the precaution of sending his eldest daughter Soudamini's son Satyaprasad with him. Satyaprasad was two years older than Robi and a very poor student having failed his exams several times. But he was a big step ahead of him in one way. He was a husband and father already. Consequently, he treated his young uncle with a mixture of affection and patronizing condescension. Satyaprasad was full of plans about what he would do on his return from England and he shared these generously with Robi during the first few hours of the journey. He would set up a practice in Sahebpara and take Robi on as his junior. He wouldn't work him too hard. He would leave him enough free time to write all the poetry he wanted. He would leave Jorasanko and rent a beautiful house, fit it up with every luxury suited to the status of a famous barrister etcetera etcetera. But, with the first cramp in his stomach, his plans were drastically altered. Moaning and groaning with every lurch of the ship he declared that he wasn't staying on the wretched boat to die of vomiting and purging. He would step ashore in Madras and make his way back to Calcutta and Robi would come with him. In vain did Robi try to make him see reason. Sea sickness, he explained over and over again, was a temporary condition and the nauseous feelings would pass. But Satya was not convinced. He declared he was dying of blood dysentery and he couldn't leave the world without seeing his beloved wife Narendrabala and his infant daughter for the last time.

The moment Satyaprasad stood on dry land and saw the boat sail away his sickness vanished. The truth was that he had realized that he would be miserable in England so far away from his wife and child. And, afraid of facing his grandfather's wrath, he had insisted on Robi's sharing the blame with him. 'Robi and I decided,' he told everyone coolly on their return to Jorasanko, 'that there was no point in going on to that *mlechha* country where people live on sandwiches and boiled mutton day after day and year in and year out. Bengalis have to have their hot rice with *musur dal* and *machher jhol* or they sicken and die. Thank God I had the sense to get off the ship in time.' And he had shuddered at the thought of his narrow escape from starving to death on sandwiches and boiled mutton.

Robi, though appalled at this falsehood, could not contradict him. His nature was such that while he was incapable of telling a lie himself, he was equally incapable of pointing it out in others. Besides, his sister Soudamini had been like a second mother to him and he did not have the heart to wound her. The best course of action, he reasoned, would be to lie low for a while. And that is why he had left Jorasanko and come to Chandannagar.

Here in Chandannagar each day floated by as light and airy as a butterfly's wing. No worries or tensions marred the bright beauty of the late autumn days. There was nothing to plan or execute and no one to fear. Robi could live as he wanted. He could wander about in the orchard with his Natun Bouthan and read poetry to her. He could go sailing on the river, pick fruit from the trees or, seating himself in the swing, hum a tune to himself for hours on end. And, if he wished, he could spend the whole day in the Round Room composing his verses.

Jyotirindranath had mastered the art of enjoyment and the three had wonderful times together. But he had to go away on business from time to time and than Robi and his Natun Bouthan were there for each other. Kadambari was only eighteen months older then Robi. She hadn't borne a child yet and because of that, perhaps, there was something youthful and unworldly about her. Her soul seemed untouched by mundane reality. Deeply sensitive to romance and beauty she sought them all the time; her yearning haunting her like a passion. And, strange though it may seem, this passion found a resting place in the person of her young brother-in-law. She reached out to the shy, sensitive boy and nurtured and cherished him as if he was her very own. Robi, on his part, could open up to her as he couldn't to anyone else.

Stepping into the garden, Robi found his Jyotidada giving some instructions to the *majhis*. 'Come Robi,' he said. 'I've decided we'll spend the whole night on the Ganga. The sky has never been so beautiful.'

'*Ki go!*' Kadambari smiled at her brother-in-law. 'You were locked up in your room all day! How much poetry have you written?'

'A little. But I've left a great deal unwritten. And that, I believe, is the real thing. I've been struggling all day to find those lines but someone casts a shadow over them and I can't see beyond it.'

Jyotirindra's boat was a two-roomed *bajra* with a square roof surrounded by a railing. Here he sat, violin in hand, on a Persian carpet his back resting against a velvet cushion. Robi and Kadambari sat facing him. As soon as the boat moved away from the shore Jyotirindranath touched the bow of his violin to the tautened strings making sky and river reverberate to the haunting melody of Raag Puravi. The sun had set but the west was luminous with streaks of gold even as the banks grew dim with twilight. And, as darkness came creeping on, other sounds came floating over the water mingling with the strains of Jyotirindra's music—a tinkling of bells from a faraway temple; the call of a muezzin, eerie and indistinct, from a distant mosque. Jyoti put down his violin and said,'Sing a song Robi.'

'Sing '*É ki é sundar shobha*,' Kadambari prompted.

'That is not Raag Puravi,' Jyotirindra smiled at his wife. 'It is Iman Bhupali Qawali and—'

'Never mind,' Kadambari cut him short. 'I want to hear it.'

Robi commenced singing, his eyes downcast. Jyotirindra poured himself a glassful of expensive French brandy and sipped it slowly. The moment the song came to an end Kadambari said, 'Sing another.' This time Robi did not wait for a request. Fixing his large, dark eyes on his sister-in-law, he sang a composition in Alaiya Jhanptal—*Tomaréi koriyachhi jeevan ér dhrubata tara, É samudré aar kabhu haba na ko patha haara*. 'It's barely dusk,' Jyotirindra laughed. 'The dhruba taara hasn't risen yet.'

The gold of the west was melting away little by little and the dark shadows of night crept slowly up the eastern horizon when, suddenly, a moon danced out from behind some clouds and flooded sky, earth and river in a torrent of molten silver. The boat floated on as if in a dream. Robi's young voice, throbbing with anguish, mingled with the yearning strains of his brother's violin.

Kadambari joined her voice to his from time to time swaying her head to the music. The three, wrapped in a mist of their own creation, had never known such ecstasy.

It was Jyotirindra who broke the spell. '*Oré!*' he called out to the *majhis*. 'We've come a long way. Turn the boat.' Kadambari's head shot up. 'So soon? But you've only just started on Behaag. I thought we would return with Bhairavi.' Jyotirindra smiled at his wife. 'What shall I play on our way back then? There is no raag after Bhairavi and I hate sleeping on a boat.'

Suddenly another whim seized Jyoti. 'We're close to Palta!' he exclaimed. 'Come Robi. Let's swim across to Gunodada's house. He'll be so happy to see us.'

Their cousin Gunendranath had bought a beautiful property at Palta and was living there with his wife and children. It was possible to row the boat to the front steps of the house but, looking on the vast expanse of swollen silvery water before him, Jyoti couldn't resist the temptation of plunging into it. 'Come Robi,' he repeated but Kadambari grasped Robi's arm and cried, 'No, Robi won't go. He won't.' Jyotirindra smiled. His wife didn't object too much to his undertaking anything hazardous. But she was overprotective of Robi. She wouldn't let him grow up.

After all-night revels such as this Jyotirindra and Kadambari slept soundly till long after daybreak. But Robi rose with the dawn and wandered about in the garden and by the side of the river. Whatever he saw–be it a flight of birds against a flame-coloured sky or an old man rubbing his back with a gamchha, it filled him with wonder. At such times he was overwhelmed by the thought that even the most trivial thing in the universe was imbued with a deep meaning. Only, it eluded him and the more he strained and agonized to give it expression in his verses the further it slipped away. Would he ever achieve fame as a poet? The thought haunted him day and night. He had authored four volumes of poetry. But, barring a few friends and relatives, no one bought his books. He knew, of course, that great poetry never won instant recognition. He would have to be patient. But was he on the right path?

Robi had achieved a measure of popularity in Calcutta and even beyond it. But it was for other things. He had a sweet voice,

67

supple and mellifluous, to which the passing years had added strength and clarity. He was also a fine actor. All the plays performed in Jorasanko had Robi in the lead role and the intellectual elite of the city flocked to see him. Reverend Keshto Banerjee had been lavish in his praise of Robi's performance in *Balmiki Pratibha* and had honoured him with the title of Balmiki Kokil. The young men of the city copied him in dress and manner. But cheap popularity of this kind could not satisfy Robi. Neither was he interested in making a mark as a singer or actor. Poetry was his first love and he wanted to be a great poet. He had written poetry from childhood upwards and rhyming words and phrases came easily to him. The trouble was that he couldn't strike the right note. Tragedy became pathos in his verses and ecstasy effusion. He was trapped in a cage of self and could not go beyond it. His poetry was too subjective. It lacked universality. Robi sensed this drawback and admitted it but he didn't know how to overcome it.

Robi's relations tried to encourage the boy with lavish praise. With one exception. Kadambari, to whom all his work was dedicated, was his sternest critic. She was always the first to read his poems, snatching the manuscript from his hand if he showed the slightest reluctance. But her comments were invariably adverse. 'Whatever you may say Robi,' she would smile and shake her head at her young brother-in-law, 'As a poet you are still far below the best. Your songs are passable but Biharilal's poetry is superior to yours.' Comparison with Biharilal Chakraborty always infuriated Robi. He would tear his verses to pieces and start all over again. Kadambari knew it and never stopped needling him in an effort to bring out the best in him. Robi, on his part, was driven by a fierce craving to win his sister-in-law's approval. He had tried emulating Biharilal's style in *Balmiki Pratibha* but was dissatisfied with the result. Surely there was some other way.

Though barely twenty, Robi had distinguished himself as a writer of prose. Unmarred by excessive alliteration and metaphorical elaborations, his language was neat, lucid, precise and incisive. There was logic in his arguments and humour and irony in his observations. His essays, ranging from subjects like World Literature, Music and Philosophy to Ancient History, Art,

Culture and Religion testified to the span and variety of his reading. Unfortunately, they brought him no fame for few were aware of his talent. The articles were printed anonymously in *Bharati*, and no one connected him with the fiery pieces that appeared week after week. Except, of course, for the few inmates of Jorasanko who knew his style and recognized it.

'O Robi!' Jyotirindranath exclaimed one morning at breakfast. 'I forgot to tell you. A man brought a letter yesterday evening. Two gentlemen from Tripura are coming to see you this morning.'

'Why?'

'How do I know? I've heard that the Maharaja of Tripura hires tutors from Calcutta. Maybe he wants you as tutor to his sons.'

'Robi a tutor!' Kadambari giggled. She was crocheting a square of lace with someone's name in the centre. Robi could discern two letters but was not sure what they were.

'Of course!' Jyoti exclaimed. 'I remember now. The Maharaja's name is Birchand. Or is it Bhiruchand? No, the kings of Tripura call themselves Manikya. Biru Manikya is the name. He has the grand design of keeping nine gems in his court—like Emperor Akbar. He has spirited Jadu Bhatta away from Bengal. Now it is your turn Robi.'

'I don't want to meet them.'

'Why not?' Kadambari cried. 'You'll be court poet. Think of the prestige. And we'll go to Tripura to visit you.' Robi fixed his eyes on his Natun Bouthan's face. There was pain in them and incomprehension.

'Of course you'll meet them,' Jyotirindra said. 'There's no harm in listening to their proposals. These native rajas are strange creatures. Some spend lakhs of rupees on a kitten's wedding; some marry five hundred women. Ghiyas-ud-din, Sultan of Mandu, kept fifteen thousand women in his harem. Even his bodyguards were women. Another raja, so I've heard, eats six parothas for breakfast fried in thirty seers of ghee. These fellows don't wage wars anymore so they don't need a defence budget. They blow up all the money of the state on their whims.'

'I'm going in,' Kadambari rose from her chair. 'The gentlemen will be here any moment now.'

'Why do you have to leave? Mejo Bouthan did not hesitate to meet the Viceroy. And you're afraid of a native king's ambassadors.'

'There are many things your Mejo Bouthan can do,' Kadambari replied striving to keep her voice under control,'which I can't. You know that very well.' And she walked away with her accustomed grace and dignity.

'Do you know what happened at the Viceroy's garden party Robi?' Jyoti asked turning his eyes away from his wife's departing back, 'Our kinsman Prasanna Thakur mistook Mejo Bouthan for Begum Sikander of Bhopal. Then, when he realized that she was a daughter-in-law of the Thakurs, he left the place in a huff.'

'Begum Sikander has named her daughter Shah Jehan, hasn't she?'

'Yes. She's very strong and masculine in looks and temperament. Though she's a Muslim aristocrat, she has shed the purdah.'

A few minutes later Radharaman and Shashibhushan came in followed by a servant carrying a basket of gifts. 'We've come to meet Rabindra Babu,' Radharaman said. 'Here he is,' Jyotirindra answered. 'This is my younger brother Robi.' The two men stared in amazement. They had heard that the poet was young. But so young? His face had the soft contours of a child and his eyes were luminous with innocence and trust. A shade of embarrassment came into them at Radharaman's greeting. 'O Poet!' the latter cried in sonorous tones, 'Most humbly and respectfully we present ourselves at the behest of his Royal Majesty Sreel Srijukta Birchandra Manikya, Maharaja of Tripura and bring to you the message that he has been deeply moved by your book of verse *Bhagna Hriday* and has sent you, as a token of his appreciation, a few gifts and a citation.'

'That's wonderful,' Jyotirindra exclaimed. 'It means Robi's fame has spread beyond Bengal to other states.'

Radharaman read out the citation and proceeded to tell the poet of the circumstances in which the Maharaja had read *Bhagna Hriday*. Robi felt his heart lift with triumph. If his verses could bring consolation to even one soul in grief there must be some good in them. And the man was no ordinary man. He was a king and a connoisseur of poetry.

After the messenger's had departed Jyoti said curiously, 'Let's see what the king has sent. Open the basket Robi.' Taking the cover off they found a shawl, a pair of dhutis and two ivory figurines wrapped in a piece of silk. Nestling underneath these presents was a small velvet pouch with five gold coins in it. 'Not bad,' Jyotirindra laughed, 'though one can hardly call it royal munificence.'

An hour later, after Jyotirindranath had left for Calcutta, Robi went into the house to look for his Natun Bouthan. But she was not to be found in any of the rooms. Then, wandering all over the grounds, he found her in the orchard sitting on a patch of grass her back resting against the trunk of a jackfruit tree. Her eyes, gazing out on the river, had a blank, dazed expression. 'Natun Bouthan,' Robi called softly. Kadambari turned her face towards him but did not speak. Robi's heart sank. He had expected her to turn eagerly to him; to ask a hundred questions; to read the citation and look excitedly through the gifts laughing and teasing him all the while.

'The Maharaja of Tripura has read *Bhagna Hriday* and liked it,' he said, adding shyly,'He has sent two of his officials to offer me a citation and some presents. Aren't you pleased?'

'Why shouldn't I be?' Kadambari replied indifferently. 'Everyone who knows you will be happy at your success.' A shadow fell over Robi's face. '*Bhagna Hriday* is yours,' he said in a pleading voice. 'If anyone deserves the citation it is you.'

'Nonsense.'

'Won't you look through the presents?'

'I will, later.' Kadambari rose and walked towards the house. 'Is anything wrong?' Robi followed her. 'Are you unhappy about something?' 'No,' Kadambari sighed and shook her head. 'There is nothing wrong.'

'Why were you packing me off to Tripura? Were you trying to get rid of me?'

'I don't have to. You'll go anyway. Your work will become more brilliant by the day and your fame will reach the ends of the earth. The wide world will claim you for its own. How can I hope to keep you to myself? And why should I?'

'I'll never leave you. Be sure of that.'

'No Robi. I'm nothing—nothing. You'll find other people

71

more worthy of reading your poems for the first time.'

'Don't talk like that. I can't live away from you. You're everything to me.'

'But you went away to England last year leaving me alone in Jorasanko. Your Natunda is so busy—he has no time for me. I was so lonely. I felt like a prisoner locked up in my room—'

'I thought of you all the time and everything I wrote was for you. The poems of *Bhagna Hriday* are all yours.'

Kadambari stood quietly for a few minutes, her face buried in her arm. Then, suddenly changing her voice and manner, she said 'Oh yes, I wanted to ask you something. Why is the dedication to *Srimati Hé*'?'

'It was meant for you.'

'You shouldn't have done that!'

'No one will guess the truth. You're Hemangini. You're Hecate. Only the two of us know that.'

'That's what you think. I was Hemangini and you were Alik in the play *Alik Babu*. A lot of people have seen it. Besides, everyone knows you call me Hecate.'

'Let people think what they will. I shall write as I please.' A note of joy crept into Robi's voice. Kadambari's mood had changed. A little smile was flickering at the corners of her mouth. He ran into the house and came back with the bundle of gifts to find Kadambari rocking herself gently from the swing and humming a little tune. Seating himself on the grass he took out the purse of gold and touched it to her feet. Then, placing the ivory figurines on her lap, he said, 'They're yours Devi. Everything I have is yours.'

'I don't want anything,' Kadambari lowered her face till it was on a level with his. 'Bhanu,' she whispered, 'Sing a song for me.'

The days passed, thus, one by one. Jyotirindranath had started a new business and was working day and night. He embarked on one project after another with tremendous enthusiasm only to lose a great deal of money each time. He was away for long stretches and Robi and Kadambari were left to themselves. They spent hours together reading poetry, singing and chasing one another around the garden. When Kadambari sat swinging by herself Robi picked armfuls of flowers and leaves and twined them around the ropes till the swing became a leafy bower. When they neither sang nor talked nor played they sat gazing into one another's eyes and their silence held a special meaning. In the evenings they sat on the steps of the river, their feet in the water, their eager eyes scanning the boats that went swaying past. Could that be Jyotirindra's boat? But, more often than not, they were disappointed. Jyotirindranath did not return.

Winter passed into spring and spring gave way to summer. And now it was the month of Ashadh. Thick dark clouds started massing over the horizon and heavy rain pelted down on the river that swelled and foamed with swift currents. Robi and Kadambari had never been happier. Sometimes a storm broke over their heads taking them by surprise. Then they ran, hand in hand, through the trees like a couple of children, their hearts pounding with fear at the sound of the thunder. But how sweet was the fear! Laughter bubbled up from within and poured out of their throats, the happy sounds mingling with the swish of swaying branches and the sweet patter of raindrops on the leaves.

One day something happened that Robi was to remember all his life. It was the middle of the morning. Robi had locked himself in the Round Room and was writing with intense concentration. He had just completed seven pages of a new novel, then taken a break to write a couple of poems in Braja Bhasha. Robi had written several poems of this kind under the pseudonym Bhanu Singh. These were in the style of his current favourite–the poet Vidyapati. Kadambari loved Vidyapati's verses and addressed Robi as Bhanu when they were alone together.

Taking up his novel once more Robi discovered that he was hungry. And, at that moment, he suddenly remembered that they had planned a picnic in the woods that morning. Kadambari was to cook under the trees and he and Jyotidada were to sing to her. Leaving his papers scattered about, he ran in the direction of the spot they had chosen. A strange sight met his eyes. Under a spreading roseapple tree Kadambari waited, her face as stark and immobile as the marble stool she sat on. A clay oven, arranged with kindling but unlit, stood in front of her and mounds of rice, dal, spices and vegetables lay scattered about. There was no sign of Jyotirindranath.

Robi's heart missed a beat. Kneeling at her feet he brought his palms together and said in a pleading voice. 'Forgive me,

73

Bouthan. I was so caught up in my writing that I forgot about our picnic. Why didn't you send for me?' Kamabari looked at him with stony eyes but did not speak a word. Robi ran into the house to call his Jyotidada but the servants told him that Natunbabu had left the house at dawn. No one knew when he would return. Now Robi was truly frightened. Natun Bouthan was very sensitive and easily hurt. She was also prone to deep depressions. At such times she withdrew into a shell refusing to communicate with anybody. A few months back she had, in a depressed state, tried to take her own life.

Returning to Kadambari he took her feet in his hands and, drawing them to his breast, begged her to forgive him. But Kadambari withdrew her feet without a word and, rising, walked into the forest. Robi followed her. 'I'll never hurt you again Natun Bouthan,' he begged. 'I promise. Only forgive me this time.'

Suddenly, it started raining, the water falling in large drops over their heads and faces. And then the shower became a torrent, drenching them to the skin. Kadambari stood under a tree her body shaking with sobs. The tears pouring down her face mingled with the raindrops and pattered silently down to her feet.

'Robi,' she called softly.

'What is it Natun Bouthan?' he whispered

Kadambari's lips moved but no words came. Robi gazed on her face like one transfixed. It had a strange, ethereal beauty. Surely no mortal could look like that 'Devi! Devi!' he cried out in ecstasy. Kadambari's eyes, pained and bewildered like those of a bird robbed of her nest, gazed into his. '*É bhara bhaadar,*' she murmured, '*Maaha bhaadar. Shunya mandir mor.* Can you sing it to me Robi? Do you know the tune?'

Robi hummed under his breath for a minute, then setting the words to the haunting melody of Misra Malhar, he started singing it in an impassioned voice.

Hand in hand they stood in the rain, wind and thunder as Robi sang.

Chapter X

As he descended the stairs one morning Shashibhushan was assailed by a strange sensation. He felt the walls go round and round as if the world was spinning furiously around him. Clutching at the stair rail he shut his eyes. He wondered if this was an earthquake. But, if it was, why was there no commotion and no blowing of conches? Hindus blew conches at such times to appease the snake God Vasuki who held the earth on his head. Shashibhushan took a few cautious steps then, without any warning, his arm was wrenched free of the protecting rail and he fell headlong down the steps to lie in a crumpled heap on the floor.

Though he lay inert Shashibhushan had not lost consciousness. His head throbbed violently and he felt as though millions of needles were being jabbed into his brain. What was happening to him? Was he dying? He couldn't bear the agony and tried to call out but his throat was dry and no sound came. And then his eyes, burning with pain and heavy as stones, beheld a strange sight. A girl stood before him; a young girl with tip tilted eyes and long thick hair that hung to her knees like a sheet. She held a bunch of white flowers in her hand. He wondered if she was real or a product of his fevered brain. If she was no illusion, where had she come from? The front door was closed and she hadn't come down the stairs. She could be a maid of the house but, if so, why had he never seen her? The girl bent over him bringing her face close to his and, looking into those long melting eyes, Shashibhushan fainted.

Shashibhushan was dangerously ill for the next few days. His brothers filled the house with doctors who tried every possible remedy. But it looked as though he was slipping away. The biggest problem was that he could not be fed anything at all. He retched and vomited incessantly bringing up even the few drops of water that were poured down his throat. His loving brothers saw him wasting away before their eyes. His emaciated body was as white as the sheets on which he lay and his voice was as feeble as a bird's. Dr Charles Gordon managed to keep him alive by a superhuman effort. But for how long? This thought was in the minds of everyone especially his sisters-in-law who nursed him with tears in their eyes. Krishnabhamini had great faith in homeopathy and nagged her husband to send for Dr Mahendralal Sarkar. But he was away in Bardhaman attending the Maharaja. A messenger was despatched with an urgent summons and was, even now, on his way.

Shashibhushan lay in a coma for days broken by small intervals of consciousness. At such times his mind was alert and awake and his eyes unclouded. But he felt as if he was floating on air; as if he had no body. His mind was clear but his limbs were inert and he felt neither hunger nor thirst. He knew he was dying. He would die the moment his heart stopped beating and that time was not far off. Tears of weakness coursed down his sunken cheeks as he thought of his happy days in Tripura. He had left everything behind—his books and his expensive cameras. Who would take care of them when he was gone?

One night he had a strange experience. It must have been well past midnight for the street noises had ceased and the house was perfectly still. The door to his room was open and, in the dim light that came from a lamp burning in one corner, he discerned a sleeping shape on a grass mat on the floor. It was a maid or a servant, he knew. Ever since his illness his sisters-in-law had insisted on someone sleeping in his room.

He lay awake for a while listening to the faint sound of breathing that filled the room. Then something happened that almost made him sit up with shock. A woman came through the door into his room and, walking past the sleeper, came straight up to his bed. A tinkling sound accompanied her movements. As she drew near he discovered that it came not from her anklets but from the bunch of keys that hung from her waist. The woman was plump and matronly. She wore a white sari of garad silk with a broad red border and her forehead was marked with a large circle of sindoor. Tears ran down her face and her body shook with sobs. Shashibhushan recognized her. She was his mother.

'Ma,' Shashibhushan whispered, 'why do you weep?'

'Bhushu,' she cried in a choking voice. 'What is this I see? My beautiful boy reduced to a handful of bones! All the blood has left your golden limbs. Oh my darling child! Why do you suffer so?'

'I can't eat anything Ma. I'm dying.'

'Hush my son,' She stroked his forehead with tender fingers as she used to in his childhood. He was her youngest child—her baby.

'Have you come to take me away with you Ma?' he asked, his hand clinging to the stroking fingers.

'Don't ever say such a thing,' the apparition trembled. 'All will be well. Tell them in the kitchen to roast some raw bel and make a sherbet with the pulp. Drink it. It will bring the taste back to your mouth. Then you can have a bowl of soft rice gruel.' Even as she said these words her voice grew faint and her form receded in wave upon wave of darkness. Shashi knew he was slipping away again. 'Ma! Ma!' he tried to cry out, 'Don't go.' The last thing he remembered before he fainted was the cool clinging of his mother's fingers and the faint fragrance of her hair. After that—oblivion.

When he recovered consciousness the room was empty and the sheets were soaking wet with perspiration. But, strangely, the limbs that had been immobile all these days now obeyed his bidding. He turned over on the other side quite effortlessly. His heart pounded furiously. His mother had died seventeen years ago when he was a mere boy. Yet the hand that he had held was warm and moist—a hand of flesh and blood. He took a deep breath. The faint fragrance of her still hung upon the air. Shashi shut his eyes to ward off the panic rising in him. His temples had started throbbing again and his throat felt dry. 'Water,' he called out hoarsely,'A little water.' The words had barely left his lips when a *jhinuk* of cool water was held to them. He opened his eyes and got another shock. A face was poised above his—not his mother's but that of the young girl he had seen the day he fell. The eyes that looked into his were dark and tender and the long hair framing her face fell in silken strands on his sheet. Was this a dream too? But he could feel the water trickling down his throat and his mouth felt cool and moist.

Next morning when his sister-in-law came into the room with his breakfast of sago and milk he raised a feeble hand and waved it away. 'Bring me a sherbet of raw *bel*,' he said, adding, 'Make

77

sure it is roasted first.' This presented no difficulty for there were several bel trees in the back garden and they were laden with fruit. When the sherbet arrived he drained the silver glass to the last drop. Next day he could swallow a bowl of gruel.

As his body recovered by degrees his mind grew clearer and sharper. He spent hours mulling over his experience of that night. He had seen not one vision but two. One was that of his dead mother. There were some who believed that the soul was immortal. Even if one were to grant that—surely the physical was not. The sari his mother had worn in life, her bunch of keys; even the thick gold bangles that now adorned the arms of his eldest sister-in-law—how had they returned in their original form? Could it be that those who professed to have seen ghosts or even gods and goddesses were not liars after all? Ramkrishna, the priest at the temple of Dakshineswar, claimed that he saw Ma Kali and even talked and laughed with her. Shashibhushan had dismissed his claims with the contempt it deserved. But now he was not so sure. Keshab Sen, he reflected, must have passed through a similar experience. Else, how had the burning flame of the Brahmo Samaj fallen under the spell of Ramkrishna? On Shashibhushan's return from Tripura he had heard that Keshab Babu had turned his back on all reason and logic and was at the beck and call of the rustic priest. Keshab Babu and his followers, Shashibhushan reasoned, must have put Ramkrishna to a severe test and been satisfied with the result.

Shashibhushan was able to sit up but was still not strong enough to stand without support when Dr Mahendralal Sarkar came to see him. Mahendralal was big and hefty in build and sported a pair of moustaches as thick and fierce as that of a Kabuli cat. He had begun his career as an allopath standing first in the MD examination. A confirmed atheist he had, in his youth, upheld the rational and the scientific and rejected gods, ghosts and homeopathy with unconcealed scorn. He had even founded a society called the Indian Association for the Cultivation of Science. Then, suddenly, at the height of his career, he had turned to homeopathy and was now its leading practitioner.

Mahendralal had been initiated into homeopathy by the great Rajen Datta himself—he who had cured Ishwarchandra Vidyasagar, Raja Radhakanta Deb and the Maharaja of Jaipur earning their gratitude for life. Radhakanta Deb had offered him a sum of twenty-five thousand rupees but Rajen Datta had refused it. He came from a very wealthy family of Taltala and didn't need the money. Besides, as he said, the fact that homeopathy had established itself as a viable alternative to allopathy was, in itself, his reward. Mahendralal's involvement with homeopathy had started as a challenge. He had set out to study its basics in order to be able to refute its claims with greater authenticity. But the more he studied the science the more it interested him. And, then, he turned to it altogether.

Mahendralal's decision sent shock waves through the medical circles of Calcutta. He was threatened with expulsion from the Bengal branch of the British Medical Association and his roaring practice sank to a whimper. But Mahendralal bided his time and, gradually, his old patients returned one by one.

Now his chambers were more crowded than those of any other doctor in the city. Keshab Sen and Mahendralal Sarkar—advocates of reason as opposed to blind faith-had been Shashibhushan's gurus in his youth. But now both had fallen from their pedestals. One was clashing cymbals and singing kirtans in a Hindu temple and the other had become a disciple of Hahnemann. Shashibhushan was appalled. What was homeopathy, after all, but glorified guess work? Some diseases left the body by a process of natural remission and the homeopaths took credit for it. The irony was that he, himself, had been brought to such a pass that he was hoping to be cured by a system in which he had no faith. It was doubly ironical that the treatment was to be meted out by none other than the erstwhile high priest of Reason.

The floor quaked under the heavy boots of the great doctor as he came up the stairs. Reaching the landing he turned to Manibhushan and asked sharply,'What is that noise? Where is it coming from?' Manibhushan smiled. 'From our puja room,' he replied. 'Our priest is making the customary offering to the family deity.' Mahendralal glanced down at his kerchief the tip of which could be seen peeping out of the breast pocket of his dun coloured coat. He drew another out of his trouser pocket and wiped the perspiration from his balding crown. 'Is your house always as noisy as this?' he asked sternly. 'We are Vaishnavs,'

79

Manibhushan replied taken aback, 'and must partake of prasad before sitting down to the midday meal. Today, of course, a special puja is being conducted for Shashi—'

'Stop it,' Mahendralal thundered. 'Stop it at once. My ear drums are fit to burst. I shudder to think of what the poor patient is going through.' Then, fixing his eyes on Manibhushan's startled face, he added, 'If you can't or won't I'll leave at once.' He turned around and began walking away. Manibhushan followed him begging abjectly, 'Please rest a while and have some paan and a smoke. The arati will be over in half an hour and—'

'I neither smoke nor eat paan when visiting a patient. I'll wait here for two minutes. Go to your puja room and get the infernal din stopped. At the end of two minutes I'll leave.'

A servant was hastily despatched with the message. The priests were loath to stop the arati and abused the man roundly. But the moment they heard that Dr Mahendralal Sarkar was in the house they trembled in apprehension. They had heard that the man was a vile heretic who did not hesitate to march into puja rooms with boots on and manhandle the priests. 'Stop the gongs and conches,' the head priest commanded. 'We will go on with the mantras. Keep your voice down or that blaspheming rogue will hear us.'

'Good riddance!' the doctor exclaimed as soon as the clamour ceased, 'Now let me have a look at the patient.' Entering the sickroom, however, he lost his temper again. 'Clear the room,' he ordered, 'There are too many people here. Open the doors and windows. Don't you know that the sick need fresh air? Ugh! This room hasn't been cleaned in ages. What is that glass of stale milk doing in the meat safe? And the dirty plates on the floor? Have them taken away at once. Has no one told you that a bedpan must be kept under the bed?' Coming up to Shashi, he placed a hand on his head and asked in a voice that had miraculously become soft and gentle. 'Where is the pain my boy? Here?' Then waving away the vast throne like chair that had been brought for him to sit on, he said, 'You come from Tripura. Are there mosquitoes there?'

'Lots of mosquitoes,' Shashi answered.

'The water of mountain streams is often infected. Do people suffer from stomach trouble in Tripura?'

'Yes. Many of them do.'

'Have you ever had a serious illness? When has a doctor last seen you?'

'I enjoy good health as a rule. The last time a doctor attended me was fifteen years ago.'

'Have you ever had an accident?'

'I fell off my horse once. I was a boy of twelve then.'

Mahendralal took Shashibhushan's wrist between his thick fingers and, shutting his eyes, seemed to go off into a trance. Then he examined, one by one, Shashibhushan's eyes, tongue, arms and legs, tapping at the joints with his knuckles. After the examination was over he called for warm water to wash his hands. 'The crisis is over,' he said abruptly, 'The boy will live. The attack was a bad one and could have damaged the brain. But, mercifully, all is well.' Glancing at the books on the shelf he said to Shashibhushan, 'You read Herbert Spencer, I see. Have you read Kant?'

Manibhushan had been fiddling with a purse in his pocket all this while. Now, as the doctor rose to leave, he drew it out. 'My fee is thirty-two rupees,' Mahendralal said. The two brothers exchanged glances. The best of allopaths charged sixteen rupees a visit. A homeopath, they had thought, would be much cheaper. The doctor looked from one face to another and said brusquely, 'You don't have to pay me now. I'm leaving some medicine which the patient will take for the next three days. He'll be up and about by then and must report to my chamber on the fourth day. If he is unable to do so you needn't pay a paisa. Mahen Sarkar doesn't take money without effecting a cure.'

As the doctor moved towards the door Shashibhushan cried out, 'Doctor Babu! May I ask you a question?'

'You may,' the doctor replied turning back. 'A doctor is obliged to answer his patient's questions.' Shashi turned pleading eyes on his brothers. 'Will you leave the room please,' he begged. After they had left, Mahendralal shut the door and came up to the bed. 'I thought I was dying,' Shashi burst out as if in desperation. 'I couldn't breathe. I couldn't eat. Then my mother came to me. She said I was to have bel sherbet and soft rice gruel. I feel much better—'

'Very well. Eat whatever you like. All food is good if the body doesn't reject it. Besides, mothers know what is good for their children.'

81

'You don't understand. My mother's been dead these seventeen years. Yet she came to me. You examined me doctor, am I going mad?'

'No. I found no trace of insanity. And your speech is perfectly coherent.'

'I can't talk about it to anyone. They'll dismiss it as a dream. But I saw her as clearly as I see you now. I touched her—'

'What of it?' Mahendralal said comfortably. 'You've seen your mother. You're the better for it. Let's leave it at that.'

'Can the dead come back to life?'

'No,' Mahendralal's voice was firm. 'No one, not even God can raise the dead. But the human mind has strange and unlimited powers. It can create everything out of nothing. When the desire is strong enough, even the dead can be seen and touched.' Patting Shashi gently on the head the doctor rose to leave. 'I have a theory on the subject,' he said, 'which I would like to share with you. But not in your present state. Come to me when you are fully recovered and we'll have a long chat. And, for the present, carry on with the diet the ghosts have prescribed. It has done you good.'

Dr Mahendralal's medicine had the effect he had anticipated. Within three days Shashibhushan was able to walk about freely and eat his meals with enjoyment. What was more the old urge to read returned. His brothers sent for all the latest papers and journals. Shashibhushan threw aside the *Englishman* and took up the *Indian Mirror* instead. But what intrigued him most were the journals of the Brahmo Samaj. He was appalled at the state into which the Samaj had fallen. Debendranath Thakur had loved Keshab Sen as one of his own sons. Yet Keshab had broken away from the Adi Brahmo Samaj and formed an association of his own called Naba Bidhan the chief activity of which was his own self projection. In consequence a third group had come into being under the leadership of Shibnath Shastri. Revolted by Keshab's behaviour, Shibnath never lost an opportunity to point out the former's contradictions and retrogressions. Keshab, who had made burning speeches against child marriage, had recently married his own ten-year-old daughter to a prince of Coochbehar. That too by Hindu rites. It was rumoured that Keshab was advocating a return to idol worship. He had put up a flag in the Brahmo prayer hall before which arati was performed every evening and at the foot of which every Brahmo was expected to knock his head in homage. Shashibhushan tossed the paper away in disgust.

One morning as Shashi sat up in bed, his back resting against the pillows and a newspaper propped up before him, he saw a girl holding a bunch of white flowers run past the door. Shashi trembled and his heart beat so rapidly that he was compelled to hold his chest tight with his arms. This was the same girl he had seen on two occasions. Calming himself with an effort he thought 'Am I going mad? Or is there a rational explanation?' At that moment Krishnabhamini came in with a glass of sherbet. Shashibhushan decided to take the bull by the horns. 'Boudimoni,' he asked, 'I saw a girl running down the veranda just now. Who is she?'

'Why that was Bhumi!' Then, seeing the puzzled expression on her brother-in-law's face, she added, 'Don't you know Bhumi? She's been looking after you in your illness.'

'Call her in. I want to see her.'

The girl came shyly to the door and stood there her eyes downcast. Shashi stared at her. She had a strange compelling beauty. Her body, draped in a plain red bordered white sari, was slim and supple as a young bamboo and her golden face gleamed as though burnished with gurjan oil. She held a bunch of white camellias to breast. Shashibhushan's heart leaped up with relief. She was real. At least one of the women he had seen had not been a vision. 'Why does she always carry white flowers in her hands?' he murmured almost to himself.

'She picks flowers for the morning puja and decorates the puja room. That is the work apportioned to her.' Krishnabhamini replied.

Now Shashi turned to the girl. 'Who are you?' he asked. 'What is your name?'

'My name is Bhumisuta Mahapatra,' the girl answered shyly but clearly. At this point Krishnabhamini took upon herself the task of enlightening her brother-in-law. A year and a half ago, she said, when Manibhushan and Suhasini went on a pilgrimage to Puri they came upon the girl near the temple of Jagannath. Her parents had just died of cholera and her uncle had sold her to a *panda* to use as a devdasi. Coming upon the scene by accident they saw the old man dragging her by the hair while she resisted with all her strength. Suhasini's heart was filled with pity. Paying the *panda* the sum he had parted with, she brought the girl to this house. Bhumisuta performed odd tasks about the house but she, Krishnabhamini said, was no ordinary maid. She came from a good family, was well educated and extremely intelligent.

From that day onwards Shashibhushan found himself watching Bhumisuta and looking out for her. He would stand on the balcony outside his room at dawn looking out into the garden. She would come, sooner or later, her basket on her arm. She would move from bush to bush picking the choicest, freshest blooms—jasmine, camellias and tuberoses. At such times she looked like a flower herself. Her sari was a spotless white and her face, framed in its halo of hair, was like a newly opened lotus. Shashi was charmed by the scene and longed to capture it on camera. How would it be, he thought, if she could be persuaded to wear a colourful sari? He could not, quite naturally, focus from the balcony. He would have to set his camera in the garden. He decided that, when he was a little stronger, he would take a picture of Bhumisuta.

Chapter XI

Robi ran lightly down the steps and round the house into the garden where Kadambari waited. She had just had her bath and her wet hair fell in long strands over her back and shoulders. A pale blue sari was draped over a simple white chemise. Her beautifully moulded arms were bare of ornament but a large, flawless diamond glittered from the middle finger of her left hand. Her feet were bare and her hands were full of *bakul*. She looked up shyly at her young brother-in-law. 'See Robi,' she said holding out her hands, 'How lovely they smell.' Robi came close to her and buried his nose in the flowers. Mixed with the scent of the newly opened *bakul* was her own distinctive fragrance.

'Look up at that tree,' Kadambari pointed a finger. 'It is covered with blooms. They fly about like tiny white stars before falling to the ground. Climb up and get me some from the top.'

'What will you do with so many?'

'I'll string them into garland and put it around someone's neck.'

'Whose?'

'Yours.' Kadambari gave a little giggle. 'You'll be king for a day.'

'I'll need a throne.'

'That can be arranged. What sort of throne would you like?'

'What better throne can I ask for than someone's heart.'

'Shh! You talk too much.' Kadambari flashed her eyes at him and continued. 'We'll stay in the garden all day. Look at that sky. See how it is darkening with cloud! It is an ideal day for spending out of doors. I won't let you mess about with pen and paper today. You'll be a *rakhal raja* and sing and play the flute. That will be a lovely game.' She turned to him eagerly as she spoke her cheeks flushed and her eyes bright. But there was no answering glow in Robi's eyes as he said solemnly, 'You play with me as if I were a doll Natun Bouthan.' A shadow passed over Kadambari's face. She stood immobile for a few seconds looking at him, her

85

eyes dark with pain and bewilderment. Then, opening her palms, she let the flowers fall to the ground. Averting her face she murmured to herself,'He sleeps till eleven, then rushes off to the theatre. The actors and actresses need him and he needs them. But don't I need anything? Anyone? Who shall I turn to Robi?'

Robi stood in abashed silence. It was true that Jyotidada had become very busy of late and was practically living in Calcutta. He was even thinking of moving out of Chandannagar and going back to Jorasanko. Natun Bouthan felt neglected. But men were like that. In wealthy households such as his, wives rarely saw their husbands except at night and that too not often. The younger generation of men, educated in the notions of the West, were pushing their wives out of purdah and bringing them within the mainstream of their lives. These women had tasted freedom and known the companionship of their husbands and were loath to go back to their lives of loneliness. It was a modern day dilemma. In an attempt to change the subject and woo his sister-in-law back to her earlier happy mood, Robi picked a handful of *kadam* and brought them to her. 'See Bouthan,' he said. 'The first *kadam* flowers of the rains.'

'They aren't the first,' Kadambari replied indifferently. 'They've been here for quite some time. The trees are covered with blossom.'

'They are my first. And they are for you. Take them.'

Kadambari took the cluster of golden globes in her hands and seated herself on the swing. 'Come and sit by me Robi,' she invited. Robi obeyed and the two sat silent for a while the swing moving gently to and fro. Kadambari seemed lost in her own thoughts but Robi felt uneasy. He kept looking at the sun and trying to gauge the time. 'Bouthan!' The words came out in a rush. 'I have to leave you now. We'll spend the whole of tomorrow in the garden together.'

'You wish to go back to your writing?' She asked gently, sensing his embarrassment. 'Which one? *Bouthakuranir Haat*? Or have you started a new poem?'

'I have to go to Calcutta.'

'Why?' Her brows came together in annoyance. 'You shan't go. I won't let you.'

'I must,' Robi cried desperately. 'I've given my word.'

86

'To whom? Why didn't you tell me?'

'You know, don't you, that Rajnarayan Bosu's daughter Lilavati is to be wed. I've been asked to compose two songs for the occasion. I'm to go today and teach them to the singers.'

'Why don't you sing them yourself?'

'Because Baba Moshai has forbidden me to go to the wedding.'

'Forbidden you!' Kadambari exclaimed, amazed. 'Rishi Moshai's daughter is to be wed and you can't go! Think how it will hurt him. He loves you so much.'

'Rishi Moshai won't attend either.'

The truth of the matter was that Lilavati's chosen husband Krishna Kamal belonged to the third group of Brahmos—those who had broken away from Keshab Sen's Naba Bidhan and formed an association called the Sadharan Brahmo Samaj under the leadership of Shibnath Shastri. The Civil Marriage Bill having been passed a few years ago, these young Brahmos preferred a registry marriage to any other form infuriating the elderly members of the Adi Brahmo Samaj who, led by Debendranath Thakur, denounced civil marriages as godless and heretical. A union which did not invoke the blessings of Param Brahma, they maintained, was no union at all. When Debendranath heard that Krishna Kamal and Lilavati were also to be married by registry he withheld his consent. Rajnarayan Bosu, though equally distressed, bowed to the inevitable. He declared that he would not stand in the way of his daughter's happiness. He would allow the marriage but not attend it. Nor would the members of his family.

When Kadambari realized that Robi was determined to go she rose to her feet. 'You must have something to eat before you leave,' she said, then turning to him eagerly, she added, 'You'll come back, won't you? Promise me you won't spend the night in Calcutta.'

In the steamer, on his way to Calcutta, Robi felt a pang of guilt. Natun Bouthan had asked him to stay back. He could have obeyed her and gone another day. Only, it gave him so much pleasure to hear someone else sing his songs! His compositions were becoming quite popular. They were being sung regularly at Brahmo prayer meetings. Only the other day his nephew

87

Satyaprasad had heard a group of boys singing one of his songs by Hedo Lake. Robi had felt a surge of triumph at the news.

Getting off the steamer at Babughat, Robi made his way to where the public carriages stood waiting. It had just stopped raining and the road was muddy and full of potholes. It was very crowded and people pushed and pummelled each other in order to get ahead. Not a single phaeton was in sight. Three or four hackney cabs, so crammed with passengers that they seemed to be bursting at the seams, were just pulling out. As Robi gazed despairingly after them someone stepped heavily on his foot coating his shining pump with horse dung. Wincing with pain Robi decided to walk.

Following the arrival of the exiled Nawab Wajed Ali Shah, Metiaburj was transformed from a marshy wilderness into a bustling Muslim colony. Shops and eateries had sprung up like mushrooms lining both sides of the road on which Robi walked. As the delicious odours of meatballs and Mughlai curries wafted into his nostrils he remembered his brother Satyendranath's khansama Abdul. Abdul's cooking had smelled just so. Satyendranath had found Abdul here in Metiaburj and taken him to Ahmedabad where he was posted as Assistant Collector and Magistrate. Robi had spent some months with his Mejodada and Mejo Bouthan in their house—an old Mughal place overlooking a river. Robi had been delighted with it. It had seemed to his newly awakened adolescent senses that here, within these high stone walls, history was trapped and stood transfixed. Walking up and down the huge terrace on moonlit nights he could swear he heard voices around him—moans and sighs and anguished whispers.

As Robi entered Lalbazar a passing carriage stopped by him. A head emerged from the window and a voice exclaimed, '*Arré*! It's Rabindra Babu. Come in. Come in.' Robi folded his hands in greeting. The man's name was Shibnath Bhattacharya but many addressed him as Shastri Moshai. He was a fine scholar and a dynamic social reformer and had done a lot to reduce the prevalence of child marriage. He had promoted widow remarriages and made burning speeches in favour of education for women. Under his leadership the Sadharan Brahmo Samaj was gaining in popularity every day. Seating himself in the carriage Robi said, 'I was on my way to your Sabha. But I'm afraid I shall be late. You see, I'm coming from Chandannagar.' Shibnath Shastri drew a watch out of the waistband of his dhuti. He noted that Robi was one hour and ten minutes late. The young Brahmos were sticklers for time. Nevertheless, he said kindly, 'I'm sure Nagen, Kedar and the others are waiting. After all, Chandannagar is a long way off.'

The bells on the horses' hooves jingled merrily and their plumes danced gaily as the carriage rolled down the road. Robi was afraid that Shastri Moshai would launch on a tirade against the members of the Adi Brahmo Samaj but he did nothing of the kind. He spoke lightly and briefly on a variety of subjects giving a patient hearing to Robi's opinions.

Dismounting at the gate Robi entered the great hall where the Brahmo prayer meetings were held. The room was empty except for a small group of young men who rose to receive him. Robi's apologies for the delay were waved away with punctilious deference and he was led to a carpet spread with white sheets at the far end of the room. Robi took his seat facing the five singers. One had an esraj in his hand and another a pair of cymbals. He knew four of them well. They were trained singers and would pick up the songs easily and quickly. But who was the fifth? He looked very young, scarcely past boyhood. His body was strong and muscular and his eyes large, dark and compelling. His name, Robi was told, was Naren Datta. The name meant nothing to him but there was something familiar about the way the boy's eyes looked steadily out of a pair of heavy brows. Of course! Naren Datta was his nephew Dipu's friend and had come to Jorasanko on one or two occasions.

After a couple of hours, when the two songs had been rehearsed to Robi's satisfaction, one of the young men said, 'Our Naren sings one of your songs really well. Can we not include it in the programme?'

'Which song is that?' Robi looked at him curiously.

'*Tomaréi koriyacchi jeevan ér dhruba taara.*' Then, turning to Naren, he added. 'Sing it Naren. Let Rabindra Babu hear it.'

Bashfulness and delicacy were alien to Naren's personality. Sitting upright and slapping his thighs vigorously to the beat he commenced singing the song in a powerful baritone. Robi listened quietly, his head bowed, his fingers etching imaginary patterns on the sheet. His chest felt tight with emotion. This song had been written for *her*. Standing on the deck of his ship on his way to England, he had missed her so desperately that the words had come rushing out of the turmoil in his breast:

> *You are the lodestar of my soul*
> *I shall follow your light*
> *Never again shall I flounder*
> *In this ocean of life*

It was *her* song. It made a secret bond between them. He wouldn't, he couldn't allow it to be dragged into the limelight. 'Naren sings it well,' he said as he rose to leave, 'But being a song of sorrow and parting, it is not suitable for the occasion.'

It was late afternoon and Robi felt prodigiously hungry. He decided to go to his brother Satyendranath's house before leaving for the steamer ghat. The children, Bibi and Suren aged nine and ten, were very fond of him. So was his sister-in-law.

Satyendranath's wife Gyanadanandini had been the first to introduce a Western style of living and etiquette into the feudal atmosphere of the mansion in Jorasanko. In this she had been supported by her husband who believed women should have equal rights. Satyendranath had tried, in his own way, to bring a breath of fresh air into the closely shuttered interiors of the Thakur household. While still a student in England he had sought his father's permission to keep his wife with him. But it had not been given. Debendranath believed that genteel women kept themselves well within the zenana. Gyanadanandini had obeyed her father-in-law but not forgiven him. As soon as her husband became financially independent she took the bold step of travelling to England and living there alone for several months with her three minor children. Such a thing was unheard of in those days. No Indian woman had ever crossed the ocean without a male escort. Gyanadanandini was twenty-six years old at the time and a dazzling beauty.

Gyanadanandini's metamorphosis from an ordinary village girl to the most advanced Indian woman of her times was like a fairy tale come true. Born in a lower middle class Brahmin family of Jessore, she had been married at the age of seven and brought to the mansion of the Thakurs in Jorasanko. The size and splendour of the apartments had daunted her so much that she had spent the best part of her first few years cowering in a corner of her room. Then, as infancy passed into adolescence, a change came over her. At first it was physical. Her frail gawky limbs filled out and became supple and voluptuous. Her skin, fair but pale and sallow, acquired the lustre of a land lotus. Then, with the passing of the years, she grew into a woman of surpassing beauty, spirit and intelligence. She spoke French and English with elegant fluency, entertained her husband's friends as a gracious hostess and attended official balls and banquets as easily as though she had been born to such things. She was the first to adapt the Western style of dress to the needs of her own country. A woman's body had, heretofore, performed two functions. It catered to the needs of her husband in his bed and to the growth of his children in the womb. What more did it require, the conservatives argued, than a length of cloth? Undergarments were considered unnecessary luxuries for creatures who spent their days huddled over their work in the dark interiors of the zenana.

Gyanadanandini found this disgusting and demeaning. She started covering her torso with chemises and jackets. She discovered that a slight alteration in the style of wearing the sari made the whole outfit more dignified and streamlined. It covered the entire body falling to the feet like a gown. The other women of the Thakur family started emulating her and thus the new style of draping a sari, with pleats in front and a brooch over the shoulder, came to be known as the Pirali style.

On her return from England Gyanadanandini had drawn a subtle but distinct line between her own family and the rest of the household. Unlike their cousins who studied in Bengali schools, Bibi and Suren were sent to Loretto and St Xavier's. They spoke in English to one another and ate off English plate and silver. Gyanadanandini kept a servant named Rama who wore shoes and trousers even in the house, and a fluffy little dog which ran about everywhere, jumped up on the beds and even entered the kitchen. The elders of the family were appalled but dared not reprove her. She had such a strong personality that the entire household stood in awe of her. Her father-in-law was the only exception but he was rarely in Jorasanko these days.

Gyanadanandini's behaviour with the other women of the family bordered on the offensive. She had travelled extensively both in Europe and India and had seen how advanced women were in other parts of the world. Compared to them her sisters-in-law seemed to her to be distressingly backward. Not only did they not emulate her as they should, they criticized her ways and called her brazen and arrogant. She had the drive and zeal of a true reformer and a proud, strong spirit besides. She ignored their barbs with a mixture of pity and scorn and lived on her own terms. She knew that women who were cooped up together like hens were bound to peck and scratch one another. Though, to tell the truth, the Thakur women were more civilized than those of the other great families of Calcutta. Quarrelling was never loud or open. Snide comments, subtle taunts and jeering and laughing behind one another's back were more in their line.

Gyanadanandini ignored everything that went on around her but felt trapped nevertheless. The environment, she felt, was not right for either herself or her children. She wrote to her husband, who was posted out of Calcutta, saying that she wished to leave Jorasanko and take up a house elsewhere. Satyendranath agreed. He was the only one of Debendranath's children who raised his voice, from time to time, against his father's tyrannical view of women. And he was ready to break with tradition. His wife would have a house of her own if she wanted it. He would support her in all her desires. Thus Gyanadanandini became not only the first woman of the Thakur clan to travel beyond India's shores but also the first to leave the ancestral home breaking up the old joint family.

The house she took up for her residence had originally belonged to the owner of the Bijni estates in Assam. It was a stately mansion facing the lake called Birji Talao and took its name from it. The house had a magnificient view of the towering domes and spires of St Paul's Church. Here Gyanadanandini lived in great style and comfort. She was a generous hostess and welcomed visitors. But, of all her relations in Jorasanko, she liked Jyotirindra and Robi best. Being nearly the same age, she and Jyotirindra were great friends and he spent a good deal of time in her company. Robi was a favourite with the children. Bibi and Suren were the only two left now, their brother having died in

92

England. They adored their Robi ka. He had stayed with them in their house in Brighton and they knew him better than their other relations. Gyanadanandini liked him too and made him welcome whenever he came to the house.

Robi entered the vast marble hall to find his sister-in-law standing on the landing of the red carpeted staircase giving instructions to a servant. She looked very handsome and stately in her cream sari of heavy silk. It was pleated in front in the Pirali style and held at one shoulder with a brooch set with rubies and emeralds. Her figure was perfect, taut and supple, belying her thirty-three years and four childbirths. Her eyes had none of the doe-like softness of the average Bengali woman. They were large and dark and flashed with spirit and intelligence. 'Robi!' she exclaimed as she came down the steps, 'Where have you been hiding? In Chandannagar?'

'I'm famished Mejo Bouthan,' Robi avoided a direct reply. 'Give me something to eat first.'

'What have you been doing with yourself? You look as though you've come through a storm. And what filthy shoes! Take them off! Take them off!'

Suren was playing tennis in the back lawn and Bibi was practising on the pianoforte in a little anteroom adjoining the hall. She heard Robi's voice and came prancing in. 'Robi ka,' she exclaimed, 'you haven't come to see us in such a long time!' Robi smiled down into the happy face tilted up to his. Bibi was getting prettier and prettier every day. In a few years she would put all the beauties of Jorasanko to shame. Following Bibi another little girl came into the room. She was Sarala, Robi's second sister Swarnakumari's daughter. The two girls dragged Robi down on the sofa and, sitting on either side of him, bombarded him with questions. Meanwhile, a servant entered the room and placed a silver dish full of pastries on a small table.

'I'm glad you've come today Robi,' Gyanadanandini said, seating herself. 'It's Suri's birthday and I've invited some friends.'

'You must spend the night with us Robi ka,' Bibi cried, 'There'll be a wonderful party with a huge big cake.'

'Natun has promised to come too,' Gyanadanandini continued. 'He's to spend the night here. Why don't you do the same? I've advised Natun to give up the house in Chandannagar and return to Calcutta. Garden houses are all very well for a few days. City people can't live in the wilds for months on end. And Robi! What are *you* doing there? Why don't you stay with us? This is such a big house. We can easily put you up.'

Robi noticed that Gyanadanandini did not enquire after Kadambari even once. He knew she didn't like her and had been opposed to the match from the start. Shyam Ganguli of Hadhkata Lane had neither wealth nor lineage. How could a daughter of his be deemed worthy of the most eligible young man of Calcutta? Mejda and Mejo Bouthan had tried to persuade Debendranath to reject the offer. But Debendranath had to be practical. Caste Brahmins of high families did not give their daughters to the Thakurs who were Brahmos on the one hand and stamped with the Pirali stigma on the other. Gyanadanandini had been outraged. Her favourite brother-in-law, so wonderfully handsome and brilliant, to be made to marry such an ordinary girl!

But Kadambari hadn't remained ordinary. She had developed and changed with the passing years and was, now, as beautiful and talented as her sister-in-law. The two women had little in common though. Gyanadanandini was shrewd, practical and worldly wise. She kept a vigilant eye on everything around her. The house ran as if on oiled wheels and she had complete control over her husband and children. She had a forceful, commanding personality and could make everyone obey her.

Kadambari, on the other hand, was dreamy and romantic. There was something wraith-like about her. It seemed as though she found reality so overpowering that she preferred to withdraw from it. She created and lived in a world of her own wherever she was, whether in the sprawling rooms and gardens of Moran's villa or in her solitary apartment on the top floor of the mansion in Jorasanko. Robi was assailed by a sense of mystery whenever he came into her presence.

In the evening the house started filling up with guests. The cake, with its eleven candles, was set out in the hall. It would be cut the moment Jyotirindranath arrived. Robi felt restless and anxious. The last steamer to Chandannagar would leave at six o clock and it was nearly six now. He had promised Natun Bouthan he would return tonight. But the children clung to him and wouldn't let him go. The way things were he might have to break his promise. To shake off the depression that overtook him at the thought of Natun Bouthan all alone in the dark, shadowy house by the river, Robi burst into song:

'Won't you tell me, Molly darling
Darling you are growing old
Goodbye sweet heart goodbye . . .'

This was a song he had picked up in England and he sang it now substituting 'Molly darling' with 'Bibi darling'. The children laughed gaily and clapped their hands to his song. Suddenly the clip clop of horses' hooves and the rolling of wheels was heard on the drive and everyone ran out to the porch. Jyotirindranath had arrived.

Stepping out of the carriage he asked anxiously, 'Am I late? Is everyone here?' He looked tired and dishevelled and the buttons of his kurta were open. Walking into the hall he went straight to his sister-in-law. 'I'm sorry Mejo Bouthan,' he said. 'I just couldn't get away from the theatre. The players are so bad—they can't even speak the language properly.' Gyanadanandini smiled up at her brother-in-law. Putting out her hands she fastened the buttons of his kurta and asked roguishly, 'Tell me the truth Natun. Which of the actresses kept you at the theatre all this while?'

After the cake was cut and eaten Robi asked his brother if he was spending the night in Birji Talao. 'Natun Bouthan will be all alone,' he said, adding, 'Have you told her what you mean to do?'

'There are plenty of servants,' Gyanadanandini spoke for her brother-in-law. 'Besides, it is only for one night. Why all this fuss?'

'Shall I return then Jyotidada?'

'That's a good idea,' Jyotirindra sounded relieved. 'Tell your Natun Bouthan I have some work here tomorrow morning. But how will you go?'

The children clamoured around Robi begging him to stay the night. The last steamer had left, they pointed out. He would have to take a boat. And that would take hours and hours. What would be the use? But Robi dismissed their entreaties with a smile and a shake of his head. Natun Bouthan had asked him to return. She was very sensitive and was easily hurt. A train left for

Howrah at eight thirty. If he made haste he would be able to catch it. Disengaging Bibi's clinging hands gently, Robi walked out into the night.

Chapter XII

Bharat felt ravenously hungry these days. There was a fire raging in his vitals from morning till night leaving him faint and dizzy. He had been scorned and neglected in the royal palace of Tripura but not starved. Here, in this house, the cooks and their attendants delighted in keeping him waiting for hours on end before doling out a few scraps that were not enough to feed a cat to satiety.

Three large clay ovens burned in the kitchen and a number of dishes were cooked every day. The head cook Nityananda took his orders, first thing in the morning, from the two mistresses of the house. Though living as a joint family the two brothers ate in their respective apartments with their wives and children. The main meals were served from the common kitchen and augmented, according to each one's taste, with ghee, butter, pickles, preserves, sweets and relishes. The servants ate coarse rice, dal and a mess of vegetables which saw a sprinkling, sometimes, of shrimps or tiddlers. The fare, though poor, was plentiful. The mistresses did not grumble even if a servant ate a whole seer of rice at a meal. Sacks of cheap rice lined the walls of the store room adjoining the kitchen and the cooks were free to dip into them whenever the need arose. But Bharat was neither a servant nor a member of the family. He had been treated with deference when Shashibhushan first brought him to the house. But since the latter's illness things had changed. Now he was seen every morning crouching outside the kitchen like a cat with its tail tucked in, waiting patiently for the two dry rutis and small dab of pumpkin stew that was his breakfast. As soon as the broken *kanshi* with these leftovers from the last night's meal was handed to him he wolfed them down with the ferocity of a starving dog, then ran to the well and drank a pitcherful of water. That quenched the fire for a couple of hours after which his stomach started rumbling again.

Bharat was almost back to normal these days. His memory

had returned and the wound on his thigh had healed. But he still couldn't recall how he had been saved and by whom. His last memory of that time was of two naked little boys throwing stones at his head, then running off into the forest. If only he weren't so hungry all the time he might remember.

Bharat roamed about in the garden all day looking for something to eat. There were bunches of green coconuts on the palms but they were beyond his reach and the trunks were too smooth for him to climb. The *bel* trees were loaded but the fruit was raw and bitter. Once he had eaten some and felt very sick afterwards. Bharat often saw a girl in the garden and it was invariably in the mornings. She was young and pretty and carried a basket of flowers on one arm. Bharat hid himself behind a tree whenever he saw her. His experience with Monomohini had been so devastating that he fell into a state of abject terror at the sight of a girl.

One day, coming into the garden from the house, he saw a strange sight. A little knot of people, with Shashibhushan in the centre, were talking and gesticulating excitedly. Shashibhushan had a tripod in front of him with a camera and he was focussing it on someone posing by a flowering bush. As Bharat watched from a distance Shashibhushan covered the camera and his own head with a black cloth and started calling out in a commanding voice. 'A little to the right. No, not that much. Look up. Lift your chin and look straight. Straight into the camera.' Bharat wondered who the object was till, coming closer, he discovered that it was the girl who picked flowers. She wore a yellow sari that morning and stood like a statue—one arm outstretched. Suddenly a cloud came over the sun and Shashibhushan was forced to take his head out of the enveloping cloth. 'We'll have to wait till the sun comes out again,' he said.

'The girl was a devdasi,' one of the men standing by Shashibhushan whispered, 'I'm sure she can dance. Why don't you take her picture in a dance pose?'

'She was not a devdasi,' Shashibhushan answered curtly. 'She was being sold as one when Mejo Bouthan found her.'

At this point the girl created a diversion. 'I can dance,' she called out in a high clear voice. 'Shall I show you?'

'No,' Shashibhushan cried sharply. 'Don't move an inch.

You'll spoil the angle.' As he spoke his eyes fell on Bharat. To his dismay he remembered that he had not spoken to him or enquired after him for months. He had seen his frightened face peering into his sick room once or twice but had been too exhausted to respond. '*Arré* Bharat!' he called out now. 'How are you? Come. Come closer.' Bharat's heart swelled with self pity and his eyes burned with angry tears. Master Moshai did not love him. He had brought him to Calcutta, then forgotten all about him. Bharat was starved in his house but Master Moshai didn't care in the least. Bharat rushed out of the garden dashing the tears from his eyes. Running as fast as his legs could carry him he came to the edge of the pond and flung himself in the long grass and reeds that surrounded it. Weeping bitterly he cried, 'Ma! Ma *go*! Take me away from here. Take me away with you.'

Then, a few days later, he came upon the girl again. He was even more hungry than usual that morning because his daily ration of rutis and pumpkin stew had not been doled out even though he had waited for it for over two hours. Seeing the tears trembling in the boy's eyes as he rose to leave, one of the junior cooks took pity on him. 'There are no leftover rutis today, boy,' he said kindly. Then, throwing a handful of muri into an enamel bowl, he handed it to him with the words, 'Make do with this till the rice is cooked.'

But the few grains of muri only added fuel to the fire. He tried to drown it with quantities of water but it raged higher than ever. Every nerve in his body, every fibre and sinew cried out for sustenance. He was a prince. Though born out of wedlock, it was a king's blood that ran in his veins. He could not beg or steal. Clutching his belly he ran out into the garden and stopped under a tamarind tree. He stared into its branches in the hope of spotting some fruit but all his eyes beheld were rich clusters of feathery fronds—green as emerald.

He jumped up and twisted off a handful from the branch just above his head and crammed them into his mouth. They tasted fresh and juicy, though a little tart. If cows and goats could survive on grass and leaves, maybe he could too, he thought to himself. Just then he heard a piercing cry, 'Ma! Ma *go*!' It was a woman's voice, loud and frightened. Bharat ran in the direction of the sound and found Bhumisuta cowering against the wall that

SUNIL GANGOPADHYAY

marked the boundary of the Singha property. From some bushes close beside her came a rustling noise. 'It's a snake,' he thought. But he didn't care to come to her rescue. He was giddy and nauseous with hunger and in no mood to take on a snake for her benefit. He looked with loathing at the shrinking girl. 'She lives like one of the family. She eats well,' was all that he could think. Suddenly there was a violent swaying in the bushes and a sound of scratching and scraping was heard. It was not a snake. It was some larger animal. What if it was a tiger? He shuddered at the thought. He had seen tigers in Tripura. They came prowling out of the forest and lurked in the tall grasses that grew by the lake. He remembered how he had dreaded being mauled by a tiger when he was buried, feet foremost, in the jungle clearing. And, then, he didn't know what came over him. Picking up a large stone he ran screaming to the spot from where the sounds were coming. There was a loud whelp as the stone hit the bush. He recognized the cry. It was a jackal's. Coming closer he found that the animal was entangled in the bushes and was struggling to break free. Bharat laughed aloud. Parting the branches he eased it out. 'Shoo! Scram!' he cried, then turning on his heel, he walked away not deigning to cast a glance on Bhumisuta.

Chapter XIII

Mahadevi Bhanumati's shraddha ceremony was performed in Brindavan with great pomp and splendour. But as soon as the rites were concluded the king rushed back to Agartala abandoning his original plan of visiting a few more places of pilgrimage. Addressing his ministers in a secret conference he revealed the purpose behind his hasty return. He wished to marry Monomohini as soon as possible. This, as he took pains to point out, was not a personal indulgence. At his age he was not eager to don a *topor* and chain himself in wedlock to a girl young enough to be his granddaughter. His late queen, just before her death, had expressed a desire that he marry her niece. It was her last wish and he had to respect it.

All this explanation was probably unnecessary because no one showed any sign of surprise. 'Let the girl be sent to her father's house then,' Radharaman said ponderously. 'We'll find a suitable date in the coming year and make the arrangements.'

'The coming year!' Naradhwaj, the king's brother-in-law, echoed sharply. 'Why not this year? Or even this month? The sooner the better. Don't you agree Maharaj?'

'The Bengalis believe in mourning their dead for a year Naradhwaj,' Birchandra smiled indulgently. 'And their brides come from their fathers' houses. Isn't that so Ghosh Moshai?'

'Why should Bengali customs be made to prevail in this country? Do we leave off eating sweets when our wives die? If a man wishes to eat a sweet, must he be made to wait a year? It doesn't make sense.'

Radharaman was silent. He knew that Naradhwaj was putting pressure on the king to marry his sister's daughter. Birchandra could have kept her as a kachhua and enjoyed her charms without getting involved in marital rites. And that is what he, Radharaman, would have advised. 'Our women don't come to us all coy and demure in their bridal finery,' Dhananjay Thakur pressed the point. 'We kidnap young girls and make them

101

our brides.' Taking his cue Naradhwaj continued, 'Let's fix the wedding for the twenty-fifth of this month. It is an auspicious day. We must get an English band from Chittagong. How much will that cost Ghosh Moshai?' Radharaman cleared his throat. 'Vast amounts of money have been spent on the two shraddhas,' he announced solemnly, 'There's very little left in the treasury. That is why I suggested postponing the wedding to a later date.'

'There's no need for an English band,' the Maharaja said hastily. 'We mustn't think of indulging ourselves at a time like this. I would like a simple ceremony with only the formal rites. The priests needn't be paid anything. They've lined their pockets thickly enough during the two shraddhas. As for the bride's jewels, Mono will get half of what Bhanumati left behind. The rest will be put aside for Samar's bride. But do we need to wait till the twenty-fifth Naradhwaj? Can't you set the date sometime this week?'

The wedding was fixed for the coming Tuesday—exactly five days away. The palace started humming with gossip and rumour. The other queens turned up their noses disdainfully at the king's choice. 'A girl like that!' they whispered to one another, 'She runs in and out of the palace as if she's a maid—not a princess. And she talks so freely with men! How can the king think of putting her on par with us?' Those of the royal women who had slandered and harassed Monomohini openly after Bhanumati's death now shivered in apprehension. She would be married to the king and enjoy his special favour for six months at the least. Who knew what revenge she would take? The only person unaffected by the news was Monomohini herself. She wandered about the palace and gardens just as she used to shrugging off all the instructions and advice showered on her by her well-meaning relatives.

Maharaja Birchandra, though fond of good food, was no glutton. In fact he was very fastidious about the taste and quality of whatever he ate. He took his meals in his own apartments as a rule but occasionally he bestowed on one of his queens, the honour of eating a meal in her mahal. The queen sought out for this distinction was overwhelmed, not so much with gratitude as with fear and panic, for the king was extremely whimsical and difficult to please.

Queen Karenuka knelt by the velvet *asan* that formed a

crimson square on the milk white marble floor of her chamber. In front of her was a vast gold thala ringed with eighteen silver bowls brimming over with curried fish, chicken, duck, mutton, vegetables, sweets and relishes. As the tapping sound of the king's khadam came down the gallery Karenuka's heart missed a beat. Would she come through the ordeal before her? Sweat poured down her face smudging the sandal paste with which she had adorned it. Birchandra glanced at the blue clad figure kneeling on the floor and his mouth trembled in a smile.

'How are you Karenu?' he asked affectionately. Then, seating himself on the *asan*, he went on, 'Hmm! You have a fine spread here I see. Which of these dishes have you cooked?'

Karenuka was the plainest of Birchandra's wives. Her body was too thin for beauty and her complexion dull and sallow. All the butter and cream she had eaten in the palace all these years hadn't made a jot of difference. Besides, she had failed to give the king a son, her only offspring being two puny daughters. No one was more aware of her deficiencies than Karenuka herself and she was very humble in consequence. She folded her hands in answer to her husband's question and murmured, 'I've cooked everything you see before you my Lord.'

Birchandra put out his hand and broke the mound of rice, white and fragrant as jasmine petals. Then, shutting his eyes, he said a little prayer. Queen Karenuka watched with baited breath as, opening them, he dipped his forefinger into all the bowls, one by one, and tasted their contents. Each time something fell short of his exacting standards he pushed the bowl away.

'What's this?' he asked at last.

'Fish balls Maharaj,' Karenuka answered. 'Made from freshly caught chital—'

'Hmm. Not bad. But Queen Bhanumati's fish balls were incomparable! The taste of it still lingers in my mouth.'

The other queens who stood crowding at the door, were delighted with the snubbing their co-wife was receiving at the hands of their common lord and master. 'Ahh! Bardidi's cooking!' they cried out in high, excited voices, 'Who can presume to compete with her?' Birchandra shot a glance at the figure kneeling beside him. The face was pale and pinched and the limbs tense with anxiety. Pointing to another bowl, he asked

103

'What's this?'

'Its brinjal, Maharaj. Cooked with garlic paste.'

'Sudakshina!' Birchandra called out to one of his queens. 'Come sit by me and have some of this.' Sudakshina tried to slip away but her co-wives caught hold of her. 'It's the king's command!' they cried. 'How dare you disobey?' Everyone knew that Sudakshina couldn't bear the smell of garlic. The very thought of it made her want to vomit. Twisting and struggling desperately she managed to free herself and ran screaming down the gallery while Birchandra roared with laughter.

The rejected bowls had been taken away, in the meantime, and replaced with others. No queen would dream of entertaining the king with a choice of less than fifty dishes ranging from the coarsest of humble fare to the most expensive and exotic of delicacies. For no one knew what he might fancy and when. It was perfectly possible for him to pass over the most succulent pieces of fat carp swimming in rich mustard gravy and dig hungrily into a bowl of sweet and sour tiddlers. Or he might, with fastidious fingers, pick out the pieces of pumpkin from a dish of mixed vegetables and put them in his mouth. After sampling all the dishes, he turned his attention on his hostess. 'Why didn't you cook jackfruit Karenu?' he asked as if surprised at this omission. 'The trees are bending over with fruit. This is just the season to eat a good jackfruit curry richly spiced and floating in ghee. Do you know that Bengalis call the jackfruit *tree goat*? If properly cooked it tastes like mutton.'

At this the sweat broke out all over Karenuka's body. All her planning, all her labour had been in vain! She had left out the one dish her husband craved. The other queens nudged one another and tried to suppress their smiles of glee.

Then something strange happened. Birchandra put out his left hand and placed it on Karenuka's head. 'You've passed the test Karenu,' he said smiling tenderly, 'You're a good girl and a good cook and I've enjoyed the meal. I'm glad you didn't cook jackfruit. My kingdom is fairly ridden with the loathesome things and I can't bear to look at them. It was very intelligent of you to keep it out of the midday meal.'

Dismissing the other queens Birchandra took a paan from Karenuka's hand and stretched out on her bed. Karenuka knelt on the floor beside it and began massaging his legs and thighs. 'Ahh!' the king breathed a deep sigh of satisfaction. 'You have a nice touch Karenu,' he said approvingly. 'The rest of you is as poky as a bundle of twigs but your hands are surprisingly soft and fleshy. How many children do you have Karenu?'

'You have favoured me with two daughters Maharaj. But, hapless that I am, I have no son.'

Birchandra could not keep count of his wives let alone his children. He hardly saw them—he couldn't bear their clamouring. 'How old are they?' he asked carelessly showing no curiosity about their names. 'They are seven and eight Maharaj,' Karenuka smiled remembering the brief months of happiness she had enjoyed as the king's new queen. Then two other women had come into his life and she had been forgotten. 'The elder one is ripe for marriage,' the king muttered yawning, 'We must start looking for a suitable match.' The words trailed away. Soothed by the gentle pressure of Karenuka's fingers on his tired muscles and tendons, Birchandra fell asleep. His breathing became regular and he snored gently. But Karenuka did not abandon her task. She went on pressing the royal limbs, a flood of gratitude and relief washing over her every time she thought of his kindness. Her lord had come to her, had accepted and been pleased with her service. What more could she want?

After an hour or so Birchandra awoke. Sitting up in bed he yawned and stretched luxuriously. 'Radhe Krishna! Radhe Krishna!' he cried flipping his fingers in front of his mouth to ward off another yawn. Then, swinging his legs to the ground, he pushed his feet into his *khadams* and said with a kind smile, 'Your apartment is so cool and airy Karenu!' He went from room to room opening windows and examining the furniture. 'Come to me Karenu,' he invited. As she advanced timidly he put out his arms and clasped her tiny bird body to his magnificient chest. 'You're a good girl Karenu,' he said tenderly. 'You serve your husband well. Your cooking is perfect and your bed as white and soft as down.' Karenuka trembled in his embrace. She had believed herself rejected for all time to come. But God had listened to her prayers. Her husband loved her and wanted her. The joy of the discovery was too much to bear. She burst into tears. 'I want something from you Karenu,' the king continued

105

stroking her back with tender fingers. 'Will you give it?' Karenuka's voice trembled with emotion. 'Ask anything of your slave my Lord!' she answered. 'Even to my life. I'll give it gladly.'

'No. No. I've no need of anyone's life.' Releasing her from his embrace the king held her by the shoulders and, looking deep into her eyes, he said 'You may have heard that I'm about to take another wife. It was your Bardidi's last wish,' he added hastily seeing the look of surprise flash across her face. 'The new queen will need a mahal of her own. Bhanumati's rooms are available, of course. But they are too full of memories. It wouldn't be fair to the new bride, would it?' Karenuka wondered if the question was addressed to her. But, before she could respond or even catch the drift of the conversation, Birchandra went on blandly, 'That is why I'm asking you to give up your mahal. A room will be found for you and we'll see that you're quite comfortable. A new queen must be given a mahal. It is her right. Don't you agree?'

Birchandra felt himself to be very noble and magnanimous as he uttered these words. He was the king of the realm and could have got what he wanted at the mere lifting of a finger. But he hadn't done so. He had wasted a good deal of his precious time on a woman who was no better than a bag of bones. He had given her the privilege of cooking for him and pressing his feet. And, far from commanding her to give up her apartment, he had begged them of her as a favour. What king would do so much for a mere wife? His royal ancestors would have been horrified at such unseemly behaviour. But that was his nature, he thought with a pleasurable sigh. He couldn't be cruel to anybody. But the moment his eyes fell on Karenuka's strained and anguished face, his mood of complacent self adulation received a rude shock. A sullen look came into his eyes. 'Get the rooms cleared by tomorrow morning,' he said walking away without waiting for an answer. 'They'll need to be painted and refurnished—'

Birchandra married Monomohini on the scheduled day with a minimum of ceremony and expense. But the nuptial chamber was magnificient with its new furniture, bright lights and masses of flowers. The vast bedstead in the centre of the room had ropes of flowers twisted about its ornate carvings and hanging in festoons from the poles. Here Monomohini stood awaiting her bridegroom. Her exquisite body, draped in red and gold muslin, made a wonderful foil for Bhanumati's jewels which glittered from her hair, neck and arms. Her eyes were not coy and downcast as those of other brides but bright with anticipation and curiosity. She tossed her head from time to time making her long diamond earrings wink and glow in the light of the many lanterns.

It was midnight by the time Birchandra entered the room. He looked fatigued and his silk kurta was soaked with perspiration. It had been a tiring day. As if the hundred and one rituals of the wedding and the entertaining of the guests was not enough, he had had to hold a long meeting with the Political Agent. Anyhow, all that was behind him now and he looked forward to relaxing with his young bride. It was not her body alone that he craved. He was enchanted by her spirit—as wild and free as one of the beautiful creatures that haunted the forests of his kingdom. In her eyes he had seen the beauty and innocence of a wild doe.

Birchandra stood at the door for a few seconds, his eyes fixed on the vision of loveliness in front of him. And, as he gazed, a film came over them. The years rolled away. This was the night of his first marriage and the girl who stood before him was Bhanumati. Birchandra had seen no resemblance between aunt and niece when Bhanumati was alive but now the latter's face came sharply before him. At her age Bhanumati had looked exactly like Monomohini. And she had worn the same jewels as a bride. Bhanumati had taken her life in a fit of anger. But now all was forgiven and forgotten. She had come back to him. He murmured beneath his breath:

'Goddess! Where lies that Heaven in which you dwell?

In close guarded silence, away from the haunts of men.

Can my hopes ever reach—'

'What are you saying my lord?' Monomohini came forward. 'I don't understand . . .'

Birchandra came to with a start. He looked wildly at her for a few seconds, then, covering his face with his hands, he burst into tears. On this, his wedding night, he truly missed and mourned his first wife.

Chapter XIV

On one side of Hedo Lake rose the imposing building of the General Assembly Institution. The lake, recently cleaned and dredged, was now part of a park enclosed with railings and set out with flowering trees and shrubs. The boys of the college had appropriated it and were seen walking about the grounds or sitting on the benches long after college hours. They smoked incessantly, quoted Shelley and Wordsworth and held heated discussions on the relative merits of Hume and Herbert Spencer. Quite often, of course, they descended from those heights. Then their talk was peppered with tales of sexual encounters with newly wedded wives or the prostitutes of Rambagan.

On this dark cloudy day the park was deserted. With one exception. Narendranath Datta, son of Advocate Bishwanath Datta of Shimle, could be seen pacing about by the lake as if lost in his own thoughts. Narendranath had been a student of Presidency College but, having suffered a bout of malaria, had been unable to take the examination. Recovering, he had joined the General Assembly Institution, passed his FA and was now preparing to appear for his BA examination. Narendranath, though still in his teens, was a fine figure of a man. Tall and strong with broad shoulders and a heavy frame, he towered over the other boys not only in looks but in energy, intelligence and spirit. His large dark eyes flashed out from his handsome face sometimes with anger and sometimes with fun and good humour. Naren was a brilliant student and a good sportsman. He could fence, wrestle and play cricket with a fair degree of proficiency. He was an excellent boxer too and had won the Silver Butterfly at a college contest. With all this he was a fine singer and could play the pakhawaj and the esraj. Very popular with the boys, he was always the centre of attention.

Yet, that afternoon, he was roaming about by himself his face as dark and sombre as the sky above his head. A strange restlessness seized him. Classes were over for the day. All the boys

108

had gone home but he had nowhere to go. He thought of several possibilities and rejected them all. He could go to Beni Ustad and practice a few taans or he could work out his frustrations with some wrestling in the akhara. But neither held any charms for him at the moment. He thought briefly of his friends in Barahnagar. He might go over for a chat. But the prospect didn't tempt him. Neither did the idea of visiting the Brahmo Mandir and listening to the prayers and singing. Above all he didn't want to go home. Ever since he had passed his FA his parents were pestering him to get married. The house was always full of prospective fathers-in-law vying with each other to catch him for their daughters. One offered a dowry of ten thousand; another twenty. One or two even offered to send him abroad to study at the Bar or qualify for the ICS. His parents were more than ready to sell him to the highest bidder. But Naren wanted to make something of his life; to gain a vision of his own before he took on the responsibility for another. Life was short. Life was precious. It was foolish to squander it away. One had to discover the truth of it, the worth of it. Eating, sleeping and proliferating were for animals.

As the sky grew darker and more menacing; as the thunder rumbled and lightning flashed, Narendra's restlessness increased till it reached a state bordering on frenzy. He walked faster and faster, shoved pinches of snuff deep into his nostrils, spat venomously here and there then, coming to the railing, suddenly started beating his head against the iron spikes. 'Arré Naren,' a voice cried behind him and two strong hands held his head in a vice-like grip, 'Are you trying to kill yourself?' It was his friend Brajendra Sheel. Brajendra was a poor student but very meritorious. He could not afford to buy many books so he spent long hours reading in the college library. He was on his way back home when he spotted Naren in the park. 'What were you trying to do?' he asked. 'Your skull would have cracked open if I hadn't caught you in time.' 'I have a headache,' Narendra answered shamefacedly. 'I thought it would help—'

'Go to a kaviraj if you have a headache.'

Naren took out his snuff box and started pushing the obnoxious stuff up his nostrils with a pencil. 'Stop it Naren,' Brajendra cried out in horror. 'It's making me sick.'

'It clears the head and relieves the pain.'

'That's nonsense. I've never heard of snuff relieving pain. Why don't you take some proper medicine? What kind of pain is it?'

'I feel an acute throbbing in the centre of my forehead—just between the brows. And sometimes I see a flame flickering in that spot. Have you ever experienced anything like that Brajen?'

'No. You'd better see a doctor. It could be something serious.'

Suddenly the rain came down in a torrent drowning his words. Brajendra whipped open his umbrella and, holding it over his companion's head, said briskly, 'Come Naren. Let me take you home.'

'I'm not going home.'

'Let's go together, then, wherever you are going. We'll part company the moment you want it.'

But the rain came on faster and fiercer as the two boys crossed the park and came on to the street. The umbrella tilted backwards in the strong wind and started fluttering like a flag above their heads. At length, thoroughly drenched and unable to combat the wind and water, the two boys took refuge under the portico of a large mansion. As Naren prepared to draw out another pinch of snuff, Brajendra said suddenly 'Naren! Kishorichand tells me that you're a frequent visitor at the temple of Dakshineswar; that you hang around Ramkrishna Thakur and have long conversations with him. Is that true?' There was no reply. 'From the prayer halls of the Brahmos,' Brajen murmured, 'to the temple of Kali is a long way! I've heard that Ramkrishna Thakur goes into a trance every now and then. You know who told me that? Our Principal, Mr Hasty. While teaching the poem "The Excursion" he was telling the boys about reverie and trance. "When a man's senses," he explained, "are suffused and overwhelmed by some phenomena, earthly or unearthly, to a point beyond his control, he goes into a trance. It happened to Wordsworth. It happens to Ramkrishna— a priest in the temple of Kali in Dakshineswar. If you boys wish to see the state with your own eyes, go to Dakshineswar." Mr Hasty believes in Ramkrishna. But quite a few others think he is a fake. You've been there several times. What do you think of him?'

'What do I think of him?' Naren turned his large eyes, burning with a strange passion, upon his friend. 'I don't know,' he said simply. 'I don't understand.' He shut his eyes for a few moments brooding on the subject, then said. 'Certain religious beliefs and customs have entrenched themselves in our culture for centuries! Can we wipe them out in an instant? And even if we could would it not create a terrible void? A vast chasm under our feet? With what would we fill it? Tell me Brajen, how would we bear the loss?'

'I see the drift of your argument Naren. And I understand your dilemma. You've read the Western philosophers—Descartes, Hume and Herbert Spencer—and have been influenced by them. But deep down within you is a core of Hindu fundamentalism that will not let you rest. What you're looking for is a God who walks the earth.'

'Aren't you?'

'No. Logic and Reason are my watch words. There's no room in my philosophy for faith. I don't need a God. But you're being driven by the question "Is there such a Being? Can we see Him?" That's true—isn't it?'

Naren was silent. He did not tell his friend that once, unable to control the curiosity that burned so fiercely within him, he had gone to Debendranath Thakur and asked him, 'Have you seen God?' But, Maharshi though he was, he had evaded the question. 'Your eyes are those of an ascetic's,' he had said. 'Abandon all else and give yourself over to Him. With prayer and meditation you will experience him some day.'

Afraid of exposing his weakness, Naren dashed out in the rain. 'Let's go,' he called out to Brajen. 'This blasted rain won't stop in a hurry. And I'm dying for a whiff of tobacco.' He started running down the street Brajen coming after him with his umbrella. As he ran he thought of the meetings he had had with Ramkrishna. The first time had been at Surendranath Mitra's house where he had been invited to sing before a gathering of disciples. It had been very hot and stuffy in the room and Naren had barely glanced at the slight dark figure in a coarse dhuti and *uduni*. He had sung a couple of songs, then slipped away. Then, last month, his kinsman Ramchandra Datta had invited him to Dakshineswar. 'Bilé,' he had said, 'I can see how harrassed you are with all the matchmaking going on in the house. Why don't you come with me to Dakshineswar? It's very pleasant there. The

111

temple stands right on the bank of the Ganga.' Naren had agreed. He had taken a couple of friends and journeyed by boat to Dakshineswar. They had been charmed with the place—the wide flight of steps rising from the river; the river itself, vast and turbulent; the *chatal* with its many temples. And then they had entered a little room in the north-west corner of the courtyard where Ramkrishna sat with his disciples. 'Thakur!' Ramchandra had introduced the boy to his guru with the words. 'This is my nephew Naren. He sings well.' As soon as they heard this the people assembled there clamoured to hear a song. Naren had no objection to obliging them. Raising his voice he sang not one but two songs. As he sang his eyes fell on Ramkrishna. Something queer had happened to the man. His eyes were open but his limbs were absolutely still. Not a muscle twitched. Not an eyelash flickered. He remained like that, in suspended animation, till the end of the song, then, suddenly came to life. Springing up, he caught Naren by the hand and dragged him out of the room to another empty room next to it. 'Oré' he cried bursting into tears. 'Why did you take so long in coming to me? I've waited such long days and nights. All these men around me with their worldly talk! I cannot bear them anymore. I'm sick to the heart. But what do you care?' Then, bringing his face close to Naren's, he muttered, 'I know you my Lord! You are an ancient Rishi. You are my Narayan in human form.' Naren was quite frightened. The man was mad, he thought. Stark, raving mad! What if he jumped on him and bit off a hunk of his flesh? He took a step backwards. 'Stay where you are,' Ramkrishna commanded. 'Wait here till I return.' He went out of the door and returned a few minutes later with a thala in his hand. It was piled high with sandesh, masses of pale yellow butter and palm candy crystals. 'Eat,' he commanded.

'All of it?' Naren exclaimed. 'How can I eat so much? I'll share it with my friends?'

'No. They'll be served later. I want to see you eat in my presence.'

Naren felt acutely uncomfortable as he stuffed handfuls of butter and sandesh into his mouth. Ramkrishna stood before him with folded hands all the time he ate, his eyes fixed solemnly on his face. When the last morsel had been swallowed Ramkrishna said, 'Promise me you'll come again. Very soon. Don't bring

112

anyone else. I want to see you alone.'

These thoughts went round and round in Naren's head as he ran down the street into Ramtanu Bosu Lane and entered his grandmother's house. His own home being too noisy and crowded for quiet study, a room had been kept for him in this old mansion. It was outside the main house, in a sort of dome, and here Naren read his books, practised his music and chatted with his friends. It was a small room but it contained all the basic essentials of living. A canvas cot with a soiled pillow on it stood in a corner. A clock ticked away on one wall. A tanpura and an esraj hung from hooks on another. There were books everywhere—on the bed, on the mat on the floor and the window sill.

Naren shed his wet clothes, wiped his head with a gamchha and wrapped a dry dhuti around him. Then, ducking his head under the string that held his few dhutis and pirans, he stood before a niche in the wall. Inside it was a hookah, a mass of coconut fibre and an earthen platter with some lumps of tobacco *gul* and a matchbox.

Naren had lit his hookah and taken a few puffs by the time Brajendranath arrived. He felt calmer now and readier to continue the conversation. 'Brajen,' he said passing the hookah to his friend. 'You wanted to know what I thought of Ramkrishna. I'll tell you. I asked him if he had seen God. And he answered that he had. He had seen God with his own eyes as clearly as he saw me standing before him.'

'Did you believe him?' Brajen gave a short laugh.

'I didn't,' Naren answered, hesitating a little. 'Yet, somehow, I'm sure he wasn't lying. What he claimed was the simple truth as far as he was concerned. The man is half mad but he is not a charlatan. I'm convinced of it. Whenever I'm with him I experience something I can't explain—even to myself. I keep racking my brains to find out what it is but the answer eludes me.' Naren's eyes clouded over and his voice shook with emotion as, having decided to open his heart to Brajendra, he recalled the strange sensations that he had experienced on his third visit to Ramkrishna. He hadn't wanted to go, he said. He had made up his mind he wouldn't. But he had promised and something, someone, seemed to be pushing him from within to redeem his promise. Finally, unable to bear the tension, he had decided to go

113

and get it over with. It would be for the last time, he had told himself. He would tell the man politely but firmly that their worlds were different and he, Naren, had other things to do.

Flushed with his new resolve Naren had set off for Dakshineswar walking at a brisk pace. But his idea of the distance from Shimle was far from accurate. In consequence he was completely exhausted by the time he reached the temple complex and entered Ramkrishna's room. He found him alone, sitting on his bed, apparently lost in his own thoughts. But his eyes lit up with pleasure the moment he saw Naren. 'Come sit by me,' he said, patting the space next to him. Then, when Naren had obeyed, he fixed his strange, sad eyes on his face and, muttering something below his breath, he raised his right leg and planted it on the boy's shoulder. Naren was frightened. He tried to move away; to throw it off but he was trapped between the wall and the leg—as heavy as stone and as implacable as death. Naren felt the blood rush to his head. Everything around him—the room, the bed, the man himself seemed to be dissolving in a mist. The walls of the room were spinning round and round, slowly at first then, gaining momentum, faster and then incredibly fast. He was being lifted out of himself into a vast expanse, a sea of emptiness which he knew was death. He would reach it soon, very soon now. '*Ogo!*' he cried out in terrible fear. 'What are you doing to me? My mother will weep. My father—' A cackle of mad laughter came to his ears. Then the weight was lifted and he could breathe again. The spinning slowed down, stopped and the walls became themselves again. Naren felt a hand on his chest. It was soothing; gentle. A voice murmured in his ear, 'Enough for now. There's plenty of time.' Naren stared in wonder at the smiling eyes that gazed with infinite tenderness into his but before he could speak a word, the moment was lost. The room started filling up with disciples and he rose and walked away.

Once home, Naren was filled with self loathing. He told himself that he had been conned, hypnotized. That was all there was to it. He had become the victim of a cheap trick that jugglers perform in the streets everyday. He hated himself because he had succumbed. Was he—the strong, brilliant, fiercely independent Naren Datta, that weak and culpable? He decided that he would go back again and expose the man for the low juggler that he was.

And he would go riding in a carriage this time. He had been fatigued by the long walk and become an easy target. This time it would be different.

On that fourth occasion Naren took a hackney cab and, when he dismounted at Dakshineswar, he felt strong and purposeful with his mind firm and his senses alert. As soon as he entered the room Ramkrishna rose from among his disciples and, putting an arm around Naren's shoulder, he said, 'Let's go for a walk.' Then leading him out of the room, he took him to a garden that stood within a stone's throw of the temple complex. After walking in silence for a few minutes Ramkrishna said suddenly, 'Do you know what I told Keshab?' Then, looking deep into Naren's eyes, he continued, 'You must know that the Brahmos believe that God is an abstraction. That we can't see him or feel him. But what I told Keshab was this: "To know God is to enter a sea of bliss. It is like floating on a vast expanse of water with neither beginning nor end. But when true faith is breathed upon these waters they congeal and turn into ice—solid, tangible. And when that happens we see God. Faith is like frosty breath; knowledge like the rising sun. When the sun of knowledge rises the ice melts and—"'

'Fine words,' Naren interrupted drily, 'but they mean nothing and prove nothing.'

'But I've seen—'

'You were hallucinating.'

'You may say what you like. But you came to me. You had to come. I haven't waited so long in vain.' His voice trailed away and before Naren's amazed eyes Ramkrishna went into a trance. He stood as motionless as stone, one hand up in the air with the fingers twirled. It lasted only a few seconds, then leaning forward, he touched Naren's brow. In an instant the world went dark and Naren fell down in a dead faint.

'I don't know how long I lay like that,' Naren concluded his story. 'But when I came to I found him bending over me. He said he had spoken to me as I lay unconscious. He had asked me a number of questions and I had answered. And for the last month—'

'Mesmerism!' Brajen cried excitedly. 'Haven't you heard of Mesmer Saheb? He used to put his patients to sleep and then draw them out as they slept.'

'Do you think that I, Narendranath Datta, could be mesmerized or hypnotized by an illiterate Brahmin? Am I sick? Am I a weakling? Besides, this happened a month ago. And I still haven't recovered. I feel different. I am different. There is a fierce throbbing in my head day and night and a flickering light before my eyes. Then, sometimes, a mist rolls over them obscuring my vision. I was knocking my head on the rails this afternoon because I couldn't see them.'

'You're overwrought,' Brajen said soothingly. 'Your brain is fevered. Forget about Ramkrishna. Sing a song instead.'

'I'm in no mood for singing.'

But Brajen would not leave without hearing a song. After a little coaxing Naren plucked his tanpura off the wall and adjusting the strings, commenced singing in his fine strong voice

'*É ki é sundar shobha*
Ki mukha héri é
Aaji mor gharé ailo hridaya nath
Prem utsa uthila aaji'

A faint rustle of garments could be heard as Naren sang. And, though it was quite dark by now, the two boys could discern a woman's shape on the veranda of the house opposite. Naren's nostrils flared in annoyance. Stopping in the middle of his song, he rose and shut the window with a bang. 'The harlot is upto her tricks again,' he muttered between clenched teeth. 'She won't leave me alone for a minute.' Then, turning to Brajen, he declared, 'I'm hungry. I'm going home.'

Over the next few weeks Naren made a desperate effort to forget his recent experiences and go back to his old life. He threw himself heart and soul into his studies poring over his books till late into the night. Then, thoroughly exhausted, he refreshed himself with singing or playing the esraj. He also took to visiting the akhara once again and practising his wrestling. Reports from Dakshineswar reached his ears from time to time. It was said that

---

* What wondrous beauty!
  Whose face is this which I behold?
  The Lord of my heart hath appeared before me.
  And the fountain of Love gushes forth.

Ramkrishna was missing him so much that he wept like a heart broken child day and night. His disciples had seen him wandering about the chatal one night, stark naked, with his dhuti rolled up under one arm, crying 'Naren! Naren! Oh! Why doesn't he come?' But Naren hardened his heart and would not go to Dakshineswar.

One night a strange thing happened. It was past midnight and, weary with long hours of study, Naren was singing his favourite compositions by the young poet Robi Thakur. He had taken the precaution of shutting the window even though the room was steaming hot and the sweat poured from his limbs. Suddenly the door burst open and the young widow who lived in the house opposite, stood in the room. She looked wild and dishevelled. Her hair streamed down her back and over her heaving bosom and her eyes burned with lust. Naren's eyes blazed with fury. 'The bitch!' he thought angrily. 'How dare she take such a liberty with me?' Harsh words rose to his lips. But, looking on her face, as white as jasmine petals and as tender, his anger vanished. She was young; very young. And she was a helpless victim of her natural instincts. Vidyasagar had had a law passed in favour of widow remarriage. But Hindu society hadn't endorsed it. A few widows had been saved. But what about the rest? They continued to live lives of acute deprivation. Scorned and despised for their widowed state, they were, nevertheless, taken advantage of by unscrupulous men from their own kin. The girl before him had evidently had a taste of sex. And now she wanted more. Could she be blamed for seeking fulfillment of a desire that was perfectly natural? Naren left his seat and, kneeling before the girl, placed his hands on her feet. 'Ma!' he cried, 'I'm your son. You're my mother.' The girl trembled and looked wildly around her. Then, covering her face with her hands, she fled from the room.

After this incident Naren left his grandmother's house and settled down in the house in Shimle. He started going to the Brahmo prayer meetings once again.

One day, as he sat singing with the others in the prayer hall, Ramkrishna came bustling in. The members looked up amazed at the little man in his soiled dhuti pulled up to his knees and wondered who he was. 'Who? What?' Voices cried out in alarm. Someone said 'Why! this is the Kali sadhu from Dakshineswar!

117

Who has invited him here?' The Acharya frowned and glared at him but Ramkrishna had neither eyes nor ears for any other than the one he sought. 'Naren! Naren!' he cried and pushed and elbowed his way through the agitated assembly causing a loud uproar. Some of the members rushed forward to grab him and throw him out. They shouted, pushed and jostled and stamped one another's feet. And in the middle of it all Ramkrishna went into a trance. Quick as a flash Naren jumped into the fray. Elbowing everyone aside with crude force, he picked up the slight body and ran out into the street. Putting him down, he asked sternly, 'Why did you come here? What if they had harmed you?'

'I miss you too much,' Ramkrishna said simply. 'My heart twists with pain and I can't bear it.'

'I'm taking you back to Dakshineswar. You mustn't come here again.'

'I won't. But I can't let go of you. Now—or ever.'

Chapter XV

Jyotirindranath took Gyanadanandini's advice. Leaving Chandannagar, he returned to Calcutta. But he did not go back to Jorasanko. He took up residence in Number 10 Sadar Street in Chowringee and moved in there with Kadambari.

Chowringhee was the most fashionable area in Calcutta. The houses were large and beautiful with neatly laid out gardens and were occupied, almost exclusively, by the British, Parsees and Armenians. It was a quiet locality and very clean. The open drains on either side of the road had been covered over recently with stone footpaths. Now the wide sweep of asphalt under bright gas lamps could match the finest street in London. Jyotirindranath liked to live in style and so vast quantities of furniture were ordered for Kadambari's new establishment. Carved bedsteads, Persian carpets and Belgian mirrors were arranged tastefully in all the bedrooms. There were pottery stands for plants in the verandas and English knick knacks in glass cupboards in the drawing room. Fresh flowers were sent in every morning from Hogg Saheb's market. These Kadambari arranged with her own hands—her floral designs changing with her changing moods.

Jyotirindranath and Kadambari had taken it for granted that Robi would move in with them. But Robi was not sure of what he wanted to do. Gyanadanandini had invited him to stay with her several times. 'You've spent quite a while with Natun,' she had said in her strident tones. 'It is time you came to us. Have you forgotten the wonderful times we had in England?' Somewhat intimidated, Robi pondered deeply over the matter and took a decision. He would move into the house at Birji Talao for the present. But he would take Kadambari's permission first.

Entering the house in Sadar Street that morning, he found his sister-in-law putting the last finishing touches to the room she had prepared for his use. It was a charming room, light and airy, with a large balcony opening out of it. And it had been furnished in Kadambari's impeccable taste. A mahogany bedstead with a

119

high mattress and snowy sheets and pillows stood between the wide windows. On tall whatnots on either side of the bed were vases with masses of white flowers in them. In one corner stood a brand new writing table and a high-backed chair. Curtains of fine white lace hung from the windows. Robi was charmed. The predominance of white in the room lent it a purity and serenity Robi had never seen in any room before.

Kadambari jumped off the stool on which she had been standing hanging up the last curtain. It was a hot airless day of late April and a metallic sun shone out of a colourless sky. Kadambari's brow was beaded over with perspiration. Untucking the end of her sari from her waist she wiped her face.

'You've made the room really beautiful,' Robi said with a naughty gleam in his eye. 'Who is to stay here?'

'Who do you think?'

'Some special guest, perhaps?'

'The guest rooms are all downstairs.'

'What if Biharilal Chakraborty decides to spend a night here? Will you send him downstairs?'

'Death be on you!' Kadambari rolled her eyes with mock severity at her brother-in-law.

'Bouthan,' Robi hesitated a little. 'Mejo Bouthan wishes me to stay with her. I was wondering if I might do so—for a while. I would spend the whole day here with you. Only at night—'

The light went out of Kadambari's eyes. 'You won't stay here?' She asked in the voice of a hurt child, 'You will go away to your Mejo Bouthan?' She gazed into Robi's face for a few moments then added, 'Very well. If you wish it.' 'Arré!' Robi changed his decision in an instant. 'You give your consent without a moment's hesitation. It means you don't care to keep me with you.' Kadambari turned her face away. 'You must do as you wish,' she said.

The consequence was that Robi moved into the house in Sadar Street. As in Chandannagar, he was very happy here. Wherever Jyotirindranath went, life, light, joy and laughter accompanied him. But whereas in Chandannagar the three had been alone, here they had plenty of society. Akshay Chowdhury, Priyanath Sen and Janakinath Ghoshal came every morning, They were Jyotirindranath's friends and on the editorial board of

120

Bharati. Although Debendranath's eldest son Dwijendranath was official editor, the actual work was done by Jyotirindranath and his friends. Robi had joined them recently and was proving to be a good worker. Animated discussions on the quality of the articles, peppered with comments on the weather, the state of the country and innumerable other subjects, were carried on over cups of fragrant, steaming tea of which there was an unending supply from Kadambari's kitchen. She, herself, was rarely to be seen at these meetings. Once in a while she would come in with something in her hands—a basket of lychees from the garden or a silver bowl full of sandesh she had made herself. Then, at some gentleman's request, she would express her opinion on the quality of some entry, startling the group with the sensitivity and sharpness of her literary judgement. But their invitation to join them in their work was invariably rejected. 'What do I know of such things?' she would say shaking her head shyly, 'I'm not learned like you.'

Another thing that Kadambari refused to do was write. There were several upcoming women writers in Calcutta now. Robi's second sister Swarnakumari and Akshay Chowdhury's wife Sarat Kumari, whom Robi had nicknamed Lahorini because her childhood had been spent in Lahore, were regular contributors to *Bharati.* Gyanadanandini, too, fancied herself as a writer though her command over the Bengali language was far from satisfactory and Robi had to rewrite her work extensively before sending it to the press. But Kadambari, who had genuine talent, refused to take up a pen.

The editorial sessions took up a good part of the day with a break for a lavish noon meal. But though the mornings and afternoons flew by as if on golden wings, the evenings in the house in Sadar Street were long and desolate for Kadambari. Jyotirindranath was never at home. Robi spent hour after hour lying prone in bed with a pillow under his chest writing incessantly. Prose, poetry, fiction or review—whatever he took up he gave it all he had. But a restlessness he could not understand seized him as he wrote. He lost track of time; of his responsibilities to others; even hunger and thirst. He wrote because he loved to write and had to write. But he was not at peace. The joy of creation eluded him. He was straining himself

121

beyond endurance; beyond his capacity even, but he was achieving nothing. A goal, shrouded in mist, glimmered before him. An urge to reach it was driving him relentlessly, cruelly. Only he didn't know what it was or in which direction he had to go.

Dusk was falling, lengthening the shadows in Robi's room. The house was absolutely still. Robi sat poring over his writing (he used a slate these days because too much paper was being wasted on cancellations) when some faint tinkling sounds, soft and melodious, wafted into his ears. He rose and, following the music, climbed the stairs to the upper floor and walked into the hall. Kadambari was seated at the grand piano and was playing with rapt attention. There was a tinge of melancholy in the tune she played, a sweet nostalgia that synchronized, somehow, with her form as it bent over the piano, dim and shadowy, in the fading light. She wore a sari the colour of incense smoke and ropes of jasmine were twined about the long strands of her open hair. A perfume, sweet and elusive, rose from her person enveloping Robi as he came up silently and stood by her. Kadambari turned her head, saw Robi, and taking her hands off the piano said ruefully, 'I've disturbed you. You had to leave your work—'

'Why do you stop? It was beautiful. What were you playing?'

'It was nothing. I thought I was playing softly. I didn't realize . . . What made you come up?'

'A flock of birds called out together just outside my window. I thought dawn had broken. I often get confused about the time. Birds call out at dawn when leaving their nests and at dusk when they return. One is a cry of welcome to the new day—the other of farewell.'

'I hear the farewell call,' Kadambari murmured absently.

'Natun Bouthan,' Robi said. 'Tell me about yourself.'

'About myself! What is there to tell?'

'Your other life—'

'You mean before I was wed? But that was so long ago! I was only a child. And I've never gone back. Your family does not approve of mine.'

'I don't mean that. I mean your earlier incarnation. When you were a goddess in Greece. One beautiful face is enough to conquer the world. And you had three.'

'Ugh! A three-faced creature! How terrible!'

'Hecate had one face turned to the world, the second to the sky and the third to the sea. She was an enchantress. When Pluto carried Persephone away to the underworld Hecate lit a flaming torch and searched for her through Heaven, Earth and Hell.'

'Why do you call me Hecate?'

'Because you have the same enchantment. Because your face is everywhere. I see it wherever I go.'

'You see nothing but the paper before you.'

'Don't I see your face there? All the time?'

'I'll go and see if the lamps are lit,' Kadambari rose from her seat. 'Don't go,' Robi took her hand in his. 'Why are you all dressed up Natun Bouthan? Is Jyotidada taking you out somewhere?'

'I wouldn't go even if he asked me,' Kadambari tossed her head making the diamonds in her ears burst into flame. 'Can't I dress up for myself?'

'Let's go up to the roof and watch the sunset. When the last streak of twilight fades from the horizon one feels one is floating in the sky—'

Jyotirindra was very busy with his new venture. He had gained quite a reputation as a playwright and people flocked to the public theatre to see his plays. This, of course, was part of a general upsurge of interest in the theatre. Conservatives frowned on this new passion and denounced it in exaggerated terms. Play acting, they declared, was shameless and godless and the antics of drunks and whores. But the public cared not a whit for these pronouncements. The actress Binodini was a prostitute but her name was on everyone's lips. Girish Ghosh was a notorious drunk and a frequenter of brothels but his popularity as an actor and playwright were phenomenal. Jyotirindranath spent all evening and much of the night in their company. And when he didn't, he was with Gyanadanandini. Gyandanandini threw a lot of parties where wine and champagne flowed freely. Entertainment of this kind was not possible in Jyotirindranath's own house. Kadambari was a good hostess but she liked a few guests at a time. Too many people and too much noise were not to her taste. Nor was it to Robi's. Yet Jyotirindranath was Robi's hero. There was not another man among Robi's acquaintance

123

who had so much talent, such capacity for hard work and so much life force. The best thing about Jyotirindranath was that when a venture failed he could cut his losses and turn all his energies on something else. Robi admired his Jyotidada immensely and tried to model himself on him.

One morning Robi woke up burning with fever. A terrible shivering took hold of him and his limbs felt cold and clammy. Wrapping himself in a thick quilt he lay in bed waiting for the fever to subside. He didn't call anyone because he didn't want to worry Kadambari. She was suffering from malaria herself. Dr Neelmadhav had taken a look at her and prescribed some medicines but she didn't seem to be getting any better.

Through that long steamy afternoon Robi lay wrapped up in his quilt. His head throbbed like a fiery coal but the rest of him was as cold as ice. These were strange sensations but he revelled in them. He felt his body had become light, so light that it could float away out of the window on the hot still air. Thoughts ran round and round his head but they had the quality of dreams. Even in that state Robi tried to compose a song. But as soon as he got to the third line he forgot the first and when, after a desperate effort, he was able to remember the first line, he forgot the rest.

A touch on the brow made Robi open his eyes. Kadambari stood before him. Her hair was dishevelled and a simple sari of yellow cotton was wrapped carelessly around her. Her face was flushed and her eyes bright with fever. 'Natun Bouthan,' Robi took her hand. It felt hot and dry in his own fevered one. 'You're burning all over,' Kadambari cried, 'Why didn't you send for me?'

'You have the fever too. You shouldn't have left your bed.'

'I'm alright. I'll send Sarkar Moshai for the doctor. And you need a cool compress on your forehead.'

'So do you.'

'Women can do without a lot of things. Your life is precious. You need to get well soon.'

'Don't you?'

'You have so much to give to the world. What have I?'

'Everyone has something to give, Natun Bouthan. Tell me, why is it that we are so close yet so far apart? Why is it that I never know what's going on in that mind of yours?'

124

'You would if you gave it a little thought,' Kadambari laughed, 'But you don't have the time.'

Robi's fever left him after two days and Kadambari's the day after. Dr Neelmadhav attended them and left medicines which effected a cure but only temporarily. And so it went on. Gradually, Robi and Kadambari got used to the pattern. Robi would write till he felt the fever coming on, then lie down dragging the quilt over him. When well, Kadambari would bathe twice a day, run up and down with tasty tidbits for Robi and take up her neglected household tasks. Then, with the first shivering, she would creep into bed or sit in a patch of sunshine. Sometimes they sat together, Robi reading out his newest poem and she listening with rapt attention. Her face had become pale and worn and her jacket flapped loosely from her thin arms and chest. But her eyes were jewel bright and her smile as sweet as ever.

Returning from Silaidaha, Jyotirindranath was appalled at what he saw. Placing a hand on his wife's brow he took a decision. Doses of quinine were not enough. Robi and Kadambari needed a change. He would take them to Darjeeling. The cool pure mountain air would do them good. Sending for Sarkar Moshai, he outlined his plans and ordered him to make the arrangements. Then he rushed off again on his innumerable missions.

That evening Robi and Kadambari sat on the roof waiting for Jyotirindranath. He had said that he would return before dusk but the hours passed and they went on waiting. And, then, before their entranced eyes, a moon huge, soft and full, rose over the horizon and turned the maidan into a sea of silver. The young pair moved closer. Their hands, hot and fevered, clasped one another's. Not a word was spoken. For the first time in their lives they had heard and spoken the language of silence.

A loud volley of shots followed by the shrill whistle of a ship leaving harbour crashed into that silence. They knew what it was. Ashley Eden, Governor of Bengal, was leaving for England. There was bound to be rejoicing in many homes tonight. Eden was hated by the natives for having foisted the infamous Vernacular Act on them. And, almost at the same time as the shots, Jyotirindra's phaeton rolled up and stopped at the door.

Robi woke before dawn the next morning. His body felt light and airy. A sweet somnolence misted his eyes and rested lightly on

125

his spirit. He wandered out into the balcony and looked up at the sky. There was a pale grey glimmer in the east against which the trees of the maidan stood etched with kohl. As he stood watching, faint streaks of mauve and pink appeared, spread over the grey, changing tints till the sky became a riot of gold, rose and pearl. Then the sun came up, a great ball of flame, and first light fell on the earth and seeped into Robi's soul. Robi gazed in wonder at the scene. A mist rolled away from his eyes and he felt as though he was seeing the world for the first time. It was bathed in light. His limbs trembled with an ecstasy he had never known before. Light—pure, clear, blinding light—was entering the innermost recesses of his being, searching out dark corners, flushing out doubts and fears. His ears were filled with the sound of rushing water as great waves of light crashed over the rocks that wombed his soul, scattering them far and wide and setting it free. Free to flow like a joyous stream towards a destination unknown . . .

Robi went into his room and started writing. His pen raced over the paper as if with a life and will of its own. Words and phrases poured out of him filling sheet after sheet without effort. It seemed to him that the muse was speaking for herself and he was only the humble medium whose hand held the pen.

He wrote all morning and all afternoon without a break, even leaving the plate of food Kadambari had sent up to his room untouched. In the evening Kadambari came. 'What is the matter?' she cried. 'You haven't washed or bathed. And you've eaten nothing. You'll make yourself ill.' Robi muttered something absently and went on writing. 'Stop it Robi,' Kadambari ordered imperiously, 'or I'll snatch your papers away.' Robi neither looked up nor answered. Kadambari took up a pencil and made a little squiggle along the margin of Robi's poem. 'What are you doing?' Robi cried out indignantly. Kadambari leaned over and ruffled his hair. Robi jerked his head away, sat up and said, 'I have written a new poem Natun Bouthan. It is called *Nirijhar ér swapno bhanga*. Shall I read it out to you?' Then, without waiting for an answer, he started reciting the lines.

'On this new morn the bird of dawn
Sings a wondrous song
From the distant sky it comes floating by . . .'

Looking up he asked eagerly, 'Do you like it?' Kadambari frowned and shook her head. 'Not much,' she said. 'I find nothing original or striking in the lines.'

'You don't understand,' Robi cried out, deeply wounded. 'There was no effort on my part. The lines poured out of me as though of their own volition.' Kadambari averted her eyes as though embarrassed at what she was about to say. 'Even if they did,' she murmured gently, 'that alone is not enough. Poetry has to be worked at like any other art form. Of course I understand very little—' Then, seeing the hurt expression in Robi's eyes, she added quickly, 'Read some more.' Robi read a few more lines and looked up hopefully. Kadambari shifted her feet guiltily. 'No Robi,' she said after a moment's hesitation. 'I think you can do better. I may be wrong of course.' At this the blood rushed to Robi's face and he glared at Kadambari in real anger. 'The woman understands nothing of poetry,' he thought indignantly. 'I'll never read my poems out to her again.' Turning his back on her he bent over his papers. 'Don't be offended Robi,' Kadambari pleaded placing a gentle hand on his back. 'Read a little more.' Robi turned over a whole page and commenced reading once again.

'At dawn I felt the sun's hand
touch my soul
Its light seeping into my very being
I heard the first bird song
Enter my cave of dark shadows
I know not how
I know not how my soul awoke
from its long, long sleep

'Robi!' Kadambari exclaimed. 'I like this bit. I like it very much.' Robi's voice changed. It became strong and sonorous as he went on —

'My soul awakes.
Passions and desires
Like a growing storm in a dormant sea
Swell and foam within me
The earth shudders beneath my feet
Primeval rocks crash down mountain slopes
First light splitting their stone hearts'

'Robi,' Kadambari grasped his arm. 'It's wonderful! It's different. You're different—somehow!'

Robi stopped. His face was flushed and his eyes shone with a strange energy. Beads of perspiration appeared on his brow. 'I am possessed Natun Bouthan,' he said quietly. 'By whom or by what I cannot say. But I'm not myself anymore. And I'll never be the same again.'

Chapter XVI

Bhumisuta rued the day that she had announced she could dance. The consequence of that careless remark was that she was sent for, every afternoon, by the two mistresses of the house and made to perform for their amusement. Since it was Suhasini who had brought the girl from Puri it was generally assumed that Bhumisuta was her personal property. But, as a matter of fact, it was Krishnabhamini who had taken the girl under her wing. Bhumisuta ate and slept in Krishnabhamini's apartments and made herself useful to her. She prepared hookahs for Bimalbhushan and picked flowers for his morning puja. She washed and mended Krishnabhamini's clothes and helped her with her toilette, grinding the turmeric and sandal for her bath.

In this household the men left quite early and the women had the whole day to themselves. Her bath and noon meal over, Krishnabhamini would sit with her sister-in-law on her high bed with a box of betel between them. Then, packing a paan into her mouth, she would call 'Bhumi! O Bhumi!' Bhumisuta knew what that call meant. As soon as she heard it she would go to her room and get ready for her part. Combing out her long hair she would twist it into a knot on the top of her head and twine garlands of flowers around it. She would darken her eyes with kohl and adorn her brow and cheeks with a design of sandal paste. Taking out an old silk sari that had belonged to her mother she would wear it in the style of Oriya dancers with the intricately woven aanchal fanning out from the waist. Bhumisuta danced well. Her movements were liquid, her feet light and her eyes effectively expressed the many moods of the dance. But the moment she started her song, her anklets jingling to the rhythm of her tapping feet, the two on the bed fell over each other laughing. The women crowding at the door—distant aunts, cousins, maids and serving women—took up the cue and rolled all over the ground in mirth. The truth was that the women of the household had never seen anyone dance before. It was something they associated with bad

129

women and licentious men.

'Who taught you to dance Bhumi?' Krishnabhamini had asked on the first day and had been horrified to hear that it was her father. She knew Bhumisuta's father had been a school master and that she came from a poor but respectable family. 'What kind of a father is this,' she had thought, 'who could train his daughter in something so wicked?' She did not know that Orissa, having escaped the influence of the Muslims, had largely retained its ancient culture. Oriya women enjoyed far great mobility and exposure to the world than their Bengali counterparts, and music and dance was an integral part of their lives. The temples of Puri and Bhuvaneshwar and the recently discovered ruins of Konarak were covered with sculpture depicting dance as an offering to the gods. There was not one temple in Bengal that could boast of such a heritage.

One afternoon, while sitting in his office, Manibhushan felt a cramp in his shoulder. He tried to ignore it at first then, when the pain became really bad, he decided to go home and lie down. As he walked up the stairs, he heard snatches of a song, the notes floating down from above. They sounded sweet but strange to his ears being sung in an alien tongue. The song was accompanied by the smart tapping of feet on the floor and the tinkling sounds of metal beating against metal. He wondered what was going on. Taking off his shoes he tiptoed, on silent feet, down the gallery till he came to his sister-in-law's apartment where a strange sight met his eyes. Eight or ten women were sitting on the floor at one end of the room and, at the other, a girl sang and danced, her body swaying gracefully to the rhythm of the cymbals she clashed with her hands. She was a beautiful girl with long, lustrous eyes fringed with thick dark lashes. Her limbs were lithe and supple and her hands slim and delicate as champak buds. He did not recognize Bhumisuta. He didn't see her much these days and she had changed a lot from the thin, emaciated girl he had brought from Puri. She was much taller now. Her skin shone like polished bronze and from under her sari he could see the triumphant swelling of her breasts. He thought her a whore brought in from a house of ill-repute for the amusement of the women of the family, and was deeply shocked. Of course he, himself, kept a woman in a pleasure house in Shankhér Bazar. But that was different. He was

130

a man. These were women, custodians of household purity and tradition. How could they, his own wife and sister-in-law among them, have sunk so low? '*Chhi! Chhi! Chhi!*' he muttered between clenched teeth, then let out a bloodcurdling roar. 'What is going on?' he thundered. 'Stop it. Stop it at once.' The women stared at him in horror. 'You've defiled the house,' he shouted at them. 'You've desecrated its sanctity. Don't we have our Radha Madhav keeping an eye on us all? Do you think—?'

'*O go! Na go!*', Suhasini cried. Her face was pale and her lips trembled. 'That's our own Bhumi. She was dancing and we were watching her—just for fun.' Now Manibhushan recognized Bhumisuta and his condemnation was complete. 'If she wanted to dance,' the inexorable voice pronounced solemnly, 'what was wrong with her being a devdasi? Why did we bring her from Puri? Once a whore—always a whore!' Then, turning angry red eyes on Bhumisuta, he said, 'I warn you. If I ever catch you at your tricks again I'll have you thrown out of the house. *Chhi! Chhi!*'

From that day Bhumisuta was forbidden to dance. Her anklets were thrown into the ash heap. But dance was in her blood and she could not live without it. It was the only way she knew to express herself. She continued to dance on the sly, away from peering eyes—sometimes in her own room, on the roof, even in the bathing-rooms downstairs. The roof was the best. It was huge and had a high wall around it. Besides, the inmates of the house rarely came up and she could dance at her ease. It was particularly good at night for everyone in the house retired early and she could dance with wild abandon under the moon and stars. At night the house was dark and silent except for one window where a lamp burned till the small hours. It was Bharat's room. Shashibhushan had returned to Tripura leaving Bharat behind. But he had given the boy the responsibility of looking after his share of the estate and had instructed his brothers to pay him a monthly salary of twenty rupees. He had also enjoined them to see that Bharat was treated with respect as befitted an employee of the estate. Radharaman had kept his word, too, and sent a stipend of ten rupees a month regularly in Bharat's name. In consequence, the quality of Bharat's life had changed. He had his own room now. Two tutors came every day to impart instruction in English, Sanskrit and Arithmetic. There were servants to clean his room, wash and mend his clothes and serve him his meals. And they vied with each other to do so for, thanks to the allowance he received, he was able to tip them generously. Bharat was a tall sturdy young man now with broad shoulders and heavy wrists and a faint dark stubble covering his cheeks and chin.

From a certain corner of the roof Bhumisuta had a full view of Bharat's room. She came and stood there often. And though he was totally oblivious of her she could not take her eyes off the handsome figure bent over his books. He was not to be seen in the garden anymore. He left his bed late these days, long after Bhumisuta's flower picking was over.

One day news came for Monibhushan that a ship carrying several tons of valuable goods, ordered by him, had been wrecked at Diamond Harbour. Monibhushan spent a sleepless night and, next morning, before rushing off to see what could be retrieved, he came to the puja room to obtain the blessings of Radha Madhav—the household deities of the Singhas. The god and the goddess were carved out of black stone and had gold eyes and gold crowns. A flawless diamond winked and sparkled from the centre of Madhav's crown.

Monibhushan stepped over the threshold and stopped short in surprise at the scene before him. On the marble floor, in front of Radha Madhav, Bhumisuta was dancing in rhythm to some *padavalis* from the *Geet Govinda* which she hummed softly. A sharp reprimand rose to his lips but remained unuttered—he didn't know why. He was a man of the world, pragmatic and materialistic with no room in him for the finer feelings. Yet he stood watching Bhumisuta dance and, for the first time in his life, his soul quivered in response to a thing of beauty. 'She's like a flower,' he thought suddenly. 'She moves as the wind breathes over her and she opens her petals to the sun.' He forgot what he had come for; forgot the loss of his property. The frown that had appeared between his brows melted away. His mouth relaxed in a smile.

Bhumisuta became aware of him in a few seconds. Turning around she gave a little cry. Her face went white. Touching her forehead quickly to the ground at Radha Madhav's feet she tried to slip out of the door. But Monibhushan wouldn't let her. He took her trembling hand in his and his eyes burned hotly into hers. 'Why did you stop?' he whispered. 'I liked it.' He pulled her closer, almost to his breast. Then, suddenly, he remembered where he was. This was the puja room and Radha Madhav were watching him. Releasing the girl abruptly he cleared his throat and muttered, 'Where's the vessel of *gangajal?*'

A few minutes later the house was filled with the sound of loud weeping. Monibhushan walked into his bedroom to find his wife rolling on the ground, cursing and tearing her hair. '*Ogo!*' she cried. 'What a cruel fate I've brought upon myself! I've been nurturing a snake on milk and honey! I took pity on the girl, rescued her from a life of shame, fed her and clothed her. And now she robs me of my own husband!' Monibhushan was aghast. He had only held Bhumisuta's hand. And that too for a few seconds. Who had seen him? A servant or a maid perhaps. Bhumisuta, herself, would not have talked about it, surely. His wife, of course, believed the worst and he would have a hard time pacifying her. '*Ogo!*' Suhasini sobbed louder at the sight of her husband. 'You've kept a mistress in Shankhér Bazar. Isn't that enough? Must you keep one in my own house?' Now Monibhushan made up his mind. 'You have only yourself to blame,' he said loudly and sternly. 'Didn't I warn you? Once a whore, always a whore? She tried to seduce me. But I'm strong and upright. I could resist her. If I were you I would get rid of her at once.'

Bimalbhushan loved good food and spent many pleasurable hours planning his meals. He had retired from active life and whiled away much of his time dozing in an armchair and sucking at the tube of his *albola*. His brother looked after the business and the estates. His wife ran the household. He, himself, was a gentleman of leisure. On this fateful morning he sat in a corner of the courtyard stroking his stomach and trying to decide what he would have for breakfast. Was it to be *chiré* soaked in rich curd with a lavish sprinkle of brown sugar and lashings of banana and mango pulp? Or did he fancy a bowl of halwa swimming in ghee and eaten with freshly puffed up *luchis* straight from the wok? But, whatever it was, it had to be preceded by a bitter draught. Bimalbhushan suffered from constipation and the kaviraj had ordered him to drink a glassful of neem juice first thing in the morning on an empty stomach. The loathsome stuff stood on a

small table at his elbow. He looked askance at it from time to time
trying to summon up the courage to put it to his lips when the
sound of a woman's voice, raised in angry condemnation,
reached his ears. Turning to his wife he said, 'Something seems to
be going on in Moni's apartment. What is it?'

'Mejo Bou is sending Bhumi away.'

'Sending who away?'

'Bhumi, Bhumi! Don't you remember? The orphan girl she
brought from Puri. Poor child! She was so useful to me. I shall
miss her sorely.'

Bimalbhushan glanced at his wife's plump face sagging with
disappointment and self pity, and his mouth curled with
amusement. He decided to humour her. And his whim of the
moment saved Bhumisusta.

'If that's the way you feel,' he said, 'why do you allow Mejo
Bou to turn her out? Who pays the servants? You or she?'

'Bhumi is not paid anything. Mejo Thakurpo bought her from
a *panda* in Puri. He spent a lot of money on her. She's theirs—'

'What money? His own or the estate's?'

'That I don't know.'

'Listen Bara Bou. I remember perfectly well that Moni
charged the estate one hundred and forty rupees against her
purchase. What right has he to throw her out? She's a family
slave—not his personal one. Besides, you are the elder of the two
mistresses. It's your word that should count.'

'Mejo Bou does as she likes. She's so arrogant—she walks
over people's heads.'

'You're afraid of her!' Bimalbhushan laughed derisively, 'You
should learn to keep her in control.'

That mocking laugh decided Krishnabhamini. It was time, she
thought angrily, that she asserted her rights as the elder mistress
of the house. She had been too kind; too easy-going. But now
things were going to be different. She shouted for her maid
Mangala and, when the woman came scurrying in, she said in a
loud commanding voice, 'Go tell Mejo Bou that she has no right
to dismiss anyone without my permission. Bhumi shall stay here
as long as I choose.'

The consequence of this message was that Bhumisuta stayed
on in the Singha household and the two sisters-in-law stopped

talking to one another.

Krishnabhamini had no sons. Of her three daughters two were wed already and preparations were on for the betrothal of the third. Being a kind, motherly sort of woman she was very fond of her sister's children, the twins Ajoy and Bijoy in particular. They were nice looking boys—plump and fair with round black eyes and shiny noses. Being identical twins they looked exactly like one another, had the same tastes and even said the same things—one echoing the other. Krishnabhamini invited them often, fed them lavish meals and gave them quantities of presents.

One day, quite by accident, the two boys saw Bhumisuta. Walking into their aunt's bedroom, unannounced, they saw her dancing for the amusement of Krishnabhamini and her maids. And, since that day, they were to be seen in the house in Bhabanipur at all hours of the day and night. Everyone noticed it except their adoring aunt who couldn't have too much of her darling Aju and Biju. The two boys never ceased to pester Bhumisuta to dance for them but she refused everytime, even risking Krishnabhamini's displeasure. And, whenever she saw them, she ran and hid herself—in the garden, the stables or the puja room. One night, in order to escape her persecutors, she crept up to the roof and stood crouching against the wall. It was a beautiful night. There was a full moon in the sky from which light descended like a silver mist illuminating every nook and corner. Bhumisuta stood enveloped in the bright haze, her entranced eyes gazing on the horizon which trembled like a sea of milky light. A cool breeze sprang up tossing the branches of the trees now this way, now that. Peace descended on Bhumisuta's soul. She was alone, truly alone at last; except for the moon who was smiling down at her.

Suddenly she heard footsteps on the stairs and her blood froze. 'She came up here. I saw her,' one voice said. 'I saw her,' the other echoed. It didn't take Ajoy and Bijoy long to find Bhumisuta. They made a rush at her and shouted in unison, 'I've found her. I've found her.' Bhumisuta slipped past them and ran towards the stairs but the two were strong young men and overtook her easily. Ajoy grasped her arm and said, 'Why do you run away from us? We won't harm you,' and the other said in exactly the same voice, 'Why do you run away from us? We won't

135

harm you.' But Bhumisuta strained and pulled against them trying to free herself. At this the boys lost their temper. One grabbed her by the hair and the other pushed her so hard that she fell to the ground. Picking herself up in a flash she ran as fast as she could, the boys chasing her like two cats after a mouse, cackling with laughter all the while. Sometimes one caught her and tried to pull her towards him but the other pulled in the opposite direction, setting her free. Bhumisuta knew that screaming for help would do her no good. She had matured considerably in the last few years and knew that men were above reproach. Males were likened to gold rings, valuable even when misshapen. No harm could come to them. But if she uttered a word of complaint against the mistress' beloved nephews she would be starved and beaten and pronounced guilty of seducing two innocents. Rushing up to the wall she considered throwing herself down. 'Let it end,' she thought bitterly, 'Let this life of misery and humiliation end. What else is left for me?' But, on the point of clambering up the wall, she thought suddenly, 'If I fall from such a great height my head will be squashed flat against the stone flags below. My legs and arms will crack and break like twigs. It will be terribly painful. Shall I be able to bear it?' She changed her mind and made a dash in the opposite direction. This time she found the stairs. She leaped down half skipping, half sliding till, missing her footing, she rolled down the rest. Amazingly, she was unhurt. Picking herself up she ran into Bharat's room—the only one in which a light burned—and closed the door. But Aju and Biju were right on her heels. The door burst open and the two ogres fell on her. 'Hé! Hé! Hé!' they cackled, 'How can you escape us now?'

Bharat had merely turned his head when he heard Bhumisuta come in. Now, seeing what appeared to be a pair of white monkeys jumping about in his room, he pushed back his chair and stood up. His blue blood boiled in his veins. Grabbing one of them by the hair he struck him on the cheek with all the force he could muster. Then, glaring at the other, he thundered, 'Get out of my room or I'll—' Picking up an iron rod he advanced menacingly. The two bullies ran out of the room like the cowards they were. Bhumisuta stood quaking in a corner, her arms covering her breast.

Bharat went back to his table without bothering to cast a glance at her. Waving a hand in dismissal he bent over his books once again. This was the second time that Bharat had come to Bhumisuta's rescue. But he didn't speak a word to her. Bhumisuta watched him for sometime then, coming up to him timidly, she said, 'You saved my honour. What can I give you in return?' Her voice was sweet and she spoke in an educated tongue. Bharat's curiosity was aroused and he turned around and looked at her. 'She can't be a mere slave,' he thought.

'Who are you?' he asked.

'I've come from Orissa. I'm an orphan.'

'You don't have to give me anything. Go to your room and don't come back.'

'If they catch me again—'

'Well, I can't protect you every time. Why don't you talk to the masters of the house?'

'They won't believe me.'

'Even if they don't—there's nothing I can do for you. I live quietly in one corner of the house. I hardly know the inmates—' Picking up the lamp from the niche in which it stood he said, a kinder note creeping into his voice, 'Go to your room. I'll hold a light for you. Don't be afraid. No one will harm you.'

The very next night Bhumisuta was back in Bharat's room. This time she came unpursued—of her own volition. Bharat looked up as she entered and his face hardened. 'Why are you here again?' he asked severely, 'What do you want from me?' Bhumisuta fidgeted a little, cleared her throat and said, 'I have a coral ring set in silver—not in gold. Will you take it?'

'A ring?' Bharat exclaimed, 'Why should I take a ring?'

'Because I have nothing else.' Bharat's puckered brow smoothened and a smile flickered on his lips. The girl was a slave in this house. Yet her sense of self respect was so intense that she would not take anything without giving something in return.

'I can sing verses from *Geet Govinda*,' she continued. 'Would you like to hear me?'

'*Geet Govinda!* Do you know Sanskrit?'

'Yes. I know English too. *A sly fox met a hen.* It means—'

'What's English for *Hathi?*'

'Elephant.'

137

'How do you say *Jagannath ér mandir* in English?'

'Lord Jagannath's Temple.'

'Who taught you all this?'

'My father. But he died of cholera. They all died of cholera. And so my lessons stopped. Will you teach me?'

'I have no time. Besides, I'm a student myself.'

Bhumisuta went and sat in a corner of the room, on the floor. 'You don't have to waste your time on me,' she said comfortably. 'I'll sit here and listen to you as you read. But if I don't understand something—' Bharat pushed his chair away and stood up. 'Please go,' he said sternly,' and don't disturb me again.'

'Then you must take this.' Putting the ring down on the table Bhumisuta ran out of the room stifling her sobs with difficulty. Bharat looked down at the ring. It was old and bent and the silver had turned black with disuse. But it was the only thing she had and she had insisted on giving it to him because she couldn't accept anything in charity.

The next morning he was awakened by the sound of a sweet voice singing outside his door. Bharat smiled to himself. The girl had evidently thought the coral ring insufficient payment for saving her life and honour. She was singing for him because that was the only other thing she could give him. Opening the door, Bharat walked up to where she sat huddled on the floor. Putting the ring in her hands he said, 'You have sung for me. That is payment enough. You must keep the ring.'

'I can dance too,' Bhumisuta rose from the floor, 'Would you like to see me?' Then, without waiting for an answer, she raised her arms above her head and swayed like a flower to the rhythm of her tapping feet. Bharat was charmed. 'Very good,' he said encouragingly, 'you dance well.'

'Will you help me with my lessons then?'

'No. I don't have the time.'

A couple of days later Bharat went to the theatre with his friends. They were showing Girish Ghosh's *Pandav ér agyatbas* at the National. It was a popular playhouse but not as popular as Bengal Theatre. The latter used more sophisticated techniques. In one of their plays they had even brought a horse on to the stage. Girish Ghosh played two roles in *Pandav ér agyatbas*. He was Duryodhan and Keechak. Amritalal was Bhim and Binodini was

138

Draupadi. Bharat wondered who Abhimanyu was till a friend whispered in his ear, 'That is Bonobiharini.' Bharat was surprised. A woman doing a man's role and that too so well! No wonder the hall resounded with claps every time Abhimanyu came on the stage. Bhushan Kumari was playing Uttara. She had to dance in all her scenes but her dancing, Bharat thought, was atrocious. Her arms and legs were as stiff as sticks. Suddenly he thought of Bhumisuta. She could sing sweetly and dance gracefully. And she was beautiful. She was ideal for the theatre. Why was she wasting her talents living as a slave in a hostile household? What did the future hold for her? Actresses, of course, were looked down upon in society. But they were rich and glamorous and admired. And they lived lives of luxury. It was much better to be an actress than a slave.

Returning home that evening he was pleasantly surprised to see that his room had been swept and dusted; his books arranged in neat piles and his clothes washed, dried and folded. The large blob of ink that had fallen on the table two days ago had been rubbed off. Not a trace remained.

Chapter XVII

Jyotirindranath's phaeton rolled majestically down the road and stopped at the gate of Number 6 Beadon Street where the National Theatre was housed. As he stepped down from the carriage the men crowding at the paan shop nudged one another and whispered, 'Jyoti Babu! Jyoti Babu!' Jyotirindranath looked splendidly handsome and elegant. Over his kurta of fine, almost translucent silk, he wore a waistcoat of shimmering blue satin. An *uduni* with a gold border rested lightly on one shoulder and the frill of his fashionably puckered dhuti was held fastidiously in one hand. As he walked through the gate the darwan, Bhujbal Singh, rose hastily from his stool. Hiding the funnel of ganja, from which he had been taking leisurely puffs behind his back, he salaamed with obsequious courtesy. Bhujbal Singh was big and fierce looking with bloodshot eyes. He was kept on purpose to intimidate, even beat up, members of the audience who disrupted performances by unruly or vulgar behaviour. Everyone feared him and he feared no one, except the owner of the theatre Pratap Jahuri and Jyotirindranath. In the latter's case, of course, it was not so much fear as awe and respect. Yet Jyotrindra was never harsh or overbearing. He smiled easily and had a kind word for everybody. Even now, he smiled at Bhujbal Singh and asked pleasantly *'Achha hai?'* before walking into the hall.

It was quite dark inside except for one gas lamp that flared and sputtered at the bottom of the stairs that led to the green room. There would be no performance tonight. The players were rehearsing and Jyotirindranath had come to watch it and offer his comments.

Jyotirindranath was accorded the respect due to a successful playwright by both management and cast. Three of his plays *Puru Bikram, Kinchit Jalajog* and *Sarojini* or *The Conquest of Chittor* had been performed several times before appreciative audiences. Of them the last was the most popular. In fact, *Sarojini* was brought back on stage whenever a new venture flopped. Of late,

140

however, the scene had changed. Girish Ghosh, the company's best actor and Jyotirindranath's friend, had left National following a quarrel with the manager. He had taken Amritalal, Binodini and Kadambini with him. Now they had set up a rival company called Star Theatre, a stone's throw away right on Beadon Street where their play *Daksha Yagna* was being performed before packed houses. The National Theatre was suffering grievously in consequence. With their best actors and actresses gone their performances were losing their public appeal. Even Bankimchandra's *Anandamath* had proved a disaster. Jyotirindra hadn't thought much of *Anandamath*. Of course, he had only seen the play. Robi, who had read the book, hadn't liked it either. The characters, he thought, were flat and wooden and the narrative marred by excessive authorial comment and instruction. It was then that Pratap Jahuri had requested Jyotirindranath to write a new play. Jyotirindra was hesitant at first. Girish Ghosh was his friend and he didn't wish to offend him or enter into any competition with him. On the news reaching the thespian's ears, he had sent word that Jyotirindra was to abandon his scruples and feel free to give his plays to anyone he wished. Consequently, Jyotirindra had given Pratap Jahuri a script that he had written three or four years ago. That play, called *Swapnamayee*, was being rehearsed that evening.

The proprietors of the two theatres, Pratap Jahuri and Gurmukh Rai, were both Marwaris. Being traders by caste and profession, they were quick to grasp the fact that theatre was a flourishing business and could bring in a lot of money—a fact that had not entered the heads of Bengali stage managers so far. The latter were usually scions of wealthy families who indulged in theatre for a sport and, far from making money, blew away a lot of their own. But now the trend was changing. Theatre management was passing into the hands of Marwaris and becoming big business.

Jyotirindranath entered the auditorium on silent feet and stood by the proscenium watching the scene that was being rehearsed. The hall was dark and empty except for a few chairs in the first row where Pratap Jahuri sat with his friends. There were two men and three women on the stage. Of these Jyotirindranath recognized only two—Mahendralal Bosu who was an accomplished actor and Bonobiharini nicknamed Bhuni. Bhuni had a good singing voice and wouldn't be too bad as Swapnamayee. She was the best actress after Binodini and, in the latter's absence, the National's leading lady. But, looking on the second woman, he got a shock. Who was this fright? She was as tall and thin as a bamboo pole and as black as coal. Jyotirindra had nothing against a dark complexion. But this woman looked hideous with her black face coated with cheap chalk. In fact, she looked like a stick wrapped in a sari with a mask at its tip. The National Theatre, it seemed, was making up its cast from the cheapest whores of Sonagachhi. What would they make of his play?

Jyotirindra's only consolation was that Ardhendushekhar had suddenly resurfaced from one of his long disappearances and was acting in *Swapnamayee*. Though the most whimsical of men, there was not another actor who could match him in a serio-comic role. *Swapnamayee* was a historical play set in the reign of Emperor Aurangzeb. Like in all his other plays, in *Swapnamayee* too, Jyotirindra had idealized the values of patriotism and loyalty to one's country and cause. There was no adequate role in it for Ardhendushekhar but his presence, Jyotirindra thought, was enough.

That evening's rehearsal was not in costume. Mahendralal Bosu, in the male lead, was wearing a *lungi* and vest and held a hookah in one hand from which he took puffs between lines. From time to time he brandished it about as if it were a sword upon which sparks and flecks of burning ash flew about the stage. Bonobiharini had a glass of cheap liquor in her hand. She drank heavily and couldn't speak a line before taking a few sips. She had left her youth far behind her but was reluctant to bid it farewell. In consequence, she tried to highlight what she considered to be her natural assets. She wore neither chemise nor jacket and took care to let her sari slip off her breasts from time to time.

'Who comes?' Bonobiharini spoke her lines. 'Whose footsteps do I hear?'

'Tish a cruel fate!' her companion took up her cue. 'A vasht army advanshes upon ush. Toushands and toushands of sholdiers!'

'Death be upon you!' Bonobiharini's plump body rocked with

142

laughter. *'Toushands of sholdiers!'* she mimicked cruelly. 'What a great actress you are Podi! You should be the heroine.'

'We'll need another play then,' Ardhendushekhar who was sitting in the front row with Pratapchand commented drily, 'A play without a single "s". Pratap Jahuri thumped him on the back and laughed. 'I'll ask Writer babu to cut out all the words with "s" in them.'

'There's Writer babu,' Bonobiharini exclaimed joyfully seeing Jyotirindranath for the first time. Then, changing her tone to one of childlike petulance, she cried, 'You haven't written my songs for me yet. We have only a week left and you promised—' Now all the men rose to welcome Jyotirindranath and begged him to sit down. But Jyotirindranath remained standing, silent, as if in deep thought. Fixing his eyes on Pratapchand's face he said gravely, 'You wish to remove all the words with "s"? I suggest you abandon my play and take up something else.'

'Arré! Arré!' Pratapchand hastened to reassure him. 'That was only a joke. You mustn't take it seriously.'

'Saheb,' Jyotirindra turned to Ardhendushekhar. 'Bad diction and mispronounciation are fatal in a play. They offend the ears of the audience.'

'That's true,' Ardhendushekhar agreed instantly. 'The wench is atrocious. We'll have to recast the role.'

'Thakur Babu,' Pratapchand tried to change the subject. Half his rehearsals were over and he was in no mind to recast the role. 'Why don't you add a few dances? Bhuni dances well.'

'Swapnamayee is a high-born Hindu woman. Dance will be alien to her character. You may add as many dances as you please. But they must come before and after my play. I'll write some songs for Bonobiharini, though.'

'They must be really good Thakur Babu,' Bonobiharini pouted her full lips at him and stuck out her bosom provocatively. 'I'll never forget *Jwala Jwala Chita! Dwigun Dwigun*. Aa ha ha! What a beautiful song that was.'

The rehearsal recommenced. Bonobiharini wasn't too bad, Jyotirindranath thought, but Binodini would have been much better. She had the ability to throw herself heart and soul into a role. But Binodini would never act in his plays again. Girish Babu was writing so many plays himself that he didn't need the services of another playwright.

'What do you think?' Ardhendushekhar asked Jyotirindranath after a scene had ended.

'Not bad,' Jyotirindra replied cautiously. 'But something seems to be missing. What the French call *joie de vivre*. The spirit—'

'That will come on the night of the performance. You'll see—'

Jyotirindra pulled a gold watch out of his pocket and pressed a tiny button. The lid flew up. He noted the time and rose to leave. But Pratap Jahuri stopped him. 'I have a plan Thakur Babu,' he said. Then, turning to Ardhendushekhar, he prompted, 'Why don't you tell Thakur Babu about Ghosh Moshai's idea? And how his *Daksha Yagna* became such a hit.'

'Girish the atheist has turned religious—as you know,' Ardhendushekhar explained. 'He keeps calling out "Ma! Ma! " between swigs of liquor and consorts with priests and devotees. He had the Naat Mandir at Kalighat cleared and conducted his dress rehearsal of *Daksha Yagna* there. Ma Kali was the sole audience. Pratapchand is convinced that that is the reason for the play's success.'

'The play received Kalimayee's blessings,' Pratapchand said, 'I've decided to seek the same for *Swapnamayee*.'

Jyotirindranath was appalled at such talk. The theatre, in his opinion, was a most powerful weapon and ought to be used to fight social and political injustice and oppression. Instead, it was being made a mockery of in front of idols of stone and clay. He couldn't, he wouldn't allow it. After all he was a Brahmo and a member of the executive committee of the Adi Brahmo Samaj. 'I'm sorry Sethji,' he said firmly. 'I have a contract with you. There is nothing in it about a dress rehearsal in the Naat Mandir of Kalighat. My play shall be staged-here and here alone.'

No other playwright would have dared to speak to the producer in that tone. But Jyotirindranath cared neither for the man nor his money. Pratapchand's fat face collapsed like a balloon. 'Then, then,' he stammered in a faint voice, 'I won't go against your wishes. You are a good writer. Your play will go down well—anyway.'

Jyotirindranath was just stepping into his carriage when another phaeton came rolling by and stopped at the gate of the

National. 'Ah! Jyoti Babu!' a face appeared at the window and a familiar voice called out in greeting. It was Girish Ghosh. There were two others with him—Binodini and a young man. The latter wore a tall turban on his head and a rope of pearls hung from his neck. But his face was so young and childlike that he looked like a child parading in his father's robes. Jyotirindranath was truly startled when Girish Ghosh introduced him as Gurmukh Rai. He had heard that the financier of Star Theatre was a Marwari businessman and that he was keeping Binodini as his mistress.

After the preliminary courtesies had been exchanged Girish Ghosh told Jyotirindra that they were on their way to a pleasure house on the bank of the Ganga where Binodini would sing before a select company. Inviting him to join them Girish, who was obviously inebriated, added in a slurred voice, 'You've given my rival company a play Jyoti Babu. But that does not mean that our friendship is at an end. Come with us. Sit for a while at least.' Jyotirindra begged to be let off but Girish would not hear of it. He kept on pressing him till Jyotirindra's resolution wore off. As the two carriages set off together Jyotirindra thought of Kadambari. He had promised her that he would come home early tonight. And, as on many other occasions, he was breaking his promise.

Chapter XVIII

Gurmukh Rai Mussadi was the son of Ganesh Das Mussadi—a wealthy industrialist who was also chief agent of Hore Miller and Company. Gurmukh lost his father while still in his teens. The loss, however, was made up for by an immense fortune of which he was sole inheritor and which he proceeded to blow up promptly on wine, women and toadies.

The theatre being the latest craze by way of entertainment, Gurmukh spent most of his evenings watching one play or another with his friends. He bought fifty tickets when he needed only ten or twelve reserving the first two rows for himself and his party for the premiere shows in all the theatres of the city. Gurmukh and his friends would sit at their ease, legs stretched out luxuriously on the seats before them, drinking whisky and cracking crude jokes to the accompaniment of loud, raucuous laughter. It was on one of these occasions that he first saw Binodini.

Girish Ghosh's *Sitaharan* was being performed before packed audiences at the National Theatre with Binodini as Sita. It had become immensely popular. One scene in particular, the abduction of Sita, took the audience completely by storm, the hall resounding with claps and cries of *Encore! Encore!* at the drop of the curtain. And, indeed, the stage decor expert Dharmadas Sur had surpassed himself in the scene. He had managed to create the illusion of a flying chariot bearing Sita away with Ravan by her side. As the chariot started winging upwards Sita flung off her floral ornaments, one by one, till, by an effect of the lighting, she appeared completely nude in the eyes of the astonished spectators. It was at that moment that Gurmukh, sodden with liquor, let out a drunken yell, 'How much is that woman worth? I want her.'

The very next evening Gurmukh Rai saw Binodini again, playing Draupadi in *Pandav ér Agyatbas*. And once again he felt overwhelmed by a passion for her. What range there was in her

146

beauty! What variety! The gentle doe-eyed girl of *Sitaharan* in her costume of leaves and flowers was transformed into a queen, stately and majestic and glittering in brocade and jewels. He understood nothing of what was going on. The sentiments of the play were lost on him. He didn't even follow the story except in fits and starts. He simply gazed, enthralled, at Binodini. He came to see her evening after evening. And, like a child, he cried out every time, 'I want that woman. I want her!' His friends told him, over and over again, that she enjoyed the protection of an immensely wealthy and powerful man and that no amount of money could woo her away from him. But Gurmukh would not give up.

One night he walked into the theatre to find it fully booked. But Gurmukh, who had drunk a lot more than was good for him, was not ready to go back without seeing Binodini. 'No tickets?' he shouted. 'I'm not used to hearing the word "no". Bring me fifty tickets this instant.' Then, digging his hands into the pockets of his kurta, he took out handfuls of currency notes and sent them flying about laughing and cursing all the while. The manager Pratapchand Jahuri could not stand the shameless disruption and, afraid for his theatre's reputation, ordered the darwans to throw him out. Gurmukh's face blazed with fury. How dare an insect like Pratapchand even dream of humiliating him so? Was he not Gurmukh Rai Mussadi the famous Kaptan of Barhtala? How much was the theatre worth? He would buy it, that very day—right under Pratapchand's nose. He left the theatre yelling and shouting abuse.

But even after he had sobered down the next morning he didn't forget his resolve. He would build a theatre, much larger and grander than the National, which was a clumsy structure of wood and tin. He would build a fine mansion of marble and concrete. He would procure the finest equipment, the best technicians and the most famous actors and actresses. And he would have Binodini.

By a strange coincidence he was able to achieve his ambition.

Pratapchand, like the mean businessman he was, decided to deduct a month's salary from Binodini's account when she went on a pleasure trip to Kashi with her Babu. He believed in the motto no work; no pay for all his employees from the highest to

the lowest. When the news reached her, Binodini was wild with
fury. She who was such a fine actress, so hard working and
committed, to be treated so shabbily! It was not the loss of the
money that infuriated her so. It was the blow to her prestige. 'Find
yourself another heroine,' she told Pratapchand arrogantly, ' I
leave your service this minute.' She then proceeded to take off the
costume she had donned for her performance. But the second bell
had sounded and there was exactly one minute left for the rise of
the curtain. Girish Ghosh hurried up to her and, placing a hand
on her head, said gently, 'The right is on your side Binod. I don't
deny it. But reflect. Your audience has not harmed you. People
have travelled long distances and spent a lot of money in the hope
of seeing you. Will you disappoint them?' Binodini could not
disregard her guru's counsel. She acted her part and, after curtain
call, she got her reward. 'Oré Binod!' Girish Ghosh cried out to
her, 'You've surpassed yourself tonight. Your acting has never
been so impassioned. You reminded me of a wounded snake.'

But Girish was not happy with Pratapchand either. The
theatre was bringing in a lot of money but the players were being
doled out the same old miserly allowances. Girish expressed his
resentment several times but was ignored. Finally, after a bitter
quarrel, Girish Ghosh left the National taking some of the best
players with him. He had heard that Gurmukh Rai was planning
to build a new theatre. When Girish approached him, he was
pleased to find Gurmukh amenable to all his conditions. But he
had one of his own—only one. Binodini had to become his
mistress.

Girish and Amritalal exchanged glances. How would they
manage that? It was true, of course, that most actresses came
from brothels and prostituted themselves for a living—their
theatre allowances being far from adequate. Some were kept by
men for several years at a stretch; some even for a life time. The
arrangement, however, was flexible. A man could change
mistresses as often as he wished. The woman, too, was free to
drop her old protector in favour of a new one with more money to
spend on her. And most of them did so—quite frequently. But not
Binodini. She received offers wherever she went but spurned them
every time. She was content with her present protector—a man of
immense wealth and noble lineage. He was extremely generous to

her, not only with his money but also with his love and attention. Cultured and well mannered, he kept his affair with Binodini strictly away from the limelight. Everyone in the theatre world respected him and, out of deference for his reputation, did not refer to him by name. In Binodini's circle he was known as *A Babu*.

Girish and Amritalal decided to work on Binodini. Their life-long dream of a theatre of their own was about to be realized. The lease papers for Kashi Mitra's land on Beadon Street were ready and awaiting Gurmukh's signature. The plans had been drawn. The only snag was Binodini. Their destiny was hanging on the whim of a common whore. It was unthinkable! They realized hectoring and bullying would get them nowhere. They would have to employ guile.

One night the whole troupe came to Binodini's house and broke the news to her. 'Binod,' Girish said in his most persuasive voice. 'I speak not for my own but our common good. Just think. A theatre of our own. Our very own. And only you can make it possible. At some sacrifice. I understand that. But it is such a small sacrifice for such a great cause! After all, who are we outside the theatre? Who cares for us? Who knows us? The theatre is our world Binod. Our life.' Now Kadambini took up her cue. '*A Babu* isn't all you think he is,' she said. 'Do you know why he isn't here in Calcutta? He's to be married! He has slipped away to his ancestral village without a word to you. Could he do that if he really cared for you?'

Binodini looked from one face to another, her eyes glazed with pain and disbelief. All the people she loved—from her revered guru to her best friend Kadambini–were bent on pushing her into Gurmukh Rai's bed only to acquire a theatre of their own! Gurmukh—who was years younger than her and a drunk and a pervert. She couldn't, she wouldn't agree. Binodini held out for a long time. Then, swamped by the collective pressure of the troupe and worn out by their emotional blackmail, she gave in.

When the news reaching *A Babu* he came rushing down to Calcutta with a band of *lathyals*. He wouldn't let that young braggart Gurmukh Rai get hold of his keep. He would kill him first. But Gurmukh had his own gang of goons. A terrible clash took place between the two in which several men were injured

before the police arrived. Like Cleopatra of Egypt and Helen of
Troy before her, Binodini had set off a trail of bloodshed.

Afraid of her being caught up in the fight and being nabbed by
the police Girish Ghosh spirited her away and kept her in hiding
for several months during which time the papers were signed and
the land acquired. Girish had written a new play called *Daksha
Yagna* and had started rehearsing it. He was Daksha and Binodini
was Sati. The rehearsals were conducted in secret in the house in
which Binodini was hidden. Except for the cast, no one knew
where she was.

Yet, one morning at crack of dawn, Binodini was rudely
awakened by a loud hammering at the door. But before she could
reach it, it crashed open and *A Babu* stood in the room. 'You sleep
too much Meni,' he remarked gravely. Then, taking a wad of
notes from his pocket, he held it out to her with the words, 'You
shan't go to that baboon Meni. I won't allow it. You'll cut
yourself off from the theatre, too, from this day onwards. There
are ten thousand rupees here. Buy your freedom with it.' But
Binodini shook her head. 'That's not possible,' she said quietly.
'I've given my word. Besides, I can't leave the theatre.'

'Not even for ten thousand rupees?'

Binodini was cut to the quick. Men thought they could buy
and sell a woman as if she was merchandize. As if she had no will
or soul or aspirations of her own. 'You can keep your money,' she
said, her face flaming. 'I can earn all the money I need. Ten
thousand rupees is nothing to me.' *A Babu* could bear it no
longer. 'Harlot!' he screamed, his limbs burning with anger and
humiliation. 'You dare raise your voice in my presence! I'll cut
you to bits with my—' Whipping a sword out of his cummerband
he brought it down heavily on her. But Binodini skipped nimbly
aside and saved herself by a hair. The sword fell on a harmonium
and got wedged in it two inches deep. While he struggled to get it
free, Binodini ran to his side and gripped his hand. '*Ogo!*' she
cried, 'Kill me if you wish. I'm a despised woman, a whore! Who
cares if I live or die? Think of yourself. You'll be sent to prison.
They might even hang you. Think of the disgrace to your family.
Am I worth so much?' Now *A Babu* flung the sword away and
collapsed on the bed. Burying his face in his hands, he burst into a
loud fit of weeping. Binodini stood at a distance shaking from

head to foot. She was tempted to go up to him, place a hand on his head and say, 'Ogo! Forgive me. Take me away with you. I won't go against your wishes ever again.' But, even as she moved to do so, a vision came before her, dazzling her eyes. She saw herself on a stage, resplendent in velvet and gold, surrounded by throngs of people. She heard frenzied clapping and strains of gay music. She knew she could not give up the theatre. She couldn't go away with A Babu. She turned her face aside to hide her tears. A Babu caught the expression in her eyes and rose to his feet. 'I release you Meni,' he said gently, 'I shan't trouble you again.'

But Binodini's dearly bought peace was shortlived. Gurmukh was extremely moody and whimsical. Within a few days he decided that he had had enough of Girish Ghosh and company. One afternoon he came huffing and puffing into Binodini's room. 'Look here Binod,' he said in his rough way. 'I want you. Only you. Why should I get caught up in this theatre nonsense? I understand nothing of it and care nothing. I'll give you fifty thousand rupees—flat. And you become mine. What do you say?'

Fifty thousand rupees! Binodini couldn't believe her ears. Her aunt, who was visiting her, stared at Gurmukh as if he had gone mad. Fifty thousand rupees! Half a lakh! For a common whore? Who had ever heard of such a thing? With a sum like that one could buy five or six large houses in the city. A prostitute's youth and beauty were her only capital. And they were lost so easily. Once they went she was worth nothing. The men wouldn't touch her with their feet. She gripped Binodini's hand. Binodini opened her mouth to speak but under the pressure of that restraining hand, she could say nothing.

When the news reached Girish Ghosh he was horrified. What would happen now? Would the boat he had steered so gently and carefully almost to the shore be swept away on the tide of a mad man's passion? If Binodini accepted Gurmukh's offer they would not only lose her for ever, they would also lose the theatre of their dreams and have to bid farewell to their hopes of independence.

Once again the whole troupe clamoured around Binodini urging her to reject Gurmukh's proposal. Amritalal took Binodini's hands in his and said with tears in his eyes, 'Will you think only of yourself Binod? Won't you think of us? Of our future?' Girish Ghosh who had stood silent all this while, watching the colour come and go in Binodini's cheeks, said in a voice as cutting as the lash of a whip. 'Stop begging Amritalal. If we don't get a theatre—we don't. That's all. If she prefers the life of a common whore; to spend her declining years as the madam of a brothel—it's her choice. People have short memories. She who is the brightest star of the theatre world and enjoys the applause of thousands will be forgotten in a few months.'

At this Binodini burst into tears. Flinging herself at her guru's feet she sobbed, 'I'll never leave the theatre! Call the Babu here. I'll tell him myself.' When Gurmukh stood before her she said plainly, 'Understand one thing clearly Babu. I'm an actress first and last. I'll come to your bed on one condition: that you build me a theatre and allow me to act. I'll leave the theatre only when I choose. Not at your command.'

Needless to say these words, though they left Gurmukh speechless, were greeted with tremendous applause by Binodini's friends. Each one vied with the other to lavish compliments and extravagant flattery on her. The only exception was Girish Ghosh. He stood a little apart, his mouth twisted in a bitter smile. 'When a bridge is built over a river,' he murmured to himself, 'a child is slaughtered and buried beneath the foundations. We've done just that tonight. We've assured the future of the theatre in Bengal. But we've sacrificed you Binod.'

The next step was the naming of the theatre. Binodini wanted it to be named after her. Her earthly form, one that had delighted so many viewers, would be burned to ashes some day and merged with the elements. But her name would live on. Binodini Natyashala. How well that sounded! Everyone agreed at first. Then the whispers started. Other theatres had such grand resounding names: Bengal, National, Great National. And theirs was to be named after Binodini! It was humiliating. Besides the public would be offended at this pampering of a common prostitute. It was tantamount to striking a blow at social norms.

Binodini ran out to meet the men when they returned from the registry office. But they had bad news for her. The theatre had been registered in the name of Star. The decision had been taken after some last minute consultations. Girish Ghosh saw her pale face and trembling lips and hastened to reassure her. 'Silly girl,' he stroked her back lovingly, 'Don't you know what that means?

Who is the star of this company? You, of course. Everyone knows that. Star means Binodini.'

Thus the Star theatre was born, famed to this day through the length and breadth of Bengal. Its founder Girish Ghosh had little idea of the revolution he was sparking off, not only in the theatre world but in the lives of the people. Play after play emerged from his fiery pen—*Daksha Yagna, Dhruba Charitra, Nal Damayanti*—each brighter and more beautiful than the last. The quality of the audience changed. The theatre ceased to be the haunt of the idle rich and their toadies; of drunks and drug eaters. The themes being culled mainly from Hindu epics, people streamed into the auditorium from all walks of life. Intellectuals from the highest rungs of the aristocracy rubbed shoulders with uneducated men from the lower middle class. People came from the furthest ends of the city and even beyond it, from suburbs and villages. And slowly, they started bringing their womenfolk with them.

Girish Ghosh was born in Bose Para of Bagbazar and was orphaned at the age of fourteen. With no one to guide or discipline him, he spent his early youth sowing his wild oats with the most depraved elements of Bose Para. Liquor, ganja and women—he had a taste for them all. Tall and powerful in frame with a magnetic personality, he was the leader of the band. Yet he differed from his compatriots in one thing. Though he had abandoned a formal education, he had retained a genuine passion for the written word. He read whatever he could find. He had even taught himself English, slowly and painfully, and had read the works of Shakespeare and Milton. And, as he grew older, his love of literature grew deeper and more intense.

At one time, in his wild indisciplined youth, he had organized a jatra party and staged the play *Sadhabar Ekadasi*. He had met Deenabandhu Mitra and Michael Madhusudan Datta. And under their influence, he had given himself over to the theatre. Drama became his burning passion eclipsing everything else. In time he rose to the position of the greatest hero of the Bengali theatre, earning for himself the sobriquet Garrick of Bengal. He was also a playwright of surpassing brilliance. He still drank heavily and surrounded himself with low women. But, mentally, he was miles above the company he kept. He was an intellectual and a rationalist. Having studied the works of Western scientists and thinkers Girish dismissed the concept of a Supreme Being standing guard over his creation. He believed that the universe moved in accordance with a set of natural laws and that religion was a manmade prop. He had no use for it.

Then, one day, he met Ramkrishna of Dakshineswar quite accidentally in the house of Balaram Bosu of Bagbazar. He was not impressed. The man looked so ordinary—no one would look at him twice. And he seemed half crazed. When the room grew dark that evening and a lamp was brought in, he kept looking from one face to another and asking the same question over and over again, 'Is this the hour of dusk? *Ogo*! Do tell me. Is this the hour of dusk?' Girish suppressed his laughter with difficulty. Was the man a lunatic? Could he not distinguish day from night? And when Ramkrishna knocked his head on Bidhu Kirtaniya's feet (Bidhumukhi had been engaged by the master of the house to sing before his guests) Girish almost cried out in disgust. They said the man was Paramhansa. Crass nonsense! He was mad; stark raving mad! Even when conversing with Keshab Sen he was giggling to himself and singing snatches of a song. Girish felt he had had enough and rose to his feet. As he reached the door he was joined by Sisir Kumar Ghosh, editor of *Amrita Bazaar Patrika*. Sisir Kumar was a Vaishnav and had no use for the Kali *sadhak* from Dakshineswar. He had come only because he did not wish to offend Balaram Bosu who had invited him. Girish saw the smile of contempt on Sisir Kumar's face and it had the strangest effect on him. He turned to go back.

'Come, come,' Sisir Kumar said. 'This is no place for you.'

'I want to stay a little longer. I want to ask the man something.'

Sisir Kumar put an arm around his friend's shoulder and steered him away. 'Are you mad?' he asked, 'What words of wisdom do you expect from him?' Girish looked back at the little man as he sat smiling and talking in his sweet sing-song voice. And, for some reason he couldn't fathom, a great wave of loneliness and despair swept over him.

Chapter XIX

Preparations were afoot for Robi's wedding. The bride, chosen by Gyanandanandini, was the only child of a wealthy landowner with an estate worth seven lakhs a year. She was beautiful too and had many accomplishments. She could converse in English, sing, and play the piano. Gyanadanandini prided herself on her find. Like the prince of a fairy tale Robi would be gaining a kingdom together with a beautiful princess. There was one snag, however. The bride's family hailed, not from Bengal but from the South of India. But Gyanandanandini swept all objections aside with her customary forcefulness. Robi deserved the best, she said, and the best was what she was giving him. The fact that the girl belonged to a different community was no consideration at all.

Although the matchmaker had described the girl in detail the women of the family wanted to see her. Gyanadanandini decided to take Robi and Jyoti along with them. As they entered the beautifully appointed salon of the house the bride's father had rented in Calcutta, they were surprised to find it full of women. The girl chosen for Robi came forward in person to greet her future in-laws. The Thakur women exchanged glances. How beautiful she was! Her complexion was like a golden champa and her eyes large and lustrous and fringed with thick dark lashes. Her hair, braided with white and orange flowers, fell to her knees. She was so vivacious and free. She laughed, talked, sang and played the piano with a gaiety and spirit that Bengali girls dared not display when being inspected by prospective in-laws. Everyone was charmed including Robi. Though he said nothing the expression on his face gave him away.

And then the bride's father walked in. Folding his hands in a namaskar he asked deferentially, 'You have met the women of my family?' Pointing to a bundle of brocade and jewels cowering in a corner, he said 'My daughter.' Then, placing a hand on the pretty girl's shoulder, he announced proudly, 'My wife.'

A stunned silence descended on the group from Jorasanko.

They sat quietly in their seats not daring to look at one another from fear of bursting out in uncontrolled laughter. Gyanadanandini rose to take her leave but her host begged her to remain seated for a little while longer. At a signal from him one of the women went out of the room. Within a few seconds several servants appeared with huge thalas piled high with sweets and savouries. The guests made a pretence of eating a few morsels then bundled out of the house as hastily as they could. Once in the carriage they could hold themselves in no longer and fell over each other laughing. 'What were you thinking of Robi?' Jyotirindranath teased, 'Abducting your mother-in-law?' To tell the truth everyone, barring Gyanadanandini, was quite relieved. 'I was on pins,' Dwijendranath declared on hearing the story, 'at the thought of conversing with my own sister-in-law in English. Why do we have to run to the south to find a bride for Robi? What's wrong with our Bengali girls?'

The search for a suitable bride was taken up once again. Around this time Jyotirindranath left the house in Sadar Street and returned to Jorasanko and Kadambari threw all her energies into redecorating her wing on the second floor. She furnished the rooms with her usual elegance and good taste and filled the verandas with potted shrubs, ferns and creepers. She instructed the servants to sprinkle rose water on the *khus punkah* every evening so that the breeze from it blew cool and fragrant. As in the house in Sadar Street, Jyotirindra's friends came over every day but now it was in the evenings. Jyotirindra was busy all day with his new enterprise—shipping. Like his grandfather Prince Dwarkanath, Jyotirindra realized that the real strength of the British lay in their ships.

One afternoon, as Robi was struggling with a review of a collection of poems called *Sindhu Doot*, Kadambari walked past him and went and stood on the veranda. From where he sat, he could see her bending over her plants. Her long dark hair, falling in silky strands over her back and shoulders, was partially concealed by a sari—the colour of the sky at noon. One arm, stark and bare of ornament, rose up and down picking out the weeds that appeared at the roots of the plants. When the sun fell on it, as it was doing now, the smooth ivory skin glittered as if flecked with mica.

Robi pushed away his papers and took up a fresh sheet. He wrote:

Amaar praan ér paré cholé gelo ké,
basantér batash tukur moto?[*]

'What are you writing Robi?' Kadambari came and stood at his elbow.

'A lyric about a spring breeze.'

Kadambari did not ask to be allowed to see it. She sighed, then seating herself, she remarked gravely, 'We don't seem to be able to find a suitable bride for you. Time is running out and—'

'What is your hurry?'

'Why, just think how nice it would be to have a little bride in the house! I'll braid her hair and dress her up in all my prettiest saris and jewels. And I'll have such lovely long chats with her.'

'Which means that you want a doll to play with.'

'Why do you say that? She'll be an outsider to begin with. I'll have to teach her the ways of the household. I'll have to make her worthy of you.'

Robi felt trapped. A few days ago his Mejo Bouthan had uttered almost the same words. She had said that she would keep Robi's bride with her. She would send her to Loretto Convent with her daughter Bibi, give her piano lessons and teach her everything she needed to know as a daughter-in-law of the illustrious Thakurs of Jorasanko. A wave of sympathy for the girl he had never seen, swept over Robi. What would her life be like with her two sisters-in-law fighting over her?

'Why are you so anxious to fasten the noose around my neck?' he asked.

'You've run free for many years now Moshai! It's time you were tied down. Your Natunda has brought a proposal for you. She's a princess. A real princess of Orissa.'

'I don't want a princess,' Robi said hastily, then rising, prepared to leave the room.

'Where are you going?' Kadambari asked.

'To Shyambazar. I have to sing at a prayer meeting.'

'There's plenty of time for that. Your brother is leaving for Orissa tomorrow. He wishes to take you with him. Shall I pack

---

[*]   Who passed over my soul,
      Like a faint breath of Spring?

157

some clothes for you?'

Robi gazed on her face for a while. 'Natun Bouthan,' he remarked gravely. 'There's something ethereal in your face and form when you seem lost in your own thoughts. But when you talk of mundane matters, as you're doing now, I don't seem to know you. You are different—somehow.'

'What is the meaning of *ethereal*?'

'Disembodied. Wrought out of some heavenly substance. It is then that you are Hecate.'

Kadambari sat in silence her eyes on the ground. Then she sighed and said, 'How can I be ethereal? I'm a flesh and blood human being. I struggle and I suffer—'

Robi had no answer to this. He walked quickly out of the room.

Soon after this Gyanadanandini decided to visit her parents in their native village of Narendrapur in Jessore. She took with her not only her own children but her two brothers-in-law Robi and Jyoti and sister-in-law Kadambari. The trip was undertaken with a certain intention. Gyanadanandini was of the opinion that Jessore girls, being pretty and submissive, made good daughters-in-law. And, indeed, many of the brides in the Thakur family had been brought from Jessore. This was the place, Gyanadanandini was convinced, from which a suitable bride could be found for Robi. Sending for all the reputed matchmakers of the district, she ordered them to scour the villages and find a bride worthy of the Thakurs of Jorasanko. They did their best bringing proposals in dozens from Dakshindihi, Chengutia and its surrounding villages. But not one girl came, even remotely, near the expectations of the party. For one thing, they were too young—between three and five years old for the most part. One had snot running down her nose; another had bundled up her sari and tucked it under her armpit and yet another burst into tears at the sight of so many strangers. Robi hated these inspection visits and begged to be let off but Gyanadanandini insisted on taking him along everywhere they went. Robi found the exercise so distasteful that he wouldn't even look up when a girl was brought in. He had decided that he would keep himself out of the whole business. He would agree to whatever his sisters-in-law asked of him. Their will would be his will.

Though they were seeing three to four girls every day, Robi found time to take long walks across the fields in company with Suren and Bibi. The children had never seen a village before and Robi was not too familiar with the countryside either. They were a strange sight and people turned to stare at them as they stumbled over the furrows between fields of golden paddy, ambled along the river that twisted and turned on its emerald banks or stood by the innumerable streams and canals that spread over the green like glittering lace. The village boys, swimming across the turgid brown waters, catching grasshoppers or fishing for shrimps and catfish, gaped at the three fair strangers—Suren in his cap and ulster; Bibi in her frock and long stockings and Robi, very debonair in his puckered dhuti and kurta, hair parted in the middle, gold rimmed spectacles and shining pumps.

On one of these rambles Robi made friends with the young postmaster of Narendrapur—a youth of barely twenty. The boy came from one of the mofussil towns of the district and was desperately lonely in this damp, mosquito ridden village. He had no family so he had to do his own cooking and look after himself as well as he could. A little girl helped him in his household tasks. He hardly had any work because the post office served seven villages, very few letters came. He spent the long hours huddled over his table writing poetry.

One afternoon, as Jyotrindranath was strolling down the village path with his wife and sister-in-law, he came upon Beni Rai—an employee of the household in Jorasanko. 'Jyotidada Babu!' the latter exclaimed wringing his hands in abject humility. 'I didn't know you were here. And the Bou Thakuranis too! I live in the next village—Dakshindihi. Now that I've seen you I shan't rest till you grace my humble dwelling with the dust of your feet. My wife and family will be overwhelmed by their good fortune!'

Next day the villagers of Dakshindihi crowded around Beni Rai's door, jostling and pushing, to catch a glimpse of the handsome, regal looking personages who were visiting their commonplace neighbour. As the party from Jorasanko took their seats, a little girl of eight or nine came in and handed round thalas of sweets and snacks and glasses of water. She was squarish in build, dark, and had a plain, homely face.

159

'Who is she?' Jyotirindra asked his host.

'Hé! Hé! Hé!' Beni Rai bared his teeth in an ingratiating laugh. 'She's my daughter Bhavatarini. *Ei* Bhabi! Touch your forehead to Jyotidada Babu's feet. And to the others.' Then, turning to his guests, he said, 'I'm looking for a suitable husband for her. That's why I've taken a month's leave.'

'Have you found anyone?' Gyanadanandini asked cautiously.

'Not yet Mejo Bouthakurani. But it is time—it is time.'

Gyanadanandini and Jyotirindranath exchanged glances.

As soon as they left the house, on their way back home, Gyanadanandini exclaimed, 'We don't need to look any further. This is the girl for Robi.'

'Do you think Baba Moshai will agree?' Jyotirindra said with some hesitation, 'The daughter of an employee—'

'We'll have to write to him and obtain his consent. Doesn't he know the difficulties of finding suitable matches for our boys? Besides, what's wrong with the girl? She's uneducated and not used to the ways of a great family such as ours. But that can be easily remedied. We'll send her to Loretto School and keep an English governess to teach her spoken English and table manners and—' Jyotirindra's objections, feebly expressed, were swept away, as usual, in the strong flow of Gyanadanandini's arguments. Her interest in the matter was calculated and clear. She wanted to remove Robi from Kadambari's sheltering wings as soon as she could. And that could only be done by foisting a wife on him. Kadambari, true to her nature, did not venture an opinion. Robi's heart sank. He was twenty-one and he was about to be tied to a girl of nine—plain, illiterate and painfully shy. What sort of companion would she make? How would he share his thoughts with her? What could she understand of his feelings and emotions? Bibi was equally upset at the idea. A girl younger than herself to be her Robi Ka's wife! Her aunt!

But, strangely enough, Debendranath, from whom the most serious objections had been anticipated, gave his consent readily. He shared his second daughter-in-law's opinion that Robi was frittering his time away in the company of his Natun Bouthan. It was time he grew up and applied himself to the serious business of life. He sent a message from Mussourie, where he was staying at the time, directing his sons to get the rites solemnized in

Agrahayan following which Robi should start work in the office supervising the accounts.

With the commencement of the preparations for the wedding, Gyanadanandini took Robi away, practically by force, to her house in Birji Talao. The children were very happy to have their Robi Ka with them and so was Gyanadanandini. As in earlier times, the days were filled with guests, music and laughter and Robi was blissfully happy.

Then, one day, he heard that Kadambari was ill; she had, in fact, been ill for quite some time. Several doctors had been called in but no one could diagnose her ailment. Robi felt overwhelmed with guilt. How could he have been so oblivious of her all these days? She was so delicate and sensitive. And she hadn't a friend in the world barring himself. How lonely she must be; how sick and desolate in her solitary apartment in the huge mansion of Jorasanko. He decided to go and see her.

But, once in Jorasanko, he felt acutely uncomfortable. It was strange to be paying a formal visit to one who was so close that she seemed part of him; one with whom words were redundant and silence spoke in many voices.

He entered the bed chamber to find Kadambari lying on her side on a huge bedstead of carved mahogany. Her form looked thin and wasted, her face pinched and her breath came in slow, painful gasps. Not a soul was in sight—not even a maid. A wave of anger rose within him and bitterness filled his heart. Jyotidada had no time for Natun Bouthan. He was lost in his new infatuation—his ship, which he was fitting up as a luxury liner. He wanted to beat the English at their own game and had thrown all his time and energy into the project. The rest of the household was equally indifferent. Robi felt the hot tears pricking his eyes as he gazed on Kadambari's face. His heart was suffused with pity. She looked so frail, so helpless—like a banished princess in a glass tower. He wanted to serve her, protect her, nurse her back to health. But he didn't know how.

'Robi,' Kadambari opened her eyes and her parched, wan lips parted in a smile. 'How long have you been here?'

'Are you angry with me Natun Bouthan?'

'No,' Kadambari's eyes widened in surprise. 'Why should I be?'

161

'Because I've left you. Because I'm staying with Mejo Bouthan.'

'No Robi. You're happy to be there and Bibi and Suren are enjoying your company. I can't expect you to be with me all the time.'

'What's the matter with you?'

'I don't know. My limbs ache terribly and my head and chest feel as heavy as stone.'

'What do the doctors say? I must talk to them.' Then, taking a quick breath, Robi blurted out the question that had been plaguing him for a long time. 'Tell me the truth Natun Bouthan. I ... the fact that I'm to be wed ... Is it ... is it worrying you in some way?'

'*O Ma!*' Kadambari sat up in her astonishment. In a voice resonant with mingled tears and laughter she said, 'Why should it worry me? I'm happy. Very very happy. Is there something wrong? Don't you like the girl? I think she's nice. A sweet, simple girl. She's young and unfledged of course. But wait and see. In a few years she'll come out of her cocoon spreading her wings like a gorgeous butterfly.'

'Get well soon Natun Bouthan. I can't bear to see you like this. I'll pack my things tomorrow and move back here.'

'You mustn't do that,' Kadambari gripped his hand with her own, light and brittle like a fallen leaf. 'It will hurt your Mejo Bouthan. And the children will be so disappointed. I'll be well in a few days. Don't worry so much.'

As the preparations for Robi's wedding rose to a crescendo some of the excitement started seeping into him as well. If he had to marry an infant, he reasoned with himself, he might as well do so gracefully. While the women got busy ordering clothes for their children and servants, and jewels for themselves, Robi turned his creative energies into composing letters of invitation to his friends. So, along with the formal card Priyanath Sen received this strange epistle.

Priya Babu,

My close relative Sriman Rabindranath Thakur is to be wed on the auspicious day of Sunday, the twenty-fourth of Agrahayan, at the auspicious hour of dusk. The members of my household and I myself will be obliged to you if you grace the dwelling of Sri Debendranath Thakur at 6 Jorasanko and witness the ceremony.

Yours humbly

Sri Rabindranath Thakur

Priyanath Sen read it through twice but could make no sense of it. Rabindranath was getting married. That much was clear. But why did he call himself his close relative? And why had he invited him to Jorasanko? The rituals of marriage always took place in the bride's house. He spoke to Nagendra Gupta to be informed that the latter had received exactly the same message.

The truth was that, in a deviation from the norm, the wedding was actually taking place in the bridegroom's house. Robi's father-in-law was a poor man and could spend very little. Clothes and jewels befitting a daughter-in-law of the Thakurs had already been sent and a house rented in Calcutta for Beni Rai and his family. As a final gesture of goodwill the Thakurs decided to spare him the expense of the wedding feast. The ceremony would be held in Jorasanko and Beni Rai and his family would attend as guests.

A Brahmo wedding is not much different from a Hindu one except in one thing—the absence of the *Shalagram Shila*. Robi's last bachelor meal was served to him with the ostentation made familiar by custom. And the following day his sisters and sisters-in-law annointed him with turmeric and oil, gave him a ritual bath and dressed him up as a bridegroom. Robi wore a silk dhuti and carried a family shawl on one shoulder. He refused to wear a crown though he allowed his forehead to be marked with sandal. Since the wedding was taking place in his own house there was no need of a ceremonial carriage. All he had to do was walk down a veranda and enter the women's quarters where the bride awaited him. After the saat paak, the bride being carried on a plank around the bridegroom seven times, came the shubha drishti—the auspicious exchange of glances. Robi peered hard, trying to catch a glimpse of her face but he could see nothing. Overcome with shyness Bhavatarini (her name had been changed to Mrinalini as more suitable to her new status) kept her head bowed beneath her heavy veil and would not look up even when urged to do so. After the shubha drishti had misfired thus, the bride and bridegroom walked into the great hall and the

163

sampradan—the giving away of the bride, began. After the sampradaan the young couple were led to the wing newly prepared for them for the *baasar*.

Debendranath did not attend his youngest son's wedding. He rarely graced his children's marriages but duly sent gifts after they were over. Many of Robi's brothers were missing too. In fact, there was a distinct lack of pomp and festivity in this last wedding of the generation. The *baasar* or congregation of women around the newly wed couple was a dim affair. The jokes and laughter seemed forced and lacked spontaneity. And no one was prepared to sing. 'O Robi!' his aunt Tripura Sundari cried, 'You're such a wonderful singer that the girls are scared to raise their voices in your presence. Why don't you break custom and sing at your own *baasar*?'

Robi did not hear her. His eyes scanned the crowd seeking a dear, familiar face. She was missing. Now that he thought of it, he remembered that he hadn't seen her at any of the rituals. She had said she was happy. But was that the truth? A vision rose before his eyes—of Kadambari standing quietly before her window, the dark chill of a winter twilight enveloping her like a mist. How different she was from Gyanadanandini! Mejo Bouthan was so strong; so superbly self confident. She had planned the wedding to the last detail and assumed complete charge. She was everywhere, resplendent in brocade and jewels, giving orders to servants, instructions to her sisters-in-law, greeting the guests, laughing, scolding—managing everything and everyone. And Natun Bouthan . . . 'Come Robi, sing.' The women sitting around him urged. Robi sighed and gave himself up to the present. '*Aa mori lavanyamayee*,' he began, '*Ké o sthir soudamini*.' As he sang this composition by his sister Swarnakumari, he cast sidelong glances at the bashful bride whose head was bowed so low that it almost touched the ground. A sense of mischief seized him. Rippling his hands in keeping with the taans he sang, he brought them close to the bride's face and repeated *Ké o sthir soudamini*, over and over again, till the company rocked with laughter. He was equally naughty during the *Bhand Kulo*, when the bamboo tray with its mound of rice and gaily coloured pots was brought in. This was a game in which the patience and deftness of the bride and bridegroom were tested. The one who could fill the pots

164

most neatly and swiftly with the rice was adjudged the winner. When Robi's turn came he took each pot and planted it upside down over the rice.

'What have you done you foolish boy!' his aunt scolded but Robi answered, 'My life has turned upside down Kakima. These are only pots.' And he laughed gaily with the cold shadow of doubt and despair falling over his heart.

Chapter XX

Naren continued to visit Dakshineswar from time to time driven there not by his own faith but the love of another. Ramkrishna loved him with a depth and passion he could neither understand nor reciprocate. But he couldn't reject it either. Ramkrishna asked nothing of him. He could argue and blaspheme all he wanted; brag about his atheism and laugh at the blind faith of ignorant folk. Ramkrishna never uttered a word of censure. Only once he had said, smiling into Naren's agitated face, 'Naren ré! Faith, unlike knowledge, is blind. You must choose one or the other but don't confuse the two.'

But though Naren found it impossible to reject Ramkrishna's love, he was embarrassed by it all the same. Ramkrishna not only singled him out of a roomful of people to ply him with sweets and fruits, he also praised him to an extent that bordered on the ridiculous. 'Naren's soul is far stronger and finer than Keshab's,' he had blurted out at a public meeting, 'Sixteen times more so.' Naren's ears had flamed with embarrassment. The news was bound to reach Keshab Babu. What would he think? It was madness to compare a man like Keshab Sen, respected and revered in the whole country and even beyond it, to a mere college student! With his disciples, he was even harder. 'You are at one level, spiritually' he told them often, 'Naren is at another.' 'All of you are flowers,' he had said once, 'Some with ten and some with fifteen or at most twenty petals. But Naren is a myriad petalled lotus.'

The disciples, quite naturally, did not like these comparisons and took their revenge by maligning Naren and spreading scandalous rumours about him. There were two passions in Naren's life. One was singing and the other the company of his friends. He enjoyed smoking and taking snuff and loved food seasoned with plenty of chillies. But he neither drank nor spent time in brothels. Yet these vices were attributed to him by some of the envious disciples of Ramkrishna. Naren was aware of it; he

166

even knew the names of the chief offenders. But he didn't care to contradict the rumours. On the contrary, he took pleasure in shocking people with statements like, 'Life is a hard and bitter struggle! If someone snatches a little pleasure out of it by drinking and whoring we shouldn't stop him, should we? I'll do the same any time I really feel like it.' Naren's detractors took care to keep their guru informed about Naren's misdemeanours—real and imagined. But none of it touched Ramkrishna. He either smiled in disbelief or flew into a temper. '*Doos sala!*' he cried out angrily when he could bear it no longer. 'Don't dare talk against Naren. He's a pure spirit—one of the seven rishis. He can never go wrong.'

One afternoon Naren and his friends were enjoying a meal at Wilson's Hotel when he suddenly rose to his feet and walked out leaving the company gaping in astonishment. Once out of the hotel he walked all the way to Dakshineswar and barged into the room where Ramkrishna sat with his disciples. Fixing his large fiery eyes on Ramkrishna's face he said aggressively, 'I've just eaten a meal in an English hotel. I've eaten what is generally termed "forbidden meat". If you have any problem with that just say so. I'll go away before touching anything in your room.' Ramkrishna gazed at Naren's face for a long time. Then beckoning him to come closer, he said, 'Eat whatever you like. It makes no difference to God. He doesn't inspect a man's stomach to see what is in it—beef and pork or vegetables and greens . He listens to the call of the heart. If God has no problem why should I?' Putting out a hand he gripped Naren's arm and said, 'See, I've touched you. Am I changed in any way?'

Naren stood as still as a block of stone. What was this man made of? Had anyone who called himself a sadhu ever said anything like this before? He knew that Ramkrishna practised many austerities in his personal life. But he allowed his disciples to follow their own inclinations. This was rare; unprecedented. Usually the opposite was true. The guru demanded many sacrifices from his disciples and indulged himself in secret. And this man? Suddenly Naren saw the truth. He had assumed that faith was contradictory to logic. That they were two opposites and one could survive only by denying the other. But Ramkrishna saw faith as empathy in any relationship, human or divine.

167

Ramkrishna saw Naren as a part of himself and so his faith in him was unassailable. There was something wonderful about the concept. Could he ever repose that kind of faith in anyone—man or God?

There was something else that puzzled Naren. Ramkrishna held him in such high esteem! Was he worthy of it? Was it true that there was something special in him? If there was why did he not feel it within himself? Again, as he groped, he arrived at an answer—dim and shadowy but consistent. He was special because Ramkrishna thought him so. Whether he liked it or not he would have to carry the burden of the latter's esteem all through his life. And become worthy of it. But how, how would he do so?

A few days after this meeting with Ramkrishna, Naren lost his father. That night, as he lay fast asleep in his room in the tower which his friends jokingly referred to as *Tong*, he heard his name being called out 'Naren! Naren!' The voice was insistent; urgent. Naren stumbled out of bed and opened his window. A boy called Hemali, their neighbour's son from the house in Shimle, stood outside. 'You must come home at once,' he cried. 'There's trouble—' Naren ran out of the house, bare chested and barefooted as he was, with Hemali by his side. 'What is it? Tell me quick,' he cried as he ran.

'Your father—'

'He's ill?' Naren gripped Hemali's arm 'Is he, is he—alive?'

'I don't know. Perhaps n-not.'

Dawn was breaking over the city when Naren reached home. He went straight to where his father lay and knelt at his feet. All around him women were weeping and men talking in agitated whispers. Bishwanath Datta had felt perfectly well all day yesterday. He had attended the court in the morning as usual and met his clients in the evening. Then, after the night meal, while smoking his *albola* and turning over some legal papers, he had complained of weariness and a slight pain in the chest. He had stopped breathing suddenly, even as his wife was rubbing his chest down with camphor oil. Naren was a strong young man of the new generation. He hated tears and emotional effusions . He sat silent for a long time his head held in his hands. Then, suddenly, a dam seemed to burst within him. Flinging himself on his father's body he burst into tears.

As the eldest son of his father, everyone expected Naren to take on the responsibility for the family. But no one was aware of the enormity of the task. Bishwanath Datta had died a pauper. What was worse, he had left behind a trail of debts. He had always lived far beyond his means, hoping with his habitual optimism, that hard work, together with a little luck, would enable him to make up the difference. Even after he was betrayed by his close associate and business partner and his firm's stock had dwindled to practically nothing, he had not panicked. He hadn't mentioned the matter to anyone—not even to his wife or his eldest son. But there was one thing he hadn't reckoned with. Death. That came so swiftly and suddenly that Naren's whole world was shattered by the blow.

Naren had never had to worry about money. Bishwanath was a generous father and gave him all he needed. His wants had always been few. He didn't care for fine clothes, fine foods or carriages. He wore a corse dhuti and *uduni* by preference and walked wherever he wished to go—sometimes ten to twelve miles a day. He knew, of course, that he would have to take up a job after his graduation. His father expected it of him. But he didn't realize that the need for it would come so suddenly and cruelly. Now, with the creditors baying like a pack of wolves outside the door, Naren was forced to run from pillar to post seeking employment. He had no idea that it was so difficult. The British had started their campaign for educating the native in the interest of building up a work force of clerks. But the number of graduates that was being churned out every year far exceeded their need and, in consequence, the streets were flooded with job seekers.

After trying his hand at translation, which brought in a few rupees from time to time, Naren approached Mahendra Gupta, whom he had met in Dakshineswar, for help. Mahendra Gupta was Principal of the Metropolitan Institution founded by Vidyasagar and, being very fond of Naren, he took him to the great man himself. Vidyasagar was so impressed with the fiery young graduate that he appointed him headmaster of one of the institution's newly opened branches. But Naren did not grace the seat for long. Destiny had other plans for him.

The school was new and so was the headmaster. Naren was

brimful of ideas for his new vocation which he proceeded to implement. Textbook education was not enough, in his opinion. What was important was personality development. His boys would learn music, excel in sports and gain a comprehensive view of the world. They would learn to think for themselves. But these ideas, fine as they were, cut no ice with the authorities. The secretary of the school, who was Vidyasagar's son-in-law, didn't approve of such unorthodox methods of teaching and instructed Naren to stick to the syllabus. Mild differences of opinion led to a severe personality clash and a complaint was lodged with Vidyasagar.

Old and enfeebled by many ailments, Vidyasagar heard his son-in-law's account and said with a trace of irritation, 'Leave every thing else for the moment. Just tell me, what sort of teacher is Naren?'

'That's crux the of the matter. He doesn't teach at all. He and his pupils spend all their time in singing and gossiping.'

The fact was corroborated by a few senior boys the secretary had brought along with him. Needless to say, they were merely following instructions. Vidyasagar was too sick and dispirited to probe further. He could have sent for Naren and heard his side of the story. But he hadn't the heart or the energy. 'Tell Naren,' he said to his son-in-law, 'that he needn't teach anymore.'

After this life became really hard for Naren. Dismissal from Vidyasagar's institution was a terrible stigma—one that no teacher could shake off easily. There seemed little chance now of his securing employment in any other school. However, one day, his friend Haramohan came bustling into his room and said 'I've news for you Naren. One of the teachers of City School died this afternoon. Why don't you go to Shibnath Shastri and ask him for the job? He knows you.' The problem of unemployment had assumed such vast proportions that young men had taken to hanging outside the *samsan* their eyes skinned for the sight of a male corpse. As soon as one was brought in they asked eagerly, 'Where did he work? Was he a clerk or a policeman?' Then, rushing home, they dashed off letters which began: *Sir, Learning from the burning ghat that a post is lying vacant in your office* . . . Naren slipped his feet into his slippers that instant and ran all the way to Shibnath Shastri's house. He had to have the job. His dependents were half starved already. If he didn't earn some money soon they would die of starvation.

Shibnath Shastri welcomed Naren with his habitual courtesy. He knew him, of course, and had heard him sing at the Brahmo prayer meetings. He had liked the young man for his intelligence and spirit and had hoped that, in time, he would become one of the pillars of the Samaj. But, of late, the boy had come under the influence of Ramkrishna of Dakshineswar. Shibnath Shastri had nothing against Ramkrishna. He was a simple unassuming man, flawless of character and truly devout. But he was a worshipper of idols and he was drawing some of the brightest boys of the Samaj into his web! There was no dearth of unemployed young men among the Brahmos. If he had a job to dispense why should he give it to a follower of Ramkrishna's and not to one of their own boys? He heard Naren out and smiled disarmingly, 'You have so many talents Naren!' he said. 'I'm sure you'll find a better job than that of a school master.' Naren got the message. It was a polite refusal. He rose to his feet. He knew that if he told Shibnath Shastri the truth about his condition the man's response would be different. But he would not do so. He would not beg for pity.

There was an easy way out, of course. He was a highly eligible young man—well born, handsome with a superb physique, and a graduate. Rich men were vying with each other to make him their son-in-law. A beautiful bride bedecked with jewels from head to foot and a huge dowry could be his if he only gave one of them an affirming nod. But that was another thing he would not do.

Naren's situation worsened day by day. There was so little to eat that he took to staying away from home during meal times so that his younger brothers and sisters could get his share. When the hunger pangs became unbearable he drank vast quantities of water to deaden them. His shoes were gone. His bare feet were covered with blisters from miles of walking and his clothes hung from his emaciated frame torn and dirty. He stopped going to Dakshineswar. He had lost faith in God and man.

As he saw it there were two options before him—marriage or escape. He could run away to the mountains and become a sadhu like his grandfather Durgaprasad Datta. An ascetic had no obligations to the world he had left behind. And the idea of moving from place to place, unfettered and free, had always

171

attracted him. People would blame him for running away from his responsibilities. They would call him an escapist. But he didn't care.

He told a few friends about his resolve. The word spread and eventually reached Ramkrishna's ears. Ramkrishna was thoroughly alarmed by the news. Naren was one of the seven rishis—destined to bring light into the lives of many. He could not be allowed to hide himself in a cave in the Himalayas. That would be selfish of him and a great loss to the world. Ramkrishna wanted to see him at once and sent a disciple with a message but Naren didn't respond. He sent several others but Naren ignored them all. The truth was that he was nervous of Ramkrishna. He couldn't make him out. He was assailed by strange sensations whenever he came into the latter's presence. His body vibrated violently to Ramkrishna's touch, his head swam and his limbs felt weightless. These feelings persisted—sometimes for days together. Then, gradually, they passed. He became himself again—his old, tormented, doubting, questioning self. Yet, despite it all, his fascination for the man remained. Ramkrishna drew him like a magnet and he needed all his strength of will to resist that pull.

One day he could fight it no longer. On hearing that Ramkrishna was in the neighbourhood he went to see him. He told himself that this would be their last meeting following which he would proceed to the next stage of his life—sanyas. But the moment he entered the room Ramkrishna jumped up from his seat and rushed to his side 'Naren ré!' he cried in a voice choking with emotion. 'It is so long since I've seen you. So long!' Taking Naren's hands in his he cried like a wilful child, 'I won't let you go home. You must come with me to Dakshineswar. No, no. I won't listen to a word you say.'

In the carriage, on the way to Dakshineswar, Ramkrishna sat quietly by Naren's side. And, once there, he spoke briefly and fitfully to his disciples. His mind seemed elsewhere and he didn't even glance in Naren's direction. Saddened and dispirited, the boy rose to take his leave and as soon as he did so Ramkrishna went into a trance. His body stiffened in the *tribhanga* pose. One hand went up the fingers twirling in the air. It lasted only a few seconds. Then, coming out of it, Ramkrishna took Naren's hands in his and burst into tears.

Something like a giant wave of light passed from those gripping hands and washed over Naren's soul. His body trembled with ecstasy and in an instant he sensed the truth. This little priest of a Kali temple knew everything and saw everything. He knew how Naren suffered and he suffered with him. This went beyond intuitive understanding. This was empathy; true empathy. Naren could hold himself in no longer. Loud sobs racked his starved body and tears streamed down his cheeks. He held on to the clinging fingers as if they were his only hope. The disciples looked on, amazed, as the two moved around the room, hands interlocked, weeping together like children. Ramkrishna was given to emotional outbursts and he wept often and easily. But Naren! He was a stubborn, headstrong youth—fiery and arrogant. What had happened to him?

Following this incident Naren abandoned his plan of escape. 'I know everything,' Ramkrishna had said to him as he wept. 'I know you're not for this mundane world and will leave it sooner or later. But don't leave *me* Naren. Stay with me till I die.'

A few days later Naren burst into Ramkrishna's room and said without preamble, 'You tell me that the idol in that temple is a living entity. That you talk to her and she responds to everything you say. Why don't you tell her to solve my problems? To arrange things in such a way that my mother and brothers needn't starve to death.' Ramkrishna burst out laughing. Stung to the quick Naren cried out, 'Why do you laugh? This is no laughing matter. I've heard you call out to her in one of your songs *I know thee O Goddess of Mercy / O Succour of the poor and wretched.* Are we not poor and wretched? Why does she not to cast her mercy in our direction? You *must* talk to her and tell her of my plight.'

'It's awkward,' Ramkrishna said timidly, 'I've never asked her for anything!' Then, his face brightening, he added, 'Why don't you ask her yourself?'

'How can I do that? I don't know her. No, no. I won't let you off that easily—'

'You don't know her because you don't care to know her. That is why you're suffering so. I have an idea. Today is Tuesday. Go to her quietly when she's all alone and ask her for whatever

173

you wish. She'll give it to you.'

Late that night when everyone lay sleeping Ramkrishna sent Naren, practically by force, into the temple of Kali. The torch of knowledge trembled in his hands as new, enlightened India took her first, cautious, hesitant steps into the realm of Theism. Logic was about to surrender to Faith. The overwhelming need for empathy and realization of something beyond the known world was driving out Reason as Naren stepped into the womb of the temple where Ma Kali stood. An earthen lamp, flickering in a corner, cast a dim glow over the naked form, black as night and of a breathtaking beauty. One hand held a bloody falchion. A garland of human heads hung from her neck and a fearful tongue, long and fierce and greedy for prey, fell nearly to her breast. A pair of glittering gold eyes gazed intently into Naren's as he walked on unsteady feet and sank to his knees before her.

Even as he did so Naren told himself that the concept of a Destroyer Goddess had not been formulated in Vedic India. There was no mention of Kali in the *Ramayan* or *Mahabharat*. It was much later that a pandit called Agambagish, inspired by the flawless body of an Adivasi woman, had formed a goddess in her image and disseminated the cult of Kali. This naked goddess was relatively unknown and unacknowledged in the rest of India. Only the Tantra-loving Bengalis were Kali worshippers. How could he, Naren Datta, accept a doll made of straw and clay as divine and all powerful? It was impossible! Impossible!

Suddenly a tremor passed through Naren's body making his blood leap up in his veins. He had seen—yes, he was sure he had seen those exquisitely chiselled lips part in a smile. He shut his eyes and opened them again. Yes—there it was. A smile of love and pity and was it triumph? He thought he saw the image sway gently from side to side. But the room was dim and hazy with incense smoke and long shadows. Perhaps he was imagining it all. His racked body and fevered brain were weakening him—making him an easy target. He tried desperately to revive all his old arguments; to summon up the logic and reason that had sustained him all these years. But he felt them slipping away. His eyes were glazing; strange currents were running in his blood sweeping him away. In the poorly lit room, swinging between patches of light and shadow, the image of the smiling goddess was

174

trembling into life.

'Ma,' Naren called in a broken whisper and then again, 'Ma!' With that one syllable, uttered twice, the Brahmo Samaj was vanquished in its entire trinity and Ramkrishna's victory was proclaimed in triumphant cries till the whole world reverberated to the sound. 'Ma!' Naren called again and again in a fever of impatience. But why was he calling out to her? What did he want from her? Oh yes. He wanted food and clothes for himself and his family. He opened his mouth to utter the words he had rehearsed so many times that evening. But they wouldn't come. She was the Mother of the world. And she had smiled on him! How could he ask her for mundane things like rice and lentils? When one has free access to a king's treasure does one beg for a pumpkin? Naren knocked his head on the floor and cried wildly, 'Give me knowledge. Give me faith. Give me light. And above all these—strength. Strength to suffer and endure. Strength to renounce.' Ma Kali continued to smile on him but made no answer . . .

Ramkrishna stood in a corner of the chatal waiting for Naren. As soon as he saw him come out of the temple he asked eagerly, 'Have you told her everything? About your troubles—I mean. What did she say?'

'I couldn't,' Naren answered in a bewildered voice. 'I couldn't utter a word. I—'

'Foolish boy! ' Ramkrishna scolded. 'After all the training I gave you! Go back again. Be sure to tell her everything and ask for her help.'

Thrice Naren went in and thrice he came out without asking for anything other than faith, strength, knowledge and conscience. 'You ask her for me,' he said at last hanging his head in shame. 'She'll listen to you.'

Exhausted in mind and body, Naren went to sleep at dawn and did not wake till late in the afternoon. It was past four o' clock when Naren rose from his bed and entered Ramkrishna's room where he sat surrounded by some of his disciples. Ramkrishna ran to his side the moment he saw him enter and, putting his arms around him, cried excitedly. 'We're one. You are me and I am you. If you throw a stick in the Ganga the waters seem to part. But that is just an illusion. The Ganga is one and

175

flows as one. It is thus with you and me Naren.' Passing Naren his hookah he said gently, 'Stop worrying Naren. Your troubles are over. Ma Kali will look after you.' Naren looked up with dazed eyes. How would Ma Kali look after him? Would money fall into his lap like rain from Heaven? Even as he reasoned thus Mahendra Gupta put some money in his hand and said, 'See how long you can manage with this.'

That evening, after many months, Naren walked into the house with a sackful of rice on his back.

Chapter XXI

Sarala and Bibi had their first real quarrel over which school the little bride was to be sent. Sarala held a strong brief for her own school Bethune while Bibi was convinced that there was no institution that could match hers. Bethune was a Bengali medium school and was situated in a predominantly Bengali locality. Yet many of its ex-students were renowned women. It was only last year that Calcutta went all agog over the case of Abala Das. Abala had passed out of Bethune and had wanted to study medicine but was refused admission by the Medical College of Calcutta which had no infrastructure for girl students. Abala had expressed her resentment so powerfully that the Bengal government had been forced to send her to the Medical College in Madras on a stipend of twenty rupees a month. The students of Bethune were taught to think for themselves particularly when it came to their own country. When the infamous Ilbert Bill was passed and the newspapers carried defaming and derogatory columns about Indians, the students of Bethune had lodged a strong protest under the dynamic leadership of a girl called Kamini Sen. They had come to school wearing black bands on their arms the day Surendranath Banerjee was arrested. The girls of Loretto House had no such awareness. The school was situated in Sahebpara and most of its students were English. There were some, of course, like Bibi who came from upper class Bengali-families. The girls learned to speak English with a flawless accent and master all the nuances of English etiquette. Girls from Loretto House made excellent wives for barristers and civil servants.

Sarala was eleven, Bibi was ten and the new bride only nine. Though they were constrained, by the rules of the family, to call her Kakima, Bibi and Sarala treated her like a friend. But Bhavatarini shrank from their friendship. She hadn't overcome her bewilderment at the turn her destiny had taken. Her situation was like that of the heroines of one of her grandmother's stories—of a woodcutter's daughter being wooed by a prince and

177

carried away to a palace high on a hill. This great house with its fine furniture and many servants intimidated her. And she stood in awe of her husband who seemed to her as fair and handsome as a prince. When he talked to her she hung her head and wouldn't reply—she felt so small and inadequate. She couldn't even remember that she had a new name now—Mrinalini.

Bibi's and Sarala's opinions were of little consequence. The decision rested with Gyanadanandini. And she had taken it. Mrinalini would stay with her and study in Loretto House. There was no question of wearing saris to school so coats and skirts of English material were getting stitched for her. Needless to say, this arrangement did not meet with everyone's approval. Kadambari had taken it for granted that the new bride would make her home in Jorasanko with Robi in the new wing that had been prepared for them. She had made many plans. She would look after the little girl, give her all the love and affection she had left behind and teach her the ways of the family. Mrinalini would be sent to school but surely she could go to Bethune along with the other little girls of the house. Bethune was such a fine school! It had been founded by one of the greatest humanitarians that had ever stepped on these shores. The great Vidyasagar himself had taken an interest in it and her own father-in-law had been one of the first to send his daughters. But the family traditions were changing. Now Debendranath allowed his second daughter-in-law to take all the decisions and make all the arrangements. He never interfered. Why, oh why, was Gyanadanandini taking Robi's wife away from her? Why did she make it a point, always, to rob her of whatever she wanted? Gyanadanandini had her own children. She had no one.

The house was still full of wedding guests and there was no scope for a private conversation. So Kadambari was forced to speak to Robi in the presence of several other members of the family. 'Why are you sending your wife to Loretto Robi?' she asked, one day, trying to make her voice as casual as she could. 'You are one of the greatest poets of Bengal. Shouldn't your wife be educated in Bengali?'

'But—but,' Robi was startled, 'I thought it was all arranged. Mejo Bouthan—'

'O Robi!' his eldest sister-in-law Neepamayi interrupted.

'Your wife doesn't know a word of English. How will she follow the lessons? It would be best if we kept her with us for a while and gave her lessons at home. Then, later, when she has learned enough she can go to school.'

'Why don't you speak to Mejo Bouthan?'

'Why should we?' Neepamayi snapped at Robi. 'She's your wife. You should take the decisions for her.'

Robi shook his head. It was evident from his face that he didn't have the courage to face his redoubtable sister-in-law. Kadambari gazed a long moment on Robi's face, then slipped away as quietly as a shadow.

Debendranath came to Jorasanko some weeks after the wedding on hearing the news of his eldest son-in-law's death. It was then that he took the opportunity of seeing his youngest daughter-in-law for the first time. Putting four gold coins into the little hand he raised his own in blessing and uttered some lines of a Sanskrit mantra. Opening his eyes he fixed them on Robi's face and asked solemnly 'What are you doing about her education?'

'Mejo Bouthan has made all the arrangements. She will join Loretto House after the Christmas vacation.'

Debendranath sat silent for a minute giving the matter due thought. 'Very good,' he said at last. 'But she may have difficulty in competing with the other girls at first. Arrange for extra tuitions in the school itself. Don't worry about the expense. I shall leave instructions at the khazanchi khana to give it to you each month.'

The wedding guests started leaving one by one. Sarala went back with her parents to their house in Kashiabagan. Gyanadanandini left for Birji Talao taking not only her own family but Robi and Mrinalini with her. Kadambari looked on with stony eyes as Robi followed his sister-in-law into the carriage like a meek little boy.

Within a few days of leaving Jorasanko Mrinalini was admitted to Loretto House. Apart from English tuitions she was given special lessons in singing and piano playing. She was constantly receiving instruction at home too. Gyanadanandini never wearied of pointing out her defects and teaching her to behave like a lady. She was to walk so and talk so. She was to sip her tea slowly without making a sound. Under the weight of so much attention the poor girl's life became hard to bear and she shed many tears in private.

Robi, who was busy correcting the proofs of his new book *Chhabi o Gaan*, saw little of what went on. He pored over his work all day and spent the evening in the company of friends that thronged to the house. Jyotirindranath came everyday. Swarnakumari Devi and her husband were frequent visitors. Of late, however, the venue had changed. The evening assemblies were now held in Swarnakumari's house in Kashiabagan.

Swarnakumari's husband Janakinath Ghoshal was an extremely handsome man with a magnetic personality. Scion of a reputed zamindar family of Nadiya Jairampur, Janakinath had, in his youth, been a close associate of Ramtanu Lahiri and Jadunath Rai of the Young Bengal movement. Under their influence and in a reaction from traditional Hinduism he had cast away his sacred thread following which his outraged father had disinherited him. Despite this fact he had been chosen by Debendranath Thakur as a husband for his second and most beautiful daughter Swarnakumari. Janakinath had agreed to the marriage on two conditions. Unlike other sons-in-law of the Thakur family he would not move into the house in Jorasanko but keep his wife with him in a house of his own. And no pressure would be put on him to become a Brahmo. This last resolve poured balm on his father's wounds and prompted a reconciliation. And, thus, Swarnakumari was enabled to move into an establishment with as many comforts and luxuries as the one she had left behind.

Several years after the marriage Janakinath decided to go to England to study at the Bar. He set sail leaving his wife, three daughters and a son at Jorasanko. During her stay in her father's house Swarnakumari's youngest child, a little girl of six, became very attached to Kadambari Devi and spent a lot of time with her. The childless Kadambari loved her dearly and treated her as her own. Then a terrible thing happened. One day, as the child was coming down the stairs from Kadambari's apartment, she missed her footing and rolled down the steps hitting her head on the floor beneath. She died after a few days and something in Kadambari died too. She withdrew, even further, into her own world coming to look upon herself as an accursed creature from whom

180

everything she loved was taken away. Janakinath returned to India, on hearing of the tragedy, and never went back. Thus, although he had passed some of the exams with distinction, his dreams of becoming a barrister remained unfulfilled.

Swarnakumari was a strange character. A strikingly beautiful woman, she was well educated with a keen interest in science and literature. There was something majestic about her personality and she took herself very seriously as a writer and intellectual. Although she had given birth to several children she refused to let her life be cluttered by them or by the needs of her household. She believed that a writer of her stature should not demean herself by domestic preoccupations. She kept a servant for each one of her children whose duty it was to minister to their needs and keep constant vigil. Sarala and her brother and sisters had no memories of their mother hugging and kissing them or telling them stories and putting them to bed. Sometimes they didn't see her for days together. Once, when Sarala was four years old, she had a nasty fall breaking two of her front teeth. All the members of the household rushed to the scene in anxious concern. The ayah wept and protested as the other servants scolded her for her negligence. Swarnakumari, who was writing in an upstairs room, heard the uproar and realized what had happened. But she did not come down to her daughter. A child was hurt. What was new about that? There were many people in the house to wash her wounds and render first aid. And if a doctor was needed her husband would send for one. She was a writer and her first commitment was to her writing.

A few days after Robi and Mrinalini left Jorasanko, preparations commenced for another wedding in the family. Swarnakumari's eldest daughter Hiranmayee was to be married to a young man called Phanibhushan Mukhopadhyay. Unlike other mothers Swarnakumari took no interest in getting a trousseau ready for her daughter or of preparing a guest list. She turned all her energies in trying to make the occasion as unique and memorable as possible. At one of the evening gatherings in her house she suggested putting up a play on the wedding night. The suggestion met with everyone's approval but some practical difficulties were pointed out. The date set for the wedding was not too far off. There wasn't enough time for rehearsing a full

181

length play. Then someone suggested putting up a musical drama on the lines of *Balmiki Pratibha*—an operatic piece that had been presented by the young Thakurs in Jorasanko some years ago. Songs were easier to learn than dialogue. And they could be sung from within the wings if the need arose. The next point to be considered was the composer. Who could do it best? Several names were put forward and rejected. Then Swarnakumari had an idea. How would it be if they all did it together? Songs could be composed by all those who had a flair for it. Akshay Chowdhury was a good composer. Jyotirindranath had a fine ear and could improvize tunes on the piano to which Robi could set the words in no time at all. Swarnakumari, herself, was no mean composer. Once the songs were ready they could be linked together by a slender thread of narrative and presented as an opera.

After this decision was taken the evenings became livelier than ever and stretched till late into the night with breaks for snacks and drinks and winding up with a lavish meal. All the mundane arrangements for the wedding were left to the master of the house. The mistress concerned herself only with the cultural side and every evening saw her sitting in state in her beautifully appointed salon with her brothers, sister-in-law and friends. Some of the younger members of the Thakur family were also admitted into these gatherings because they would be the ones to come on stage in action or dance.

Till lately Robi had been a frequent visitor at Swarnakumari's house. But he was rarely there these days being totally preoccupied by his newest venture *Chhabi o Gaan*. The publication process was over. All that was left now was the dedication about which he couldn't make up his mind. Should he dedicate it to his wife? A shadow fell on his face at the thought. She wouldn't read the poems. And, even if she did, she wouldn't understand them. There was one, only one, who read his work from cover to cover and understood it; who praised and criticized with honesty and true knowledge. She was the source of all his joys. She was the source, too, of his most exquisite pains, touching the deepest chords within him with a gentle and unerring hand. She was his sole inspiration! Delving into his memories he found that each of the poems in *Chhabi o Gaan* had its genesis in some moment or other with her—sad, joyous,

182

thoughtful or romantic. He had dedicated many of his books to her. He would like to dedicate them all. Frowning and biting his pen for a few moments he wrote: This garland of songs is woven from the blossoms of last year's spring. I place it at the feet of her in the light of whose eyes, the flowers opened, each dawn, one by one.

Leaving the Brahmo Samaj Press Robi came straight to Jorasanko and, stepping through the open door, entered Kadambari's room. She sat at a window with her back to the door through which Robi had entered. She didn't rise at his entrance or even turn her head. She went on sitting, a listless immobile figure, her eyes fixed on the evening sky over which a stream of white cranes were gliding past. Dusk was falling outside and shadows were lengthening in the room. Just outside the window a bakul tree, dark and gnarled with age, was swaying gently in the breeze sending showers of blossoms into the room which danced about the air like tiny white stars before falling into Kadambari's lap.

'Nathun Bouthan,' Robi called softly.

Kadambari turned her head and looked at him. But her eyes conveyed nothing—not joy on seeing him nor pain at his prolonged absence. Her lip quivered a little but she didn't speak. Not knowing what to say next Robi asked awkwardly, 'Are you well?' Kadambari swayed her head gently and said, 'Yes!' Robi tried again. 'Why is it so dark in your room?' he asked,'Why don't you light the lamp?' Kadambari did not answer. She turned her face again to the window and gazed out at the darkening sky.

'Here is my new book Chhabi o Gaan,' Robi said after a while. Kadambari put out a hand and, taking the book, glanced briefly at the dedication. Then, ruffling the pages absentmindedly she placed it on a small table beside her. Robi thought he heard her murmur 'last year's,' before she put it aside. The complete absence of interest in his book shocked Robi and wounded him deeply. Tears pricked his eyelids. Mixed with the pain of his rejection was a touch of guilt. He knew that Kadambari had been deeply hurt the day he had gone away with Gyanadanandini. A wave of anger and frustration rose within him. Mejo Bouthan had forced him to go with her! Not content with taking Natun Bouthan's husband away from her she was doing the same with Robi. She seemed to enjoy pushing Natun Bouthan deeper and deeper into her dark, lonely world. And Kadambari! Robi sighed. Why didn't she fight for her rights? Why didn't she go with her husband wherever he went? Instead she sat hour after hour, day after day, night after night, waiting for him to return.

Looking on that still, sad figure sitting at the window in the twilight Robi's heart twisted within him. He longed to return to Jorasanko and spend all his time with her. But he knew that the moment he did so tongues would start wagging. The house would echo with whispers some of which might even reach his father's ears. Besides he was very busy now and had little leisure. The long golden days and starry nights at Moran's villa were like a dimly remembered dream!

'Why don't you go with Jyotidada to Swarnadidi's house Bouthan?' Robi said at last, 'We have such fun every evening. There's singing and—'

'I can't go there,' Kadambari answered in a stifled voice. 'I'm an accursed creature with an evil eye—'

'What nonsense!' Robi cried. 'Why do you say that?'

'Thakurjhi's daughter Urmilla used to come to me. I would wash and feed her and put her to bed. Everyone says she died because of me. They say such things because I'm a sterile woman—incapable of bearing a child in my womb.'

'*Chhi! Chhi!* Don't ever utter those words again. That was an accident. It could have happened anywhere. Besides no one says such things about you.'

'Don't they? But I seem to hear them all the time. The air is thick with whispers —'

'You're imagining things. You sit locked up in this room day and night. You don't go out anywhere. You don't talk to anyone. If you did you would know how much everyone loves you. Come with me to Swarnadidi's house tonight. You'll feel much better.'

Kadambari hesitated a little then said softly, 'No Robi. They may not . . . The truth is I don't like going anywhere. I don't belong—' she turned her face away fixing her gaze, once more, on a sky now black with night and sprinkled all over with stars. Robi decided to be firm. Taking her by the shoulders he turned her around. 'Come with me Bouthan,' he said with a desperate edge to his voice. 'You must. They'll all be so happy—' Kadambari shook her head. Putting his hand gently away she said evenly,

'You're getting late. Go Robi.'

Robi stood uncertainly for a few moments. He realized that pleading with her was useless. She had made up her mind. Besides he *was* getting late. The group in Kashiabagan would have assembled by now and must be waiting for him. He had promised to write two songs and bring them along but he hadn't even thought of a line. Stifling a sigh he walked quietly out of the room.

The moment he entered Swarnakumari's house he was greeted by a chorus of voices. 'Robi!' 'Why are you so late?' 'We've been waiting and waiting.' Robi removed his shoes and socks and took his place on the carpet along with the others.

'Explain the situation to Robi,' Swarnakumari prompted Akshay Chowdhury who hurried to do so. 'It's like this,' he explained, 'The hero sees the heroine for the first time and is enchanted by her. We need a song to convey his feelings.' Jyotirindranath rose from his seat at the piano and picked up his esraj. 'I've set the tune,' he said. 'What do you think of this Misra Khambaj Robi?' Robi sat in dazed silence. An image rose before his eyes—the same image that had haunted him all the way to Kashiabagan—of a slender figure sitting in a room full of shadows . . . her hair lifted softly in the breeze . . . flowers falling into her lap. He murmured as if in a dream,

'She sits silent by that window
Cheek resting on one hand
Her lap is strewn with flowers
Her garland lies unwoven . . .'

Then, as the soft nostalgic strains of Jyotirindra's esraj floated into his ears he lifted his voice and sang

'Clouds glide before her eyes
Birds go winging past
All day long the falling blooms . . .'

The hot tears welled into Robi's eyes and his voice was charged with emotion as he sang. Why had everything changed so? Natun Bouthan was desperately unhappy and he could do nothing about it. He felt powerless; trapped. Till the other day he had spent all his time with her without experiencing a twinge of guilt. Why was he being assailed by such feelings now? Why was he considering what other people would think and say? Nobody loved her. No one cared for her. There was not one person in this

185

room who ever asked Jyotidada, 'Why don't you bring Kadambari?' And Robi! He too had deserted her. Here he was sitting and singing with this lively group while Natun Bouthan—
          'She sits silent by that window
          Cheek resting on one hand . . .'

Chapter XXII

Working with Binodini was getting more and more difficult day by day. She was invariably late for rehearsals and Girish and his cast had to sit idle for hours waiting for her. On a couple of occasions he had sent a servant to call her but she had expressed her resentment so openly that he dared not repeat the attempt. When she did come, she expected the entire cast to fawn over her, fussing and pampering. And she was very autocratic in her manner. 'That light is bothering my eyes,' she might say sharply in the middle of someone's lines. 'Will someone take it away?' She thought nothing of humiliating her co-actresses. 'You smell so foul Jadukali,' she said once to a young actress, 'that I'm about to vomit. Go take a bath and change your clothes before coming near me.' Such comments were not only extremely offensive—they ruined the tempo of the rehearsal. She even took on Girish Ghosh from time to time, something she had never dared to before. 'This speech has too many difficult words in it,' she said on one or two occasions, 'Can't you make it simpler?' Though couched in the form of a request it sounded like a command. Her behaviour set Girish's blood on fire but all he would do to assuage his feelings was to open a brandy bottle and pour the contents, neat, down his throat. Never had he felt so helpless.

In his long career as director and playwright Girish Ghosh had trained many women picking them up from among the lowest of the low if they so much as had a presentable face. These girls, when they first came to him, had neither grace nor poise and spoke in atrocious accents. But Girish worked so hard over them that many were metamorphosed from cocoons to butterflies. Some, of course, couldn't make the grade and fell by the wayside. Binodini, who had won acclaim early in her life becoming a star before she was twenty, was a supreme example of his skill as a trainer. But now he had lost his power over her. She was the proprietor's mistress and he ate out of her hand. If Girish attempted to discipline her as he had done in the past he might lose his job. He knew the reason for the change in her. She hadn't forgotten or forgiven the fact that he had played on her emotions and pushed her into Gurmukh's bed. This was her revenge. She was sending a clear signal to him and to the others that the theatre had been bought with her blood and tears and that she wouldn't let them forget it.

The play that was being currently performed was *Nal Damayanti* with Binodini playing Damayanti. It had proved vastly popular and sales were soaring every day. The acting was brilliant, Binodini playing her part with a sensitivity unusual even for her. The stage effects were spectacular. There was a scene in which a bird flew away with Nal's garment in its beak. In another, dancing apsaras emerged from an unfolding lotus.

Yet, even though *Nal Damayanti* was running to packed houses, Gurmukh Rai wanted a new play. He cared little for the money that was coming in—he had so much. His burning ambition to cripple the National Theatre and bring Pratapchand Jahuri to his feet was well on its way to realization. The reputation of the National Theatre was declining everyday. Soon it would have to wind up.

Goaded by Gurmukh, Girish Ghosh put together a new play called *Kamalé Kamini* and commenced taking the rehearsals. But Binodini, flushed with the success of her Damayanti, turned up her nose at the part assigned to her. It was, she complained, unworthy of her talent at an actress. She wanted a role equal in passion and power to Damayanti. Girish tried to reason with her. Could two plays be identical? But she continued to sulk till Girish was driven to a fury he could barely conceal. He wanted to shut her up with a sharp rebuke but he dared not. He was afraid of Gurmukh. In an effort to hide his anger and frustration he would walk away from the stage and, sitting in a dark corner of the wings, take a long draught from the brandy bottle. He also took to reciting stotras in praise of Kali, his voice growing louder and more sonorous with every line. At such times no one dared go near him—not even Binodini.

One day Mahendralal Sarkar caught him in this mood. Although a very busy doctor Mahendralal was a great theatre lover and was often seen among the spectators at the Star. That evening, after watching a performance of *Nal Damayanti*, he hurried backstage to congratulate Girish whom he had known for several years. 'Girish! *Ohé* Girish!' he called out in his booming voice as, crossing the stage, he stepped into the wings. Then he got a shock. Girish was sitting crosslegged in a dark corner. His eyes were closed and tears streamed down his face as he rocked to and fro reciting verses in praise of Kali.

Girish was particularly upset that day. Binodini had gone to the green room to change her costume, and had taken up her cue seven minutes after the due time. The other actors and actresses had covered up for her and the spectators had not sensed anything out of the ordinary. But Girish was furious. He felt like slapping her across the face but he didn't dare even rebuke her. Gurmukh was waiting in the wings watching over her. Girish felt his heart thumping so hard with agitation that it threatened to burst out of his rib cage. But all he could do was drink and sing stotras to Kali.

'*Oré baap ré*!' Mahendralal Sarkar exclaimed on seeing him there. 'Here is another one devoured by Kali.' At the sound of his voice Girish opened his eyes. 'Daktar Moshai!' he said. 'Come in and sit down.'

'Is this a joke? Or have you really turned religious?'

'I'm trying hard to. But it's difficult—'

'I thought you had a scientific bent of mind.' Mahendralal said staring at him in dismay. 'You said you believed in Kant's doctrines. What has happened to you? Since when have you become a devotee of Kali?'

'What did you think of the play?' Girish tried to evade the question.

'The play was excellent. Not a dull moment. But to go back to my point. I had an idea that there were two aspects to your personality. The real you—I mean the man—is an atheist; an unbeliever. But the artist in you brims over with religious feelings. Something like your heroines. The actress is a goddess—the real woman a whore. The playwright is also an actor. Ha! Ha! Ha!'

'You are right Daktar Moshai!' Girish said softly. 'I was an atheist not so long ago. Then something happened. Ever since then—'

'What was it? Tell me.'

At that moment Binodini and Gurmukh came in. Girish

189

sighed and said, 'Some other time Daktar Moshai. I'll come to you myself.' Mahendralal Sarkar rose to his feet. He realized that this was neither the time nor the place for the kind of confession Girish wished to make. Besides, a performance had just been concluded. The producer and director, quite naturally, had important matters to discuss. His curiosity unsatisfied, he walked down the hall out into the street where his carriage stood waiting.

Mahendralal was wrong. Gurmukh had not come to discuss anything but to have a few drinks with Girish. He kept a bottle with him all the time and took swigs from it from early afternoon onwards. His eyes were red and slightly unfocussed already, although the night was still young. Suddenly a whim seized Girish. He would drink this arrogant brat out of his senses. A boy, barely out of his teens, pretending to be a man! He would show him what a man was truly like. He would show him what Girish Ghosh was!

Brandy bottles were brought in, one after another, and emptied with astonishing rapidity. As the night progressed Gurmukh got so drunk that he could barely keep his eyes open. But he wouldn't give up. He was determined to outdrink the old rascal who had so much power over Binodini. Then, just as dawn was breaking over the city, Gurmukh fell with a thud on the floor and passed out. Girish, sitting straight as an arrow, glanced at the figure lying prostrate at his feet. His lip curled in a little smile. Draining the rest of his glass to the dregs he let out a thundering belch and called in a booming voice, '*Oré*! Pick up the drunken clown and take him home.' Gurmukh's servants hurried in and carried their master out of the theatre.

Gurmukh fell seriously ill after this incident and was confined to bed for ten whole days. During this period the doctors discovered that some of his organs were in a state of decay—a natural consequence of the kind of life he led. Gurmukh's mother, who had no control over her son, sent for her brother from Lahore. The latter, a huge hefty man with a towering personality, took over Gurmukh's life and commenced steering it with an iron hand. He decided that his nephew would, henceforth, have no contact with Binodini or the theatre. Gurmukh, who had no fight left in him, was forced to obey.

One morning, several days later, a pale enfeebled Gurmukh

Rai tottered into his theatre with a proposal for Girish. He would gift half the ownership of Star to Binodini. The rest could either be sold in the open market or bought over by the rest of the troupe. But before anyone could say anything Girish rejected his proposal. Fixing his eyes on Binodini's face he said solemnly, 'The offer is generous Binod, but don't give way to temptation. You're an artist—a great artist. You must throw everything you have in your acting—your heart, soul, mind and senses. If you start counting rupees, annas and pies it will be the end of your acting career. I wouldn't take on a business if someone gave it to me free. And running a theatre is no different from running any other business.' Turning to Gurmukh he continued, 'You must reconsider your proposal. If you give half the ownership to Binodini the theatre will be ruined. She's a member of the troupe. The others will refuse to work under her.'

Gurmukh had neither the strength nor the desire to fight Girish. He had to get rid of the theatre, at whatever cost. After a little haggling a deal was struck. It was decided that the troupe would buy it from Gurmukh at the cost of eleven thousand rupees—a mere fraction of what he had spent on it. The money was collected in a few days and the papers signed. Four men, nominated by Girish, were to have the ownership rights and represent the troupe in everything. Thus the STAR passed into the hands of Girish and his cronies and Binodini was reduced to working on a monthly wage. However, her unquestioned obedience to Girish did not go unrewarded. Those of her colleagues who had hated and envied her all these years felt a softening in their hearts. 'Poor girl!' they whispered to one another, 'She has given up a king's ranson. Would you or I have done it?'

Binodini was now free of a protector and her house was her own. It was a good place to spend time after performances and Girish and his friends were there most evenings drinking and chatting about this and that. Binodini still held the opinion that her role in *Kamalé Kamini* was not worthy of her. She was also bitterly jealous of Bonobiharini who had left National Theatre for STAR and was playing Srimanta Saudagar. Binodini continued to complain but now Girish could shut her up with a sharp reprimand. One evening, while pouring out his brandy, she turned a pair of large pleading eyes on Girish and said 'Everyone says that Bhuni will get more claps than me in *Kamal é Kamini*.'

'They must be mad,' Girish took the glass from her hand. 'On your first entry as Chandi the walls of the theatre will burst with applause.'

'Yes, because of the costume. But Bhuni's role is much better. It has so many beautiful songs. Why didn't you give it to me?'

'But she's acting a man —'

'I can too. Don't I have the ability?'

'Of course you do. But who wants to see you as a man? Bhuni is much older than you and not half as beautiful. That's why I've given her the part of Srimanta. But the spectators want to see Binodini all dressed up in silks and jewels—flashing her eyes, laughing, weeping, singing, dancing. They come in hundreds to see your beautiful face and voluptuous figure. Can we disappoint them? After all they provide us with our living.'

'Let me play Srimanta for one night,' Binodini begged. 'I know all the songs and —'

'Stop nagging, woman,' Girish snapped at her. 'How can I change parts at this eleventh hour? Besides Bhuni won't agree.'

'Then leave me out of the play.' Tears glittered in Binodini's eyes and her voice trembled in disappointment. 'I don't want to act anymore.'

Girish gazed on her face for a long moment. An idea started forming in his head. Suddenly, his eyes glowing with enthusiasm, he said, 'I've just thought of a subject—a historical drama in which you will play the male lead. It will be a long part and a serious one. No coquetry and tricks. Can you do it?'

'Why not?'

'It's settled then. I'll start writing tonight. You'll have to put all you have in it, Binod, because you'll be solely responsible for its success or failure. Another thing. It'll be the most difficult role you've played in your life—a role that will test your acting ability as no other role could ever do.'

Chapter XXIII

One morning Bhumisuta was on the roof putting out some clothes to dry when her eye was caught by a scene in the woods, opposite the house, that made her run to the edge for a better view. On a reed mat, spread out in a little clearing between the trees, Bharat and a young man, who from his goatee and fez appeared to be a Muslim, sat peeling potatoes. A little distance away two other boys were struggling to light a fire. They puffed and blew till they were red in the face but all that rewarded their efforts were clouds of thick smoke that sent tears pouring down their cheeks. Bhumisuta giggled. The wood had been packed two tightly between the stones and had no room to breathe! A few vessels and baskets lay scattered about. It was obvious that Bharat and his friends were picnicking in the woods and were planning to do the cooking themselves. But how would they manage without help? Who would grind their spices and fetch them water? Bhumisuta needn't have worried. As a matter of fact, the boys had organized themselves quite well. Dwarika had done all the shopping and borrowed cooking vessels from his mess cook. He had even bribed the servants to grind several kinds of spices. He would do the cooking and Bharat, Irfan and Jadugopal would assist him.

Dwarika came from an orthodox Brahmin family, Jadugopal was a member of the Sadharan Brahmo Samaj, Irfan was an Ali Sunni Muslim and Bharat didn't know what he was. Yet the four were knit together in a bond of friendship that was as tenacious as it was strong. Dwarika was so fond of Irfan that he often remarked regretfully, 'If you weren't born a Muslim, you ass, I would have married you to my sister.'

Bharat was a king's bastard; Irfan an orphan from a very poor family of Murshidabad. But they had a lot in common. Both were mild in speech and introverts by nature. And both lived on sufferance—Bharat in the house of the Singhas and Irfan under the roof of an employee of Janaab Abdul Latif. They shared a passion for learning and a burning ambition to make something worthwhile of their lives. However, there was one big difference between them. Bharat's soul was corroded with bitterness—against his father, against the ways of the world and against women. Irfan, despite all the humiliations he suffered as a poor relative, had a nature as sweet and trusting as a child's. Dwarika had taken off his shirt and tied a gamchha around his waist. His face was red and hot and his hair dishevelled as he lay flat on the ground blowing at the fuel that refused to catch fire. With the thick white *poité* resting on his bare chest he looked more like a Brahmin cook than a student of Presidency College.

'Shall I hang up a sheet on this side?' Bharat offered, 'It might keep out the breeze and—'

'Don't keep out the breeze for God's sake,' Jadugopal quipped. 'It might be all we'll get this morning.' Then, prodding Dwarika's back with a bony finger, he continued, 'Do you hold out any hope Dwarika? The rats are wrestling with each other in my stomach already.'

'Tell them to call a truce,' Dwarika replied. 'There's plenty of time.'

Suddenly, a rustling in the bushes a few yards away made all the boys spin around. 'What was that?' Jadugopal cried out in a startled voice. 'I hope it's not a jackal. All we need now is a pack of jackals springing on us.' The rustling sound was now accompanied by a violent swaying of leaves and branches. Bharat ran towards the spot and, parting the bushes, saw a girl crouching on the ground. It was Bhumisuta. Bharat's brows came together in distaste. 'What are you doing here?' he asked sternly. Bhumisuta rose from the ground and, ignoring him completely, walked towards the others.

'Who is the girl?' Jadugopal asked curiously.

'She's . . . she's someone who lives in the same house—' Bharat couldn't bring himself to say, 'She's a maid.'

Bhumisuta walked straight to the fire, and, pulling out some of the sticks and rearranging the others, commenced fanning it with the end of her sari. Within seconds the wood burst into flame. 'Wonderful!' Dwarika exclaimed. Bhumisuta lifted the lid of a pot and tried to peer inside but Bharat stopped her with a gesture. 'That's enough Bhumi,' he said with all the dignity he could muster. 'Go home now.'

'Why not let her stay?' Jadugopal urged. 'She can help Dwarika.'

'Is this the girl you told us about?' Dwarika asked curiously. 'The one who can sing and dance.'

'Yes,' Bharat replied cautiously. 'She's from Orissa. I'll tell you more about her later. She must go now. It's not proper for her to be seen with us.'

'Why not?' Jadugopal persisted.

'Because people in the road have already started staring at us,' Dwarika replied.

'Let them,' Jadugopal said stubbornly. 'There is nothing wrong in men and women mixing as friends. We of the Brahmo Samaj believe women to be equal to men in all respects. We are urged to work for their uplift and—'

'Stop nattering about your Samaj,' Dwarika snapped irritably. 'How many Brahmos do we have in our country? This is a land of the Hindus. Our traditions decree that women be confined to their homes and look to the comfort of their husbands and sons.'

'Our traditions!' Jadugopal exclaimed angrily. 'You're talking rot Dwarika. What do you know about our traditions? Have you read ancient history?'

Bhumisuta turned her head to have a good look at Jadugopal. Her father used to talk exactly as this young man was doing. She hadn't heard anyone say that women were equal to men ever since she had left home. But, for all the strength of Jadugopal's arguments, Dwarika was proved right. A little knot of people could be seen on the road whispering to one another and pointing out to the group in the woods. A couple of carriages had halted, too, and curious faces peered from the windows. 'Go home Bhumi!' Bharat ordered in an ominous voice. Bhumisuta glanced briefly at his red, angry face and, putting down the ladle she held in her hand, walked meekly away. 'What cowards you are!' Jadugopal cried. 'Are we doing anything wrong? Are we drinking or dallying with the girl? How long can people stare at us? After sometime they will understand that this is an innocent picnic and go away.'

'The mutton is nearly done,' Dwarika said by way of reply.

'I'll start boiling the rice. We can eat in a few minutes. I'm cooking this meal for my friends and I don't need a woman to help me.'

Bhumisuta was flogged the next day. Word had spread, through what source she did not know, that she had been seen laughing and flirting with Bharat and his friends. When the news reached Monibhushan's ears his lust for the girl, suppressed with difficulty, was metamorphosed into a murderous rage. The thought of Bhumisuta smiling on another man set his blood on fire. '*Haramzadi*!' he cried hoarsely between clenched teeth as he struck the delicate body, over and over again with a whip, 'I'll put an end to your harlot tricks . . . I'll make the flesh fly off your bones before I've done with you . . .' Monibhushan's eyes rolled and foam gathered at the corners of his mouth. His heart beat so heavily that he felt it would burst. But he went on striking the girl screaming 'Bitch!' and 'Whore!' between blows till Bhumisuta fell at his feet in a dead faint. The mistresses of the house stood at a distance watching the flogging but did not come forward to stop him or protect Bhumisuta.

Bhumi lay like a bundle of bloodsoaked rags for hours in the sun. Then, after all the household tasks were done, two maids picked her up and carried her to her room. She lay there for four days. Not a soul came near her. Her back, thighs and breasts were covered with angry red welts. The skin on her long delicate fingers was cut to ribbons. But her face was untouched. The most vicious of Manibhushan's blows had failed to leave their mark for she had covered it with her hands. 'I should have died,' she thought over and over again. 'Why didn't I? Why do I go on living? Shall I kill myself? I can set my clothes on fire and—' Her lips, cracked and swollen with thirst, trembled in self pity and tears oozed painfully out of her eyes.

No, Bhumisuta could not die. Strange though it was, it was hunger and thirst that drove her out of her isolation and brought her back to the scene of her humiliation. She was young and strong and her body craved food and drink.

There were changes awaiting her. A middle-aged widow had been appointed to take over her duties in the puja room. Henceforth, she was not to go near the gods lest she pollute their air with her sinful breath. The most menial of tasks were allotted to her. She was set to scrubbing kitchen vessels, washing clothes and wiping down the floors of the rooms and verandas. Bhumisuta accepted her new role without a murmur. She didn't want to get beaten again.

In the evenings, after the beds were made and her work done for the day, she would go up to the roof to catch a breath of air. She dared not look in the direction of Bharat's room though it drew her irresistibly. Bharat hadn't been let off either. Monibhushan had threatened him with expulsion from the house if he was caught anywhere near Bhumisuta. Bharat had stood his ground. He had said that he was answerable to Shashibhushan and to no one else. He was here as Shashibhushan's representative and would leave the house only on his command.

The days passed. Bharat and Bhumisuta did not even exchange a glance. Then, one evening, as Bharat was walking up the stairs to his room, he chanced to look up at the roof. As soon as he did so someone glided away from his line of vision as swiftly and imperceptibly as a shadow. Bharat stood undecided for a moment, then made up his mind. Running up to the roof he came and stood by Bhumisuta. 'I have something to say to you,' he said. Bhumisuta stood silent, her eyes fixed at her feet. 'I understand your predicament,' Bharat went on. 'But there is nothing I can do to help you. I'm a dependent myself. Mejo Karta has threatened to throw me out if he catches me anywhere near you. It won't do you any good either. He'll treat you even more cruelly. You must stop coming up to the roof and peering into my room. Do you understand me?' Bhumisuta nodded. Bharat lit a cigarette and paced up and down for a while. Then, clearing his throat, he continued, 'This country is governed by the British according to a rule of law. Mejo Karta may have paid your uncle a few rupees but you are not his slave. He can't keep you here against your will. You can leave this house any time you wish. The police will help you. A friend of mine has told me that the Brahmos have opened an ashram in Kolutola where girls like you can find a home. Not only that, they are given an education and taught some skill enabling them to earn their own living. Would you like to go there? Do you have the courage?' Bhumisuta lifted her eyes and, fixing them on Bharat's face, said steadily, 'Yes.'

'Can you leave this house?'

'I can.'

'You'll have to go in secret. I'll help you. But only to the extent of taking you there. After that you're responsible for yourself. You'll never see me again.'

Two days later Bhumisuta left the house of the Singhas. Pushing her way out through a patch of broken wall she walked on silent feet to the corner of the road where Bharat stood waiting. It was late evening and the shadows were closing around them. Bharat tried to peer into Bhumisuta's face but he couldn't see it. The edge of a pink sari was drawn over her head so low that it fell to her breast. But he recognized her from the way she walked. And he also noted the small bundle she carried under her arm.

The hackney cab that carried Bharat, Bhumisuta and two other passengers, went clattering along by the side of the Ganga. It was a risky venture, for at this hour of twilight, drunken goras often came out from the Maidan, waylaid innocent passengers and robbed and molested them. The nervous driver urged his rheumatic horse on with alternate shouts of encouragement and cruel cuts with his whip till, reaching Janbazar, everyone heaved a sigh of relief. Bharat and Bhumisuta stepped down and started walking towards Kolutola where Jadugopal would be waiting for them. 'Careful! Careful!' Bharat scolded as Bhumisuta slipped and stumbled over pits and ruts. 'Push the veil off your face and mind where you're going. Who knows you here?' Bhumisuta did not reply. Nor did she unveil her face. Her heart beat fast with trepidation. Had she done right? She was a doomed creature. Who knew what destiny had in store for her now?

As they reached the mouth of Hadhkatar Gali a group of men came rushing out of it brandishing swords and flaming mashals and yelling at the top of their voices. Before either of them could react another group emerged from Malanga Gali also carrying lights and weapons and shouting obscenities. Sensing a communal clash was about to break out, people screamed and ran this way and that. Bharat stretched out a hand to pull Bhumisuta away to a place of safety but before he could reach her he was felled to the ground by the butt of a sword and the rampaging horde passed over him stamping and kicking till his body became a mass of cuts and bruises. As soon as he could, Bharat gathered himself slowly together and, rising to his feet, looked around for Bhumisuta. She had disappeared.

By now a cavalcade of mounted policemen had come riding in. Doom! Doom! Shots were fired into the air and the confusion increased a hundred fold. Bharat found himself wedged in a mass of human bodies running towards Sealdah and there was no option for him but to run along with them. But he kept his eyes skinned for Bhumisuta and called out, 'Bhumi! Where are you?' till his voice was hoarse and cracking. But there was no answering call. There were some women in that sea of humanity but they were either serving women or prostitutes.

The riot was quelled in an hour. The crowd dispersed and Bharat returned to the scene of the clash. The police had gone and so had the rioters but the injured and the dead still lay where they had fallen. Bharat peered into each face but they were all the faces of men. Then he examined the nullahs by the side of the road. Bhumisuta may have lost her footing and fallen into one of them. Then she had either fainted or twisted her foot so badly that she had been unable to climb on to the road again. But, though he combed the entire area with dogged perseverance he found no trace of Bhumisuta. Bharat's heart beat heavily within him. What had he done? He had persuaded Bhumisuta to leave what was, after all, a secure shelter and expose herself to the outside world. And, in the process, he had lost her. What was happening to her now? Had she been abducted and carried to a cheap brothel in the red light area which was only a few yards away?

Suddenly a ray of hope irradiated Bharat's soul. Bhumisuta knew they were going to Kolutola. What if she had managed to find her way to the spot where Jadugopal stood waiting. As soon as the thought struck him he started running like one possessed down the dark deserted streets till, reaching Kolutola, he stopped short. What was that shape sitting huddled by the side of the road? Was it human or animal? He slowed his steps afraid of frightening it away. Then, coming closer, his heart gave a tremendous bound of relief. It was Bhumisuta. Bharat felt himself lifted on a great wave of happiness. It gushed out in a quick warm flood from eyes spent with hours of searching for a dearly beloved face. 'Bhumi! Bhumi!' he cried in a voice choking with emotion. 'I've found you. Thank God I've found you!' But the eyes that looked steadily back into his burned with hate. 'So this was your plan?' There was a vicious edge to her voice. 'To lure me out of the house and then leave me to my fate. Go back to those sheltering walls where you belong and be happy.'

'You wrong me Bhumi!' Bharat cried passionately. 'I didn't leave you on purpose. I was thrown down—trampled on. I've walked miles and miles looking for you.'

'Why? What am I to you? What do you care if I live or die? Go back. I'm an orphan and the street is my home!'

Bharat stood still for a few minutes. He felt his heart twist cruelly within him. And, suddenly, he knew the truth. He loved Bhumisuta and couldn't live without her. 'Take my hand,' he said gently but firmly. 'And come with me. I won't leave you . . . ever again.'

Chapter XXIV

One of the doors in Kadambari's bedroom was hung with a mirror of valuable Belgian glass—so large that it stretched across a whole panel affording a full view of her form from head to toe. Here Kadambari stood one afternoon, combing out her long wet hair and humming a little tune to herself. Her heart felt light and free. She had whiled the whole morning away curled up on her bed reading Robi's *Sandhya Sangeet*. She had become so immersed in it that she hadn't heard the maid calling out to her that it was time for her bath and meal. It was past noon when, aware of the lateness of the hour, she had scrambled to her feet and dashed off to take a bath. Unlike her other sisters-in-law she didn't bathe in the bathroom downstairs. Her husband had built one adjoining her apartment for her exclusive use.

Smearing a little sindoor on her forefinger she ran it along the blunt edge of the comb. Then, with meticulous care, she drew a red line down the parting of her hair. As she did so she glanced at herself in the mirror. The dark circles under her eyes were gone. Her face had filled out and the skin on her neck and arms stretched taut and smooth as satin. She was so tired of being ill. Thank God she felt well these days—really well.

'Boudimoni!' her maid called from outside the room. 'The cooks have brought up your meal. Shall I bring them in?'

In the cavernous kitchens below, a dozen cooks sweated from dawn till dark cooking enormous quantities and varieties of food. Rice was boiled in huge pots, drained in baskets and poured over clean white cloth, mound over mound till it rose to a mountain. Chunks of fish, rubbed all over with salt and turmeric and fried to a golden crispness, were piled in wooden basins in hundreds. Some were eaten plain—others cooked in sharp gravies of mustard and chillies or ginger and cumin. Some were even mixed in a sweet and tart sauce of tamarind and molasses to tempt the jaded palate. The men of the house were hearty eaters and demanded variety. The mistresses were good cooks too and stirred up a dish occasionally as and when the fancy took them.

Till quite lately the women of the house had assembled every morning in the great veranda adjoining the storeroom with baskets of vegetables and *bontis*. It was a pleasant hour to which everyone looked forward. Tongues wagged pleasurably while hands peeled potatoes, sliced brinjals and shelled peas. But now many of the women were gone. Most of Debendranath's married daughters had left Jorasanko and made homes for themselves with their husbands and children. His daughters-in-law, too, were as strangers to one another. Gyanadanandini had her own establishment in Birji Talao and Mrinalini, the youngest of them all, had been whisked away from Jorasanko even before she had made proper acquaintance with her sisters-in-law. The small knot of women that huddled together over their bontis these days was only a pale shadow of the old throng. In any case, Kadambari was not invited to join them anymore.

As Kadambari turned away from the mirror her glance fell on the table in one corner of the room, where last night's meal lay uneaten. Her nostrils flared in distaste. The maid was new and unused to the ways of a great family like the Thakurs of Jorasanko. She should have removed it hours ago. 'Come in Halor Ma!' she called out, 'And take last night's thala away.'

Halor Ma entered the room and lifting the cover off the thala sniffed delicately at the pile of luchis and bowls of curried fish and vegetables. 'What shall I do with this Boudimoni?' she enquired.

'What else can you do but throw it away?'

'Throw it away! But stale luchis are good to eat.'

'Eat them then!' Kadambari laughed lightly and turned her attention to what the cooks had brought in.

Kadambari ate little as a rule and even less when she was distressed or unhappy. Her night meal was left untouched more often than not as waiting for her husband to return strained her nerves so unbearably that the finest of delicacies tasted like sawdust in her mouth. It had been so last night. But today was different. Her husband would come for her in the evening and take her with him to his ship where a grand celebration had been arranged. And there she would meet Robi. A wave of happiness swept over her and her stomach heaved pleasantly, craving food. Turning eagerly to the thala just brought in she lifted the cover. A mound of white rice rose in the centre, fragrant and steaming with melted ghee trickling down the sides. Several bowls surrounded it. One had finely sliced bitter gourd fried to a crackling crispness with pieces of *bori*. Another was filled with golden moong dal. Two others contained tender pumpkin stew and delicious smelling *patal posto*. And the highlight of the meal—a pair of huge lobsters in a thick coconut cream gravy—rested in an enormous bowl on one side.

Till a few years ago the Thakurs had eaten their meals sitting on velvet asans on the marble floor. On Gyanadanandini's return from England she had had a dining table and chairs set up in her apartments and Jyotrindra, who approved of everything his Mejo Bouthan did, followed suit. Thus Kadambari was constrained, against her wishes, to eat at a table. But unlike Gyanadanandini she didn't use crockery and cutlery but ate from a thala using her fingers.

Kadambari mixed some of the ghee soaked rice with the bitter gourd and ate it with relish. Then she had some dal and rice and a bit of the pumpkin stew. Suddenly an idea crossed her mind making her hand pause on its way to her mouth. There was to be a great dinner on the ship tonight. Jyotirindra had told her that he was ordering an array of delicacies from an English hotel. If she filled herself up with all this homely food now she would have no appetite left for the evening. And her husband and Robi would scold her for not eating enough.

Putting down the rice she held in her hand she rose to her feet. She washed her hands and popping a paan into her mouth, came and stood on the veranda. She smiled wryly. The rest of the meal including the succulent lobsters would be enjoyed by Halor Ma.

Returning to her bedroom she glanced at the clock. It was two. Her husband would come for her at six. There was plenty of time. She lay on her bed and opened *Sandhya Sangeet*. Turning the pages one by one, her thoughts went back to her life in Chandannagar—those long, lazy days and starry nights when a young bud was unfolding its petals gently, timidly, under her tender care. The bud had bloomed now and many bees and butterflies hovered over it. These thoughts went round and round her head till, wearying of them, she fell asleep. She woke with a start as the cuckoo in her English clock chimed the hour. One,

203

two, three, four, five. *O Ma*! It was five o' clock already. Scrambling out of bed she ran to the bathroom. She would have to get ready in a hurry. Her husband must be on his way.

Jyotrindranath had managed to set his ship afloat after a mammoth effort and after parting with enormous sums of money. Named after the heroine of his most successful play *Sarojini*, it rested now in the waters of Srirampur ready to embark on its maiden voyage down the Ganga to Khulna with goods and passengers. There would be a full moon tonight and the whole family would congregate on the deck to celebrate the success of this unique venture. When first conceived the idea had been unique but, not being secretive by nature, Jyotirindranath had been unable to keep it to himself. In consequence, a British concern called the Flotilla Company had beaten him to it and their ship was, even now, carrying cargo between Khulna and Barisal.

Gyanadanandini had already taken possession of a couple of cabins in *Sarojini* and had settled in with Robi and her children. Jyotirindranath had requested her to supervise the furnishings and decor bypassing his own wife Kadambari whose taste, everyone had to admit, was impeccable. But though Kadambari had not asked for an explanation Jyotirindra had hastened to supply it. He told her that, being in competition with a British company, he had to have everything in *Sarojini* very westernized and modern. And, having lived in England for several years, Mejo Bouthan knew best what that was. Kadambari hadn't uttered a word of reproach. But every time she thought of them all together, busy and happy, she felt a stab of pain in her heart, so sharp it was almost physical.

Kadambari bathed herself in cool scented water, then opening her cupboard began to look through her saris. She had so many of them! Silks with heavy gold borders, dhakais, muslins and balucharis with elaborate motifs and intricately worked anchals lay folded in neat piles—untouched for the most part for she hardly ever went out. The last time she had worn one of these was at Hiranmayee's wedding. There was a little prick in her heart at the memory. She hated going to Swarnakumari's house and avoided it whenever she could. But she could hardly escape a family wedding. She had been miserable. She had stood by herself all the time while the others were rushing about laughing and talking and enjoying themselves. Even Robi seemed to be avoiding her. Suddenly she discovered a profound truth. When alone with her there was no one warmer and more understanding than Robi; no one more deeply sensitized to her feelings. But, in the presence of others, he felt guilty and ashamed and couldn't look her in the eye. She pushed the thought aside. It was unbearable.

Discarding one sari after another Kadambari finally chose a nayan sukh sari of kingfisher blue silk. The colour would look lovely in the moonlight. Sending for her *alta dasi* she had her feet painted with vermilion. Next she lit a dozen sticks of incense and let the fragrant smoke flow over each strand of her hair. She brightened her eyes with surma and darkened her brows with kajal. Then, taking up handfuls of champa flowers, she pressed them under her armpits and between her breasts. She braided her beautiful hair and, twisting it into an elaborate *khonpa*, fixed it in place with a jewelled comb and gold-headed pins. Finally, after draping her sari to her satisfaction, she wound a rope of fragrant *juin* in the blue black masses of her hair. Then, shyly, hesitantly, she approached her mirror and looked at herself. The face that looked back satisfied her and she smiled a little smile of contentment. She was looking her best and her husband was coming for her. He would bring his steamer all the way from Srirampur so that she could join in the revels by the light of the moon. Suddenly a thought occurred to her making her blood run cold. What if he didn't come in person? What if he sent Robi? Kadambari made up her mind. She wouldn't go with Robi. She would go only with her husband. And she would have him by her side all night. She would show Gyanadanandini . . . Kadambari was startled out of her thoughts by the chime of her cuckoo clock. One, two, three, four, five, six. It was six o clock. Was that a footstep she heard on the stairs? Bursting with excitement she opened the door and called out to her maid, 'Who's that coming up the steps Halor Ma?' Halor Ma went to have a look but came back shaking her head. There was no one. Kadambari sat on her bed prepared to wait. Her husband was a busy man. He might be a little late but he would come . . .

But the cuckoo, the cruel cuckoo, called out to Kadambari

relentlessly hour after hour. Spring had come and gone but the cuckoo would not cease her song. Nine chimes! Ten! Eleven! Halor Ma had gone away and the house was dark and silent. How much longer would he be? She clung to her hopes still. He would come. He must . . . Only she couldn't endure the waiting much longer. Suddenly her eyes fell on her own reflection and, in the bright light that spread from the crystal chandelier she saw the other Kadambari smile mockingly at her. 'He's forgotten you, you fool!' the other one said. 'They've all forgotten you. Look at you! All dressed up in your finery like a young bride about to meet her bridegroom. But you're not a young bride. You're a witch—an ugly, old witch and everyone despises you.'

Kadambari covered her face with her hands and flung herself on the bed. She had been longing to do so for sometime now but hadn't from fear of dishevelling her hair. She wanted to weep but the tears wouldn't come. She stared up at the ceiling her eyes hard and dry. And then she did the strangest thing. She started humming to herself, her voice low and husky at first then rising to a crescendo as she gave herself up to her song:

'The hours go by in waiting.
Come to my bower dear one!
I had hoped to string a garland
And hang it around your neck
But alas! you came not to me
And my flowers wilted in the waiting'

Suddenly she stopped her song and giggled. Then, getting off the bed, she came and stood before the mirror once again. Rolling her eyes at her reflection, she hissed in a passionate voice, 'Get out of my room you slut! Don't dare look at me with those eyes. All dressed up too! Shame on you! Shame! Shame!' She whirled around and, picking up Jyotirindranath's silver-headed cane, she struck the mirror over and over again with all her might making the glass rain about her in splinters. Then, when the panel stood stripped, dark and empty, she heaved a sigh of relief. 'Good riddance,' she muttered to herself. 'I'll never have to see her again.' Then, raising her voice, she started singing her song once more.

After a while she thought she heard a sound outside the door. 'Who's there?' she called eagerly. But no one answered. She

206

waited a while, all her senses alert—her eyes sharp and piercing as an eagle's. 'It's only the south wind,' she murmured. Craning her neck she squinted at the darkness outside. 'Wild wind!' she cried aloud, 'You're not for me. And you, you moon of the night—you're not for me. And all you flowers! You're not mine. No—not one of you!' She jumped off the bed and paced restlessly up and down the marble floor stamping her feet in her agitation. 'If I were a bird,' she thought whimsically, 'I could fly out of that window. I could go to my loved ones winging my way out of this great city and across the wide river. That would be best. To have no body, only a soul; a soul set free to wander at will.'

Upon this thought she ran to the adjoining room and stood before the cupboard that was set into one wall. Turning the key with a trembling hand she wrenched the lock open and drew out, from a secret recess, a sandalwood box inlaid with ivory. It was full of jewels—diamond bracelets, a heavy moon necklace of rubies and emeralds, chokers and strings of pearls hung with jewelled pendants and many other exquisite pieces. Pushing them aside with an impatient hand she pulled out a small paper packet and tipped its contents into her palm—four balls of some sticky black substance that Bishu the weaver's wife had given her. Bishu, from whom Kadambari bought her saris, was also a *deyashini* and dabbled in roots and herbs. She had given her these balls of opium to soothe her nerves and help her sleep, warning her that an overdose might bring on the sleep of death. This box also contained three letters. Kadambari had found one of them in the pocket of her husband's *jobba*. The other two she had discovered tucked away between the pages of a voluminous dictionary. They were all written in the same hand—a woman's hand. They bore no signature and no address. All three commenced with the phrase—*More precious to me than my life itself.*

Kadambari read the letters, one by one, as she had done so many times in the past. Her breath came in short gasps and her eyes glittered as her lips mumbled forming the words. And as she read, the slow burning in her breast became a raging fire—the flames licking her body and engulfing her soul. She tore the letters into pieces; the pieces into fragments, and tossed them into the air till they flew about like snow flakes. She watched her handiwork, laughing for a while, then tipping the contents of her palm into her mouth she swallowed them with great gulps of water.

Peace! Peace at last! She sighed a deep sigh of contentment. She was free. Free from doubt and torment. Free to go where she liked; to do what she liked. There were no walls before her now. Spreading her arms as though they were wings she darted this way and that round and round the room. But though she flew about as though she were, in truth, a gorgeous blue humming bird the white marble of the floor, littered with fragments of glass, told another story. It bore the imprints of her feet—etched not in vermilion but in blood. Kadambari felt nothing; saw nothing. She whirled on and on dancing her dance of death. Her sari impeding her movements, she pulled it off her body and flung it into a corner. Then she took off her jewels, one by one, and tossed them, laughing, into the air. Her diamond *kankan* hit the chandelier and fell to the floor in a shower of crystal flakes. Next she attacked her hair tugging at the comb and flower-headed gold pins till the braids, released from their confinement, fell over her back and shoulders like twisted, wounded snakes. Panting with the effort she came and sat at the table where Jyotirindranath did his writing. It was littered with his papers. She glanced at them from the corner of her eye. What was she doing here? Oh yes! She had to write a note. People always did that before they took their lives. Thank God she had remembered in time. She picked up a pen and drew a sheet of paper before her. To whom would she address her note? To Robi, of course. But, even as her pen touched the paper, two lines of poetry came to her mind. They had been written by Robi soon after the wedding. She had came across them by chance when preparing the bridal chamber.

Depart from hence—the old
For the new hath begun her game . . .

How true it was! Women grew old and were discarded. But men! Why did they never grow old and useless? Was it because they lived in a larger, more expansive world and could constantly renew themselves? She shrugged off the thought and turned to the more urgent matter at hand. She would write a note—not to Robi but to her husband. How would she address him? *More precious to me than my life itself*? She giggled at the thought wondering what such words really meant. Her head was growing lighter and she had difficulty in keeping her eyes open. She realized that she would have to hurry for soon darkness would engulf her. *Beloved*, she began then, hastily, she scribbled a few lines ending *From one who has yearned for you all her life*. The pen slipped from her fingers that felt, by now, as though weighted down with lead. 'Robi! she cried aloud, frightened. 'I'm going! Your Natun Bouthan . . .' Suddenly, without any warning, her body twisted sideways and, slipping from the chair, fell in a huddled heap on the floor.

The thirty lamps in the chandelier burned on, the candles sinking slowly in their sockets. The diligent cuckoo kept vigil breaking the silence of the night, hour after hour, with her ecstatic cry. And from the open window a wild sweet wind blew in and danced around the motionless form sprawled on the white marble . . .

Kadambari was, by habit, an early riser. She left her bed, each day, with the first glimmer of dawn and watered her plants with her sprinkler. That morning Halor Ma waited till the sun was up then knocked on the door. But it did not open. Thinking her mistress to be still asleep she went away and came back some time later. She came and went thrice and though her gentle knock changed, with the passing of the hours, into a furious rapping all was silent within. Frightened, Halor Ma alerted the women of the house. Now everyone came crowding to Kadambari's apartment. Her sisters-in-law called out to her. The servants banged on the door till their arms ached but there was no response.

Of the two mansions that stood side by side in Jorasanko one belonged to the Brahmo and the other to the Hindu branch of the Thakur family. From one of the wings of this Hindu house a portion of Kadambari's apartment could be seen. Now everyone came crowding here pushing and jostling. But though the window was open wide all that was visible was Kadambari's bed—the sheets and pillows smooth and unslept in. She, herself, was nowhere to be seen. Then one of the women had an idea. Pulling a high stool as close to the window as possible she propped Gunendranath's youngest daughter Sunayani on it and bade her look inside. 'What do you see Sunayani?' the women urged. 'Tell us—tell us quick.' But the little girl said nothing. Her face grew pale and his lips trembled. For child though she was, she knew instinctively that what she had seen was death. That twisted unnatural form that was her Natun Kakima's lay on the floor—not in sleep but in death.

The next thing to be done was to inform the menfolk and get the door broken. But who would take the responsibility? The dead woman's husband was away. Suddenly the women remembered that their father-in-law was in the house. He had arrived suddenly last night on one of his brief unannounced visits.

Debendranath was in the middle of his morning meditation when two of his sons came into the room and broke the news. Debendranath heard their account in silence. His eyes were closed; his lips kept moving with the mantra he was repeating but his ears took in each minute detail of what was being said to him. Not a muscle twitched in the smooth white marble of his face and form.

After a while he sighed and rose to his feet. Motioning to the boys to leave the room he sent for his intrepid and trusty attendant Kishori. 'You must have heard the news,' he said with his habitual directness, as soon as Kishori had shut the door behind him. 'My sons tell me that Natun Badhu Mata has taken her own life. Act quickly and with discretion. Get the door broken down but let no one enter the room—not even my sons. You alone should go in. Keep a sharp look out and remove all traces of anything suspicious that may be lurking there.' Frowning in thought for a few moments he went on, 'It is not seemly that the remains of a daughter-in-law of this house be sent for a post mortem. Have a coroner's court set up in this house and see that a verdict of natural death is given.' He shut his eyes as if in weariness, then opening them again he went on, 'No newspaper, Indian or English, national or international, must be allowed to carry the news. Call a meeting of all the editors and make my wishes known to them. All this will cost money but that is of no consideration. Take a thousand rupees from the khazanchi khana for the present. You may submit the accounts later. May the blessings of the All Merciful Param Brahma be with you! Go!'

It took four sturdy men servants over an hour to break open the door which was of solid mahogany. When it gave way, at last, Kishori asked everyone who stood about it to leave for such was the Maharshi's command. Then, stepping into the room, he got a shock. The floor was littered with fragments of glass, overturned furniture and splotches of blood. Kadambari lay in the middle of the wreckage. Her body clad only in a silk chemise and jacket, lay on the floor twisted unnaturally, one arm sprawled out, the other resting on her breast. The soles of her long slim feet were coated with clotted blood. But her face was as luminous and tender as though bathed in moonlight and her lips were parted in a smile.

The first thing Kishori did was to pick up a sheet from the bed and cover the body. Then, casting his sharp eyes around the apartment, he noticed that the floor of the adjoining room was strewn with shreds of paper. He swept them up in his hands. He knew what they were instinctively, even without glancing at the writing. Stuffing them into his pocket he turned to the cupboard which stood wide open, the key still hanging from the keyhole. A sandalwood box with jewels spilling out of it and stared him in the face. But he felt not even a prick of temptation. Sweeping its contents back into the box he closed it and locked the cupboard. Then, he came back to the room in which the dead woman lay. There was a letter on the table. He picked it up and read it. Then, tearing it across, he shoved the pieces into his pocket with the other fragments. The room was in a mess. He would have to sweep up the glass and wipe away the bloodstains.

Looking around for a broom he nearly jumped out of his skin. He had heard a sigh, clear and audible, and it seemed to come from the dead woman. The thought made his heart beat so fast that he thought it would burst. He didn't want to look in her direction but something, he didn't know what, impelled him from within. Kadambari lay in the same position but now her eyes were open. Hard and glittering like jewels they stared steadfastly into his. It was only for a few seconds, then the lids fell over her eyes once more. Sweat streamed down Kishori's face and neck. Trembling like a leaf he sank to his knees on the floor. Picking up her hand he examined her pulse. It was feeble, very feeble, but not gone. She was alive.

Now everything changed swiftly. Kadambari was lifted from the floor and laid on the bed. Her sisters-in-law washed and tended her. And the best doctors of the city were sent for—Indian as well as English. A messenger was despatched with the utmost haste to the *Sarojini* and Jyotirindranath and his entourage came rushing back to Jorasanko.

Kadambari lay in a deep coma, the doctors battling for her life. She never knew that her two dearest ones were by her side through day and night. And then, two days later, she drew her last breath.

Kishori had made all the arrangements with his habitual sagacity. A coroner's court had been set up in the house with the magistrate, a chemical examiner and a couple of clerks in attendance. They were treated to excellent food ordered from an English hotel and the finest of wines and liquors. Satisfied, they went away certifying her death as owing to natural causes.

The cremation was to be performed according to Brahmo rites by Hemchandra Vidyaratna. Vast quantities of sandalwood, incense and pure ghee were sent for in conformity with the status of the deceased. But who would light the pyre? Kadambari was childless and her husband was prostrated with shock. He hadn't been able to come for her because the tide had run out. Some of his guests had suggested that she be brought by road but it had become too late for that. Had he known that she would take his breach of promise so much to heart he would have surely come for her. Resolving to bring her the very next day he had flung himself into the celebrations. He felt overwhelmed with guilt every time he remembered that he had been singing and laughing and enjoying himself the very moment that his wife was taking her own life. He was so distraught that Gyanadanandini, fearing for his mental and physical health, took him away from Jorasanko to her own house even before the cremation.

As for Robi—he was too dazed by what had happened to feel sorrow or pain. He saw Kadambari's body being laid out on the bier. He watched his nephew Dipu light the pyre. The smoke from the leaping flames stung his eyes and the combined odours of burning wood, incense and ghee assailed his nostrils but he felt nothing. After the cremation, through the days of mandatory mourning, he sat on a reed mat, hour after hour, his back resting against a wall, his eyes hard and dry. And all the while he thought of the days he had spent with his Natun Bouthan in Moran's villa in Chandannagar. A series of images flashed before his eyes—picking flowers with Natun Bouthan on bright autumn mornings; swinging together on long shadowy afternoons under a sky dark with monsoon cloud; gazing out on the river sitting side by side in the twilight; Natun Bouthan holding his hand and gazing deep into his eyes. There had been silence between them—a silence that spoke more than words. His new book *Prakritir Pratishodh* was coming out in a few days. Would he have time to add a new lyric? *Mori lo mori amai banshi té dékéchhé ké.* He might have to alter the text a little. But would he have the time?

Robi sat up with a jerk. His limbs quivered with shock at the realization that he had started thinking of other things. And that before Kadambari's ashes had barely cooled. He was already planning his new book. How could he have done that?

And now, the hot tears, so long unshed, coursed down Robi's cheeks.

Chapter XXV

That night Bharat brought Bhumisuta back to Bhabanipur. They had left the house at dusk and returned after midnight. Bharat had anticipated a lot of trouble. They would be denied entrance—he was sure of that. But he was determined to stand his ground. He was Shashibhushan's guest and he would leave the house only on Shashibhushan's command. If Bhumisuta was thrown out he would keep her with him in his own room. But, by a strange coincidence, his fears turned out to be without foundation. Shashibhushan had arrived suddenly that very night and all the members of the household were so busy buzzing around him that they failed to note their absence. Bhumisuta slipped quietly into her own room and so did Bharat. Without knowing it, Shashibhushan had saved Bharat once again.

It had suddenly dawned on Birchandra Manikya that many of the native rajas, Raja of Mysore, Jaipur and Patiala among them, had their own mansions in Calcutta. It was but right that the Maharaja of Tripura have one too. His young queen was bored in the palace of Agartala and was clamouring to see the sights of the premier city of which she had heard so much. Besides, the monsoon months were hot and sticky in Tripura and brought on various disorders of the spleen and stomach. The Maharaja had suffered several bouts of sickness and had been advised by his physicians to try a change of scene and climate. The English doctors of Calcutta, he had heard, had eradicated malaria and controlled cholera and other enteric fevers. If he had a place of his own in the city he could spend the monsoon months, each year, away from Tripura. So Shashibhushan was despatched post haste to look for a suitable house and have it fitted up with furniture and servants in preparation for the royal visit.

From the next day onwards Shashibhushan spent his mornings looking for a house, Bharat accompanying him everywhere he went. Returning home they had their noon meal together in Krishnabhamini's apartment—the two being served

214

side by side as if they were brothers. Bharat was surprised at this elevation in his status. He did not know that Manibhushan was planning to touch his brother for a loan and couldn't afford to displease him by treating Bharat in a cavalier fashion. Now that he had easy access to the inner apartments he came across Bhumisuta often. Though he rarely spoke to her he never failed to note the pallor of her cheeks and the sadness in her eyes. And his determination to look after her grew in intensity.

After several days of search a house was eventually found—a large mansion standing on one and a half acres of ground in Circular Road. It had a well laid out garden with some fine old trees and was surrounded by high stone walls. The house had two storeys with two separate wings. This was as it should be for the Maharaja was coming with his wife and would need an andar mahal for his privacy. The front wing had six rooms. Here Shashibhushan would take up residence, permanently, for such was the king's command. One of the rooms would be fitted up as an office. The inner wing was much grander. It had verandas on all three sides, floors of Italian marble and glass windows with wooden shutters.

Shashibhushan and Bharat went from room to room then came up to the roof. On one side lay a vast track of marshy land with stretches of water gleaming between clumps of reeds and mangroves. Some fishermen could be seen dragging a heavy net out of the still brown waters. On the other side were rice fields emerald green in the morning sun. Facing them were the dwellings of the fashionable rich—tall three-storeyed mansions set in landscaped gardens.

'Bharat,' Shashibhushan put an arm around his shoulder. 'Now we need to look for a place for you.'

'For me! Shan't I be staying here with you?'

'Have you taken leave of your senses? I don't want you within miles of anyone from Tripura. Someone might recognize you and inform the Maharaja. And then—' Shashibhushan laughed ruefully and continued, 'I mean to get you out of the house in Bhabanipur. You won't be safe there. One can never tell with the Maharaja. He might walk in, without prior notice, upon a whim.'

'When he does that I'll hide—'

'That may not be possible every time. He may catch you

unawares. Why don't you rent a room in Shyambazar? He'll never get that far.' Then, seeing the stricken look on Bharat's face, he added hastily,' You needn't worry about the expense. I'll look after all that. Concentrate on your studies and leave everything else to me.'

The proposal was excellent. Bharat would have a place of his own for the first time in his life. He would be independent. His friends could visit him freely. And he could live as he pleased. Yet Bharat's heart sank at the thought. If he left Bhabanipur what would become of Bhumisuta?

After some search a place was found. Two small rooms with an adjoining terrace over a godown stocked with spices was rented for him in Hari Ghosh Lane—one of the smaller lanes that meandered out of Beadon Street. The area was respectable and the rent only eight rupees. Shashibhushan even found a servant for him—a young man named Mahim who had worked for the previous tenants. Everything was arranged quickly and efficiently and Bharat was instructed to pack his things and leave in a couple of days.

Bharat obeyed but with a heavy heart. He had promised Bhumisuta that he would look after her and he was abandoning her. What was worse, he hadn't even told her he was leaving. She would think him a liar and a cheat and she would be justified in doing so.

Bharat hung about Krishnabhamini's apartment hoping to get a few moments alone with Bhumisuta. He paced up and down the veranda outside his room in order to catch her on her way up to the roof. But Shashibhushan's presence in the house had added to her duties and she had no time for herself. And, then, on the day of his departure he got his chance. Returning from college that evening he saw a palki waiting at the gate. It being the night of a lunar eclipse one of the mistresses was going for her ritual dip in the Ganga. Presently three women, heavily veiled, came walking out of the house. He couldn't see their faces but he could swear that one of them was Bhumisuta. 'Bhumi!' he called out in his desperation. Startled, she turned her head towards him but only for a few seconds. Then, hurrying, she stepped into the palki. But in that brief instant Bharat raised his hand as if to say, 'I am with you Bhumi. However far I may go I shall always be there for you.' But he couldn't tell if Bhumisuta understood.

Bharat left the next day his heart heavy with guilt. How could he have done this to Bhumisuta? He was a fraud and a coward. He should have made his feelings public. He should have taken Bhumisuta away by force if necessary. He should have kept her with him; looked after her. But how? Shashibhushan would never allow it. And he was dependent on Shashibhushan.

It took Bharat about a month to settle down in his new lodgings. Shyambazar lay to the north, in a much older part of the city. In comparison with Bhabanipur the streets here were narrow and heavily congested with pedestrians and traffic and the houses stood packed together in close proximity. The atmosphere was informal and congenial. The men called out to their neighbours in greeting and stopped to spend the time of day while passing one another in the street. Women leaned out of their windows and exchanged gossip and news. Everyone knew what was being cooked in their neighbours' kitchens, the maladies their babies were suffering from and the problems they had with their maids and servants. Bharat looked on interestedly from his veranda each morning on the streams of people who passed up and down—pedlars hawking milk, fish, fruit and vegetables in strange sing-song voices; women with head loads knocking on doors, offering *alta*, sindoor, bangles, saris and ribbons.

But even as the days flew by, Bharat was unable to rid himself of his sense of guilt with regard to Bhumisuta. Now, all his hopes of meeting her and begging her for her forgiveness were gone, for he had heard from Shashibhushan, who had visited him once, that Bhumisuta had been removed from Bhabanipur and was now employed as a maid in the mansion at Circular Road. That meant he would never see her again. What was worse, she was in greater danger then ever. Suhasini, in an effort to remove her from her husband's proximity, had thrown her from the frying pan into the fire. The Maharaja's mansion was a lion's den with himself as the most powerful and ferocious of all the animals that lurked there. The Maharaja appreciated beauty and talent in women. He was sure to notice Bhumisuta and then who could stop him from taking her as his kachhua? Certainly not Bhumisuta herself. What power could the poor girl wield against the selfish, tyrannical king? Every time he thought of Bhumisuta in the Maharaja's bed-chamber his blood boiled with fury. And his inability to protect her stung him like a thousand scorpions.

Bharat was too overwrought these days to concentrate on his studies. He turned the pages of his books without taking in a word and wondered why he was wasting his time with them. What he needed was not a college degree but a means of making a living. For a man was not a man while he depended on another.

One evening Bharat sat in his kitchen making tea. Mahim had disappeared a few days ago with Bharat's savings and a couple of vessels and Bharat had decided not to employ another servant. He drank a lot of tea these days. It helped to keep him awake and it also dulled the appetite.

Placing the kettle on the blazing wood he put in the tea leaves, milk and sugar and waited for the mixture to boil. Then he strained it over a piece of rag into a glass. The kettle was large enough to make three glasses at a time. As he was pouring out his second glass he heard a sound; a thud as of something falling from a height. Turning around he got the shock of his life for standing at the door, partly concealed by the shadows, was a man. Bharat hadn't lit the lantern for it wasn't quite dark yet and the light coming in from the gas lamp in the street was enough to work by. 'Who? Who's that?' Bharat cried, his voice faint and trembling a little.

'Namaskar go Dada. Namaskar,' the man came forward grinning amicably. 'I caught the smell of your tea and couldn't resist the urge to have a few sips.' Bharat stared at him. He was fairly young with a tall gaunt body and a long nose sticking out of a thin bony face. His head was shaven in front and a thick *shikha* sprang up from behind. He wore neither vest nor shirt. A fold of his frayed dhuti was wrapped around his chest and shoulders. Bharat breathed a sigh of relief. If he wasn't a ghost Bharat had nothing to fear. He could fell the weak, malnourished body to the ground in a few seconds. '*Ki go* Dada!' the man laughed, 'Did I frighten you?'

'N-no . . .' Bharat stammered. 'How did you get here?'

'I live next door. Our roofs touch one another.'

'But this house doesn't have a roof.'

'Can a house be built without a roof? What you mean is there are no stairs to your roof. But there are footholds and I can climb

218

like a cat. I used to come to this house often when Nitai Babu lived here. I called his wife Bara Mami. However, all that is of no consequence. Won't you offer me some tea?'

Bharat lit his lantern and poured out a glass of tea for his guest. Cradling it in both hands the man drank great gulps from it with noises of relish, talking all the while. 'My name is Bani Binod Bhattacharya. My grandfather named me Bani Binod. My neighbours call me Ghanta Bhatta and look down on me because I'm a priest by profession. If they could see the respect I get from my *jajamans*! Rich, fat Kayastha *kartas* touch my feet in veneration. There's a Basak family in Shobha bazar, very wealthy, where the *ginni* washes my feet with her own hands and drinks the water. Can I have another glass? Do you know that I can't get a drop of tea in my own house? My wife refuses to make it. She says it's a *mlechha* drink . . .'

This was on the first day. After that Bani Binod came often and sat with Bharat in his kitchen chatting and drinking tea. Gradually Bharat came to know all about him. Though less than thirty years old he had two wives and seven children already. His first wife lived with her four children in Halisahar. His second wife was here with him in Calcutta. He hadn't much learning. His Sanskrit was faulty but he had a few rich *jajamans* nevertheless. With his sharp features, fair complexion, long *shikha* and thick white *poité*, he was quite impressive looking and had access to the women's quarters of several distinguished houses of Calcutta. The family priest was the one male with whom women from even the most conservative families could talk freely, for they had to assist him in his work. They picked flowers and bel leaves, washed the vessels, prepared the sandal paste and sat by while he recited his mantras. Bani Binod knew a lot about what went on in the inner quarters of wealthy families—gossip which he shared freely with Bharat. In such families the men often kept mistresses and spent the nights away from their wives. Bored and unhappy, these women formed relationships—with cousins, brothers-in-law and even friends of their husbands. And they used the family priest as their go-between, paying him handsomely for his services. This, according to Bani Binod, brought him more money than his appointed salary. Without it, in fact, he would have difficulty feeding his family.

219

When Bharat heard this he had an idea. 'Bhattacharaya Moshai!' he said, 'Many rajas and maharajas have taken up residence in Calcutta. Why don't you work for one of them?'

'I would jump at it if I got the chance. But why should a maharaja employ me? The city is full of priests—far more learned than me. They come buzzing like flies at the smell of a job. Why, last Thursday they were feeding Brahmins in Rani Rasmoni's house in Janbazar. I went in the hope of a good bellyful and a gift. But what I saw there made my head reel! *Oré baap ré*! About a thousand Brahmins were sitting in rows waiting to be served. The competition is getting tougher everyday. Soon I'll have to starve with my wives and children—'

'The Maharaja of Tripura is here in Calcutta. He's very religious and will need a family priest. Why don't you try your luck there?'

'What kind of maharaja? Where is Tripura?'

'Tripura is an independent kingdom. Haven't you heard of it? The Maharaja is very generous. If he's pleased with you he'll think nothing of taking off his diamond ring and putting it on your finger.'

'Really!' Bani Binod said excitedly 'Where is the house? I'll go tomorrow. Do they speak Bengali?'

'Yes, of course. The Maharaja is very fond of hearing the *padavalis* of the old Vaishnav *pada kartas*. If you can recite a few—'

'Wonderful. I know *Chandi Mangal* by heart. Would you like to hear a few lines?'

Bharat took it for granted that Bani Binod would be employed by Maharaja Birchandra Manikya and gain access to his andar mahal. And then—he would surely meet Bhumisuta! Bhumisuta had made all the arrangements for the daily puja in the house of the Singhas. Surely she would be given the same duties in the Maharaja's mansion. Bharat could send her a letter through Bani Binod.

Bharat imagined her standing on the landing outside the puja-room. She wore a white sari and held a basket full of flowers in her hand. Her face was like a flower too—a new-blown lotus. There was a startled expression in her long dark eyes and drops of dew in her hair. 'Do not misunderstand me Bhumi,' he started

220

composing the letter in his mind. 'Don't turn away from me in disgust. I'm helpless. I have to live by the will of others. But, one day, when I'm my own master I shall come to you. I shall stand by your side and . . .'

Chapter XXVI

One Friday morning in early May two carriages set off from Jorasanko towards the river where the *Sarojini* lay anchored in midstream. Jyotirindranath and Gyanadanandini occupied one of them. Robi and Jyotirindranath's friend Akshay Chowdhury sat in the other with Gyanadanandini's children. The ship was to sail that day for the first time and Gyanadanandini had insisted on accompanying her brother-in-law on her maiden voyage. Jyotirindranath had tried to discourage her. He had pointed out that this was a test venture undertaken with the goal of identifying defects in the vessel. It would be risky taking women and children along. But Gyanadanandini had dismissed his feeble protests with her customary force. She had crossed the oceans to England, she reminded him. That too alone, without a male escort. What danger could there possibly be in a mere river journey? If the worst came to the worst they all knew how to swim.

The carriages clattered out of Chitpur Street past the mosque and shops and came to a stop at the ferry in Koilaghat. The passengers had barely descended when several boatmen came running up to Jyotrindranath who, with his gold pince nez, pleated dhuti and silk kameez was immediately identified as the leader of the group. Like *pandas* at a place of pilgrimage they swarmed around him pointing out the merits of their respective crafts and offering to row the party to where their ship was anchored. Pushing their way through the crowds Bibi and Robi walked down to the edge of the river where a number of boats bobbed up and down in the murky water. 'Just like banana flower husks,' Bibi turned to her uncle eagerly. 'Isn't that so Robi ka?' Though twelve years old Bibi wore a frock over long stockings. She still hadn't learned to manage a sari.

'The ones with the *chhois* look like vamped slippers,' Robi answered, 'Giants like Meghnad could wear a pair of them.'

The two burst out laughing. After a while the others caught up with them. The crowds at the ferry ghat stared at the sight of so many good-looking men and women together. The men, in particular, couldn't take their eyes off Gyanadanandini. She wore a Benares silk sari of a rich ghee colour which set off her golden skin to perfection. The diamond flower in her enormous *khonpa* glittered like a starry constellation. She looked as beautiful and majestic as a queen.

A boat was finally selected and they all climbed in. The children's faces paled a little as it rocked violently over the great waves that came rolling up with every movement of the large vessels around them. Gyanadanandini laughed their fears away. 'You know how to swim,' she reminded them, 'Why are you scared?' They were all good swimmers, Robi and Jyotirindra in particular. All except Akshay Babu. 'I should have learned to swim,' he muttered clinging to the side of the boat with both hands. Then, suddenly, he gave a cry of alarm. '*O ki! O ki!* A ship is coming straight towards us. O Jyoti Babu! We'll all be crushed to death.'

'Why that's my *Sarojini*!' Jyotirindranath stood up in his excitement. '*Oré!* Stop the boat. Stop it!'

'Don't worry Karta,' the boatman answered coolly. 'We're taking you to your ship. You'll be there in a few seconds all safe and sound.'

The party looked on in expectation as the *Sarojini* glided towards them. They could see her clearly now. In her gleaming white paint with the two lifeboats by her side, she looked as beautiful and stately as a swan floating over the water with her cygnets. The boatmen maneuvered the craft with their accustomed skill and brought it to a halt alongside the ship. As soon as they did so a rope ladder was unwound from the *Sarojini* and thrown into the boat. The children clambered up easily enough. Now it was Gyanadanandini's turn. The men looked on with worried expressions but Gyanadanandini was unfazed. Tucking the end of her sari firmly into her waist she took off her shoes and placed a foot, as pink and tender as a lotus bud, on the first rung. Robi and Jyotirindra put out their hands to help her but she pushed them away. 'I used to climb trees as a child,' she said laughing, making her way up on firm and fearless feet. Akshay Babu was a different proposition altogether. '*Oré baba*

223

ré,' he cried out with every step. 'This rope is swinging like a coconut palm in a storm. I'll fall. I'm falling. O Jyoti Babu!'

The lower deck was for ordinary passengers. Three cabins, lavishly appointed, for the use of the master and his friends, stood on the vast upper deck set out with chairs under gaily striped umbrellas. Here the whole party relaxed after their climb while the servants served them hot tea and freshly made *nimki*. It was a bright morning with a strong wind. Gyanadanandini's hair flew out of its restricting pins and she had difficulty in keeping her sari in place. Akshay Babu's cigar was blown away from his mouth and fell into the water at which everyone laughed gaily. Looking at them no one could have guessed that a violent tragedy had disrupted their lives only a month ago. They were aristocrats and didn't display their emotions like ordinary people. It seemed as though Kadambari's memory had faded from their minds. No one had taken her name even once so far.

Robi stood on the deck clutching his flying hair with one hand and the rail with the other. As his eyes looked out on the vast stretch of water a wave of nostalgia swept over him. He had seen the Ganga in her many moods—dark and sullen before an impending storm; rose-flushed at sunset; and a ribbon of silver under a radiant moon. And always, always, Kadambari had been by his side—her face bright and eager, her eyes entranced. 'Look at that tree Robi,' she would cry out, 'Look how the branches are bending over the river, as if they are whispering deep, dark secrets in her ear.' She had loved trees and taught Robi to love them.

A kite, circling above the water, gave a piercing cry startling Robi. And, suddenly, the sky resounded with the call of Robi's own heart, 'Natun Bouthan! Natun Bouthan.' The hard knot in his throat melted and quick warm tears rose to his eyes.

'Robi,' Gyanadanandini had come quietly up to him. She caught the expression in his eyes and her face hardened a little. Putting her hand on his arm she said softly. 'It's beautiful—isn't it?' Robi turned to her, trying to smile.

'What are those boats?' Gyanadanandini pointed a finger. 'They all look the same. Where are they going?'

'Those are passenger boats. They ferry Babus to and from their offices in Calcutta.'

'You must write a description of this voyage Robi—a

day-to-day account. Like you did on your trip to Europe.'

At this moment Bibi and Suren came running up to their mother clamouring to be allowed to go down and see the rest of the ship. 'Go,' Gyanadanandini gave her permission. 'But only with Robi Kaka. Robi!' She threw him a meaningful glance. 'Take the children with you and show them the ship.' Robi hastened to obey.

Now Gyanadanandini made her way to Jyotirindranath's cabin. She stood for a moment, her hand on the door. Then, making up her mind, she turned the knob and walked in. Jyotirindra lay on his bed but not in sleep. Stretched out on the milk white sheets he looked like a Greek god; a figure of sculpted marble. But the lines of his face were drawn and melancholy and his eyes were dazed and expressionless. He saw his sister-in-law walk in and take her place by his side but he said nothing. Neither did Gyanadanandini. She stood in silence for a few minutes allowing him to imbibe her presence. Then, very gently, she placed her soft moist palm on his forehead.

Her touch had the strangest effect on Jyotirindranath. It seemed as though the marble figure quivered into life. He sat up, his face working, harsh dry sobs racking his chest. ' Why did she do this to me Mejo Bouthan?' he cried turning to her desperately. 'Why didn't she tell me how she felt? If she had even hinted I would have . . . I would have. I never knew she was so unhappy. I thought she liked to be by herself; to think her own thoughts. I never dreamed. People look at me . . .' Gyanadanandini allowed him to rave for a few minutes. He needed to unburden himself. And he could only do so before her. They were both the same age and she was his friend and confidante. 'Don't blame yourself Natun,' she said after a while, her voice soft but firm, 'It was all her own fault. She could have done worse. She could have ruined our family's reputation. Thank God that was averted. Her death has been a blessing to her and to us all.'

Jyotirindranath stared at her in amazement. Her face, radiant and beautiful as the Goddess Durga's with the same golden complexion, arched eyebrows, red lips and flashing eyes smiled down on him. Taking his face between her hands she pressed it to her breast murmuring sweet endearments in his ears, 'Natun! Natun!' she whispered, running her fingers through his hair.

'Don't grieve Natun. You have a whole life to live. You have so much to achieve. You must be strong. She's gone but *I* am here with you. Your Bardada lives in his own world. Your Mejdada is busy furthering his career. Baba Moshai depends on you. Besides you have your own work now. You have to compete with the British and beat them at their own game. I'll help you. I'll stay by your side—always.' Jyotirindra's tears fell thick and fast dampening the satin that covered her soft breasts. Taking his chin in her fingers she raised his face and wiped the tears tenderly away. The two gazed deep into one another's eyes.

Suddenly a sound of footsteps running on the deck was heard and Akshay Babu's voice called out 'O Jyoti Babu Moshai! Do you know that your ship doesn't have a captain? There's no one to guide it. Heaven knows where we are going!' Jyotirindra ran a hand over his face and hair and rose hastily to his feet. Stepping out on to the deck he found Robi and the children. They, too, had discovered that the captain, a Frenchman, was absconding and the ship was now being steered by a couple of common sailors.

Jyotirindranath had employed the Frenchman not merely because he had a preference for the race but because the man was skilled at his work, and knew a great deal about the ship's mechanism. But he had one grave defect. He drank heavily, not everyday, but once in a while and then passed out. Doubtless, that was what had happened. He had been celebrating on the eve of his maiden voyage on the *Sarojini* and had drunk himself into a stupour. Jyotirindra looked on the frightened faces around him and sat down—his head between his hands. It was too late to go back. On the other hand, a ship without a captain was like a boat without oars. Who knew in which direction the ship was heading?

At this time two sailors came up to the deck and assured the master that there was nothing to fear. They had learned the art of steering from the captain and were confident of being able to take the ship, without any hazard, to Barisal. Jyotirindra heard them out. He had no other option but to let them continue. Calling upon the All Merciful Param Brahma to protect them in this fearful hour he said, 'Let's go on, then.'

The steamer chugged on, cleaving the breast of the Ganga and darkening the sky with the smoke from her chimneys. The afternoon passed peacefully but towards evening a clamour arose of many frightened voices crying out together, 'Stop! Stop! Turn it! Turn it quick!' Jyotirindra and the others ran out to the deck to see a vast iron buoy rushing towards them from the middle of the river. What it meant, of course, was that the ship was racing madly towards it. The sailors tried their best but could not change direction and, even as everyone looked on fearfully, the catastrophe occurred. The ship crashed into the buoy and nearly keeled over. The impact was so strong that Akshay Babu, though clutching the rail with all his might, was thrown to the ground. The children would have fallen too if they hadn't been holding on so tightly to Robi.

Pale faces looked on one another anticipating a watery grave. The vessel was rocking violently and things were crashing to the ground—crockery, cooking vessels and furniture. However, the worst was averted. The ship recovered her balance after a while and Jyotirindranath, who had rushed down to the engine room, was informed that the damage was less than they had expected. The vessel was intact. There were minor breakages in some parts of the machinery which could be repaired. It would be best to cast anchor here and let her rest for the night. Then, tomorrow, they could repair the ship and set sail once more.

Their worst fears over, the party cheered up. Sitting together on the deck they fell to hungrily on the hot luchis, *mohanbhog* and *kheer* that were brought up by the servants. Sipping tea out of elegant porcelain cups they looked out on the river which was so wide here that her banks were barely visible. Gradually, before their admiring eyes the sun, huge and soft with evening, sank in a haze of rose and gold.

'Robi,' Gyanadanandini called out to her brother-in-law. 'You seem rapt in your own thoughts. Won't you share them with us?'

Robi stood a little apart, his hand on the rail. He remembered an evening just like this one. He had been sitting with Natun Bouthan on the steps that went down to the river from the garden of Moran's villa. Her eyes on the setting sun, Natun Bouthan had said softly, 'Sing a song Bhanu! A new one.' And Robi had instantly composed and sung *Marana ré tunhu mama Shyam samaan*. He hummed the sweet, melancholy strains below his

227

breath and turned to Gyanadanandini.

The sailors kept their word. Repairing the ship the next morning they set sail and reached Barisal by way of Khulna. As the steamer made her way into the harbour a strange sight met their eyes. There were crowds everywhere cheering and waving out to them. People from all walks of life—mukhtiars and lawyers, hakims and zamindars, teachers and students, shopkeepers and customers—pushed and shoved in order to get a better view. The passengers on board were puzzled. What were the people so excited about? Surely they had seen vessels like the *Sarojini* before. The ships of the Flotilla Company had been ferrying passengers between Barisal and Calcutta for quite some time now. Then, suddenly, the truth dawned on them. *Sarojini* was the first native ship to sail on the Ganga. It was a proud moment for all Indians! The crowds at the harbour were expressing their joy and triumph. Gyanadanandini turned a bright, laughing face towards her brother-in-law and said, 'Your dream has been fulfilled Natun.' Jyotirindra was so overcome with emotion that tears rose to his eyes. In an effort to hide them he lowered his head and started polishing his pince nez.

The ship belonging to the Flotilla Company was docked a little distance away and people were being carried to it in little boats. Suddenly, to Jyotirindra's surprise, a young man ran up to them with folded hands crying out, 'Listen brothers! Heed me for a moment. Don't travel in the foreigner's ship. You are Bengalis. There's a Bengali ship waiting to take you to Calcutta. Board it. Don't use your money to enrich the foreigners. They think nothing of us. They hate and despise us and call us bloody natives. The Thakurs of Jorasanko have brought their ship *Sarojini* to Barisal. Will you not give them a chance to serve you?'

The passengers looked at one another doubtfully. The British ship had been tried and tested. Besides, the British could be relied upon to conduct whatever business they undertook with consummate skill. Who knew what this native ship was like? What if it capsized in midstream? Some pretended they hadn't heard and stepped quickly into the waiting boats. But, by now, others had come forward. They begged and pleaded—even pulled some passengers by the hand. A boy of about twelve stood in waist deep water and cried, 'Babu *go*! The saheb's ship is unsteady. It sways this way and that. Our ship is as firm as a rock. It cares little for storms and winds. *O Karta*! Don't step into the saheb's ship. You'll fall into the river and drown.'

The party on the deck burst out laughing as did many others who stood nearby. But not Robi. The impassioned plea of the little Muslim boy in his torn lungi set him thinking. The possibility of competition with the sahebs had penetrated into the consciousness of the common folk. When did this happen and how? After the dismal outcome of the Sepoy Mutiny the natives had come to think of the whites as invincible; as born to rule the dark-skinned natives. When did that mindset begin to change? From where did the poor peasant boy get the courage to speak as he did?

Two Englishmen standing on the deck of the ship belonging to the Flotilla Company watched the scene with interest. One was an old India hand; the other had recently arrived from England. 'What do you think?' the latter asked puffing at his pipe, 'Can Bengalis compete with us in business?'

'Pooh!' the other replied dismissively. 'Natives have neither the brains nor the patience for business. We have nothing to fear from them. But they must be punished for trying to take our passengers away. We should inform the police.'

'No, no. There's no need to call in the police just yet. That will only excite them further. It might even lead to a mass boycott of our ship. Let's wait and watch.'

The sahebs looked on as half the passengers in the quay side climbed into *Sarojini* and the ship sailed triumphantly towards Khulna. It was a great victory for Jyotirindranath. Two days later he was felicitated at an impressive function attended by all the important residents of Barisal, both Hindu and Muslim.

The French captain returned a couple of days later and the ship went up and down the Ganga as scheduled. Within a few months Jyotrindranath acquired two more ships—*Banga Lakshmi* and *Swadeshi*. The common folk lined up on both sides of the river waving and cheering every time one of these ships passed. Flushed with his success, Jyotirindranath started working harder than ever.

After his return from that first trip Robi did not accompany Gyanadanandini to her house but took up residence, once more, in Jorasanko. Back in his own wing he found masons and carpenters at work renovating the premises. It was difficult to concentrate with workmen all over the place hammering at doors and walls. But Robi had tremendous will power. Sitting at a table, in the midst of all the activity and commotion, he pored over his proofs. And at night he slept on a mat spread out on the floor.

Prakritir Pratishodh had come out exactly seven days after Kadambari's death. *For you* the dedication had run. It was followed by the play *Nalini*. And now Robi had corrected the proofs of *Shaishab Sangeet*, a volume of poems written during his boyhood, and was wondering whom to dedicate it to. Could books be dedicated to the dead? Upon an impulse he picked up a pen and wrote, *I used to sit by your side and write my poems. You were the first to read them. You will still be the first for my poems will reach you wherever you are . . .'*

Suddenly Robi pushed his papers away and rose to his feet. Then, running up the steps to the second floor, he came and stood outside the apartment that had been shared by Jyotirindranath and Kadambari. It was kept locked these days. Jyotirindranath hadn't stepped into it even once after Kadambari's death. Robi lowered the latch and pushed the door open. The room looked just the same as always. The bed was made up, and on a small table by its side, a copy of Robi's *Bou Thakurani'r Haat* lay open. But Kadambari had kept her rooms spotlessly clean, and now dust lay thick on everything. It was clear that no one had entered these rooms after her death.

Robi walked up to the window at which Kadambari was in the habit of sitting, looking out at the bakul tree. He recalled the evening when he had come up here with his *Chhabi o Gaan* in his hands. It was the same hour of dusk. The lamp was unlit and the room was full of shadows. 'Natun Bouthan,' Robi called softly, then again, 'Natun Bouthan.' One part of his consciousness told him that she would not answer. She was dead. He had seen her being burned to ashes with his own eyes. But something, someone, deep down within him, told him that she was there, close beside him, guarding him, guiding him as only she could.

Robi wandered from room to room then came out to the veranda. Here were rows of pots with plants that she had tended with her own hands. Even in this fading light he saw that some of

230

them were dead, others wilting and dying. Robi walked into her bathing room and found a tub full of water. It had obviously stood stagnant for days and had specks of dust floating on its surface. It was probably the water she had bathed in last. Dragging the heavy tub to the veranda he splashed the water on the plants stroking the leaves lovingly. And, in doing so, he felt Kadambari's touch.

Going back to her bedroom he stretched himself out on her bed and murmured, 'Natun Bouthan.' Suddenly he heard footsteps and a tinkle of jewels and started up in surprise. Someone stood at the door—a figure bundled up clumsily in a heavy brocade sari the edge of which fell over her face. It was Mrinalini.

'You?' Robi cried out amazed. 'How are you here?'

'I came away with Bolu dada. I don't want to stay there any more.'

'But why? They all love you. Besides your school—'

'I don't want to go to school.'

Robi smiled. He, too, had hated school as a child and had run away whenever he could. He was hardly the right person to lecture her on the advantages of a formal education. Nevertheless he said with an effort, 'Bibi and Sarala go to school —'

'The school is closed.' Mrinalini said desperately.

'How can that be? The vacations are over.'

'But today is a *chhuti*. A *chhuti*. Don't you believe me? It is. It is.' Mrinalini burst into tears.

'*Chhuti*? How sweet that word sounds when you say it. I have a new name for you. From today I shall call you *Chhuti*.'

Robi walked up to his child bride and placed a hand on her head.

231

Chapter XXVII

Shashibhushan had organized a band party from Mechhuabazar for the royal welcome. And now its pipes and kettle drums burst into a lively rendition of 'For he's a jolly good fellow' as the equipage carrying the king and queen rolled up to the gate. Shashibhushan hastened to open the door, then called out in a sonorous voice, '*Swagatam*, Maharaj. *Swagatam*.' Behind him the servants stood in two neat rows on either side of the path made bright and gay with red gravel, garlands and potted plants.

Birchandra stepped out of the carriage looking as unlike a Maharaja as anyone could imagine. He wore a fatua over a dhuti and a *muga* shawl was flung carelessly over one shoulder. He looked weary and travel stained. Passing a hand over his rumpled hair he looked around at the house and grounds and nodded his head in approval. Then, turning to the bundle of rich brocade and jewels that was his queen, he put out his hand and said, 'Come.'

The royal pair walked up the path to the house followed by Radharaman Ghosh and Kumar Samarendra. Shashibhushan led them to a room on the ground floor, arranged with sofas and chairs, so that they could rest a while before being taken to their apartments. As soon as she had set foot in the room Monomohini pushed the veil away from her face and announced in her clear, strident tones, 'I want some water. I'm thirsty.' A servant hurried to a table on which a silver pitcher of water and crystal glasses stood arranged on a tray. Monomohini drank two glasses in quick succession and asked, 'Which one is my room?' Then, on being led to it, she ran up the stairs as playfully as a fawn her brocade aanchal trailing after her.

The Maharaja watched her go, his lips curled in amusement. Then he turned to Shashibhushan with an enquiring glance. Shashibhushan was nonplussed. The Maharaja was obviously asking for something. What could it be? Radharaman put an end to his dilemma by booming out the question, '*Ki hé* Shashi! Where's the hookah baradar?' Shashibhushan turned red with

232

embarrassment. How could he have forgotten? He ran out of the room to make the arrangements without delay. But the Maharaja could not enjoy his smoke. After taking a few puffs he clutched his abdomen, his face twisting with pain. 'What is it Maharaj?' Radharaman asked anxiously.

'I don't feel too well. I get these sudden cramps in my stomach. The quacks in Tripura stuffed me up with pills and mixtures but couldn't cure me. I hear Calcutta doctors are wizards. You'd better get one of them to see me Shashi.'

'Would you like to try homeopathy Maharaj?'

'What is that?'

'It's a new branch of medicine and yields very good results. I can send for Dr Mahendralal Sarkar. He is considered a *dhanwantari*.'

'That would be best,' Radharaman Ghosh said. 'Dr Mahendralal Sarkar is very famous. Besides he practises both allopathy and homeopathy.' Birchandra nodded in approval. 'And send for that boy from the Thakur family,' he said, 'The young poet. What's his name? Ah, yes. Rabindra Babu. The doctor's pills may have no effect, but Rabindra Babu's poetry is bound to cure me.' He rose and commenced walking towards his private mahal. At the foot of the stairs he paused and said over his shoulder, 'And don't make my illness an excuse to feed me green bananas and *singi* fish broth. I can't stomach the stuff. Send a servant to Bagbazaar Ghat for a basket of freshly caught ilish. I fancy thick wedges of ilish fried crisp in its own fat. And hot rosogollas from Nabin Moira's shop.'

Shashibhushan went to Dr Mahendralal Sarkar's chambers that very evening to find it overflowing with patients. But the doctor was not to be seen. Mahendralal's interest in pure science was turning into an obsession. He had founded the Vigyan Parishad for research and spent a good deal of his time in organizing its activities. In consequence his own work was neglected. But, despite the fact that his patients often had to go back untreated, his clinic was always full.

Shashibhushan had to wait forty minutes before Dr Sarkar put in an appearance, then another twenty minutes while he went from patient to patient barking at one, soothing another. At last Shashibhushan's turn came. He had hoped for a smile of

233

recognition but was disappointed. 'Don't beat about the bush,' he was told curtly. 'I don't have time to waste. Just tell me the symptoms.'

'I haven't come for myself,' Shashibhushan said humbly. 'I'm here on behalf of another. My name is Shashibhushan Singha and—'

'Shashibhushan Singha! Ah yes. I remember now. You came from Tripura. You had a mental problem did you not? What's the matter? Has there been a recurrence?'

'No. Thanks to your treatment I'm fully recovered.'

'Is that so? Sit down my boy. I was thinking of you only the other day. In fact, it's the strangest coincidence. Do you know the playwright Girish Ghosh?'

'No. But I've heard of him. He's very famous.'

'He'll be here at seven thirty. I'll introduce him to you. Well, as you probably know, Girish was an atheist for a good part of his life. He had read Bentham, Mill and Kant and was influenced by their philosophies. Then, suddenly, he turned religious—a Kali worshipper. Do you know how? It's quite a story. Listen carefully. Once Girish fell ill; very ill. The doctors did their best but couldn't help him. Driven desperate with pain he went to the temple at Tarakeswar and prostrated himself at the feet of the idol. Such things happen. People turn to blind faith when logic and reason can't support them. He returned—his suffering unabated. But that same night he dreamt that his mother stood by his bedside. Of course he denies that it was a dream. He says he heard his mother's voice; felt her touch. She told him what medicine to take. And he obeyed her and was cured. Rather like your experience is it not?' Shashibhushan nodded his assent. 'Do we take it then,' the doctor continued, 'that the dead come back to life? That mothers become doctors after death?'

'No,' Shashibhushan murmured solemnly. 'The dead cannot return to life. I know, now, that what I saw was a dream. My brain was fevered and my body weak. In that state the dream acquired a special potency. It seemed real.'

'Auto suggestion,' the doctor wagged his large head. 'You created her out of your own imagination to fulfil an overwhelming need. I didn't tell you at the time but—' Suddenly he gave a great bark of laughter, 'Mothers may become doctors after death but they don't attend their sons more than once. Girish is ill again but now he's under my treatment—not his mother's.'

A few minutes later the curtain was pushed aside and Girish Ghosh entered the room. His eyes were red, his feet unsteady and his breath reeked of alcohol. But he came in with the air of a hero making a stage entrance. '*O hé* Daktar,' he called in the deep, wonderful voice that had held audiences in thrall for over two decades. 'Your medicine isn't working. I had a terrible attack last night. I nearly fainted with the pain.'

'What can you expect with all the brandy you pour into your stomach? What power do my poor little homeopathic doses have against that noxious stuff? I've told you again and again—'

'I drink a little when the pain is bad. It's the only way I can bear it.'

'The relief is temporary. In the long run alcohol can only worsen your condition. If you want to kill yourself it's your decision. But don't blame me.'

'Why do you call it alcohol? I drink Ma Kali's prasad! Ambrosia! Jai Ma Kali! ' Then, suddenly losing his temper, he banged his fist on the table and cried, 'You have no right to lecture me. You're a doctor. You're supposed to give me medicine that will cure me.' His red eyes looked angrily into the doctor's implacable ones. But only for a few moments. Then a wistful look came into them like that of a little boy begging for a toy. 'Won't you?' he asked in a pleading voice.

'I will on two conditions. You won't touch a bottle while under my treatment. And you'll walk to the Ganga everyday and take a few dips.'

'Very well,' Girish answered. 'Can I recite mantras in praise of Kali while I take my dip?'

'Mantras or Shakespeare—you may recite what you will. It makes no difference to me. What you need is some exercise and I'm determined that you get it. By the way, I hear very good reports of your new play. When can I come and see it?'

'Come this Saturday. I'll reserve a box for you.'

'I'll bring this young man along,' Dr Mahendralal Sarkar announced. 'Take a good look at him. He's your dream cousin—Shashibhushan Singha.'

235

A few days later, Maharaja Birchandra lay sprawled, half
naked, on his bed while two maids wiped him down tenderly with
gamchhas wrung out in hot water. Monomohini stood by his side
holding his silver hookah in her hands. Birchandra had to have a
pull, now and then, even while performing his bodily functions.
'Another three days Mono,' he said, 'And I'll be as good as new.
This doctor's medicine has worked wonders, I must admit. I like
the fellow. He knows his job.'

'Daktar Babu's voice is so loud and deep—it booms like
thunder.' Monomohini said, quite unexpectedly, 'And his face!
How red and angry it is! I was frightened to death.'

'When did you see him?' Birchandra's brows came together in
disapproval. Monomohini was so childish and wayward. She ran
about everywhere instead of keeping herself decorously within
the zenana as befitted her status. He didn't know how to control
her. Frowning over these thoughts he suddenly fell asleep.
Monomohini smiled wickedly and, putting the hookah to her
lips, took a deep pull. Coughing and spluttering, she ran out of
the room into the next. Flinging open her cupboard she pulled out
all her saris and threw them on to the floor. Then she went and
stood before a portrait of Queen Victoria. Glaring at it for a long
moment she put out her tongue and grimaced at Her Royal
Majesty. Next, she fell to pulling the books from the shelves,
tearing out leaves and scattering them around the room. She felt
bored and restless in the tiny apartment. There was no one to talk
to or play with. The Maharaja was sick and slept most of the time.
Prince Samarendra was busy with his new hobby—photography.
She, who was used to a palace, felt she was living in a hen coop.

After a while she could bear it no longer. Slipping out of her
apartments she went down the stairs to the front wing where
Shashibhushan's office and private rooms were housed. As she
crossed the veranda a melodious sound wafted into her ears.
Someone was singing. The voice was low and husky and
incredibly sweet. Following it she came to a door and pushed it
open. In a tiny room, dark and damp, a girl sat crosslegged on the
floor combing her hair before a small mirror propped up in front
of her. She was obviously a maid of the household. But how
sweetly she sang, swaying from side to side, as she drew the fine
comb down the long strands! Monomohini stared in surprise.

Maids were not allowed to raise their voices even in speech. And this one dared to sing! Besides she was obviously well trained. From where had she learned the art? For, though Monomohini knew nothing about music, she knew instinctively that what she was hearing was very superior indeed. 'Who are you?' she asked abruptly as the singer, startled by her entry, sprang to her feet. 'What's your name?' She had never seen the girl before but the latter evidently knew who she was. For she knelt, very respectfully, at the young queen's feet and touched her forehead to the ground. 'My name is Bhumisuta,' she said shyly. Monomohini decided that she liked her. 'Sing some more,' she commanded. Then, when the singing was over, she took her by the hand and dragged the protesting girl to her own room.

One morning, a few days later, Birchandra stood outside Monomohini's apartment a puzzled frown on his face. The sound of a sweet voice singing in an alien tongue came floating out of the closed door. He wondered who it was. Pushing the door open he walked in to see a strange sight. On the flowered Persian carpet covering the floor Monomohini sat at her ease, her legs spread out before her. And kneeling by her side was a girl. She held a pair of cymbals in her hands which tinkled delicately to the rhythm of her song. Her eyes were closed and her head swayed to the music like a flower on a stalk. The Maharaja was charmed.

Monomohini turned eagerly to her husband as he walked in. 'This girl's name is Suto,' she announced. 'She's my friend. She's teaching me to sing.' Bhumisuta rose and prostrated herself at the Maharaja's feet. The puzzled frown on Birchandra's face deepened. 'I've seen you somewhere,' he murmured. 'Where do you come from?'

'From Orissa, Maharaj.'

'Stand up and let me see you properly. Raise your face to mine. Hmm! I have seen you somewhere. I know your face.'

Bhumisuta felt quite alarmed. Why did the Maharaja insist that he had seen her? She knew, for a certainty, that she had never seen him in her life. Seating himself on a sofa Birchandra commanded. 'Sing a song. It's time for my bath. I can't stay long.' Bhumisuta knelt at his feet and commenced singing

'Madhava bahut minati kari toi
Déhi tulasi til déha samarpalun
Daya jani chhodbi moi'

237

Birchandra wagged his head from side to side calling out 'Bah! Bah!' from time to time. 'Who taught you to sing?' he asked at the conclusion of the song. Bhumisuta lowered her eyes and murmured, 'My father, Maharaj.'

That evening Birchandra sent for Shashibhushan. '*Ohé* Shashi,' he greeted him heartily as soon as he entered, 'My wife has discovered a gem this morning. She was hiding in your household like a pearl in an oyster.'

'Hiding in my household? I don't understand you Maharaj.'

'Her name is Bhumisuta and she says she comes from Orissa. She's a lovely girl and has the voice of a cuckoo. The moment I saw her face I felt I knew her. I was sure I had seen her before. I thought and thought and suddenly I had the answer. You remember the bunch of photographs you sent me last year? She was in one of them. Standing in a garden with a basket of flowers over one arm. I remember commenting: "This is excellent Shashi. Good enough to win a prize in a competition." It was the same girl—was it not?'

Shashibhushan was astonished. What a memory the king had! He had recognized Bhumisuta from a photograph taken over a year ago. But what was Bhumisuta doing in the royal apartments? She had been sent by his sister-in-law to look after him. She wasn't the king's servant.

'Now tell me frankly what you propose to do with her,' the Maharaja continued. 'Do you wish to marry her or to keep her as your concubine?' Shashibhushan blushed to the roots of his hair. 'Neither Maharaj,' he answered. 'She's a servant in my household. That's all.'

'That's the trouble with you Bengalis. You haven't learned to value women. A girl as pretty as that one and with such a voice, shouldn't be allowed to remain a servant. She's a jewel that a man should wear on his neck. If you wish to marry her I can make all the arrangements.'

'No Maharaj. I have no wish to marry just now. I'm enjoying my freedom.'

The Maharaja frowned, obviously following a train of thought. Then, shaking his head sadly, he murmured, 'All my life I've cherished the wish that someone, a woman with a lovely voice, would sing me to sleep with the verses of the ancient *pada*

238

kartas. But I never found such a woman. My queens know
nothing of music. I try to teach them but they are too stupid to
learn. Excepting Bhanumati of course. She was a queen among
queens. So beautiful and talented! Such a fine singing voice!
Many were the Manipuri ballads she sang to me. But alas! She
went away leaving me desolate. She thought I had ceased to love
her. But that wasn't true. I've cared for her son Samar—have I
not?' Birchandra's eyes misted over and he covered his face
dramatically with his hands.

This mood, however, did not last long. Like a ripple in a river
it disappeared after a few seconds. Uncovering his face he turned
eagerly to Shashi. 'I wish to take Bhumisuta with me to Tripura.
She can live in the palace and sing me to sleep every night. Go
Shashi. Bring her to me. I am in a fever of impatience to hear that
melodious voice again. And Shashi—buy her some colourful saris
and a pair of earrings. Take the money from the khazanchi.'
Shashibhushan was thoroughly alarmed. The Maharaja had
decided to appropriate Bhumisuta; to take her to Tripura and
keep her as his concubine. But Bhumisuta did not belong to
Shashibhushan. She belonged to Monibhushan. What if he
refused to release her? The king, for all his easygoing nature, was
very stubborn. If he fancied a thing he wouldn't rest till he had got
it. How would Shashi manage to fend him off? Biting his lips
worriedly he went in search of Bhumisuta. He found her at the
bottom of the stairs lighting the lamps. She wore a faded blue
cotton sari torn in places and smudged with lamp black. Her hair
was loose and hung untidily down her back.

'Why is your sari so shabby and dirty?' Shashibhushan
snapped at the girl. 'Change into something else and come at
once. The Maharaja wants to hear you sing.' Bhumisuta raised
her large dark eyes to his and shook her head. 'What do you
mean?' Shashibhushan cried. 'The Maharaja commands you.
How can you refuse?'

'I won't go,' Bhumisuta said steadily her dark limpid gaze
fixed on Shashibhushan's face. 'I'm not a baiji that I'll sing before
strangers.'

'Why did you go to his room then?' Shashi gnashed his teeth at
her. 'You went creeping into his rooms like a greedy cat. And now
you shake your head with chastity and virtue. That won't

239

do—you know. It's the Maharaja's command. You'll have to obey.' Shashibhushan caught Bhumisuta's unflinching gaze and lost courage. 'Please come,' he begged humbly, 'Just this once.'

Bhumisuta laughed. 'Tell him I'm not well,' she said softly, feeling sorry him. 'Tell him I have a headache and am lying in my room.' Then, turning, she walked away her hair swaying, her *alta*-covered feet flashing white and crimson on the marble floor.

Chapter XXVIII

Star theatre in Beadon Street was full to overflowing. Girish Ghosh's *Chaitanya Leela* had been running for two months now and was still drawing packed houses. Hindus, riding triumphantly on the crest of a religious revival, were pouring into the theatre every evening from the most obscure lanes and by-lanes of Calcutta as well as from suburbs and villages. It was rumoured that the god of love, Sri Gouranga, had appeared on earth in person and was making himself known to his worshippers.

Sitting in his room in Dakshineswar, Ramkrishna heard his disciples talk animatedly about the new play. Unlike the ashrams of most holy men where only the guru's voice was heard, raised solemnly in prayer or oration, Ramkrishna's room echoed with noise and laughter. The half-crazed priest of Kali encouraged all manner of talk, even going to the extent of exchanging crude jokes with his disciples. And now, after hearing them praise the play to the skies, he declared his intention of going to see it. This put his disciples in a quandary. They stole furtive looks at one another and fell silent. How could they take their guru to a common playhouse? There were rogues, lechers and drunks among the audience. And the actresses were whores. The playwright himself was a notorious alcoholic who got so drunk during the course of the play that he had to be carried home every night. Ramkrishna's disciples hastened to dissuade him pointing out that men of his stature did not visit such dens of iniquity. Even Vidyasagar, who always saw women as victims, had turned away from the theatre when he learned that the actresses led loose, unchaste lives. Keshab Sen and Shibnath Shastri did not step, even by mistake, into a public theatre considering it the deadliest of sins. But all this advice rolled off like raindrops from a yam leaf. Ramkrishna paid no heed to them. 'I won't see them as whores!' he exclaimed with a radiant smile. 'In my eyes they'll appear as pure and chaste as my Ma Anandmayee!'

241

Unable to fend him off the disciples had to agree. It was decided that Mahendra Mukherjee would send his carriage to pick him up from Dakshineswar from where he would journey to Calcutta with some of his followers. He would stop at Mahendra Babu's flour factory at Hathibagan for a brief rest after which they would proceed to Beadon Street.

When the carriage came Ramkrishna clambered in grinning from ear to ear. Then, as the horses clattered out of the temple premises, he sat quietly by the window observing the landscape and humming a little tune. After a couple of hours the followers, who had dozed off with the movement of the carriage, were startled to hear an angry snarl. 'Hazra says he's going to teach me a lesson. *Sala!*' They glanced at one another maintaining a studied silence. They knew, from experience, that their guru became a trifle disoriented and spoke out of context just before a *bhav samadhi*. This time, however, Ramkrishna pulled himself out of it with an effort and announced, 'I'm thirsty.'

'We should have brought some water,' one of the disciples exclaimed, 'And some food.' 'Thakur won't eat anything now—,' another began but Ramkrishna stopped him with a muttered, 'Yes I will. But I must empty my bowels first. The urge is growing stronger every moment.' The disciples stared at one another in dismay. What would they do now?

Fortunately they were close to their destination and arrived there in a few minutes. As soon as they descended Ramkrishna was bundled off to the lavatory from where he emerged, after a while, smiling broadly. He had had a wash and drops of water still clung to his hair and beard. 'Ahh!' he sighed in deep satisfaction, then taking the green coconut that was offered, he drank the sweet milky water at one draught.

That evening, the street outside Star theatre was choc-a-bloc with landaus, phaetons and hackney coaches. Pacing up and down at the entrance Girish Ghosh eyed the crowd at the ticket counter with satisfaction. Soon they would put up the HOUSE FULL sign as they had been doing for the last two months. Girish felt too old and ill to prance around on stage these days. He made it a point, instead, to stand at the gate every evening and welcome all the distinguished personages who came to see his plays. Colonel Alcott, leader of the Theosophical Movement, had arrived already accompanied by the eminent professor from St Xavier's College—Father Lafon. Bijay Krishna Goswami of the Brahmo Samaj had followed them. Girish had just ushered in Mahendralal Sarkar and Shashibhushan Singha when he saw a carriage roll up and stop at the gate. A couple of men leaped down from the box and, opening the door of the carriage, helped someone to alight. Though it was getting dark Girish recognized the man. It was Ramkrishna of Dakshineswar.

Before Girish could get over his astonishment Mahendra Mukherjee came bustling up to him and announced ponderously, 'Our revered preceptor Sri Ramkrishna Paramhansa Deb has expressed a desire to see your *Chaitanya Leela* and is here tonight. Do we have to buy tickets?' Girish frowned. He had seen Ramakrishna twice and been unimpressed. And, even more than the holy man, he found himself out of sympathy with his band of followers. They buzzed around him like flies and constantly expected favours from others. 'I'll give him a pass,' Girish said, his jaw hardening, 'But the rest of you will have to buy tickets.'

Girish was flattered, of course, by Ramkrishna's arrival. Groups of Vaishnav pandits from Nadia Shantipur were coming every day the subject being close to their hearts. But to be able to entice a Kali Sadhak to see *Chaitanya Leela* was a great victory! The fame of his play had clearly spread far beyond Calcutta! His heart swelled with triumph. Greeting Ramkrishna with polite deference he escorted him, personally, to a box upstairs. Ramkrishna looked around with lively interest marvelling at the bright lights, the velvet curtains and the crowds of people. He had never seen anything like this before. The pit downstairs was crammed with spectators—talking, laughing and gesticulating. And, upstairs, in boxes similar to the one in which he sat, were ensconced the wealthy elite of Calcutta. Servants fanned their masters with wide palm leaf fans and held out elegant *albolas* with long silver pipes. In some of the boxes he even saw cases full of bottles, crystal decanters and long-stemmed glasses.

Seeing Ramkrishna sweating profusely on that warm September evening, Girish Ghosh sent for a servant and bid him fan his guest. Then he went away reappearing, a few minutes later, with a dark red rose in his hand. As he handed it to Ramkrishna the latter stared at him in bewilderment 'Ogo!' he said in his quaint sing song voice, 'What shall I do with this? Flowers are for gods and rich babus.' Girish Ghosh hurried away without answering. The orchestra had started playing the Overture and the curtain would rise any minute. Besides, he had started to feel the familiar spasms slowly contorting his insides. They would grow in intensity, as he knew from experience, till his abdomen felt as if on fire. The best thing for him would be to go home. Amritalal would take care of any emergency that might arise in his absence. Hurrying across the courtyard and out of the gate he hailed a hackney cab and went home.

Ramkrishna moved excitedly in his chair rolling his eyes and wagging his head in delight. 'Bah! Bah!' he cried. 'It's a grand house! What shining furniture! What carpets! What curtains! I'm glad I came.' Then, shutting his eyes, he murmured, 'People! So many people. When many human beings congregate in one place He manifests himself. I see Him clearly. One becomes All and All become One.' Then, opening his eyes, he turned to one of his followers and asked in an everyday voice, 'These seats must be expensive. How much will they charge?'

The curtain rose, at this point, to reveal a pastoral scene. Outside a small hut, in the heart of a forest, a group of rishis and prostitutes were celebrating the birth of Nimai, the child who would grow into the legendary Sri Chaitanya Mahaprabhu. Beating their drums and cymbals they began chanting the one hundred and eight names of Krishna whose incarnation had just been born.

Keshava Kuru Karma Deené
Madhava Manamohan, Mohan Muralidhari
Hari bol, Hari bol, Hari bol mana amaar

Sitting in the first row downstairs Mahendralal hissed in Shashibhushan's ear, 'Girish has stolen this from the Bible. The Bible tells us of three wise men who followed a star to Bethlehem to offer gifts to the newborn Jesus.' The spectators sitting around him threw burning glances in his direction but he ignored them completely and went on in his very audible whisper, 'No one had the slightest inkling when Nimai was born that he would grow up to be someone special. For many years he was considered to be nothing more than his mother Sachi's spoiled brat.'

But the scene that drew these adverse comments from

244

Mahendralal had quite the opposite effect on Ramkrishna. He folded his hands in reverence to the bearded rishis and, swaying his head to the music, went into a trance.

A few scenes later, Binodini made her first appearance in the role of the adolescent Nimai. She had wanted to do a man's role wishing to break Bhuni's monopoly. She had thrown the challenge to Girish Ghosh and he had taken it up. He had created a role that was as difficult as it was demanding. And Binodini had risen handsomely to it justifying his choice of her. She had immersed herself so completely in her new character that even those who had been seeing her every evening for over a decade could not recognize her. It seemed as though she had taken a vow to shed her old image of the beautiful coquette who sang and danced with such grace and ease. Sloughing off her old identity she was taking on a new one. She rose at dawn each day and bathed in the Ganga. She spent the whole day in prayer and meditation, ate simple food and spoke as little as possible. And day by day she found herself changing. She was not only acting Nimai. She was becoming Nimai.

The Hindus, whose religion had taken a severe beating at the hands of the Brahmos and Christian missionaries, felt elated. Here under the bright lights of the proscenium Hinduism was manifesting itself—not as a religion of narrow creeds and dark superstitions but as catholic and humane.

Sitting in the first row Colonel Alcott and Father Lafon watched the play entranced, not at the glory of Hinduism, but the acting ability of Binodini. 'I've seen performances in England by the best of actresses,' Colonel Alcott murmured in his companion's ear. 'I've seen Ellen Terry in the roles of Portia and Desdemona. But I'll say, without prejudice, that this actress' performance is not a whit inferior. I hadn't expected anything like this. Most amazing!' Father Lafon did not reply but his eyes shone with pride. He loved India and Indians. Triumph surged within him at the thought that the much despised natives had proved themselves equal to the British in one field at least. And, that too, in the highly sensitive, creative field of the theatre.

Upstairs, in his box, Ramkrishna became more and more emotional as the play wore on. And now the curtain rose on the highly acclaimed scene of the Ganga puja at which Nimai, unable

245

to bear the pangs of hunger, snatches up handfuls of sweets and fruits from the thalas laid out on the river ghat at Nabadweep. The devotees, chanting the mantras with their eyes closed, get a rude shock at this violation of their offerings and stare in astonishment. The irate pandits chase the lad shaking their fists at him and cursing him with death and destruction. But Nimai is not afraid. Wiggling his thumbs mockingly at the outraged Brahmins, he runs away. But the women among the devotees cannot bear to see him go. ' *Nimai ai, Nimai ai,*' they cry begging him to return. Then one of them rises to her feet. She knows the mantra that will draw Nimai like a moth to a flame. Raising her arms above her head she starts swaying from side to side singing *Hari bol! Hari bol!*

At this point the music director Benimadhav Adhikari, who was standing in the wings watching the scene, gestured to the musicians whereupon a flood of music burst forth from pipes and drums and the whole cast started singing *Hari bol! Hari bol!* Nimai stopped in his tracks, undecided, for a few seconds then gradually his feet started tapping the floor. His arms rose above his head and his body started whirling in a slow circular motion.

'Aaha! Aaha!' Ramkrishna cried wiping his streaming eyes. His followers immediately took up the cue and a torrent of aahas issued from their lips. And, indeed, looking on Binodini, there were many who had tears coursing down their cheeks. Her eyes had the glazed look of one who knew not who or where she was; of one who was floating on a sea of bliss. Her limbs dancing to the beat of drums and cymbals, had lost their languorous grace. It seemed as though, filled with a divine frenzy, she had surrendered body and soul and was dancing her way to God.

The scene was so moving that many among the audience burst out weeping. Some chanted *Hari bol* with the singers on stage; others swayed their heads eyes closed in ecstasy. One man stood up on his chair and started dancing in rhythm to the drumbeats. '*A molo ja!*' Mahendralal Sarkar cried out irritably, 'The man's stone drunk. Why don't they throw him out?'

'Shh!' A fellow spectator hissed from behind. 'Mind your language Moshai. He is the revered Sri Bijay Krishna Goswami.'

'Revered by whom? What does he do?'

'He's a leader of the Brahmo Samaj.'

246

'A Brahmo!' Mahendralal grimaced. 'All the Brahmos I've met keep running their mouths about the Abstract and the Formless. What's a Brahmo doing here chanting *Hari Bol* and weeping buckets with Nimai?'

'That's just it Dada,' another spectator put in his bit. 'The lost sheep are returning to the fold. Those who denied Hinduism and strayed away are coming back.'

'Nonsense,' Mahendralal cried explosively. 'What about those who became Christians and Muslims? Are they returning? And if they did would the Hindus take them back?' Then, turning to Shashibhushan, he demanded angrily, 'What's amusing you, young man? I've been watching you. I just have to open my mouth and you start to snigger.'

'I'm being doubly entertained Moshai! By Girish Ghosh and by you. Can you blame me if I'm unable to hide my delight?'

At the end of the first act, when the curtain had descended for a brief interval, a man came huffing and puffing up to Mahendralal. 'Would you come to the green room for a moment Daktar Babu,' he whispered urgently. Mahendralal rose to his feet instantly and followed him. As soon as they were out of earshot the man hissed in his ear, 'Binod has fainted Daktar Babu. She came tottering out of the stage after the *Hari Bol* sequence and fell down in a heap. We'll have to stop the play if you can't revive her in a few minutes.'

'But I haven't brought my box of medicines,' Mahendralal exclaimed. 'And the shops must have shut by now. It's past eleven o' clock.' Then, seeing the stricken look on the man's face, he added quickly, 'Take me to her, anyway, and let me see what I can do.'

Binodini lay in a dark passage behind the stage her head cradled in the lap of a white man in a cassock whom Mahendralal recognized instantly as Father Lafon. Binodini's cheeks were pale and marked with tears. Her hair spilled out of the priest's lap and fell to the floor in rich curls as he massaged her head vigorously with long white fingers. Lying like that she looked young and vulnerable and every inch a woman. Even as the eyes of the two men met Binodini's lips trembled into life. 'Ha Krishna! Ha Krishna!' she muttered. Mahendralal smiled wryly. The crisis was over. Father Lafon had done whatever there was to be done

247

and his presence was not required. He knew what had gone wrong of course. The girl had pitched her emotions too high and had cracked under the strain. Anyway, she would recover very soon now and the play could go on.

'What happened? Was someone taken ill?' Shashibhushan enquired as soon as he had returned to his seat.

'If every little whore from the back alleys forgets she is Khendi or Penchi and starts believing she's truly the queen or goddess she's enacting—it poses a problem, does it not? The theatre is an artificial world, all glitter and no gold, and actors and actresses cannot afford to forget the fact.' Taking a breath he continued with his characteristic forcefulness, 'Tell me. Why are all these people weeping and beating their breasts for a glimpse of Krishna? What can he do for them even if he does appear in their midst? Can he cure their illnesses? Or feed their wives and children?'

'You're a practical man and you talk of worldly things. But in this play Girish Ghosh has tried to instill other feelings—'

'What other feelings?'

'Well! Detachment from worldly desire and . . . and a passion for realizing God. And he has succeeded as you can see.'

Mahendralal craned his neck to get a better view of the audience, then snorted his disgust and disbelief. 'Detachment from worldly desire indeed! The people you see here wouldn't give a copper coin to a beggar if he saw him starving in the streets. They are the ones who kick their servants about and treat them like slaves and come to blows with their neighbours over an inch of land. And look at them now—sighing and snivelling. The hypocrites!'

'Don't you like the play at all sir?'

Mahendralal seemed taken aback by the question. He rubbed his nose and said almost shyly, 'The songs are truly melodious. And I must admit, the girl, Binodini I mean, is a great artist. She has kept the audience in thrall ever since she stepped on the stage. Do you know Shashi? I'm not religious in the least. I don't believe in gods and goddesses and I despise those who do. In fact, they make me vomit! Yet, whenever I hear good music, religious or otherwise, I feel my heart twisting with the strangest sensations. There's a sort of pain and also . . . also . . . a wild ecstasy. I can't explain it. All I can say is that Girish is wonderful. Oof!'

The playgoers refused to leave even after the play was over. 'Encore! Encore!' they shouted clamouring to see Binodini. She had appeared before them twice already but they kept calling. To prevent the frenzied men from mobbing her, the guards formed a ring around the stage that left the rabble out but not the wealthy and the powerful—rajas, zamindars and rich babus on whose patronship the company depended. These men insisted on seeing Binodini and showing themselves to her and had to be allowed entrance. Strangest of all, the shaven-headed, *shikha*-waving pandits from Nabadweep too expressed a desire to see Binodini and give her their blessings.

Up in his box Ramkrishna sat as still as a statue even after the play was over. His eyes were shut as if in a trance. 'Thakur!' his followers prompted softly. 'The play is over. It's time to go home.'

'Gour Hari! Gour Hari!' Ramkrishna opened his eyes. They were glistening with tears. Suddenly he stood up 'Sri Gouranga!' he cried, 'Take me to Sri Gouranga! *Ogo.* I want to go to Him.' He hurried out of the door, his disciples running after him trying to stop him. Ignoring them he ran down the steps weaving his way in and out of the press of people till he came to the stage, crying, 'Gour Hari! Gour Hari!' all the while. The guards did not know him but, for some reason, they allowed him to pass.

Inside, Binodini sat on a stool surrounded by her admirers. She was weary to the bone and her limbs trembled from exhaustion. A little distance away Amritalal Bosu sat drinking brandy and snapping every time someone came to inform him about the presence of some great man in the theatre '*Ja! Ja!*' he cried dismissively. 'Actors are drunks and actresses are whores! Haven't they being saying that all these years? What's happened to them now? Now they are crying all over us. But they won't be the only ones. We'll take the play to the suburbs and villages through the length and breadth of Bengal. We'll make all the bastards cry—'

'Ramkrishna Thakur is here,' a man said, 'The priest from Dakshineswar. Won't you go to him?'

'What do I care for priests? Or for gods or goddesses? I'm no devotee. If he's here, he's here. It has nothing to me. I'm a lecher

249

and a drunk. And an outcaste from society. All decent people look down their noses at me—'

Even as he spoke Ramkrishna came hurrying on to the stage crying *'Gour Hari! Gour Hari!'* Binodini saw him and rose to her feet. She was a prostitute, unchaste and impure. Touching the feet of a sadhak was a privilege denied to her. She folded her hands and lowered her head over them in reverence. But Ramkrishna ran towards her. His eyes were glazed and his voice cracked with emotion, as calling out 'Gour Hari! Gour Hari!' he flung himself at her feet. The disciples, who were out of patience with their guru already, couldn't bear this last, monstrous aberration. He who was Paramhansa; he who never touched his own father's feet had prostrated himself before a depraved creature—a loose, immoral woman, a whore! Hauling him roughly to his feet they cried out, 'What are you doing Thakur?'

That brought him to his senses. Looking into Binodini's face he realized that he had made a mistake. The one at whose feet he had knocked his head was not Sri Chaitanya. It was a woman. The knot of hair on the top of her head had come loose and rich dark tendrils crept down her neck and shoulders. Her painted cheeks were streaked with black from the eyebrows which had been darkened with kajal and were now beaded over with sweat. She was weeping as if her heart would break.

'Prabhu,' she cried as she wept. 'Will you not give me your blessing?' Ramkrishna smiled. Placing both his hands on her head he said softly, 'May Chaitanya be yours.' Then, as he prepared to depart, someone asked, 'What was the play like Thakur?' Ramkrishna laughed. It was his normal high-pitched laugh. 'I saw the true and the false as one and the same,' he answered.

Mahendralal and Shashibhushan stepped aside to let him pass. As he did so Shashibhushan whispered in his companion's ear. 'That was Ramkrishna—the Kali sadhak from Dakshineswar.'

'Hunh!' Mahendralal grunted indifferently.

'I've never seen him before. People say he is an avatar.'

'That's nonsense! How can a man be an avatar? He was born from a woman's womb, was he not? He feels hunger and thirst and the pains of the flesh, does he not? And I'm sure he yearns for sexual gratification as we all do—' Frowning a little, he added

250

after a few moments, 'Yet, there's something in his face that is different. I can't put my finger on it but he's not like other men. I'm sure of it.' Walking up to Binodini he said to her, 'You performed very well tonight. Girish should be proud of his training. But there's one thing you should remember. You're an actress acting a part. You're Binodini Dasi—not Nimai of Nadiya.'

Binodini, who was still in a daze after her encounter with Ramkrishna, was brought sharply down to earth. The doctor's words, though kind, hurt her deeply. She turned her face away to hide her tears.

Chapter XXIX

It was a cold windy morning in early winter. Jyotirindranath stood on the deck of his ship *Banga Lakshmi* gazing out on the Kirtan Khola river. The sky was blue and cloudless but a thin mist, rising from the water, obscured the horizon, clinging to it like a glimmering web. Jyotirindra's eyes were still heavy with sleep and he shivered a little under his expensive jamawar. The river was dotted with boats of different shapes and sizes most of them laden with grain. The land was fertile in these parts and this year the harvest had been even more bountiful than usual.

As he stood surveying the scene a boat moved rapidly over the water and stopped alongside the *Banga Lakshmi*. A man stepped out and, climbing the ship's ladder, came up on deck. He wore a dhuti of fine Farashdanga cotton with the *kachha* tucked securely in the small of his back. Over it went a coat of black china silk. 'Good morning!' he called out heartily in English. 'I hope I'm not disturbing you.' Puzzled though he was at this intrusion, so early in the day, Jyotirindra was his usual courteous self. Leading the man towards a chair, he enquired if he would like some tea.

'Frankly I would be glad of a cup,' the man answered, seating himself. 'I drink a lot of tea—up to twenty cups a day. But let me introduce myself first. I'm a lawyer and I go by the name of Abhaycharan Ghosh. My name, of course, will mean nothing to you. But you must have heard of my senior partner Pyarimohan Mukhopadhyay.' Jyotirindra's brow, till now furrowed in thought, smoothened. So that was who the man was. A lawyer. He should have guessed it from the way he was dressed. 'I've heard of him,' he answered. 'He's the son of Raja Jaikrishna Mukhopadhyay of Uttarpara is he not? He's a brilliant lawyer and very famous. But what can he want of me?' The man coughed delicately and averted his eyes. 'I've seen you before,' he said avoiding a direct answer. 'Your skin had the colour and radiance of beaten gold. Now it is burned to copper. You spend all your time on your ships. It's a hard life—one to which men from

252

families such as yours are not accustomed. Your health is breaking—' Then, his glance falling on Jyotirindra's face, he added quickly, 'How much longer do you wish to run this business?'

'What do you mean?' Jyotirindra felt himself reddening with anger at this invasion of his privacy. 'I'll run it as long as I like.'

'Can you do it? The shipping business is not a soft game. You're a zamindar. Collecting rents will be more in your line.' Jyotirindranath opened his month in indignant protest but the man stopped him with a gesture. 'Just hear me out Jyoti Babu,' he pleaded. 'I've come here on behalf of the Flotilla Company—a client of our law firm. I have a proposal which I've been instructed to place before you. The company is willing to buy you out—your ships and everything in them, tools, furniture, equipment—at a fair price. The matter can be settled in a day or two, as soon as you are ready.'

Jyotirindra's face flamed with indignation. He felt like ordering the guards to throw the man out. The dirty rascal with his glib, oily tongue had come pimping for the British! How low could his countrymen stoop? But men of his breeding did not display their feelings. He controlled himself with an effort and said quietly, 'If a dwarf has a fancy to pluck the moon from the sky that's his problem. One cannot put a rein on fancies. But the owner of the moon may have a different idea. Kindly tell your client that I didn't buy my ships to sell them. This conversation need not go on any longer. Namaskar!'

But Abhaycharan did not take the hint. He kept sitting in his chair his mouth curled in a self-conscious smile. 'You promised me a cup of tea,' he said. 'So I needn't leave till I've had it. And since it will take a few minutes to arrive let me ask you a question How long can you hold out against overwhelming odds?'

'I don't have to answer that question.'

'It was in bad taste—amounting to probing in your personal affairs. I admit that. Let me ask you another. If the Flotilla Company were to reduce the fare by two pice they will get all your passengers. What will you do then?'

'Reduce the fare! Why would they do that? There's not much profit in the business as it is. Why would they want to run it at a loss?'

253

'To break you. Theirs is a large company with ships sailing in many parts of the world—England, Africa and other places in India. They can afford to lose a couple of lakhs here. They can easily make it up somewhere else. Their idea of doing good business is removing all obstacles and acquiring a monopoly. You're the obstacle and they'll squeeze you out even if it means incurring a loss. Then, when you're out of the picture, they can raise the fares as and when they please.'

'They will never squeeze me out! I didn't start the business to wrap it up at a threat.'

'Look Jyoti Babu. You're gifted and creative and you have the artist's vision. We are humble, ignorant folk and see things as they really are. The people of our country are poor; constrained to save every pie they can. Why will they pay more if they can help it? They'll abandon your ship before you have the time to blink. That's why I say it will be far better for you to sell out now while the going's good.'

Jyotirindra fixed his large dark eyes on the man's face—not in anger but in sorrow. Compassion stirred in his heart—compassion and understanding. 'Your words imply that I dwell in an ivory tower,' he said, his voice deep and resonant and tinged with melancholy. 'But let me tell you something. I am in close touch with the people of the land. And I know that though our rulers strike us mercilessly our backs are still unbroken. My passengers will not be fooled by the white men's wiles. They'll gladly sacrifice the two pice incentive to keep their native industry alive.' Abhaycharan shook his head. 'I'm a Bengali too Jyoti Babu,' he said sadly. 'And I would be glad to see you win. But the sahebs are too clever for us. Business runs in their blood. We'll never beat them.'

The Flotilla Company reduced its fare the very next day. At first the difference was not perceptible. There were plenty of passengers on Jyotirindra's ships. Jyotirindra's heart swelled with triumph. He had been proved right. His countrymen were with him. Then, after a week or so, things began to change. Jyotirindra's ships left Barisal laden with passengers but returned with a mere handful. Unlike Barisal, Khulna did not have a band of students making patriotic speeches at the ghat exhorting passengers to board the native ships. Gradually the numbers began to dwindle even in Barisal. Passengers looked this way and that and, ducking them heads guiltily, ran towards the foreign ships. Within a month Jyotirindra's ships were going up and down practically empty while the ships of the Flotilla Company were bursting at the seams.

One day, as Jyotirindra sat booding over the disaster that had overtaken him, his manager came up and said, 'This cannot go on any longer, sir. We'll have to do something. Why don't we reduce our fare by two pice?'

'Two pice!' Jyotirindra thundered banging his fist angrily on the table. 'I'll reduce it by four pice. Put up the notice this instant.'

And now a tug of war ensued the like of which had never been seen before. With the reduction in the fare the passengers abandoned the Flotilla Company and came crowding into Jyotirindra's ships. Within a few days the Flotilla Company had reduced its fare still further and Jyotirindra had followed suit. He gave orders for sweets and fruits to be distributed among the passengers and, when even that ceased to work, dhutis and saris. Travellers commuting between Khulna and Barisal had never had it so good. A four anna ticket not only took them to their destinations but took care of their breakfast as well with the added bonus of a dhuti or sari. People started travelling just for fun, the numbers swelling so greatly that Jyotirindranath was forced to employ guards who monitored the crowds and kept discipline on the ship.

Riding high on the crest of this wave of excitement Jyotirindranath was totally unprepared for the blow that fell. Caught in a violent storm, on its way to Calcutta, Jyotirindra's prized ship *Swadeshi* capsized and sank pulling down with it the entire future of the swadeshi enterprise its owner had struggled so hard to preserve. Mercifully there were no passengers on the boat. The crew managed to save their lives but the expensive cargo with which it was laden found their way to a watery grave. Jyotirindranath had sunk all his assets in the business and borrowed heavily from friends and relatives. He had been running it at a loss for the last few months. Now he found himself a pauper. Reeling under heavy debts, and broken in mind and body, Jyotirindra had to acknowledge defeat.

This time Pyarimohan Mukhopadhyay came to see him in

person. The Flotilla Company, he said, was ready to buy the rest of his ships and he would see to it, personally, that Jyotirindra got a fair price. Jyotirindra signed the contract and returned to Calcutta like a weary soldier scarred and mutilated after years of gory battle.

Avoiding Jorasanko he went straight to his Mejo Bouthan. There was a time when he would come to her house, striding in with the majesty of a prince, his face glowing with health and energy, his magnificent figure draped in silks and velvets and the finest of Cashmere shawls. Now his face was drawn and haggard, the eyes sunk deep in their sockets and his clothes hung limp and worn on his bony frame. Gyanadanandini had heard everything. She didn't ask any questions. Taking him by the hand she led him gently into the house.

From that day Jyotirindra ceased to speak except in monosyllables. He kept the door of his room locked and sat in it day after day unbathed, unshaven and muttering to himself. Bibi and Suren were shocked and frightened at the change in their uncle and took furtive peeps through the windows only to find him sitting in his chair staring at the wall or the ceiling. No one knew that, for the first time in his life, he was obsessed by thoughts of Kadambari. All through his busy life his awareness of her had been shadowy; almost elusive. Now he thought of her all the time. He remembered her tender solicitude, her grace and elegance, the beauty of her mind and spirit. Who was responsible for the way her life had ended? He asked himself the question, fairly and squarely, for the first time after her death. And, diving deep into his soul, he knew he could not be exonerated. He had taken her for granted. He had judged her wrong.

Although Jyotirindra had paid out every rupee he had received from the Flotilla Company it had not been enough to clear his debts. Now his creditors hung around Gyanada-nandini's house baying for his blood. Gyanadanandini was worried on another account. Jyoti's behaviour was getting more and more abnormal every day. Was he losing his mind? There was a history of insanity in the Thakur family. Two of her brothers-in-law were not normal. Would Jyoti, her bright, beautiful, beloved Natun end up like them? She was too distressed even to weep. Her husband was away from Calcutta.

256

Her father-in-law had not been told anything of what had happened. To whom could she turn for advice? After some deliberation she decided to consult the famous barrister Taraknath Palit who was also their family friend.

Taraknath Palit was Satyendranath's closest friend and a man of phenomenal wealth. He had always looked upon Satyendranath's family as his own and treated Jyotirindranath as a younger brother. Now, at this hour of need, he truly proved himself. Calling all the creditors together he took stock of the situation. Assessing the exact amount of damages he made Jyotirindra sign a bond promising to pay back whatever he owed in easy instalments. A good amount he disbursed initially from his own pocket and stood guarantor for the rest.

But though one part of Gyanadanandini's worry was over the other remained. Jyotirindranath sat, hour after hour, sunk in gloom refusing to communicate with anyone—not even his beloved Mejo Bouthan. Taraknath, who visited them often, suggested a change of scene. A few days in Jorasanko might be good for him, he felt. After all, that was his home. He had been born there and had spent the best years of his life in that house. There he might be able to come to terms with himself and with the changes that his destiny had wrought for him.

Jyotirindranath stepped into his apartment and looked around with disinterested eyes. The mirror on the door had disappeared but everything else looked the same. He came and sat in a chair by the window. It was a hot, still afternoon and gusts of wind, warm and laden with the scent of bakul from the tree outside, came drifting in. And, sniffing that air, he was transported into the past. He saw himself lying prone on the bed writing . . . Kadambari opening her cupboard with her silver keys her slender form draped in a blue sari, her bangles jingling. And suddenly the face that had become a blur swam into view. He saw it clear and whole; the long neck, the proudly raised chin, the eyes—dark, vibrant and fringed with thick lashes—in a face that seemed cut out of marble. He knew, of course, that it was not her he saw. It was his memory of her. Memory deepened. The face came closer. And then he saw an expression on it that he couldn't fathom. It was not anger. Nor sorrow or reproach. Only a deep yearning and melancholy. The blood pounded in his heart and

257

SUNIL GANGOPADHYAY

great waves of it beat against his brain. That face told him, clearer than words, that he had failed her. But how? How? It was true that he had neglected her sometimes but that was only because he was busy—too busy. But he had been a good husband to her. They had had their good moments together. Sailing on the Ganga in Chandannagar; singing to her; reading out his poems and listening to her comments. Why couldn't he see her face as it used to be then—rapt and bright and suffused with love?

Jyotirindra stood up. He couldn't stay here to be haunted by that long pale face and yearning eyes. He ran down the steps shaking his head like one possessed. 'No! No!' he cried as he ran. 'I'll never come back here. No. Not as long as I live.'

258

Chapter XXX

Dwarika had recently come into a fortune and had changed a great deal in consequence. He used to be a good student, an enthusiastic litterateur and an ardent patriot. But now, with the arrival of a thousand rupees a month from the estates he had inherited from his maternal uncle, he started neglecting his studies and everything else connected with it. And, as was to be expected, he started looking for ways of spending his money. Bharat watched him with dismay. He knew that a sudden change in fortune had disastrous effects on some people, but he wished it hadn't happened to Dwarika.

'Bharat,' Dwarika said, walking into his house one evening, 'Get ready quickly. I want to take you somewhere.'

'Where?' Bharat looked up timidly.

'Don't ask silly questions. Simply follow me.'

Out in the street, Dwarika hailed a cab and ordered the coachman to drive in the direction of Boubazar. Coming to the end of Hadhkatar Gali he stopped before a house whose front door stood hospitably open. Dwarika paid the fare and taking Bharat by the hand, ran up the stairs. 'I spend the night here sometimes,' he said by way of explanation. 'My father used to come here too. I've heard people say that he ran away from home two days before he was to be wed. After a frantic search he was discovered in this house and brought back just in time.'

Reaching the top floor Bharat and Dwarika stood before a closed door. Dwarika gave it a push and it opened easily, the hinges groaning a little. Inside, the room was flooded with light from the candles burning brightly from the eight brackets set in the walls. A huge bedstead of carved mahogany stood in the middle of the room. And, on its high mattress spread with snowy sheets, a girl, young and slender and of a dazzling beauty lay on her back, her eyes closed and her hands crossed over her breast. Her delicate limbs were draped in a heavy sari of Benares brocade and her arms and neck were weighted down with gold. The door

259

had creaked with an agonized sound but the girl did not open her eyes. There was something unreal about the scene. *A sleeping princess.* The thought came into Bharat's head as Dwarika, raising his eyebrows in mock dismay, leaned over the girl and sang softly —

'Kunchita Késhini nirupam béshini
Rasa—abéshinibhangini ré
Adhara surangini anga tarangini
Sangini naba naba rangini ré'

The girl opened her eyes but did not sit up. She let her soft warm gaze rest on Dwarika. 'She's my friend,' Dwarika explained to Bharat. 'Her name is Basantamanjari.' Then, turning to the girl he asked, 'Why were you sleeping at this hour Basi?' Basantamanjari yawned revealing a soft pink mouth. 'I have a fever,' she said in a complacent voice. 'No you haven't,' Dwarika placed a hand on her brow, 'And if you do, why are you all dressed up? And why is there so much light in your room?'

'I like dressing up. And I hate sleeping in the dark. I visit so many places in my dreams. I meet so many people—' Waving a dazzling white hand in Bharat's direction, she asked, 'Who is he?'

'My friend. His name is Bharat. He's a good boy, wonderfully innocent!'

Basantamanjari fixed her eyes, large, dark and shadowed with long lashes, on Bharat's face. There was a slight quiver in her voice as she asked, 'Who are you? Have I seen you before?' Bharat shook his head. 'But I know you,' the strange girl continued. 'It happens with some people. You recognize them even if you haven't seen them before. I have seen you in my dreams.'

'What rotten luck!' Dwarika exclaimed rolling his eyes comically. 'I squander all my money on you; buy you saris and jewels. And my friend becomes your dream companion! Are you tired of me and want a change?'

'But it's true. I see him in my dreams. I see a falchion hanging over his head. Death is stalking him!' Her eyes fixed his with a compelling gaze, 'Isn't that true?' she asked.

Bharat felt his heart thumping against his ribs. Who was this girl and why did she look at him so strangely? There was something mysterious about her not only in what she was saying but in her manner. There were two men in her room and she went

260

on lying on her bed. 'What nonsense you talk!' Dwarika scolded her tenderly. 'Don't listen to her Bharat. She says the strangest things at times'

'It isn't nonsense. Ask him if what I've said isn't true.'

'I must go,' Bharat rose to his feet.

'Why?' Dwarika clutched his shoulder. 'We've only just arrived. Let's have some brandy. I keep a bottle here—'

'No. I can't stay. I'm going.' Bharat flung off the restraining hand and rushed out of the room. His face was on fire and his breath came in gasps. The blood pounded in his heart. He ran down the steps and out of the open door into the street ignoring the drizzle that soaked him to the skin. He hated himself. The girl's beauty had drawn him like a magnet and he had nearly succumbed. How could he have forgotten Bhumisuta even momentarily? Wasn't it somewhere here, in Boubazar, that he had promised Bhumisuta he would look after her all his life? He hadn't kept his promise. He had abandoned her. And now she was lost to him. She was in the king's custody and he dared not go near her.

Chapter XXXI

In the paved yard that fronted the mansion of Jorasanko a brand new phaeton stood waiting. Its bright ochre varnish shone like gold in the morning sun. The morocco leather of the upholstery was of a rich plum colour. Two jet black horses snorted and pawed the air nervously as grooms and servants crowded around asking eagerly, 'Whose carriage is this? Which babu's?'

They were not kept in the dark for long. From the side door of the *khazanchi khana* a young man stepped out and walked briskly towards them. He was tall and well built with a narrow beard and dark hair waving down to his neck. He wore a puckered dhuti and banian and had a shawl on his shoulders. On his feet were English socks and shining pumps. It was Robi. He was twenty-four years old and this carriage was his father's gift to him.

Debendranath spent most of his time in his house in Chinsura. But he kept a stern eye on everything that went on in his family. More and more people were referring to him as Maharshi these days, seeing, in his self-imposed exile from Calcutta, a parallel to the lives of the ancient rishis. Yet Debendranath was an extremely calculating, pragmatic, man of the world. He had taken the deaths of his daughter-in-law, two sons-in-law and son Hemendra with exemplary calm. But, faced with the ignominious failure of Jyotirindranath's shipping venture, he found his patience at an end. It was not only the loss of the money that he regretted. He looked upon it as a blot on his family's honour. People would be laughing at the Thakurs of Jorasanko. And his own son was responsible. He could hardly believe it. Jyoti—his favourite, the boy on whom he had set his highest hopes, had let him down. Not once, but again and again. He wouldn't, he couldn't forgive him. He decided to mete out the severest punishment.

Within days of Jyotirindranath's return to Calcutta Debendranath proceeded to strip him of all his offices. The

262

charge of the estates was passed on to Dwijendranath and the
secretaryship of the Adi Brahmo Samaj was conferred upon Robi.
Some of the family's well wishers advised Debendranath against
such a course. The boy was shattered in spirit already. He needed
support and encouragement from his father—not vindictiveness
of this kind. But Debendranath was unmoved by these entreaties
and went on calmly with his plans.

He raised Robi's allowance and even arranged for a sum to be
paid to his wife each month. He gave orders for the redecoration
of their wing. And now he had given Robi this new carriage. The
secretary of the Brahmo Samaj had to move around, meet people
and organize meetings. He needed a carriage of his own. But,
Debendranath's generosity notwithstanding, he was a hard task
master. Robi had to visit him every week with a report of all the
activities of the Samaj and its expenses. Though pleased with his
youngest son's hard work and dedication he made it a point to
chide him from time to time. 'You did well to purchase a new
harmonium,' he had said on one occasion, 'It was needed. But
why did you send the old one for repairs? That is waste.' Robi
never answered back. He obeyed his father's commands without
question though he felt rebellious at times. He hadn't approved of
his father's treatment of his Jyotidada. But he was powerless to
protest. In his embarrassment he had stopped going to Gyanadanandini's house.

Of late Robi was straining every nerve to bring the three
groups of Brahmos under one banner. Hinduism, riding on a high
new wave, was threatening to crush the Brahmo Samaj whose
members were small in number and hopelessly divided. If
something was not done to unify the Brahmos, he was never tired
of pointing out, the Samaj would disintegrate. But, though
everyone agreed with him, each section dictated its own terms
and would not be swayed. Thus a consensus eluded them. But
Robi did not lose heart. He went on trying.

Now, on his way to Pratapchandra Majumdar's house, he
suddenly remembered something his father had said at their last
meeting. He had been holding Robi's *Shaishab Sangeet* in his
hand when Robi walked into his study. Looking up from the
dedication which he had obviously been reading, he had asked
sternly, 'How many books a year do you mean to print from the

263

Brahmo Press?' Then, without waiting for a reply, he had walked out of the room. Robi had stared at the departing back in bewilderment. He thought his father liked his poetry. He had complimented him often and given him presents. Why, then, did he ask that question? Was he annoyed because the poems in the book were love poems? Or was he hinting that Robi was taking unfair advantage of the press which was public property? Or was it the dedication that had offended him? Robi shivered a little at the thought. He had tried, genuinely tried, to forget Natun Bouthan and get on with his life. He had succeeded too. Except when it came to writing a dedication. Then he could think of no other person. Natun Bouthan's face looked unfailingly out of the innocent white sheet before him. For *Prakritir Pratishod* he had taken care not to put down her name. 'To you' the dedication had run. Yet he had seen members of his family exchange meaningful glances. Gyanadanandini's face had hardened and Swarna-kumari had passed a snide comment. In consequence he had left the dedication page blank for his next volume *Nalini*. And, now, he was about to publish *Bhanu Singhér Padavali*. Bhanu was *her* name for him. But for her the poems would never have been written. Not taking her name he had written: 'You entreated me often to publish these poems. I have done so. But you are not here to see them in print.'

The horses stumbled over a rut in the road making the carriage rock precariously and startling Robi out of his thoughts. Then, when the vehicle started running smoothly once again, the words he was struggling to shut out clamoured in his brain, 'How many books a year do you mean to print from the Brahmo Press?' Why had Baba Moshai asked that question? Was it because his books didn't sell? They lay in piles in the shops of the People's Library, Sanskrit Press Depository and Canning Library and didn't bring in a pie. Bankim Babu's books sold like hot cakes and were even pirated. Perhaps Baba Moshai was hinting that there was no point in publishing book after book if no one was interested in buying them! Robi's heart sank at the thought.

Suddenly an idea struck him. A gentleman called Gurudas Chattopadhyay had recently opened a shop called Bengal Medical Library which sold poetry and fiction along with medical books. He would go and see him. Leaning out of the window he instructed the coachman to drive to College Street where the Bengal Medical Library was housed. Entering the shop Robi inspected the shelves with interest. Bankim Babu's novels took up the maximum space. Michael Madhusudan's and Hem Banerjee's works filled a couple of shelves. There were copies of Tarak Ganguli's *Swarnalata*, Kaliprasanna Singha's *Hutom Pyanchar Naksha* and Nabin Sen's *Palashir Judhha* but not one of his books. Robi sighed. People did not care to read lyrics. They liked narrative and action.

Gurudas Babu greeted Robi with the deference due to him. Though not much of a writer he was, after all, Deben Thakur's son. Leading him into a small anteroom he invited him to sit down and ordered the servant to bring an *albola* and paan for his refreshment. These initial courtesies over, and after some preliminary discussion, he came out with a proposal that startled Robi. He would buy the eight thousand unsold copies of twelve of Robi's books for a fixed sum of money. Thereafter, he would sell them at his own price. Robi would have no claims to royalty or commission. The sum he mentioned was staggering. After some calculation he offered Robi the princely sum of two thousand three hundred and nine rupees.

So much money! From his books? Heaps of paper that would have turned to food for termites in a few months! Robi could hardly believe his ears. The thought of bargaining never even occurred to him. Thanking Gurudas Babu profusely he rose to leave. After many days his heart felt light and free. Yet—not quite. 'If only *she* were here to share my triumph!' The thought cast a shadow over his happiness.

On his way back home Robi started making plans. He would celebrate this great event in his life by inviting his friends for a feast. He would call Priyanath Sen, Shreesh Majumdar and Akshay Choudhary. His little bride was growing into quite a good cook. She was still attending school though she hadn't gone back to Gyanadanandini. She was taken to Loretto House every morning in the carriage dressed in a frock and long stockings. But back home she was often seen in the kitchen wearing a sari and giving instructions to the cooks in the voice and manner of a middle-aged matron. Then she didn't seem so young anymore.

After dinner that night the discussion veered around the

subject of Bankimchandra's writing. The latter's son-in-law had recently started a newspaper called *Prachaar*. Bankimchandra was writing regularly for it as well as for Akshay Sarkar's *Nabajeeban*. And, lately, both his columns and novels were displaying a Hindu chauvinism that Robi found distasteful. *Anandamath* was bad enough, in his opinion. *Debi Choudhurani*, which followed, was even worse. Hitherto he had restrained himself from expressing any derogatory remarks. But today he felt free to do so. They were both writers and his books were selling too. Why should he continue to stand in awe of Bankimchandra? 'I consider *Anandamath* a very mediocre work,' he announced gravely. 'The characters are flat and boring. And it is full of melodrama.' Shreeshchandra, a great admirer of Bankim, took umbrage at this remark and a lively argument ensued lasting far into the night.

After the guests had departed Robi came into his apartment. Despite the long day he felt wide awake and far from weary. He was sleeping less and less these days and he hated lying in bed staring into the dark. He came and stood on the veranda and gazed out into the star filled sky. Suddenly he heard a sigh that seemed wrenched out of a suffering soul. He turned around his heart beating swiftly. 'Where did that come from?' he thought. 'It sounded like Natun Bouthan!' And, at that moment, he thought he saw something slip past like a shadow. A tremor of fear passed through him. Was Natun Bouthan's ghost hovering around him? Nonsense! Robi gave himself a little shake and walked purposefully into the bedroom.

On the vast bedstead Mrinalini lay fast asleep curled up in a corner. She looked very young and vulnerable as she lay there. Her pink sari was pulled down to her feet and strands of hair clung to her face. Robi looked down on the little figure with tenderness in his eyes. 'Poor girl,' he thought. 'She's worn out with the labours of the day.' And, indeed, Mrinalini had played hostess to her husband's friends like any grown wife. She had cooked some of the dishes and served them with her own hands. Suddenly a realization dawned on Robi. They hardly ever spoke to each other. There was no possibility of doing so during the day and she was, invariably, fast asleep when Robi came in at night. Robi took a decision. He would bury the past once and for all.

Moving swiftly towards the bed he lifted the mosquito net and lay
down beside her. On other nights he did so softly, stealthily, so as
not to wake her. But, tonight, he took her face in his hands and
pushed the clinging strands of hair away from her face. Mrinalini
opened her eyes. He saw no awe or fear in them—only an eager
longing. Tenderly, with his forefinger, he outlined first her
mouth, then her eyes and chin as though he was etching her face
on paper. Mrinalini put out a little hand and closed her soft damp
palm over those long sensitive fingers. Robi took her in his arms
and clasped her to his breast. 'This is right,' he thought. 'This is as
it should be. It is far better to live with flesh and blood than with
shadows.'

Chapter XXXII

Maharaja Birchandra Manikya was returning from a social visit to Sir Rivers Thompson, the Lieutenant Governor of Bengal. Monomohini had been invited too and had clamoured to go but Birchandra had snubbed her into submission. Queens of the Chandravansha dynasty didn't show their faces in public. He had taken Shashibhushan instead. He could converse in English after a fashion but not too well. He could do with Shashibhushan's help.

Now, sitting in the carriage on the way back, Birchandra's face looked grim and sullen and angry tears glistened in his eyes. He felt hurt and humiliated. He hadn't, of course, been mistreated in any way. He had been received with due deference and no political pressure had been inflicted on him. His host had given him tea and enquired politely after his wife and they had chatted briefly on several subjects for about twenty-five minutes. The humiliation lay in the look the white man had given him. Rivers Thompson was a very tall man and erect in his bearing. While shaking hands he had looked down from his great height at the portly little specimen of royalty he was entertaining. The pale blue eyes had looked pointedly at Birchandra's stomach and the lips had twitched a little. So little—it was almost invisible. But Birchandra was no fool. He recognized contempt when he saw it. And he was very, very sensitive. 'I shouldn't have gone,' he thought bitterly. 'After all I am king of a realm, however small, and he's only a civil servant.' But in his heart he knew that a refusal was out of the question. An invitation from the Laat Saheb was like a royal command. It was a reminder that the British had it in their power to whisk his crown off his head at any time they chose.

Birchandra had a happy disposition in general. But once thwarted or humiliated he brooded over his wrongs for days. In order to cheer him up Shashibhushan organized a symposium of letters. Well-known poets and prose writers like Sisir Kumar

Ghosh, Rabindranath Thakur and Dineshchandra Sen, were invited to read from their works. The king sat in state amongst them in the durbar hall on the second floor but his face remained drawn and his manner abstracted. After a while he rose and left the room.

The next day Shashibhushan invited a group of kirtaniyas. They were the top performers of Calcutta and were invited often by the Raja of Shobhabazar who was a connoisseur of music. But though Birchandra loved listening to kirtan he didn't seem to think much of them. After sitting quietly for a few minutes he poked Shashibhushan in the ribs with his elbow. 'Where is that girl?' he asked quite out of context. Shashibhushan was so startled by the question that though he opened his mouth to speak no words came. 'You know who I mean,' the king persisted. 'That Suto or Suta—whatever her name is. Send for her. I want to hear her sing tonight in my bedchamber. She has a good voice.' Shashi drew a deep breath and said, 'She's ill Maharaj.'

'What!' the Maharaja exclaimed. 'She's been ill for so long and you've done nothing about it! Do you want to kill her? Send for the doctor at once. What are her symptoms?'

'Fever Maharaj. It comes and goes.'

'That's a bad sign. She needs treatment immediately. Come,' he rose to his feet. 'Take me to her. I wish to see her with my own eyes.'

Now Shashibhushan's face turned pale. If the king saw Bhumisuta he would know that Shashibhushan had been spinning a web of lies all these days. 'Why should you go Maharaj?' he cried out in his desperation. 'I'll bring her to you.' But the king shook his head. 'There's no need to pull her out of her sickbed,' he said. 'She needs her rest. I'll look in on her and give her some medicine.'

Shashibhushan hurried after the king as he walked purposefully towards the stairs his shoes clacking loudly on the marble floor. Downstairs all was dark and silent. Birchandra stood for a moment at the head of the stairs a queer smile on his lips. 'Wait a little Maharaj,' Shashibhushan said. 'Let me fetch a light.' But the king put out a hand and stopped him. 'You know Shashi,' he said conversationally, 'I thought nothing of barging into the servants' rooms when I was young. If I saw a pretty

269

wench I would carry her upstairs however much she cried and protested. But I'm older and wiser now. I realize that it is not proper for a man in my position to enter a maid's bedchamber. You should have stopped me. I'm your master and your king. How could you forget your duty to me?'

Shashibhushan stood silent, his head bowed. He knew that whatever he said would be misconstrued. To keep mute was best. 'Get the wench out of her sickbed and send her to me. She's too precious a gem to be thrown carelessly into the ash heap. Send for the best doctors. And don't stint on the expense. I give you three days,' Birchandra wagged his forefinger at Shashibhushan threateningly, turned around and made his way back to the durbar hall. Shashibhushan breathed a sigh of relief. It had been a close shave. But the danger hadn't passed. The Maharaja was determined to have Bhumisuta and she was equally determined not to let him. 'Send me away from here,' she repeated like a parrot every time he told her that the king wanted to see her. But where could he send her? To his ancestral home in Bhabanipur? He could do that but what would he tell the king when he asked for her? What if he came to know that Shashibhushan had removed her to his own house? The king and queen had been invited to Bhabanipur once by his brothers. What if the invitation was repeated?

Bhumisuta! Bhumisuta! A fierce resentment rose in Shashibhushan's breast. He was being forced to think of her day and night. No woman had occupied his thoughts to such an extent after Suhasini's death. He had been married to Suhasini for five years when she died of cholera. She had been a beautiful woman and well educated. He had poured out his soul to her in love. He had given her everything she had ever wanted. Ignoring the frowns of his sisters-in-law he had taken her with him wherever he went. They had enjoyed holidays in Darjeeling and Nepal. And, every night, he had sat with her teaching her Sanskrit and English. He had placed a standing order in Cuthbertson's Perfumery. A bottle of every new perfume that arrived from France was to be sent to his wife. But despite everything he did, he hadn't won Suhasini's heart. That had been given to another. He had come to know, some months before she died, that she was deeply involved with her cousin Anangamohan and had been so

270

from before her marriage. Shashibhushan hadn't said a word to Suhasini. He had simply withdrawn from her. She hadn't seemed real anymore and when she died he had felt no grief.

Anangamohan couldn't have felt much grief either. Shashibhushan knew that he had transferred his affections to Suhasini's sister Tarangini before her ashes had cooled. Yet he was the one Suhasini had loved. The thought was too humiliating; too hard to bear. His brother Monibhushan had suggested that he take Tarangini as his second wife. Horrified by the idea Shashi had escaped to Tripura. He had made up his mind. He wouldn't marry again—ever. He had lost his faith in women.

That night Bhumisuta came into his room as usual with the glass of hot milk he drank just before going to sleep. She placed the silver glass on a little table and was about to leave the room when Shashibhushan stopped her. 'Wait,' he called out imperiously, 'I wish to speak with you.' Bhumisuta turned around but stood where she was. She didn't approach him. 'The Maharaja was enquiring about you this evening,' he said. 'How much longer can I go on telling him you are ill? What is wrong with singing for him?'

'I can't do it,' Bhumisuta answered. Her voice was soft but firm.

'But why?' Shashibhushan persisted. 'You must give me a reason. The Maharaja is determined to hear you sing. You'll have to satisfy him—'

'Send me away.'

'Don't be stupid. The Maharaja has given me three days. At the end of it you'll have to go to him.'

'No one can force me.' Bhumisuta's eyes flashed. 'I'll slit my throat first. I've managed to get hold of a knife.'

Shashibhushan stared at her in shock and horror. And suddenly he recognized the alien streak in her. She looked and spoke like an average middle-class Bengali girl. But she wasn't that. What Bengali girl could express herself with so much power and passion? He went on staring at her. For the first time since Suhasini's death he had actually looked at a woman. 'She can't be what she appears,' he thought. 'She can't be an ordinary maid.' He put out his hand saying, 'Let me see it.' Bhumisuta stared back at him. 'I don't have it with me,' she said. 'I've hidden it in my

271

room.'

Shashibhushan knew he ought to go down, inspect her room and take the knife away. But he made no effort to do so. 'I've never heard you sing,' he said instead.

'I sing only for myself and God.'

'I won't force you Bhumisuta,' Shashibhushan heard himself saying. He was amazed at the tenderness in his voice. 'Don't sing for the Maharaja if you don't want to. But will you sing for me? Just one song—?'

272

Chapter XXXIII

The devout Rani Rasmoni's spirit had left her mortal frame these many years. And her faithful servant and son-in-law Mathur had passed away. The present owners of the estates had neither the time nor the inclination to worry their heads about the temple their ancestress had created and cherished and nurtured with her life blood. Consequently they did not even know that Ramkrishna Thakur was seriously ill.

He had been suffering from a bad throat and violent fits of coughing for a long time now. The disciples had called in several doctors most of whom were of the opinion that the malady was not serious. Clergyman's Sore Throat some of them called it. They recommended a diet of strengthening meat soups and left medicines. But none of it seemed to help. The pain in his throat increased day by day and his limbs felt weaker and weaker. His disciples were growing in number and he had to sit with them and talk to them even when the pain in his throat was excruciating. During one of his *bhav samadhis* he had called out to the Goddess in a sullen voice, 'Why do you send so many Ma? They crowd around me so—I don't get a moment's peace. It's only a cracked drum as it is. How much longer can it withstand so much battering?'

Though the owners of the temple took no notice of his illness his disciples did all they could to alleviate his sufferings. It was decided that the damp rising from the Ganga was doing him no good. He ought to be shifted to a warmer, drier place. Thus, Ramkrishna was removed from Dakshineswar, where he had lived for thirty years, and brought to Balaram Bosu's house in Ramkanta Bosu Street in Calcutta. Ramkrishna was pleased to be there. Balaram Bosu was one of his favourite disciples. Besides there were many others living close at hand. Vidyasagar's Metropolitan College being only a stone's throw away, Mahendra Mukherjee could visit him several times a day. Girish Ghosh, at Bagbazar, was within walking distance.

After that first visit to the theatre Ramkrishna had gone there often. And he had drawn the blaspheming atheist, Girish, to him like a magnet. Girish, who had rejected the concept of the guru being the medium through which one reached the divine, felt himself drawn into Ramkrishna's web slowly but surely. He tried to disentangle himself from time to time much as a drunk tries to shake off his intoxication. 'What is a guru?' he had enquired once of Ramkrishna. Ramkrishna's lips had twitched with amusement. 'You should know,' he had answered, 'You have one.' Girish was horrified. What was the man saying? Who was his guru? This illiterate yokel in his coarse dhuti and *uduni*? Impossible! In order to shake off Ramkrishna's spell Girish started misbehaving with him. He would walk into his room in Dakshineswar whenever he felt like it, stone drunk, trying to pick up a quarrel. But even though he reviled the priest and his fourteen generations hurling the foulest expletives in his vocabulary, he failed to get a reaction from him. Ramkrishna smiled as if at a little boy's tantrums and looked at him out of loving eyes.

His every move defeated, Girish tried to rationalize the situation. No human being, he reasoned with himself, should be exalted to the level of a spiritual medium between Man and God. Ramkrishna claimed to be such a medium. Girish could not admit his claim. Yet, he couldn't deny his power over him either. There was some force in him that defied definition. Therefore, it was obvious that Ramkrishna was no ordinary man. He was an avatar of the Divine. Ram and Krishna were twin incarnations of that one single Power and they had come together in the person of Ramkrishna. Having admitted this Girish surrendered himself body and soul to the priest of Kali. And thus he found peace.

But Naren and several others could not admit that Ramkrishna was anything other than an ordinary mortal. If he was an avatar of God, they argued, why was he suffering in the flesh? Avatars were untouched by sickness and old age. Who had ever heard of Lord Krishna of Mathura and Lord Ram of Ayodhya suffering from fever or dysentery. Ramkrishna was a victim of both. He had a weak digestion and felt the urge to empty his bowels several times a day. And he caught chills and fevers often. Only the other day he had fallen and broken his arm and had to have it plastered. And, now, the pain in his throat was so bad that he spent his nights tossing and turning in his bed moaning in agony.

Of late Ramkrishna had started behaving like a child. If the doctor was late by even a few minutes he would sulk pettishly, 'Oh why doesn't he come? Why doesn't someone go and fetch him?' And every time anyone came near him he asked eagerly, 'I'll get well, won't I? Do you think this new medicine will cure me?' Allopathic medicines being too strong for him his disciples had called in the renowned homeopath Pratapchandra Majumdar. His pills brought the patient some relief but it was only temporary. The disease that racked him continued to grow insidiously within. He started coughing up bits of blood and found it more and more difficult to swallow. Now the doctors had to admit that what he suffered from was something more serious than Clergyman's Sore Throat.

One day the famous kaviraj Gangaprasad came to see him. After examining the patient's throat, he shook his head. 'He is suffering from rohini,' he said, 'We have no cure for it.'

'What is rohini?' the disciples surrounding him asked.

'The sahebs call it cancer.'

Those among Ramkrishna's followers who lived by the assumption that faith was superior to logic were convinced that he could shake the disease off his system if he so wished. Pandit Sasadhar Tarka Churhamani accosted him one day with the words, 'How is it possible that a saint like you suffers thus?'

'It is not I who suffer,' Ramkrishna replied, 'It's this wretched body.'

'But surely you have control over your body. The shastras say that men like you have the power to dismiss the ills of the flesh. If, during a *bhav samadhi*, you concentrate on the organ that is troubling you; if you focus your whole mind and spirit on it you will be enabled to overcome the disease.'

'What!' Ramkrishna cried passionately, 'You, a pandit, ask me to do such a thing! My mind and spirit have been consecrated to God. Would you have me turn them away from Him to this broken cage of bones and flesh?'

Sasadhar did not say any more. But he thought Ramkrishna's argument a feeble one. He was convinced that Ramkrishna's

---

illness had robbed him of some of his powers. If his broken cage of bones and flesh meant nothing to him why was he describing his symptoms to one doctor after another and asking them if he would live? Why was he taking medicine?

A week after this encounter Ramkrishna left Balaram Bosu's house and took up residence in a rented house in Shyampukur Street. Balaram Bosu was a devout and faithful follower of Ramkrishna. But he was somewhat of a miser. He didn't mind spending on his guru. He was prepared to give him all the comforts his house could offer and also pay for his treatment. What he grudged was the expense he had to incur on the crowds who came to see him every day. Ramkrishna had other wealthy followers who were prepared to spend money on him. It was decided to keep him in a rented house.

At dusk, on the ninth day of the waning moon, Ramkrishna stepped over the threshold of the house in Shyampukur Street and looked around him with interest. A neatly made up bed stood ready in one corner. On the walls were several pictures. Ramkrishna examined them by the light of a lamp held up by Ramchandra Datta. There was one of Balgopal with Jashoda Ma and another of Sri Gouranga dancing with his disciples. As Ramkrishna peered up at them one of his followers whispered to another, 'See! He is looking at himself.' The very next moment the man got a shock. Ramkrishna turned around and asked fretfully, 'Why have they kept the window open? I feel a draught coming in. I'm chilled to the bone.'

In the house in Shyampukur Street Ramkrishna's condition started deteriorating at an alarming pace and his disciples were at their wits' end. So many doctors had come and gone but not one had been able to alleviate his sufferings let alone effect a cure. The only doctor left was Mahendralal Sarkar. But Ramkrishna cried out fearfully every time his name was mentioned. 'No. No. Not him,' Ramkrishna found Mahendralal Sarkar an extremely alarming personality. Once, several months ago, he had been taken to the doctor's house in Shankharitola. Mahendralal Sarkar had been very short with the disciples who had brought him. Bundling them out of the room, most unceremoniously, he had fixed a stern eye on the priest and motioned him to a chair. 'Open your mouth,' he had commanded in the tone he used for all his patients. On Ramkrishna's doing so he had snapped, 'Wider! How can I look down your throat if you don't open your mouth properly?' Ramkrishna had tried to tell him that he was doing his best but that had brought on the most shocking response. 'Quiet!' the doctor had thundered, 'Don't move your tongue.' And he had held Ramkrishna's tongue firmly in place with a spoon. It had been a painful experience for Ramkrishna both physically and otherwise and he didn't care to repeat it.

Now, of course, the pain was much worse. He felt as if a knife was sticking in his throat cutting into his palate and food pipe every time he swallowed. Of late even his ears had started hurting. And he had started vomiting blood. The disciples couldn't afford to take their guru's terror of the great doctor seriously any more. They sent for Mahendralal Sarkar.

That evening Dr Sarkar came to the house in Shyampukur Street. Entering Ramkrishna's room he looked around for somewhere to sit. The disciples were alarmed at the sight of him striding in arrogantly on leather shod feet into a place consecrated by the presence of their guru. But Ramkrishna merely patted one side of the bed on which he lay and motioned to him to sit down which he did without hesitation.

'Where does it hurt?' the doctor asked with a rare gentleness.

'I feel a swelling in my throat the size of a roseapple. The air is pushed back into my mouth whenever I try to swallow.'

'Do you have a cough?'

'I cough all night. Then the pus pours out of my mouth as thick as castor oil.'

'Do you have any pain?'

'I feel as if a knife is sticking in my throat. I can't sleep for the pain.'

'Open your mouth. Let me have a look at your throat.'

Ramkrishna obeyed, his eyes fixed fearfully on the stern face just above his. Looking down into the torn, bleeding ravaged organ the doctor murmured, 'Why are you afraid of me? I'm a doctor. I try to cure people—not kill them.'

After a while he stood up, his face grave. 'I'm leaving medicines,' he said with a return to his habitual curtness. 'Take them regularly. And talk as little as possible. The world can do without your eloquence—for the present at least.'

On his way out he turned to the men accompanying him and asked, 'Does this house belong to Rani Rasmoni?' 'No sir,' one of them hastened to inform him. 'This is a rented house. Some of Thakur's disciples pay for it.'

'Disciples!' Mahendralal Sarkar exclaimed, 'Does this man have disciples? I thought he was being kept by the Madhs of Janbazar. Which ones among you are his disciples?'

On being told that they were all Ramkrishna's disciples including Naren and the other graduates, the doctor's brows rose in astonishment. He could understand semi-literate men in their prime looking for a prop on which to rest their burden of sins. But that young men like Narendranath Datta—educated, rational and Westernized in their thinking—could be drawn into the web of the rustic he had just left behind was unthinkable! And Girish. That self-proclaimed atheist! Mahendralal was shocked at the transformation in him. The disciples, in their turn, were shocked when he returned the fee they offered.

'What is this for?' he asked sternly.

'Your fee, sir' one of them replied. 'Thakur's disciples are paying for his treatment.'

'I'm not a disciple,' Mahendralal said shortly, 'But you may add my name to the list of contributors. I don't need to be paid any fees. Nor anything for the medicines I leave. I warn you though. The patient is in a very serious condition. He needs rest and quiet. Stop outsiders from coming in and disturbing him.'

After the doctor had left the men looked at one another in dismay. How would they fend off the crowds that gathered at the door at all hours of the day? Thakur had been relatively undisturbed in Dakshineswar—it being a good distance away from Calcutta. But, here, word had spread that a fragment of dust from the feet of the Paramhansa would ensure a smooth passage to heaven. After a lot of discussion, it was finally decided that the younger disciples would keep vigil outside Ramkrishna's door and try to prevent people from entering his room.

One day a follower of Ramkrishna's named Kali Ghosh brought a young man with him. He looked like a foreigner in his impeccable Western suit and rimless glasses. Niranjan, at the door, tried to stop them from coming in but Kali Ghosh waved aside his protests. After being locked in an argument for over an hour Niranjan had to surrender and allow the older man entry. The foreign gentleman took no part in the exchange. His face was serene and unruffled and his gaze elsewhere.

But the moment he stepped into Ramkrishna's room he took off his glasses and his hat. Everyone looked on him, amazed, for out tumbled a cloud of silky black curls. 'Pardon me, Prabhu,' a woman's voice cried, 'I wanted to see you once—for the last time.' The stranger sank to the floor and placed her head on Ramkrishna's feet. Ramkrishna recognized the voice instantly. It was Binodini's. Ramkrishna laughed—peal after peal of delighted laughter. 'This is true love,' he cried out in a hoarse, cracked voice, 'True yearning!' But, looking on his emaciated face and body, Binodini wept as if her heart would break. Resisting Ramkrishna's feeble efforts to raise her she pressed her face on his feet and washed them with her tears.

On her way home, in the carriage, Binodini drew out a little mirror from her pocket. Her face was a mess. The paint she had applied for the part was running in streams down her cheeks. Taking a kerchief from her pocket she proceeded to wipe it off when she noticed a spot on her chin—unnaturally white. She had seen it earlier and ignored it. But now, peering closer, she thought it had grown larger. Something else was growing within her—a conviction that her acting days were coming to an end. She wondered what her affliction was. Was it leucoderma? Or leprosy? 'Why am I being punished thus?' she thought, fresh tears pouring down her face, 'What sin have I committed?' And, at that moment, she took a decision. She would give up the stage. Her admirers had idolized her for years. She wouldn't show her cursed face, marked by the hand of God, to them ever again.

Chapter XXXIV

It was a hot moonless night of early summer. Beads of sweat dotted Bharat's bare back as he stood on the balcony gazing out into the night. The gas lamps had not been lit, for some reason, and the city was in darkness. Dwarika had left him a while ago after a futile effort to make him a partner in his nocturnal ventures. He had tried every wile. He had told him that Basantamanjari was pining away for love of him. But Bharat had stood firm. This was not for the first time and he knew it wouldn't be the last. But though he resisted Dwarika's persuasions every time, he hadn't forgotten Basantamanjari. Her face swam before his eyes day and night and he couldn't understand why. Was it because she reminded him of Bhumisuta? But Bhumisuta's gentle loveliness was in total contrast to Basantamanjari's startling, exotic beauty. And she lacked the latter's gorgeous plumage. Bhumisuta was a servant maid and her clothes, though clean, were well worn and frayed in places. It was the voice perhaps—low, musical with a haunting quality . . .

Dhoop! Bharat turned his head at the familiar sound. The priest living next door was here. He jumped down from his window to the tiny terrace adjoining Bharat's kitchen whenever he wanted some tea. 'Why haven't you lit the lantern brother?' Bani Binod's voice came to him from out of the dark. 'I'll light it in a minute,' Bharat answered. He was pleased to see Bani Binod. Listening to his jabber he forgot his cares for the present. 'And make some tea,' he added. 'There's no need to rush,' Bani Binod answered with a chuckle. 'Today I have something for you.' Setting an earthen pot on the floor he put his hand in and brought out a sandesh which was at least six times bigger than an ordinary one. 'Come brother, eat,' he said, pressing the sweetmeat into Bharat's hand. 'It's excellent stuff I assure you. Especially ordered by royalty.'

'Was there a feast at Rani Rasmoni's palace today?'

'No, no,' Bani Binod waved his hand dismissively. 'The

Madhs of Janbazar have become very tight fisted. Besides, they aren't royalty. This one is a true king. Big and strong and fair with moustaches that stand up on both ends like tongues of flame.'

'Are you a royal priest then?'

'I'm filling in for the priest who has gone back to Tripura to see his ailing son.' Then, noting Bharat's shocked look, he added, 'It was you who told me about the Maharaja of Tripura. Have you forgotten?'

Bharat's heart started thumping so hard that he could hardly hear the rest of Bani Binod's story. Bani Binod was the performing priest in Maharaja Birchandra's household and was seeing Bhumisuta every day. He could think of nothing else.

'What is the house like?' he asked when the drumbeats in his blood had subsided a little.

'You've never seen anything like it. All the floors—even the stairs and verandas are covered with red velvet. Except the puja room of course. And that is gleaming white marble. As for the statues and chandeliers—'

'How big is the puja room?'

'At least four times the size of both your rooms put together.'

'Does someone help you with the puja?'

'Two women are in attendance all the time. They keep flowers, tulsi, sandalpaste and gangajal in readiness and hand me whatever I need. I don't have to move from my asan.'

'Are they the king's wives?'

'You're a numskull. Why should queens do menial work? Besides, the present queen is very young—I'm told. I've never seen her. Of the two maids who attend me one is an elderly woman. The other is in her thirties. They are good women and very respectful. They make it a point to touch their heads to my feet every morning.' Bharat's heart sank. Where was Bhumisuta then? Why was she not working in the puja room as she had done in the house of the Singhas? Had the king made her his mistress already?

The thought depressed Bharat so much that he could barely eat or sleep for the next few days. And so, when Jadugopal invited him to visit his maternal uncle's estate in Krishnanagar he accepted with alacrity. He needed a change badly. If he continued brooding over Bhumisuta's fate any more he would go mad.

'Look here, Bharat,' Jadugopal eyed him sternly on their way to the station. 'If you think I'm going to pay for your ticket you're mistaken. And I'm not paying for your cigarettes either. And if you think you'll be treated like a royal guest in my grandmother's house—you can think again. You'll get your meals of course—gram and ginger for breakfast and rice and dal twice a day. Don't expect delicacies. My grandmother is an old lady and is often confined to bed. When that happens you'll have to lend a hand with the cooking.'

'I'll do that,' Bharat said in a relieved voice. 'The fact is that the thought of being treated as a royal guest gives me the shivers.'

All this was a joke as Bharat realized the moment he stepped out of the carriage which had been sent to the station. Looking up he saw a huge mansion, somewhat old and decayed, but still grand enough to compel respect. The two friends looked at each other and laughed as they were ushered in by the servants of which there seemed to be plenty.

After a wash the boys settled down to eat their breakfast which was not gram and ginger by any means. Two huge thalas piled with hot luchis, fried vegetables and a variety of sweetmeats were set before them together with tall glasses of milk—thick and sweet as kheer.

'Let's go see my grandmother,' Jadugopal said when the meal was over. 'She's a tough old lady and sharper even than her lawyer husband was. Don't get into an argument with her. You'll be sure to lose.' The two friends walked up the wide staircase and crossing innumerable wings and galleries, came to the old mistress' apartment. Walking in they found a tiny, dainty looking old lady sitting very upright on a red velvet chair shaped like a throne. Her hair was snow white and so was her sari. Her skin was the colour of old ivory. But despite her fragility there was something imperious and indomitable about her bearing. 'Who's that?' she called in a voice of command the moment the boys stepped into her room. 'It's I—Jadu,' Jadugopal answered coming forward, 'Didn't Nayeb Moshai tell you I was coming?'

'Leave us Saro,' the old lady ordered the maid who sat on the floor pressing her feet. Then, without moving her head, she said, 'Come child,' and clasped Jadugopal to her breast. Bharat, who stood at the door watching the scene, realized with a shock that she was blind. 'I've brought a friend with me Dimma,' Jadugopal said after his grandmother had covered his face with kisses. 'We have come here to study. The exams are drawing near and we need peace and quiet. Calcutta life is too hectic. Come Bharat.' Bharat advanced and stooped to touch her feet. But she withdrew them hastily saying, 'I've just had my bath. I don't care to be touched by a non-Brahmin. What caste are you?'

'Dimma!' Jadugopal exclaimed. 'You can't talk to my friend like that!'

'Mind your tongue,' the old lady said sharply. 'Who are you to tell me what I can or cannot do? You live the way you like. Do I interfere? Why should you interfere with me?' Then, addressing Bharat, she repeated her question, 'What caste are you?'

Bharat didn't know what to say. If he went by the caste of his natural father he was a Kshatriya. There was no such caste in the Bengali order. Besides, he did not wish to carry the burden of his relationship with the Maharaja of Tripura any longer. 'I have no caste,' he answered firmly. 'I'm a human being.'

'That's funny,' the old lady chuckled. 'You were born of human parents, weren't you? Or did you drop from the sky?'

'Dimma!' Jadugopal broke in impatiently.

'Quiet,' the old lady said sharply then addressing Bharat she continued, 'Come forward Bharat. You say you're human. Let me check if that is true. For all I know you may be a monkey.' Though thoroughly startled Bharat obeyed. The old lady put out her hand and drew him to her. Stroking his face and head lovingly she murmured, 'Listen son. All men are not human beings. Not even all Brahmins. You claim that you are. May you succeed in asserting this claim all your life. My blessings are with you.' Then, addressing her grandson, she said sternly though not without an undertone of indulgence. 'As for you and your big talk! If you're against caste distinctions why are you marrying a Brahmin girl? If you practised what you preach you would have brought home an untouchable. Then I would have been truly impressed.' Suddenly, before Jadugopal could react, she waved a tiny hand in dismissal. 'Go now,' she said imperiously, 'and send Saro to me. I feel a little tired.'

On their way out of the room Jadugopal glanced at Bharat's bewildered face and laughed, 'My grandmother enjoyed a little joke at your expense. She's like that.' Then, sobering down, he continued, 'She's wonderful! Do you know that her only son was Vidyasagar's follower and was one of the first to marry a widow? My grandmother accepted her daughter-in-law without the slightest fuss and stood firm when her action was criticized and she was ostracized by her family and friends. She's a tower of strength. Do you know that she runs three estates singlehanded? Even after she lost both eyes after an attack of small pox? Nothing can break her. She's invincible!'

That evening the two friends went for a walk. 'Look Bharat,' Jadugopal said. 'There was an intention behind my bringing you here. Of all our classmates I fear you most as competitor. I want to come out of this examination right on top. Ramkamal is not a threat anymore. He keeps thinking of his new bride and sneaks off to Bardhaman whenever he gets a chance. Neither is Dwarika. He is too busy looking for ways to spend his new-found wealth to attend to his studies. Bimalendu is a slogger but he lacks imagination. The only one left is you—'

'Why do you *have* to come out on top?' Bharat smiled at his friend. 'Not that you need fear any competition from me.'

'I wish to go to England to study at the bar. I have to return a barrister.'

'You don't need to be first for that. All you need is money of which you have plenty. And why do you *have* to be barrister anyway?'

'Hmph!' Jadugopal cleared his throat embarrassedly. 'The truth is—I'm getting married as you probably know.'

'Yes. A Thakur girl I believe.'

'It has been one of my cherished dreams to marry a girl from the house of Jorasanko. You haven't seen them. They are as talented as they are beautiful. It's the most wonderful luck that the matchmaker brought the proposal. Baba has agreed and—'

'I understand. The Thakurs look for barristers and ICS officers for their girls. That is why you have to go to England to study at the Bar. Was it one of their conditions?'

'Oh no. They're quite happy with me as I am. I shall soon be a graduate from Presidency College and I shall inherit all my grandfather's property. In fact they are pressing me for an early marriage. But I've said I shall marry only on returning from England. All my other brothers-in-law are high officials. I shall not be content to remain a mere country gentleman.'

'Have you seen the girl?'

'Only once. She acted in a play they performed at Swarnakumari Devi's daughter's wedding. I have a photograph though.'

'I still don't understand why you have to top in the examination.'

'I want to carry the insignia all my life. Another one of my cherished dreams is to step off the ship at the port of London to the cries of "He's here! He's here! The first class first from Presidency College, Calcutta. Welcome! Welcome!" The two friends laughed gaily. By this time they had reached the river. Jadugopal made his way to a boat tied to a tree and loosened the rope.

'Let's go for a ride—shall we?' he said.

'Whose boat is this?'

'It belongs to the estate. The boatman should be around somewhere. But we don't need him. I'll take you myself.'

It was the month of Asadh and the sky was dark with monsoon cloud. A sweet wind blew and the boat skimmed smoothly over the water which was much clearer here than in Calcutta. Handling the oars lightly and easily Jadugopal sang:

'*Dil dariyar majhé dekhlam aajab karkhana*
Déhér majhé barhi aachhé
Sei barhi te chor legechhe
Chhoi jana té sindh kétechhé
Churi karé ek jana'

'Did you make this up?' Bharat asked curiously. He knew Jadugopal wrote poetry from time to time and composed songs extempore.

'Don't you know anything?' Jadugopal exclaimed. 'This is a song by Lalan Fakir. I'll take you to his aakhra one day. He has many followers both Hindu and Muslim. Lalan doesn't preach or dole out instruction. He just sings one song after another. And

---

* I looked into the sea of my heart
   And saw a queer workshop
   A house within the body
   Six burglars had broken into it
   But only one was doing the stealing

285

though he doesn't know one letter from another his songs are brilliant compositions. The man is truly gifted.'

Chattering of this and that the two friends reached the ghat at Nabadweep. Looking around him Bharat felt overwhelmed with the realization that he had come to the spot where Chaitanya Mahaprabhu was born. It was here, perhaps at this very ghat, that he had romped and played with boys of his own age, teased the maidens and thumbed his nose at the curses of the old crones. Tying the boat to a banyan tree so ancient that the aerial roots hanging from it shrouded it like a curtain, the two friends walked up a little knoll on top of which stood a thatched hut with a cow tethered to a tamarind tree by its side. Outside the hut a man sat oiling himself in the sun.

'Horu Jetha!' Jadugopal called out, 'How have you been?'

'Who is it?' The man crinkled his eyes against the sun, then recognizing Jadu, smiled a welcome. 'Oh! It's you—Jadu. When did you come from Calcutta? Is Ma Thakrun well?'

They spoke for some minutes and then Jadugopal led his friend back to the boat. Glancing at his companion's face Bharat was surprised to see his brow furrowed as if in thought and his nose wrinkled in distaste. Then, before he could ask him the reason, Jadugopal supplied it. 'The man's a scoundrel,' he cried angrily. 'Worse than a murderer. He deserves death by hanging.'

'Why?' Bharat was startled by the passion in Jadu's voice, 'What has he done?'

There was no answer. Jadu seemed to be wrestling with his thoughts. 'Haramohan was the performing priest in my grandmother's house,' he said after a few minutes. 'He had a daughter of about seven or eight whom he would bring with him quite often. She was a beautiful girl and to hear her talk was like listening to music. But she had strange spells from time to time. She would stop still wherever she was and, fixing her eyes on a tree or a stretch of water, she would mutter to herself. Many of the things she said at those times actually came to pass. People said she wasn't quite right in the head. But that wasn't true—as I realize now. The truth is that she had a lot more imagination and insight than ordinary people. My grandmother recognized this quality in her. She wanted to keep her in the house and give her an education. But Haramohan would not allow it. He believed his daughter to be abnormal and was anxious to give her away in marriage before people found out. Dwarika used to come up here with me on holidays the way you've come this time. On one of his visits he saw the girl. She was eleven years old at the time and a radiant beauty. Dwarika was so charmed he wanted to marry her but Haramohan rejected his offer.'

'Dwarika wanted to marry her!' Bharat exclaimed. 'Why didn't her father agree?'

'He had promised her to an old man who held a mortgage on some of his property. Dwarika was a poor boy then. Haramohan turned down his request on the pretext that he was a Bhanga Kulin and therefore unfit to wed his daughter.' Jadugopal shook his head sadly and went on, 'The girl's name was Basanti. "Basi," I said to her one day, "You can look into the future. You've said so many things that have actually come to pass. Can you see what's before you? Do you think you'll be happy?" Basanti stood still at my words. Her eyes, fixed on a clump of marigolds, glazed over. "I shall float away over the river," she murmured. "I shall be carried from this Ganga to another Ganga—wider, fuller and more turbulent . . ." And that is exactly what happened. The old man died within two years of the marriage. You know how widows are treated in this country. Particularly when they are young and beautiful. They are banished to Kashi or they fall victim to human predators who use them for a time then abandon them when the charm wears off. Basi passed through several hands before she ended up in the red light area of Calcutta—a city by the bank of a wider, fuller, more turbulent Ganga!'

'Why didn't you stop the marriage?'

'How could I? There's no law in the country that punishes a father for victimizing his daughter. You know why I went there today? I wanted to tell him that his daughter is a prostitute in Hadhkatar Gali. I wanted to see the look on his face. But, somehow, I couldn't bring myself to do it.' Bharat had been staring at Jadugopal all this while. Now he asked in a wondering voice. 'Is her real name Basantamanjari?' Then, when Jadugopal nodded in affirmation, he murmured. 'Dwarika keeps her—in a house in Hadhkatar Gali. Did you know that Jadu?'

'Yes,' Jadugopal murmured. 'He took you with him one night. I know that too. Isn't it a pity, Bharat, that they've come

287

together at last but only in sin?'

'Can't they marry? Even now?'

'How can they?'

That evening Bharat took a decision. He would return to Calcutta as soon as he could. He had to get back to Bhumisuta. She would suffer the same fate as Basantamanjari if he didn't save her from the king's clutches. Dwarika had failed Basantamanjari. But Bharat wouldn't fail Bhumisuta.

Chapter XXXV

Swarnakumari Devi had taken charge of *Bharati* and changed its entire character. She had a strong personality and acted on her own inclinations dismissing the advice of others. The immediate effect of the journal passing from Jyotirindra's hands to hers was a marked decline in Robi's contributions. Robi sensed, instinctively, that his sister did not think much of his creative abilities. At the literary meetings held in her house, which Robi attended from time to time, he found himself at the periphery. Swarnakumari dominated the scene and occupied the position of honour.

Swarnakumari's house was permeated with the breath not only of literature but of politics. Her husband Janakinath Ghoshal was an enthusiastic supporter of all his wife's cultural endeavours but his own inclination was towards politics. The term Indian National Congress was being bandied about more and more but few knew precisely what it was or how it had come into being. Janakinath hadn't enrolled himself as member but he had attended its first meeting in Bombay quite recently.

The unrest following Surendranath Bandopadhyay's arrest hadn't quite died down and the student community was straining at the leash to become part of a larger movement. Their heroes, Surendranath and Anandamohan Bosu, were travelling extensively all over India trying to bring the people together. Meeting leaders of various parties in the different provinces they endeavoured to integrate them into a homogeneous whole. The Indian Association, whose members came from the upper middle class and from the intellectual community of Calcutta, was drawn in. There were two other associations—the British Indian Association of the industrialists and zamindars of Calcutta and the Central Muhammedan Association of the Muslims. Surendranath realized that a sense of nationalization could be aroused in his countrymen only if all these groups could be merged and given a common identity. It was thus that the Indian

National Congress was formed and two meetings had already been held—one in Bombay and the other in Poona.

Robi gathered all this information from his brother-in-law but it left him unimpressed. It seemed to him that the leaders of the Congress were only interested in displaying their superior English education in fiery speeches. They were not addressing themselves to the real problems of the country. The pleas of the Congress leaders for an extension of the age limit for the Civil Service Examination and their insistence that a centre be opened in India seemed, to Robi, to be ridiculously out of context. These advantages, if acquired would benefit only the tiniest fraction of the nation. What use were they to the common man? He hated the way his countrymen were always begging the rulers for something or the other. When would they acquire some self respect?

The great educationist and reformer of yesteryears Ishwarchandra Vidyasagar was of the same opinion. Soon after the party was founded some Congress leaders had requested him to join them. He had given them a patient hearing then asked with his usual candour, '*Bapu hé*! Are you prepared to cross swords with the British for the independence of your country?' The men had glanced at one another in dismay. What kind of traitorous talk was this? Who had said anything about independence and crossing swords? Smiling at their discomfiture Vidyasagar had said, 'Leave me out of it then and do what you have to do.' When the men had left he had muttered to himself disdainfully, 'Congress! Leaders of the nation! Will big talk and fiery gestures save the country? What good is politics in a land where thousands starve to death every day?'

Robi, of course, was not in favour of taking up arms against the British. He knew that Indians could never do what the Irish were doing. Aggression, of any kind, went against the grain of the Indian people. What they needed was a sense of self respect and that could only be obtained through the achievements of some of their own people. Robi was a writer. It was his duty to address himself to his writing with all the devotion he was capable of. And, if in the process, it became good enough to instil a sense of pride in his countrymen it would be a job well done.

But, travelling through the small towns and villages of Bengal as he was doing quite extensively as secretary of the Brahmo Samaj, Robi's views were changing. Everywhere he went he found his countrymen reeling under the pressure of poverty and ignorance. Famines were endemic in the country. Only a short while ago the districts of Birbhum and Bankura were devastated by a terrible famine. Passing through these areas Robi's heart was wrenched with pain. He realized, as never before, that it was not enough to write about the sufferings of the poor. Action was necessary. And he tried to do all he could. He offered to settle the famine ridden in the newly-acquired estate of the Thakurs in Sunderban. Each family would be given a plot of land and farming implements free of cost. Their housing would also be taken care of. But the Bengalis are a peculiar race. They would rather bite the dust of their ancestral villages and stare death in the face than move out and start a new and better life. Rani Swarnamayee Devi had the same experience as Robi. Moved by the sufferings of the peasants of Birbhum she opened public kitchens in her state of Kasimbazar and kept them in readiness to feed up to two thousand people a day. But hardly anyone came. And this was after travelling expenses had been offered them by the Rani. Looking on their starved, pinched faces and hearing their repeated pleas for 'a little rice water' Robi understood, as never before, what a terrible opponent hunger was. Unlike other forms of suffering which rendered a man finer and stronger, hunger devastated him, robbing him of his humanity and bringing him down to the level of an insect. He saw another thing for the first time—the amount of food that was wasted in households such as his. The sight of mounds of rice and vegetables and baskets full of luchi being thrown out on the streets after a wedding or thread ceremony was so common in Calcutta that it made not even a dent on anyone's conscience. It appalled Robi to think that the same people who lived lives of such opulence and indulgence were the ones who were weeping copious tears on the fate of the poor and deprived. Politics was such a dirty game and bred hypocrites so easily!

After his near banishment from the realms of *Bharati* by his sister, Robi directed all his energies on *Balak*—a periodical started by Gyanadanandini Devi. Along with the task of contributing a large member of articles a lot of the editorial responsibility also passed into his hands. Robi enjoyed going to Gyanadanandini's house. His niece Bibi loved him deeply and couldn't pass a single day without seeing her Robi Ka. She had turned thirteen now and was growing lovelier and lovelier every day. She was a meritorious student too and had a fine singing voice. She still wore skirts at times and behaved like a child particularly with Robi. She had a number of nicknames for him of which one was Buji. She would fling her arms around him the moment he arrived with cries of 'Buji! Buji! Where have you been all this time?'

Of late Robi had started taking her along with him to his literary meetings. And, wherever she went, Bibi became the cynosure of all eyes. People stared, fascinated, at her dazzling beauty, grace and elegance. The girls from the house of Jorasanko were renowned for their beauty and charm but this one seemed to outstrip them all. Unlike others from the first families of Calcutta, the Thakur girls were not being given away in marriage before they attained puberty. Swarnakumari Devi's daughter had passed her Entrance but her parents weren't even thinking of a suitable match. Another of Robi's neices, Pratibha, a girl of extraordinary beauty and talent, was twenty and still unwed. Robi had turned matchmaker these days. He wanted his friend the barrister Ashu Choudhury to marry her.

Bibi and Mrinalini were of the same age but Mrinalini was no companion to Robi. She was shy and retiring by nature and preferred staying within the confines of her father-in-law's house to going out with her husband. In consequence, she was totally unknown outside the family. But Robi's nights with her were tender and pleasant and between them Bibi and Mrinalini kept Robi floating on a sea of bliss. Kadambari's memory had almost faded, only appearing in fits and starts in his poetry.

One night Robi had a strange dream. He had been returning by train from Deoghar where he had gone on a visit to his father's closest friend Rajnarayan Bosu. The latter had been seriously ill and it was a duty visit. But Robi had enjoyed his few days in Deoghar. His host was a charming old man and had entertained Robi with lively stories about the old days. Michael Madhusudhan Datta had been a class friend of Rajnarayan Bosu's in Hindu College and, although Robi did not think much of Michael's poetry, he enjoyed listening to the anecdotes of which the old man had a goodly stock. 'Madhu had a very dark complexion,' Rajnarayan said wagging his snowy beard, 'and a voice that cracked easily. If anyone referred to the fact he invariably said, " I may be a voiceless cuckoo but at least I'm not a white duck and I don't quack." Madhu had turned native in his old age. If anybody, from old habit, called him *Saheb* he said, "*Ohé* I happen to have a mirror in my house and I can see my colour for myself. I'm not a saheb and will never become one except perhaps in the hereafter."'

Seeing that his host's condition had improved considerably, Robi left Deoghar and returned to Calcutta. After getting into the train he climbed up to his upper berth in a second class compartment and prepared to go to sleep. But one of the lamps was right above his head and shone uncomfortably into his eyes. Putting out a hand he clicked the cover in place. There was an immediate reaction from some Anglo-Indian passengers in the compartment. They had been drinking all this while and talking in loud excited voices. Now one of them strode purposefully up to the lamp and, glaring balefully at Robi, clicked the cover open. The others rose to their feet and started flexing their muscles. Robi knew that they were getting ready for a fight. Sun-heated sand, he thought whimsically, was hotter than the sun itself. Robi returned the man's stare for a few seconds then turned his eyes away. He wanted to blot the man's face from his consciousness; wipe out the ugly compartment in which he was trapped with these drunken beasts. He shut his eyes and tried to sleep but sleep would not come. He tried to think of a plot for a story. Mental exercise of this kind always soothed his nerves and calmed his spirit. But that night his mind was in a whirl and would not focus on anything. He tossed and turned on his bunk for some hours then drifted into a fitful slumber. And, then, he dreamed a strange dream. He saw a man standing outside a temple holding a little girl by the hand. They were both staring at a stream of dark fluid trickling from the door of the temple down to the steps where they stood.

Suddenly the girl gave an agonized cry, 'It's blood! Blood!' The man tried to pull her away but she kept on crying in a frightened voice, 'But it's blood! It's blood!' Robi woke up with a

293

start. What was the meaning of this dream? He suddenly remembered something he had seen many years ago. He had been passing by the Kali temple at Thanthan. A goat had been slaughtered before the goddess and the blood was pouring out, over the threshold and on to the steps. Even as Robi watched in horror a low-caste woman bent down in reverence and, dipping her forefinger in the sacrificial blood, marked her infant's forehead with it. Robi shivered as he remembered the scene.

Returning to Calcutta Robi started writing *Rajarshi*, a historical novel depicting the life and times of Maharaja Gobindamanikya of the royal dynasty of Tripura. *Rajarshi* started appearing in serial form in *Balak*.

One day Gyanadanandini said to him, 'I've decided to put an end to Mrinalini's education. There's no sense in wasting money on her fees.' Robi felt somewhat peeved. 'Why?' he asked defensively. He knew Mrinalini was not very keen on her studies. But surely that was no reason for putting an end to them. One had to go on trying. 'It's better for her to stay at home,' Gyanadanandini laughed and flashed her eyes at her brother-in-law. 'She shouldn't move about too much in her present condition. What if she feels unwell in school?'

'Feels unwell!' Robi exclaimed, startled. 'Why, what is wrong with her?'

'As if you don't know.' Gyanadanandini laughed once again.

'I don't,' Robi said. There was a trace of anxiety in his voice. 'I really don't. No one told me she was ill.'

'What an innocent little boy he is!' Gyanadanandini leaned forward and pinched Robi's cheeks. 'You're about to become a father. Don't you understand?' Seeing the blood rush to Robi's face in embarassment she added kindly, 'Take your wife away somewhere for a change of air Robi. It will do her good.'

But fate was against poor Mrinalini. Before Robi could make any plans news came from Bombay that his father was seriously ill. Debendranath had been spending the last few years either in the hills or by the sea. Looking out of the window from his sick bed he had hoped that this illness would be his last and that his soul would float away over the vast expanse of water to be merged with the Eternal and the Infinite. But that was not to be. Robi arrived at his father's Bandra residence to find him considerably better and after a few days Debendranath left for Calcutta. Robi did not accompany him. Instead, he accepted his brother Satyendranath's invitation to spend a few days in Nasik where the latter was posted.

Once in Nasik he felt overwhelmed with remorse. Why hadn't he thought of bringing Mrinalini? Mrinalini was nurturing his unborn child with her life blood. Who knew what she was going through? Poor girl! She asked for nothing and received nothing. He had never taken her out with him except for one brief visit to Sholapur where Satyendranath had been posted. And this time he had come away in such a hurry that he hadn't even exchanged a few words with her before leaving Calcutta. The more he thought of his young wife the more he missed her. He remembered their days together in Sholapur. They had been alone for hours together, every day, for the first time and it was there, in Sholapur, that they had consummated their marriage. It had been a wild rainy afternoon and they had loved each other with all the frenzy and passion of youth. Shutting his eyes he could still feel her warm young body throbbing against his.

Taking up his pen he wrote:
Cast off your garment!
Strip the veil away from your face
Wear only the beauty of your nakedness.

Robi had never written such words before but now they came to him easily.
Girl Goddess!
Wrap yourself in moonbeams
Through whose clear light is visible
The unfolding lotus of your corporeal form.

Chapter XXXVI

The sunshine streaming into the room awoke Shashibhushan. Opening his eyes with difficulty he discovered the figure of a young woman framed against a square of white light which was a window. It was only when she moved away to the next and proceeded to open it that he saw it was Bhumisuta. Shashibhushan was puzzled. Why was Bhumisuta opening his windows? He had never seen her doing so before. And then he remembered that he always slept with his windows wide open. He wondered who had closed them and why.

After Bhumisuta had left the room he rose from his bed and walked over to the window. The trees and grass outside were wet and the air was cool and moist. He realized what had happened. A shower of rain had come while he slept and someone had closed the windows to keep out the gusts of wind and rain. Who was that someone? Bhumisuta?

Shashibhushan went back to his bed. He could do with some more sleep. The Maharaja had invited some singers last night and the performance had gone on till the small hours. The Maharaja loved music and could listen to it for several days and nights at a stretch. But Shashibhushan had started dozing off soon after midnight. Laying his head once again on the pillow he thought, 'The Maharaja will rest all day. There'll be nothing for me to do. I'll go back to sleep.'

At this moment Bhumisuta entered the room bearing a tray on which was placed a cup of tea with a couple of biscuits in the saucer, and half a glass of lime water. Shashibhushan drank lime water before his tea every morning. It helped to clear the bowels. Putting the tray down on a small table Bhumisuta said softly, 'Your bath water is ready. Shall I tell them to send it in?'

'There's no hurry,' Shashibhushan answered, 'I wish to sleep a little longer.' Bhumisuta hesitated a little. 'You have an appointment with the lawyer at eleven,' she murmured, her eyes on the floor, 'It's nearly ten o clock.' Shashibhushan sat up in astonishment. It was true. There was an important case pending in the High Court and Radharaman had sent an urgent message to him to meet the lawyer. How could he have forgotten?

Shashibhushan had a hurried bath and sat down to his breakfast of luchi and mohanbhog which Bhumisuta served to him, piping hot from the kitchen. He thought of how useful she was to him. Her service was perfection itself. She had only one defect. She would not communicate. She answered his questions with brief nods or at most a few words. He had not an inkling of what went on in that pretty head. And she was stubborn. The way she was putting off the king was becoming acutely embarrassing.

The queen was getting bored with Calcutta and was urging her husband to return to Tripura. The king, too, had had enough of the premier city, it seemed. He had sent for Shashibhushan only yesterday and asked him to make arrangements for their return to Agartala. And he hadn't forgotten Bhumisuta. 'I wish to take the girl with me,' he had said. 'She's been ailing here and a change of place will do her good. I'll send her to Jompui for a few days. The keen, bracing mountain air will revive her—' Shashibhushan looked at the door behind which Bhumisuta stood in readiness to serve him whatever he needed. 'Get ready to leave for Tripura,' he said. 'The king will be leaving in a few days and wishes to take you with him.' Then, without waiting for a reply, he rose and, gathering his papers, left the room.

In the carriage, on his way to the High Court, Shashibhushan felt a trifle uneasy. The man he was about to meet was a pukka saheb named Umeshchandra Bandopadhyay popularly known as WC Bonnerjee. Would Shashibhushan's knowledge of the English language and English etiquette stand the test of WC Bonnerjee's exacting standards? He had a reputation for socializing only with Englishmen and speaking nothing but English. Yet, Shashibhushan knew for a fact that though his wife had converted to Christianity, he hadn't. He was also an ardent champion of the country's causes and had chaired the first meeting of the Indian National Congress in Bombay.

Entering Umeshchandra's chamber Shashibhushan saw him sitting at a table with four or five gentlemen facing him. He was a man in his early forties and wore a three-piece suit and rimless glasses. His hair was parted in the middle and combed neatly down the sides. He appeared to be amused by what was being said for a little smile quivered about his mouth. Shashibhushan recognized two of the other gentlemen. One was Maharshi Debendranath's son-in-law Janakinath Ghoshal and the other was the lawyer Atulprasad Sen.

The conversation, as he realized in a few minutes, centred around a marriage that had recently taken place in Calcutta. A young man named Tejeshchandra Ganguly, scion of a Kulin Brahmin family and a doctor with a medical degree from England, had married a Shudra nurse. A large section of society viewed this marriage as a shocking aberration and some of the gentlemen present were voicing the same opinion. But Janakinath Ghoshal seemed to be holding a staunch brief for the errant lovers.

'Do you suppose for a moment,' one of the gentlemen present questioned derisively, 'that this man Ganguly married a Shudra in order to set an example and thereby help to remove caste prejudices? Nothing of the kind. He was in love with the woman and he married her to legitimize their shameful affair.'

'What is so shameful about it?' Janakinath took him up. 'Europeans fall in love and marry after a period of courtship.'

'This is not Europe,' another man cut in sharply. 'This is India. If men and women are allowed to mix freely our society will disintegrate and our moral values will be devastated.' Everyone burst one laughing. Janakinath controlled himself with an effort and said, 'We are not keeping our girls confined to the zenana anymore. We're sending them out to get an education. How can we prevent them from meeting men? We have to move with the times.'

Surprising Shashibhushan considerably, Umeshchandra Bandopadhyay spoke for the first time in flawless Bengali. 'I've been hearing both sides of the debate for some time. And, now, I have a question for anyone who chooses to answer. In which caste category do the memsahebs belong? Our men have been bringing mem wives to this country for years now. I've heard no public outcry against them. Michael Madhusudan Datta married not one but two European ladies. But no one thought of treating him as an outcaste. Some of the leading men of Hindu society have wined and dined with him. Why all this fuss about a

Shudra?'

'Hear! Hear!' Janakinath clapped his hands in applause, 'Excellent verdict! All's fair in love!' The gentleman who had been arguing shook his head smiling, 'We don't accept it. Umeshchandra is not a judge and delivering a verdict does not fall within his powers. He can ask questions—as many as he likes.'

After the gentlemen had left Umeshchandra turned his attention to Shashibhushan and proceeded to brief himself about the case which the Maharaja had filed against a British company. It was a complicated case concerning the lease of one of the king's tea gardens.

Returning home Shashibhushan changed his clothes and waited for Bhumisuta to bring him something to eat. He usually had a small snack at this hour and Bhumisuta served it to him with her own hands. He waited for half an hour but she didn't come. Perhaps she was unaware that he had returned. He went to the door and called, 'Bhumi! Bhumi!' but there was no response. Shashibhushan was puzzled. This was quite unlike her. Was she unwell? Really unwell this time? He came down the steps and stood outside her door. One of the panels was open and he could see the scene within. Rani Monomohini sat on the bare floor with her back to the wall and her legs stretched out in front. She had something in her hand which looked like tamarind pulp. From time to time she put out a little pink tongue and licked at it. Bhumisuta knelt in front of her. She was beating a pair of cymbals and singing softly. Shashibhushan knew that spying on the Maharani was the height of insolence but he couldn't move from his place. It drew him like a magnet. Listening to the sweet voice for a while, he realized that Bhumisuta was singing one line over and over again as if she was teaching it to Monomohini.

With a tremendous effort Shashibhushan wrenched himself away and came back to his room. A new fear assailed him. Monomohini had seen Bhumisuta and would tell the king that there was nothing wrong with her. The king would call Shashibhushan and demand an explanation. Why had Bhumisuta exposed herself to the queen? Was she, after all, keen to go to Tripura? To become the king's mistress? The thought was unbearable—though he did not know why.

Bhumisuta came in after a while. She had a plate of

sweetmeats in one hand and a glass of water in the other. Glancing at the dish Shashibhushan saw his favourite sesame balls and coconut half moons. 'Wait,' Shashibhushan commanded as, placing them on a small table, Bhumisuta proceeded to leave the room. Bhumisuta turned around and looked enquiringly as Shashibhushan's eyes raked her form. What an unusual way she had of wearing her sari! The upper half was wound tightly over her bare breasts and the lower half fell halfway between her knees and ankles. Her hair was twisted into a knot which swung loosely on the nape of her neck. Her eyes had the soft, moist look of one in a dream. 'Get ready to go to Tripura,' he said though that had not been his intention a moment ago. Then, seeing the look of surprise in her eyes, he added desperately, 'You will need some saris. The Maharaja likes Murshidabad silk. I shall buy some and you can pick out what you like.'

'I don't need any saris and I'm not going to Tripura.'

Shashibhushan's heart gave a bound of relief but he knitted his brows and said in a stern voice, 'The queen knows there is nothing wrong with you. What excuse can you give now? Don't you realize that I'll have to answer to the king for the lies I've been telling?'

'I won't go to Tripura. The Maharaja needs someone to sing Vaishnav *padavalis* to him every night. I'm teaching the queen a few songs. That will serve the purpose.'

Shashibhushan burst out laughing. What a silly girl she was! Didn't she realize that the king wanted her? He wanted *her* sweet voice to put him to sleep—not Monomohini's. Besides, Monomohini couldn't sing to save her life. She had no interest in learning either. He remembered how Monomohini had sat licking at her tamarind pulp with noises of relish all the time Bhumisuta was trying to teach her. Sobering down in a few moments he said gently, 'The king wants you and no one's word is above the king's. He can take you away by force and no one can stop him. Even if he doesn't, what will became of you? You can't stay here after flouting his orders and I can't give you my protection. Where will you go?'

'I don't know,' Bhumisuta sighed and left the room.

Watching her slender form move away Shashibhushan

300

suddenly remembered the time he had fallen down the stairs. It was her face his eyes had beheld before darkness had overtaken them. And then, that night when in the throes of a deadly disease, he had whispered through his cracked lips, 'Water! Water!' it was she who had heard. It was she who had come to him. The scene swam before his eyes. A face, lovelier than a flower, had hung above his. He had seen tender concern in the long dark eyes and a gentle hand had held the water to his lips. He sat up with a start. What had he been about to do? He had been about to give away a jewel like Bhumisuta to a lecher and a tyrant who would have his fill of her, than toss her away like a soiled rag, without a moment's hesitation. No, never! He wouldn't, he couldn't allow it—he would rather change the course of his own life. And, then, an idea struck him so suddenly that his head started reeling. He would marry Bhumisuta.

There would be an uproar. He knew that his family would oppose it and so would his friends. But, after listening to the conversation in the lawyer's chamber that morning, he didn't care. He would have the support of men far superior to the carpers. He would resign from the king's service. He didn't need the money. He wouldn't stay with his brothers either. He would take up a house somewhere and give Bhumisuta the full status of a wife. He felt so elated with his new idea that he had to share it with Bhumisuta that instant. Rushing out of the room he accosted her on the stairs, 'You don't have to go to Tripura Bhumisuta,' he burst out, 'You don't have to do anything you don't like. I'll make you mine. I'll leave my job here and we'll go away together—' Bhumisuta's face grew pale and her eyes widened in fear. She didn't know what to make of this sudden change in Shashibhushan. But Shashibhushan noticed nothing. Bursting with excitement he went on outlining his plans to her, 'We'll have a registered marriage which is perfectly legal and then we'll move to our own house. We could stay in Chandannagar. Or, if you prefer it, we could move to Cuttack or Puri.' Still Bhumisuta did not speak. Carried along on the tide of his own elation Shashibhushan took no notice. 'Ahh!' he breathed deeply. 'Freedom! Freedom at last! I've been only half a man Bhumi. My life has been arid, barren—without the love of a good woman. But now everything will change. You'll be my queen; my only love. Flowers will bloom on these dead branches. Why don't you speak Bhumi?'

Bhumisuta sat down on the steps and covered her face with her hands. Tears trickled through her fingers and fell to the floor.

The next morning Shashibhushan woke up earlier than usual. A strange restlessness seized him. He had to see Bhumisuta at once. There was so much to do and so little time. Walking over to the stair landing he called out her name and waited, in a fever of impatience, till she came. He noted, with surprise, that she did not look her usual self. She hadn't bathed and her uncombed hair hung in tangled strands over her back. Her sari was crumpled and the end of it was pulled carelessly over her shoulders. He had never seen her like this. Looking down on the pale unhappy face raised to his, Shashibhushan felt overwhelmed with regret. She had done so much for him but he had given her nothing in return. He had never even said a kind word. All he had done was try to push her into the arms of a man she loathed. Vowing that he would make up to her for all his sins of omission and commission he said gently, 'Bring in the tea. I have something to say to you.'

His tea arrived shortly afterwards but it was brought in by a middle-aged serving maid called Sushila. Shashibhushan detested her. Her teeth were black from the *mishi* she rubbed into them all the time and her hair crawled with lice. 'Why? Where is Bhumisuta?' he asked sharply resisting the impulse to dash the tray to the ground. He wondered what had happened. Why had Bhumisuta ignored his call? 'She's just gone for her bath,' the woman replied and went on with her usual garrulity, 'There's something wrong with her, Babu. She didn't sleep a wink the whole night. Everytime I opened my eyes I saw her sitting with her back to the wall crying as if her heart would break. I asked her if she had a stomach ache but she didn't reply.' A cloud came over Shashibhushan's face. Was Bhumisuta ill? She certainly hadn't looked her usual neat, serene self. Or could it be that she was offended by what he had proposed? Why should she be offended? He had offered her marriage. She, who was a slave, would be elevated to the status of a daughter-in-law of the Singhas. Her children would carry the family name. Was he too old? Shashibhushan rose and walked over to a mirror hanging on the wall. The face that looked back was rugged but not unpleasant.

302

There was a little grey at the temples but the hair was still strong and thick. And, though considerably older than Bhumisuta, he was not too old. Men, much older than him, took second or third wives.

An hour or so later Bhumisuta came into the room with his breakfast. She was freshly bathed and her long hair, dripping water, hung down her back. She looked stark and ascetic in a plain white sari. Shashibhushan saw that her feet had no vermilion and the sandalpaste was missing from her forehead. Her eyes had the resigned melancholy look of a girl widow. 'I hear you've been crying all night,' Shashibhushan said tenderly, 'Is anything wrong? Do you feel unwell?' Bhumisuta shook her head. 'Why were you crying then?' Shashibhushan persisted, 'Has anyone said anything to hurt you?' Bhumisuta shook her head again and said, 'I'll fetch you some water.' But Shashibhushan stopped her with a gesture. 'I don't need water,' he said, 'Sit down. I need to talk to you.' Bhumisuta moved some distance away and sat on the floor. 'No. Not on the floor,' Shashibhushan commanded. 'Come and sit here in this chair.' Bhumisuta rose and came to the chair but did not sit down. She stood behind it, her eyes on the ground. 'I don't understand you,' Shashibhushan said, 'I wish to give you my name and status. But the prospect seems to make you unhappy. Why? No, silence will not do. You'll have to answer me.'

'I'm not worthy of your offer.'

'Who says so? You're more than worthy. You're peerless among women. Tell me Bhumisuta, don't you trust me? Do you think I'm trying to deceive you? That I have some evil intention?'

'No. You're great and noble—'

'Then why do you not respond to my call?' The words burst from Shashibhushan like a cry of agony. 'Why? Why? I love you and desire you as I've never desired a woman. I want you for my life companion. These bonds of slavery are not for you.'

Bhumisuta trembled but did not speak. Throwing all caution to the winds Shashibhushan rushed forward and grasped her hand. Bhumisuta gave a little cry and shook it off. Then, running to the other end of the room, she cowered against the wall, crying, 'Forgive me. Please forgive me.' Shashibhushan stared at her in wonder. Why was she asking for forgiveness? She had done no

303

wrong? 'Don't you understand?' In his desperation he almost
shouted the words. 'There's no other way before you. It is only as
your husband that I can protect you from the king. He is
wayward and dissolute but he will not touch another man's wife.
That much I know.' Then, in a gentler tone, he added, 'This is no
time for tears, Bhumi. We must make our plans quickly. I've
found a place in Taltala where we can go tonight. We'll get
married tomorrow then move to Chandannagar. It is a very
pretty place right on the river. You'll love it there.'

Before Bhumisuta could respond the maid named Sushila
walked in. She had a sealed envelope in her hand. 'You're here
Bhumi!' she exclaimed. 'I've been looking for you all over the
house. Purohit Moshai has brought a letter for you.' A letter for
Bhumisuta! Shashibhushan's brows came together. 'Who is this
Purohit?' he asked sternly. 'Why would he bring her a letter?'
'That's just what I've been wondering,' Sushila cried, 'We're
maids of the house—unlettered and ignorant. Who would write
to us? Perhaps it is for you Babu. Perhaps he was looking for
Bhumi so that she could give it to you.'

Shashibhushan took the envelope from her and turned it over
in his hands. There was no address. Motioning to the woman to
leave he tore it open and drew out a sheet of notepaper which he
proceeded to unfold. His eyes fell first on the name of the sender.
A tremor ran through his body and he sat down heavily on the
bed. Suddenly all the pieces of the puzzle came together and, in a
startling moment of clarity, he knew the truth. He knew why
Bhumisuta was eluding him. 'Bharat!' The name came through
his clenched teeth in a harsh whisper. Controlling himself, he read
the letter, line by torturing line:

Hé Bhumisuta,
I gave you my word that I would release you from your life
of humiliation. I have not kept it. Doubtless you think me
a coward and deceiver. You have a right to think so.
But the truth is I am powerless to do anything for you at
present. You are in the service of the Maharaja of Tripura.
And, for a reason that I cannot disclose just now, I dare
not go anywhere near him. But I think of you day and
night. I keep seeing you everywhere—in whatever I do
during the day and in my dreams at night.

I've heard that the Maharaja is leaving for Tripura in a few
days. He will want to take you with him. Don't go
Bhumisuta. Don't ever, ever, go. If you do you'll never see
me again. Purohit Moshai is a friend of mine. Send me a
reply through him. I'm in a fever of anxiety to hear from
you.
Yours for ever
Bharat Kumar

Shashibhushan crushed the letter in his hands. A fire, such as
he had never known before, rose in his limbs. His dream, his
beautiful dream had been burned to ashes. And by whom? By that
worm Bharat! That half crazed, emaciated spawn of a king that
had sat among the beggars muttering gibberish to himself. Where
would he have been if Shashibhushan hadn't rescued him; hadn't
fed him and clothed him and given him his protection? He had
quarrelled with Radharaman Ghosh over him and brought him
to Calcutta. Even now the boy lived on Shashibhushan's charity.
To think that he had to give up Bhumisuta to such a one! It was
like hanging a string of pearls on a monkey's neck. 'Bharat!' he
said again. His eyes burned into Bhumisuta's. 'It was for him that
you wept all night. It was for him that you denied yourself to the
king.' Bhumisuta did not speak. Her eyes were fixed on the letter
in his hand. 'Are you mad Bhumi?' Shashibhushan continued,
'You're relying on Bharat to save you? He has nothing—nothing.
He lives on my charity. He'll starve in the streets if I withdraw my
protection.'

Tearing his eyes away from Bhumisuta's serene, unyielding
ones he looked around him wildly. He had to cling to his hopes.
He couldn't give up his cherished dream. He couldn't give up
Bhumisuta. He had believed the king to be his rival and had made
preparations to snatch her away from his grasp. Who had ever
thought that an insect like Bharat would stake a claim to the
lovely creature he desired with all his heart and soul? Who was
Bharat? A lowly ant that Shashibhushan could crush under his
foot if he so desired.

He glanced at Bhumisuta's face and was surprised to see the
change that had come over it. She hadn't read the letter but the
very knowledge that Bharat had written to her had, obviously,
imbued her with hope and strength. The frightened doe eyes of a

few moments ago now looked straight, unflinching and unafraid,
into Shashibhushan's. There was determination in every line of
her lovely face and form. Tossing the letter angrily to the ground
Shashibhushan muttered through his clenched teeth, 'Bharat will
never disobey me. He'll wash your feet and knock his head on
them if I command him.' Bhumisuta did not reply. Swift as an
arrow she sprang on the piece of paper and, picking it up, held it
to her breast.

Chapter XXXVII

Dr Mahendralal Sarkar was in a foul mood. He scolded the servants, snapped at his wife and strode from room to room on heavily shod feet. It was morning and he was preparing to leave for his chamber in Bhabanipur. But everything in his household appeared ugly and shoddy in his eyes and he took care to express his disgust with all the viciousness of which he was capable.

Sitting down to breakfast he eyed his toast and omelette scornfully, and announced to the world at large that the first was scorched and the second had the look and texture of a piece of shoe leather. Then, very grudgingly, he put a spoonful of fried liver into his mouth. Next moment he spat it out venomously nearly exploding with fury. The fool cook, he shouted, had drowned it in chilli paste. He gave his plate such a hard shove that it went spinning to the other end of the table. Not deigning to cast a glance at it he rose and marched out of the house. His wife ran after him begging him to eat something before he left. She could, she said, tell the cook to make some luchi and mohanbhog if he preferred it. But he answered rudely. 'Eat it yourself. Stuff the luchi and mohanbhog down your own throat like the glutton you are. Don't bother about me.' Then, getting into his carriage, he ordered the coachman to drive to Sukia Street.

The carriage clattered down the road and stopped outside the house of the famous lawyer Durgamohan Das. Mahendralal, his face as dark and ominous as the Shravan sky above his head, strode into the house with the air of one marching into battle. 'Durga! Durga!' he called in a voice of thunder. Durgamohan, who was sitting with his clients in the front room, rose hastily, 'Mahendrada!' he exclaimed in hearty greeting. 'What brings you here?' Mahendralal eyed the men in the room as if they were insects. 'Get rid of these fellows,' he said, 'I have something very important to discuss with you.'

'Come this way,' Durgamohan took him by the elbow and guided him into another room. Then, smiling at his visitor, though inwardly apprehensive, he said, 'What brings the great Dhanwantari to my door? No one is sick in my house.'

'Who says no one is sick?' Mahendralal stood with his arms akimbo and glared at Durgamohan. '*You're* sick. You have a fever in the brain.'

Durgamohan burst out laughing. And that enraged the good doctor more than ever. 'You laugh at me!' Mahendralal thundered. 'You're more shameless than I thought. Anandamohan informed me last evening that you've decided not to send Abala back to Madras. Is that true?'

'It is true. But why do you remain standing? Sit down. Sit down. I'm not sending my daughter back because she is to be wed.'

'To be wed! Have you gone mad?'

'Why do you lose your temper Dada?' Durgamohan cried good humouredly, 'Don't fathers find husbands for their daughters?'

'Let the whole world run around looking for sons-in-law. Why should you?'

'What sort of talk is this Dada?' Durgamohan was dying to laugh but he managed to control himself, 'My daughter is sixteen. I'm not violating the Marriage Act. What's wrong with getting her married?'

'There's everything wrong with it. Is your daughter an ordinary girl who has nothing to look forward to but a husband and brats? She's one in a million with a brilliant career ahead of her. I felt as if the sky had fallen on my head when I heard the news. Have you forgotten with what difficulty we managed to send her to Madras? How proud we were when she set off to study medicine? If you had allowed her just two more years she would have been the first lady doctor of India.'

'Dada,' Durgamohan said gently. 'It was on your advice and that of Shibnath Shastri Moshai that I sent my daughter. But she isn't keeping well in Madras. The climate doesn't suit her and she doesn't like the food. She misses the *machher jhol bhaat* she's eaten all her life—'

'That's nonsense!' Mahendralal spluttered with rage. '*Machher jhol bhaat* indeed! People don't die of eating the food they don't relish. How do Indians manage to survive in England?

Let her get her degree, then she can eat all the *machher jhol* she wants.'

'But Abala doesn't wish to go back.'

'I don't believe it. It is you who is putting all these ideas in her head. You're like all fathers. You can't rest in peace till you've pushed your daughters into other men's kitchens. I won't hear another word. I'll break your head if you try to contradict me.'

'We are of the Brahmo Samaj. We don't marry off our daughters without their consent. Abala has met the boy and approves of him. If you don't believe me let me send for her. You can talk to her and find out the truth for yourself.'

Abala came in a few minutes later. Touching Mahendralal's feet she asked softly, 'How are you Jethamoni?' Mahendralal's anger had spent itself by now and a great sadness had taken its place. His eyes clouded over as he looked at the girl. He had cherished such great hopes of her. Whenever he met young girls, in the houses of his friends and relatives, he had one mantra for them, 'Work hard my dears,' he said over and over again. 'Do well in school and then study for a medical degree. Our mothers, sisters and daughters die everyday for want of medical attention because male doctors are not allowed inside the zenana. So many children are stillborn and so many women die at childbirth. Don't you see? Only women can save women.' Most girls were frightened by such talk but not Abala. She had agreed enthusiastically and even after being denied admission to the Medical College of Calcutta, she had not given up. She had prevailed upon her father to send her to Madras. Placing a hand on her head in blessing, Mahendralal said sadly, 'I'm as well as I can expect to be at my age, Ma. What about you? I hear you've decided not to go back to Madras.'

'I didn't like it there Jethamoni.'

'You were doing well. Your results show it.'

'I wasn't happy. I had no friends. The girls there are all Christians and they keep to themselves.'

'What sort of talk is this? Success doesn't come easily in this world. One has to struggle hard to achieve it. If you persevere just another two years you'll be the first lady doctor of India. Just think. Your name will go down in history. You'll be the pride of the country.'

309

'I'm not meant to be a doctor Jethamoni. My head spins whenever I enter the operation theatre.'

'That's quite normal. Everyone feels like that in the beginning. You'll get used to it. Everyone does.' Then, making his voice as soft and persuasive as he possibly could, he almost begged. 'Go back child. It's only for another two years. Tell your father you don't wish to marry just yet. There's plenty of time . . .'

Abala stood silent and unyielding. Her eyes were on the floor and she drew patterns on it with her toe nail. Suddenly Mahendralal lost his temper, 'Get out of my sight then,' he shouted. 'Stubborn girl! If you were my daughter I would have slapped your cheeks. You've dashed all my hopes. Go. I don't want to see your face ever again.' Durgamohan motioned to his daughter to leave the room. Then, turning to his guest, he said, 'Why do you lose your temper Dada? The girl's to be wed in a few months. Give her your blessing.'

'I can't dole out false blessing,' Mahendralal Sarkar rose from his chair. 'I'm leaving this house never to return. Send for some other doctor when anyone is sick.'

'That's not fair Dada. I heard all you had to say. Now you must hear me out. Tell me. Would I have sent my daughter so far from home if I was not keen to see her a doctor? Now she has changed her mind. She's of marriageable age and wishes to get married. Shall I thwart her?'

'Who is the boy? Some rich man's worthless offspring, I presume.'

'Do you know Anandamohan's father-in-law Bhagaban Bosu? He was deputy magistrate of Bardhaman. A very fine, upright man and well known all over East Bengal. When I heard that he was looking for a suitable match for his son I sent a proposal. The boy has approved of Abala and—'

'But what does he do? Fly pigeons like all spoiled brats of rich fathers?'

'Bhagaban Babu is not a rich man. In fact he is quite heavily in debt. He lost quite a lot of money trying his hand at tea planting in Assam. The boy was also studying medicine but he had to give it up.'

'Bravo! The ideal couple! Both half doctors! Phoh! I detest people who can't complete what they've started. Spineless

310

cowards! No spirit. No endurance. I spit on them!'

'Listen to the whole story first. Jagadish—that's the name of the boy—was a brilliant student and doing very well in medicine. But, unfortunately, while in Assam he had contracted the disease kala azar and hadn't quite recovered. The fever kept breaking out from time to time. Finally his own teachers advised him to give up medicine and study something else.'

'I understand now. Abala has seen the boy and is totally infatuated with him. And because he gave up studying medicine halfway she decided to follow suit. Woe to the woman who is more qualified than her husband! *Chhi*! *Chhi*! To think that Abala could be so stupid!'

'Do hear the rest Dada. Then deliver your verdict. Jagadish couldn't become a doctor but he's become a scientist. He got his degree in Physics from Cambridge University. And, while in England, he recovered from kala azar. The air in that part of the country is extremely healthy. He's back now with a teaching assignment in Presidency College.'

'Aaah!' Mahendralal's eyes nearly bulged out of his head. He stood up in his excitement, 'A Bengali boy teaching Physics in Presidency College! That's a white man's aakhra. How did they allow an infiltrator?'

Astute lawyer that he was, Durgamohan knew how to build up a case. The trump card had to be hidden in the sleeve to be brought out with a flourish right at the end. Smiling at the older man he said gently, 'Consider the boy's calibre Dada. Has any Bengali achieved what Jagadish has? You are doing so much for the spread of science in the land. Have you received any recognition? Yet, do you know who recommended Jagadish for the post? Lord Ripon himself.'

'What!' Mahendralal almost screamed the question. He started pacing feverishly up and down the room. 'You know Father Lafon, don't you Dada?' Durgamohan went on. 'Jagadish was his favourite pupil in St Xavier's College. When Jagadish left for England Father Lafon gave him some letters of introduction one of which was for Mr Fawcett—the famous economist and now Post-Master General of England. Mr Fawcett helped the boy in many ways. Just before Jagadish was to return to India Fawcett sent for him and said, "You've done exceedingly well, my boy, and I'm proud of you. I would like to make sure that you get the job you deserve." Then, handing him a letter he added, "The Viceroy is a friend of mine. Go to him as soon as you reach India and give him this." Jagadish did as he was told. Lord Ripon examined his papers and interviewed him for over an hour. He was obviously impressed because he sent a communication to the Education Secretary to find suitable employment for the boy.'

'I've never heard of the Viceroy recommending a native. It's unbelievable!'

'It happened, nevertheless. But there is more to come. The Education Secretary, Sir Alfred Crawford, was of the view that a native had no head for science. He might be allowed to teach Bengali or Sanskrit or Philosophy at the most. But Physics was out of the question. Charles Tawney, Principal of Presidency College, was of the same opinion. Yet they couldn't ignore the Viceroy's recommendation either. Crawford offered Jagadish a job in the Provincial Service on the pretext that there was no vacancy in the Imperial Service. But why should Jagadish, with all his qualifications, accept a post in a lower service? He turned down the proposal.'

'He was right. Absolutely right!'

'But Lord Ripon had remembered his promise. When, on examining the *Gazette*, he found the boy's name missing he sent for Crawford and demanded an explanation. Crawford hastened to make amends. He offered Jagadish a teaching assignment in Presidency College. But the white race cannot overcome its contempt of the dark under any circumstances. The post was not only temporary—the salary offered was a third of what the white teachers received. Jagadish wrote to the Education Department saying that he would teach without an honorarium till such time as the Department deemed him fit to receive equal salary with the rest of his colleagues.'

'Wonderful!' Mahendralal exclaimed. He was so moved that tears stood in his eyes. 'The boy is one in a million. A true diamond! Marry him to Abala at once Durga. Only a mad man would let such an opportunity slip through his fingers.'

'Do I take it, then, that you are not angry anymore? With me or Abala?'

'Angry! I'm so happy I could dance with you on my head.'

Then, sobering down he continued, 'I wasn't angry Durga. I was disappointed. I had set my heart on Abala becoming a doctor. There are so many women doctors and nurses in Europe. We don't have even one. You must have heard of Florence Nightingale? The nurse who performed such wonders in Crimea? Can't our girls follow her example?'

'Of course they can and will. Abala is not the only girl in India, Dada. She has failed but others will succeed.'

'Will Jagadish object to Abala taking her degree? Dwarkanath Ganguly is allowing his wife Kadambini to continue—'

'That I can't say Dada. It's up to him and her.' Then, lowering his voice, he added, 'They're not well off. Jagadish doesn't earn anything as yet and his father is heavily in debt. Jagadish is so high principled—he won't take a pie from anyone. Not even from me. I don't know how they'll manage.'

'Don't worry!' Mahendralal patted the younger man on the back. 'Everything will come out right. You've taken the correct decision. It is the man that counts—not his money. I'll go see Jagadish this evening and try to persuade him to let Abala take her degree. A doctor wife will be of great help to him.'

Mahendralal kept his word. Walking into Jagadish's room that very evening, he saw a young man of about twenty-seven, big and dark with curly hair and a bushy moustache. Jagadish, who had taken a camera apart and was trying to put it together again, looked up to see a tall, portly, middle-aged man in an impeccable three-piece suit and English boots.

'You're Bhagaban's boy are you not?' The stranger said roughly. 'Do you know how to tote a gun?' Jagadish stared at him, his eyes wide in surprise. 'Of course you do,' the strange man went on, 'I remember now. You went tiger shooting when you were little. But I hope you are not out of practice. You see, I wish to fight a duel, with you. You may choose the day and time—'

'I beg your pardon, sir. I don't quite understand—' Jagadish replied politely although he had serious doubts about the man's sanity.

'Don't you? You're marrying Durga's daughter Abala—are you not? The fact is that I wished to marry her myself. I was waiting for her to complete her education when you suddenly

313

appeared out of the blue and snatched her away from right under
my nose. Well, if you wish to marry the girl you'll have to prove
you're the better man of the two.' Then, seeing the bewildered
look on the boy's face, he burst out laughing. Coming forward he
clapped Jagadish heartily on the shoulder and said, 'Just a joke.
I've heard all about you, my dear boy. You've set the sahebs by
the ears and the whole country is proud of you. Abala is just the
girl you should marry. By the way—you probably don't know
me. I'm a doctor. My name is Mahendralal Sarkar.' Jagadish rose
hastily and touched the older man's feet. 'Who doesn't know you
sir?' he exclaimed. 'As a student I often visited your Institute for
the Cultivation of Science and listened to the lectures.'

'Well, you're not a student any more. You're a brilliant
scientist. I invite you to address the gatherings from time to time.
On a remuneration, of course. No. No. Shaking your head won't
do. I insist on paying you what I pay the others.'

Two days later Mahendralal Sarkar received a doctor's call
from the house of Janakinath Ghoshal of Kashiabagan. Walking
into the drawing room the first person he saw was Janakinath's
daughter Sarala. Sarala sat at the piano playing a little tune and
singing the words over and over again. 'Bandé Mataram,' she
sang, 'Sujalang Suphalang, malayaja sheetalang shasya
shyamalang . . .'

'Good! Good!' the doctor cried appreciatively, 'A very pretty
verse! Did you write it yourself?' Sarala bit her tongue and shook
her head. 'You don't know anything Jethamoni!' she cried. 'This
was written by Bankimchandra. Robi Mama set the tune for the
first two verses and asked me to do the rest.'

'Why couldn't Bankim set the tune himself?'

'He didn't intend it to be a song.'

Seeing Sarala, Mahendralal was struck with an idea. 'Sarala,'
he asked in his sweetest, most persuasive voice. 'Would you like
to study medicine after you pass out?'

'Why medicine?' Sarala's brows came together.

'Why not? A doctor's profession is the most noble in the
world.'

'I want to do my graduation first. After that I'll decide what to
do.'

Sarala was about to appear for her Entrance examination.

There were several years before she would graduate. Mahendralal decided that he would keep drilling the idea of becoming a doctor into her head for the next four years. He wouldn't give up.

At this moment Janakinath Ghoshal walked into the room. His face was flushed and his eyes bright with fever. 'You seem to be fine,' Mahendralal began, eyeing him aggressively. 'Why did you send for me? I don't like wasting my time.'

'I'm far from fine. The fever refuses to leave me. Come Mahendra, don't scold. Give me some of your excellent medicine and get me back on my feet. I have a lot of work before me.'

'You *are* on your feet. Unless, of course, I'm seeing a vision.' Then, banging his fist on a table he cried out angrily, 'Why aren't you in bed? Don't you know that no medicine in the world will work on a person who moves around with fever burning his limbs? Even God can't help you.' His eyes fell on Sarala as he said these words and his mood changed. 'Aren't you planning to get your daughter married Janaki?' he asked, quite forgetting his indignation of a moment ago. 'You married your elder daughter off at her age.'

'Don't talk to me of Sarala! She's taken a vow to work for her country and that's not possible, she says, unless she remains a spinster. Marriage, a husband and children are not for her. The amazing thing is that her mother agrees with her!'

Mahendralal was charmed. A girl like Sarala—young, beautiful, talented and admired by so many young men—had taken a vow never to get married! To devote her life to her country! What could be more moving? His eyes misted over. Sarala was a gem; a pearl among women. She would make a fine doctor. Abala had let him down. And Kadambini! He sighed deeply as he thought of Kadambini.

Kadambini was the most beautiful girl Mahendralal had ever seen. She was also the brightest—the first female graduate of Calcutta University, sharing the distinction with another girl called Bidhumukhi Bosu. That was a few years ago. Mahendralal Sarkar had advised her to study medicine and she had agreed. Then, suddenly, out of the blue, she had decided to marry Dwarkanath Ganguly—a man seventeen years her senior. Dwarkanath, who had been her teacher in school, was a widower with two children. His daughter Bidhumukhi was of the same age as Kadambini and engaged to be married to a very bright young man called Upendrakishore Roy Choudhury. The other child, a boy, was both spastic and mentally retarded. Dwarkanath was very poor and extremely unattractive in appearance being tall to a fault, gaunt and totally without grace or charm. Everyone had been aghast at Kadambini's choice. She, who could have had her pick of handsome young men from the first families of Calcutta, had chosen to fall in love with a poor widower twice her age. Mahendralal knew that it was neither love nor infatuation that had prompted her. They had a shared ideal. They were both committed, heart and soul, to the education and upliftment of women. Kadambini knew that marriage with anyone else would put an end to her medical career. Dwarkanath would not only allow her to continue, he would support her in every way he could.

Mahendralal liked the couple so much he visited them often. On one occasion he had gone to Dwarkanath's house to find Bidhumukhi rocking Kadambini's baby in her lap and trying to put him to sleep. The baby was screaming lustily and poor Bidhumukhi was having a hard time of it. Dwarkanath, wrapped in an enormous gamchha, was in the kitchen struggling with the evening meal. All this was surprising. But most surprising of all was the sight of Kadambini, poring over her books in a corner of the room, totally oblivious of her surroundings. So great was her concentration that she didn't even raise her head when Mahendralal entered the room with his heavy tread singing one of her husband's songs in a cracked and tuneless voice.

Bharat sleeps . . .
    Ah! Bharat sleeps and will sleep on
    Till her daughters wake and rise.

Chapter XXXVIII

Ashutosh Chowdhury's ancestral house was in Krishnanagar but he had rented a small house in Scott Lane, near City College, where he lived with his brothers and sisters. A brilliant student, Ashutosh had set a record in Calcutta University by taking his BA and MA degrees in the same year. Immediately afterwards he had left for England where, after obtaining a Tripos in Mathematics from the University of Cambridge, he had studied at the Bar and returned to India a qualified barrister. But though Law and Mathematics were his professional pursuits his first love was literature. He was an avid reader of poetry—Bengali, Sanskrit, English and French—and had excellent discrimination and a fine ear for the nuances. It was this trait that had endeared him to Robi. They had first met on board ship during Robi's second voyage out to England—an abortive attempt that had ended in Madras on the whim of his nephew Satyaprasad. But those few days were enough to establish a friendship that lasted a lifetime. The two were men of the same age and had a great deal in common.

From Ashutosh Robi learned that evaluating poetry was a special skill—one that had to be developed with care. It was not enough to express appreciation or dislike. The serious reader needed to prepare himself for the task of evaluation by acquainting himself with the tradition to which the poem belonged. To take an example, as Ashutosh pointed out, it was imperative to have some knowledge of the work of the Vaishnav *pada kartas* in order to receive the full impact of a modern lyric such as the kind Robi wrote. Ashutosh was a brilliant critic. He could take up a poem, analyse it line by line and point out parallels in ideas, images and forms with other older sources.

Robi liked Ashutosh immensely and was proud to be his friend. Consequently he was a frequent visitor to the house in Scott Lane. Ashu's fifth brother, Pramatha, a boy of seventeen, was his ardent admirer. Not daring to intrude in the

317

conversations his eldest brother had with his poet friend, he often stationed himself outside the door from where he gazed with admiring eyes at his hero. Robi Babu, Pramatha thought, looked like a Greek god. And, indeed, Robi had grown into an extraordinarily handsome man. He wore his hair long these days. The thick locks that flowed down to his shoulders were a rich glossy black as were the soft masses of hair that covered his cheeks and chin. His skin was burnished gold and his features seemed carved out of marble. His body was tall and well formed and radiated with health and vitality. In the heat of the summer Robi wore no shirt. Above his dhuti he wrapped a fine *uduni* loosely around his back and chest.

After Ashu's return from England an idea started forming in Robi's head. How would it be if Ashu was promoted from a friend to a relative? He was such an eligible young man and there were several unmarried girls in the house in Jorasanko. Robi's third brother's daughter Pratibha was twenty-one—a beautiful girl with many accomplishments. Hemendranath had died a year ago and the responsibility for settling her had fallen on his brothers. Robi considered a match between the two an excellent idea. But he foresaw a couple of obstacles which needed to be overcome. The Thakurs belonged to the Rarhi Sreni of Brahmins and the Chowdhurys to the Barendra. Baba Moshai was bound to object. Again, Ashu's father might demand a large dowry for his son was, indeed, a great catch. But Baba Moshai, though he had retained a number of Hindu customs in his personal life, was dead against dowry. He would be more than generous in what he gave his granddaughter but he would brook no demand from her in-laws.

One evening Robi invited Ashutosh to tea. Mrinalini, who was shy with strangers at the best of times, was more so now for her pregnancy had started to show. Consequently the task of pouring the tea and handing out the cakes and sandwiches fell on Pratibha. Pratibha was as open and friendly as Mrinalini was shy and reticent and soon the three young people found themselves engaged in lively conversation. The talk veering on the possibility of blending Indian and Western tunes in modern compositions, Robi requested Pratibha to demonstrate that it was possible by singing some of his songs. Pratibha rose instantly and, opening

318

the piano, played and sang with unaffected ease. The beauty of her voice and the grace and charm of her manner affected Ashutosh deeply. Robi caught the glances his guest kept stealing at his beautiful niece and knew that his mission had succeeded. Pratibha, he was certain, would make Ashu an excellent wife. As a brilliant barrister with an increasingly flourishing practice he needed a partner well versed in the social graces.

The first step concluded, the next one was to tackle Baba Moshai. With this end in view Robi proceeded to visit his father in Chinsura. Debendranath heard Robi out patiently though not without some surprise. He kept a close watch on each one of his children and was well aware of their merits and defects. Over the last few years he had come to the conclusion that Robi had shaped up better than his other sons. His skill in the composition of Brahmo Sangeet and his hard work on the estates had won him a grudging respect from the old patriarch. Now Debendranath saw another side to Robi's character—his commitment to the family and his sense of duty. Although the youngest it was he who had taken upon himself the responsibility of finding a husband for his fatherless niece, not the others. Debendranath asked several questions regarding the boy's qualifications and family background. Then, to Robi's surprise, he announced heartily, 'It seems an excellent match. See that it takes place without delay.' Robi was elated. His father hadn't even touched on the question of Rarhi and Barendra and he had expressed no curiosity about the family's financial position. He knew, though, that dealing with Ashu's family wouldn't be quite so easy.

He was right. As soon as he took the proposal to Ashu's father the latter started asking questions about the extent of the dowry he could expect. In vain did Robi try to assure him that the Maharshi's gifts to his granddaughter would far exceed his expectations. But the old man wanted a clear commitment which Robi was incapable of giving. When Robi had almost given up hope of a satisfactory conclusion to the matter, Ashutosh took it up himself. He came to Jorasanko one evening and said without preamble, 'Bhai Robi! My brothers and sisters are pestering me to get married. Why don't you set a date? I have one condition, though. I want a simple ceremony. No ostentation. No dowry. I hope you agree.'

319

The wedding took place, according to the tradition of the Thakur family, in the house of Jorasanko. The groom's father stayed away but his siblings were all there. They were a jolly lot and kept the nuptial chamber enlivened all night with their jokes and laughter. Since there was no question of Ashutosh living in Jorasanko as a resident son-in-law, Pratibha made the move from her father's palatial home to her husband's humble one. And, belying everyone's fears, she quickly adapted herself to her new surroundings. Robi visited her every day. *Balak* had recently been merged with *Bharati* and he had plenty of time.

One day two students of Presidency College came to the house in Scott Lane. One of them, a young man called Jadugopal, was an old acquaintance of Ashu's from his Krishnanagar days. Accompanying him was his friend Bharat. Bharat, Robi observed, was as silent and withdrawn as Jadugopal was loud and garrulous. He sat quietly in one corner, his eyes fixed on Robi's face, while Jadugopal did the talking. Declaring himself to be a great admirer, Jadugopal bombarded Robi with questions. Robi didn't mind. The boys of Presidency College, he had heard, were highly politicized. It amused him to find that they read poetry on the side.

'Robi Babu,' Bharat took advantage of a lull in the conversation and said softly. 'I've read your *Rajarshi*. Have you ever been to Tripura?'

'Not yet,' Robi answered smiling. 'But I hope to—some time.'

'You've described the country so well. It's difficult to believe that you've never seen it.'

'That's the advantage of being a poet,' Ashutosh commented with a laugh. 'Poets write confidently about all the places they've never seen. Don't forget Dante wrote a whole poem set in Hell.'

'Bharat comes from Tripura,' Jadugopal offered the information.

'Is that so?' Robi enquired with interest. 'May I stay in your house, then, when I visit Tripura?'

A shadow came over Bharat's face. He shook his head sadly and said, 'I don't have a house in Tripura.' Before Robi could react Jadugopal fired his next question. 'Achha Robi Babu,' he said with a degree of familiarity unwarranted on such a slight acquaintance. 'You do so many kinds of work. You work for the

Brahmo Samaj, edit a journal, look after your father's estates and write poetry. Which of your activities gives you the greatest pleasure?' Robi fixed his large, dark eyes on Jadugopal's face. 'Do you know,' he said with a disarming smile, 'I've never really thought about it.'

But, in his heart, he knew the truth. He did a number of things because he had to do them. But what he liked best was to lie in bed all day and write poetry. Writing a poem was like building a house. Setting word after word, carefully selected, like brick by brick, till an idea took shape and form! What could be more wonderful or more fulfilling!

321

Chapter XXXIX

Chaitanya Leela was followed by a series of religious plays—*Prahlad Charitra*, *Nimai Sanyas*, *Prabhas Yagna* and *Buddhadev Charit*—but none of them did well at the box office. The spectators dwindled in number so alarmingly that the manager and cast were forced to admit that Girish Ghosh had lost his touch. After his involvement with Ramkrishna he refused to write on subjects other than the religious. *Chaitanya Leela* had entertained while evoking religious sentiments. But the ones that followed, they admitted among themselves, were as dry as dust.

At length even Girish Ghosh had to sit up and take notice. He had hoped that his *Buddhadev Charit*, based on Edwin Arnold's *Light of Asia*, would bring in the audience. But though the songs gained popularity, the play didn't. Girish was very disappointed. He had taken great pains with it and Sir Edwin Arnold, while on a visit to Calcutta, had seen it and praised it. Yet it failed to enthuse the general public.

One day Girish Ghosh entered Ramkrishna's room to find him telling his disciples a story. It was about a religious charlatan and he was enacting the character with such vitality and humour that his audience was convulsed with laughter. At that moment an idea came to Girish. He would write a story based on the life of Bilwamangal. It would have a moral ending but the focus of the play would be on the love between Bilwamangal and Chintamoni. The play was written and staged within a few days with Amritalal playing Bilwamangal and Binodini Chintamoni. It became extremely popular. The HOUSE FULL sign, which had been collecting dust for so many months, was hung up every evening. The Star had come into its own again.

But Binodini was not happy. The press was enthusiastic but not about her. The columns were full of praise for Gangamoni who played a madwoman and sang her way into people's hearts. Binodini got only two rounds of applause whereas Gangamoni got eleven. Binodini's disappointment gradually worked itself up into a terrible fury. She couldn't bear the thought that Gangamoni, a plain, middle-aged strumpet who played maids and aunts in other plays, was outstripping her, Binodini, the acknowledged queen of the theatre world! It was insupportable. She was convinced that Girish Ghosh had deliberately given Gangamoni the better part to spite her.

One evening, after the first bell had sounded, one of the actresses tiptoed up to Amritalal and told him in a whisper that Binodini hadn't donned her costume or put on her make-up. Amritalal came rushing into the green room to find her sitting on a stool in front of her mirror in an attitude of complete lethargy. Shocked and anxious he cried, 'Why aren't you getting ready, Binod? Do you feel unwell?' Binodini looked up. Her eyes held his, unwavering, for a few moments. Then, turning away, she said, 'Stop the show. I'm not appearing tonight.' Amritalal was not unprepared for a scene of this kind. Binodini had been acting very oddly of late. But he felt uneasy. Girish Ghosh had left and he would have to deal with her all by himself. He would have to get her back to the stage by a combination of flattery, persuasion and threats. He wondered if he would succeed. Sidling up close to her he placed a hand on her back. 'You don't know what you're saying, Binod,' he said making his voice as sweet as honey. 'How can we stop the show? The hall is so packed—there's no room for a pin. Take a peek if you don't believe me. People have come from far and near to see you. They've spent a lot of money.'

'Return their money. I'm going home.'

'We'll have to give them a reason.'

'I don't wish to appear tonight.' Binodini stood up and flashed her eyes arrogantly at Amritalal. 'That's reason enough. Don't my wishes count for anything? Who created Star? It was I, Binodini Dasi, who procured the money. I sold my body to do it. Have you forgotten that already?'

'I haven't forgotten,' Amritalal replied humbly. He had heard these words so often in the last few months that he was sick of them. But, making a prodigious effort, he bared his teeth in a smile and said ingratiatingly, 'How can I forget what you've done for us all? You're Star and Star is you. But surely that doesn't mean that we can let down our spectators upon a whim. They are our gods. We are pledged to serve them and not to serve is to sin.'

323

'You keep saying the same thing over and over again. But my mind is made up. I'm not acting tonight. In fact I'm not acting in *Bilwamangal* any more. The shows must stop.'

'Are you crazy?' Amritalal was so shocked that he shouted the words at her. 'The play is a hit. We're making good money.'

'*Chaitanya Leela* was a hit too. You can start running it. Or *Daksha Yagna*.'

'Those plays have had a long run. Who will see them again? *Bilwamangal* has just started making waves. People are flocking to the theatre. This is no time to stop.'

'Look here Bhuni Dada. I don't like *Bilwamangal* and I've told you I shan't act in it. But I may consider changing my mind on one condition. Get that slut Gangamoni out. In fact cut out the part. Are you ready to do it?'

Amritalal sighed and said, 'Who am I to cut out any part? Have you forgotten that the play has a writer and a director? Could you have made such a demand on Girish Babu? Besides, this is the best play he's written. And it has been written for you. Consider the depth of the character you're portraying. Consider the length of the part. People clap for Gangamoni because they're amused by the funny songs she sings and the faces she makes. But it is your part that they'll remember forever.'

'That's nonsense,' Binodini cut in sharply. 'We both know that our guru wrote Ganga's part with the intention of humiliating me. And you're all in the plot. Do you think you can get rid of me this way?'

'I don't know what has got into you Binod. Why should we wish to get rid of you? You're our best, our most valued asset. Don't we all know that it is you who pulls the crowds? But there's something you must understand. We are players. Our job is to work together and make a success of whatever role is given to us. We have no right to interfere with the playwright's work or make demands on him. Look at me. I accept any part. I don't complain even if it's a small one—a servant's or a thief's.'

'The theatre was built with my money. You didn't even name it after me—'

'That's an old story. What's the sense in raking it up now? There! That's the second bell. Put on your costume like a good girl and—'

'I've told you my condition. Cut out Ganga's part. From tonight—'

Amritalal's patience was at an end. 'No' he said firmly, 'I won't cut it out. In fact I won't change a word. Her role will remain exactly as it is. If you're determined not to play tonight I'll make the announcement and return the ticket money. I'll tell the audience that Binodini does not wish to act in *Bilwamangal* any more.' Amritalal rose. Binodini's face crumpled like a scolded child's. 'Wait Bhuni Dada,' she called after him. 'I'll play the role. But just for tonight. This business has got to be thrashed out. I won't allow anyone to humiliate me.'

The matter was reported to Girish Ghosh in due course. 'Tch! Tch!' he clicked his tongue in derision. 'Envy!' he cried contemptuously. 'It's plain and simple envy. These theatre sluts are all the same. Can't bear it if someone else gets a few claps. An actress of Binodini's stature feels threatened when a paltry whore like Gangamoni gets a bit of applause! It's unbelievable! *Striyascharitram!*'

Next morning he sent for Binodini, 'It amazes me Binod,' he said, 'that a great artist like you, one who has been the reigning queen of the theatre for so many years, cannot overcome your fascination for a few claps. Haven't I told you about the famous English actress Ellen Terry? She didn't get a single clap when she acted Lady Macbeth. The spectators were terrified of her. Yet they couldn't forget her. Out of all her performances that was the best and most memorable. Don't you remember what Bankim Babu said when he came to see, um, what was it—? Ah yes, *Mrinalini*. His own *Mrinalini*. Seeing you play Monorama he exclaimed, "But this is a real, living Monorama! Far superior to the one I created." A compliment of this sort from Bankim Babu is not to be taken lightly. You don't know your calibre as an actress, Binod. That is why you need constant reassurance. Let me tell you something. When I created Chintamoni it was your face that floated before my eyes. But what you've made of her goes far beyond the pages of my script.'

Binodini was mollified for the time being and the shows went on as usual. But her frustration and discontent kept smouldering within her erupting, suddenly, from time to time. Gradually her colleagues started finding her intolerable. Her tempers and tantrums; her whims and sulks; her total disregard of theatre discipline and her constant harping on the fact that it was with her money that Star had been purchased were getting on everyone's nerves. Girish Ghosh felt it too but even in his indignation and disgust he could find a ripple of sympathy. The girl had sacrificed her own self interest for the collective good. There was no doubt of that. 'Bini,' he said to her one day, 'I'm writing a play called *Bellik Bazar*. It's full of fun, music and laughter. No more religion and morality for a good long while. You shall be playing Rangini. The spectators like to see you in gorgeous costumes singing, dancing and coquetting. You'll get so many claps—your ears will burst.'

'From Nimai and Chintamoni to Rangini!' one of the bit actors commented snidely, 'What a come down!' 'We have to save the theatre, don't we?' Girish Ghosh snapped. 'What good will ideals do when we're all starving to death? Bini is a great actress. She acted Bilasini and Nimai at the same time, didn't she? A few light roles for the present will do her good. I'll get her on to serious ones again.'

Bellik Bazar was a success and Binodini got all the applause she wanted. Her anger had simmered down and, to the ordinary eye, all seemed to be as before. But there were changes in her personality that didn't go unnoticed. Amritalal saw, to his surprise, that she, who had always used the lightest make up possible, was covering her face with layers of powder—not only during performances but during rehearsals. Around the same time rumours started going round that a white spot had appeared on Bini's chin which might be leucoderma. Binodini had always kept herself aloof from Gangamoni but now she started avoiding Bhushan Kumari, Kshetramoni and all the other women as well. She started coming in late for rehearsals and leaving early. Sometimes she wouldn't make an appearance at all. Her absence at rehearsals didn't affect her own acting but it created problems for the others. Girish Ghosh was wild with fury when, coming in one day, he found her missing. 'Who does she think she is?' he thundered, 'The Lady Vicereigne? Come Bhuni. Let's go to her house and drag the little bitch in here by the hair.' Then, seeing Amritalal hesitate he cried angrily, 'What's wrong with you? You look as if I'm pushing you into a lion's den. Are you that scared of

Bini?'

'No Gurudev. The fact is—things have changed. We can't walk into her house as and when we please any more.'

'Why not? Has she turned ascetic?'

'Far from it. She's got a new babu.'

'What?'

'He's immensely rich. And he has a title. He is a raja. A real raja.'

'This country crawls with real rajas. What's his name?'

'I can't tell you that. I'll have his paw on my neck if I do. He is no ordinary raja. He is a king lion—'

'Bini! Bini!' Girish Ghosh sighed and shook his head. 'When she first came to me she was like a doll. She simpered self-consciously and moved her hands and feet with jerky little movements. I made her into the woman she is today. I breathed fire and passion into her. I gave her depth and character. But she has no use for me any more. She didn't even care to tell me about her new babu.'

'You can't blame her Gurudev. A woman can't survive by herself in this wicked city. She needs a man to protect her. You're totally wrapped up in your Ramkrishna and have no time for her. What is the poor girl to do? Her present protector, I've heard, is a good man and treats her well.'

'Let's go to her. I must see her at once.'

Amritalal tried to prevent Girish Ghosh from undertaking this foolish venture but the latter had made up his mind. Hastening to his carriage he drove like the wind till he came to his destination. Stepping down, he walked with his accustomed arrogance towards the looming mansion ahead but was stopped roughly by the sentries at the gate. There were two of them—huge, strapping northerners with tall turbans and fierce mustaches. But Girish Ghosh was not intimidated. He had had a lot to drink and was in a fighting mood. 'Let go of me, you rascals,' he thundered in his deep rich voice, 'Let me pass.' The men didn't understand. They merely repeated, in their unintelligible tongue, that they had orders not to let anyone in. Frustrated in his attempts to enter the house, Girish turned his face to the window of Binodini's bedroom and yelled, 'Bini! Binod! Come down. Come down at once.' Binodini did not come but a maid called Padmabala, did. '*Ogo* Babu!' she said, 'Didimoni can't see you today. She's ill and—' Girish glared at her. 'Tell me the truth Podi!' he asked severely, 'Does your mistress know I'm here? Did she hear me call?'

'That she did. She's even seen you from her balcony. She sent me to tell you that—'

Girish Ghosh turned away. There was a great sadness in his heart. Helping him into the carriage, Amritalal said gently, 'Don't be too hard on her. Perhaps her babu was there.' Girish made no reply. After a while, when the carriage had started moving, he muttered sullenly, 'Pride goes before a fall. She forgets that it was I who made her. And that I can break her whenever I wish. I can drag her from the limelight and throw her down into the deepest of shadows.' Suddenly he took Amritalal's hands in his. 'Can you get me a lump of clay Bhuni?' he cried feverishly. His lips twitched with excitement and he ran his tongue over them, 'I'll teach it to speak; to sing and dance. And like the Greek sculptor Pygmalion, I'll breathe life into it. I'll make it into a greater actress than Binodini ever was! Get me a new girl. As young and raw as you can find. I want to try my hand at it again. I want to feel the joy of creation.'

Chapter XL

Ramkrishna's health was deteriorating rapidly. There were days, now, when he felt so weak that he needed help to perform his bodily functions. He had virtually stopped eating. His tongue was bloated to twice its size and covered with sores. And his throat hurt so badly that to swallow a drop of water was agony.

Dr Mahendralal Sarkar advised a change of scene. Calcutta, with its pall of dust and smoke, was a polluted city, extremely harmful for the patient who had lived in Dakshineswar for many years and was used to breathing the pure, clean air of the Ganga. It was imperative, he said, that Ramkrishna be moved to cleaner, quieter surroundings.

Ramkrishna's disciples discussed the matter amongst themselves. The best places for recouping health were, of course, Darjeeling and Puri. But they were a good distance away and far too expensive. It was necessary to look for some place nearer home. One of them suggested a return to Dakshineswar. But Ramkrishna shook his head. Mathur Babu's son Trailokya, the present owner of the temple, had never shown the slightest interest in Ramkrishna. He must have heard of his illness but hadn't come to see him even once though he stayed right here in Calcutta. The disciple tried to push his proposal by pointing out that Ramkrishna's adored Ma Kali was in Dakshineswar. But Ramkrishna retorted sharply, 'Is she not everywhere? Even here in Calcutta?'

After some search a house was found in Kashipur on the Barahanagar Road. A pleasure mansion, standing on eleven bighas and four kottahs of land, it belonged to Rani Katyayani's son-in-law Gopalchandra Ghosh. It had sprawling gardens filled with fruit trees, shrubs and flowering vines—somewhat tangled and neglected but still beautiful. There were two ponds with ducks and geese. The whole property could be rented for eighty rupees a month. Since it was not possible for Ramkrishna to live there alone it was decided that a good part of his entourage would move with him. The rest would come and go at their convenience. The house would be taken for six months to begin with and all the expenses would be met out of a common fund to which everyone would contribute. Ramkrishna, though seemingly indifferent to all things other than his own illness, kept himself informed about everything that went on around him. Calling Surendranath Mitra to his side one day he said, 'Look, Surendra, you're the most well-to-do among my disciples. The others are clerks and schoolmasters—hard put to fend for themselves and their families. Between them they'll manage the other expenses. But you must offer to pay the rent.' Surendranath agreed and within a few days the whole party moved to Kashipur.

One day Mahendralal Sarkar came to see Ramkrishna. He was in a foul mood. He had spent the morning in the house of a patient—an elderly lady with a huge establishment in Boubazar. The exercise of examining the patient had proved so futile that it left him fuming with rage. Flinging the fee offered to him by the lady's son in the boy's face he had stormed out of the house. 'What's the matter, sir?' his compounder Jaikrishna asked in dismay, 'Has your patient expired?'

'The old hag won't die in a hurry,' Mahendralal huffed and puffed on his way to his carriage, 'She'll kill everybody off first . . . Bit by bit,' he added as an afterthought.

'Why didn't you take your fee then?'

'What did I do that I should take a fee? The old bitch wouldn't let me touch her. She lay in bed with the curtains drawn, as coy as a new bride, while her maid applied the stethoscope. I couldn't even see if it was touching her back or her bum. An old hag of sixty with a rump like an elephant's and breasts the size of pumpkins! What had she to fear from me? Would I have eaten her up?' The good doctor snorted in his indignation. Jaikrishna gave a cackle of laughter and got a box on his ears for his pains. 'Why do you laugh, you rascal? Is this a laughing matter?' Then, sobering down, Mahendralal clicked his tongue and muttered sadly, 'We need women doctors in this country. I keep saying so but no one heeds me.'

When the carriage had started moving Jaikrishna consulted a notebook and said, 'Your next appointment is at the Medical College. There is a meeting at—'

'I'm not going to any meeting,' Mahendralal announced firmly, 'I'm sick and tired of them. I've a mind to visit the old man at Kashipur. I sense a beckoning within me . . .'

Walking into Ramkrishna's room the doctor was surprised to see him sitting up in bed chatting and laughing with his disciples. '*Ohé* Master!' he was saying to Mahendralal Mukherjee, 'The boys are tired of eating *dal bhaat* day after day. Send out for some mutton. You needn't spend more than five or six annas. The cook can make a good, rich curry and serve it with hot—' Seeing Mahendralal at his door, he gave a start and left his sentence in mid air. Mahendralal shot a sharp glance at his patient's face. It was smooth and unlined and bore not a trace of the agony that had etched deep marks on it over the last few months. His body, too, seemed relaxed and comfortable in a dhuti wrapped loosely around his middle and an *uduni* covering his bare back and chest. In his eyes was an expression the doctor could not fathom.

A tremor passed through Mahendralal's frame as he looked into those eyes and a deep depression assailed him. Conquering it with the force of character that was natural to him, he sat in the chair that was brought for him and asked brightly, 'I hear Dr Coates came to see you. He's a fiery old saheb with a violent temper. Was he rude to you?' The disciples shifted their feet and looked pointedly at Shashi. Prior to examining his patients Dr Coates had asked Shashi to hold his bag but Shashi hadn't touched it. He was an orthodox Brahmin and wouldn't touch anything belonging to a *mlechha* Christian. 'You, you! Go from here you *ullu*,' the old man had shouted, his face red and angry. Mahendralal laughed on hearing the story and, turning to Ramkrishna, asked, 'And what about you? Are you not an orthodox Brahmin? How could you allow a *mlechha* foreigner to touch you?'

'I . . . I don't know,' Ramkrishna replied, stammering a little. 'Something happened . . . I'm not quite sure what. I wasn't quite aware of what was going on till after he left. Then I purified myself by sprinkling gangajal on my bed and chanting *Om Tat Sat.*'

'You contradict yourself Moshai!' Mahendralal Sarkar said shaking his head severely at Ramkrishna. 'Only the other day you told us the story of Shankaracharya of Kashi. Of how, as he walked down the street one day, a Chandal bumped against him by mistake. "Why did you touch me?" he asked the Chandal angrily. But the Chandal replied, "I didn't touch you and you didn't touch me." Then, seeing the look of surprise on Shankaracharya's face he explained, "It is the soul that is important is it not? And the soul is not contaminated by touch. Our souls are as pure and untainted as ever they were." Didn't you tell us this story? Then why all this purification? All this gangajal and *Om Tat Sat*?' Ramkrishna grimaced and made a gesture of helplessness. Then he said, 'You are right, doctor. I don't practise what I preach. I can't help it. I'm a victim of my conditioning. For centuries we Brahmins . . .' His voice trailed away for a few seconds, then he continued, 'The other day Latu was standing by my side holding on to my bed when my meal arrived. How could I eat with him holding me. So I asked him to leave the room. Naren was very angry, "You don't believe in untouchability," he scolded, "Why then did you ask Latu to leave the room?" To tell you the truth, doctor, I don't know what I believe and what I don't. I can't make myself out. We Brahmins . . . generations of conditioning!'

The disciples looked nervously at the doctor. They were all afraid of him. He was so fierce and unpredictable. And so rude to their guru. Yet Ramkrishna Thakur never seemed to take offence. He did not brook argument from others. He either snubbed them into silence or changed the subject. But with the doctor he was different. He heard him out patiently and tried to answer his questions. They remembered an argument that had taken place the last time he was here. Ramkrishna was trying to explain the difference between faith and knowledge. 'Faith is like a woman,' he said. 'She's allowed to enter the innermost sanctum of the house. Knowledge is like a man. He has to wait in the outer rooms.

'Not all women are allowed to enter the innermost sanctum,' the doctor had punctured the beautiful argument with his accustomed crudity. 'What about prostitutes?' Ramkrishna and his disciples were tense with anxiety every time the doctor came on a visit. He found fault with everything he saw and was quite vocal in his criticism. If he caught sight of a disciple touching his head to his guru's feet he snarled angrily, 'Why do you addle his brains with all this sycophancy? He is a good man. Don't worship him as a god. This is how Keshab Sen was ruined.' He attacked Ramkrishna quite mercilessly whenever he felt like it. 'Why do you place your foot on people's chests during your famous trances?' he demanded once, 'Who do you think you are?' Ramkrishna looked guilty and ashamed. '*Ogo*! I'm not myself when I'm in samadhi,' he answered humbly. 'God enters me and takes possession of my body and soul. I lose all control. I have no knowledge of what I'm doing. It's a kind of madness. It is this madness, perhaps, that is killing me—little by little.' Mahendralal gave a snort of contempt at which Naren took him up. 'If you can devote your life for the spread of science,' he demanded, 'Why can't he risk his for the grandest of all sciences—the discovery of God.' Mahendralal's face turned a fiery red. 'Discovery of God indeed!' he muttered. 'Why can't each man do his work on earth with sincerity and commitment and leave God alone? But no. Everyone aspires to be a religious reformer! Has any man who is obsessed with God been content to live with his personal quest or discovery—as you put it? Every one of them—be he Jesus, Chaitanya, Buddha or Muhammud has had to pull crowds along with him. "What I say is right. Everyone else is wrong." Is this not a shameless proclamation of the self?'

Today, however, he did not seem to be in a fighting mood. Fixing his eyes on the sick man he said softly, almost tenderly, 'I couldn't sleep very well last night owing to the storm. And I kept worrying about you. You're apt to catch cold easily. So I came this morning to see how you were.'

'O *Ma*!' Ramkrishna exclaimed with an ecstatic smile. 'These are words of love. Your soul has caught colour after all. You have imbibed faith and—' 'No' the doctor interrupted hastily, 'Not faith. Only love. Love is beyond all reason. I love you, so I keep coming to you. Your disciples hate me. If they had their way they would kick me out of your presence. Everyone hates me. Even my wife and son think I'm hard hearted; devoid of love and mercy. But I'm not. It's only that . . . that I don't display my emotions.'

'But you should,' Girish Ghosh advised. 'You should open the doors of your heart from time to time.' Embarrassed by his own sentimental outpouring Mahendralal said gruffly, 'Let's change the subject. Let's have some singing. Sing a song Naren.' Ever willing to oblige, Naren burst into song. '*Prabhu main ghulam/main ghulam/main ghulam téré*,' he sang in his rich baritone, '*Tu dewan/Tu dewan/Tu dewan méré.*' Carried away by the power and melody of Naren's voice Ramkrishna rose from his bed and started swaying and pirouetting but, unlike other times, the doctor made no move to stop him; not even when his body became still and stiff in a *bhav samadhi*. It lasted only a few moments, then exhausted, Ramakrishna sank down on the bed with a sigh. For the first time that morning he looked straight into the doctor's eyes. 'Why!' he exclaimed, 'I see tears. You weep—' Mahendralal shook his head helplessly. The hard knot in his throat melted into a gush of tears that rolled down his cheeks and chin. 'My heart twists with pain whenever I hear sweet music,' he said. Ramkrishna clapped his hands like a child. 'You've caught the fever of the divine.' he exclaimed. 'There's no escape for you now.' Then, as if cracking a joke, he winked and added, 'You should thank me for it.' The doctor looked steadily into his eyes. 'Do I have to do it in words?' he asked. The voice was husky and tender—quite unlike his usual strident tones. 'What am I but an ordinary physician? I've been given the privilege of coming to you. I've learned so much . . .'

He rose and left the room. Girish Ghosh accompanied him to the door. 'How is Paramhansa Dev?' he asked. 'Much better—wouldn't you say? At least seventy-five per cent better.' Mahendralal placed a hand on Girish's shoulder. Shaking his head sorrowfully he muttered, 'No. He's not well. Not well at all.'

'Why do you say that?' Girish exclaimed, shocked. 'He's moving around without help. And he's eating better. I can guarantee that he'll be out in the streets in a couple of days.' Still shaking his head Mahendralal murmured, 'No one will be happier than me if your words come true.' He walked down the stairs not on heavily resounding feet, as was his wont, but with a muffled tread.

Two days later Ramkrishna vomited blood—great globs spattering his clothes, bed and floor. The cancer in his throat had spread its tentacles right across his head and lungs and excruciating pain shot through them in spasms. Groaning in agony Ramkrishna muttered, 'Avatar! Avatar! If I am one why do I suffer so? It's these people—Master and Girish and the others—who are responsible. If they hadn't insisted on deifying me this would never have happened.' But the very next morning he sent for Naren. Asking all his disciples to leave the room he beckoned to the boy to approach him. Then, taking his hands in his, he whispered, 'I give you . . . all that I have. From this moment I'm a fakir. I have nothing left. Nothing.' Then, his glance falling on his wife Saradamoni as she stood weeping in a corner of the room, he said, 'I leave her in your care. I leave them all in your care.' Naren stood like an image of stone, his large, lustrous eyes fixed on the dying man's face. 'Who is this man?' he thought. Ramkrishna seemed to hear the words that beat in Naren's head and heart, 'You still don't understand,' he said sadly. 'I'll tell you the truth. The absolute Truth. He who is Ram is Krishna. And they dwell in this body mingled together! Ramkrishna! Your Vedantas of course will tell you different—' He glanced once more at Sarada and said, 'The boys will look after you as they've looked after me. Don't weep. You know how I hate a glum face.'

On Sunday morning a man called Rakhal Mukherjee came to see him from Bagbazar. The man was a pukka saheb and he started berating the disciples the moment he entered the room. The soup they were feeding their guru had no strength in it, he said. Chicken broth was what he needed. Ramkrishna shrank a little from the idea of eating the unholy fowl. 'I have nothing against it personally,' he said his voice faltering, 'Our religion forbids it and . . . We'll see about it tomorrow.'

But the same evening, while chatting with his disciples, he gave an agonized cry, 'I burn! I burn!' he shrieked, 'My lungs are on fire. Is this the end? *Ma go!* Is this the end?' Two of his disciples ran to fetch the local doctor who came in a few minutes. All through the examination Ramkrishna tossed and turned in agony, 'I feel as if boiling water is shooting through my veins. Will I get well doctor?' Then, seeing that the doctor's face was serious and he made no answer he nudged the disciple closest to him and asked in a bewildered voice, 'Does that mean I won't get well? After so many months of agony they say I'll never get well! I'm not afraid of death. But, can anyone tell me from where the breath of life escapes? And how?'

No one could tell him. The terrible spasms died away in a while and Ramkrishna felt much better. 'I'm hungry!' he declared after the doctor had left. 'I would like to eat some *payesh*. I haven't eaten *payesh* in many months.' But when it was brought to him he couldn't swallow even a spoonful. It trickled out of his mouth and ran all over his chin. 'My belly is empty,' he said sadly, 'So empty—it aches. I feel like stuffing it with big handfuls of *bhaat* mixed with *dal* and *alu posto*. But Mahamaya is cruel. She denies me even a few grains.' Sighing, he chanted *Hari Om Tat Sat* and, turning over on his side, fell asleep. Relieved, the disciples went down to have their own meal.

A few hours later Latu came up. Ramkrishna lay on his side exactly as they had left him. But he moaned in his sleep so piteously that Latu ran down to tell the others. As soon as they came into the room Ramkrishna opened his eyes and smiled. 'I'm hungry,' he said. 'Won't you give me something to eat?' The disciples looked at one another in dismay. He was finding it impossible to swallow. Even water was being fed to him drop by drop through a wisp of cotton wool. What could they give him? A bowl of rice mush was brought in and, quite amazingly, Ramkrishna was able to eat it without any difficulty. After one bowl—another. 'Ahh!' he said with a deep sigh of satisfaction. 'Peace at last! Now I feel well. Truly well!' He lay down and went to sleep once again.

Night came. The household noises ceased as the inmates fell asleep one by one. Only Latu and Shashi kept vigil in the sick man's chamber. It was pitch dark outside. From time to time the baying of jackals broke the silence of the night. A few minutes after one o' clock Latu heard a strange sound—a thin, whirring noise like that of a clockwork toy. It was coming from where the patient lay. Latu jumped up and ran to his guru. Ramkrishna lay in an unnatural position. His body was stiff and twisted sideways and his head was hanging out from the edge of the bed. The sound came from his open mouth. Latu had seen his guru in *bhav samadhi* several times and recognized the symptoms down to the goosebumps that had broken out all over his body.

The disciples crowded into the room a few minutes later. Many of them believed, like Latu, that their guru was in a trance and would return to normal in a while. They moved around the bed chanting mantras and singing kirtan while they waited and waited . . . All except Naren. He sat, motionless, at the foot of the bed—his guru's feet clasped to his breast. After a while, he placed the feet back on the bed and ran out of the room.

As soon as dawn broke a messenger was despatched to Mahendralal Sarkar. He heard the account carefully but made no comment. His face was impassive and his voice sombre as he explained that he was on his way to a patient in Duff Street and that he would come to Kashipur as soon as he was free.

Mahendralal Sarkar reached Ramkrishna's bedside around one o' clock. He didn't even have to touch the patient. A glance at the face, eyes staring as though he had been loath to lose sight of his beloved world even in death, was enough to apprise him of the truth. The mouth was half open as though he had been trying to speak; to communicate with someone—anyone, till death had overtaken him. Avatar or otherwise he had had no yearning for heaven. It was this world of earth and dust that he had loved.

'He's been dead for about twelve hours,' Mahendralal Sarkar murmured. Then, addressing the disciples, he said, 'It was expected. Every effort had been made to save him but cancer is beyond our reach. Stop grieving and start making arrangements for the funeral.' Taking out a ten-rupee note he handed it to one of them with the words, 'This is a small contribution from me. See that a photograph is taken—of his last journey.'

It was five o' clock by the time the body was brought down. The disciples smeared sandalpaste on the limbs with loving hands and laid their guru reverently on a new bedstead spread with dazzling white sheets. Masses of white flowers were placed at his feet and over his breast.

Not many people knew Ramkrishna. Consequently, the number that wended its way to the burning ghat was pitifully small. The funeral processions of some other sadhus of the city had thousands of mourners whereas Ramkrishna's numbered a hundred and fifty at the most. But, of them, eleven were young men and one, at least, was equal to a million . . .

There were a few distinctive features about the procession. One mourner carried a Hindu trident; another a Buddhist spud. A third had a Christian cross in his hands and a fourth a replica of the crescent moon and star—symbol of Islam. Ramakrishna had preached the concept of *Jata Mat Tata Path* (there are as many ways to God as there are faiths) and, even in this hour of sorrow,

SUNIL GANGOPADHYAY

his disciples hadn't forgotten it.

Among the mourners was a small knot of actors and actresses from the Star. Behind them, keeping a studied distance, a solitary figure walked alone. It was a woman wrapped in widow's white. No one saw the tears that rolled silently down her cheeks as she walked and no one heard her sobs. The sound of her weeping mingled with the patter of the rain that fell from the sky as softly and sweetly as flowers on the parched earth below.

Chapter XLI

Bharat and Irfan sat watching the rain from an upstairs veranda of Dwarika's house in Maniktala. The exams were over and the boys felt relaxed in mind and light of heart. They had the house to themselves. The other inmates had gone home to their parents and Dwarika was out on his nocturnal jaunt. He had coaxed and cajoled them to accompany him but both Bharat and Irfan had stood firm.

It was a pitch black night. The gas lamps had been blown out by the violent gusts of wind and rain that had been sweeping the city for the last few hours. But, right in front of them, a large mansion was ablaze with light. There had been a recent invention called the dynamo by the aid of which one could have the strongest of lights. And these, indeed, were so strong that they dazzled the eyes.

The two boys sat smoking cigarettes and discussing an incident that had taken place in their college only a few days ago. Two eminent professors of the Philosophy department, both Englishmen, had started an argument which had taken such an ugly turn that the Chief Secretary of the Education Department had been forced to intervene. Irfan had seen the whole incident and he was describing it to Bharat. One of the two men, Edgar B Brown was small in build, mild and gentle of speech and sympathetic to native causes. The other, George O'Connor, was tall and powerfully built with a rich resonant voice which had all the power and passion of a seasoned actor's. Though the latter was more popular with the boys the former was considered the better scholar. Irfan had watched, amazed, as the two men rushed out of the hall arguing in loud voices. He hadn't understood everything they said because the exchange was heated and excited. But he heard O'Connor use the word 'Scoundrel' several times and saw Brown retaliate by grinding his teeth and muttering 'Stupid' and 'Blockhead'. None of the other professors had tried to resolve the quarrel or pacify the two men. John Reed, the Chief Secretary, had investigated the matter and suspended Brown for fifteen days at the end of which he was to tender a written apology to O'Connor. The principle behind the judgement was that George O'Connor's abuses had been aimed at an absentee individual—a man named Charles Darwin. But Edgar B Brown's had been hurled at his own colleague directly to his face. But who was this Charles Darwin? And why was George O'Connor so incensed against him? Only Irfan knew the truth.

Irfan was a favourite student of Edgar B Brown and visited him often in his house in Bentinck Street. Their association had begun long ago—from the day Irfan had saved the Englishman's life. Brown was the epitome of the proverbial absentminded professor. One day, as he walked down the street, puffing at his pipe and frowning in habitual abstraction, a pair of horses had come galloping by and knocked him down. Irfan saw the old man fall and, quick as a flash, he leaped forward and, picking him up, made a dash for the pavement. A second's mistiming and both would have been trampled under the dancing hooves. Recovering his breath Brown looked Irfan up and down, 'Why did you risk your life for me young man?' he demanded sternly. 'Is it because I'm an Englishman?' Irfan was startled at this strange reaction. 'I saw the horses coming towards you sir and ran to save you.' he answered. 'I didn't have time to think. Besides, I didn't even recognize you then.' Brown shook his head doubtfully. 'I don't believe you,' he said, 'People don't rush to one another's rescue in this country. They prefer to stand by and watch. I'm an Englishman. Do you expect a reward for saving me?'

Irfan was so disgusted by this question that he didn't even bother to answer it. Turning his back on the old man he walked rapidly away. But the professor ran after him and grabbed him by the arm. 'You've given me my life. Won't you take me to the hospital and get my wounds dressed? I have been badly injured. Look at the blood on my back and shoulders!'

After this incident Brown started inviting Irfan to his house. He lent him books and cooked meals for him. And, despite the vast disparity in age, race and scholarship the two became very good friends. Brown was a philosophy teacher by profession but he took tremendous interest in new science and kept himself informed about all the latest developments. He found in Irfan a willing and intelligent listener and began sharing all his ideas with him.

That evening, as Bharat and Irfan sat smoking their cigars and listening to the concert of rain, wind and thunder Irfan asked suddenly. 'Have you heard of Charles Darwin, Bharat?' Bharat frowned, trying to remember. The name was familiar. 'I seem to have heard it or rather seen it somewhere,' he answered, 'In *Englishman* perhaps. Why? Is he coming out to India?'

'Oh no. He died four years ago. He was a scientist.'

'Why do you talk of him now?'

'Because he's been on my mind for over a month. If what he says is true then what we've believed in all our lives is false.'

'What does he say?'

'Darwin denies the concept of Creation. We all believe that a Supreme Power (Muslims call him Allah, Christians God and Hindus Ishwar) created the world and all things in it. But Darwin says nothing was created. All natural phenomena—from the firmament to the human form—evolved over a period of time.'

'We don't have to believe everything a scientist says.'

'But he has given proof. Proof so conclusive that the Western races are facing a serious crisis of faith. Doubt and speculation are rife and men's minds are troubled. Because, you see, for all intents and purposes, Darwin is denouncing the Bible as myth.'

'Aah!' Bharat exclaimed, startled.

'According to the Bible God created the earth and firmament out of Chaos. And it took him six days to complete his creation—the last item of which was man. A couple of theologians have, after serious research, calculated the date on which man was created as 23rd October 4004 BC. Brown Sir told me that. We are now in the year 1886 which means man was created exactly five thousand eight hundred and ninety years ago. But we know for a certainty that men walked the earth before that. There were Hindus in India more than six thousand years ago. The Chinese are an even older race. There were people in Arabia and Persia. And even before that there were men living in caves and forests who hunted using stone implements.'

'Who was this Darwin anyway?'

'He was an Englishman—a doctor's son. His father sent him to study medicine but he found the subject drab and uninteresting

341

and left in a few months. His real interest lay in the study of flora and fauna and he had a truly scientific mind. When he was twenty-two he was invited by the British Government to sail on board ship *The Beagle*, which was being sent out on a survey of some islands in the Pacific archipelago. There were many who wondered at the choice. Why was such a young, half-baked scientist being sent out on such an important mission when there were botanists and biologists far more experienced? The reason was that the expedition was to last five years and it was to be a labour of love. The crew was to be paid nothing. What senior scientist would agree to those terms? Anyway, Darwin roamed the islands for five years collecting samples of plants and insects. Then, after extensive research, he wrote a book. I forget the full name which is very long. But it may be summarized as *The Origin of Species*. Brown Sir has lent me the book. Would you like to read it?

'What is it about?'

'I couldn't understand all of it. But at the centre of the book is the concept of Evolution. Darwin says that man evolved from a being something like a monkey. It was this that had led to the quarrel between the two professors. O'Connor was so incensed by the thought that his ancestors were monkeys that he called Darwin a scoundrel. And, Brown, who accepts Darwin's theory called O'Connor a blockhead who refuses to keep an open mind.'

'Galileo was imprisoned for going against the Bible. Giadarno Bruno was burned at the stake. How did Darwin manage to escape unscathed?'

'The age of the inquisition is over. We are living in a modern age. An age of science. The book raised a storm of controversy, of course. The clergy and the traditionalists heaped abuse on Darwin. But eighty per cent of the world's scientists have accepted the theory of Evolution. So have the enlightened sections of the West. The book is being sold in thousands and the veracity of the Bible is being seriously questioned.'

'If a scientist propogated the view that the Quran is a myth—what would be his fate?'

'He would be exterminated. We Muslims lack the scientific approach. We treat a code of laws written nearly two thousand years ago as sacrosanct and morally binding to this day. That is

342

why our society is so retrogressive. You Hindus are not much better.'

'Tell me Irfan, why do you agitate yourself over something that is happening in the West, so far from our own present reality? You are being unduly influenced by Brown Saheb.'

'You may be right. But some of Darwin's ideas have stuck in my head so firmly, that I can't root them out. One of the things he says is that a struggle has been going on from time immemorial and is still going on among all living creatures—a struggle for survival. And only the strongest, the fittest, win. The weak and vulnerable are wiped out. If it weren't so the earth would be teeming with every kind of plant, animal and insect. There would be no room to breathe. Floods, famines, pestilence and disease take toll of some. But how many? Some species die out because they don't have the will or the endurance to stay alive. *The Survival of the Fittest*. That's the key phrase. Does it make sense?'

'Hmm. It sounds right . . . somehow.'

'Do you see what that leads to? It shatters our age-old belief that Allah stands guard over us; protects our interests and looks after our welfare like a benign father. If we accept Darwin we have to deny Allah's role in our lives as both creator and nurturer.'

'Even so why does it upset you?'

'You don't understand Bharat. I'll have to go back to Murshidabad—to my own people for whom the dictates of the Maulvi are more important than those of the Viceroy. I'll have to read namaaz five times a day and fast during Ramzaan. I won't be able to utter a word of what I think. How shall I endure such a life?'

'Now let me tell you about myself Irfan. I was born in a Hindu household and I followed Hindu ways of worship till a man I respect above all others taught me otherwise. He was my tutor—Shashibhushan Singha. He told me that the entire pantheon of gods and goddesses were wrought out of the human imagination. They were mere idols of stone and clay and the breath of God did not pass through them. I was so shocked when I first heard this that I felt my head would burst. My whole world seemed to disintegrate. Then, little by little, I started accepting it . . .'

343

SUNIL GANGOPADHYAY

'Islam, as a religion, is more advanced. Our prophets have taught us that Allah is an abstraction defying description and formation. Don't mind my saying so Bharat, but I've always been amused by the way you Hindus laugh and weep and go into a frenzy over a bundle of straw and clay. It makes me think of little girls playing with dolls.'

'Not all Hindus worship idols. The worship of an abstract, omnipotent omniscient presence has also gone on for centuries. The Param Brahma of the Brahmos is no different from your Allah or the God of the Christians. The three great religions of the world are agreed that there is one Supreme Power presiding over the universe. But each insists that theirs is the true one. Isn't this amusing too? I haven't read Darwin's book but I agree with him. I believe that even if there is such a power he has nothing to do with man. The problem, Irfan, is that man needs something physical to hold on to. If you—I mean Muslims, Christians and Brahmos—really believe God to be an abstraction why do you sing hymns in his praise, mutter prayers and cry *Allah hu Akhbar*? Would an abstraction have ears to hear? And speaking of idols—don't Christians have idols too? What are the images of Christ, Mother Mary and the Angels? What about your mosques? There are no figures in mosques—true. But what about the carving and frescoes with their rich inlays of ivory and precious stones? Do you really need all that for the worship of an abstraction? Do you really need to worship Him at all? Wouldn't He know what was in your hearts without your putting it in words?'

'*Baap ré!*' Irfan exclaimed. 'I've never heard you talk like this Bharat.'

'I don't—usually. But have you considered, Irfan, that innumerable men and women have worshipped God in their innumerable ways through the centuries? Do we really have the right to dismiss their faith as worthless? True faith should command respect—no matter to whom it is addressed. Whenever I see someone wrapt in meditation of his God I bow my head in reverence.' Bharat rose to his feet as he spoke these words adding in a lighter tone, 'I have to walk home in the rain. Won't you give me something to eat before I go?'

'Of course,' Irfan rose too. 'Everything is ready. All I need to

344

do is warm up . . .'

The two friends proceeded to the kitchen. 'I hate the thought of going back,' Irfan muttered as he lit the fire. Bharat laughed, 'It was an evil day for you when you saved Brown Saheb's life,' he teased. 'From Brown to Darwin! From the frying pan into the fire! But don't distress yourself. You'll forget them both the moment you see your new bride's face. You'll say your namaaz, observe Ramzaan and become one with your family, clan and community. And quite rightly, too. Why should you alienate yourself from all you've held dear all these years? Living in isolation is terrible, Irfan. Particularly in a village—'

Irfan stood up suddenly and took Bharat's hands in his. 'What if I go mad Bharat?' he asked in a dazed, wondering voice. 'My head feels as though a storm is raging through it day and night. I see nothing but darkness before me.'

'Shove Darwin's book into the fire, Irfan. And stop going to Brown Saheb. Why do you torture yourself? Hang on to life and sanity. They are more important than knowledge.'

Bharat had to wade through knee deep water on his way back. Irfan had begged him to stay the night. His brain was agitated and confused, he said, and he was in desperate need of company. But Bharat declined. He couldn't sleep except in his own bed, head resting on his own pillow. His friends teased him about his insistence on getting back home. 'You don't have a wife waiting for you,' they grumbled, 'Why do you have to rush back?' Bharat smiled and answered invariably, 'My pillow is waiting for me.'

The rain had stopped falling and a few stars were twinkling in the sky when Bharat set off. Walking past Hedo Lake he started humming to himself. When alone his memory of Bhumisuta became sharper and more poignant. Reaching home he unlocked the front door and lit the lamp. He had talked more than he usually did and the exercise had robbed him of all desire to sleep. His brain was teeming with thoughts and he felt wide awake. He decided to make himself a cup of tea. Lighting the fire he was filling up the kettle when he heard a carriage roll up to the door and an angry voice call out, 'Bharat! Bharat! Open up at once.' Bharat ran to the veranda. It was very dark outside and all he could see were two dim shapes and the silhouette of a carriage. Even as he called, 'Who is it?' one of them lifted a walking stick and rapped loudly on the door. Bharat ran down the steps and opened it. And now he recognized them. One was Shashibhushan and the other, her veil pulled down to her chin and hands crossed over her breast, was Bhumisuta.

Shashibhushan ascended the stairs without a word, then, reaching Bharat's room, snapped angrily, 'Why haven't you lit the lamp?' Bharat ran to the kitchen and brought it. Raising the wick till a golden glow filled the room he looked up at Bhumisuta. And then he saw, with a shock, that a large bandage covered one side of her head. It was soaked with blood. There was blood, too, clotted in the long strands of her hair and her sari was streaked with red.

Shashibhushan waved his stick angrily in the air and said in a harsh whisper, 'I have brought her to you. You may do what you like with her. I won't be there to see it. As of today I have nothing to do with either of you.' He stopped, frowning, for a few moments, then continued, his voice changing a little, 'I didn't believe in destiny ever in my life. But I do now. We are powerless before her.' He turned to go. Bharat ran after him. 'Master *Moshai*!' he cried. Shashibhushan couldn't control himself any longer. 'Silence! You base ingrate!' he shouted. 'I saved you from a terrible death. I fed you, gave you shelter and educated you. And you! You betrayed me! You kept me in the dark. You wrote her letters. Yes—love letters. And she? I pulled her out of the lion's jaws. I offered her everything any woman could ever want. Independence, a life of dignity, a beautiful house by the river, wealth, status, prestige. I offered to marry her and give her my name. But she wanted none of it. You two have conspired together behind my back. You've made a laughing stock of me and—'

'I know nothing of what you say. Believe me—' Bharat cried, his face twisted with pain.

'He is not to blame,' Bhumisuta murmured. 'It's all my fault.'

Shashibhushan didn't even glance at her. 'You live on charity yourself,' he curled his lip derisively at Bharat. 'How do you propose to give her your protection? The Maharaja will make enquiries. If you are caught—it will be the end of you. You'll have to spend the rest of your life as a fugitive. I wanted to give you a new life. A pure, clean life. But your own blood has betrayed you.

346

How can you escape it? The fount from which it flows ... I should have remembered—'

'Sir please. Please sit down and tell me—'

'No. I can't endure your presence another minute. I can't breathe the polluted air. I feel choked, suffocated . . .'

Bharat fell to the ground and clasped Shashibhushan's feet with both hands. Shashibhushan stepped back hastily as if recoiling from a snake. 'Don't touch me haramzada!' he snarled. 'I'll break your head if you do.' And he raised his stick as though he would actually strike Bharat. Then, trembling all over, he lowered his arm and turned to the door. 'It's no use,' he muttered. 'Violence is not for me.' He stopped once again and said as if pleading with Bharat. 'I didn't strike her. She jumped from the balcony in an effort to escape and hit her head. But where was the need? I wouldn't have kept her against her will. I only wanted . . . Never mind. It's of no consequence.' He went rapidly down the stairs his English boots creaking loudly as he went. A door slammed in the distance followed by the sound of wheels rolling down the road. It grew fainter and fainter and gradually faded away . . .

Bharat turned slowly to Bhumisuta. She was sitting on a frayed *mora* at the doorway leading to the other room, her elbows on her knees and her chin resting in her hands. Her veil was pushed back from her face and her eyes looked compellingly into Bharat's. The minutes passed as though they were hours. When Bharat spoke it was quite out of context. 'Will you have some tea?' he asked. Bhumisuta shook her head. Bharat wondered why he had asked her that. Then he remembered that he had been about to make tea for himself. Groping in the maze of his agitated mind he sought desperately for something to say. 'Your . . . your head,' he stammered. 'Does it hurt . . . badly?' Bhumisuta shook her head again. Then she stood up. 'The Maharaja wanted me to go with him,' she said.

'To Tripura?'

'Yes. But I didn't go. If I went with him I would have had to stay there forever.'

'That is true,' Bharat agreed thoughtfully. 'No woman has ever returned from the king's palace.'

'I don't know if he meant to keep me in the palace.' Bhumisuta could see Bharat's awkwardness and tried to ease the situation by carrying on the conversation. 'He wanted me to sing to him every night.'

'Sing to him!' Bharat echoed then asked curiously, 'How did he take your refusal? What did Master Moshai say?'

'He said that the only way he could save me from the king was by marrying me. I shut my ears when he said that—not with my hands but with my mind. I do that whenever I don't want to hear—'

They sat in silence after that listening to the rain which had started to fall again. The wind rose and howled around the house. 'Shall I shut the door?' Bhumisuta asked softly, 'The rain is coming in.'

'Bhumi!' Bharat cried out in the voice of a drowning man. 'Why did all this have to happen?'

'I had written an answer to your letter. But I didn't know how to send it. Then I decided to come to you. I couldn't stay there any longer.'

'I promised to look after you. I wanted to—desperately. I've thought about you day and night. But I didn't want you this way. I owe Master Moshai everything. Everything, Bhumi, down to this life itself. He loves you. He wishes to marry you. How can I . . .? No, no Bhumi. I can't. You shouldn't have come—'

'I wouldn't have married him even if you hadn't written. But I don't want anyone's pity. I . . .'

'Bhumi!' Bharat cried out in his agony. 'Don't you understand? He loves you. I've never heard him speak of any woman . . . He was determined never to marry again. Then he saw you and loved—'

'I've waited for you. Day after day and night after night. I knew you would respond some day.'

'You've come to me. This should have been the happiest day of my life. But the cost . . . The cost is too great. How can I think only of myself? Master Moshai has been cruelly hurt. He loves you—'

Bharat and Bhumisuta stood facing one another. One step forward and they could have been in each other's arms. But no one took that step. 'What shall I do now?' Bharat, in utter helplessness, turned to the very woman who had come to him in the hope of protection. She had no answer to give him. Raising the edge of her sari she wiped the tears that streamed silently down her cheeks. Bharat shook off his indecision with a tremendous effort and said, 'We cannot sleep under the same roof. And marriage is out of the question. I cannot live with my mentor's curses ringing in my ears to my dying day. I have nothing; nobody. I'll starve in the streets if Master Moshai withdraws his protection. And you'll starve with me. Go back to him. He's worth a hundred of me Bhumi. He'll make you a good husband. You'll be happy and I'll be happy in your happiness.' Bhumisuta shrank from these words. Cowering against the wall she looked at him with the eyes of a dumb animal. 'There's a bed in the other room,' Bharat continued. 'Go—get some sleep. I'll spend the night with my friend.' Slipping his feet into his shoes he murmured, 'I'll take you back tomorrow morning. When Master Moshai hears we have spent the night apart from one another he'll forgive us.' Unhooking his *piran* from a nail in the wall he slipped it over his head and went on, 'There's wood and water in the kitchen. I'll bring the milk with me when I come. Don't be frightened if you hear sounds overhead. There are large rats on the roof and they scamper about all night.' He felt his heart bursting with pain as he uttered these mundane words. Hot, bitter tears rose to his eyes. He ran out of the house, into the wind and rain, sobbing loudly as he went.

Irfan opened the door to find Bharat standing outside dripping from head to foot, his clothes caked with mud and slime. He was shivering violently and his teeth chattered so that he could hardly speak. Irfan put down the candle and drew his friend into the room. 'You're soaked through!' he exclaimed. 'And what is this on your clothes? Did you fall on your way home?' Bharat made no answer. Irfan fetched a gamchha and lungi, fussing all the while. 'Now rub your head dry. And take off your wet clothes. What happened? You couldn't reach home? Where were you all this time?'

'Will you let me stay with you tonight Irfan?'

'Of course. I told you not to attempt going back in this terrible weather and—' He peered into Bharat's face and got a shock. Bharat's lips were twisted in an effort to keep himself from crying and his eyes were as red as hibiscus. 'What's the matter with you?'

Irfan asked anxiously. 'Tell me Bharat.' But Bharat only shook his head. 'You should have some brandy mixed with hot water,' Irfan said. 'It will warm you up.' Now Bharat spoke, for the second time after his return. 'Can I have some tea?' he asked. Tea! At this hour? Irfan was nonplussed but he went into the kitchen and made a big glassful. Bharat drank it in great, thirsty gulps and felt better. 'Irfan,' he said. 'We were talking about Reason and Logic only a couple of hours ago. But they don't work in the life of a human being. I—' Irfan cut him short with a great yawn. 'We'll resume our conversation tomorrow,' he said. 'I'm so sleepy I can hardly keep my eyes open.'

But for Bharat there was no sleep. He kept sitting in the outer room staring into the dark. And before his eyes he saw—no, not Bhumisuta's face, pale and soft as a wilting flower, but Shashibhushan's—dark and fiery with suppressed anger and humiliation. Bharat had lost his mother in his infancy. His father had sent him to a cruel death. No one loved him. No one had ever spared a thought for him. Except Shashibhushan. He had to prove to Shashibhushan that he was no base ingrate; that he valued his affection and protection above everything else in the world. Even life and . . . and love. A wave of salt water welled up in his eyes at the thought of losing Bhumisuta. But he stood firm. He would give her up. He would take her back to Shashibhushan and then—he would go away. From everything and everyone who reminded him of her.

Across the street, in the weaver's colony, a cock crew heralding the approach of dawn. Bharat rose to his feet. His clothes lay in a soiled, dripping heap in a corner of the room. There was no question of wearing them. But he couldn't walk the streets in Irfan's lungi. He entered Dwarika's room. Dwarika's clothes hung on a wooden *alna* folded neatly in stacks. Bharat picked out a dhuti and a *piran* and put them on. Then, walking into the kitchen, he picked up a large meat knife and stuck it at his waist. If Shashibhushan doubted his words he would slit his throat in his revered guru's presence and prove his fidelity.

Bharat closed the door gently behind him and walked out of the house. It was very early and the streets were deserted except for some bathers who were making their way to the Ganga with their *ghotis* and gamchhas. Bharat walked rapidly past them, stopping only once—at a sweet shop.

Over a clay oven a vast vat of rich milk simmered, creaming and frothing and emitting clouds of fragrant steam. In another a fat cook was frying *jilipi*. Bharat watched the golden strands curl and twist crisply in the hot ghee. The delicious odour assailed his nostrils and he felt a sharp pang of hunger. He bought a pot of milk and a basketful of jilipi. Bhumisuta would be hungry, he thought. He would have to give her something to eat before he took her back.

Climbing up the steps to his apartment he was surprised to find the front door wide open. Bhumisuta must have forgotten to shut it after he left last night. 'Bhumi! Bhumi!' he called, peering into the bedroom. But there was no one there and the bed was neat and smooth. No one had slept in it. Bharat was frightened. What had happened to Bhumisuta? He went from room to veranda and back again. He peeped into the kitchen and lavatory and even climbed up to the roof. But there was no sign of Bhumisuta.

Where could she be? Had she gone back to Shashibhushan? Hurt and humiliated by Bharat's betrayal she hadn't waited for his help. But would she be able to find her way? Bharat had to find out. He had to take her back, in safety, to Shashibhushan. If he started right now he might overtake her. He rushed down the steps and ran down the street. Banibinod was cleaning his teeth with a neem twig a few yards away. He grinned at him but Bharat had no eyes to see. Jerking his head like a madman he muttered as he went, 'You risked your life in coming to me Bhumi. You hurt yourself. But I couldn't give you my protection. I'm not worthy of your love Bhumi. Forget me. Be happy in your new life.'

Arriving at his destination, Bharat stood at the gate to recover his breath. He had avoided coming within miles of this house for death awaited him here. But, at that moment, he had no fears for himself. He only thought of Bhumisuta. Stepping through the gate along with a pedlar who had been allowed entry by the gatemen, Bharat came to the great hall where a flight of stairs curved upwards. Banibinod had described the house to him in detail so he knew where to go. Skipping nimbly up the stairs he came to Shashibhushan's chamber. Shashibhushan sat in a chair by the window—his face tense and preoccupied. Then, before the latter could stop him, Bharat fell to his knees on the floor. 'Don't misunderstand me, sir,' he cried wildly, rubbing his face on his mentor's fair feet. 'I didn't want her. I didn't keep her. I sent her back to you.' Shashibhushan felt the warm tears trickling between his toes and tried to rise. But Bharat clutched them like one possessed and went on. 'She has realized her folly and come back. She wants you—only you.' Now Shashibhushan withdrew his feet and said sternly, 'I told you I'll have nothing to do with either of you. Why do you come here to torment me?'

'I haven't touched a hair of her head. I swear it before you Master Moshai. I left home last night. I sent her back . . .'

'Sent her back! Where?'

'To you. Isn't she here?'

'Why should she be here? I don't want her any more. No—I don't want her.'

'She isn't *here*?' Bharat raised his head. His eyes stared wildly out of his pale face at Shashibhushan. 'Where is she then? She isn't in my house.'

Shashibhushan had lifted his arm to strike Bharat the night before and had checked himself in time. But now he lost control. Gripping Bharat's hair with one hand he twisted it mercilessly. 'You've lost her you scoundrel!' he cried in an agonized voice. 'You coveted her but you couldn't keep her.' His eyes, flaming with rage and hate, glared at Bharat. 'Get out of my sight you worthless bastard. Get out!' He pushed Bharat away with all his might, then rose and left the room.

The rest of the day was spent in looking for Bhumisuta. Shashibhushan sent a messenger to the house in Bhabanipur. But she hadn't come there. Enquiries were made in all likely and unlikely places. But Bhumisuta was nowhere. She seemed to have vanished altogether. And she had gone empty handed. Her clothes had been left behind in the Maharaja's house. Even the bandage on her head was found, thrown in a corner of Bharat's bedroom.

Bharat walked all day through the lanes and alleys of Calcutta looking for Bhumisuta. Then, in his wanderings, he reached the river. He peered into each ghat in the light of the setting sun. Then, completely exhausted, he sank to the ground beneath a tree. A little breeze, dancing in the leaves above his head, played sweetly over his heated, fatigued limbs. His eyelids slipped over his burning eyes and sweet sleep, the balm of hurt minds and bodies, overtook him. Crowds of people passed him by. Memsahebs in gorgeous gowns promenading with their companions, Eurasian girls, arm in arm with their escorts, walked up and down the Strand. They cast curious glances at the fair boy lying asleep on the bare ground. But no one cared to find out why. The city was a cruel place.

A few minutes later the rain came—in a little drizzle at first, then, gaining momentum, it became a torrent. The tell-tale marks of suffering and anguish on Bharat's face were washed away. Drenched with rain drops it looked like a newly blown flower— unbruised by time and the hands of men. Bharat slept through the rain—a deep, restful sleep.

Book II

Book II

Chapter I

It was the month of Ashadh. In the sky the newly darkening clouds played hide and seek with the sun, chequering the earth with light and shadow. Occasionally a light rain winged past like a flock of twittering birds. The zamindar's bajra floated proudly on the breast of the wide river. The banks on either side were so far away that they seemed etched in water, which changed colour with the changing sky.

The bajra was not too large and was being manned by only six boatmen. Two guards with guns sat on top of the boat under a huge umbrella and kept their eyes skinned for any danger that might lurk in the waters. The two puffed at their hookahs and spoke in low voices. They had received instructions from the steward to be as quiet as possible.

There was only one passenger within. He lay prone on his bed in the luxuriously fitted out state chamber, a pillow under his chest and a slate in his hand on which he scribbled something diligently. He was Rabindra, the youngest son of Debendranath Thakur of the Thakurs of Jorasanko. That hoary patriarch had many sons yet he was hard put to find someone who could tour his vast estates, scattered all over the districts of Bengal and Orissa, and collect the taxes. His eldest son Dwijendranath was a scholar and philosopher—totally out of touch with the mundane affairs of life. His second, Satyendranath, was a busy civil servant. His third, Hemendranath, was dead and two others were insane. The son in whom he had reposed the greatest faith had disappointed him most bitterly. After the disastrous crash of his shipping business Jyotindranath was reduced to a lamp without a flame. Robbed of all his light, he had crept under the sheltering wings of his Mejo Bouthan. He was afraid of facing his father and his father had lost all interest in him.

Dwijendra's eldest son Dwipendranath had assumed a fair degree of responsibility for the family on reaching adulthood. But Dipu was a city boy and used to its luxuries. He didn't mind supervising the accounts in the khazanchi khana but he drew the line at travelling all over his grandfather's estates in boats and bullock carts. Yet it was imperative that someone do so. The presence of the zamindar or a member of his family, from time to time, kept the peasants reminded of their obligations. Debendranath's sons spent lavishly but didn't care to ask where the money was coming from. And so he had no option but to put his youngest son to the test. Rabindra was intelligent and gifted but he had been whiling his time away in Calcutta writing poetry. Determined to give him some responsible work that would wipe his silly fancies away, Debendranath had sent him on a tour of the estates. He had received reports that the boy was doing the work allotted to him with seriousness and commitment and was pleased.

Rabindra was thirty-two years old, a man in his prime, strikingly handsome and of robust health. He was, now, on his way to Sajadpur or Shahjadapur which lay in Pabna of the Yusufshahi pargana.

Though there were *kuthis* everywhere he went, Rabindra preferred sleeping in the bajra, which he did often. In consequence, everything he could possibly need was stocked in the boat. Sacks of fragrant Kaminibhog rice, golden moong dal, almonds and raisins, baskets of apples, oranges, bananas and coconuts, oat meal and quaker oats, jars of oil and spices, mango pulp dried in sheets, pickles and preserves, earthen pots full of sweetmeats, scented soap, hazeline, cream, tooth powder—the list was endless. There were, besides all these, cases of brandy, champagne and wine. The last three items were of no use to Rabindra. Unlike his peers from other wealthy families of Calcutta, Rabindra did not care for alcoholic drinks. But he had to keep them in his boat, for entertaining English and Indian officials in high positions was part of his job.

It was late afternoon. The bajra was skimming, like a stately bird, over the wide expanse of water clear as glass. The zamindar's son was in his chamber reclining on the bed. But his hand neither held a glass of wine nor the tube of an *albola*. Nor were his eyes rivetted on a dancer or singer performing before him. He was alone, quite alone. He wore a simple dhuti and nothing else. His elaborate costume of choga, chapkan and turban hung from a bracket on the wall. The sun coming in from the window fell on his bare back and feet bathing them with sweat but he would not move away. Heat didn't bother him. His mind was on the poem he was writing. He thought of nothing else. At this moment he was not a zamindar. He was a poet—the finest and most illustrious poet of Bengal.

All through boyhood and youth Rabindra had written his poems with one, dearly beloved face floating before his eyes. For years after her death that face had haunted him but now, in his prime, he saw another—constantly, invariably. She had left her childhood behind her and was now a young woman, exquisite of face and form and keen and sensitive of mind and spirit. Indira and Mrinalini were of the same age. But what a world of difference lay between them! Mrinalini's husband had tried hard to educate her, to instil in her a love of poetry, art and music. But his efforts had been wasted. He had never seen her face glow with empathy when he read out a favourite piece. Once or twice she had even fallen asleep. She was no companion to him except in bed where, of course, she was all that he desired. She had given him three lovely children whom he adored. And she was an excellent housewife. She was an ideal daughter-in-law for the family but no soulmate for her poet husband.

Of late Rabindra couldn't rest till he had shown what he had written to Indira. Indira was not only the most beautiful of the Thakur girls, she was also the most talented. She had recently been awarded the Padmavati Suvarna Padak for standing first among the girls who appeared in the University examination. She spoke and wrote English and French with a competence that matched her performance in her mother tongue, Bengali. She also read all three literatures with avid interest. She was an accomplished musician too, excelling equally in Indian and Western classical forms. Her latest craze was her uncle Rabindranath's songs for which she could set the notations in the twinkling of an eye. But despite her beauty and many talents she was twenty and still unwed, though not from any lack of suitable proposals. She rejected each and every one of them—why she wouldn't or couldn't explain. Was it because she couldn't bear to leave her Robi ka?

Indira had been deeply attached to Rabindranath from her

childhood and he had returned her love with tender affection. Now, it truly seemed as though they couldn't live without one another. Not one of the suitors she met came anywhere near the standard she had set for herself. Robika was her ideal man. He was so brilliant; so handsome and distinguished looking and had such a large heart. Where was the man who could match this ideal, even remotely? When in Calcutta she had to see him every day. And when he was away, she spent her days writing him letters which he replied faithfully filling sheet after sheet with his elegant flowing hand. Writing to Indira was the work he loved best and, in doing so, he often set aside other, more important tasks. Her mind was so receptive; so attuned to the most delicate nuances of his thoughts and feelings that he could open up to her as he could to no one else.

A couple of years back Rabindra had sailed to England borrowing the passage money from his nephew Satyaprasad—his father having turned down his request with the statement that he was not sponsoring any trip abroad for any of his sons. Satyaprasad had become quite calculating of late. He lent money to his uncles and cousins and took care to retrieve it with interest. Rabindra had not undertaken this voyage for purposes of study. He had planned it as a pleasure tour. He proposed to travel to Europe and gain exposure to Western music, art and theatre. His friend Loken Palit was going with him. He liked Loken's company. Loken had a brilliant, analytical mind deeply sensitized to the fine arts. Rabindra's Mejda, Satyendranath, was also travelling with them which meant that he would be saved the trouble of making arrangements and taking decisions. Rabindra looked forward to the delightful time ahead of him but no sooner had he reached London than he started feeling homesick. He longed to go back to Calcutta and to India. The longing changed into a sick desperation as the days went by.

England is lovely in September. The air is soft and mellow and the leaves of the trees turn russet and gold against an azure blue sky. But all this beauty eluded Rabindra's eyes. He had no thoughts at all except for the letters that arrived regularly from Indira. Every morning, on waking up, he rushed to the letter box and was in a fever of impatience all day if he found it empty. He was equally distressed when letters came, for Indira begged him to return in every line. 'I hate everything here,' she wrote, 'I can't bear to live here any more.'

In one letter Indira threatened to stop writing if he didn't come back immediately, and declared that she would have nothing to do with him in future. She kept her word. She didn't write for a whole week and then sent a brief note inserted in a letter written to her father. Rabindra's face turned pale with shock and humiliation. She had never done such a thing before. Did she really mean to sever all connection with him? The thought was too painful to bear.

That day he took a decision. He would return as soon as he could. Loken and Satyendranath were nonplussed when he told them of his intention. 'Are you mad?' they cried in unison. 'We meant to spend three months here and it is only a few weeks since we've arrived. We haven't seen anything of Europe yet. And everything's well at home. You had a letter from your wife only yesterday. You said so yourself.' But Rabindra was desperate. He had to go. He started making preparations secretly, quietly, and within six weeks of his arrival in England he started on the journey back.

Reaching Bombay he boarded a train to Calcutta. Two months and eleven days on the boat and another three days on the train! Rabindra could hardly conceal his impatience. After aeons, so it seemed to him, the train puffed its way into Howrah Station. Rabindra breathed a sigh of relief. Engaging a hackney cab he ordered the driver to drive straight to Birji Talao. In his eagerness he forgot his duty—to make his first obeisance, after his return, to his father.

The light was fading by the time the carriage entered the gate of Gyanadanandini's house. Rabindra looked out eagerly. A young woman stood in the garden her eyes fixed on a flock of birds circling and twittering about the dome of St Paul's Cathedral. The sound of carriage wheels on the drive made her turn around. She saw a young man descending from the carriage. He was tall and handsome with a dark beard and wavy hair and he was smiling at her. She stared in wonder. Was she seeing a vision? Was this truly her Robi ka or was it a phantom wrought out of her desperate longing? The figure spread out his arms and called 'Bibi!' Indira forgot everything—her misery and indignation of the past and her doubt and dismay of the present—and ran like a fawn into those waiting arms . . .

One good thing about a bajra was that it didn't jump about like a horse carriage. One could read and write at one's ease. Sometimes the gentle swaying of the boat lulled one to sleep. Rabindra slept little but he dreamed many dreams. Some of them provided him with plots for his short stories. Others carried a whiff of the essence of poetry. He had started writing narrative poems these days and found himself enjoying the experience.

Evening had come. A servant entered the room with his cup of tea. Sipping delicately from the porcelain cup Rabindra looked out of the window. The sky was a riot of red and gold and so was the earth. The trees and shrubs growing by the river seemed to have shed their green and imbibed the colours of the sky. The sun was setting and the boat would soon be anchored at some village ghat to rest for the night. Even as he thought so he heard the splash of heavy metal in water and cries of 'Careful! Careful!' from the boatmen. Rabindra rose and, leaving his room, came up on deck. He loved looking out on the river at this hour. So many people could be seen at the ghat! Women with mud pots on their hips, men in caps making their way to a tumbledown mosque, children playing about in the water. So many sights! So many sounds! The shrill call of birds winging their way back to their nests, the quick, clear voices of mothers calling out to their children, the call of the azan, heard a thousand times yet eerie and unfamiliar. All these never failed to touch an answering chord in Rabindra's soul.

'We have reached Sajadpur Huzoor,' an employee of the estate murmured. His manner implied something more. Rabindra's brow furrowed in thought then, suddenly, he realized what it was. He had come out of his room, his torso and feet bare. But here in Sajadpur he was not a mere poet. He was Raja Babu, a zamindar. And he had to appear as one. He descended the steps quickly and entered his room

The next morning was lovely, cool and bright. Rabindra stood on the balcony of the *kuthi* listening to the music that came wafting over the air. It was the morning raga of Bhairavi being played on the shahnai. As the sweet, poignant strains entered his ears he felt his heart twist with nostalgia. It was a familiar sensation. He often found himself assailed thus in the presence of something overwhelmingly beautiful.

Today was *Punyaha*, the day fixed for the landlord to commence collecting rents for the ensuing year, and his subjects could see him for the first time. Though, to tell the truth, they were not his subjects. Sajadpur lay within his uncle Girindranath's estates. Girindranath had died many years ago when his grandsons Aban, Samar and Gagan were minors. Debendranath had looked after their property along with his own. They were adults now, but still refused to take up their responsibilities. They liked nothing better than to keep themselves within the house and idle the hours away in music and painting. Thus Rabindranath was constrained to play zamindar on their behalf.

All was in readiness for this first meeting between tenants and zamindar. The shahnai players had taken up their positions on a machan above the lion gates. Banana saplings had been planted around the *mangal ghat* and the front of the kuthi had been hung with garlands of bright yellow marigolds. Within, the big hall had been converted into a reception room. A chair, vast and elaborate as a throne and covered with red velvet, stood at one end. The rest of the floor was covered with coloured dhurries, bamboo mats and sacking.

Though Rabindra had toured these parts before, it was his first visit to Sajadpur as an adult. He had come here once, many years ago, with his brother Jyotirindranath. Jyoti dada, who did everything in style, had brought a large company of friends and family members, servants and maids and a band of musicians. Jyoti dada had taken him tiger shooting one day and put a gun in his hands. Rabindra had pulled the trigger at his brother's insistence but his hand had trembled so badly that the bullet had flown wide off the mark. Rabindra was thankful for that to this day. No, hunting and shooting were not for him.

'Huzoor!' The manager came and stood at his elbow. 'Your subjects are waiting. It's time to go down'. Rabindra sighed and, going indoors, struggled into his official costume of china silk kurta and pyjamas, high turban with jewel and feather and nagras for his feet. As he walked down the steps a guard called out ponderously: '*Of the long line of the illustrous Thakurs of*

363

Jorasanko Sreel Srijukta Rabindranath Mahimarnav . . .'
Rabindra felt as though he was acting a part in a play; a part he
had performed often on stage and with which he was familiar.
His entry into the hall was greeted with a dozen conches being
blown together, the piercing sounds drowning the soft crooning
of the shahnai. The assembly stood up, their hands folded in
humility. As Rabindra took his seat on the false throne all the men
fell to their knees and knocked their foreheads on the ground.

Events such as these invariably began with the offering of
arati to the zamindar by the priest of the local temple. But this
particular zamindar was a Brahmo who believed in inaugurating
every auspicious occasion with prayers to the All Merciful Param
Brahma. Accordingly, an Acharya came forward, read some
prayers, then garlanded the zamindar and anointed his brow with
sandal. The manager of the estate now took up his cue. Rising to
his feet he read out a long eulogy praising the zamindar in terms
that made him appear like a god newly descended from heaven.
Rabindra's lips twitched with amusement. The innocent villagers
believed every word that was being said. They thought him a real
king who sat on a throne and wore silks and jewels and had the
power to change their lives. Little did they know that he was as
false as false could be: that he hated sitting on this throne and that
his costume was hot and uncomfortable and he longed to throw it
off. He had written a poem recently which ran *The caged bird sat
in her golden cage/the wild bird in the wood.* At this moment he
felt like a caged bird.

His thoughts had wandered and he came to with a start. The
manager had finished his speech and was garlanding him. It was
now his turn to speak; to bless the assembly and begin the
Punyaha. Every year, on this occasion, one of the tenants received
the zamindar's special benediction. The idea behind this practice
was to send a signal to the gathering that the zamindar was
committed to nurturing and cherishing his tenants; that he took
from them but he also gave. It was a symbol of his magnanimity
and love. The man selected to receive the *Punyaha* this year was a
middle-aged Muslim who appeared from his looks to be well
born and wealthy. Rabindra garlanded the man and put the mark
of sandal on his brow. Then he handed him his gifts—a gold
chain, a new dhuti and *uttariya*, a big fish, a pot of curd, paan,

tobacco and fruits. The man touched each item to his forehead and put it aside. Then, lying prostrate on the ground, he clutched Rabindra's feet with both hands. Rabindra stepped back hastily but this form of salutation was customary and the man was determined to do his duty. He crawled on his chest towards the unwilling feet and placed a pouch full of gold coins on them. After this the other tenants came up with their gifts one by one. This went on for such a long time that Rabindra got quite bored. His eyes wandered away and rested on the gathering in front of him. And it was then that he noticed something odd. There were several distinctly separate groups in the room. The Hindus sat on one side—the Brahmins on spotless white sheets spread on carpets and the lower castes on cotton mats. The Muslims, who were the largest in number, sat on the other side on strips of sacking.

Two days later Rabindra left Sajadpur and sailed towards Shilaidaha. His mission had ended successfully and he felt pleased with himself. The tenants seemed contented; the manager and servants of the estate were working well and enough rents had been collected to satisfy even Baba Moshai.

On the way, in the boat, he wrote two short stories. They were coming as naturally to him these days as poetry. He had been contributing a short story to each of the issues of *Hitabadi* till the editor Krishna Kamal Bhattacharya commented that his stories were too heavy for the ordinary reader. 'Write something in a lighter vein Robi Babu,' he had advised. That had incensed Rabindranath. Was he to adapt his style to the whims of editors? He stopped contributing to *Hitabadi* giving his stories, instead, to his nephews Sudhindra and Nitindra who were looking after the family journal *Sadhana*. One of the two stories he wrote on this journey was called 'Kabuliwala'. For some reason he kept remembering his little girl Beli all the way to Shilaidaha. She had just learned to talk and was talking all the time.

Shilaidaha of the Birahimpur pargana was situated at the mouth of the Gorai, one of the tributaries that branched out from the Padma. The name had an interesting history. During Muslim rule this ancient village had been called Khorshedpur after a pir named Khorshed who had appeared from no one knew where and built a hut in the woods. Then, with the coming of the British, he had suffered the indignity of being forgotten. A fiery indigo planter, who went by the name of Mr Shelley, built a kuthi at the fork of the two rivers. Gradually the village acquired the name Shelleydaha, corrupted in the vernacular to Shilaidaha. Needless to say, the cruel, oppressive Mr Shelley was no kin to the dreamy, romantic, tender-hearted poet of England.

When the fortunes of the planters had dwindled, Rabindra's grandfather Dwarkanath Thakur had bought the enormous kuthi for a song. Ever since then it had served as an office not only for the estate of Shilaidaha but for Kaya, Janipur, Kumarkhali and Punti Mahal. It was also used as a holiday resort by the Thakurs and Rabindra remembered many happy boyhood days spent in it. However, over the years it had fallen into a decline and had to be demolished. A new kuthi had been built in its place and it was there that the *Punyaha* would be conducted. But on reaching Shilaidaha, Rabindra decided not to move into the kuthi. He preferred to stay on the boat in full view of the river which had swelled to twice its size with the monsoon rains and acquired a wild terrifying beauty.

The *Punyaha* took place the next day. The arrangements were somewhat different here. The zamindar was welcomed not with the sweet, throbbing strains of shahnai but with a volley of gunshots. The distance between the river ghat and the kuthi was less than a hundred yards but a palki had been arranged to carry the zamindar. It was not meet that he walk the path like a peasant. But Rabindra waved the palki away and declared that he would walk. The nayeb was dismayed, more so at the fact that Rabindra had discarded his princely costume. He wore a simple dhuti and achkan and carried a shawl over one shoulder.

Inside the hall, Rabindra noticed the same pattern in the sitting arrangements. In addition, there was a row of chairs presumably for the important officials of the estate. He had held his tongue in Sajadpur but here he decided to protest. 'Why are they sitting in separate groups?' he asked the manager gravely.

'It's been the custom for years, huzoor,' the man replied. 'The Hindus pay first. That is why they sit in front.'

'But the Muslims are greater in number. They should be allowed to take precedence. Besides, why are they sitting on sacking? Why have no sheets been spread for them?'

'Each man is seated as per his caste. The Brahmins are highest. Then come the Kayasthas. It's the custom—'

'All customs are not good or just,' Rabindra cut him short. 'Many need to be changed with the changing times. Please alter the arrangements. Let everyone sit together as friends.'

'You don't know what you are saying huzoor,' the manager smiled indulgently as if dealing with a recalcitrant child. 'That will convey a most disastrous message. The lower castes will think they are just as good as their superiors. Come, sit on your throne and start the *Punyaha*. It is getting late.'

'I don't believe in caste distinctions and I won't accept them. I won't sit on the throne either. Take it away. I'll sit on the floor with the others.'

'No, huzoor,' the manager shook his head and bit his tongue. 'We can't change the rules of centuries so easily. Come, let's begin. It will take a long time and—'

Rabindra fixed his large dark eyes on the manager's face hoping to shame him into obedience. But the man was an old hand, hardened and astute. He had ruled the estate with an iron hand for many years and he was not about to lose his authority on the whims of a youngster. He had heard that this youngest son of the Karta's was as unlike a zamindar's son as possible. He didn't ride or shoot or keep company with singing and dancing girls. He didn't even drink. Instead he wrote poetry and sang songs. He was determined not to stand in awe of such a one.

'I'm sorry,' he said firmly, 'but I can't alter the arrangements without the zamindar's permission.'

'I'm the zamindar here,' Rabindra replied equally firmly, 'and my command is above all others. If you choose not to obey me you'll have to leave.'

'I'm not the only one. All the officials of the estate will resign if you force the issue.'

'So be it,' Rabindra replied coolly. 'Anyone who wishes may leave my service. I've brought my own khazanchi from Calcutta. He'll look after the estate.' With these words Rabindra picked up the heavy throne-like chair and placed it in a corner of the room. Then, turning to his subjects, he said 'Today is *Punyaha*—a day of rejoicing and union. We will set aside all caste distinctions and sit together like brothers.'

His words created quite a stir in the assembly. It took the members some time to understand the purport behind the zamindar's pronouncement. Then, when light had dawned, the Brahmins started muttering their disapproval and the Muslims looked shamefaced. 'We are quite comfortable where we are,' they said. But a band of young men had risen on the zamindar's command and they came forward to help him. Together they picked up the chairs and placed them outside the hall. Removing the sacking they spread white sheets all over the floor. When all this was done they turned to the now standing assembly and cried, 'Huzoor has said all his subjects have the same value in his eyes. All men are equal. You may sit where you like.'

After all the men were seated, Rabindra sat down facing them and the *Punyaha* commenced. The manager and his officials stood standing for a while. The former looked angry and perplexed. He hadn't expected such firmness from one who looked so soft and gentle. It was a highly embarrassing situation, and he didn't know how to deal with it. Matters became worse when a couple of officials looked at one another sheepishly and decided to sit down. But Rabindra put an end to his dilemma by smiling kindly at him and saying, 'I request Manager Babu to withdraw his resignation. And the others too,' he added.

After this incident other changes were ushered in easily and painlessly. Rabindra went walking by himself, dismissing his guards and attendants. He met the villagers and apprised himself of their problems and needs. Not everyone opened up before him though. Many still stood in awe of the zamindar.

But though Rabindra was busy all day with his estate officials and subjects, the nights were his own and he spent them in the bajra, huddled over a lamp and writing poetry far into the night. When weary he would stroll on the deck and look out on the river, vast as a sea and swelling and foaming with deadly currents. He loved the Padma. She whispered to him at night and many were the thoughts she shared with him.

Looking out over the dark expanse of water, that night, he remembered the mysterious woman he had come across at the river ghat. She had a pleasant face and a tight well-knit body draped in a saffron sari. Her anchal was tucked into her waist and it was full of white flowers. Nayeb Moshai had told him about her. She lived in a leaf hut under a *tamal* tree by the little green pond that belonged to the Basaks. No one knew where she had come from but many stories were whispered about her. 'Don't look into her eyes huzoor,' Nayeb Moshai had warned him, 'She has strange powers.' Rabindra had suppressed his amusement with difficulty and when he saw her at the river ghat, he looked straight into her eyes. Sarbakhepi, for that was the name the woman went by, stopped short and returned stare for stare. Then, taking up a handful of camellias from her anchal, she put it in his hands murmuring softly, 'Gour. My heart's treasure! The jewel of my eyes! My beautiful, beautiful Gour!' Rabindra felt the soft hand brush against his and a shudder passed through his frame. Sarbakhepi held his eyes with her own dark ones and song in a sweet clear voice:

'*Morè jè bolo sè bolo sakhi*
Sè roop nirakhi nari nibaritè
Majilo jugal ankhi
O na tanukhani Keba sirojilo
Ki madhu makhiya tai'

Rabindra wondered if this was Sarbakhepi's own composition or that of some ancient *padakarta's*. He left her and came away but her song wouldn't leave him. He kept humming it all day.

Boats went up and down the river even at night, their lights flickering over the dark water like glow-worms. In the sky the moon played hide and seek with the clouds. A soft breeze, laden with the scent of flowers, blew into his face and lifted his hair. His ears were filled with melody from the voices of the boatmen who sang as they plied their oars:

'*Jyobati!*
Kyan ba karo man bhari
Pabna thèkè ènè dèbo
taka damèr motri'

Rabindra was charmed. This was a song of love and separation;

---

* You may chide me as you will my friend
But my eyes beheld his beauty and stood transfixed
Ah! who created that beauteous form
And anointed it with honey?

369

emotions as old as the human race itself! The traveller had left his young beloved far away in a distant village and set sail over the Padma on a long uncertain voyage. She had wept and sulked and he had tried to comfort her with the promise of bringing her a *motri* from Pabna. What tender pathos there was in the lines! What nostalgia in the tune! Rabindra wondered what a *motri* was! What was that invaluable something that cost only a rupee but would bring a smile to the face of the beloved?

Rabindra hurried to his room and wrote down the lines in an exercise book he kept for the purpose. He couldn't allow this charming little song to be borne away over the river and be lost to him. It was better than many compositions of so-called poets. He decided to send for the runner Gagan Harkara next morning. Gagan had a fine collection of songs which he sang as he ran with the post, from village to village. Rabindra would copy them in his book. Bengalis were so musical!

His sojourn by the villages of the Padma was coming to an end and he would be leaving for Calcutta in a few days. He had collected a substantial amount of money in taxes and Baba Moshai would be pleased. But his personal collection of experience was his own and he hugged it in secret. So many faces! So many songs! Sights, sounds, scents! He was taking back a treasure trove.

Chapter II

The evening teas at Janakinath Ghoshal's house were famous, practically on par with the Governor's 'At Homes'. Receiving an invitation to one was considered a status symbol and anybody who was anybody in Calcutta had attended them at some time or the other. The gatherings were presided over, not by the master of the house but by the mistress. It seemed to be an age of women's empowerment. Queen Victoria ruled England, and Swarnakumari, the Ghoshal family of Kashiabagan.

Swarnakumari took care not to invite more than seven or eight guests at a time but they all had to be distinguished in some field or other. Thus bureaucrats, politicians, poets, playwrights, doctors and journalists rubbed shoulders with one another at the gatherings in her house. Unlike other high-profile parties a fair sprinkling of women could also be seen in Swarnakumari's drawing room. The furniture in the room was Western, the ambience Western but the conversation that went on was strongly national in spirit. The master of the house was an ardent patriot and though he kept a low profile, it was his personality that imbued the assembly. He resented British rule as fiercely as he hated the traditions that created and nurtured disparities between man and man. His crusade against the caste system was far from theoretical. He had brought it right into his own kitchen by employing cooks from the lowest stratum of the caste hierarchy—the untouchables. His passion for the upliftment of Indian women was manifested in the freedom and status enjoyed by his wife and daughter.

Today, of course, the untouchable cooks had been replaced by Brahmins of the highest order as was evident from their thick shikhas and dazzling white *poités* swinging from bare torsos. A special guest was coming this evening from Bombay about whom many stories were circulated. It was rumoured that he was a rabid Hindu who wouldn't deign to wash his feet in a non-Brahmin house.

371

Swarnakumari cast a final glance at the arrangements before going up to her room to dress for the party. She was satisfied. Everything was in place. The couches had small teapoys in front of them with a glass of water, a silver cigar box and brass ashtray, long and slim and shining like gold, on each. The sixty-four-lamped chandelier was ablaze with its wealth of candles and the grandfather clock was polished to perfection. Little lace fans were scattered about, there being no *punkah* in the room. Swarnakumari put up her hand to straighten a picture on the wall, then turning to her daughter she asked, 'What songs have you prepared for this evening Sarala?'

'Two songs of Robi Mama's,' came the reply. 'Don't ask me to sing any more.'

'Mr Tilak doesn't know Bengali. Why don't you sing something in Sanskrit?' Sarala had a large repertoire of songs. She could sing in English, Bengali, French, Sanskrit, Hindi—even Karnataki. 'People from other parts of India think Bengalis have faulty diction when it comes to Sanskrit,' Swarnakumari continued. 'Show Mr Tilak how good your Sanskrit is.'

'Why should I? I don't care to put my accomplishments on display for anyone—not even Mr Tilak.'

'That's a very foolish attitude Sarala,' Swarnakumari said severely. 'You must sing Bankimbabu's *Bande Mataram* at the very least.'

Sarala and her mother often got into arguments. But they were never loud or aggressive. Their family culture drew a firm line against the rude and the vulgar. Besides, offending your elders was considered the height of bad breeding. 'I'll sing *Bande Mataram*,' Sarala conceded sullenly, 'but if we can learn Hindi, surely they can learn Bengali?' Sarala was a rebel. She had wanted to take up Physics as her subject in college but Bethune didn't even have a Physics department. The best they could offer by way of a science course was Botany. But Sarala had not want to study Botany. She decided to attend the evening lectures at the Indian Institute of Science and take the exam in private. Her parents and relations advised her against it but Dr Mahendralal Sarkar backed her up. 'We'll make special arrangements,' he declared joyfully. 'In any case, the boys are not tigers. They won't eat her up.' The special arrangement was the placing of three chairs in one corner of the hall. At the commencement of each evening's lectures Sarala was escorted there by her two brothers who sat by her till they were over. 'Bodyguard! Bodyguard!' the boys whispered loudly enough for her to hear but she didn't condescend to cast a glance in their direction.

Sarala had passed with distinction and been awarded a silver medal. Following that she had completed her graduation and was now studying for her postgraduation in Sanskrit. This shift from Physics to Sanskrit had surprised many. 'It won't be that easy,' an eminent professor of Sanskrit College had said on hearing that she proposed to take the examination on the strength of instruction from a private tutor, 'We'll see how she gets through.' Sarala had taken up the challenge and was working day and night. Her pandit was very pleased with her efforts, and had declared that out of all his pupils Sarala and Hirendra Datta of Hathibagan were the most meritorious. Sarala had two other preoccupations these days. One was editing the family journal *Bharati* and the other was keeping her numerous suitors at bay. She was determined not to marry and become a housewife. One had only a single life, which was too precious to waste. Her parents were not putting pressure on her either.

The sound of carriage wheels on the drive made Swarnakumari beat a speedy retreat. She couldn't let anyone see her as she was. She would come down the stairs after all her guests had arrived and taken their seats, and make her entrance into the hall as dramatically as a queen. Sarala, unlike her mother, paid little attention to her dress or to the effect her presence would have on the guests. She wore a white silk sari, this evening, held at the shoulder with a brooch set with a large ruby the colour of pigeon's blood. She wore no other ornament. She hastened to the door, just as she was, to see her father descending from his carriage. 'There won't be any bachelors this evening Solli,' he smiled at his daughter. 'No one will pester you to marry him.' Even as he spoke another carriage rolled up the drive and, within a minute, two men entered the hall. One was Motilal Ghosh, brother of Sisir Kumar and editor of *Amrita Bazar Patrika*. His companion was also a journalist. He came from Bombay and was the editor of the famous Marathi journal *Kesri*. He was a fiery pamphleteer and wrote both in English and Marathi. His name

373

was Balgangadhar Tilak.

Balgangadhar was about thirty-six years old. He had a very fair complexion, a strong muscular body and a face in which pride and arrogance were ill concealed. He belonged to the caste of Chitpavan Brahmins who considered themselves to be the highest in the Brahminical order. Sarala was familiar with the legend associated with the Chitpavans. Centuries ago, after a shipwreck in the Arabian Sea, a number of bodies had come floating over the waves and been cast ashore on the Konkan coast. Presuming that these were dead bodies, the villagers had prepared a giant pyre for their cremation. But the moment the flames touched them the corpses rose and leaped to the ground. That they belonged to some white race was evident from their exceedingly fair complexions and grey-green eyes. They were accepted by the community and given the status of Brahmins for were they not twice born?

Balgangadhar was well educated but his views, on some subjects, were astonishingly traditional—even retrogressive. He advocated Western education but was against widow remarriage. He favoured the caste system and was against a law being passed denying conjugal rights to a husband till such time as his bride reached the age of puberty. Reports were constantly coming in of girls as young as five or six being raped by husbands in their prime and of being badly injured; of even dying from pain and shock. All enlightened, forward-thinking men of the country had welcomed this move of their rulers. But not this lion of Maharashtra. He had protested against the bill with a passion bordering on frenzy.

Balgangadhar took off his shoes on entering the room and expressed a desire to wash his feet. Sarala led him to the courtyard and poured water on them with her own hands. He allowed her to do so but did not condescend to address her with a word. The other guests arrived. Swarnakumari made her appearance and, after exchanging the preliminary courtesies, commenced arranging the refreshments on plates and handing them out one by one. Out of deference to Mr Tilak all the food served was vegetarian. Rosogollas had been ordered specially from Nabin Moira's shop. The Brahmin cooks had prepared luchi, mohanbhog, nimki and sandesh. Motilal Ghosh, in whose house

Mr Tilak was staying, whispered in his hostess' ear, 'Don't serve him anything.'

'Why not?' Swarnakumari asked, astonished, 'Everything has been prepared at home by Brahmin cooks.' But Motilal shook his head. 'Mr Tilak has no faith in Bengali Brahmins,' he said. 'I, too, had engaged a Brahmin to prepare his meals but he has brought his own cook from Bombay.' Swarnakumari felt deeply offended. Tilak noticed her expression and said, 'I'll have some tea. But please tell your servants to bring the liquor, sugar and milk in separate vessels. I'll mix them myself.' Motilal stared at him in surprise. 'I'm amazed that you've consented to drink tea here,' he said. Then, taking his guest's permission, proceeded to tell the gathering of an incident that had taken place some years ago in Poona. A Christian missionary and his sister had invited Tilak, Ranade and Gokhale to address a meeting. After the speeches were over he had taken them home and served them tea and biscuits. Next day their host had leaked the story to the press and it had appeared in the local newspaper. The Shankaracharya, incensed by the fact that these distinguished Brahmins had not only drunk the alien concoction but that too in the house of a *mlechha* foreigner, had delivered an edict ostracizing them from the Hindu community. Tilak had appealed to him to withdraw his edict promising to pay a fine and to perform whatever penitential rites were asked of him. He had kept his word and been forgiven. At this point in the story the barrister Ashutosh Chowdhury fixed his eyes on the Maratha's face and asked gravely, 'Why did you agree to pay the fine Mr Tilak? Do you really believe that drinking tea in an Englishman's house is a sinful act?' Tilak wagged his head from side to side. 'No,' he said solemnly.

'Then why—?'

'You won't understand. You, in Bengal, have changed many of your social laws. That's because your social discipline is not very tight. You have no moral leader of the stature of Shankaracharya. It's different in Maharashtra. Besides, the common folk believe that one loses caste by eating in a foreign household. Had I not performed penance they would have rejected me. I couldn't risk that. You believe in social reform first and political change afterwards. I believe in working in the

375

opposite order.'

'I've heard you're against widow remarriage,' Sarala said somewhat edgily.

'Yes.'

'Why? Widows in this country suffer such pain and deprivation. Are you not aware of it?'

'I am. But I believe they should continue to do so. They should give up all the pleasures of the world and spend their lives in selfless service to the members of the family in which they live. By doing so they'll be setting a great example. If they stray, rot and decay will set in—not only in their families but in our entire society.'

'Wonderful Mr Tilak!' Sarala laughed. 'Women must suffer and set examples. But a man may marry one woman after another and —'

'You seem to have only a partial knowledge of my views daughter,' Tilak interrupted. 'I oppose the remarriage of widowers just as I do that of widows.'

At this the whole gathering started twittering with suppressed laughter. Janakinath felt uncomfortable. The man was a guest in his house. It was in bad taste to needle him or laugh at him. He thanked his stars he hadn't invited Dr Mahendralal Sarkar.

'Mr Tilak,' Anandamohan Basu took him up next. 'I've heard you're against the Conjugal Rights Bill but I don't understand why. Do you really condone the cruelty that goes on in the name of conjugal rights?' At this Sarala rose and left the room. It wasn't proper for a young unmarried girl to hear such talk. 'If I catch one such beast of a husband,' Tilak muttered between clenched teeth, 'I'll give him such a shoe beating that he'll remember it all his life.' Anandamohan was surprised. 'But I've heard just the opposite!' he exclaimed. 'I'm told that you've written burning articles against the bill. You've collected signatures. I've even heard that you and your supporters disrupted a public meeting in Poona called in favour of the bill.' But Tilak was unfazed. 'All this is true,' he announced calmly. 'I *am* opposed to the bill. It should never have been passed.' Then, looking straight into Anandamohan's eyes, he said tersely, 'I wish to make my views clear before you gentlemen this evening. I am totally opposed to child marriage. I believe that girls should reach the age of sixteen and boys the age of twenty before they are wed. I also believe that there is a good deal wrong with our society and many of our laws need to be changed. But why should we allow the British government to interfere? It is our problem and we will solve it whenever we can. You Bengalis are incapable of doing anything yourselves. All you do is draw the attention of your foreign rulers to your weaknesses. They mock and revile us and pass laws. We in Maharashtra are trying to take away their powers while you are putting more and more power in their hands.'

'There are several Bengalis who share your views,' Anandamohan replied. 'But have you considered the fact that social evils are perpetuated unless a law is passed against them? Could we have prevented the burning of widows without a law? Or the selling and buying of human beings as slaves? We are a dependent nation. What power do we have to bring reform from within? Going by what you said just now you would have preferred to wait till these heinous customs changed by themselves. In the meantime thousands of women would be burned alive and thousands of men, women and children would be bought and sold like sheep and goats in the marketplace.'

Janakinath rose from his seat. 'Some more tea?' he asked in an effort to steer the conversation away to a more neutral area. Motilal Ghosh came to his aid. 'Let's have some music,' he said, 'Call Sarala Ma.'

Sarala came into the room and, taking her place at the piano, sang the three songs she had prepared. The guests expressed their admiration of her singing in glowing terms. All except Mr Tilak who looked totally unimpressed. He had the same expression on his face when Swarnakumari presented him with two of her books. It was an honour she bestowed on very few. But her special guest just turned them over in his hands briefly before putting them away. Then he rose to his feet. 'Friends of Bengal,' he began in the voice and manner he used when addressing a public meeting. 'I wish to place a certain proposal before you this evening. That is why I am here in Calcutta.' Then, taking a deep breath, he continued, 'We, the members of the Congress, meet once a year and mouth fiery speeches, needless to say, in English. Do these speeches or meetings have any impact on the masses? Do they even know what we are trying to do? Our trouble is that we are hopelessly divided, hopelessly rooted in our own provinces and in our own small cultures. We need to come together; to bring the common folk together. But how? Not through meetings and speeches. And we don't have a national festival. The need of the hour is to organize a festival in which everyone will join. We have started celebrating Ganesh Chaturthi in Maharashtra and received excellent response. Why don't you introduce it in the Bengal Presidency? The idea is to get the common man in the streets on any pretext.' Mr Tilak's co-guests looked at one another. Sarala's mouth twitched with amusement. She found the Hindu god Ganesh with his protruding stomach and elephant head very funny. 'Mr Tilak,' one of the guests pointed out. 'You said Indians don't have a national festival. What about Muharrum? There are crowds in the streets throughout the length and breadth of India.'

'Is that an Indian festival?' Tilak asked testily. 'Or Arabian? I agree that the Muslims are united. But what about the Hindus? Are they not Indians? Why do they dwell in groups like frogs in their separate wells? If all Muslims can join in a Muharram procession why can't all Hindus do the same for Ganesh—the granter of boons?' Now Motilal Ghosh said with a little smile, 'You're talking to the wrong people. This is a group of Brahmos who have rejected idol worship. They duck their heads and hasten away when passing a temple. And you're asking them to celebrate Ganesh Chaturthi!' Tilak was silent for a few moments. When he spoke there was a slight sneer in his voice. 'Very well,' he said. 'You Bengalis are very superior beings and don't have religious festivals. So be it. Let's think of something else. Can we not organize a festival around the birth of a great warrior? A national hero? The British think we are a weak and cowardly race. Let's show them that brave men have been born in this land. The only way we can fight our rulers is by organizing ourselves into a strong race of warriors and patriots.'

The others looked at one another in dismay. Bengal barely had a history leave alone a great king. Then one of them spoke. 'He needn't be a Bengali. Why don't we take Emperor Akbar?' 'Yes! Yes!' the others echoed. 'Akbar would be acceptable to everyone.' Tilak looked steadily into the face of the man who had spoken first. A queer light flickered in the slate-coloured pupils of his eyes as he said, 'Was Akbar a great warrior? All he did was subdue a few native rajas and chieftans. Besides, can Akbar be called an Indian? Did he not have the blood of Timur and Chengiz running in his veins? I know my history. Akbar's grandfather Babar wrested the throne of Delhi from Ibrahim Lodi in the year 1526. And Akbar mounted it in 1556. Are you suggesting that it took only thirty years for an alien dynasty to turn native? If we consider the Mughals to be Indian what's wrong with the British?'

'The Mughals made this country their own,' someone murmured. 'They married Indian women and became Indian.'

'By that logic we should wait another two or three centuries. By the end of that time, doubtless, the British would have married Indian women and become Indian.'

Following this an argument ensued in which everyone took part. Some maintained that the Mughals could not be compared with the British—Akbar in particular. He was secular at heart. He had even advocated a coming together of the two religions—Hinduism and Islam. Other names were also suggested. What about Porus? But he was a Greek. Sangram Singha? No one had heard of him. Nana Saheb? Guru Gobind Singh? Tilak rose to his feet and, in a voice that quelled the clamour, announced a name. 'Chatrapati Shivaji Maharaj.'

Chapter III

Sarala was bored. Her magnificient home, filled with beautiful objects, had hardly any human beings in it. Her brother was in England; her father in the mofussils. Her sister, her closest friend and confidante, had recently left for Rajshahi with her husband. Her mother was at home, of course, but she had never been very communicative with her children. Besides, she spent most of her time writing and disliked being disturbed. The mornings and evenings were bad enough, but the afternoons were the worst. The hours crawled by, maddeningly slow. How much could one study? One could sleep, but Sarala hated sleeping during the day. Sitting on a mat spread out on the floor she pored over her lessons. When she got tired of Sanskrit she would take up a volume of Bengali poetry and read it aloud. Sometimes she even composed verses of her own. Every now and then she walked into the adjoining room. This room had been her sister's. Hironmoyee was very fond of mirrors and she had had a huge one put up on her wall. Sarala often stood before it examining herself. She saw a young woman, wrapped carelessly in a cotton sari with a face in which the eyes were the most prominent. They were large and bright and heavily outlined with kajal. Sarala dispensed with chemise and jacket during the hot afternoons but took care to adorn her eyes with kajal or surma. Standing, thus, before the mirror she asked herself, 'What do I look like, really and truly? Am I beautiful?' The young men who visited her in the evenings, the ones her father called her 'suitors,' never tired of telling her how beautiful she was. One said she looked like a princess; another like the Goddess Saraswati. But she shrugged off their compliments with a laugh. She knew that they said the same things to all the girls they met. If they were to see Bibi they would compose paeans in paise of her loveliness. Bibi was far more beautiful than she was.

Sarala was incapable of taking any of her suitors seriously. Without exception they all made her laugh, particularly when they tried to become intimate with her. One afternoon a young man called Jogini Chatterjee came bursting into her room. It was a highly improper thing to do but he didn't seem to be aware of it. This Jogini was the brother of Mohini Chatterjee who had married Saroja the eldest daughter of her uncle Dwijendranath. On the strength of this relationship Mohini's four brothers had easy access into the houses of Dwijendranath's siblings. Jogini and his brother Sajani were head over heels in love with Sarala. But Sarala couldn't return the compliment and had evolved a method of dealing with them. The moment one of them tried to get too familiar she would say, 'Let's play cards.' Then, shuffling the pack with deft fingers, she would deal and start the game. She was very good at it and invariably won.

That afternoon, however, she was so taken aback that she didn't know how to react. She was lying on the bedstead in Hironmoyee's room her eyes on the other Sarala who looked at her out of the sheet of Belgian glass on the wall. She started up at Jogini's entry. He hesitated at the door for a moment, then rushed up to her and thrust a blue velvet case in her hands. 'Sarala! Sarala!' he cried theatrically, 'I've been wanting to give you this for months. But I couldn't muster up the courage. There's a phial in it filled with *attar* of roses. And mixed with it is the essence of my heart. I beg you to anoint your limbs with it.' Jogini was young and handsome and Sarala was just blossoming into womanhood. But, far from being moved by this romantic declaration, Sarala burst out laughing. '*Oki*! *Oki*!' she exclaimed, 'Why are you using such fancy language?' Jogini's ardour collapsed like a deflated balloon. He moved back, step by step, till he reached the door. There he stood for a while watching her as she rolled on the bed in helpless mirth.

Jogini didn't come near her for the next ten days. Sarala realized that he was hurt but she couldn't help it. Declarations of love made her laugh. She found them silly and theatrical.

Jogini's closest rival for Sarala's attention was Abinash Chakravarty, son of the famous poet Biharilal Chakravarty. When the two were visiting together each wanted the other to leave first and consequently both stayed on and on. Sarala yawned and looked bored but they paid no attention. Instead they measured each other up with wary eyes and urged one

381

another to go home. Jogini might say to Abinash, 'It's getting late. Sarala looks tired.'

'You're right,' pat would come the reply, 'You start off. I'll follow you in a minute.' Or, if Abinash muttered meaningfully, 'It's going to rain', Jogini was quick with the suggestion, 'You'd better hurry home. My carriage is coming for me.' Though not a poet himself Abinash looked like one with his long hair, soft dreamy eyes and a silk *uduni* on his shoulders. He even spoke like one. One evening, hearing Sarala play Beethoven's Moonlight Sonata on the piano, he rushed up to her and caught her hand. 'Ah me!' he exclaimed. 'What ethereal strains! What stream of nectar gushes forth from heaven! What waves of sound pass through groves and gardens; over flowers and leaves! Don't stop Sarala! For God's sake don't stop. Play more . . . more!'

'Yes I will,' Sarala said solemnly, 'But how can I if you keep holding my hand?'

Abinash released her hand with a jerk. Sarala resumed her music her mouth twitching with suppressed laughter as Abinash went on murmuring extravagant compliments in her ears, 'Sarala! Sarala! Your fingers are the colour and shape of champak buds. Your teeth are as lustrous as pearls. Your cheeks have the delicate flush of the pomegranate seed. You're no ordinary mortal. You're an apsara Sarala! A goddess!'

At this point Jogini's brother Sajani walked in. He couldn't stand Abinash and tried to frustrate his attempts at coming closer to Sarala in every way he could. Now he made a dash for the piano and exclaimed, 'Let's have a duet Sarala! I'll sing and you play.' Abinash and Sarala were both alarmed at the prospect of hearing Sajani sing. 'Brother Sajani,' Abinash said quickly in the voice mothers use with troublesome children, 'Why don't you go out into the garden and sing? Sarala was playing an exquisite piece of music for me and—'

'Look here Abinash,' Sajani turned angry, red eyes on his rival. 'I'm not your brother—in the first place. In the second—why should I go out into the garden? I shall sing right here.'

'You can if you so wish. No one can stop you. But Sarala was playing classical music. That won't blend with your brand of music, will it brother?'

'Why not? Classical means ustadi music—does it not? I can sing ragas.'

'The two classicals are not the same. *East is East and West is West. And ne'er the twain shall meet.* They won't blend. They can't.'

'They can and they will,' Sajani declared stubbornly. Abinash pursed his lips and whistled a bar from the work of some European composer. And all the while he eyed Sajani as if egging him on to battle. Sajani stood with his mouth open glaring at his opponent. Sarala found the scene so comic she had to clamp a hand on her mouth to keep herself from laughing. Then, controlling herself with an effort, she said. 'I have a suggestion. Why don't you two gentlemen go out into the garden and get your blending done? Then we can take up the duet here and—'

'You're right,' Sarala's two suitors agreed instantly and marched out of the room arm in arm. Sarala looked after them, a quizzical gleam in her eyes. They were nice young men; well born, well educated and good looking. Why did they not put their assets to better use? Did they really imagine that playing this silly game of love was the way to win a girl's heart? Women liked men of character and purpose. All the young men who came to her house were so petty; so wishy washy; so caught up in their own rivalries and jealousies. They never gave a thought and, consequently, had no opinion on real problems like the state of the country, the presence of the foreign rulers and the need for social reform. There was only one of her acquaintance who fitted her mental picture of a real man. He was Loken Palit—son of the barrister Taraknath Palit.

Sarala had met Loken in Rajshahi when she and her mother had gone on a visit to her sister. He had just returned from England after passing his ICS examination and was posted in Rajshahi as Deputy Magistrate. He had plenty of time on his hands and spent several hours each day in the company of the two sisters. Sarala had liked him very much. He was not only smart and handsome, he had a keen, alert mind and was wonderfully articulate. Extremely well travelled and well exposed to other countries and cultures, he could engage Sarala in conversation for hours on end. He was also very well read and had a vast knowledge of literature both Indian and Western. He was Robi

Mama's friend, as she knew, and that fact endeared him even more to her.

'Loken Babu,' she had said to him one day. 'Being a deputy magistrate you are surely expected to socialize with the British; to attend their parties and to drink and dance. But I never see you go. Haven't you made any English friends?'

'How can Indians be friends with the British? It's not that I never go to parties. I do, sometimes. But I don't enjoy them. I feel I don't belong. As a student in England I had several English friends. We studied together, chatted for hours on end and really enjoyed each other's company. One day we were in a singing mood so one of the boys, a Scotsman, began singing and the others took up the chorus, *"Rule Brittania, Brittania rules the waves, Britons never, never never shall be slaves"*. That day I got a jolt. I realized that they belonged to a race of rulers and I to a race of slaves. After that I have never been very comfortable with the English.'

One day Loken asked the two sisters to define the difference between love and friendship. Hironmoyee blushed to the roots of her hair at the question and nudged her sister. But Sarala looked Loken straight in the eye and said, 'Love and friendship are closely related emotions. But love has wings. Friendship doesn't. Friendship is love without its wings.' Loken was suitably impressed by her definition and told her so. Then he made a suggestion. 'Hironmoyee has an opinion, too, I'm sure,' he said, 'Only she's too shy to speak out. Why don't you two sisters write a few lines on the subject. I'll mark the exercises and the winner will get this.' He drew a spectroscope out of his pocket, as he spoke, and showed it to the girls.

Sarala and Hironmoyee wrote their pieces and handed them over. Loken read them through and announced in a mock ponderous tone, 'In my capacity as Deputy Magistrate of this district I declare Sarala to be the winner.' Sarala took the spectroscope he put in her hands and opened it. There was an inscription inside. *To Sarala*, it ran, *From a dear friend*. Hironmoyee bent over it eagerly then, raising an indignant face, she cried out. 'This is very unfair. You had made up your mind to give it to her.'

'I knew hers would be best.'

'It *is* unfair,' Sarala said quietly. 'You should give the prize to Didi.'

But Hironmoyee, though annoyed at being tricked, had no grudge against her sister whom she loved dearly. Needless to say the matter was resolved in a few minutes in Sarala's favour.

The three loved going for long walks. Sometimes they left the town and walked over fields and meadows or by the thick jungles that skirted them. Sarala and Loken were so wrapped up in one another that they often forgot Hironmoyee who was left lagging behind. 'You two walk on,' Hironmoyee said one day. 'I'm going back home.'

'Why?' Loken asked, 'Are you tired already?'

'I'm not tired in the least. But I realize that three is a crowd. You don't need me here.'

'But we do. Three is a safe number. It spells friendship. Two might signify love.'

'What's wrong with that? I'm sure both you and Solli are ready to put out your wings.'

Hironmoyee had barely finished her sentence when a shout came from behind them. Looking around they saw Jogini puffing and panting towards them. 'Sarala!' he exclaimed. 'Thank God I've found you. I was so bored in Calcutta without you—I had to come. I've just arrived. Phanidada said you were out walking. How are you Sarala?'

With Jogini's arrival the equations changed. Loken reduced his visits to Hironmoyee's house. His withdrawal from Sarala was subtle, almost imperceptible. In consequence their friendship remained where it was and could not blossom into love.

During the long lonely afternoons at home in Calcutta, Sarala often recollected the days she had spent in Rajshahi. And, sometimes, her thoughts were so unbearable that she felt like running out of the house into the hot empty streets and go wherever her feet took her. That, of course, was not possible. The next best method of escape was to visit one of her relatives. But she had to take her mother's permission first. One afternoon Sarala walked timidly into her mother's room and called softly, 'Ma'. Swarnakumari was sitting at her desk with some papers spread out before her. She couldn't have heard Sarala for she did not look up.

'Ma,' Sarala called a little louder. 'I would like to go to Jorasanko. May I take one of the carriages?' Now Swarnakumari raised her face and looked coldly at her daughter. 'You saw I was at work Sarala,' she said, 'Did you really need to ask me such a trivial question just now? Couldn't you have waited till the evening?'

'I'm bored and lonely. I want to go now.'

'Go if you wish. But you shouldn't have disturbed me while I was writing. You've spoilt the flow.'

Sarala put on her chemise and jacket her breast swelling with indignation and self pity. Her mother had no time for her. All she thought about was her writing. She had often seen Bibi go up to her Robi Mama when he was writing and ruffle his hair or snatch his manuscript away. But he never reprimanded her. He was ever ready to put away his work and have a chat. Was her mother's work superior to Robi Mama's? Sarala took a decision. She would leave home and go away somewhere; anywhere. She might even go to England, like her brother. But she was a woman. Would her parents agree to send her? She would work on them and make them change their attitude. But, before she did so, she would have to go to her grandfather, the head of the vast clan of Thakurs, and take his permission.

Sarala was lucky. On reaching Jorasanko she found that Debendranath had arrived that very morning from Chinsura. She went straight to him and, after touching his feet in the customary greeting, told him what she had decided. Debendranath was surprised but not angry. 'Times are changing,' he said solemnly, 'And there's little sense in holding on to ancient traditions. Whatever you do; wherever you go—my blessings will be with you. Have you decided on a place?'

'Not yet.'

'Let me know when you do.' Then, smiling a little, he added, 'I hear you are resisting marriage. Why is that? You have attained marriageable age for quite some years now. Soon you'll have crossed it.'

'Everyone tells me that. Bibi isn't married yet and she's the same age. But no one—'

'Bibi is a memsaheb. They marry when they please. Besides Bibi doesn't come to see me anymore. Listen to me Sarala. It's not right for a girl to remain unwed all her life. If you don't wish to marry a man I shall marry you to a sword.'

Sarala came home her heart dancing with joy. Her grandfather had been so kind and understanding. And he had actually joked with her. Marrying a sword! What a romantic, exciting idea! The sword would lie beside her all night and no man would dare come near her. She lay sleepless that night for hours fantasizing about her future. She would go away to a far country. She would work hard, like a man, and return home at the end of the day tired and spent. She would spend her evenings alone, quite alone, singing and playing the piano. She wouldn't have to endure the company of silly, foppish young men who hadn't a single, sensible thing to say. She would be free of them forever.

But in a couple of days Sarala had changed her mind. She couldn't; she wouldn't live alone all her life. She wanted a companion—someone brave and strong and sensible. Someone she could love and respect. If some such person came into her life she would not turn her back on him. If she never knew love she would never know anything. Poetry, art, music would turn to dust within her. Love was the fount of all inspiration; of all creativity. She would seek love and find it—no matter how long, how arduous the search.

Chapter IV

Girish Ghosh tiptoed out of the green room and came to the yellow wall that separated it from the stage. On it hung a portrait of Ramkrishna Paramhansa Deb. Girish Ghosh stood before it, eyes closed and hands folded in reverence. His attitude of humble submission was at variance with his appearance which was that of a dashing Englishman of several centuries ago. He wore velvet trousers with a sword at the waist, a ruched silk shirt and high-laced boots. His face was painted a bright pink and his salt-and-pepper whiskers were dyed a jet black hue. A curled wig covered his bald pate. He was making a comeback to the stage at the age of fifty and he needed the blessings of his guru.

Tonight was the opening night of an adaptation of Shakespeare's *Macbeth*. Girish, who had written the play and was playing the title role, had serious apprehensions. He had been out of the theatre circuit for years. How would the audience receive him? There were many among them who hadn't even heard of him. He was also worried by the fact that a raw, untrained, bit actress was to perform the female lead. Teenkari Dasi, the girl he had trained for months to play Lady Macbeth was suffering from an attack of vomiting and purging and hadn't yet recovered. A strong, young, healthy woman like Teenkari! Who had ever dreamed that she would be so ill that she couldn't raise her head from the pillow for days together? Consequently no one had been trained to replace her in an emergency.

The crisis upon them, some members of the cast suggested that he send for Binodini. There was only one actress in Bengal, they pointed out, who could learn a part in a couple of days and play it to perfection—and that was Binodini. But Girish Ghosh shook his head. Seven years ago, at a rehearsal of *Roop Sanatan*, Binodini had quarrelled bitterly with some of her colleagues and swept out of the Star theatre never to enter it again. Girish Ghosh had been shocked. He couldn't believe that an actress of her standing and reputation could put her personal emotions above her commitment to the theatre in such a blatant, shameless way! He had been so hurt and offended that he had resolved never to see her face again and had severed all connection with her. But much water had flown under the bridge in those seven years. At a time when the fame of the Star was at its height with play after play emerging from Girish Ghosh's powerful pen; when the competition with Star was so tough that other companies were hard put to scrape their production costs together, suddenly, like a bolt from the blue, a lawyer walked into the theatre and addressed Girish Ghosh thus: '*Ohe* Ghosh ja! Start packing and get ready to quit. My client is buying up your land.'

Girish Ghosh and his friends thought it a joke and burst out laughing. But within a few days truth dawned. Though the theatre was their own, the land on which it stood was not. The land, taken on a lease, had been bought by Gopal Lal Sheel, grandson of the immensely wealthy Motilal Sheel, in a secret deal. The latter's toadies had been urging him to open a theatre pointing out that it was not only sound business but would provide a lot of entertainment as well. Gopal Lal was tempted but he was astute enough to realize that if he wanted to run a theatre successfully he would have to mow down the Star first.

Girish and Amritalal were completely flummoxed by the situation in which they found themselves. What would happen now? Would they be forced to abandon their theatre? Moving the courts was possible but they dared not take on an opponent as rich and powerful as Gopal Lal Sheel. They decided to settle the matter out of court. After a great deal of bargaining an agreement was reached. Gopal Lal would buy the auditorium for a sum of thirty thousand rupees but the name Star would remain the property of Girish Ghosh and Company. With the money received the latter bought land in Hathibagan following which they got busy raising funds with which to build a new Star theatre. The old theatre, renamed Emerald, underwent extensive renovations before Gopal Lal's' first play *Pandav Nirvasan* was launched. But it fell flat. Despite the bright lights, the expensive decor, the brilliant actors and actresses—Mahendralal Basu, Ardhendushekhar, Bonobiharini, Kusum Kumari—the audience found it disappointing. The play lacked life and verve. It was like a sky without a moon; a *yagna* without a presiding deity.

389

Now the toadies started pressing Gopal Lal to rope in Girish Ghosh. He was the one, they said, who held the strings of the theatre in his hands and could make a play come to life. The players were puppets who responded only to his pull. Moved by these arguments Gopal Lal sent a messenger to Girish Ghosh with an offer. He would make the latter manager of Emerald at a monthly salary of two hundred and fifty rupees and a ten thousand rupee bonus. But it didn't take Girish even a second to reject the offer. He wouldn't; he couldn't leave Star. He had created it. From the biggest star in the cast to the humblest dresser and promoter—he had trained them all. The messenger came back the next day. This time Gopal Lal was offering three hundred rupees a month and a bonus of fifteen thousand. Girish folded his hands and said humbly, 'Give Sheel Moshai my thanks and tell him that I'm unable to accept his most generous offer. I cannot leave Star.' But the following day the man returned. This time he had a lawyer with him and a couple of guards with guns. 'Ghosh Moshai,' the lawyer said weightily while the guards stroked their whiskers and looked fiercely at Girish. 'My client has sent me with a final offer. Three hundred and fifty rupees a month and a bonus of twenty thousand. I urge you to accept it. Who, barring the Laat Saheb, earns this much? Besides, if you live in the river you cannot afford to quarrel with the crocodile. You know how powerful Gopal Lal Sheel is. He can buy up your entire cast if he so wishes. What will you do then? Can you build your precious Star and run it all by yourself? He has made up his mind to employ you as his servant and he will. You cannot escape him.'

Girish Ghosh was trapped. Not so long ago Binodini had sold her body to build Star. Now Girish had to sell his soul. Calling his colleagues together he explained the situation to them. Then, handing over sixteen thousand rupees out of the twenty he had received, he gripped Amritalal's hands and said, 'Build the theatre and get it going as soon as you can. But see that everyone associated with it, from the highest to the lowest, gets fair and equal treatment.'

And so Girish Ghosh became the manager of Emerald. His first play *Purna Chandra* was staged with a lot of fanfare and was very successful. But, though Girish did everything that was expected of him, his heart was not in his work. The new Star theatre in Hathibagan had been completed and his old colleagues were visiting him in secret. They needed a play. Who would write for them? Girish Ghosh shook his head. As per the terms of his contract with Gopal Lal Sheel he could not write for any company other than Emerald. Besides, Gopal Lal's spies kept a strict watch on his movements.

One day, Girish draped a sari and went out of the house. He was a great actor and walking like a woman was not difficult for him. He had to hide his whiskers, though, and to that purpose he pulled the veil on his head down to his breast. Watching him walk away no one could dream that he was a man. He went to the house of a friend and dictated the play *Nasiram*. It was performed at the Star but no one knew who the playwright was. The name appearing in the titles was a pseudonym—Sevak.

The two plays were performed night after night at their respective theatres. Both were doing well but Girish Ghosh was happiest when the sales at Star outstripped those of Emerald Already people were saying to one another. 'Oré *bhai*! Have you seen the new play at Star? There's a new playwright called Sevak whose work puts Girish Ghosh's to shame.'

A year or so went by in this manner. Then, one afternoon, Gopal Lal Sheel stormed into his manager's office and said, 'I've had enough of this theatre nonsense Ghosh Moshai. It's a low business—not worthy of a man with a lineage like mine. I want you to shut up shop. Right from tomorrow.' Gopal Lal was a rich man. He had launched the project upon a whim. Now he was abandoning it upon another.

The theatre was sold, in due course, and the new owner proceeded to run it. But Girish Ghosh had no contract with him. He was free. Bursting with joy he returned to the Star to be installed as manager in place of Amritalal. He felt like one, exiled for many years, returning to his motherland.

But Amritalal, though he had conceded his post to his erstwhile mentor, was far from happy at his return. He didn't see why he should spend his whole life in his guru's shadow. Had he not proved his worth as manager of Star when Girish Ghosh was away? And now, even after his return, was it not he, Amritalal, who was bearing the heaviest load? Girish Ghosh wrote play after play—*Prafulla, Haranidhi, Chanda*—but did not attend the rehearsals barring one or two right at the beginning.

'Get them into shape Bhuni,' he would instruct Amritalal briefly before vanishing from the scene. Amritalal had to take care of everything but, when the play was a success, the credit for it all went to Girish Ghosh. 'Girishchandra Ghosh Mohodai,' a newspaper column ran, 'has written a very superior play. The excellent production and flawless acting is all owing to his tireless training and scrupulous attention to detail.' Although an intelligent man, Girish hadn't a clue as to how all this was affecting Amritalal. He persisted in his naïve conviction that Amritalal was perfectly content to bask in his reflected glory.

Around this time Girish was overtaken by a domestic crisis. His second wife passed away after a prolonged illness and he had no one to help him take care of the sickly child she had left behind. This boy was the apple of his father's eye. Once, in a drunken state, he had begged his guru Ramkrishna to be his son. Then, when the child was born, he fondly believed he was his guru come back to life. He was completely wrapped up in the child and wouldn't leave him for a moment. He spent all his time caring for him, consulting doctors and trying out new remedies. He hardly ever came to the theatre. If they needed a new play he dictated something hurriedly to whoever came to ask for it. He was the manager of the theatre and took a monthly salary. But he wasn't there—either physically or in spirit.

Discontent had been simmering in Amritalal and his cronies for quite some time. It now rose to a raging fire. What was Girish Ghosh doing for Star, they asked each other, except writing a few plays? Anyone could write plays. Amritalal's own *Sarala* had proved more popular than Girish Ghosh's *Nasiram*.

Gradually the resentment started expressing itself. Words were exchanged, first mild, then heated. 'You dare to talk to me like that,' the impulsive, egoistic Girish Ghosh cried out one day, 'because I take a salary. Well—I won't take a paisa from this day onwards. And I won't write for you. Fend for yourselves as best as you can.' Girish Ghosh was sure Amritalal and his group would come to their senses and beg him to continue as before. But nothing like that happened.

The doctors having advised a change of climate for the sick boy, Girish Ghosh proceeded to leave Calcutta for Madhupur.

But he was very short of money. Nothing was coming in and he had spent most of his savings. Around this time a man named Neelmadhav Chakravarty approached him with an offer. Neelmadhav had recently purchased a theatre named Bina and started running it under the new name of City Theatre. He wanted to stage three of Girish Ghosh's old plays—*Bilwamangal, Buddhadev Charit* and *Bellik Bazar*—and was prepared to pay a fair sum for them. The terms were acceptable to Girish and the deal was concluded.

With the money received Girish rented a house in Madhupur and threw heart and soul into nursing his son back to health. The air of Madhupur was clean and unpolluted. The vegetables were fresh and eggs and mutton were plentiful and cheap. The boy improved slowly and Girish Ghosh felt greatly relieved. Then, suddenly, a message reached him that Star had brought a suit against Neelmadhav Chakravarty for appropriating plays Girish Ghosh had written for Star as its paid employee. The management had also made a public announcement of Girish Ghosh's dismissal as manager of the company.

The news was so unbelievable that Girish Ghosh shrugged it off at first. It just couldn't be true! Star was his. He had created it with his blood and tears. How could they sack him as though he was any paid employee? How could they bring a case against him? Then, gradually, he saw the truth. Amritalal was the leader of the group that wanted him out. And he had worked silently and stealthily. Amritalal—his favourite student whom he had loved as a son! Only the other day, it seemed to him, Amritalal had brought him home, dead drunk, practically carrying him on his back. What had happened? Why had everything changed so drastically?

But Amritalal and his friends had their own arguments. Girish Ghosh had worked hard for the theatre in the past. No one denied it. But how long could he cash on that? For several years now he had done nothing but take a salary. Didn't Binodini have to leave? Had her contribution been less than that of Girish Ghosh?

The realization that he was truly in trouble brought Girish Ghosh post haste to Calcutta. Amritalal came to see him. Although he was the prime instigator of the present crisis Amritalal was the soul of courtesy while addressing the older

man. 'Gurudev,' he began humbly, 'I wish to say a few words to
you. If you find them offensive you may punish me as you will.
But hear me out first. I've observed that, for some years now, the
bonds between you and the theatre have slackened. First you
stopped acting. Then you gave up directing and training
newcomers. Your heart is elsewhere. You've lost interest—'

'Lost interest!' Girish Ghosh burst out angrily. 'You're telling
me I've lost interest in the theatre! It's like telling a fish it's not
interested in water; like telling a bird it's not interested in the sky.
Where has my interest gone—may I ask?'

'Beyond the pale of the Earth. The day you accepted
Ramkrishna as your guru you gave up the theatre—in spirit at
least. Try to recall the past Gurudev. You were present in the
theatre every single day. Your wife's illness; your eldest son
Dani's near death; your own diseased liver—nothing, nothing
could keep you away. But ever since Ramkrishna fell ill and you
started visiting him in Kashipur—' Amritalal did not complete
the sentence. He didn't need to. Girish Ghosh sighed and was
silent. After a while he raised his head and asked with a great
sadness in his voice, 'What do you want of me?' Amritalal
hesitated a little, then said softly, 'You've loosened your link with
the theatre little by little. Let the break be final. You're still a great
playwright. If you sign a new contract with us promising to give
us everything you write I'll persuade the others to withdraw the
suit.' Girish Ghosh laughed—a hard, dry, mirthless laugh. 'You
want to get rid of me, don't you Bhuni?' he asked bitterly. 'You're
an important man now. Manager of Star and a playwright
besides. My presence is a thorn in your side. But, rest assured, I
won't dream of entering into competition with you. In fact, my
sincerest blessings are with you. Be a big man—bigger than your
guru. May your fame spread throughout the land and far beyond
it.'

The contract form arrived the next day. Girish Ghosh was to
have nothing to do with Star from henceforth, but he would not
join any other theatre company, either, for acting, directing or
training. He would be obliged to offer anything he wrote first to
Star, for which he would receive a monthly salary of one hundred
rupees. If Star rejected a manuscript he was free to give it to any
other theatre company. In short, as per the terms of the new

contract, Girish Ghosh could not enter a theatre except as a member of the audience. Girish Ghosh signed his name with a flourish, then, throwing the pen away, said whimsically, 'I'll never take up a pen again. I won't act, direct, train or even write anymore. That should make you happy Bhuni.'

With his occupation gone, the Garrick of Bengal didn't know what to do with himself. 'Binodini's curse has fallen on me,' he thought. Life became even more unbearable after his little boy's death. The thought that he hadn't been able to save the child even at the cost of giving up his life's mission tortured him day and night. In this mood he longed to get out of Calcutta. But where could he go? Suddenly an idea came to him. Saradamoni was still alive. He would go visit her and see Ramkrishna's birthplace.

As the bullock cart wended its way slowly towards Kamarpukur Jairambati, Girish looked out eagerly. He had lived in the city all his life and had never seen a village as primitive and backward as this one. He was charmed, nevertheless. Meadows, green as emerald, stretched far away merging into the horizon. The sky was blue and cloudless and the air fresh and pure. There was not a brick structure to be seen anywhere. Little homesteads built of bamboo and straw dotted the landscape appearing between fields of golden paddy and waving palms.

Saradamoni was very happy to see him and Girish, who had been orphaned as a child, experienced a mother's love for the first time in his life. Saradamoni cooked delicious meals for him and sat by while he ate waving away imaginary flies with a palm leaf fan. She washed his clothes and made his bed smoothing down the sheets with gentle hands. When he lay down to sleep he felt her touch, warm and tender, soothe and caress his tortured body and mind. 'You're my mother,' he said to her one day in a gush of sentiment. 'I'm your son. I left you and was miserable—'

'You've come back haven't you?' Saradamoni smiled at him, 'Stay as long as you like.'

Girish, who had come to spend a week, stayed on for two months. Then he left for Calcutta with a new resolution. He would take up his pen again, but not to write plays. He would write a book based on the lives of his guru and guru ma. This would be his new mission in life. On his return Girish gave himself up to the task with a singlemindedness that was quite

unusual for him. He didn't go near the theatre again. Not did he
care to hear about it. In fact, whenever some of his former
colleagues came to see him, he abused them roundly and drove
them out of the house. The only people he associated with were
Ramkrishna's disciples.

One day a gentleman called Nagendrabhushan mukherjee
came to see him. Girish knew him slightly. He was the grandson
of the famous Prasanna Thakur of the Pathuriaghata branch of
the Thakur family. It was hardly possible to turn away a man
with such a distinguished lineage, so Girish Ghosh was obliged to
give him a hearing. After the initial courtesies were over
Nagendrabhushan came to the point. 'Girish Babu,' he said
shaking his head in a dejected manner, 'Are you aware of the
depths of depravity to which the Bengali theatre has sunk? Cheap
dialogue, obscene gestures, titillating song and dance sequences
are being offered to the public in the name of the theatre. You're
still alive, Girish Babu, and here in Calcutta. How can you be so
indifferent? You must find a way to curb this disgusting trend and
bring the glorious age of the Bengal theatre back again. Don't you
realize that it is a blot on the reputation of the entire race? Do you
know what was reported in *Englishman*—?'

'Nagendra Babu,' Girish interrupted. 'You're probably not
aware that I've snapped my links with the theatre. I have nothing
to do with it anymore.'

'I'm aware of the fact. But I don't see why I should accept it.
The reputation of our whole nation is at stake. How can you have
the heart to hold yourself so aloof when the fabric you wrought
with your blood and tears is falling in shreds about you? The
sahebs were forced to admit once that our theatre was not a whit
inferior to theirs. Now they laugh and pass snide comments.
Won't you do anything about it?'

'Why do you come to me? Ardhendushekhar is your man. If
anyone can stand up to the British—he can.'

'Ardhendu is as slippery as a fish. He's here today—there
tomorrow. No one can get hold of him. Besides, his brains have
addled with the passing years. No, Girish Babu. You're the only
one who can grasp the oars firmly and bring the floundering boat
back to the shore. The need of the hour is a new hall and a new
play of such excellence that even the sahebs will have to sit up and

take notice.'

'Who will pay for the new hall?'

'I will. I've bought up the land on which the Great National stood and I've started building a new auditorium. It's a fine imposing mansion fitted with the most modern equipment. I'm calling my theatre Minerva. Do you like the name?'

Girish Ghosh sat silent, frowning in thought. No one had come to him with such a proposal for years now. People thought he was finished. He had thought so too. But the fire of his ego, reduced to ashes by domestic cares, heart break and humiliation, now roared into life. His breast heaved as though huge breakers of salt water were pounding against it. He was Girish Ghosh and he could still show the world what was what. Then, suddenly, he remembered the bond he had signed. Shaking his head sadly, he sighed and said, 'My contract with Star debars me from joining any other company. I'm sorry. I must respect my own signature.'

'Nonsense!' Nagendrabhushan cried out angrily. 'No one has a right to put in a clause like that. It has no legal standing. You're Girish Ghosh—not a man to be trifled with. Let me have a look at the contract—'

'No, no,' Girish said hastily. 'I've no wish to embroil myself in legal wrangles any more. I'm at peace now. Leave me as I am.'

However, he handed the document over and Nagendra-bhushan read it carefully. Presently his lips twitched in a smile. 'Have you gone through this contract?' he asked. 'I don't need to,' Girish shrugged his shoulders. 'I was told what it contained.' Nagendrabhushan shook his head in admonishment. 'If you had taken the trouble to go through it you would have realized that you had nothing to fear. The men who drew it up knew that it would have no standing in a court of law. They've taken the precaution of adding a line right at the bottom. It says that you'll have to pay five thousand rupees in case you break the contract.' Girish Ghosh stood up in his excitement. 'Really? Let me see,' he cried, bending over the paper. Nagendrabhushan ran his forefinger over the line and said, 'I'll send five thousand rupees to the manager of Star this very evening. Consider yourself released from your bond and get busy writing a crackling good play. We must remember that we are undertaking an important mission—that of reviving the reputation of the theatre in Bengal.'

Girish Ghosh hadn't touched a bottle for many months but that evening he sent for one. His mind was in a whirl. Sitting before his writing table he hesitated a few moments before taking up his pen. He had known peace and tranquillity for the first time in many years. Did he really wish to exchange them for the strains and anxieties of his old life? The backbreaking work, the hard drinking, the sleepless nights, the endless bickerings and jealousies. He closed his eyes in weariness at the thought. Then, suddenly, he felt the blood leap up in his veins and pound in great waves against his heart. He remembered the bright lights, the gorgeous costumes, the crowds, the music. What glamour! What excitement! He had lived without them for many months. But could he call it *living*?

Girish drew a sheet of paper towards him. Picking up a quill he dipped it in ink and wrote MACBETH. The idea of an adaptation of this great play had been simmering in his head ever since Nagendrabhushan had told him that they needed a script that would shock the sahebs out of their complacence. He would begin with Shakespeare; with one of his greatest tragedies. Girish's pen raced over the paper for an hour or so. Then he rose and, taking a swig from the bottle, paced up and down the room with the air of a caged lion. His eyes burned and he breathed heavily. 'They tried to get rid of me,' he muttered between clenched teeth, 'But they forgot who I am. I am Girish Ghosh.' And that moment he took a decision. He would not only write and direct. He would act once again. He would play the lead role. He would be a Macbeth that people wouldn't forget in a hurry.

But who would play Lady Macbeth? Girish considered Promoda Sundari at first then rejected the idea. She was a good and experienced actress but she had grown quite obese of late and waddled like a duck. Next he considered Teenkari. Teenkari was much younger and far less experienced. But she had promise. Besides, she would look right in the role. She was tall and gaunt and there was something decidedly masculine in her voice and manner.

Girish's calculations were proved right. The first two nights went off without a hitch and Teenkari received several rounds of applause. Then the blow fell. Teenkari was taken ill and there was no one to replace her. Disaster stared Girish in the face. He had

invited the press and some distinguished gentlemen of the city,
several Englishmen among them, for the Saturday night's
performance. And he didn't have a Lady Macbeth.

Ardhendushekhar came to him where he sat disconsolately
with his head in his hands. It was lucky for Girish that
Ardhendushekhar had suddenly surfaced from heaven knew
where and had offered his services. He was playing several
characters in the play—one of the witches among them. 'There's a
girl in the cast Gurudev,' he said, 'who knows the whole play by
heart. Why don't you try her out?'

'Don't talk nonsense,' Girish lashed out at him. 'Simply
learning the part by rote means nothing. Can she act? And that
too—Lady Macbeth?'

'There's no harm in trying her out, seeing as we have no other
option.'

Girish sat abstracted in thought for a few minutes. Binodini
was out of the question. Should he send word to Bonobiharini?
Or Kusum Kumari? They were too old. They had retired from the
theatre ages ago. Promoda Sundari? He shook his head. 'Call the
girl in,' he muttered. 'Let me have a look at her.'

Ardhendushekhar left the room and reappeared a few
minutes later bringing a young girl with him. Girish recognized
her. She was playing Lady Macduff's son. She was tall and slim
and had long tip tilted eyes with a clear, unflinching gaze.

'What's your name?' Girish asked.

'Nayanmoni,' the girl replied.

'That's the name we've given you. What's your real name?
The name your mother calls you by. Is it Penchi, Khendi, Dekchi,
Podi? Which is it?'

'I don't have a mother and my name is Nayanmoni.'

'Where were you born? Sonagachhi or Hadh Katar Gali? Or
was it Goabagan or Ulta Dinghi?'

'In none of those places. I was born very far away.'

Now Girish looked the girl up and down appraising her
carefully. 'You're very thin,' he said disapprovingly. 'Don't you
get enough to eat? I hear you know my whole play by heart. Let
me see. Can you recite Lady Macbeth's *Come, you spirits that
tend on mortal thoughts?*' The girl not only recited the lines with
a rare fluency—she even enacted the part. Girish Ghosh heard her

399

out his brow creased in a puzzled frown. 'There's something alien in your pronunciation—a tendency to enlarge the vowel "a". Tell me truly. Where were you born?'

'Very far away' Nayanmoni repeated, then hastened to add, 'I'll correct my pronunciation and—'

'Can you walk like an Englishwoman? Show me.'

Nayanmoni drew herself to her full height. Then, head held high, she walked with arrogant strides across the stage. Girish turned to Ardhendushekhar. 'Where did you find this girl Saheb?' he asked.

'From the ash heap you might say. She has many other talents. She can sing and dance. She hasn't had a proper break so far. She's done bit roles—mostly of little boys.'

'Do you have a regular Babu?' Girish asked the girl.

'What?' The girl didn't seem to understand the question.

'I mean, are you free to spend the night with me?'

A deep flush rose in Nayanmoni's cheeks. Her eyelids quivered a little as she stood silent, eyes downcast. Girish, who was in a fever of anxiety, couldn't brook her silence.

'Do you imagine?' he shouted rudely at her, 'that I'm asking you to spend the night cavorting in my bed? We'll have to rehearse the part of Lady Macbeth every minute of the time left to us. Can you do it?'

'I can.'

Over the next three days Nayanmoni worked on her role with a dedication and perseverance that surprised Girish. Under his expert hands she blossomed into a wonderful actress. Girish was overjoyed. Her acting was excellent—far beyond his expectations. But he felt a faint stab of worry from time to time. Performing well during rehearsals was one thing. Facing an audience was another.

Just before the first bell, on the opening night of Nayanmoni's performance as Lady Macbeth, Girish Ghosh sent for her. When she walked in, he stared in amazement. He hardly recognized her. He hadn't realized that the girl was so beautiful. Her arched neck rose like a marble column above the collar of her black velvet dress whose voluminous skirt and elaborate sleeves hid the thinness of her legs and arms. Her lustrous eyes with their fringe of deep lashes had a faraway look in them—as though they beheld another world. Her lips were painted a pomegranate pink and her cheeks were the colour of cream tinged with vermilion. Rich, black hair knotted at the nape hung to her waist. 'Come Nayan,' he said, 'Seek the blessings of my guru.' Nayanmoni knelt before the portrait of Ramkrishna and touched her forehead to the ground. She stayed like that for quite a while, then lifting her head, brought her palms together. Her lips moved a little as though she was muttering something below her breath. Then she rose and took the dust of her own guru's feet. 'Nayan,' Girish's voice trembled as he placed a hand on her head in blessing, 'You won't let me down, will you?'

Girish was totally unprepared for the extent of the evening's success. He had heard that the editor of *Englishman* had remarked to a colleague before the event: 'A Bengali Thane of Cawdor! What can be more amusing? Let's all go and see the natives perform *Macbeth* and have a good laugh.' But that same gentleman was sitting in the audience with several other Englishmen. And no one was laughing. In fact they were clapping with a frenzy that was a rarity even at their own plays. Girish noticed that most of the applause was for Nayanmoni. He was amazed to find that she was performing even better than during rehearsals. The girl seemed to be a born actress.

A number of Girish's erstwhile colleagues from Star and the other theatres had bought tickets in secret and come to see Girish Ghosh make a fool of himself. They were in for a shock. Never had they seen such brilliant costumes, such wonderful lighting and authentic sets. As for Girish himself—who could ever guess, from the vigour and vitality of his speech and movements, that he was so old and had so many ailments?

After curtain call all the players received a standing ovation. Girish introduced the members of the cast one by one. When Nayanmoni's turn came a member of the audience, a wealthy zamindar, announced that he would present her with a gold medal.

Next morning, all the newspapers carried favourable reports of the play. The players were mentioned by name—all except Nayanmoni for Girish had forgotten to change the name in the handbills. Teenkari Dasi's performance as Lady Macbeth

401

received a great deal of praise. As if that was not disappointing enough for Nayanmoni, Teenkari returned to the theatre after three or four days. She had recovered and wanted her role back. Girish and Nagendrabhushan exchanged glances. As per the conventions of the theatre she had every right to make such a demand. But Nayanmoni's performance had been so much better! Nagendrabhushan and Ardhendushekhar were of the opinion that Nayanmoni should be allowed to continue. But Girish shook his head. It would create bad blood between them and the cast would be divided. 'Explain the situation to Nayanmoni,' he told Ardhendushekhar, 'and tell her not to mind. We'll give her the lead role in the next play.'

'Mind! The girl is mad. She wants nothing for herself. She'll do whatever you tell her.'

Still Girish sent for Nayanmoni and said, 'You came to my rescue when I was in trouble, Nayan, and I won't forget it. You not only saved my reputation—you glorified it. The *Englishman* carried two paragraphs on your acting though the credit went to Teenkari. But these things happen in our profession. You mustn't take them to heart. I promise to give you better roles in future. I've a mind to take up *Hamlet* next. You'll be Ophelia.'

'I don't mind doing small roles. I'm quite happy as Macduff's son.'

'You'll do better than that. We'll split up the shows between the two of you. Teenkari can be Lady Macbeth some nights and you—'

'Let Teenkari Didi have the role. She's very good. I love watching her. What a beautiful voice she has!'

Girish laughed. 'I've never heard anything like this before,' he said. 'Tell me truly. Who are you and where do you come from? I hear you can sing and dance as well as act. Will you sing a few lines for me?'

Nayanmoni sang a verse from *Geet Govind*. Girish stared at her in amazement 'Where have you been hiding all these years, Nayan?' he asked softly. Nayanmoni did not answer. She stood silent, looking down at her feet. A tear trickled down her cheek and fell to the floor.

Chapter V

Gangamoni had her own three-storeyed house in Rambagan. Having retired from the theatre she was constrained, now, to live on her savings and the rents collected from the tenants she had installed on the ground floor. These were mainly women from her own profession. Kusum Kumari (Khonra), Harimoti (Dekchi), Tunnamoni and Kiran Shashi didn't have regular Babus and earned too little from the theatre to be able to afford houses of their own. Gangamoni had divided up the rooms downstairs among them and charged a nominal rent. She was a soft-hearted woman and, being familiar with the line, knew how hard it was to make a living from it. The rest of the house she kept for her own use barring a tiny room on top. A young actress called Nayanmoni had recently taken possession of it for a monthly rent of twenty rupees.

Gangamoni hadn't let go of the theatre without a struggle. After all, she wasn't that old. The trouble was that she had started bloating and that too at an alarming pace. She had been quite sought after even till lately and could pick and choose her roles and change her loyalties from Star to Emerald and back again as often as she pleased. But now her waist was like a cow's, wider in circumference than her back and breasts put together, and her stomach protruded from it like a drum. How could she expect to play heroine with a figure like that? She had tried hard to fight the obesity that seemed to have overtaken her like a disease. She hadn't touched a drop of liquor for months and had practically given up eating. She bathed in the Ganga every morning and prostrated herself afterwards before the image of Ma Kali in the temple of Ahiritola begging her to restore her lost looks. But nothing happened. She swelled steadily like a summer fruit, till, her patience exhausted, she surrendered to the inevitable. She gave up the theatre for good and settled down to a life of ease and enjoyment. Now she ate and drank as much as she pleased and whiled the hours away fondling and playing with her seven cats.

Of all her tenants she liked Nayanmoni best. The girl was strange—quite unlike others of her profession. She was beautiful and she seemed well educated. She read the newspaper, every morning, with a fluency that surprised Ganga. And she could sing and dance. But she made no effort to push herself forward and make a mark in her profession. Only the other day she refused an invitation from Mahendralal Bosu to sing at a mehfil in his pleasure house in Barahnagar. A renowned actor like Mahendra Babu! He had so much clout and could have helped her in so many ways! Ganga tried to teach her the tricks of the trade. It wasn't enough to be beautiful and talented. To succeed one had to have the top actors and managers on one's side. And it could only be done by making oneself available. A bit of coquetry and flirting together with discreet promises of other, better things would do the trick. Hadn't Gangamoni gone through it all? She had sidled up to the chief whenever she could, flattered him coyly, prepared his hookah, pressed his legs and even let him have his fill of her. And look at the heights she had reached! But Nayanmoni laughed her counsel away. She was quite happy, she said, doing bit roles. And the money she earned was enough for her. She didn't need more.

Though in the same profession there was a world of difference between Nayanmoni and the residents of the ground floor. Nayanmoni lived very simply. Her room was tiny and she had neither a kitchen nor a water tap. She carried up water in pails from the tap downstairs and cooked a simple meal, once a day, on a bucket oven in a corner of the terrace. Unlike the other rooms of the house, which were overflowing with furniture, pictures, birds in cages and gold fish in bowls, her's was stark, almost bare. A neatly made up bed spread with a spotless sheet stood at one end of the room. In a corner, at the other end, was a statue of a smiling Lord Krishna playing the flute. On their free evenings, when the other girls' rooms were ablaze with light and ringing with music and laughter, hers was dark and silent for she never had a visitor. On some such evenings Gangamoni had huffed and puffed her way to the top floor to find her sitting before her god, eyes closed in reverence, singing verses from *Geet Govind*. Once she had even seen her dance before him. He seemed to be the only male she knew or cared for.

404

Being kindly and easygoing, Gangamoni didn't mind the clamour downstairs even when it became loud and violent. High-pitched singing, raucous laughter and the sound of shattering glass often crashed into the silence of the night, waking her rudely out of her sleep. But she didn't put a stop to it. The girls were young and youth was fleeting. They earned a bare pittance from the theatre. If they could make a little money on the side and have a good time as well—she wouldn't stop them. She tried to tell Nayanmoni all this but in vain. Nayan was not only not interested in making more money—she didn't even care to conserve what she had. She insisted on paying rent when Ganga would have been glad to let her off. She also, quite firmly though sweetly, turned down Ganga's offer of feeding her from her own kitchen.

Nayanmoni's resistance to all her overtures saddened Ganga but she admired her for it. Nayan seemed to achieve, quite effortlessly, what Ganga had never even dreamed of. Ganga had spent the best years of her life flattering and wheedling men and giving in to their basest desires. She had been tossed from one hand to another, often against her will, ever since the age of ten when her mother had wanted to sell her to a wealthy businessman of Lahore. Ganga had wept and pleaded to be allowed to remain in Calcutta for the stage had already cast its spell on her. But both mother and daughter knew that the theatre, for all its glamour, wouldn't put rice in their mouths. For that they had to look elsewhere. And so poor Ganga was forced to join the throng of women who were borne on the current like dead flowers to wherever their fate took them. She learned to fight for her rights at an early age; to coax and cajole the men at the helm; to spy on her fellow actresses; to squabble and abuse and carry tales. She never forgot an injury and waited patiently for her turn to take revenge. When Bonobiharini got rid of Binodini it was Gangamoni who had helped her.

But Nayanmoni did none of these things. She had cheerfully given up her part to Teenkari even though she had received seven rounds of applause and Teenkari only three. And she didn't seem to need men, either. Looking on her Ganga realized, for the first time in her life, that it was possible for a woman to survive without a man; to live by herself with pride and dignity.

405

Nayanmoni said something to Ganga one day that she was to remember all her life. Coming into her room that evening Ganga found Nayanmoni dancing before the image of Lord Krishna. '*Olo* Nayan!' Ganga cried. 'Have you no fear of the hereafter? Do you want to go straight to hell?'

'Why Didi?' Nayan fixed her clear, limpid gaze on Gangamoni's face. 'Why should I go to hell for worshipping the Lord?'

'You were dancing—'

'Dance is my worship. What else do I have to give him? Besides, doesn't the priest dance while performing arati? He holds a five-wick lamp in one hand and a bell in the other and dances—'

'Silly girl! Comparing yourself to a priest! Are you a Brahmin?'

'But God belongs to everybody. Not Brahmins alone. He was raised in the house of a cowherd, remember? Besides, he created us too, did he not?'

'But you don't know the mantras.'

'I don't need mantras. I speak to him through my songs. You sing so well yourself Didi. Why don't you do the same?'

'You'll be the death of me some day. You shouldn't have kept an image of the deity in your room in the first place. We sinners are debarred from doing so.'

'I don't know why you keep calling yourself a sinner. I'm no sinner—'

'When anyone asks you who your parents were you tell them you fell from the sky. Now, I didn't fall from the sky. I know who my mother was. She was an actress and a prostitute. My father didn't marry her so I'm a sinner, doomed from birth.'

'How can you be blamed for what your parents did? Did you ask to be born? Why should you carry their sin on your shoulders? Don't call yourself a sinner ever again—'

Hearing these words Ganga burst into tears. Embracing the younger woman tenderly, she cried, '*Olo* Nayan! If someone had told me this when I was little I would have lived a different sort of life. I would never have allowed myself to become a pawn in the hands of those bastard men. I might have starved but I would

406

have kept my head held high. I didn't know there was another way.'

One evening three gentleman came to see Gangamoni. Ganga knew one of them. He was Neelmadhav Chakravarti—the one who had bribed a number of players away from Star and engaged them in his new City Theatre Company. With him was a man who wore several diamond rings on his fingers. From his looks and bearing he seemed important and wealthy. Handing her an enormous box of sandesh Neelmadhav began in a patronizing tone, 'You've got yourself a nice little nest Ganga. I hear an ex-Babu of yours has sold it to you for a song.' Then, hesitating a little, he added 'Won't you offer us some tea?'

The scene was a familiar one. This was the tone theatre managers used when they wanted to lure an actress away from another company. Ganga had been in great demand particularly after *Bilwamangal* in which she had played the part of a madwoman. But now she was old and couldn't sing and dance with ease. Perhaps they wanted a fat woman for a comic role. She didn't mind doing it if it wasn't too small or too insignificant. The men drank tea, chatted of this and that but wouldn't come to the point. At last, unable to bear the suspense, Ganga put out a feeler. 'Ogo!' she addressed Neelmadhav, 'Which board do you work on these days?'

'Some of us have decided to join Emerald. We wish to breathe fresh life into it. It is the old Star after all. You worked in Star for many years. You must have a soft corner for it?'

'What play—?'

'Robi Babu's *Raja Basanta Rai*. You've heard of Robi Babu, haven't you?' Gangamoni shook her head. She hadn't heard of Robi Babu. Someone called Atul Krishna Mitra, she had been told, was writing for Emerald. 'Robi Babu is Jyoti Babu's brother,' Neelmadhav continued. 'Don't you remember Jyoti Babu Moshai? Author of *Sarojini*?' Now Ganga brought her palms together and touched them to her forehead. 'Who can forget him?' she said. 'He carried himself like a prince. I've never seen a more handsome man.'

'Robi Babu is the youngest scion of the Thakur family of Jorasanko and a great playwright. His *Raja Rani* had a good run. *Raja Basanta Rai* will fare even better I'm sure. There are many

407

songs and—'

'How many scenes do I get?'

The gentlemen exchanged glances. There was a minute's silence, then Neelmadhav cleared his throat embarrassedly and said, 'The problem is—there's no suitable part in it for you. After all,' he hastened to add, 'We can't give you just any role, can we? The audience loves your singing. In our next play we'll give you one with plenty of songs.'

'But you said this play has many songs!' Gangamoni sounded truly bewildered. 'They're to be sung by the hero,' Neelmadhav said hastily. Then, with the desperation one feels just before swallowing a bitter draught, he added, 'And by a young woman. We came to you in the hope . . . in the hope that the girl who lodges with you . . . you know the one who works for Minerva. This Nayanbala or whatever her name is, is doing quite well I hear. The fact is that I saw her one night in the role of Lady Macbeth. She was superb. I watched her entranced. Performing against Girish Ghosh is no joke! There's a fire in her that is seen only once in a while —'

'O Hari!' Gangamoni thought. 'They don't want me. They want Nayanmoni. Why couldn't Neelmadhav Babu have said so right in the beginning instead of hemming and hawing and spinning a foolish web of lies and contradictions?' Had such a thing happened a year ago she would have been wild with fury. She would have chased the whole party out of her house at the end of her broomstick. But now she smiled at her own foolishness. She had been lured, momentarily, by the glamour of the stage. She had thought that her youth had returned. But that was not to be. Never again would she stand in the wings, just before a scene, her heart beating with trepidation. Never again would she know the heady excitement of frenzied applause.

'The girl is whimsical,' she began tentatively, 'not like the others.'

'Call her in.' His worst fear over Neelmadhav's voice rang out loud and strong. 'Let us talk to her. How much does she get in Minerva? Twenty-five or thirty rupees at the most? Rajen Babu here is prepared to pay her one hundred rupees a month. He's our new financier. Apart from that she'll get an annual bonus of five hundred rupees. She'll have a carriage of her own.'

Gangamoni was so happy for Nayan that she ran all the way up to her room and cried, 'Come quickly Nayan. Some gentlemen have come with an offer for you.' Then, seeing her stand motionless, she added. 'Don't you hear me? Change your sari and come down at once. They want to make you the heroine. They're offering lots of money.'

'How can I join another company Didi?' Nayanmoni's eyes looked stricken like a frightened doe's. 'Girish Babu will scold me.'

'Death be on you, you foolish girl! Why should Girish Babu scold you? You haven't signed a bond with him, have you? You're free to go to whichever board offers you a bigger part. And you should go. The bigger the part the better known you'll be. How long can you remain content with playing boys' roles in Minerva? As for your precious Girish Babu—hasn't he changed companies? I wasn't born yesterday. I've seen all there was to see. Come, wash your face and run a comb through your hair.'

Holding her by the hand Gangamoni dragged the reluctant girl into the gentlemen's presence. Neelmadhav whispered to his companion, 'Do you see how she walks. I can swear she knows how to dance.' Then, scrutinizing the girl carefully from head to foot, he asked, 'What's your name?'

'Her name is Nayanmoni,' Ganga answered for her much as though Nayanmoni was a would-be bride on display and she the bride's mother.

'We'll have to change the name. It's too old fashioned. We'll call you Panna Rani.'

Ganga gave a shriek of laughter. 'The Monis are out, are they Chakravarty Moshai? The Ranis are in. Well, call her whatever you like. Only —'

'Ahh! Ganga. Can't you let the girl speak for herself? Listen child. We've come to you with a proposal. We've made a script out of Robi Babu's historical novel *Bou Thakuranir Haat*. It has two female roles of which we are offering you one. It's practically the heroine's role.' He paused, waiting for some response. But Nayanmoni turned her face away. *Bou Thakuranir Haat*! She had read the book in her other, previous life. She pushed the thought away. It brought back too many memories. 'Ganga must have told you how much we are offering,' Neelmadhav

409

SUNIL GANGOPADHYAY

continued, ignoring her silence. 'I'm sure it satisfies you. Friday is a good day according to the almanac. We'll start the rehearsals from that day. By the way, you don't have to stay here any longer. Rajen Babu has a house on the river where you can live like a queen. He's a very generous man and will think nothing of covering you with jewels from head to foot.'

As she heard these words scenes from Ganga's own past swam before her eyes. She had been in the first flush of her youth when men had come to her mother with similar proposals. She could still see the greed and triumph which had leaped into the ageing eyes. But, however generous the offer, her mother would haggle over the terms and try to better them. And then, she would hand her over . . . Ganga sighed. She was playing her mother's role tonight.

'A house by the river,' she muttered. 'Is she to live in it alone?'

'Quite alone. It is to be hers exclusively. It is fully staffed and there's a watchman at the gate. She'll be well protected. Why don't you say something Rajen Babu?'

But Rajendra Babu only grinned self consciously and looked down at his feet. 'It's settled then,' Neelmadhav rose to his feet. Now Rajen Babu drew a velvet purse from his pocket and thrust it into Nayanmoni's hands. 'I've brought two hundred rupees as advance,' he said. 'Don't worry about money,' Neelmadhav purred like a cat. 'Or jewels. Please Rajen Babu and he'll give you everything you could possibly want.'

Nayanmoni dropped the purse on the *chowki* on which she was sitting. Then, with her hand, she pushed it away, till it hit the wall. 'I don't wear jewels. They prick me,' she announced, rising to her feet. 'I'm not leaving Minerva.' The other four persons in the room froze in their places. There was a stunned silence. Then Neelmadhav burst out. 'Not leaving Minerva! Why? What are they paying you that —'

'I don't care about money,' Nayanmoni replied. 'I'm happy with what I'm getting. I wish to sit at Girish Babu's feet and learn acting from him.'

The men coaxed and cajoled, even scolded and threatened her but to no purpose. At last, admitting defeat, they walked away in a huff. Gangamoni stood with her arms akimbo and rolled her eyes at her. 'You're the stupidest, stubbornest girl I've seen.

410

You're being your own worst enemy. And for what? For Girish
Babu! What will Girish Ghosh do for you pray? You don't know
him. He's the most selfish, the most callous man on earth. He's
making much of you now. But he won't think twice before
flinging you off like a dirty rag the moment he has no use for you.
Youth and beauty don't last forever. Make money now while the
going's good and stock up for the future.' But Nayan didn't seem
to be listening to a word. The moment Gangamoni paused for
breath she giggled and cried, 'O Didi! That Rajen Babu or Fajen
Babu whoever he was, was scared to death. Did you see how he
was sweating? I can bet he has a harridan of a wife at home. As for
that Neelmadhav—he looks like a wild cat. His whiskers —' She
could hold herself in no longer and rolled all over the *chowki*
laughing.

Gangamoni forgot to scold. She gazed at her in amazement.
Tears shone in her eyes as, springing forward, she clasped the girl
to her breast. 'How do you do it Nayan?' she cried over and over
again, 'From where do you get the strength?'

411

Chapter VI

It was exactly four hundred years ago that Columbus had discovered America. To mark that epoch-making event a mammoth festival was being organized in the city of Chicago of which an important feature was the congregation of religious leaders from all parts of the world. Such a coming together was unheard of. For centuries the word *religion* had been synonymous with intolerance, hatred and distrust. The European Church, dismissing the claims of all other religions, had sent and were still sending their members to the ends of the earth on a mission to convert the heathen. It was no wonder that the Archbishop of Canterbury was horrified by the idea. Particularly incensed by the news that spiritual leaders had been invited even from India he had declared his intention of not attending the conference. 'Natives,' he had exclaimed angrily, 'are like our slaves. To share a platform with them would be as good as admitting that they are our equals.'

But America was not Europe. Americans were less conservative, broader in outlook and more open to other cultures. Being the richest nation in the world they were consumer oriented and materialistic. Darwin's theory of Evolution had struck at the roots of Christianity. He had proved, conclusively, that the Bible was a myth. Being, scientifically, the most advanced among nations and nurturing a spirit of enquiry Americans, by and large, accepted Darwin's theory. And doing so, they saw no harm in exploring other religions. Who knew but they might have something to offer?

Invitations to speak at the Congress had been sent to spiritual leaders from all parts of the world. Jews, Muslims, Buddhists, Confucians, Taos, Shintos and the fire worshipping Zoroastrians of Persia were to give discourses on their respective faiths side by side with representatives of the Catholic, the Greek and the Protestant Church. Even Brahmos and Theosophists had been invited. The only religion left out was Hinduism. And that was because Americans knew nothing about it. From what they had heard it could hardly be called a religion. It was a savage, primitive cult in which women were burned alive on the funeral pyres of their husbands; which encouraged mothers to throw their suckling infants into a so called holy river to be devoured by crocodiles. It contained a strange sect called Brahmin, the members of which considered themselves polluted by a non-Brahmin's touch. These Brahmins, it was said, were revered like gods and were so powerful that they could burn down the houses of anyone who incurred their wrath with impunity. And, once a year, the rolling chariot of a monstrous god named Juggernaut mowed down hundreds of people in its triumphal progress.

The day set for the inauguration of this Parliament of Religions was Monday, the eleventh of September and the venue Chicago's Hall of Columbus. On a vast iron throne, in the centre of a hundred-foot long dais, Cardinal Gibbons—the Head of the Catholic Church of America—sat in state. On both sides of him, in rows of chairs, the other speakers sat awaiting their turn to speak. There were quite a few Indians among them—the Buddhist leader Dharampal, Veerchand Gandhi of the Jain community, the Theosophists Jnanendra Chakravarty and Annie Besant and the Brahmos BB Nagarkar and Pratapchandra Majumdar.

On first entering the hall, Pratapchandra's eyes had fallen on a young man in a strange costume who, from his features and complexion, seemed to be an Indian. Pratapchandra noticed that several other Indians were also staring at him. 'Hindu! Hindu!' Dharampal whispered in his ear as he took his seat. 'He wasn't invited. He came on a recommendation.' Pratapchandra stole another glance at the stranger. He was quite young, in his twenties perhaps, with fair, handsome features and bright flashing eyes. He wore a long, loose robe of bright orange silk and a tall orange turban that looked as though it had been pulled off the head of a native raja's dewan. 'What kind of Hindu?' he whispered back. 'Is he from Nepal?'

'No. No. I've heard he's from Madras. Or Calcutta.'

At this moment the young man caught Pratapchandra's eye and smiled at him in recognition. There was something vaguely familiar about him now. Pratapchandra knew he had seen him

413

somewhere but where or on what occasion he couldn't remember.

After a couple of hours Dr Barrows, one of the organizers and a friend of Pratapchandra's, came up to him and whispered.

'It's your turn next Majumdar. Start getting ready.' Gathering his papers together Pratapchandra asked, 'Who is the man in the turban, Barrows?'

'He's from India. Don't you know him?'

'I don't seem to remember. What's his name?'

'His name . . . his name . . . It's quite a tongue twister. Let me see. It's Soami Viv Ka Nand.'

Pratapchandra's brows came together. He had never heard such a name in his life. Soami was obviously Swami but what was Viv Ka Nand? The man was not a Bengali. That much was certain.

Pratapchandra's lecture drew a lot of applause. His English was excellent and the parallels he drew between the Bible and the Upanishads demonstrated the extent of his learning. In between reading from a prepared text he spoke fluently, explaining the Sanskrit verses and quoting large portions from the Bible. Applause, of course, was a form of politeness in the West and all the speakers got it—even the Chinaman whose discourse was totally incomprehensible owing to his odd accent. The morning passed. Pratapchandra noticed that the young man in the turban was being approached by Dr Barrows several times. But he declined each time, shaking his head with a smile. He was not yet ready, it seemed, to speak.

During the lunch interval, when Pratapchandra was scanning the crowd for a glimpse of Jnanendranath Chakravarty a voice called out in Bengali, '*Ki go* Pratapda! How are you?' Pratapchandra turned around to see the young man in orange smiling warmly at him. He was a Bengali then! A Bengali sanyasi in a turban.

'Who are you?' Pratapchandra began tentatively. 'I don't quite —'

'You've seen me before. You don't recognize me because of my costume.'

'I've seen you before? Let me see. What's your name?'

'I'm a sanyasi now. I can't pronounce the name I went by in

my life as householder. I am Ramkrishna Paramhansa Deb's disciple. I was a regular visitor at the meetings of your Nababidhan.'

'Ramkrishna! I knew Ramkrishna. Our Keshab Babu thought very highly of him. It was he who introduced Ramkrishna to the elite society of Calcutta. I didn't know he had disciples. I heard of his illness, of course, and subsequent death. But —'

'He did not initiate anyone formally. Some of us are trying to cling to his memory and live the way he would want us to.'

'What sect are you representing? Who has sent you here?'

'No one has sent me. In fact I wasn't even invited. Yet, I'm here. How—it's difficult to say.'

'Wait a minute. I remember you now. You used to sing at the Brahmo prayer meetings. Your name was . . . your name was Naren. You're from the Datta family of Shimle. You were a graduate—were you not?

'You remember me then.'

Pratapchandra's attitude underwent a sea-change from that moment onwards. The boy was not only a Bengali—he was one of their own boys. They had hoped that he would, in time, become a pillar of the Brahmo Samaj. But that hadn't happened. He had gone over to Ramkrishna. But that didn't matter. The Brahmos had nothing against Ramkrishna. The two were Bengalis, together, in a foreign land and that forged a bond between them.

'I'd heard about the financial troubles you had to face on your father's death,' he said, 'but I had no idea you had become a sanyasi. Now tell me. Why are you here?'

'I wished to speak a few words in support of Hinduism. But now I'm not so sure. After hearing your discourse and that of some of the other speakers I'm afraid to open my mouth from fear of being booed out. I doubt if anyone will care to listen to me.'

'Everyone will listen to you.' Pratapchandra patted Naren kindly on the shoulder. 'I'm sure you'll do very well. Think of your guru and speak from the heart.' Then, turning to Jnanendranath Chakravarty, who had materialized among them, he asked, 'Do you know this boy Jnan Babu? He's from Calcutta.'

'Ah! Yes,' Jnanendranath replied. 'I've been hearing about him for the last three or four days. He's Vivekananda—is he not?'

'So that's the name!' Pratapchandra exclaimed. 'Vivekananda! The swamis of Bankim Babu's *Anandamath* are, each of them, some kind of Ananda—Satyananda, Jeebananda, Dheerananda . . . You too are an Ananda. Good! Good! Now tell me how you came to America—'

'It's a long story and will take some time in the telling. The second session is about to begin. You'll have to wait for another day Pratapda.'

Naren's metamorphosis from a whimsical lad to a spiritual leader was owing not to his own efforts but to a sequence of events that had carried him on their wings. One of the ten or twelve boys who had stayed on in the house in Barahnagar after Ramkrishna's death, he had spent his time reading Sanskrit texts, singing kirtans and reminiscing about the old days with the others. Since they had no source of income the richer among Ramkrishna's disciples sent them money from time to time. When they forgot and there was no rice in the pot the boys went begging from door to door. There were days when Naren and his friends had one meal a day and that too only boiled rice mixed with a soup made of chillies that grew wild in the garden. Their parents couldn't understand what their sons were gaining from this self-inflicted torture and insisted on their returning home. The boys held out for as long as they could but, gradually, the group started disintegrating. This happened not because of the hardness of the life or of the pressure parents and guardians were putting. The truth was that they were getting bored. There was nothing to do; nothing to look forward to. One by one, they started leaving. Some returned to their families and others took off on pilgrimages. Naren tried to keep the flock together for as long as he could, agonizing over each departure, till one day, after the youngest of them all, a boy called Sarada, had left, he wondered why he was doing so. 'Who am I and what am I doing with my life?' he asked himself. And, in a moment of clarity, he got the answer. He was not for this world. That much was clear to him. He had left his home, his mother and younger siblings. Why, then, was he clinging to this house? Why was he worrying about Sarada's youth and ignorance of the ways of the world and fearing the possibility of his getting hurt? Had he exchanged one family, one set of responsibilities, for another? The ascetic was

416

like a river which had to flow to keep its waters pure and clear. That day he took a decision. He would leave too. He would explore this country, inch by inch, and see what it was like.

Having acknowledged to himself that he was a sanyasi who should keep himself rootless and free, Naren left the house quietly one night without announcing his intention to anyone. In appearance he was a traditional ascetic. He wore a saffron loin cloth and carried a lathi and brass pot. The only jarring note was the bundle of books he carried on his back. Reading was a habit Naren could not and would not give up. He read whatever he could lay his hands on—from the Vedantas to the adventure novels of Jules Verne.

And thus Naren's travels began. He went from place to place without aim or direction, equally eager and excited about the prospect of seeing the Taj Mahal as Lord Vishwanath's temple in Kashi. If someone gave him food he stuffed himself greedily. If he didn't get any he went hungry equally cheerfully. Sometimes, someone was kind enough to buy him a ticket which enabled him to sit in a train. But, oftener than not, he had only his legs and lathi to take him forward. And, just as he hadn't surrendered his aesthetic instincts, he had no intention of giving up his thirst for knowledge. He visited Paohari Baba's ashram in Gazipur but spent an even longer time with Pandit Bhudev Mukherjee in Varanasi arguing about some ancient texts.

He found Bengalis everywhere he went. They had been the first to learn English and were, in consequence, India's first lawyers, doctors, journalists, schoolteachers and railway officials. In many of the places he visited Naren found his fellow students from Presidency College. They were in high positions and were appalled, at first, by the sight of him in his filthy loin cloth, his hair long and tangled and his eyes sunk in their sockets. But they took him in, kept him in their houses for as long as he cared to stay, then gave him addresses and letters of introduction. Wherever he went Naren made a mark. From the meanest cobbler in the street to the highest official in the Town Hall he impressed everyone he met with his dignified bearing, fluent English and knowledge of innumerable subjects. Gradually his fame spread. More and more people were talking of the scholarly, handsome young sadhu who was steeped in the ancient wisdom

417

of the country yet as enlightened and liberated in thought and spirit as any European.

He began receiving invitations from several royal families of India—from Alwar, Kota, Khetri; from the Nizam of Hyderabad and even the Maharaja of Mysore. After seeing him and hearing him speak many of them expressed their bewilderment at the life he was leading. 'Swamiji,' the Raja of Alwar asked him once, 'You were one of the brightest students of Calcutta University. You could have taken your pick of lucrative jobs. Why do you choose to roam about the country in this manner?'

'Why do you spend your time hunting and shooting like the sahibs instead of looking after your state?' Naren asked smiling.

'Why?' The raja spluttered in astonishment. 'Well . . . I can't say why except . . . because I enjoy it I suppose.'

'That's exactly why I wander about like a common fakir. Because I enjoy it.'

'But why the saffron?'

'That's for self protection. If I went about in a dhuti beggars would ask me for alms. I would have none to give and that would have pained me. Dressed as I am people recognize me for a bhikshu and treat me as one.'

Some of the royal personages he visited invited him to stay on in their palaces as tutor to their sons. Others offered him expensive presents. But Naren wouldn't take anything from anyone. 'You may buy me a ticket to my next destination,' he would say if pressed too hard. He took only one gift and that was from the Maharaja of Mysore. Picking out a small sandalwood hookah from the array of costly presents set before him, he packed it in his bundle. Smoking was another habit he couldn't give up.

From Haridwar to Dwarka; from Trivandrum to Rameswar; from the Himalayas to Kanyakumari—Naren wove back and forth like a shuttle over the vast tapestry that was India. And wherever he went he saw sickness and hunger; illiteracy and superstition; poverty and abuse of power. He realized, little by little, that in this country the pursuit of Faith, Knowledge, Reason and Logic had been abandoned ages ago. The only pursuit left was that of power. The caste system was like an insidious web trapping and choking the life breath out of its members with its poisoned filaments. 'Hinduism be damned,' Naren muttered bitterly when what he saw became unbearable, 'What is the worth of a religion which draws no one to it? Which humiliates and rejects its own followers? True morality lies in feeding the hungry, nursing the sick and bringing comfort to the comfortless.'

It took Naren four years to tour the whole country. Then, one day, he came to the end of his journey. Reaching Kanyakumari he sat on a rock jutting out of the sea. A vast expanse of blue green water stretched out on all three sides as far as the eye could see. Behind him was India . . . Covering his face with his hands he wept, deep harsh sobs racking his starved, fatigued body. He had lost the path he had known so far and his peace of mind with it. But there was no other path before him. What would he do now? Where would he go from here? Back to Barahnagar to read the Vedas and sing hymns? No, that was not possible anymore. Having seen the suffering millions of his country he could not turn his back on them. The first task before him was to find food for his fellow men. He could think of their souls and his own afterwards. But how was that to be done? Science was the answer. Scientific knowledge and modern instruments had to be imported from the West and used for growing food for the masses. But no one gave anything for nothing. What could India give in return? Suddenly he got the answer. Weak and enfeebled though she was, India had something the countries of the West had lost. Their religion was under severe stress. Doubt and speculation were rife and despair was setting in, slowly but surely. India had a spiritualism that went back thousands of years; one that had withstood the shocks and tremors of innumerable invasions and still stood firm. *Give us food and we'll give you a philosophy.* That could be India's slogan. The more Naren thought about it the better the idea seemed to him. He would take this message to the West. But how? It was not possible to announce it in the streets. Then, suddenly, an idea struck him so forcefully that he stood up in his excitement. He would go to Chicago where representatives of all the religions of the world were meeting under one banner, and address the people of the West.

Returning to Madras Naren disclosed his intention to his friend and admirer Perumal Alasinga. Perumal thought the idea

419

an excellent one and got busy organizing the trip without delay. The first thing to do was to raise funds for the journey. Perumal and his friends started a collection but the amounts that came were small and trickled in very slowly. Chicago was an expensive city and a great way off so a good deal of money was needed. Fortunately some of Naren's royal friends now came forward. All of them contributed generously but the largest donation came from Ajit Singh—the Raja of Khetri.

Ajit Singh also designed the costume Naren was to wear at the conference and it was he who chose his name. Naren had taken the name of Vivishananda, just before setting out on his travels, but it was such a mouthful that he, himself, had difficulty pronouncing it. Ajit Singh toned it down to Vivekananda. Thus Naren became Swami Vivekananda.

One cold frosty morning Naren's ship docked at the port of Vancouver in Canada. After that it was a three-day journey by train to Chicago. It had seemed an exciting adventure when being planned and executed but every day in this new country made Naren more and more aware of the foolishness of the undertaking. He had thought himself well prepared but, in reality, he was not prepared at all. He didn't have an invitation to the conference. He didn't even have letters of introduction from important men in his country. He had come on an impulse and hadn't even thought of these things. How would he prove to the organizers that he was representing India? Why should they take him at his word? Besides, the stock of money he had brought with him, which had seemed so large in India, was worth very little in this country, and was dwindling at an alarming rate. And worst of all was the news that the conference was a month away. Like a naïve fool he had rushed over without checking the dates. Naren's heart sank and his limbs started trembling in trepidation. What would he do now? He knew no one here and no one knew him. Where would he live for a whole month and how? Seeking alms was out of the question. In this country begging was a legal offence.

Naren stood on the pavement of Chicago's South Wabash Avenue bracing himself against the icy blasts of wind that threatened to sweep him off his feet. That was another point he hadn't considered—the climate of the country towards which he was headed. He was totally unequipped for the bitter cold in which he found himself. People turned to stare at him as they walked past, much as if they thought him a being from another planet. And, indeed, he presented a strange sight. His orange silk robe fluttered like a banner in the strong wind and he had difficulty keeping his turban in place. His feet in their open sandals were blue with cold.

As he stood, uncertain, wondering what to do, a group of children ran up to him clapping their hands and crying out some words in a tongue that seemed completely alien to him. Americans spoke English. He knew that. Why, then, didn't he understand what these children were saying? After a few minutes they got bored with their game and started pelting him with pebbles which they picked up from the street. Now Naren started to walk away from them. The children, delighted at having evoked a reaction, ran after him. Naren ducked his head to avoid the shower of stones that was being aimed at it and ran towards a hotel that stood in a corner of the street.

Entering it he realized that it would be expensive but Naren was too desperate to consider that now. Chilled to the bone, hungry and exhausted in mind and body, he needed a roof above his head, a hot meal and a warm bed in which to rest his limbs. If he didn't get them soon he would die of cold and exposure.

Naren spent three days in the hotel trying to pull himself together and take a decision. Going back to India was out of the question. He didn't have the money for a ticket. He could have hung around the dockyard begging for a free passage. Anyone else in his position would have done just that. But Naren was made of different mettle. Deeply ingrained in his character was a streak of pride and stubbornness that would not allow him to admit defeat. He had come here with a purpose and he would follow the purpose to its logical end or die in the attempt.

Ajit Singh had given him a suit of Western clothes to wear on the ship. Naren decided to put aside his ascetic's orange for a while and don the suit. It would keep him warmer and would make him less conspicuous. Attired thus he started moving about the city trying to study the country and its people. America was a vast country and everything in it was immense. The buildings were like palaces and the roads the longest and widest he had

421

seen. But, to his dismay, he found that the minds of the people were narrow and closed. He had believed Americans to be open and receptive to other cultures. But the openness, he discovered, was confined to one section of society—the scientists and intellectuals. The rest were as bigoted and chauvinistic as their English forebears. Colour was the test of worth even in this country. The coloured races were to be considered inferior to the white; to be despised and treated with contempt. This was an unwritten rule which the majority of Americans followed. Naren had come with such high hopes of this newly discovered land. The reality left him shaken and depressed.

In his rambles through the streets of Chicago he found out that Boston was a cheaper city in which to live. Naren decided to move there and return to Chicago a day before the conference was scheduled to begin and, with that end in view, he boarded a train to Boston. As luck would have it, the man sitting next to him was an Indian called Lalu Bhai. As they chatted of this and that a lady rose from her corner seat and came up to them. 'Excuse me gentlemen,' she said, 'What country do you come from?'

'From India,' Naren answered.

'From India!' the lady echoed. 'Can Indians speak English?'

'Of course. India has many provinces and many languages. But English is spoken everywhere. In fact, even when conversing with one another in our mother tongues, we often fall back on English. Sanskrit is another language of ours, a very old one from which most of our modern languages are derived. It is kin to English too—a kind of aunt or grandmother.'

The lady didn't press him further and returned to her seat. But as they were stepping off the train at Boston station she asked him, 'Where do you plan to stay?' On being told that he would look for a hotel, she said, 'Why not come with me to my farmhouse instead? You'll be quite comfortable there. My friends have never seen an Indian. They would like to meet you.' Her words fell like music on Naren's ears. If he accepted her offer he would be saved the trouble of counting cents and worrying about expenses for some time at least. Smiling in agreement he followed her as meekly as a lamb.

The lady's name was Katharine Abbott Sandbourne and she was both educated and wealthy. Her circle of friends were curious about her new find and came rushing over to see him. They had many questions to ask about his country, its culture and religion. And they were amazed to find that the strange specimen of humanity who sat on Katharine's sofa looking like some exotic bird of paradise in his orange silk, had not only read the Bible but many other books besides. He could converse in English as fluently as any Englishman born to the soil. He was witty and amusing as well as knowledgeable but he could also be razor sharp in his criticism—be it of his own country or of the West. Gradually curiosity changed to respect. More and more people invited him to their houses and the *Brahmin Sanyasi* from India began occupying the centre of attention in upper-class Boston society.

A member of Katharine Sandbourne's circle was Henry Wright, a Professor of Greek studies in the University of Harvard. This gentleman, thoroughly impressed by Naren's scholarship and enlightened outlook, took him to his house for a visit. To his amazement he found that the Indian swami was as liberated in his personal habits as he was in his opinions. He sat with them at their dinner table and ate whatever was served, be it fish, fowl, venison or even beef. It was, indeed, a coming together of two kindred souls. Naren and Henry Wright spent hours discussing Greek and Hindu philosophy, British imperialism, ancient history and a number of other subjects.

On learning that Naren had come to America to present his views at the Parliament of Religions but would not be able to do so because he had no invitation, Wright urged him not to give up hope. Dr Barrows, the secretary of the Organizing Committee, was a personal friend of his. He would write him a letter requesting him to allow Naren to speak at the conference and also make arrangements for his stay. Wright also took upon himself the task of preparing Naren's biodata. Handing over all the documents he had prepared, Wright bought Naren a first-class ticket to Chicago and put him on the train.

Unfortunately all these efforts were wasted—not from any fault of Wright's. It was entirely owing to Naren's carelessness. On reaching Chicago he realized that he had only one of the envelopes with him—the one containing his biodata. The letter of introduction to Barrows was missing. It must have dropped out

423

of his pocket on to the floor of the compartment. But the train had left and there was no way of recovering the letter. Naren was so frustrated that he felt like banging his head against the wall. He had, by an amazing stroke of luck, managed to bring his battered boat almost to the shore. Would he lose it now and his life with it? The conference was due to begin in a day or two. There wasn't time to go back to Harvard and bring another letter. On the other hand, he couldn't abandon his resolve after so much effort on Wright's part.

Coming out of the station he saw that it was raining heavily outside. The air was bitterly cold. The evening was drawing to a close and soon darkness would set in. Naren dashed out in the wind and rain and ran hither and thither trying to find a room in a hotel. But the city was bursting with strangers, newly arrived from other places to attend the conference, and the hotels were full. Unable to secure shelter anywhere Naren returned to the station where, looking around him moodily, he observed a large wooden crate standing abandoned in one corner. He was so cold and exhausted by now that he didn't even think of the consequences. He climbed into the crate and lay down. It was small for him and he had to lie on one side his legs drawn up to his chest. Fortunately the night passed uneventfully. He wasn't taken for a vagrant and hauled off to jail. When he rose, the next morning, he had made a resolution. He would go to Dr Barrows and beg for an audience. But from where was he to get the address? He decided to go from door to door and ask the question. Surely someone would know.

But, as it turned out, no one knew. Naren went from one house to another—huge mansions set in several acres of beautiful gardens around Lake Michigan—the owners of which were the wealthy industrialists of the city. Some told him that they didn't know; hadn't even heard of the conference. Others, mistaking him for a lunatic, drove him out like they would a stray dog.

After many hours of trying Naren gave up the attempt and sat down on the road faint with hunger and exhaustion, his limbs stiff with cold. And then, when all hope was gone, an angel of mercy descended from heaven and saved him from sure death. A lady had been observing him from an upstairs window of a three-storeyed house. Now she opened her door and approaching him, where he sat in the dust, asked an unexpected question. 'Have you come as a delegate to the Parliament of Religions?'

Everything was smooth sailing after that. Mrs Hale, for that was her name, took him home with her. After a hot bath, a good meal and rest, Naren was escorted by his benefactress to Dr Barrows' office. Fortunately, Henry Wright had taken the precaution of sending a letter by post to his friend and all the arrangements had been made already. Naren was given a delegate's badge and conducted to the quarters he would occupy. Naren's troubles were over at last . . .

Naren had put off speaking for a long time but he couldn't do so indefinitely. Finally the hour came when he had to take up the task for which he had undertaken such a long journey and so many hazards. He rose and walked towards the rostrum. Pratapchandra had told him to take his guru's name before he began his speech but the blood was thudding so violently in his heart that his mind went blank. He couldn't remember a single name—neither Ramkrishna's nor Ma Kali's. He looked with glazed eyes at the sea of human faces in front of him. Beyond them was a statue of white marble; a female figure—her hand stretched out as if in blessing. It must have been the representation of some Greek goddess but, in his overwrought condition, he thought it was the goddess Saraswati newly descended from heaven. 'Ma Saraswati!' he murmured 'Have mercy on me. Unlock my tongue and give me speech.' Then, taking a deep breath, he began: '*Sisters and Brothers of America.*'

As an opening sentence this was an unusual one. People started clapping—a few at first. Then more and more joined in till the hall echoed with applause. Naren stood, nonplussed, for a while. Western audiences were generous with their applause—he knew that. But the kind he was getting wasn't a form of politeness. It seemed to be something else—a frenzied endorsement of his sentiments by a gathering of which the majority were women. Stirred by an emotion he couldn't explain, even to himself, his fear vanished. His voice rose, strong and clear, and rang like a sonorous bell through the length and breadth of the room:

'I thank you in the name of the most ancient order of monks in the world . . . I am proud to belong to a religion which has taught

425

the world both tolerance and universal acceptance. We believe not only in universal toleration, but we accept all religions as true ... As the different streams having their sources in different places all mingle their water in the sea, so, O Lord, the different paths which men take through different tendencies, various though they appear, crooked or straight, all lead to thee ...'

The applause rose to a crescendo. Like a mighty storm, it washed over the vast hall, in wave after deafening wave. People started leaving their chairs and running towards the rostrum at which he stood. The other speakers stared at one another, dumbfounded. What had the young man said that they hadn't? They had all, at some point or the other in their discourses, advocated tolerance of other religions. What they didn't realize was that their discourses had been academic exercises. Naren had had no written text before him. He had spoken from the heart and, in doing so, he had won over the hearts of the Americans. He hadn't extolled the virtues of his own religion. He had pleaded for a Brotherhood of Man. 'The boy spoke well,' one of the organizers whispered to another, 'but who could have thought he would receive an ovation such as this? If he can keep his head in the right place after today he's a remarkable young man indeed!'

Chapter VII

A little distance away from Bharat's lodgings in the town of Cuttack was the residence of the district judge Biharilal Gupta. Biharilal and his wife Soudamini were warm and sociable in temperament and very hospitable. Consequently their house was packed with guests at all hours of the day and the air redolent with the aroma of delicious food. The evenings, in particular, rang with music and laughter for Biharilal liked to relax in the company of his friends after a gruelling day in court. Soudamini was a motherly sort of woman who loved feeding her guests. Though she had many servants she insisted on cooking some of the dishes herself and serving them with her own hands. She was small and slight in build and ate very little herself. But she loved the sight of others enjoying a meal and that included birds and beasts. Her heart sang with joy, each morning, as she threw handfuls of grain to her pigeons and pushed the tenderest of leaves into the mouth of the doe in her garden. She even looked on with pleasure at the sight of the syce giving the horses their gram.

Biharilal and Soudamini were Brahmos and intimate friends of the Thakurs of Jorasanko. Soudamini had once been a member of Swarnakumari Devi's Sakhi Samiti. Now, having moved to Cuttack, she had opened a branch for the women of the town. Classes in music, painting, dancing and needlework were held in her house and she encouraged all the young girls she knew to come and join them. She was dead against the notion of purdah and could be sharp in her criticism. 'Are you a doll?' she would scold if she found a girl sitting timidly, her eyes on the ground, 'Haven't you learned to talk?' And if anyone covered her face before a man she would rail at her, 'Why has god given you a pretty face if you don't show it?'

Bharat, though only a bank clerk, had managed to find a place in these gatherings. Biharilal and Soudamini made no distinction between people. They kept open house and made everyone welcome—Bengali or Oriya, rich or poor. Bharat liked Orissa

427

and felt a strange bonding with her country and people. They were Bhumisuta's and since Bhumisuta was his he felt they were his too. After scouring the streets of Calcutta for months, trying to find her, he had decided to come to Orissa. She might have, in her disgust and disappointment with Bengal, gone back to her roots. He had roamed from place to place—Puri, Baleswar, Cuttack—his eyes strained for a glimpse of her. Finally, worn out with physical and mental exhaustion, exposure and starvation, he had fallen in a dead faint outside the temple of Jagannath in Puri. No one had picked him up. No one had extended a helping hand. Puri was full of lepers, beggars and lunatics. Who had the time to glance at them? Pilgrims crowding into the temple had thrown a brief glance at the fair youth lying on the ground and, thinking it to be a novel way of begging, had flung a few paisas in his direction before walking on. How Bharat had come out of that faint he did not remember. But he had not only survived—he had managed to make a living in Puri. Sitting under a tree outside the Post Office, he had filled out money order forms, at the rate of one paisa per form, for those who could not read or write. With the ten or twelve paisas he made each day he could buy himself two coarse but nourishing meals, for Orissa was a cheap place. And at night, he slept under the stars on the vast *chatal* of the temple.

He lived like this for a year clinging to the hope that he would find Bhumisuta. All Oriyas visited the temple of Jagannath some time or the other. She might be married, by now, of course. He didn't mind that. All he wanted was to meet her and beg for her forgiveness. But Bhumisuta eluded him and the hope died slowly in his breast.

Then, one day, a gentleman offered him a job. He had seen Bharat several times sitting outside the Post Office filling forms and been surprised by the neatness and elegance of his hand. Lloyd's Bank, he told Bharat, had recently opened a branch in Cuttack and was looking for young men who knew English. Bharat was obviously well educated. Why didn't he send an application? Bharat took the man's advice and got the job. That was six years ago. Now he had risen to the post of Chief Accountant and was a regular visitor at the house of Biharilal Gupta.

One day Soudamini said to him, 'Do you know how to sing Bharat? We are putting up Robi Babu's *Balmiki Pratibha* this Maghotsav and are short of a male voice.' Bharat blushed and protested. He had never sung in his life, he said, and didn't know one note from another. But Soudamini wouldn't let him off. Thrusting the role of the first dacoit on him she started training him for the part. Within a few minutes she realized that he hadn't exaggerated. But there was no one to replace him so, comforting herself with the thought that a dacoit's voice needn't be very sweet or tuneful, she started working on him harder than ever. As for Bharat, his original reluctance wore off in a few days and he started enjoying the rehearsals.

Doing the female lead was a girl called Mohilamoni. She was a child widow, beautiful and intelligent. Having received some education she was a great help to Soudamini in running the Samiti and spent most of her day in Biharilal's house. Bharat had been struck with her beauty and charm the first day he had seen her which was over a year ago. Now he marvelled at her singing voice. She sang the songs of the 'little maid' with so much feeling! And her enunciation was perfect!

'I saw *Balmiki Pratibha* for the first time in Jorasanko,' Biharilal said during one of the rehearsals. 'Robi Babu played the male lead and a niece of his, a girl called Pratibha, played the heroine. In fact the opera was named after her. She was a beautiful girl and had the sweetest voice I had ever heard. But, to tell you the truth, our Mohilamoni is doing even better than Pratibha.'

'Mama Babu!' Mohilamoni laughed and shook her head with mock severity at Biharilal. 'You mustn't flatter me with all these lies. I'll stop acting and go home if you do.'

'I'm not flattering you child. It's nothing but the plain truth I'm telling you.'

A few days later news reached the players that Robi Babu was coming to inspect the family estates in Balia and would not only be visiting Cuttack but would actually be staying in the house. It was instantly decided that a performance would be put up expressly for him and his opinion on its quality sought. It was a rare opportunity and should not be missed on any account. This decision threw everyone in a flurry of preparation. Rehearsals

429

began an hour earlier and went on till late into the night. Bharat could come only after the bank was closed for the day but he stayed on right till the end.

It was during one of these rehearsals that Bharat had a strange experience. His role over for the time being, he was sitting with the others looking at Mohilamoni as she sang her lines. Suddenly she turned her face away from him and he saw it in profile for the first time. His heart gave a tremendous leap. It was Bhumisuta's face. He almost stood up in his excitement but, before he could do so, Mohilamoni was facing him once more and the resemblance was gone. Now Bharat started watching her covertly and, after a while he realized that though their figures, colouring and facial expressions were dissimilar their right profiles were uncannily alike. That and a trick both women had of lowering their lashes and fixing their eyes on the ground. Whenever Mohilamoni turned her face to the left and lowered her glance she looked exactly like Bhumisuta. Was there some relationship between the two, Bharat asked himself feverishly. Were they sisters? No. That was not possible. Bhumisuta's parents had died long ago. Were they cousins then? If that were so Mohilamoni would have news of Bhumisuta. Should he talk to her and try to find out?

Next evening Bharat was even later than usual for the rehearsal. An angry Soudamini railed at him for not taking the show seriously. But her complaints and criticisms made not a dent on his consciousness. His eyes, his mind and spirit were fixed on Mohilamoni as she sat, her face turned to one side, her eyes on the carpet. He had seen that expression so many times before that it seemed as familiar to him as the beat of his own heart. He felt Bhumisuta's presence, in this room, as he hadn't felt it in these seven years since he had lost her. Bhumisuta was here and she was trying to reach out to him . . .

Chapter VIII

The two friends bumped into one another outside Bankimchandra's, house in Pratap Chatterjee Street. They had been students in college together. Now Dwarika was a wealthy landowner, stout and handsome in his tussar kurta stretched tight across a great expanse of chest. An expensive Kashmiri shawl sat carelessly on one shoulder and a pair of magnificent whiskers waved luxuriously above his upper lip. Dwarika visited his estates in Khulna once a year. The rest of his time was spent in Calcutta running a journal called *Nabajyoti* for Dwarika had retained his love of literature. Jadugopal had fulfilled his life's ambition of going to England and returning a barrister. And having married a daughter of the illustrious house of Jorasanko was, now, numbered among the elite. He wore a faultless three-piece English suit and shining boots.

'Why Dwarika!' he greeted his old friend facetiously, 'Can't you let the poor man alone? Must you wrest a story for your infernal magazine even from his sick bed?'

'No brother,' Dwarika's face looked pale and worried. 'Bankim Babu is in no condition to write—for me or for anyone else. The doctors say he's critical. Besides, he left off writing years ago.'

'Why? He's not that old. Fifty-five or fifty-six—at the most. That's no age to retire. He's the king of Bengali literature. He should go on and on.'

'His spirit is broken. After his daughter's death he—'

'Ah yes! I remember. His youngest daughter Utpalkumari committed suicide, didn't she?'

'It wasn't suicide. I'm close to the family so I know the truth. Utpala's husband Matindra is a beast in human form. Wine, women, gambling, ganja—he indulges in every vice you can find on this earth. He has a gang of toadies who feed on him constantly and egg him on. Naturally, it didn't take him much time to run through his own money. Then he started pestering

431

Utpala to give him her jewels. But Utpala was a strong woman and denied him resolutely. They were her own *Stridhan*, given to her by her father. Why should she let her husband squander them away? He harrassed her in every way he could but didn't succeed in getting them out of her. Then, with the help of a doctor friend of his, he got hold of a drug and poured it into her bottle of medicine. He had no idea of the potency of the drug. So he may have put in more than he was supposed to. He said he hadn't meant to kill her, only to make her unconscious. Anyhow, Utpala died and Matindra, in a panic, hung her body from a beam and made it look like suicide. It was later, during the post mortem, that the poison was discovered in her system.'

'But the court gave a verdict of suicide.'

'Bankim Babu didn't contest the case. After all, his family honour was at stake. To prevent the ugly story from coming out into the open he supported his son-in-law.'

'Kundanandini!' Jadugopal breathed.

'Exactly. He was haunted by that thought himself. "I poisoned Kundanandini," he said over and over again. "I killed her. And now my own daughter—" Is it not tragic, Jadu, that such a fiery pen has been extinguished? The doctors say he has lost the will to live.'

'I've come to him with a proposal. You must help me get his permission. Some of my friends in England wish to translate Bankim Babu's works and publish them.'

'You won't get his permission.'

'Why not? He won't have to do anything himself. All the work will be done by others. If translations of his books are available they'll be read by people of other countries and his fame will spread far beyond Bengal. Besides, he'll get a lot of money.'

'He's a proud, stubborn, bitter man. He doesn't permit translations because he's convinced that the sahebs won't read his work. And, even if they do, they won't understand it. He has translated his own *Debi Choudhurani* but hasn't published it. He detests the English and won't have anything to do with them.'

The two friends were sitting in the drawing room with the other visitors—all waiting in the hope of seeing the great man. No one was being allowed into the bedroom for Dr Mahendralal Sarkar was examining the patient. Bankimchandra had been suffering from diabetes for quite some time. He had recognized the symptoms—a raging thirst and frequent urinations—but hadn't called in a doctor. Then, one day, he suffered a violent attack of pain in his underbelly. The pain was so agonizing that he twitched and flung his limbs about like a newly slaughtered goat. There was no question of fighting it alone. The best doctors of the city were sent for and, after careful examination, a large boil was discovered in his urethra. The doctors advocated an operation but Bankimchandra would not hear of it. 'I know I'm doomed,' he told Dr O'Brien. 'What's the use of cutting me up? Operation or no operation—I won't survive. I feel it in my bones.' Now the family had sent for Dr Mahendralal Sarkar.

After a while the doctor came down the stairs his great boots clacking noisily. He stood with his arms akimbo, thumbs thrust in the pockets of his waistcoat, and looked solemnly at the waiting men. 'You'll have to go back—all of you,' his big voice boomed. 'The patient can't see anyone. He needs his rest.' Jadugopal and Dwarika sprang forward to help carry his bag but he waved them away imperiously. 'I can do all my own carrying, thank you,' he said and strode out of the room. Jadu and Dwarika ran after him crying, 'How is he Daktar Babu? Do tell us.'

'Why don't you ask him?' Mahendralal snapped. 'He's a bigger doctor than I am. He knows everything. He informed me that if we cut out the abcess the pus will mingle with his blood and contaminate his whole body. As if we doctors don't know what we're doing.'

'You mustn't listen to him,' Dwarika cried, 'You must force him; threaten him. Everyone is afraid of you.'

'He's not. Besides, no doctor should use force on a patient. Particularly on one as famous as he is.'

'Have you given him medicine?'

'No. There's no sense in mixing homeopathy with allopathy. His present treatment can continue for what it's worth.'

Leaving the two young men staring after him, Mahendralal Sarkar climbed into his carriage. Poking his head out of the window, immediately afterwards, he added, 'I've learned one thing in my many years of doctoring. And that is, if a patient has lost his will to live no doctor can save him. No—not even if Dhanwantari visits him in person.'

Mahendralal's carriage clattered down the road. Dwarika watched it go, his eyes blank with despair. Then, suddenly, he burst into tears. 'I can't bear it Jadu,' he wept, his face working like a child's. 'I can't bear the thought of Bankim's death.'

'*Arré*! *Arré*!' Jadugopal clasped his friend in his arms, 'He's still with us. Besides, doctors are not gods. They may be wrong.' He took Dwarika's arm as he spoke and dragged him to his carriage. 'Go home and don't worry,' he said helping him in. But Dwarika clung to Jadu's hand. 'Come with me Jadu,' he pleaded. Jadugopal hesitated for a moment, then climbed in after Dwarika. The coachman whipped the horses and they set off at a fine canter. Jadugopal noticed that the coachman didn't wait for instructions. He seemed to know where to go. At the mouth of Hadh Katar Gali Jadugopal cried, 'Stop! Stop! I must get out here.' But Dwarika grasped Jadu's arm and begged, 'Come with me Jadu. I'm going to Basantamanjari. Do you remember her? She talks of you often and will be delighted to see you.' Jadugopal had never entered a red light area before. He took a strictly moral view of such matters. But he couldn't find it in his heart to shake off the clinging fingers. People believed Dwarika to be a man of loose morals. But Jadugopal knew that he loved Basantamanjari and had loved her from the first flush of his manhood. His love was like a pure, shining flame which had endured through the ups and downs of his life. He couldn't make her his wife but he honoured her more than many men honoured their wedded wives.

As Jadugopal stepped gingerly on the steps leading to Basantamanjari's room Dwarika said, 'Basi has a strange gift. She can look into the future. Did you know that Jadu?'

'Can she see her own future?'

'She never talks about herself.'

Basantamanjari was sitting on the floor plucking at the strings of a tanpura and singing softly to herself. Her voice was husky, sweet and deep. She didn't hear the two men enter at first and went on singing. Then, sensing their presence, she rose to her feet with a cry, 'Jadu Kaka! It's been so long. So long!' Running up to him she fell at his feet and burst into tears. Jadu let her cry. He knew how she felt. He had brought her childhood, long lost and forgotten, back to her and the experience was painful.

In a little while she collected herself and started plying him with questions about everybody and everything she had known in the village. The only names she didn't bring to her lips were those of her father and mother.

Dwarika poured himself some brandy and muttered, almost to himself, 'We lost Vidyasagar three years ago. And now Bankim—' It seemed he could think of nothing else. Even Basantamanjari's storm of weeping had gone unnoticed. 'Vidyasagar suffered agonies before he died,' Dwarika continued. 'He had lost his speech near the end and kept looking blankly from one face to another while the tears streamed out of his eyes. He was trying to say something —'

'I was in Allahabad at the time,' Jadugopal murmured, 'So I couldn't go and see him.'

'I remember it as if it was yesterday.' Dwarika's voice rose, loud and full, as though suddenly enthused. 'It was the thirteenth of Sravan. I remember the date clearly. Basi and I were sitting on the terrace and she was singing . . . It was well past midnight when she pointed to the sky and cried, "Look! Look at that beam of light moving slowly across the sky! A great soul is leaving the earth." I looked up but could see nothing. Next day I heard Vidyasagar Moshai had breathed his last in the middle of the night—at two-thirty to be precise.'

'*Ogo!*' Basantamanjari interrupted Dwarika's reminiscences with a sudden question. 'Where is that friend of yours? The one called Bharat.'

'I have no news of him. Irfan says he disappeared one morning and was never seen again.'

'He's gone far—very far,' Basantamanjari murmured dreamily.

'When did this happen?' Jadugopal asked curiously.

'It's been many years now. Six—no seven years. Basi keeps asking after him even though she has seen him only once in her life. I used to feel jealous at one time. But it's over now. He may be dead for all I know.'

The two friends chatted for a while longer then Jadugopal rose to his feet. He had a long way to go.

Dwarika went to Bankimchandra's house religiously every day. The great man was adamant in his refusal to have the operation preferring to die of the pain than suffer the indignity of being cut to ribbons by the surgeon's knife. Fate was on his side for, quite miraculously, the boil burst on its own and the blood and pus drained away out of his body. The wound healed and he felt much better. Now he could sit up and talk to his visitors.

'Why do you haunt my bedside you foolish boy?' he asked Dwarika one day. 'Are you still hoping to get a novel out of me?'

'You mustn't give up writing,' Dwarika begged, clasping the sick man's feet with his hands. 'Don't write for my journal if you'd rather not. Write for *Bharati*. Or for *Sahitya*. You are our pride and strength. We won't let go of you that easily.'

Bankimchandra smiled wryly. The end was coming near slowly but steadily. He knew it. He felt it in his bones. Around the ruptured boil others were rearing their heads—a whole crop of them, small as pimples but filled with a deadly poison. Pain lashed his worn body once again; excruciating pain that drove him into a coma. Then, one day in late Chaitra, between sleeping and waking, Bankimchandra passed away. It was not only the end of the year; it was the end of the century. A new age was being ushered in. It would dawn in a few days but Bankimchandra would not be there to see it.

Chapter IX

Macbeth, though hailed by critics as the best play of the year, was not a box office success. The public didn't take to it and the audience dwindled in number so rapidly that the management was alarmed. Running a theatre was a business after all. What was the point of staging a play, however good it was, if only a handful of intellectuals came to see it? At length, even Girish Ghosh was forced to admit the truth. People didn't want to see a serious play. He felt so frustrated that he was tempted to give it all up and go back to writing his book on Ramkrishna. But he had signed a contract with Minerva and couldn't quit upon a whim. Besides Nagendrabhushan was a perfect gentleman. It was but fair to consider his interest. Abandoning his grand plan of adapting and staging Shakespeare's plays one by one, Girish turned his hand to writing little pieces full of fun and froth with no substance. One by one they emerged from his pen—*Mukul Manjura, Abu Hossain, Baradin ér Baksheesh, Saptami té bisarjan*—farce, not even comedy, full of slapstick humour and laced with erotic songs.

After the box office had revived a little Girish set himself seriously to writing a new play. He had been hurt and offended by some newspaper reviews which had likened his latest work to the 'dancing of buffoons'. The need of the hour was a play which would have quality as well as general appeal. He decided to fall back on the Mahabharat as he had done so often before. For the new venture he selected the story of Jana. The audience hadn't seen a mythological play for many years now and would welcome the rich sets and gorgeous costumes. Besides *Jana* had a strong story line and a variety of characters. Into this blend Girish mixed a little of his own philosophy. But he took care not to serve it up neat. He coated it in humour, subtle but pungent.

This time Girish decided to stay out of the stage and gave his son Dani the hero's role. Dani had a wonderful voice, even deeper and richer than his father's. In fact many people said that, in a few years, Dani would outstrip his father as an actor. Teenkari Dasi was Jana and Ardhendushekhar the clown. This last role was really the most important one in terms of the theme. The clown had all the punch lines.

Jana was a great success and ran to full houses night after night. Then, when its popularity had reached its zenith, the blow fell. Ardhendushekhar came to Girish Ghosh's house one morning and, after a hearty breakfast of kachuris and rosogollas and several cups of tea, he broke the news. 'You'll have to let go of me,' he announced calmly, 'The bird is poised for flight.' Girish Ghosh froze at these words. He knew Ardhendushekhar. He was an extremely gifted actor but moody and impulsive. The love of roving was in his blood and he couldn't put down roots. Nothing and no one could pin him down. He was indifferent to wealth and fame and could abandon them on a moment's whim. He had a fascination for the occult and took off from time to time in its quest. He had spent several months in the mountains learning Hatha Yoga from a sadhu and he had taken lessons in hypnotism from Colonel Alcott.

'Why! Where are you planning to run off this time?' Girish cried, making his voice loud and jocular. 'Just when we are starting to make waves! Now, listen to me brother. We need you in Minerva. You can't abandon us.'

'That's exactly what I propose to do.'

'Are you leaving Calcutta?'

'No. But I'm leaving Minerva.'

'Why? Has anyone offended you? Who would have the guts? Besides, everyone loves you.'

'No one has offended me. And even if they had—I have a thick skin. The truth is —'

'Has Star recalled you?'

'No. Besides, I wouldn't go back to Star if they begged me on their knees.'

'Go home Saheb,' Girish cried in a burst of irritation, 'and stop bothering me. No one has hurt your feelings! No theatre has offered you a job! Your role in *Jana* is being acclaimed by one and all! Yet you wish to leave. It doesn't make sense.'

Ardhendushekhar took the *albola* from the older man's hand and put the pipe to his lips without troubling to wipe it. 'Let me be frank with you then,' he said, 'I've got a worm stirring in my brain. I keep trying to shake it off but it won't go. I want to be Number One.'

'What do you mean?'

'You write the plays. You direct the actors and actresses. You even compose the music. I leap and prance upon the stage at your command.'

'Is that all?' Girish Ghosh sounded relieved. 'Very well then. I put the next play in your hands. Write, direct—do everything. You be Number One. I'll keep out of the way.'

'That's easier said than done. Wherever you are you'll predominate. Do you know what decided me? I had a queer dream last night. I dreamt I was a tiger in a jungle roaring at the top of my voice. When I awoke I understood what it meant. I may be a tiger but you are the King Lion. If I mean to be king I must find another jungle.'

'Indigestion!' Girish gave a great cackle of laughter. 'You must have stuffed yourself with pulao and mutton curry floating in ghee and spices. That's why you had this silly dream. Go home and drink some lime water, then get back to bed. You've had a disturbed night and —'

'No, Girish. My mind is made up. Emerald has been lying vacant for several months now. I'm going to rent it and start a company of my own. I've made all the arrangements.'

'Who is the producer?'

'No one. I'm putting in my own money. I don't want anyone holding a stick above my head. I'm going to be Number One. Remember?'

Now Girish was truly alarmed. Taking Ardhendu's hands in his he pleaded, 'Don't do such a thing Saheb. It's a terrible risk to take. We are artistes. What knowledge do we have of financial matters? Look at me. I could have been manager of Star had I wanted to. But I steered clear of all that. I know you. You have the spirit of a true artist. Be Number One if you wish. Go anywhere you like. But don't try to run the business yourself. You'll be ruined.'

'Un hunh,' Ardhendushekhar shook his head. 'I've told you the worm in my brain won't let me rest. I'll have to try it out. After all, all I'll lose is a little money.'

439

'What about the play? *Jana* will crumble to pieces without you. No one can do your role.'

'You can.'

'I'm too old.'

'Why? You played Macbeth only the other day.'

'But the part was written for you. The audience adores you. They won't accept a substitute.'

'They'll accept you alright.'

Ardhendushekhar left Minerva after three days and a number of the company went with him. Just before he left he sent for Nayanmoni. 'Will you come with me Nayan?' he asked her then went on in the forthright manner that was habitual with him. 'You'll never play heroine in this theatre. Be sure of that. Teenkari is Girish's favourite and you'll never take her place. I've studied you. You have the potential. All you need is a little spit and polish.' Nayanmoni didn't know what to say. She revered Girish Ghosh like a god and had resolved to learn the art of acting at his feet. But Ardhendushekhar was like her father. It was he who had picked her off the streets and brought her to the theatre. She owed him her very existence. Coming home she consulted Gangamoni. 'Take his offer. Take it,' Gangamoni was quick to advise. 'It's a great chance. Don't lose it. One should never stay in one place too long. The more one moves the higher one reaches. Besides,' and here she dropped her voice though no one was listening, 'Ardhendushekhar is a better trainer than Girish Ghosh. I've spent a lifetime in the theatre. I know what I'm talking about.' Then, raising her voice, she cried, 'If you refuse this offer I'll drive you out of my house at the end of my broomstick. I swear I will.'

The next day Nayanmoni left Minerva and joined Emerald. The first play Ardhendushekhar chose for performance was Atul Krishna Mitra's *Ma*. Nayanmoni was to play the female lead. She was to get one hundred and fifty rupees a month, free meals during rehearsals and a carriage to fetch her to the theatre and take her back. Ardhendushekhar was a generous man.

But though kind and fun-loving in general, Ardhendu was a hard taskmaster and extremely strict during rehearsals. No one dared utter a sound or move from his place from fear of provoking a sarcastic comment. He also took a lively interest in each one's personal habits and gave good advice. 'What do you eat during the day Nayan?' he asked her one day, 'Begin with breakfast.' On hearing her account he flung his hands in the air with a cry. 'You mean to tell me you eat no fish or meat? You're not a widow, are you? Even if you are let me tell you something. An actress has no social obligations. Your job is to sing and dance and entertain the public, sometimes for hours at a stretch. How can you hope to do that on a diet of rice and greens? From where will you get the energy? No, no Nayan—this won't do. You must eat some fish or meat everyday to keep up your strength. Do you drink?'

'No.' Nayanmoni shook her head.

'Is anyone keeping you? I mean, do you have a Babu?'

'No.'

'Do you have a lover then?'

'No.'

'Are you married? Do you have a husband?'

'No.'

'No! No! No!' Ardhendu echoed angrily. 'Is that all you can say? I hope you are lying because if you aren't it's something to worry about. A woman needs to sleep with a man from time to time. The sap dries up in her body and her face becomes hard and brittle if she's left alone for too long.' Then, winking at her, he whispered, 'I can help you out you know. But doubtless you think me too old. We must find a young buck for you.'

The play was staged after two months of rigorous rehearsing. The critics were thrilled with it and so was the audience. Nayanmoni's role was praised to the skies and she was referred to in newspaper columns as the 'rising star in the horizon of the Bengali theatre'. But though playgoers were flocking to Emerald, night after night, it was obvious that the expenses incurred went far beyond what was coming in. Ardhendushekhar's own investment had been swallowed up and he was heavily in debt. It seemed as though Girish Babu's prophecy was coming true. But Ardhendushekhar would not give up his dream. He decided to take on a partner, a businessman called Harishchandra Malakar, and set about signing a contract with him. Harishchandra would not only pay off Ardhendushekhar's debts, he would finance the new play and take charge of the accounts in future.

On the day the contract was to be signed Harishchandra

brought his legal advisor with him—a young barrister, newly returned from England, named Jadugopal Roy. One by one the members of the cast came up to him and signed their names or put their thumb impressions on the papers spread out before him. When Nayanmoni's turn came the barrister looked at her curiously. He had seen the play twice and had been fascinated by her beauty and histrionic ability. Now, in her simple sari of striped cotton with her hair tied carelessly in a knot at the nape of her neck, she looked a different person altogether. Yet, there was something vaguely familiar about her. He was sure he had seen her somewhere; somewhere other than the theatre. The more he looked at her the surer he was. Moved by an impulse he blurted out, 'Nayanmoni Dasi must be your stage name. What's your real name?'

'Nayanmoni is my name. I have no other.'

'You can't fool me. I've seen you before—many years ago. I have a good memory and forget nothing. While in College I had a friend called Bharat. One afternoon some of us were picnicking in the woods in front of his house in Bhabanipur. A young girl came and lit the fire for us. She was a pretty girl, well educated and could sing and dance. As far as I remember the girl's name was Bhumisuta. Am I right?'

Nayanmoni froze where she stood. Her lips went dry and drops of sweat broke out on her forehead. 'Bharat was my friend,' Jadugopal went on, relentless in his probing. 'I hear he has disappeared from Calcutta. Do you have news of him?'

'No,' Nayanmoni's voice was no more than a whisper. Then suddenly she started screaming, 'No! No! No! I know nothing. Nothing.' Turning, she ran out of the room, out of the theatre and climbed into her carriage. Reaching home she flung herself on her bed in a storm of tears. 'What's wrong with you child?' Gangamoni asked over and over again. 'Has any son of a bitch said anything to you?' But Nayanmoni did not answer. She buried her head deep into her pillow and wept as though her heart would break.

Chapter X

It was past midnight and the house was dark and still. All the inmates were asleep barring one. Rabindra stood by the window, his hand gripping a bar. The knuckles were clenched and the veins stood out over the fair skin. A terrible rage had taken possession of him. His eyes burned and the blood thudded against his heart in angry spurts. It was an unusual condition for him. Rabindra was patient and tolerant by nature and rarely allowed himself to lose his cool. A poet couldn't afford to. Anger clouded a man's imagination and blunted his creative powers. He kept telling himself this but it wasn't helping. Not this time.

This trip to Orissa seemed to have been jinxed from the start. He had come, ostensibly, on a tour of his estates but in reality he had wanted a change. He had wanted to get away from the pulls and pressures of Calcutta and to spend a few days relaxing with his friends and enjoying the spectacular beauty of the sea and lush green land. The sea, in particular, drew him like a magnet. He had crossed the Atlantic on his way to England. He had spent several holidays by the Arabian Sea. But he had never seen a more awesome; a more wondrous sight than the sea of Puri. He could stand on the sands for hours on end feasting his eyes on the breakers that swelled so high they seemed to touch the sky before rolling majestically to the shore. The deafening roar threatened to tear his ear drums. The water, warmed by aeons of tropical sun, curled and foamed about his feet. The wind all but knocked him down with every gust. But he never had enough of it. He stood gazing at the great expanse, hour after hour, his heart as light as though transported into another world. Yet it was in this very paradise that Rabindra had had a bitter experience.

His host and hostess Biharilal Gupta and Soudamini were old friends and excellent people, but having brought him to Puri for a holiday, couldn't bear to leave him to his own. His soul cried out for seclusion but he had to endure their company and that of their friends every single minute of the day. Even that wasn't so bad.

Rabindra didn't mind meeting the local people who were simple and unassuming and came in small groups. But he drew the line at meeting the big officials of the town particularly if they were British.

Biharilal didn't know Rabindra's bashful nature and couldn't understand his need for privacy. He thought it was his duty as host to introduce him to important people. Rabindra's presence was a feather in his cap and he liked to show him off. But it wasn't only that. He was thinking of the boy's welfare. Rabindranath was a scion of the noble house of Jorasanko and a poet. But who knew him outside Bengal? It was important that he met people wherever he went and, to this end, Biharilal insisted on taking him to the house of the District Magistrate. Rabindra begged to be let off but Biharilal pointed out that, as a zamindar come to tour his estates in Orissa, it was his duty to call on the DM. Protocol demanded it.

Flushed with his plan Biharilal sent a letter to Mr Walls informing him that he was bringing his distinguished guest to meet him that evening. But when they reached the saheb's bungalow they were surprised to find that there was no sign of a welcome. A chaprasi made them wait on the veranda and went inside to inform his master and mistress. He came out in a few minutes with the message that the saheb and memsaheb were busy and couldn't see them. However, they could come back the next morning. Rabindra's face turned pale with humiliation. Biharilal, though considerably mortified himself, insisted that the saheb and memsaheb were decent people and wouldn't misbehave with him. There must be some communication gap, he assured Rabindra, over and over again.

As indeed there was. An hour or so later a servant came from the District Magistrate's bungalow with a letter from his mistress. Apologizing for what had happened she explained that it was owing to the fact that her bearer had forgotten to give her Biharilal's letter. The District Magistrate was ready to meet the District Judge and would do so gladly. To make up for the faux pas she invited them over for dinner the next day.

The letter failed to assuage the indignation that swelled in Rabindra's breast. He felt extremely slighted. It was clear that the lady had no compunction about turning a zamindar and famous poet out of her house. It was the affront to the District Judge that she regretted. Rabindra declared he wouldn't go but Biharilal was horrified at the idea. The magistrate's lady had invited them; there was no question of refusing her. She would feel hurt and humiliated. 'We are natives,' he pointed out. 'We can swallow our humiliation and keep a straight face. But they belong to the race of rulers. Besides, she has apologized for the misunderstanding. What more can you expect?' It was not in Robi's nature to wave aside other people's wishes and stick stubbornly to his own. He obeyed his host and went but his mood was spoilt and he felt edgy and uncomfortable. Everything his host or hostess said affected him adversely. When Mrs Walls led them to her table saying, 'You may partake of everything freely, gentlemen. There's no beef in any of the preparations. You are Hindus and may be afraid to lose your caste,' he thought he saw a sneer on her elegantly powdered face. He was convinced that she had not said what she had out of concern for the tastes of her guests. There was a movement going on, in many parts of the country, for the preservation of the cow. Her words, he was sure, was a snide comment on a race so barbaric as to deify an animal and make an issue out of the eating of its flesh.

Rabindra's uneasiness increased after dinner when the insensitive though well-meaning Biharilal informed the company that his guest was a fine singer. Mr Walls was fond of music and instantly requested Rabindra to regale them with a few songs. Rabindra knew that they would neither like his singing nor understand it and he hated himself for getting into such a distasteful situation. He tried to cry off but Biharilal couldn't understand his reluctance and pushed and prodded till he was forced to sing. His audience clapped dutifully at the end of each song much as though they were encouraging a child in his recitation of nursery rhymes.

The dreadful evening was over at last. Once home, Rabindra told Biharilal, very firmly, that he was not meeting any more British officials and made him promise not to force him. He didn't care if he was breaking protocol. He was determined.

But Biharilal and Soudamini couldn't live without company. Back in Cuttack their hospitality increased ten fold and, with the great poet Rabindranath Thakur in the house, a lot of parties were organized. A large reception had been held, that very evening, to which a number of people had been invited. Among the guests was Mr Hallward, Principal of Ravenshaw College. On Rabindra's reminding him of his promise Biharilal said hastily, 'You said you didn't want to meet British officials. This man is an intellectual. You're bound to like him.'

But Rabindra didn't like him one bit. He was a monstrous hulk of a man with a face as broad and flat and red as a slab of beef. Rabindra privately thought he looked more like a policeman than the principal of a college. From the moment Hallward entered the room he dominated the conversation as though by divine right. Rabindra, who was the chief guest and whom he had come to meet, was addressed in a booming, authoritative voice with a 'You're a poet are you? A Bengali poet! Why don't you write in English?' before being passed over in favour of other more important men of the city. Rabindra gritted his teeth at the sound of that voice. It went droning on and on, not allowing anyone else to put a word in edgeways. It was so harsh and grating and had such a peculiar intonation that Rabindra couldn't understand half of what was being said. Rabindra had met many Englishmen and women on his two trips to England. They were courteous and pleasant and he had felt comfortable with them. What happened to the British when they came out to India? Why did they change so drastically? Or was it that the crudest, the most unpolished of the race was shipped out to the dark continent? He couldn't find the answer.

Two topics of discussion took precedence over all others at the dinner tables of the whites these days. One was the infighting among the natives over the killing of the cow. The other was the Lieutenant Governor's decision to dismiss juries in some districts of Bengal. This last had provoked considerable agitation and burning articles had been published by the native intelligentsia in newspapers and journals. Sipping from his glass of wine Mr Hallward addressed his host in a voice both ponderous and patronizing. 'You are a judge yourself, Gupta. What is your opinion of the dismissal of juries?'

'If juries are considered useful in England I see no reason why they shouldn't be so in India. We have the same laws.'

'Same laws!' Hallward threw back his head in a loud guffaw.

'Do you mean to tell me that what's good for the English is good for the natives? The English race has a moral standard, a sense of responsibility.'

'Don't Indians—?'

'Show me one native who isn't corrupt; who doesn't take bribes?' Then, realizing that he was surrounded by Indians, he added quickly, 'Present company exempted of course.' Then, warming to his theme, he carried on, 'I'm the principal of a college. Hundreds of Indian students pass through my hands each year. Don't I know the Indian character? Cheats and rogues—every man jack of them! To think that they aspire to sit in judgment on white men and women. What audacity!'

Rabindra tried to protest a couple of times but his soft, low-pitched voice got totally lost in the torrent of sound that issued from the white man's lips. He looked around for the reaction of the other guests. And, to his horror, he found some of them nodding eagerly, obviously agreeing with everything the man was saying, and the others sitting shamefacedly, their eyes on the ground. The blood rushed to Rabindra's head and pounded in his temples. He felt sick; physically sick. A terrible fury stormed his being. These were his country men. These . . . these animals who sat passively while a foreigner, an interloper, abused and insulted them in their own country! That fury was still with him and wouldn't let him rest. He paced up and down the room, ears tingling, face flaming with shame and rage. Then he made up his mind. Waking up his nephew Balendra, who had accompanied him on this trip, he ordered, 'Start packing Bolu. We leave for Balia tomorrow. Not another night under this roof.'

Once out of Cuttack Rabindra recovered his composure. It was raining heavily in Balia; had been doing so for several days. The sight of monsoon clouds and pelting rain always did something for Rabindra. The bitterness and frustration he had brought with him were washed away and peace descended on his soul.

From Balia Rabindra went to Bhubaneswar and thence back to Cuttack via Khandagiri and Udaigiri. The sight of the fine old temples and ancient rock edicts soothed his spirit and revived his pride in his heritage. He forgot the unpleasant episode in Cuttack and forgave Biharilal and Soudamini. They were old friends of

447

the family, he reminded himself, and patriotic at heart. Biharilal's profession required him to interact with the British and pay them lip service and that was all he was doing.

Biharilal had also learned his lesson. This time he didn't organize any parties or receptions. The evenings were now spent in rehearsing *Balmiki Pratibha* and its author was requested to inspect the production and point out its defects. Rabindra was happy to oblige. Needless to say, he felt a thrill of pleasure when he heard that his play was being staged in Cuttack. It meant that his works were being read and his songs sung even outside Bengal. Could he dare to hope that, some day, his songs would be equated with those of Chandidas, Vidyapati, Ramprasad and Nidhu Babu? The prospect left him tingling with anticipation.

Watching the rehearsal, that first day, Rabindra noticed that Herambachandra, the young man who was playing Balmiki, was rather stiff and awkward in his movements. He had a strong voice but it lacked flow. The others in the cast were just about passable. But the heroine, a spritely young woman called Mohilamoni, was very good indeed. Rabindra was charmed by the grace of her movements and the beauty of her voice. Her intonation was perfect and she sang spontaneously with deep feeling. He noticed another thing. She had not only rehearsed her own part to perfection, she knew everyone else's too. Whenever one of the cast faltered she was quick to prompt.

'You could play Balmiki if you wished,' Rabindra said to her with a smile. 'You seem to know all the songs.'

'That's true,' Soudamini caught the drift of his words and turned upon Herambachandra. 'What's wrong with you Heramba?' she cried. 'You usually do better than this!'

'The presence of the playwright is making me nervous,' the young man answered ruefully. 'Besides, the knowledge that he has played the role himself is turning my limbs to water. I have a suggestion Rabindra Babu. Why don't you play Balmiki again? In our play, I mean. It will be a thundering success with you in the lead role. I'll step aside gladly. I know I'm no good.'

The others looked on hopefully but Rabindra shook his head. 'Oh no,' he said firmly.' I haven't committed a crime by writing the play, have I? Why should I be punished by being made to act in it? I wish to sit in the audience and enjoy the performance.

Don't feel discouraged Heramba Babu. You aren't bad at all. You just need a little more practice.'

The rehearsals took place each evening and Rabindra attended them with clockwork regularity. Gradually he came to know all the members of the cast. He was particularly intrigued by Mohilamoni. Soudamini had told him that she was a child widow and had been confined to the women's quarter of her father's house till Soudamini had pulled her out of it. She enjoyed some freedom now because her father had immense respect for Biharilal and Soudamini and didn't go against their wishes. Rabindra caught himself thinking about her a good deal. He wondered what her life would be like once Biharilal was transferred out of Cuttack.

'That boy Bharat,' he said to his hostess suddenly one day. 'You know the one who sits right at the back and hardly ever speaks. Is he married? If he isn't why don't you marry him to Mohilamoni?'

'Marry him to Mohilamoni!' Soudamini was startled by the idea. 'Widows don't get remarried in Orissa.'

'Someone has to start. The first thing to do is to find out if the boy has the courage.'

'Why don't you talk to him?'

But Rabindra decided against broaching the subject directly. He sent Balendra instead with the offer of a job. They needed a clerk in the cashier's office of the mansion in Jorasanko. Bharat was well educated and understood accounts. He would be an ideal choice.

Balendra went to Bharat's house the next day and was amazed to find him wrapped in a gamchha swatting at a cockroach with a besom. 'Oh! It's you Bolu Babu,' Bharat exclaimed on seeing him. Then, waving a hand across the room, he continued with an embarrassed smile, 'The room is in a mess as you can see. I meant to tidy it this morning but I've been killing cockroaches. The place is simply ridden with insects. I killed a scorpion last night.' The word *scorpion* sent a shiver down Bolu's spine. He was a city boy and had a horror of creepy crawly things. He was sure that the spouse of the deceased scorpion was lurking nearby, getting ready to dig her poisoned fang in his ankle. He glanced quickly around the room and shifted his feet.

449

Bharat shed his gamchha and washed his hands. Then the two boys sat on the veranda and chatted of this and that. Balu made his offer but Bharat turned it down. He had a good job already and was not interested in going to Calcutta. 'You'll have to talk to him directly Robi,' Soudamini said on hearing Bolu's account. 'There's no other way.'

The next day Rabindra had a wonderful experience. It had been raining since morning, the showers falling heavy and incessant out of a sky as dark as night. Rabindra was locked up in his room reading a book called *Nepalese Buddhist Literature*. He was sure there would be no rehearsal that evening. Who would care to come in the pouring rain? Even thought this, he heard a woman's voice lifted in a song whose tune was sweet and solemn and familiar—too familiar. It seemed to be coming from the long low room at the back of the house where the rehearsals were held. He rose to his feet and walked towards it. At the door he stopped short. Mohilamoni was in the room. She was standing by a window looking out into the grey expanse of sky and land. Her open hair, soft and moist as a monsoon cloud, hung to her knees. Her sari, damp with rain clung to her back and hips. She looked unreal, somehow, as she stood framed by the window like a painting done in sombre hues against a background of cloud and rain and gathering twilight. But she was singing in a human voice. It was one of Rabindra's compositions:

'*Emono din è taarè bala jai*
Emono ghana ghor barishai˚

Rabindra felt a surge of happiness pass through his soul. He gazed entranced at the picture before him. She was like the heroine of Kalidas' *Meghdoot*, he thought. The universal woman grieving for her absent lover! So they might have looked—all those maidens of yore who stood by the banks of the Reba or Sipra communing with the clouds. 'Beautiful!' he murmured, 'Beautiful!'

Mohilamoni turned around, sensing Rabindra's presence. A faint blush rose in her cheeks and she lowered her eyes. 'Why do you stop?' Rabindra prompted gently. 'You were singing well.'
'I don't know anymore.'

˚   On such a day I might let him know
    On such a day dark with pouring rain

'Come. I'll teach you the rest.'

The preparations for staging of *Balmiki Pratibha* were under way. Invitation cards had been sent out to all the distinguished citizens of Cuttack. A pandal was being erected in the immense courtyard of the residence of the District Judge and Balendra, who had been put in charge of the stage, was busily making props. On the evening of the dress rehearsal the blow fell. Mohilamoni did not put in an appearance. Everyone was surprised. She was so regular; so dedicated. What could have happened? Could she be ill? An orderly was sent post haste to her house to find out. He came back with the news that he hadn't been allowed to see Mohilamoni. A member of her family had met him and told him she wouldn't be coming. He had asked for the reason but none had been given. The next day Biharilal went himself and returned his face pale with shock and disappointment. Mohilamoni had been forbidden by her father to act in the play, he told his wife and the others. It had to be cancelled. There was no way out. There were only three days left and no other girl could be trained for the part in such a short time.

Mohilamoni's father Sudamchandra Naik was a fairly rich and well-known businessman of Cuttack. Five years ago he had married his eleven-year-old daughter to a fine boy from a good family of their own caste and status. But the ill-fated girl had lost her husband within two years of the marriage. The young man had gone swimming in the Mahanadi, swollen to twice her volume with the heavy rains of the monsoon, and been drowned. It was predestined, everyone said. Only those guilty of a terrible sin in their previous lives were punished with widowhood. Chastity and abstinence was the only way for them. If they followed the rules laid down by their wise ancestors rigidly and meticulously in this life, they would be able to rejoin their husbands in the next. No one gave a thought to the fact that the girl was only thirteen and hadn't lived with her husband for a single day; hadn't even seen him after the ceremony.

Sudamchandra, though a conservative man in general, had been fairly lenient with his daughter. He had kept a tutor for her education and a music master to teach her to sing. He had allowed her to become a member of Soudamini's Sakhi Samiti and help her in her work. The District Judge and his wife were

451

highly respected people in Cuttack, he told the women of his household. What harm could come to her while under their roof? Though not a Brahmo himself, he liked the Brahmos of the city. They were moral, high-minded people. They didn't drink or keep mistresses and were cultured and polished in their speech and manners.

But associating with a Brahmo family was one thing. Acting in a play to which the whole city was invited was quite another. Acting with men, too! On a public stage! His clan and community would spit on him if he allowed it. Folding his hands humbly before Biharilal he said, 'Don't make such a request Judge Saheb. I cannot grant it. Shall I push my widowed daughter on the path of perdition?' Biharilal tried to explain to him that they were not professionals performing in a public theatre. They were just a group of like-minded people enjoying themselves together. In Jorasanko, he pointed out, the daughters and daughters-in-law of the household acted in plays along with their brothers, brothers-in-law and husbands. But Sudamchandra would not be convinced. There was no such precedence in his society. Orissa had an ancient tradition of theatre but men acted all the parts—even those of women.

But strangely, miraculously, everything changed over the next two days. Soudamini and the others had sat, sullen and downcast, listening to Biharilal's account. The whole house seemed to be plunged in grief like a house of mourning, Then Rabindra had sighed and said, 'So much talent is wasted in this country every day! So much unhappiness can be spared and isn't . . .' Soudamini had raised her head sharply at those words and said, 'This is not to be borne! Why should the poor girl be thwarted and punished all her life for no fault of hers? Your idea of marrying her to Bharat is an excellent one Robi. We must see it through.'

Everything moved swiftly after that. Two girls were sent to Mohilamoni to find out how she felt. Biharilal met the distinguished Oriyas of the city and sought their help in persuading Sudamchandra to agree. They had all heard of Vidyasagar and his life-long struggle for bettering the lot of widows. They were educated and enlightened people and did not see why something good could not be introduced into their own society and culture. Bharat was not even given time to consider the proposal. Like a strict yet benevolent mother Soudamini took him in hand and virtually forced him to give his consent. Perhaps the idea had occurred to him already. It certainly didn't come as a terrible shock. Bhumisuta was lost to him forever. That much was clear. Why not the next best then? Mohilamoni, with her lissome figure and charming profile, reminded him of Bhumisuta and aroused within him the same feelings. Marrying her was almost as good as marrying Bhumisuta. Mohilamoni, when she heard it was Rabindranath's idea, assented shyly. Two days later Bharat and Mohilamoni were converted to the Brahmo faith and married according to Brahmo rites in Biharilal's house. And the following evening *Balmiki Pratibha* was staged—the first play with a mixed cast to be seen in Cuttack.

Chapter XI

Maharaja Birchandra Manikya arrived at Sealdah station by special train with his retinue of courtiers and bodyguards. His health was declining fast and he had to come to Calcutta several times a year to consult his physicians. Rani Monomohini was not accompanying him this time. She was, now, the mother of two small princes and couldn't leave Tripura.

Birchandra stepped off the train leaning heavily on the shoulder of his chief bodyguard Mahim Thakur. Mahim was a fine young man of twenty-eight with a strong athletic body and a keen, alert mind. Over the last two years Birchandra had come to rely on him a great deal.

'No land is dearer to me than Tripura, Mahim,' he said as he walked towards his carriage. 'I revel in her clear sunlight and soft breezes. They soothe my very being. But there is something about this city that draws me like a magnet. The air here is far from pure. There is too much sound and too many people. Smoke pours out of factory chimneys and fouls the atmosphere. Yet, I feel a lifting of the heart the moment I arrive. So many great men have lived in Calcutta! So many are still living here—poets, scholars, composers! Their breath is mingled in the air, however polluted. Where in the whole of India will you find such a city?'

'Why are your palms sweating Your Majesty?'

'That's one of my symptoms. The nuts and bolts of my body must be rusting and falling off. Yet I'm only fifty-nine. Mahim! Send for that doctor, will you? That famous homeopath Mahinlal or Mahenlal—whatever his name is.'

'You mean Dr Mahendralal Sarkar?'

'That's the one. I don't know if it's his medicine or his manner that does me good. But I do feel much better after he's had a go at me. He's the only man in the world who dares to insult me.'

The carriage clattered into the driveway of the Maharaja's house in Circular Road. Birchandra looked out eagerly, remembering his first visit. Shashibhushan, who had been in his service then, had organized a royal welcome. Shashibhushan had left him several years ago. He and the servant maid who sang *padavalis* had disappeared together one night. He wondered why they had thought it necessary to elope. He would have arranged their marriage and given them his blessings if they had only asked him. He thought of Shashibhushan with fondness and nostalgia. He was a fine, intelligent young man, devoted to his master's service. And he had an excellent hand with a camera.

Dr Mahendralal Sarkar came to see Birchandra the next day. He stood at the door for a while, thumbs in the pockets of his waistcoat, frowning and looking around the room. Then, striding forward, he announced rudely, 'You look terrible! Much worse than last time. Your complexion is sallow and there are dark rings around your eyes. What have you been doing with yourself?'

'Nothing much,' the king's lips twitched with amusement. 'I do what my ancestors did.'

'Your ancestors!' Mahendralal snorted in contempt. 'Royals have the most atrocious habits. You must have some too. What are they?'

'I write poetry.'

'What!' Mahendralal nearly jumped out of his skin, 'Why?'

'Because . . . because I like to, I suppose.'

'A king has no business to addle his brains with poetry,' Mahendralal told him severely. 'He should concentrate on governing his state. Whenever kings have written poetry it's been the end of them. Look what happened to Bahadur Shah of Delhi and Wajed Ali of Oudh. They lost their kingdoms and died in exile.'

'I'm not a great poet so I don't run that risk. I only scribble a few verses for my own pleasure. The British don't know about it and never will.'

'Well! You know best about that. However, if you must indulge yourself with that nonsense it must be during the day. No burning the midnight oil.'

'I don't write at night. But I listen to music—till the dawn breaks, sometimes.'

'What sort of a king are you? You write poetry all day and hear music all night. When do you work for the welfare of your subjects? They should hound you out of the kingdom.'

455

'They seem quite satisfied with me. I have another bad habit. I do photography. I'm planning to do a series on the Ganga while I'm here.'

'Ah! You're a modern maharaja! Good, good. These interests, worthless though they are, are better than oppressing the subjects. How much do you drink each day?'

'Not a drop. I don't touch alcohol.'

'Aah!' Mahendralal exclaimed, startled 'This is the first time I've met a maharaja who doesn't drink.'

'I smoke a lot, though. I have to have a pipe at my lips all the time. My hookah baradar follows me about even when I'm walking or riding.'

'How many queens do you have?'

Birchandra frowned. 'I can't tell you the exact number. I'll have to do some calculations. I can answer your question in a day or two.'

'What do you eat? And how much?'

'I used to eat a lot. I loved khichuri and could polish off a whole basin at one sitting. But I've lost my appetite over the last few years. I eat twenty to twenty-five luchis for my mid-day meal. Dinner is even lighter. Some rice, a bowl of mutton curry, a fish head and half a dozen pieces of sandesh. That's all. While in Calcutta I eat a pot of rosogollas. The rosogollas here are excellent.'

'Hmph!' Mahendralal grunted. 'I get the picture. Now sir, you'll have to change some of your habits if you want me to treat you. You may carry on writing poetry and taking photographs if your subjects have no objection. But you'll have to reduce your diet. I forbid you to eat more than four luchis a day. As for the fish head, it would be better for you to pass it on to one of your sons. You'll have to reduce your tobacco intake and your passion for listening to music through the night. I'm fond of music too but I draw the line at midnight. We are getting on in years, king and commoner alike. We need our sleep.' The doctor rose to his feet and, picking up his bag, delivered his parting advice. 'A spell in the mountains will do you good. High mountains with snow on them. Why don't you go to Darjeeling? Or Kurseong?' He walked to the door, then turned back and said, 'Oh! By the way, my friend Anandamohan Bosu was telling me that *satidaha* is still

456

practised in Tripura. Is that true?'

'No it isn't. I banned it a couple of years ago.'

'But you've been on the throne for several decades now. Why did you allow it to continue all these years?'

'It is an ancient custom with its roots in the religion of our land. My subjects believe in it. How could I tamper with their faith? My secretary Radharaman Ghosh has been after me to put an end to the practice for some years now. But I hesitated . . .'

'What happened a couple of years ago? Why did you change your mind?'

'My Senapati, Charan, died of a sudden illness and his wife Nichhandavati, a woman of surpassing beauty, declared her intention of becoming a sati. I had no knowledge of it. And even if I had, it would have made no difference. Women burn with their husbands everyday in Tripura. I was out in the forest taking photographs when I came upon the scene by accident. What I saw gave me such a shock that I banned *satidaha,* there and then.'

'What did you see?' Mahendralal came closer to his patient. His eyes glittered with an unholy light.

'I saw a crowd of men beating drums and clashing cymbals and calling out *Jai Sati Ma* at the top of their voices. Nichhandavati stood in the centre. She looked like a goddess of beaten gold. She wore a red-bordered white sari and garlands of hibiscus hung from her neck. Her hair rippled like a dark river over her back and hips. Her large doe eyes were glazed with bhang. I shut my eyes. I imagined the greedy red flames licking that exquisite body, charring it, changing the hue from gold to ash. I couldn't bear the thought. "Stop!" I cried out like a madman. "Stop it at once." From that day onwards no woman has been allowed to burn on her husband's pyre. Not even voluntarily.'

'And after that?' Mahendralal prompted with a mocking smile. 'You married the beautiful Nichhandavati and added her to your harem?'

'*Arré*! no, no,' the Maharaja smiled coyly.

'It was because she was beautiful that you were moved was it not? Would you have had the same feelings if you saw an ugly old woman being pushed into a flaming pyre? You would have walked away from the scene without a moment's regret wouldn't you?' Leaning over, he grasped the king's arm pinching the skin viciously between his thumb and forefinger. 'Imagine Maharaj,' he said in a harsh whisper, 'that one of your wives is dead. Your relatives drag you to her funeral pyre and push you in with her. People call out encouragement. I don't know if there is a term for male sati. But, whatever it is, you're one now. Your hair disappears in a cloud of flames. Smoke, thick and acrid, rises from it. Your skin pops and crackles and bits of it dance about in the leaping flames. Your eyes melt in their sockets. There's a hissing sound as the fat pours from your pampered body, and feeds the fire. The stench is overpowering . . .' Mahendralal gave a final twist to the soft flesh between his fingers and flung the arm away. 'Sati!' he spat out the word as if it tasted foul in his mouth. 'A lot of vicious, evil, dung-eating bastards of priests started this practice. And you encouraged it. You and your dung-eating ancestors!' Mahendralal's face was twisted with hate. His hands trembled and his eyes burned like live coals. Birchandra stared at him in shock and horror. No one had ever had the audacity to touch his royal limbs in that rough manner. No one had ever talked to him in that voice. This was British territory. If he had stood on the soil of Tripura he would have fed this man to the dogs.

Mahendralal controlled himself in a few seconds. Straightening up he said coolly, 'If you wish to receive my treatment you must practice the austerities I have mentioned. If you can't, there's no need to send for me again.' He walked out of the room with his heavy tread leaving the king sitting on his bed motionless as though turned to stone.

Birchandra rose after a while and walked about the room, up and down, up and down, like a caged lion. He felt as though tongues of fire were running through his veins and threatening to engulf his head and heart. He couldn't believe what he had just seen and heard. Had it really happened or had he imagined it? 'Mahim! Mahim!' he called out in a high, cracked voice. Mahim hastened to his side and stood with his hands folded. 'You heard what that bastard of a doctor said to me? He had the audacity to . . . to.' Mahim nodded, his face pale and eyes staring in horror. 'You had a pistol!' the voice shouted. 'You should have shot him like a dog.' Mahim scratched his head in silence and lowered his eyes. 'Who does the son of a bitch think he is? A doctor! Hmph! There are scores of doctors in Calcutta who'll come crawling on their knees at my command. Don't dare call him again. I'll kill you if you do.' The king strode up and down the room, faster than before, fuming with indignation. Suddenly he stopped short and his lips curved in a smile. Mahim turned cold with fear. Was the king contemplating a terrible revenge? But this was not Tripura. This was . . . His fears were belied by the kings words. 'Do you see what I see, Mahim?'

'What is it Your Majesty?'

'Don't you have eyes? I was unable to walk without support for the last two months. I couldn't put a foot on the ground without getting the most terrible palpitations. My legs felt like water. But now, I'm not only walking—I'm striding about.' He threw back his head and gave a roar of laughter. 'That doctor is really something. I have to admit it. He has cured me without a drop of medicine. Simply by annoying me! It's amazing. I haven't even had a puff of tobacco smoke since he came.' He thought, frowning, for a few moments, then added, 'Forget my previous command and send for him again. Use force if necessary. But take care that no one is lurking about when he's talking to me. They'll lose respect for their king. As for you, if you so much as breathe a word of what happened today, I'll have your tongue pulled out.'

Birchandra improved steadily after that first visit and soon he felt well enough to pursue his other interests. Sending for Rabindranath, one morning, he ran his fingers through the poet's latest volume of verse, *Chitra,* and said, 'These poems are excellent Robi Babu. The best you've written yet. They deserve to be printed in gold lettering and bound in morocco leather.' Rabindra smiled ruefully. The Brahmo Mission Press had very little money. In consequence, their paper and binding were cheap and coarse. But he was lucky to get even that. So many poets couldn't find publishers. 'I'd like to sponsor a publication of your complete works,' Birchandra continued. 'Everything you've written till today—in one elegant volume. What do you say?' Rabindra nodded shyly. 'Thank you Maharaj,' he said 'But I have a request to make to you. Thousands of verses have been written by *padakartas* in this country. Many are lost and the rest are scattered about in obscure manuscripts. If you were to use your

patronage to bring out a volume of Vaishnav *padavalis*—' He
looked up eagerly into the king's face.

'A wonderful idea!' Birchandra cried out enthusiastically.
'Start the work of compilation without delay. I'll meet the
expense—even if it runs to a lakh of rupees.'

Birchandra Manikya met Rabindranath several times after
that, discussing their new project and exchanging ideas. The king
had read some poetry but he had little knowledge of what was
going on in literary circles. He had a lot of questions to ask his
young friend and Rabindra was ever ready to enlighten him.
Radharaman Ghosh joined them frequently. He, too, had a
passion for Vaishnav literature and could give them a lot of
practical advice.

'Robi Babu,' Radharaman said to him one day. 'I've heard
that a young man from Krishnanagar is writing good poetry these
days. I come from those parts myself. His name, I believe, is
Dwiju Babu and—'

'Yes! Yes,' Rabindra recognized the name instantly.
'Dwijendralal Roy is my friend and an excellent poet. He sings
very well too.'

'Why don't we send for him one day?'

'You send for him if you like,' Birchandra snapped. 'I'm a one-
poet man. For me there's only Robi Babu.'

'No Maharaj,' Rabindra admonished him gently. 'You must
keep an open mind. Dwijendralal's compositions are of a very
high order. You will like them.'

Birchandra was soon well enough to indulge his third
passion—the theatre. The city was humming with dramatic
activity. Girish Ghosh and Amritalal were churning out play after
play in their respective theatres. Ardhendushekhar Mustafi had
lost all his money, and the business as well. Emerald had passed
into the hands of a wealthy Marwari named Benarasi Das. The
latter had retained the old cast, however, and Ardhendushekhar
as director. He who had owned the company was now a paid
employee.

Birchandra sat in his box watching the play being currently
performed in Emerald. It was called *Banga Bijeta*—a historical
drama written by Ramesh Datta. He looked up startled the
moment the leading lady began to sing. He was sure he had heard

the song before. But where? He racked his brains but couldn't come up with an answer. He searched her face with a scrutinizing glance. But it told him nothing. He didn't have a good memory for faces but once he heard a song he never forgot it. The heroine was quite popular, it seemed. The audience applauded enthusiastically every time she came on stage and at the end of each song. Suddenly he got it. It was not the song that was familiar. It was the voice. He had heard it before.

During the interval he asked Radharaman. 'Do you recognize the leading lady Ghosh ja?'

'No. I'm seeing her for the first time.'

'She was a maid in our house in Circular Road. Can you recall her name?'

Radharaman shook his head. He had never interested himself in the maids and servants of the royal household. Looking down at the handbill on his lap he said, 'Her name is Nayanmoni.'

'Un hunh!' the king frowned and shook his head. 'That's not the name. It's something else. Aa ha ha! Don't you remember the girl Shashi master brought to the house? He ran off with her too.'

'Do you mean Bhumisuta?' Radharaman remembered the name at last. 'Shashi didn't run off with her. He's married to someone else and has two children. I went to see him once, not so long ago. He has bought a nice little property overlooking the river in Chandannagar. He has no news of Bhumisuta—so he told me.'

'Shashi married someone else!' Birchandra looked at Radharaman, his eyes wide with pain and surprise. 'Why didn't he give her to me then? I wanted her.' He spoke in the bewildered voice of a child who had begged for a toy and been denied it by an adult he loved.

After the play was over Birchandra expressed a desire to meet the actors and actresses and reward them for the pleasure they had given him. The entire cast lined up to receive the honour in a room at the back of the stage. Birchandra greeted Ardhendu-shekhar first. Putting a diamond ring on his finger he handed him a velvet purse with one thousand silver rupees in it. Then he walked down the line nodding and smiling and murmuring compliments as each member of the cast stooped to touch his feet. When Nayanmoni's turn came he turned to Radharaman.

461

SUNIL GANGOPADHYAY

'Ghosh ja!' he said pleasantly. 'Ask this girl if she was once a maid in my household.' Nayanmoni's face turned pale and her heart beat fast with fear. She had recognized the king of Tripura but hadn't dreamed that he would recognize her in her ornate costume and painted face. Before Radharaman could react to the first command Birchandra made another. 'Ask her why she left without informing me.' Nayanmoni turned and ran out of the room. Birchandra stood looking after her, an enigmatic smile on his lips. Then, addressing Ardhendushekhar, he said carelessly. 'Do me a favour Mustafi Moshai. Send the girl to my house tomorrow evening. I wish to hear her sing.' He moved towards the door then turned back and added, 'In the privacy of my apartment.'

After an hour or so Ardhendushekhar sent for Nayanmoni. She entered the office room to see him lounging on an armchair his legs propped up on a small table in front of him. In one hand he held the stem of his *albola*. The other was raised in the air. Nayanmoni saw that his gaze was riveted on the diamond ring that sat on his finger. The velvet purse the king had given him lay on the table. It was nearly empty.

'Come Nayan,' he invited. Nayanmoni had changed her gorgeous costume for a simple cotton sari and had washed away the paint along with the tears that had poured down her cheeks ever since her encounter with the king. Ardhendushekhar threw a brief glance at her pale face and reddened eyes and murmured, 'I've given away most of the money. There's hardly anything left for you.'

'I don't need money. If there's some left over give it to Uddhab. His wife isn't well and—'

'She's had another child!' Ardhendushekhar exclaimed angrily. 'This is her seventeenth isn't it? That rascal Uddhab ought to be whipped till the blood runs down his back. Does he want to kill the poor woman? Whatever you may say, Nayan, that bugger won't get another pie out of me. I've already given him five rupees.'

'It isn't for him. The infant needs to be fed. The mother can't suckle him. She has no milk.'

'Naturally not. Does he give her enough to eat? He squanders all his money away on ganja. Don't I know it? Why do you always

462

plead for others Nayan and never for yourself?'

'My needs are few and my salary generous. I can manage quite well.'

'I want to give you something Nayan. The success of the play is almost entirely owing to you. Here, take this ring.'

'Oh no!' Nayanmoni recoiled from it as if from a snake. 'The Maharaja gave that to you. It's yours.'

'Hmph!' Ardhendushekhar grunted. 'Do I belong to the class that wears diamonds? That's Bel Babu for you. You've seen Amritalal Mukherjee, haven't you? He's a great *kaptan* of Calcutta and wears diamonds on all his fingers.' He turned his hand this way and that as he spoke. The stone caught the light of the many lamps in the room and flashed and sparkled wickedly. 'This is a fine gem Nayan,' he looked down, squinting, at it. 'A truly flawless diamond. Take it. I want you to have it.'

'I've said I don't want it.'

'Why not?'

'I hate jewels. They poke and prick me.'

Ardhendushekhar stared at her in total bewilderment. Then he tapped his forehead and sighed. 'You're the strangest girl I've ever seen,' he said. 'A woman who hates jewels! Where in the world will you find another? Who are you? Tell me the truth Nayan. Were you an apsara dancing in heaven before you came to us?'

'I was a maid. A lowly servant maid in a rich household.'

'A maid! Hmm. That's what the king said. But hardly lowly—I should have thought. He wants to hear you sing. You know what that means.'

'May I sit down for a while?'

'Yes of course. Make yourself quite comfortable. We haven't had a chat in months. And you've forgotten your promise to invite me to a meal. Can you cook vindaloo? No? It's a sort of mutton curry spiced with mustard.'

'You just said that I always pleaded for others—never for myself. Well, I'm doing so now. I'm not going to the king's house tomorrow. Or ever. Don't make me.'

'You won't go!' Ardhendushekhar took his feet off the table and sat up in astonishment. 'Why not? He's a very big man. Monarch of an independent kingdom. It's an honour he's

463

bestowing on you.'

'I'm an actress, an artiste—not a singing girl. I don't perform mujras. Nor do I sing for the entertainment of a single man.'

'But he's no ordinary man. He's a king. Don't behave like a child Nayan. You'll go tomorrow. I'll take you myself.'

'I'll kill myself first.'

Ardhendushekhar narrowed his eyes and searched Nayanmoni's face for any tell-tale marks. 'You're from Tripura,' he said severely. 'You made us believe—'

'I'm not from Tripura. I've never been there in my life. I was born in Orissa.'

'How did you come to be in the king's service?'

'I wasn't in his service. I served one of his officials.'

'It's the same thing.'

'It isn't. I've never received a pie from the king as wages. And I wasn't his slave either. He didn't buy me.'

'He has declared before everyone in the cast that you were his maid. Who will believe your story? If he is frustrated in his desire he might take a terrible revenge. He can accuse you of stealing from the royal household. What will you do then?'

'I'll go to jail. But I won't go to him.'

'You're overwrought. Go home now. Think it over and come back to me tomorrow.'

But Nayanmoni didn't go back to Ardhendushekhar. She rose very early the next morning and, hiring a cab, drove to Jadugopal Roy's house. She was met at the gate by a servant who informed her that the barrister was out riding in the maidan but would come in presently. She could wait for him if she so wished. Nayanmoni entered the house and, seating herself on a chair in the veranda, pulled the end of her sari over her head and face down to her breast. Coming in, a few minutes later, Jadugopal looked curiously at the blue-clad figure sitting alone on the veranda. He had many women clients but they always came with male escorts.

'Who are you?' he asked bluntly.

'I'm a poor woman in dire need of your help.'

Jadugopal nodded. Instructing his servant to open up his chamber and take the lady there, he went into the house. Flinging off his steaming wet riding clothes he took a shower, changed, and went to meet his client.

'Have you come alone?' he asked. 'Who is with you?'

'No one.' Nayanmoni lifted her veil and looked into his face for the first time. 'I'm in grave trouble and need your help. I'll pay whatever fee you ask.'

'Bhumisuta!' Jadugopal exclaimed. 'You're as pale as a ghost! What is it? Some trouble at the theatre?'

Nayanmoni shook her head, then told him what had happened. She kept back nothing—not even the fact that she had been a maid in the king's household. Jadugopal gave her a patient hearing. Then, when she had finished, he commented wryly, 'One thing is not clear. Actors and actresses vie with one another for royal patronage. Why are you resisting it?'

'I don't need that kind of patronage. And I have no wish to oblige him. He may be a king and I a pauper, but if he insists on gratifying his wish I can do the same.'

'So it's a battle of egos!' Jadugopal laughed. '*Rex versus singing girl.* Sounds like a fairy tale to me. Is it only that or something else? Is your husband against it?'

'I don't have a husband.'

'Your protector, then?'

'There is no such person.'

'Why not?'

'Because I cannot sell myself for money.' Her voice trailed away. She murmured almost to herself. 'If I found someone I could love . . .' Stopping short she pulled herself together, then looked full into his face and demanded, 'Can you help me?' Jadugopal frowned. While in England he had come in close contact with an organization whose members were followers of a German economist and philosopher called Karl Marx. Marx expounded the doctrine of equality and dreamed of a classless society. *Workers of the world unite* was his slogan. Looking on the wan, troubled face before him Jadugopal felt the full force of those arguments for the first time.

'Of course I can help you,' he said firmly. 'A king of Tripura! What right has he to throw his weight about here? This is British territory—governed by a rule of law. If he tries to use force on you he'll have to go to jail.'

'Suppose he abducts me and packs me off to Tripura? Can the

465

law reach him from so far?'

'Is there such a possibility?' Jadugopal looked startled.

'I don't know,' Nayanmoni shuddered at the thought. 'He has dealt much worse with others.'

'Leave him to me,' Jadugopal rose to his feet. 'I'll deal with him. But you must take some precautions. Don't go back either to the theatre or to your house. Stay here with us for the next few days. My wife will look after you.'

'Stay with you?' Nayanmoni stared at him scarcely believing her ears. 'I'm an actress; a low woman on whom everyone looks down. Yet you . . . you.' She couldn't complete her sentence. Dropping her face into her hands, she burst into tears.

'I've just returned from the West where singers and dancers are respected for their art. They occupy the highest rungs of society. Don't worry Bhumisuta. Stay here and forget all the unpleasantness.'

'Bhumisuta's dead. Call me Nayanmoni.'

That evening the king sat in state over a small durbar consisting of a few distinguished men of the city. He wanted to show off his new acquisition; to apprise the world of the fact that the famous actress Nayanmoni Dasi had been a maid in his house and still enjoyed his patronage. He had, by constant self deluding, managed to persuade himself that he had done it all. That Nayanmoni was his discovery; his creation. He felt a surge of triumph at the thought.

But the hours passed and there was no sign of Nayanmoni. Birchandra sat sweating in his royal robes, his head weighted down by the crown of his ancestors. He kept glancing at his watch. At about seven o'clock a messenger arrived from the theatre with the news that Nayanmoni had disappeared. She was not to be found anywhere—not at home, not at the theatre, not even at the house of the few friends she had. Birchandra's face went white—not with anger but with disappointment and sorrow. He rose to his feet and paced about the room. 'I only wanted to hear her sing,' he kept saying over and over again. 'What was wrong with that? She sings for everybody. Why not for me? I would have treated her like a queen. I would have covered her with jewels.' Turning to Mahim, he asked in a forlorn voice, 'Was she afraid I would hurt her Mahim? Punish her for running away? But everyone knows my kindness and generosity with erring subjects.'

'Everyone does Your Majesty. She's a foolish girl and doesn't deserve your patronage. Shall I send for someone else?'

'No. My mood is spoiled. Why do Calcutta people have such twisted minds? There's no warmth in them; no trust, no spontaneity. I'm sick to death of this artificial city. Let's get out of here. The doctor advised me to go to Darjeeling or Kurseong. I'll do that. I'll spend a whole month among the trees and mountains.' Then, his voice faltering like a pampered child's, he added, 'But who will sing to me there Mahim?'

'There's no dearth of singing girls in Calcutta Maharaj. We'll take one with us.'

'No', the king waved the proposal away with an imperious hand. 'No more women. Go to Jorasanko to Robi Babu and tell him that I would be delighted if he agreed to accompany us to Darjeeling. To hell with the girl! I'm glad she disappeared. Now I can hear Robi Babu's singing to my heart's content.'

Chapter XII

Swami Vivekananda was in a fix. Fame and popularity have their side effects and he found himself hopelessly embroiled in the latter. When it became evident that the young ascetic had the power to draw crowds, the go-getting Americans lost no time in making a few dollars out of it. A Chicago firm named Sleighton Lysium Bureau approached him with an offer. They would organize tours to various towns and cities of the United States where he could address the gatherings and make known his message. All the arrangements would be made by the company and all the expenses paid. The money garnered through sales of tickets and donations would be shared equally by the speaker and the organizing firm. The contract would be for three years. Vivekananda thought it an excellent proposal. After all he had come to America with the objective of disseminating Hindu philosophy. There was no sense in going back with his mission unaccomplished. And if a third party took on all the organizational responsibility, what could be better? Vivekananda signed the agreement with alacrity. But soon second thoughts came creeping in.

Was it morally correct for a sanyasi to receive money for spreading the word of God? He had had no time to consult with anyone before signing the agreement. He knew no one in America. And he had lost contact with his fellow disciples in India many of whom had heard of Swami Vivekananda but did not know that the conquering hero of America was their own Naren. The question tortured him till he eased his conscience by telling himself that America was not India. If had been perfectly possible for him to beg for a meal and spend the night under a tree in India. If he tried it here he would be taken for a vagrant and clamped in jail. He needed money to keep himself in this cold and hostile country. He had to book himself into a hotel wherever he went and it had to be a big hotel. The managers of smaller, cheaper places were racist in their attitudes and wouldn't take in coloured people. Apart from that he needed money to fulfil his dream of opening charitable institutions in his own country. He had come to America not to enjoy her splendours or win fame for himself. He had come to earn money, a lot of it, and take it back to India.

But, within a couple of months, Vivekananda realized that he had made a mistake. What began as a joyous interaction gradually became a painful drudgery. His managers drove him relentlessly from city to city; from forum to forum, making him speak for hours on end till he was ready to drop down with fatigue. From Chicago to Madison, Minneapolis, Iowa City and Memphis and back again to Chicago. Then to Detroit, Ohio Ada and Bay City of Michigan and from there to several cities of the South—it went on and on. Vivekananda went spinning like a top till he thought he would die of cold and weariness. He had tremendous life force but his constitution was weak and he fell ill from time to time. But there was no respite for him. Sick or well he had to honour his commitments. He was given money, of course. He received as much as nine hundred dollars from one day's work in Detroit. But soon he became aware that he wasn't getting his full share. He was becoming a controversial figure and supporters and detractors were flocking to his meetings. At one place tickets worth two thousand five hundred dollars were sold but he was given only two hundred. He realized that the company was lining its pockets at his expense but he didn't know what to do about it. He had signed a contract for three years. If he broke it he would have to return every cent he had received and that was not possible. So the grind went on, getting more and more excruciating day by day.

Vivekananda also found himself out of tune with the American mind set. They attended his meetings in thousands but, barring a few, most of them came out of curiosity; in the same spirit as they would come to see a rare, exotic animal in a zoo. He found it impossible to relate to them or tell them anything worthwhile. 'Hey Mr Kanand!' they would call out to him. 'Don't bore us with all that philosophy stuff. Tell us about the strange customs practised in your country. We've heard that mothers throw their babies to the crocodiles. Is that true?'

'Well!' Vivekananda answered on one occasion, mustering up a smile with difficulty. 'If my mother had done so I wouldn't be

469

standing here before you.'

'Boys are not thrown,' another voice was heard, 'Only girls—'

Vivekananda's lips twitched. 'That may be because crocodiles love female flesh. It's softer and sweeter.' Then, as if worrying over a fine point, he added, 'If all girl children are thrown to the crocodiles I wonder how males take birth. Perhaps one of you can enlighten me.'

'You're evading the question,' an angry voice came from the audience. 'But even if you deny female infanticide you cannot deny the custom of Suttee. Widows are burned with their husbands in your country. We know that for a fact.'

'I admit it—up to a point,' Vivekananda conceded. 'The burning of widows is punishable by law now, but at one time it was widely prevalent. But let me tell you that in most cases it was voluntary. Force was used but only occasionally. Now I have a question for you. You must have heard of Joan of Arc who was accused of being a witch? She was burned at the stake not so long ago. In France.' He looked enquiringly but no one had heard of Joan of Arc. 'In Christian Europe during the Middle Ages,' Vivekananda continued, 'thousands of women were branded as witches and burned to death. You haven't heard of them either?' A ripple passed over the assembly as people whispered to one another. 'Blind faith and superstition have been the bane of all religions at some time or the other,' Vivekananda's voice grew louder and more sonorous. 'The people of the West have, very conveniently, forgotten their own past. An Englishman will never ask a Frenchman about Joan of Arc. But the moment he sees an Indian he'll make it a point to remind him of the custom of Suttee. Why is that?'

What Vivekananda felt worst about was the fact that such questions came not only from crude, uneducated miners and factory workers. Wherever he went, be it to an elite club, a church meeting or an university seminar, someone or the other was bound to fling these accusations at him. These pin pricks notwithstanding, Vivekananda's following was rapidly growing in number. Of all the Indians who had come to speak at the Parliament of Religions, he had become the most famous. He was speaking everywhere and being quoted every day in newspapers and journals. The extent of his success gradually became a thorn in the side of his fellow Indians. Pratapchandra Majumdar, who had been so kind to him, turned into his bitterest enemy. Launching a slander campaign against the young ascetic he spread the word that Vivekananda was a fake and a fraud; that he had neither been invited by the organizers of the Conference nor been sent out as a representative of the Hindus. He was a trumped up charlatan who was hogging the limelight by unfair means. Back home in India, he gave statements to all the newspapers that, cloaked in the garb of an ascetic, Vivekananda was living a life of sin and perversion. He was not only smoking and drinking—he was eating beef and pork and cohabiting with American women. Some of this news trickled into Vivekananda's ears from time to time but he shrugged it off. Only when he thought of his mother and how these reports would affect her, his heart was saddened and despair, at the state of the world, filled his soul.

However, fortunately for Vivekananda, his contract with the Sleighton Lysium Company was terminated within four months of signing it. This came about through the intervention of some powerful people he had drawn into his orbit. He had to pay a heavy price for it though. Every cent that he had saved went into his release. Yet he welcomed it. He was physically worn out with all the travelling he had to do and mentally, too, he was exhausted. Besides, the question of where he was to stay was not so acute anymore. Many of the men and women he met were only too happy to keep him in their houses. One of these was the ex-Senator Mr Palmer, an extremely wealthy man who owned a ranch where he bred the finest race horses and Jersey cows. He was about sixty years old and a man of strong appetites who loved eating and drinking and making merry with his friends. He had heard Vivekananda speak at a church meeting and, much impressed with the originality of his ideas, had invited him to his ranch where he commenced showing him off to his friends at one party after another. At one of these gatherings a journalist accosted Mr Palmer with the question, 'Have you converted to Hinduism, Mr Palmer?'

'If I have,' Palmer replied in a clipped accent, 'Do you have a problem?'

'No no. Why should I have a problem? I've heard you're

migrating to India. Is that true?'

'I might if I feel like it.'

'What will you do with your horses? And your cows? You're so attached to them—'

'I'll take them with me to India. Who can stop me?'

Next morning the newspapers carried a report that Mr Palmer had embraced Hinduism and was leaving for India shortly. He was taking his horses and cows with him but on one condition. His horses would be used only for pulling the chariot of Juggernaut and his cows would be venerated as *Go Mata* according to Hindu tenets.

Among the others who took an interest in Vivekananda was a wealthy widow called Olé Bull. She had a large house in Cambridge in the outskirts of Boston where she held several soirées every year at which all the intellectuals of the city were invited. Olé Bull's parties had a distinctive character. There was lavish eating and drinking but the conversation was not confined to gossip and small talk. Serious discussions were held on the state of the world; on politics, literature, the arts and religion, and she often invited a speaker to address the gathering. Having discovered Vivekananda she lost no time in bringing him home and introducing him to her friends. In doing this she was following a fashion she had picked up on her European travels. European women of the wealthy upper classes were no longer content with running households and entertaining their husbands' friends. They kept themselves abreast of the latest developments in the fields of art, music, religion and literature and acted as sponsors to young aspirants.

Bessy Sturges and Josephine Macleod were two sisters who also fell under the spell of the Indian yogi. Born of wealthy parents, they enjoyed a privileged position in the highest rungs of American society. But they were much more than pretty socialites. They had been well educated and, having lived in France for a number of years, were cultured and artistic in consequence. Bessy had been widowed some years ago and was now engaged to a prosperous corn merchant of New York named Francis Leggett. Josephine, named after Napoleon's beautiful wife, was still a spinster and beleaguered by suitors. Vivacious and charming, she attracted attention wherever she went and, though she had formed attachments from time to time, not one had lasted. For the present she seemed quite content to pass her days visiting art galleries and exhibitions and attending theatres, concerts and lectures by well-known speakers.

One day Bessy and Joe were persuaded by their friend Dora to accompany her to New York to hear a lecture by an Indian yogi called Vivekananda. The name meant nothing to them nor did they have an inkling of what Hinduism was all about. Nevertheless they went and took their places in a dingy little hired hall big enough to accomodate about fifty people. The fifteen or twenty chairs that lined the walls were occupied so the girls were forced to sit on their haunches on the bare floor. But to their surprise, the hall started filling so rapidly that within a few minutes there was no room to insert a pin, and the audience started spilling out on the verandas and stairs and even stood about in the street below. Presently the speaker came in and took his place at the lectern. He was a man of medium height with a thickset somewhat portly figure in a bizarre costume consisting of a bright orange silk robe and turban. He stood with his arms folded across his chest and his eyes, beneath a noble brow, looked straight into the eyes of his audience.

Joe felt a roll of thunder pass through her soul. The holy man's dark, unflinching gaze held hers, commanding; compelling. At that moment she knew, as sure as she lived and breathed, that this was the man she had waited for all her life. And when he started speaking she listened to him, all her senses alert—the blood flooding and receding by turns in her cheeks. His words fell on her heart and it cried out with every beat, 'True! True! Every word this man is saying is true. Follow him and he will lead you on the path of Truth.' When the lecture was over Joe rose, trembling, to her feet. Her mind was in a whirl. She hadn't exchanged a word with the strange man. Why, then, did she feel that he held her soul in his hands? These peculiar feelings persisted even after she reached home and for days afterwards.

Now Joe started attending Vivekananda's lectures whenever she could. Bessy, though not quite so keen, accompanied her wherever she went. Vivekananda noted their presence and one day, after six or seven meetings, he came forward and asked pleasantly, 'Are you two sisters?' On Bessy's nodding in the affirmative, he added, 'Do you come from far?'

'From Dobb's Ferry,' Bessy replied. 'A village by the bank of the Hudson river thirty miles from here.'

'Wonderful!' Vivekananda exclaimed genuinely impressed. 'That's a long way off.'

This was the first exchange—that too with Bessy. But Joe's chance to speak to Vivekananda came within a few days. One evening, while dining with Francis Leggett at the Waldorf Hotel, the two sisters kept fidgeting and glancing at their watches. On Leggett's enquiring if they had another appointment they answered that they had intended to attend a lecture and were getting delayed. Mr Leggett called for the bill and, after paying it, asked if he could come along. The girls were only too delighted and the three of them set off together. But by the time they reached the hall there was no place to sit. Bessy and Joe were worried. What was Francis Leggett thinking of them? Being dragged away from the bright lights of Waldorf Hotel and brought to a dark, poky room in which he had to stand for over an hour listening to a lecture on Hinduism was surely not his idea of a pleasant evening. They kept stealing sidelong glances at his face trying to gauge his mood. Was he bored? Was he getting irritated? They needn't have worried. Leggett listened to the entire lecture then, pushing his way through the crowd, said to the speaker, 'I would be extremely grateful if you came and had dinner with me one night. I would like to introduce you to some of my friends.'

The friends turned out to be only two in number—his fiancée and her sister. But the evening was a great success. The wall of reserve broke down on both sides. Joe and Bessy chatted animatedly and Vivekananda proved himself as charming and witty a dinner companion as he was a powerful speaker.

After a week or so Leggett invited Vivekananda to spend a few days in his country house in New Hampshire. It went by the modest name of Fishing Tent but was, in reality, a large, two-storeyed wooden bungalow overlooking a beautiful blue lake and surrounded by acres of woods and meadows. Vivekananda was charmed with the place. He spent hours swimming in the crystal waters of the lake and rowing to and fro in a small boat. Occasionally he took long walks in the woods with Bessy and Joe.

The evenings were spent in reading portions of his Sanskrit texts aloud to his friends. Joe loved the sound of the words though their meanings eluded her. Something deep down in her responded to this ancient language, the sounds plucking at her heart as though it were a stringed instrument.

One morning Vivekananda had a strange experience. It happened just before breakfast. 'Joe,' he had said to her, 'I'm sitting out in the garden under the pine tree. Call me as soon as breakfast is ready.' Then, shaking his head at her in mock severity, he had added, 'It had better be a good one.' Then, leaning against the trunk of a giant pine that grew in a sunny corner of the garden, he had read the Gita for a while. Suddenly something came upon him. He shut his eyes and started murmuring to himself. 'What am I doing in this country? I've come all the way from my native land, crossing seas and rivers and mountain ranges. But for what? I'm telling the people of America about our religion and philosophy. But do my words mean anything to anyone? Are they making a dent anywhere? I wanted to help my countrymen; to find a way of removing their miseries. But what have I done about it? Do I even remember them? I'm on the wrong path. Yes, without a doubt, I'm on the wrong path. My place is with my own people; in my own country. I've a new mission before me. It is not enough to feed the hungry and clothe the naked. The fetters that bind their souls are sharper, more cruel than hunger. I must teach my people to rise; burst their bonds and demand their right to live . . .'

A few minutes later Joe came out into the garden to call Vivekananda. But reaching the pine tree she got a shock. He sat, still as a figure of stone, eyes closed, not a muscle twitching in his face or form. The book he had been reading lay on the ground, open and awry, as though it had fallen from his hands. Terrified, Joe ran back to the house crying distractedly, 'Francis! Bessy! Swamiji's dead. He's gone from us. Gone!' The three ran back to where Vivekananda sat. 'Shall I shake him to see if there is any sign of life?' Francis asked. Suddenly Joe remembered something Vivekananda had told her—about a state called *bhav samadhi* that holy men experienced from time to time. It was a state in which the motions of the body, even the circulation, were temporarily suspended and the yogi became a living soul. 'No,' she cried. 'No. Don't touch him. He's in *bhav samadhi*.'

She was right. After a few minutes Vivekananda's eyelids fluttered. His lips parted. 'Who am I?' he murmured, 'Where am I?' Then, opening his eyes, he saw the three anxious faces bending over his. 'Why do you look at me like that?' he asked, 'What has happened?'

'Swamiji! Swamiji!' Joe burst out weeping. 'You frightened us so. We thought . . . we thought—'

'I'm sorry Joe,' Vivekananda rose to his feet. 'I didn't mean to frighten you.' Then resuming his usual, teasing manner with her, he added smiling, 'Be assured of one thing. I shan't go away leaving this body in your country. What about breakfast? Isn't it ready yet? I'm starving.'

Chapter XIII

Maharaja Birchandra Manikya was gravely ill. Following Mahendralal Sarkar's advice he had journeyed to Kurseong with a small retinue which included the poet Rabindranath Thakur and his eldest son Rathi. Though winter was quite a long way off it was very, very cold. Rain and hail fell incessantly and a dense fog shut out the sun for the better part of the day. It was impossible to step out. But, inside, the house was made warm and cozy with log fires blazing in every room exuding the fresh sweet smell of resin and pine cones. The Maharaja had never been happier in his life. He spent his mornings and evenings in the company of the young poet, listening to him reciting his verses and singing his songs. From time to time they discussed the details of the volume of Vaishnav *padavalis* they planned to bring out together. Rabindra, on his part, had found in the king his most ardent and intelligent admirer and was thrilled to spend time in his company. But, unfortunately, the good time didn't last very long. The king's health started deteriorating in the damp mountain air and clammy fogs of Kurseong. He caught a severe chill which spread to his lungs and, one afternoon, in the middle of an animated discussion on the machinery which would be required for the new printing press, he fainted.

A local doctor was called in who revived him somewhat but he was so weakened by the infection that it was no longer expedient to keep him in Kurseong. The group returned to Calcutta. The best doctors were sent for and with their combined efforts, together with his tremendous life force and will to survive, the sick king gradually came out of the valley of death. Kumar Radhakishor begged him to return to Tripura but Birchandra was not ready to do that. Instead, he sent for Kumar Samarendra.

While in Kurseong Rabindra had recited portions of his novel *Rajarshi* and his play *Bisarjan*. The king, deeply moved by this story set in his kingdom, had begged the poet to put up a performance. 'You stage so many plays in the mansion of Jorasanko. Can you not do *Bisarjan*?' he had asked wistfully. Looking on the pale, puffy countenance and dark ringed eyes Rabindra made up his mind. *Bisarjan* had been performed once and could easily be revived. There was a permanent stage in the courtyard of the house. His nephews Aban and Gagan were good painters and could take care of the backdrop. Bibi would play the harmonium. There was no one to touch Bibi with a harmonium. She had magic in her fingers. Rabindra set a date and rehearsals began in right earnest.

But while the players were rehearsing, Birchandra, who was the chief guest, was also getting ready to play his part. He wanted to make on impressive entry into the famed house of the Thakurs, and to that intent, was determined not to lean on the shoulders of his bodyguards or display any sign of weakness—physical or mental. He sent for an elegant walking stick of finely carved rosewood with an ivory handle and started practising walking without help. On the evening of the performance he arrived at Jorasanko well before the prescribed time and, instead of taking his place with the audience, walked into the green room where he commenced an inspection of the costumes. He had sent Mahim over, a few days ago, to apprise Rabindra of the kind of dresses worn by Tripura royals during the period in which the play was set. Now, even at the last moment, he made minor changes in the costumes of Nakshatra Rai and Gobinda Manikya. Authenticity had to be maintained at all cost for the audience would be a distinguished one. And for some reason, unknown even to him, he felt responsible for the success of the play. 'Where is Robi Babu?' he asked after a while.

'Why!' A member of the cast exclaimed. 'Here he is—standing right beside you.'

Birchandra turned his head and got the surprise of his life. Rabindra, as Raghupati, was unrecognizable in his dark red dhuti and wig of tangled locks. His eyebrows had been darkened heavily with kajal and met, fierce and strong, above a pair of blood flecked eyes. Under the *namabali*, flung carelessly across his shoulders, his broad, bare chest gleamed as though carved from a block of white marble. Rabindra smiled and his eyes twinkled. He had been standing by the king all this while but the latter hadn't even glanced at him.

The play caught the imagination of the audience right from the first scene. They looked on, amazed, at the transformation of the sensitive poet with his liquid eyes and gentle voice into the ruthless, scheming Raghupati. And, indeed, it was a fact that Rabindra underwent a metamorphosis every time he stood on a stage. He forgot himself and took on the persona of the character he was enacting, be it fictitious or historical.

In the third scene, in which Raghupati is alone in the forest addressing the idol of Kali, Rabindra got so carried away that he lost all sense of time and place. According to the story Raghupati, incensed with the goddess for her demand and acceptance of human sacrifice, lifts the idol in his hands and flings it into the waters of the Gomati. But, since it was not possible to show that on stage, a rope was tied to the base of the statue the end of which was in Aban's hands. As per the stage directions Rabindra would pretend to lift the image; the lights would go out and the statue would be pulled into the wings. But Rabindra got so excited while shouting his lines:

'Bloodthirsty demoness
Return thy prey
Dost thou have ears to hear?'

that he actually picked up the heavy block of stone in his hands and was about to hurl it into the wings when the sight of Bibi sitting there with her harmonium, brought him to his senses. Another moment and she would have been crushed to death. Rabindra trembled from head to foot. Sweat ran down his limbs. Finally, with a tremendous effort, he put down the stone image. The audience shouted 'Bravo! Bravo! A superb performance,' and the entire auditorium rang with applause.

At the end of the play Maharaja Birchandra Manikya presented a gold mohur apiece to each of the players. Then, without lingering any further, he hurried to his carriage and seated himself. Mahim ran after him and peered curiously into his face. It looked sullen and angry. Back home, Mahim's enthusiastic appreciation of the play was cut short by a imperious wave of the royal hand. 'Shut up!' The king snapped, then giving full vent to his ill humour, he shouted, 'Why is everything so much better in Calcutta? Why can't we do what they do? What's wrong with us?'

Taken aback by this attack, Mahim stuttered, 'But . . . there's no tradition of theatre in Tripura. Calcutta—'

'Why didn't you start a tradition you fool?' Birchandra thundered. 'Haven't you received an education? Can't you see what's lacking in your country's culture? Get out of my sight. I can't bear to breathe the same air as you.' But, though ordered to get out, Mahim couldn't. It would be unseemly. He stood quietly, his head bowed in humility, ready to receive whatever further chastisement the king thought fit to mete out to him. Insult after insult was hurled at the bowed head, then, his anger spent, Birchandra muttered moodily, 'Make all the arrangements for going back to Tripura. I wish to leave in a day or two. We'll start a theatre in Agartala, in my palace courtyard, and put up one play after another. We'll begin with *Bisarjan*. Now, who do you think should act in it?'

'We must look for an actor,' Mahim answered, his face brightening visibly. 'I'm sure we'll find—'

'Don't be stupid! Where do you mean to look? It's not a lost cow that you'll make discreet enquiries at the abattoir. We have actors right in the palace. You can be Jai Singh and Radharaman—Gobinda Manikya. No, that won't do. He's too thin. He can be the minister. We could try out Naradhwaj. And I'll be Raghupati.' He drew himself to his full height as he said this and stroking his moustaches, added, 'I'll act even better than Rabindra Babu. You'll see.' Birchandra walked up and down the room excitedly, stroking his chest from time to time. Turning, he ordered sharply, 'Bring the book!' Mahim ran out of the room and reappeared after a few moments, a copy of *Bisarjan* in his hands. Birchandra opened it at random and began declaiming:

'The truth?
Why shall I not speak it?
Am I afraid?
A craven coward?
The demon goddess . . .'

Suddenly the book slipped from his hands and Birchandra Manikya fell, face foremost, in a crumpled heap on the floor. Mahim ran to him and, kneeling on the ground, turned him over. Blood was flowing from his nostrils in a thin stream and the corners of his mouth were laced with foam. But his senses were intact. 'Take me home Mahim,' he whispered. 'Back to Tripura. My chest hurts so . . . it's about to burst . . . Take me . . . before it's too late.'

It *was* too late. With these words the king fell into a stupour from which he came out, from time to time, after long intervals. And then he would call out to his first queen Bhanumati. But the moments of consciousness were few and far between. Five distinguished physicians took turns in watching over him day and night. But no one could hold out any hope.

Seventeen days after his fall Birchandra opened his eyes and spoke for the first time. Seeing Samarendra leaning anxiously over him, he placed a trembling hand on his head and whispered, "I promised your mother you would be king. Take the throne and don't let go at any cost.' Then, smiling wanly at the worried faces around him, he asked, 'Am I well enough to go back to Tripura?' The members of the king's household were delighted at his recovery but the English doctor looked grave. 'This is a precarious time,' he warned Mahim. 'He may slip away any moment. Exercise the utmost caution and care.'

Next day Birchandra felt well enough to sit up for a while leaning against masses of cushions. He even took a few sips from the cup of fruit juice offered to him. Then, addressing Mahim, he said, 'I've lived a good life and kept the throne of my ancestors with strength and policy. I've subjugated rebellions and kept peace in my country. And though I've indulged in the pleasures of the flesh, I haven't neglected the spiritual side. I've been to Brindaban on a pilgrimage.' He sighed contentedly then, as if suddenly remembering, he commanded, 'Take care of my photographs. They mustn't get lost. And look after my youngest queen. She's still a child. She mustn't suffer in my absence.' Dim, ageing eyes held Mahim's for a long moment. Then he said almost shyly, 'Only two of my desires will remain unfulfilled. One is to draw my last breath in the air of Tripura. The other . . . the other . . . is to hear that maid . . . Nayanmoni . . . sing to me while I'm dying. I've longed to hear her sweet voice sing *padavalis* at my bedside for so long—I can't even remember. I want to hear that voice . . . the last thing . . . before I die.'

Mahim rose and, wiping his eyes on his sleeve, ran out of the

481

room straight to Ardhendushekhar's house. Nayanmoni had left the theatre, he was told, but she had come back home. Together they went to Gangamoni's house and sought audience with her lodger. This time Nayanmoni did not refuse. Changing into a garad sari, and covering her shoulders with a shawl, she accompanied the two to the king's mansion—the house she had lived in and left so suddenly so many years ago. Entering the royal chamber, she seated herself at the king's bedside. Birchandra was breathing with difficulty. But the moment he saw her a smile of triumph lifted the blueing lips. He was a king, used to getting what he wanted. He had wanted her and here she was. Even while passing into death his heart swelled with a sense of victory. 'Why did you go away?' he whispered, 'I might have lived a few more years if you had . . . if you had . . .' His voice trailed away.

'What shall I sing?' Nayanmoni asked softly.

'Anything you like.' Then, gasping for air, he continued, 'Live Bhumisuta. Live long and be happy. My time is over. I'm going . . .'

Nayanmoni began her song but before she could complete a full verse, Mahim burst out weeping . . .

In a few hours Birchandra's house was filled with mourners. With one notable exception. Rabindranath Thakur could not come. While the king had been ill Rabindra had been confined to bed. He had strained his back muscles, while lifting the heavy statue, so badly that he found it difficult to stand—leave alone walk. And when news came that Birchandra Manikya of Tripura was dying, his wife Mrinalini started her labour pains. She was giving birth to Rabindra's fifth child. Next morning, after seeing his newborn son, he hurried to the burning ghat at Keoratala and laid a bunch of flowers at the dead man's feet.

Chapter XIV

Exactly eighteen months after their marriage Mohilamoni gave
birth to a son. Bharat looked on as the baby lying in the chamber
was put up in the courtyard and marvelled at himself. Mohilamoni was in labour but he felt nothing—nothing at all. Not
apprehension or anxiety on her behalf nor elation at the thought
of becoming a father. But when it started to rain, the water
lashing mercilessly at the flimsy structure of grass and bamboo,
he suddenly woke up to a sense of impending doom. Mohilamoni
was in there, tossing and turning in agony, sweating and struggling to bring forth his progeny, while he stood helpless. The water
was seeping through the grass and soaking her to the skin. He was
sure of it. What if she caught a chill and died and the unborn babe
with her? He ran into the courtyard and started pacing up and
down in a fever of anxiety, oblivious of the rain that fell on him in
torrents. The midwife and the two women who were assisting her
railed at him for his foolishness and bade him to go back to his
room and wait. But he turned a deaf ear. He stayed out in the
wind and rain till a cry, much like a night bird's shriek, entered his
ears. He breathed a sigh of relief. His child was born and, like
every other human being, was weeping its way into the world.

Bharat came back to the house and, entering Mohilamoni's
puja room, knelt before the images of Radha and Krishna.
Knocking his head on the floor he wept in gratitude to that
Supreme Deity who, in his infinite mercy, had thought fit to bless
him with a child. He who had never known a father's love now
had a son to love and protect; to nurture and cherish. He vowed
to keep the tiny flame alive through all the winds and storms that
might buffet it. He had suffered excruciating agonies at the hand
of god. But now he had his reward.

God had rewarded him in other ways too. His hard work at
the bank had been recognized and he had risen step by step. Soon
after his marriage the agent of the bank, Mr Ferguson, had sent
for him. 'Babu,' he had said, 'You will need to improve your

financial situation now that you're married. I'm elevating you to the status of a manager. I could send you to Calcutta if you so wish. Alternatively, you could go to Puri. We are opening a new branch there of which you could take charge.' Bharat had no desire to return to Calcutta. He had promptly accepted the transfer to Puri and moved there with his wife. Opening a new branch and getting it going was strenuous but he didn't mind. He worked hard all day then went back to the house he had rented near Singhadwar, with a sense of eager expectancy. He love his home. It was the only home he had ever known. Mohilamoni kept it very neat and pretty with a few pieces of elegant furniture, lace curtains and flowers. She, too, had never had a home of her home and gave it all she had. With her good sense and natural good taste she had created a haven for Bharat to return to at the end of each day. And it was here that God had blessed them with a son.

Mohilamoni recovered from her ordeal in a few days. And to Bharat's amazement, the child seemed to be growing by the hour. His features were taking shape and the mottled redness of his skin started disappearing leaving it as smooth and silky as a rose petal. His eyes were like two spoonfuls of the clearest sea water and he kept turning them this way and that exploring his surroundings. He didn't cry so much these days. He had learned to laugh and he did so frequently, opening his little mouth wide and displaying a tiny tongue and palate as fresh and pink as a kitten's. Bharat wondered at the child's innocence. What did he see in this miserable world that made him so happy?

The neighbours were dropping in every day and commenting on the child's beauty. He was exactly like his mother, they said, except for the chin which was like that of his father's. Bharat laughed at these remarks. He saw no resemblance to anyone. But one day he got a shock. The cash clerk at the bank, a conservative Brahmin, came to see the child. 'He is like his mother,' the man remarked, 'Happy is the son who has his mother's face. But his brow is like yours. It bears the royal stamp.' Bharat's heart quaked and a shudder passed over his frame. 'Why did he say that?' he thought frightened, 'Does he know the truth?' But the very next moment he laughed in relief for the man continued, 'This boy will grow up to be a judge. Or at the very least—a magistrate.' It was true, Bharat thought. Judges and magistrates magistrate.' It was true, Bharat thought. Judges and magistrates were treated like kings these days.

Bharat caught himself staring at mother and babe particularly when Mohilamoni was suckling him. He found the scene incredibly beautiful. Her face, turned sideways to her son, had a radiance—a rare beauty. Her long eyelashes quivered; her lips shone. The breast, pushed out of her jacket, gleamed as lustrous as mother of pearl. He wondered if anyone had ever held him like that. His mother had died when he was born. Had any other breast given him sustenance? Now, more than ever, he saw Mohilamoni's resemblance to Bhumisuta. Her new motherhood made it sharper; more poignant. And, looking on his son, he saw the same tilt of the eyes and curve of the mouth. The child could have been Bhumisuta's! He caught himself sharply. What was he thinking of? Bhumisuta was lost to him. That phase of his life was over. He must try and forget her. He owed it to Mohilamoni.

One day Mohilamoni said to her husband, 'We call him Sona but the boy must be given a proper name. You must choose one for him. I have no idea of the kind of names men have in Assam from where you come.' Bharat was silent. He had told everyone here that he came from Assam because his mother had been Assamese. He hadn't breathed a word about Tripura or Calcutta. He didn't feel as though he belonged to either of those places. His natural father had banished him from Tripura and his surrogate father Shashibhushan, who had brought him to Calcutta, had told him that he didn't want to see him ever again. It was only here, in Orissa, that he felt loved and wanted. He worked here and had married here. He would spend the rest of his life here and his son would be Oriya. 'We'll call him Jagannath,' he said on an impulse then, correcting himself, he added, 'No, Jagannath is too common. Jagatpati is better. I am Bharat Singh. My son will be Jagatpati Singh Deo.'

When Jagatpati was a year and a half, word came that Mohilamoni's father was seriously ill and wished to see his daughter. Making arrangements at the bank took three days and, at the end of that period, Bharat set off for Cuttack with his wife and son. There was a train to Cuttack but it had to be caught from Khurda Road. Thus the first phase of the journey had to be undertaken by palki. It was a winter morning and bitterly cold.

485

through a deep forest. Bharat had been warned that it was infested with brigands who waylaid travellers and robbed them of their lives and valuables, and had, in consequence, taken the precaution of travelling with two armed guards. He had no fears that bright winter morning particularly in view of the fact that it was only a day's journey. They would reach the rail station well before sundown. Husband and wife sat facing one another in the palki taking turns in holding the child. Bharat's heart was fit to burst with pride as he looked on his little family. The aanchal had slipped from Mohilamoni's head and her face was open to view. Her fair cheeks glowed in the winter sunlight and a sweet fragrance came from the flowers that adorned the knot of rich hair on top of her head. She had dressed the boy with special care in a red velvet coat, white woollen cap and socks and gold bangles on his tiny wrists. They laughed and chatted as they went along. And then . . .

The bearers screamed in terror and dropped the palki. Bharat thought they had seen a wild animal and, opening the door, he stepped out to see them fleeing into the forest. He tried to call out to them but before he could do so three men, terrifying in aspect with swords in their hands, bore down on him. One of them touched the tip of his sword to Bharat's chest and hissed, 'Shut your mouth, bastard. Utter a word and you sign your death warrant.' Bharat could hardly believe his eyes. It was broad daylight. How could this be happening? And the guards—the armed guards he had brought to protect them! Where were they? He turned his head to find one of them lying on the ground threshing his limbs in agony. The other had disappeared. 'Don't take our lives,' he entreated his captor in a hoarse whisper, 'We'll give you everything we have.' A harsh command from one of them compelled Mohilamoni to come, trembling, out of the palki—her baby clasped tightly to her bosom. The men dragged her forward by the hair and proceeded to strip her of all her jewels, from the gold pins in her hair to the rings on her toes. But they wanted more than just her jewels. Their eyes burned with lust. One of them snatched the baby from her breast and flung him into a bush. Another grabbed her by the arm and pulled her towards him. Mohilamoni screamed. And, hearing that scream,

486

something snapped inside Bharat. It was happening again! His cursed destiny was dogging him, threatening to take all he had. Over and over again he built up something only to lose it. He wouldn't allow it. Not this time. Without stopping to think he flung the sword aside with a powerful thrust of his arm and leaped on his captor. The strength and frenzy of seven devils seemed to have entered his body as he rolled over and over and, reaching the sword, took it in his hand. Then, springing up, he cried out in a terrible voice, 'Let go of her, sons of bitches, or you die!' Bharat had never uttered a term of abuse in his life. He never raised his voice. But now, he wasn't himself. He was someone else. He knew only one thing. He had to save his wife and child or die in the attempt.

But, however desperate he was, he couldn't have fought the three men single-handed for long. Luckily for him, two more palkis appeared on the scene. The armed guards accompanying them rushed towards the brigands crying 'Ré ré ré!' at which the three bandits dropped their weapons and fled. Bharat chased them through the woods for a while, then turning back, he fainted. He was revived and taken to the rail station by his saviours where he caught the train to Cuttack. He had averted the disaster that threatened to engulf him and in the process he had learned a lesson. He realized that he had to fight his destiny; to resist it. He decided to buy a gun and keep it with him all the time. But the next blow came so swiftly and suddenly that he got no chance to retaliate.

Three or four days passed. The child, having fallen inside a leafy bush, had escaped unhurt. And Mohilamoni, except for being dragged by the hair and pushed to the ground, hadn't suffered any physical injuries. The wound was to her spirit, and that refused to heal despite the love and affection that was showered on her and her child by her parents and siblings. Everyone went into raptures over the boy's beauty. Mohilamoni's ailing father, though he hadn't fully endorsed his daughter's second marriage, softened towards her on account of the child who was his only grandson. All the other children of his generation were girls. Pressing five gold guineas in the little hands he blessed the boy. But none of this had the power to soothe

487

Mohilamoni and make her forget. It was only when she thought
of how her husband had taken on three armed men, single
handed, in an attempt to save her, that balm fell on her lacerated
soul. Bharat often found her weeping into her pillow. 'Forget it
Moni,' he told her, stroking her head tenderly. 'It won't happen
again. No one can touch you while I draw breath, ever again.'

Somewhat stifled in the cocoon of love and warmth that
enqulfed him Bharat escaped, now and then, to Biharilal Gupta's
house and to those of some of his old friends. One morning he
decided to visit the bank in which he had worked and meet his
ex-colleagues. While they sat drinking tea and talking shop a
servant came running in with the news that Bharat was wanted in
the house immediately. Mohilamoni had had a fall, while
bathing, and lost consciousness. Bharat came rushing back to
find a kaviraj sitting by his wife's side, a finger on her pulse, while
she lay as pale and still as if in death. The man looked up as Bharat
entered and shook his head helplessly. She was still alive, he said,
but in a state of acute danger. A vein had ruptured in her head and
was haemorraging into the brain.

Three days went by with no change in Mohilamoni's
condition. More doctors were sent for but not one—not even the
English civil surgeon—held out any hope. They all had the same
prognosis. Death was only a matter of time. Only a miracle could
save her.

Bharat couldn't believe what he heard. Mohilamoni was only
twenty-three. Why should she leave the world? What had she
done? What kind of judgment was being passed on her? And
why? He could fight life but how could he fight death? Standing
by her bedside he broke into a violent fit of weeping, calling out
her name, again and again, with the passion of a madman, till her
brothers were forced to take him away.

After that Bharat, who had been taught to shun idol worship
by his mentor Shashibhushan, went from temple to temple
offering prayers and begging the gods for Mohilamoni's life. 'Hé
Ma Kali!' Hé Ma Chandi!' he cried, 'Save my wife. Return her to
me. Take everything I have except her.' On hearing that there was
a tantrik somewhere near Udaigiri who had miraculous powers,
he went rushing there. Three whole days he waited outside the

tantrik's cave, shivering and calling out, 'Save Mohilamoni! Take my life but save hers. She's my son's mother. Have mercy! Oh God have mercy!'

Chapter XV

It was the end of April—a season of hot winds and blazing sunlight; of desperate longings and thwarted hopes when the eyes are turned involuntarily upwards, over and over again, in the hope of a speck of cloud; when the parched earth lies open and waiting for a shadow to pass over it; when even the blue of the sky is burned out to ashes . . .

Fortunately for him, Rabindra did not feel the heat all that much. Or the cold. When other people smothered themselves in caps, coats and mufflers all he needed was a light shawl flung carelessly across his shoulders. And on summer afternoons, when his brothers and nephews lay sleeping in darkened rooms under undulating punkahs, he went about his work walking or riding down the burning streets with not even an umbrella to protect his head. He spent his mornings and evenings writing in the covered veranda on the second floor. It had no punkah and since Rabindra was not in the habit of using a palm leaf fan sweat poured down his limbs in streams. But it didn't bother him one bit. He filled page after page with his flowing hand stopping only to brush away the drops that fell on the paper.

Rabindra often wrote far into the night after everyone was asleep. Poetry seemed to come unbidden to him when the world was dark and silent. Of his five children Rathi and Madhuri were old enough to sleep in a separate room, apart from their parents. The three youngest still slept with their mother on her vast bridal bed. They were fast asleep by nine o'clock after which Mrinalini took up some sewing for an hour or two. Rabindra had told her several times that sewing by candlelight was bad for the eyes but Mrinalini ignored his advice. For one so quiet and placid she had a strong will and could be quite stubborn on occasions.

Mrinalini had tried, in the past, to sit by her husband at this hour, when they were alone together, and engage him in conversation. But, though Rabindra never reproved her for disturbing him and answered her questions patiently, there was

490

something missing in the exchange—something that she felt should have been there and wasn't. Though neither analytical nor brooding by nature, she sensed a gap in their relationship. He was a good husband and father—kind, gentle and caring but he had nothing to say to her. It was true, of course, that he was a reticent man and didn't open up easily. He treated everyone, including his wife, with the same formal courtesy. He changed only in the presence of Bibi—her second brother-in-law's daughter. Mrinalini had seen them sitting together talking animatedly for hours together. The women of the household had told her that her husband wrote masses of letters to Bibi whenever he was out of Calcutta, touring his father's estates or for any other purpose. But to Mrinalini, his own wife, he only sent a few lines and that too at long intervals. And all they contained were polite enquiries after her health and that of her children. Mrinalini had accepted the fact that she was no match for her brilliant, famous husband; that she could never share his thoughts. She knew she had no role in his life barring that of ministering to his physical needs and giving birth to and nurturing his progeny. But, still, the thought that he preferred another woman's company to hers hurt her, sometimes so cruelly that the scalding tears oozed out of her eyes and burned their way down her cheeks.

One night Robi sat writing a song. He had begun by humming a tune in Hambir and gradually it had fallen into rhythm with Teora Taal. And now he had found the words:

How far?

How far away lies that land of Joy?

Blinded and weary I grope my way . . .

Suddenly he felt a cool breeze at the back of his head. He turned around startled. Where had that come from? The night was stiflingly hot. Was a storm brewing at last? He rose from his chair and walked to the veranda. There wasn't a breath of wind. Not a leaf stirred in the potted plants. He came back to his room and recommenced his work. Again! Again he felt the cool lifting of his hair as though touched by a gentle hand. 'Natun Bouthan,' he murmured involuntarily. She used to steal up behind him, on hot still afternoons, as he wrote industriously and ruffle his hair or fan him with a palm leaf fan. But she had been gone these twelve years!

Soon after Jyotirindra's self-imposed banishment from Jorosanko, Rabindra had moved into his rooms, partly because they were the most beautiful in the house but even more so because, in them, he felt his Natun Bouthan's presence. He often saw her shadow lurking behind a door or gliding past the gallery or washroom. And it didn't frighten him. If anything, he welcomed these visitations and looked forward to them. He felt as though Kadambari's wounded, tortured spirit was struggling to attain human form again; to come close to those she loved. But every time she attempted it, it shattered to splinters like a sheet of clear glass. He knew he was imagining it all but he clung to the idea out of a strange desperation and hope. What if her efforts bore fruit, after all, and she came back to him? The thought sent a tremor of happiness through him. He had been very young then; a young, unknown poet struggling to attain fame and recognition. The dead woman had been his only admirer and he had wanted to cling to her memory. But the situation had changed. He was, now, the brightest star on the horizon of letters in Bengal and had thousands of admirers. Besides, he wielded power as administrator of the Thakur estates, practically ran the Brahmo Samaj, was a husband and father to five children.

Rabindra recalled an experience he had had exactly two years ago. It was another April night, not hot and still like this one but wild and stormy. Rabindra had been sitting at his table, writing, when the storm broke. A wild wind, moist with approaching rain, came lashing in making his papers fly about the room. He rose and shut all the windows, then came back and took up his pen. But one of the windows had a loose latch, perhaps, and rattled noisily every time the wind blew on it. Looking at that window Rabindra had the strangest feeling that Natun Bouthan stood outside it, and that she was rapping on it begging him to open it and let her in. He knew that was nonsense. The room stood on the second floor. No one could come in that way. Nevertheless, he rose and, walking over to the window, opened it wide. There was no one there. A gust of wind blew in and a flower fell on the floor. Rabindra picked it up. It was a *juin*—her favourite flower. He shut the window and went back to his table. A memory stirred deeply within him. Natun Bouthan used to attract his attention, when he was engrossed in his writing, by throwing flowers at him. It was her soul, he thought whimsically, that had come flying in on the wings of the wind and startled him out of his abstraction. Pushing aside the work he had been engaged in, he took up the pen and wrote:

'You come too late
Now, when the door is barred against you.
Dark is the night and the street deserted,
The lost wind howls its way along the path
Begging sanctuary . . .'

Suddenly, it seemed to him, the rapping grew louder and a voice sobbed piteously, 'It's not the lost wind. It's me! Me!' A shudder passed over Rabindra's frame. But he didn't move from his place. He turned his eyes this way and that and looked around the room. This was Natun Bouthan's apartment. Her plants were still here and her books. It was her hand that had hung those lace curtains and put up the pictures on the walls. He wrote:

'Why do you wait forlorn and destitute
Outside a door that was your own?
For whom this thwarted love? For whom this pain? . . .

Let sleepers sleep
Why wake them from their slumbers?
Seeing your anguished face this sudden night . . . .'

The suckling infant, sleeping with his mother in the next room, gave a startled cry shocking Rabindra out of his reverie and bringing him back, sharply, into the real world. Rabindra took hold of himself. What was he thinking of? He had actually believed Natun Bouthan . . . It was only a storm outside—a phenomenon quite usual during this season. And the rattling of the window was clearly owing to a loosened latch. He must get it fixed tomorrow. And then, suddenly, he remembered. Exactly twelve years ago, on this night, Natun Bouthan had taken her own life . . .

Rising from his seat he walked to the veranda and, leaning on the balcony rail, yielded himself up to the elements. The driving rain soaked him to the skin. Thunder roared all around him accompanied by flashes of lightning. He stood there for a long time. But, for some reason, he didn't think of Kadambari or feel her presence. He thought, instead, of the diseases that had broken out in the city. Cholera and chicken pox were usual at this time of the year but, to add to people's woes, plague had come sweeping in from Maharashtra and was killing thousands of men, women and children. Rain was needed—a lot of it. Rain washed away the germs and cleared the atmosphere.

Next morning Rabindra instructed the servants to bring his writing table and chair down to a room on the first floor. The inmates of the household were puzzled and asked him, repeatedly, why he was exchanging his beautiful room on the highest floor of the mansion for one so ordinary. Rabindra smiled shyly. The children disturbed him as he wrote, he explained, and Mrinalini had a hard time keeping them away. He needed quiet and seclusion for, without them, he couldn't concentrate . . .

Clinging to the past was useless. Rabindra realized that he had to let go. He had to turn his face to the future and go on with his life. Besides, he was growing busier by the day and the demands on him were endless. Over the last few years the Congress had been gaining popularity with the masses, evoking the interest and curiosity of the common man. More and more meetings were being organized all over the country. That winter a session was to be held in Calcutta and several members of the Thakur family were caught up in the preparations. Rabindra, who was to be a delegate, had been given the responsibility of composing the invocation song.

One morning, Bipin Pal came to Jorasanko with a strange request for Rabindra. He had heard that Ganesh Puja was being celebrated with great success in Maharashtra every year with vast numbers of people participating in it. Something like that, in his opinion, was needed here in Calcutta. The most prominent deity of the Bengalis was Durga. The thing to do was to bring the festival out of the mansions of rajas and zamindars and hold it in the streets where the masses could congregate. With a different focus, of course. The public needed a symbol for their country;

one with which they could identify. What could be better than worshipping Ma Durga as *Desh Mata?* That would arouse patriotic feelings among all sections of people. Could Robi Babu write a lyric in praise of the Mother Goddess which could be sung as the invocation song at the meeting of the Congress?

Rabindra heard him out quietly but was shocked at the proposal. An invocation in praise of Durga! Was the Congress a Hindu party? Had it not been formed to bring all the people of India—Hindus, Muslims, Parsees, Buddhists and Christians together? Noting the expression on Rabindra's face Bipin Pal added quickly, 'I'm not asking you to write a religious poem. All I want you to do is compose a paean in praise of our country in the Mother image. Just looking at a map tells us nothing. Visualizing the country as Mother will have a powerful effect on ordinary people. Don't be so finicky Robi Babu. After all we are not asking Muslims and Christians to perform puja. We're only asking them to look upon the country as their Mother.'

'Bankim Babu's *Bande Mataram* should serve your purpose,' Rabindra said quietly. 'It expresses both devotion and patriotic fervour. We could sing that.'

'The language is too high flown, beyond the comprehension of the common man. If you could give us a simplified version perhaps—'

'Forgive me,' Rabindra said, shaking his head. 'I can't do that.'

Bipin Pal's face fell. He hadn't anticipated such a reaction. Making his displeasure obvious he rose and left the house. Rabindra sat, frowning, for a while pondering on the subject. He was a Brahmo; a member of a sect that rejected the worship of images. How could he compromise his deepest sentiments by composing a paean of praise to Durga? And sing it at the Congress meeting, of all places? Impossible! He could write a different kind of lyric though; one that could be understood by the entire gathering. People were coming in from all parts of the country. He had to find a common language and sentiments that were universal. Taking up his pen he wrote:

'Oi bhuvan man mohini

495

Oi nirmal surya karajjwal dhwani
Janak janani janani . . .
Neel sindhujal dhauta charan tal
Anil vikampit shyamal anchal
Ambar chumbit bhaal himachal
Shubhra tushar Kiritini . . .'

He frowned and put down his pen. There were too many
Sanskrit words in the poem. But Sanskrit was the only Indian
language common to the diverse people of the country! All the
languages of India were derived from Sanskrit barring Tamil and
Telugu. But all educated Indians knew Sanskrit—even Muslims.
Rabindra completed the lyric oblivious of the fact that it, too,
evoked an image—a woman's image. The invocation song, the
elders decreed, was to be *Bande Mataram* after all. As Robi Babu
had said, a song in Sanskrit would be more acceptable to the
entire gathering. But when Rabindra took up the task of training
the singers he found that it was too difficult a composition to be
sung by a group. After some deliberation he picked out a song
written and set to music by his brother Jyotirindranath:

Chal re chal sab é bharat santan
Matribhumi kare ahwan

A huge pandal was put up on Beadon Square for the twelfth
session of the Indian National Congress. Chaired by the famous
lawyer Janaab Rahim-u-tulla M. Sayani, it was represented by
the eminent elite from all parts of the country. After the
invocation was sung the crowd cheered lustily and called out,
'Robi Babu! We want to hear Robi Babu!'

Robi stood on the stage facing the audience. It numbered
more than two thousand. He took a quick decision. He would
sing *Bande Mataram*. Beckoning to Sarala to accompany him on
the organ he commenced singing in his rich baritone. There was
pin drop silence as the impassioned voice, throbbing with
powerful feeling, rang around the auditorium. This was the first
time that people from all over India heard *Bande Mataram* and it
left every man, irrespective of region, religion, caste and creed,
moved beyond his wildest imaginings. Tears stood in every eye
and a hush fell on the assembly to be broken, at last, by a storm of

applause that went on and on.

Any song after this one was bound to come as an anti-climax, so *Oi bhuvan man mohini,* which Rabindra had taught to the group who sang the invocation, had to be dropped, to the great disappointment of one of the boys. 'Robi Babu,' he asked wistfully 'Are we not to sing your new song?' The young man was a barrister newly returned from England. His name was Atul Prasad Sen.

Atul Prasad got his chance a few days later, when the delegates were invited to dinner at the house in Jorasanko. As soon as the guests were seated a group of boys and girls, dressed in spotless white, stood in a half circle in front of them and sang *Oi bhuvan man mohini.* Rabindra stood in the centre and sang with them. The response was overwhelming. Many of the delegates said they had never heard a composition more beautiful and stirring. Others expressed their satisfaction at having understood every word.

Rabindra's involvement with the Congress session had kept him so busy that he hadn't written for nearly a month. And now a restlessness seized him. He felt as though his spirit would sicken and die if he kept himself away from pen and paper any longer. Late that night he came up to his room on the first floor and took up his pen. While waiting for an idea to come he began doodling on the paper in front of him. Suddenly, a face took form rising, trembling, to the surface—a long, pale face with anguished eyes. 'You're here again!' Rabindra muttered, hardening his heart against her. 'It's over between us. Whatever there was is over. I've forgotten you. You're false; false . . .' Suddenly his head slipped down to the table and he burst into a storm of tears. 'No! No!' he cried aloud, oblivious of who may or may not be hearing him. 'I haven't forgotten you. No, not for a day. Praise is meaningless; adulation worthless since you're not here to see it. I'm your creation! You put the crown of love on my head with your own hands.' Rabindra sobbed like a broken-hearted child for some more time then, lifting his head, took up the pen. And, now, words flowed out of him on to the paper. The pen raced on, ahead of his thoughts, as though it had a life and will of its own. He wrote—

> Render me oblivious
> Of all things true and false.
> Set me afloat on a sea of happiness.
> Madness and reason; freedom and captivity
> Are one and the same to me.
> May only thy desire.
> Enveloping the universe,
> Rise and engulf my soul.

Chapter XVI

Jadugopal sat on an upstairs balcony of his house in Janbazar sipping tea from an elegant porcelain cup. He had just returned from court and this was his hour with the family which consisted of his wife, two children, a widowed sister, an old aunt and her son. They all sat together drinking tea and talking of this and that when the orderly entered with a card on a silver salver. Jadugopal frowned at the old retainer. 'Not now,' he said waving his hand in dismissal. 'I won't see anyone now.' Even as he said this his eyes fell on the name. It was that of his old friend Dwarika. 'I'll see him,' he amended hastily then, turning to his wife Sunetra, he asked 'Shall I send for him up here? You know Dwarika.' Sunetra nodded. She came from a Brahmo family and was used to conversing freely with men.

Looking at Dwarika's shaved head, as he was being ushered in, Jadugopal felt a pang of guilt. Dwarika had lost his mother three months ago and Jadugopal had neglected to meet him and condole with him. He hadn't even attended the shraddha. He had been very busy at the time with a case in Nator. But Dwarika was a good friend. He hadn't held that against him.

'Come Dwarika,' Jadugopal rose to receive his friend. 'I'm so ashamed of myself. I heard about your mother's passing away but I couldn't attend the shraddha. Do forgive me.'

'You were in Nator at the time were you not?' Dwarika asked. Then, seating himself, went on to say, 'I hope I haven't come at the wrong time.'

'Not at all. You've come at a very good time. You'll have tea with us, won't you?'

'Of course. I never say "no" to tea.'

Sunetra poured out a cup of tea and placed a plate tastefully arranged with ham sandwiches, salted cashewnuts, biscuits and barfi before him. Dwarika's eyes brightened. He loved good food and could put away masses of it at any time. But Jadugopal punctured his enthusiasm by saying to Sunetra, 'Don't give him

499

ham sandwiches. Tell the cook to make some with cucumber.'

'Why?' Dwarika asked, surprised.

'You're not supposed to eat meat or fish during the period of *Kalashouch*. Aren't you following the traditional customs?'

'You're a Brahmo and a barrister from England,' Dwarika bit into a ham sandwich. 'You're not supposed to know all this.'

Dwarika finished everything on his plate then, leaning back, began sipping his tea with relish. 'The food was marvellous Bouthan,' he said smiling at Sunetra. 'I've never eaten better sandwiches in my life. As for the tea—'

'I'm very sorry about your mother Dwarika,' Jadugopal said. 'She was a great lady. A towering personality! Yet so kind and loving to us all.' Dwarika nodded in affirmation. 'I heard you spent a fortune on the shraddha,' Jadugopal went on. 'Once here and once in your native village. You distributed clothes to five hundred Brahmins and two thousand destitutes—'

'I didn't do so because I wanted to. Zamindars are expected to spend lavishly on weddings and funerals. If I didn't rise to people's expectations they would think me miserly and unused to the ways of a great family. And they would be right. As you know I'm not a zamindar by virtue of my birth. I inherited the zamindari by a fluke.'

'Are you involved in a lawsuit?' Jadugopal asked curiously, 'Has another heir to the estate appeared on the scene?'

'Why do you ask that?'

'Because people are too busy to visit friends these days, except when they need help. If you are in some legal trouble don't hesitate to tell me. I'll help you all I can.'

'Wherever there's property there's wrangling and dispute. But nothing's so wrong with my affairs that I'll need the services of a big barrister like you. No, I haven't come to you for legal advice.' Dwarika frowned as though deliberating his next move. Jadugopal waited for him to say something more then, nothing forthcoming, he said, 'Do you remember Irfan, Dwarika? I helped a relative of his win a case some years ago. He has been sending me clients ever since. In fact my Muslim clients outnumber my Hindu ones—thanks to Irfan.' Dwarika grunted, apparently absorbed in his own thoughts. Jadugopal waited a few moments for a response, then went on, 'You'll never believe what happened the other day. I was preparing a case for a Muslim tanner when I discovered that the defendants were some members of the Thakur family. Robi Babu's name was on the list. You know Robi Babu, the poet? We were such fans of his in our college days! It was terribly embarrassing for me. I had to prosecute members of a family of which I was a son-in-law. Luckily, I managed to get both parties to agree to a mutual settlement out of court.'

'Look Jadu,' Dwarika said suddenly, interrupting Jadugopal's train of reminiscences, 'I saw you sitting with your son on your lap as I came in. Your wife was by your side serving the tea. The scene was so beautiful—it brought tears to my eyes. But it made me a little envious too. I have no one—neither wife nor child. A home is not a home without them.'

'That's entirely your own fault. You chose not to marry. However, there's still plenty of time. Find a girl and make her your wife.'

'That's exactly what I plan to do. But I need your advice and support.'

'Wonderful! Have you set a date? No, of course you haven't. Your mother passed away only three months ago. You'll have to wait until the year is out.'

'You seem to know more about our Hindu customs than I do,' Dwarika said with a touch of asperity. 'Which Shastra decrees that a man may not marry for a year after his mother's demise? Can you name it?'

'Of course I can't. I'm only telling you what I've seen all my life.' Jadugopal was silent for a moment then said cautiously, 'Don't take offence, Dwarika, if I ask you a question. You were a conservative Hindu once. What has made you change so?'

'I haven't changed at all. I was and still am a Hindu and I'm proud of being one. I'm inheritor to one of the noblest, the most catholic religions of the world. But I can't accept the trappings that have fastened themselves to it—the hateful customs sanctified by usage, the primitivisms, the superstitions. None of them are found in the Shastras.'

'You may be right,' Jadugopal said hastily for Dwarika was getting quite worked up. 'Now tell me. Have you chosen the girl? What is her name and where does she come from?'

501

SUNIL GANGOPADHYAY

Dwarika hesitated. 'Jadu,' he said after a while. 'You know my feelings for Basantamanjari. I've loved her ever since I was a boy. But fate was against me. She was given away to another. When I found her again I wanted to make her my wife but my mother wouldn't hear of it. She made me swear a solemn oath and threatened to take her own life if I broke it. My mother's dead now and I'm free. Free to marry Basi and—'

'Oh my God!' Jadugopal cried in a stricken voice.

'Why!' Dwarika exclaimed, startled. 'Aren't you on my side?'

'Dwarika,' Jadugopal answered in measured tones. 'Your father may have been an ordinary man but your mother was a zamindar's daughter. She was an intelligent woman and knowledgeable in the ways of the world. The oath she made you swear was for your own good. As a zamindar you can keep ten concubines if you like. No one will point a finger at you. But if you give a soiled, unchaste woman the status of wife you'll set every one of your subjects against you.'

'Basantamanjari is neither soiled nor unchaste.'

'We know that—you and I. But who will believe us? People will judge her by what they see. To all appearance she's a widow who ran away from home and lived with several men before winding up in a brothel in Hadh Katar Gali. Don't take such a drastic step Dwarika. Look after Basi as you've been doing all these years. But marry another. You need a wife who can take her rightful place by your side and give you children.'

'Wonderful!' Dwarika sneered at his friend's counsel. 'Marry an innocent girl knowing fully well that I can never give her the love she deserves! And deny the woman I love the status of a wife! You'll make a great judge Jadugopal. You're so upright and noble!'

'Why are you mad at me?' Jadugopal cried, 'I'm a Brahmo and have no social constraints to fight against. You are a Hindu. Hindu society holds its members in a vice-like grip and compels submission to its norms. You may have to pay a heavy price if you go against it.'

'I must follow my conscience Jadu. Even at a price. If society decrees that an innocent girl be pushed into a living hell for no fault of her own—I reject that decree. If anyone deserves to be punished, it's her father. Yet he escapes unscathed! What kind of

502

judgement is this? What is the moral worth of such a decree?'
Rising to his feet Dwarika continued, calmly, without any
bitterness, 'I see that you don't agree with me Jadu. But,
irrespective of whether you stand by me or not, I shall marry
Basantamanjari.'

Jadugopal put out a hand and pushed him back into his chair.
'When, in God's name, did I say I won't stand by you?' he
demanded. 'Why should I object? I don't want you to suffer any
ill consequences. That's all.'

'I'm really impressed by your attitude Dwarika Babu,'
Sunetra spoke for the first time that evening. 'You show
exemplary courage and consideration for the poor girl.'

'You've changed a great deal from the old Dwarika of our
college days.' Jadugopal said solemnly. 'You have gained
confidence and consistency of mind. I respect you for it. Go ahead
with your plan of marrying Basantamanjari. I'll help you all I can.
There are bound to be repercussions and we must be ready for
them. I'll take care of the legal implications—if any. But the
resistance put up by your family and society—you'll have to fight
alone. You and Basi.'

'I'm determined to do this thing Jadu and do it I will. No one
can stop me. But thank you for your support. It takes a great load
off my chest. I'm trying to get back in touch with all my friends.
Do you have Bharat's address? The boy from Tripura?'

'No. Even Bhumisuta had no news of him.'

'Who is Bhumisuta?'

'The girl who helped us light the fire when we picnicked in the
woods outside Bharat's house. Don't you remember? She's an
actress now.'

Dwarika nodded. 'I'll invite her to the wedding,' he said. 'I'm
making it a grand affair with thousands of guests. No hole and
corner business for me. I want the whole world to know I'm
marrying the woman I love.' He rose to leave and Jadugopal
followed him down the stairs. At the carriage door Dwarika put
his arms around Jadugopal and said with a break in his voice,
'I've suffered such agonies Jadu! I couldn't bare my soul to you
before your wife. But, do you know, we've never come together in
a physical union? We've lived in the same house, eaten together
and slept on the same bed but I've had to deny myself night after

503

night.'

'Why?'

'Because Basi wouldn't allow it. She said she couldn't endure the thought of her children being born out of wedlock; to be called bastards and to live out their lives under a cloud of humiliation. Can you imagine the agony of lying beside the woman you love and not being able to touch her? And all for a stupid oath made under a domineering woman's threat!' Jadugopal stared at his friend too overcome to speak.

Dwarika had geared himself to topple over all the impediments that stood in the way of his gaining his heart's desire. But he hadn't dreamed that the greatest resistance would come from Basantamanjari herself. He had kept the marriage a secret from her with the idea of giving her a wonderful surprise. But Basantamanjari came to know of it in a devious way. Her maid Moofi had a flirtatious relationship with Dwarika's watchman and had heard from him that the Babu was to be wed shortly. Preparations had already commenced in the house and the cards printed. This information Moofi duly passed on to her mistress. Basantamanjari, truly happy on hearing that Dwarika was settling down at last, gave her two silver rupees for bringing her the good news and, when Dwarika came to her that evening, she ran eagerly to the door crying out, '*Ogo*! I'm so glad you've decided to get married at last. I've told you again and again that you need a wife who can give you sons to carry the family name. I only wish you had taken this decision while your mother was alive. Poor lady! My heart goes out to her.' Dwarika tried to put in a word of explanation but Basantamanjari swept on, 'I can't be present at the wedding, of course, but I'll string the garlands for the *mala badal*. Promise me that you and your bride will wear my garlands.'

Dwarika gave a great shout of laughter. 'You can't be present at the wedding!' he cried, 'Whom shall I marry then?' Basantamanjari's face paled. 'What are you trying to say?' she asked in a faltering voice. 'Whatever's between us—'

'You thought I was marrying someone else? Am I a scoundrel? A cheat? My mother is dead and I'm free of my oath. You shall be my wife in the eyes of God and man. I shall marry you according to Brahmo rites.'

Basantamanjari moved quietly away, her silver anklets chiming softly as she went and stood by the window. The last rays of the setting sun fell on her exquisite profile and glowed richly in the folds of her ruby red silk sari. The waxy petals of the *champa,* nestling in the masses of her blue black hair gleamed luminous, as mother of pearl. Her long eyelashes rested, in a curve, against a cheek as delicately pink as a pomegranate seed. She looked like a painting, wrought in dim, rich colours, of a woman of yore—unreal, untouched, unearthly. Her low musical voice was husky with tears as she murmured. 'I cannot be your wife. Fate does not will it. But I'm yours and will be yours forever. I'll sing for you as I do now and pour wine for you to drink. I'll even dance when happiness wells up in my heart. That role is enough for me. I seek no other.'

Dwarika rose from his seat and, stealing softly up to her, placed his hands on her shoulders. 'Basi,' he said, his voice cracking with emotion, 'I've never forced you to do anything against your will. I've never touched or caressed you because you didn't wish it. Even when I was driven mad with desire—I kept away. But I'll use force now. You must agree to marry me. All the arrangements are made. I've told everyone I know—'

'You've told everyone!' Basantamanjari murmured in a strange, wondering voice. 'Everyone—except me.'

'I wanted to surprise you. I never dreamed—'

'People will scorn you if you don't marry me now. They'll call you a cheat and a hypocrite. You're afraid of that—aren't you? But I'm afraid too. I'm afraid people will think me a scheming harlot who enticed you into marrying her; a worm from the gutter aspiring to fly to heaven.'

'Why should we care about what people think? We love each other. That's all that matters. I want you to be my wife and the mother of my children.'

Basantamanjari turned her face to the sky, now dim with twilight. 'I see nothing written there,' she said in a passionate whisper. Then, turning to Dwarika, she cried, 'Why don't you understand? I'm a whore. Men don't marry girls like me.'

'I do and I will. My seed will flower only in your womb. Look into my eyes Basi! Look deep into my soul. Do you not see a fire burning it to ashes, bit by scorching bit? Can't you leap into the

505

flames to save me? I won't take you in secret. I won't take you out of a sense of guilt. I'll proclaim to the whole world that you are the queen of my home and heart. I want you by my side not only through this life but in all our lives to come.'

Chapter XVII

It was Swami Vivekananda's second visit to England. On his journey out to the West he had sailed by way of Japan, over the Pacific, and had landed in Vancouver. Then, after winning a good measure of acclaim in America, he had been persuaded by the Macleod sisters to accompany them to Europe. Francis and Bessy had set the date for their wedding and the venue was to be that most elegant and sophisticated of European cities—Paris. A Hindu ascetic was debarred from participation in wedding celebrations—even of those of his nearest kin. Yet Swamiji came to Paris. Was it because he had found it impossible to shake off the entreaties of his dearest Joe? Or was it because his wanderlust and love of beauty, suppressed for so long, were asserting themselves and he felt irresistibly drawn to the art and architecture of the most civilized city in the world? All this was true but only up to a point. The intention behind his European visit was deeper and more significant. While in America he had taken a decision. His next step would be to spread the message of Hinduism among the English people. France and England were separated by the thinnest strip of water. Once in France it would be the easiest thing in the world to move on to England. He had good friends there who would be only too happy to put him up.

One of them was Henrietta Müller whom he had met in America. Another was ET Sturdy. Sturdy had spent some months in an ashram in Almora and was fascinated by Indian ascetics. Both of them had invited Vivekananda, several times, to be their guest.

At the conclusion of the wedding festivities Vivekananda had left Paris and come to London. He hadn't stayed long but his sojourn, short though it was, had taught him a good deal about the English people. The English, he had discovered, were far less racist than the Americans. He had walked the streets of London without children running after him crying 'Blackie! Blackie!' It was possible for a coloured person to book himself into any hotel or walk into any shop. No one looked askance at him or ordered him out. The men and women who came to his lectures took him seriously and heard him out with patience unlike the Americans who were facetious and offensive by turns. The English had far greater exposure to cultures other than their own and were civilized, in consequence. Compared to them Americans were frogs in a well. Interacting with English men and women, in their own country, he marvelled at the difference between them and the ones who came out to India.

That, however, had been a short visit undertaken with a view to test the country and its people's powers of receptivity. This time Vivekananda had come with a purpose. He wished to open some centres from which knowledge of the Vedantas could be disseminated. His English disciples would see to the running of the institutions but who would take the responsibility of delivering the addresses? He, himself, couldn't be in two places at the same time. He took a decision. He would send for some of his fellow disciples from India. Young men like Sarat, Kali Vedanti and Shashi were well versed in Sanskrit and could read and explain the texts. Besides, they also had a smattering of English.

The last few months in America had been very productive. It was obvious to everyone that the mockery and hostility with which Vivekananda's discourses had been received, in the beginning, were considerably diluted by now. More and more people, in search of a spiritual solace their own religion could not give them, were coming to his meetings. His followers were growing in number and a band had emerged, the members of which had declared their intention of devoting their lives to the proliferation of the humanistic ideals of the Vedantas. It was at this juncture that Swamiji had started giving *deeksha* and receiving the people of the West into the Hindu fold. Herr Leon Landsberg and Mary Louis, among the first to be initiated, were renamed Kripananda and Abhayananda and became disciples of Sri Ramkrishna—the same Ramkrishna who had lived out his life as a humble priest in the temple of Dakshineswar, unknown even in his own country, except to a handful of people.

In England Vivekananda's reception was even better. Within weeks of his arrival, the numbers that flocked to his meetings proliferated to such a great extent that he was forced to seek out a bigger place. In this he received immense help from Mrs Müller and Mr Sturdy. Not only did they make all the arrangements, they even alerted the Press and saw to it that he got a fair degree of coverage in newspapers and journals. The Press was more than favourable. One newspaper carried the report that the English hadn't heard a better speaker than the Indian ascetic after Ram Mohan Roy and Keshabchandra Sen.

Vivekananda had started out with one discourse a day held in the form of a class each morning. Then, on growing public demand, he began addressing large gatherings, every evening, from some well-known forum. These evening lectures were on a variety of subjects—religion, history, philosophy, even current affairs. They were never planned or prepared in advance. The moment Swamiji stood on the podium words poured out of him as spontaneously as rippling water from a mountain stream. And he didn't hesitate to speak his mind. The same venom with which he had criticized the consumerism of the Americans was now spewed out on the British for their policy of 'divide and rule' in India. In his flame-coloured silk robe, held at the waist with a cummerbund, his glowing, vibrant face and deep, passionate voice, he held his audiences in thrall. They stared at him entranced. Many declared that they saw in his face and form an uncanny resemblance to Gautam Buddha.

The morning sessions were mostly attended by women from different walks of life and different sections of society. Teachers and nurses rubbed shoulders with wealthy widows, housewives and divorcees. From the highest to the lowest they were bound by common needs. Some came for a dash of excitement and variety in otherwise boring, humdrum lives. Others found an escape from loneliness and stress in the presence of the Swami which, though temporary, gave them strength to go on. Most of them were regular visitors at Vivekananda's meetings yet one of them drew his attention as no one else did. The moment he stepped into the hall his eyes skimmed over the sea of faces coming to rest, at last, on the face of the one he sought. She was a young woman and her name was Margaret Noble.

Margaret was thirty years old and the daughter of an Irish clergyman. Her father had died when she was only ten, following which event she had moved with her mother and siblings to the home of her maternal grandparents. Here she had received an education but very little love and affection and had been constrained to earn her living and take charge of her family from the age of seventeen. Love had come to her drab, lonely existence soon after she had taken up a post as a teacher. She had met a young man from Wales, a handsome, charming engineer, and they had had a lot in common. But just as their friendship started flowering into love, the youth died, suddenly, of a single day's illness leaving the young Margaret shattered and disconsolate. Unable to bear her life in a place so full of memories Margaret had left her native habitat in the suburbs of London and come to the great city.

Margaret was a good teacher and the children loved her. She loved them too and it was only in their midst that she could find solace. She felt this to be her true vocation—this moulding of young minds. But, as the months passed, she discovered other qualities in herself. She had ideas, interesting and original, and the ability to implement them. People took her seriously and were influenced by her. She decided to put these qualities to use by opening a school of her own—a new kind of school. Unlike other institutions there would be no common curriculum and no capital punishment. Each child had differing needs and aspirations and different talents. It was necessary to study each child's psyche and help him to find his moorings; to take care of his needs and find an outlet for his talents.

Once in London, however, Margaret got caught up in other things as well. London was not only the capital city of England. It was the heart of a vast empire on which the sun never set. A truly cosmopolitan city it was full of clubs and associations which hummed with activity from dawn till dusk. Margaret got quickly absorbed in the life around her. She became a member of the elite Sesame Club and later its secretary. She organized lectures and symposia, took an active part in discussions and also started contributing to newspapers and journals. It was thus that she met Bernard Shaw, Aldous Huxley and many other literary giants.

Living her full and busy life Margaret got over her heartbreak quite quickly and, within a few months, had formed a new attachment. The young man was a fellow member of the Sesame Club and his past was not unlike hers except for the fact that his beloved had not been snatched away from him by death but had moved away of her own volition. The two drifted towards each other, their common suffering creating a bond between them. But as soon as Margaret began dreaming of wedded bliss the blow fell. The young man disappeared without a word to her. A few days later Margaret learned the truth. His old love had sent for him and he had hastened to obey her summons. What was more, they were married already and on their honeymoon.

This blow was even harder to bear than the last. In a state of shock, and reluctant to face her friends and acquaintances, Margaret fled from London and took refuge with her friend Miss Collins in the town of Halifax. Miss Collins welcomed her to her house and soothed and comforted her. But it was not for long. After her initial breakdown Margaret took herself firmly in hand and, within a few days, announced her plan of returning to London. She was missing her school and the children. Back in London she threw herself into her work. While in this frame of mind she first came in contact with Vivekananda.

One day Margaret received an invitation from Lady Isabel Ferguson to attend a discourse by Swami Vivekananda in the drawing room of her house in the West End area of London. Margaret had never heard of Vivekananda and knew very little about India. Yet she felt a bond of sympathy with the country. Like her own country, Ireland, India lay under the domination of the British.

It was a chill damp evening of late November. Swami Vivekananda sat with his back to a roaring fire in Lady Ferguson's drawing-room, his audience facing him in a semi-circle. There were about sixteen people in the room—all scientific minded, enlightened intellectuals without a trace of blind faith. Yet there was pin drop silence as the Swami carried on his discourse. From time to time he recited Sanskrit mantras which no one understood. But the alien sounds, pronounced in the deep, sonorous voice, fell like music on the ears.

Margaret sat in a corner by the window, shrouded in winter twilight. The lamps had not been lit and the room was dark except for the glow that came from the fire. Gazing at the speaker for a long while, Margaret had a strange and wonderful experience. She felt as though her soul had left her body and gone winging across half the world to a little Indian village. She saw herself standing by a well beside a giant banyan tree. Beneath the tree, irradiated by the last rays of the setting sun, an ascetic in an orange robe sat murmuring verses in a strange, exotic tongue . . .

The spell broke in a few moments. The discourse ended and the company rose to their feet. Over tea the guests muttered comments and exchanged their views in whispers. It was generally felt that the Indian yogi hadn't said anything that could be deemed original or significant. Margaret thought so too. She left the house without exchanging a word with Vivekananda.

Yet, through the week, his face kept coming before her eyes—a bright, golden face with large, dark eyes burning with power and passion yet wonderfully innocent and child like. She wondered why she thought of Baby Jesus in Mother Mary's arms every time she saw that face in her mind's eye. She shook her head impatiently but couldn't dispel the illusion. It kept coming back . . .

Margaret decided to go to another lecture and test him out once more. Though he hadn't removed her doubts or answered any of the questions that plagued her he had held her attention all the time he was speaking. There was no doubt that he was a learned man. He had touched on a variety of subjects with the confidence of sure knowledge. Margaret scanned the newspapers and, having found a date and venue that suited her, went to hear Vivekananda once again. Once again she was disappointed. It was a good speech, scholarly and analytical, but what was there in it for her? Back home, she suddenly remembered that she had sat speechless all the time he was speaking, her eyes fixed on his face. The memory made her blush but she hastened to tell herself that that was because of his outstanding personality. And his voice, even in remembrance, sent a thrill down her spine.

The next thing Margaret did was to get hold of his address and write him a letter. And, to her delight, she received an answer long before she expected it. It was a warm, friendly letter and it filled her with a sense of well being. He didn't know her yet he had addressed her as though she was an old friend. He had consoled her with the advice that purity, patience and perseverance would enable her to overcome all the obstacles that stood in the way of her happiness. 'With all my love,' he had ended, 'Yours

Vivekananda.' Margaret was amazed. She had been distinctly cold to him. She had attended two of his lectures but had neither wished him nor uttered a word of praise. Yet he had sent her his love.

After that Margaret started going to all his discourses even though she wasn't at all sure of what she was receiving from them. Her education had given her rational views and she was atheistic by temperament. Her father and grandfather had been clergymen but she disliked the Roman Catholic Church with its narrow prejudices and ostentatious rituals. She wasn't impressed by Hinduism either. She attended Vivekananda's lectures but not in a spirit of acceptance. Vivekananda never complained. He accepted her non-acceptance and welcomed her to his meetings. Perhaps he heard, in this young woman's vehement denial of faith, an echo of his own—not so long ago. He had doubted Ramkrishna; even hated and despised him. He had raved and ranted against him. But he hadn't been able to keep away. Margaret was going through a similar experience. She rejected Vivekananda's doctrines but couldn't stay away from him.

There was something about him that set her wondering. In all his discourses he never once touched on the negative aspects of the human race. To hear him one would think that his vocabulary did not contain the word *Sin*. He appealed, always, to the highest and noblest in human nature and his confidence in his fellowmen was phenomenal. Of late he had been speaking a great deal on the value of sacrifice. 'The world needs men and women,' he had said once, 'who can find the courage to leave their homes and come out into the streets with the slogan, "I know no other than God. And God dwells within my fellowmen." Who is ready to abandon his own small family and seek a larger one? To nurture and cherish; to serve and to comfort . . .?'

These words fell like blows from a hammer on Margaret's heart. She had wanted a husband and children, a small family of her own, but they had eluded her. She had no desire for them now. She would answer Swamiji's call. She would walk in his footsteps and seek out a larger world.

Chapter XVIII

Ardhendushekhar Mustafi had been removed from the post of director of Emerald and was, in consequence, left without a job. He had sold off all his medals along with his wife's jewellery to pay the creditors, who had hounded him like a pack of wolves, and was now penniless as well. Fortunately, his son was grown up now and in a position to support his parents.

Ardhendushekhar hated sitting at home all day. He found it boring and stifling. Having nothing else to do, he found a novel way of passing his time. He walked aimlessly in the streets from dawn till dusk stopping here and there as the fancy took him. He would sit for hours under a tree on the bank of the Ganga or look on interestedly as a snake charmer played his pipe to the dance of a hooded cobra. Or he would even take sides in a street brawl. But he never went anywhere near a theatre. Ever since he had left Emerald he kept away from everything and everyone connected with the acting profession. But there was one habit, picked up during his heydays of acting and directing, that he couldn't give up. And that was drinking. He had to have at least three bottles of whisky a day. And it had to be a local brew. He wouldn't drink Scotch if it was offered to him on a silver platter. He had told his friends that he had no desire to be cremated with sandalwood and incense and made them promise to pour some bottles of liquor on his corpse before setting it alight. Only then, he declared, would his soul find peace and wing its way straight to heaven.

One morning, Ardhendushekhar sat at a table in Piru's Hotel when a couple of young men sidled up to him with an effusive, 'Namaskar Guru! What great good fortune is ours that—'

'I'm no one's guru,' Ardhendushekhar snapped, turning his face away. He recognized the boys. They were Byomkesh and Neeladhwaj—bit actors without looks or talent who spent their time drifting like river moss from one bank to another in search of roles. They had worked for some months in Emerald. Byomkesh, he had heard, had tried to worm his way into Nayanmoni's heart but she had sent him packing.

Turning his back on the pair Ardhendushekhar fell hungrily on the two boiled eggs a waiter set before him. They were duck's eggs—huge and soft and emitting clouds of fragrant steam. But it took more than a mild snub to subdue the enthusiasm of the two yokels. 'Do you know what we did the other day Guru?' they continued, unabashed. 'We went to Girish Babu and said to him, "You must do something about the jumped-up fop that's taken possession of Emerald. He's getting too big for his shoes. Why don't you and Mustafi Moshai get together and kick him out?" "Don't talk to me of Ardhendu," Girish Babu brushed us away as though we were flies. "He's finished. Even God cannot resurrect him."' Ardhendu threw a burning glance in the direction of the two boors and attacked his eggs with renewed vigour. 'Girish Babu is jealous of you,' Byomkesh tried again. 'He can't bear the thought of your popularity. He's an old horse who can't pull the cart any more. You're young and the public wants you.' Ardhendushekhar finished the eggs and rose to his feet. 'I pity you two,' he said clicking his tongue sadly at them. 'You've learned nothing. Nothing at all. Not even the basic courtesy of looking the other way when someone is eating. You think I don't know what you're like? You come toadying up to me trying to set me against Girish. And you do exactly the same with him. *Oré haramzada!* If Girish is jealous of me he's paying me the compliment of my life! He wouldn't stoop to envying you, would he? But let me tell you this. If I die today, he'll weep more than any of you. And if, God forbid, he goes before me I'll be shattered with grief.'

Byomkesh and Neeladhwaj looked at one another then, their faces crumpling with disappointment, they abandoned the game. 'Save us Guru,' they cried, hurling themselves at Ardhendushekhar's feet. 'We've been without roles for two months now. Our families are starving. We are the dust of your feet. Take us with you wherever you go. It you're not teaming up with Girish Ghosh you must be joining Classic and—' Ardhendushekhar withdrew his feet in alarm. '*Arré arré!* What is this?' he cried. 'You're in a hotel—not in a playhouse. Who told you I'm joining Classic?'

'Everyone in the line is saying so. "Do you think Classic will let Saheb Mustafi fade away into oblivion?" they say. "They'll drag him out of his hideout and reinstate him as director with full honours."' Ardhendushekhar smiled wryly. Far from reinstating him with full honours, the new proprietor of Emerald, renamed Classic, hadn't even sent a feeler. The young man had dismissed all the old members of the troupe—actors and actresses as well as technicians. Why would he bother with the old director? 'You may be the dust of my feet,' he said jocularly, 'But if anyone wants me they'll have to bow their heads humbly before me and wash my feet clean of all impurities before I condescend to go with them. Now stir your behinds and get going. I'm sick of the sight of you.' Ardhendushekhar brushed past them and came and stood on the street. His pretended nonchalance, notwithstanding, their words had set his senses tingling with pain and humiliation. No one had sent for him. No one wanted him. And he had no money with which to start something of his own. He was now numbered among the has-beens.

Once an actor—always an actor! Although he had lost his audience Ardhendushekhar couldn't rid himself of the urge to act. He walked about the city streets singing snatches of song and muttering whole pages of dialogue as he went along. And he always had a bottle with him. From time to time he would take it out of his pocket and, refreshing himself with a swig, start his mutterings all over again.

One night he fell asleep under a tree by the river. He was woken, at crack of dawn, by the loud whistle of a ship casting anchor a few yards away from where he lay. He sat up with a jerk and stretched his cramped limbs till the joints, jammed with hours of inactivity, crackled into life. 'Aah!' he cried in a tone of mingled pain and pleasure. 'Aah!' a voice echoed a little distance away. Ardhendushekhar glanced in the direction of the sound and saw a man lying on the ground, further up the bank. He looked at Ardhendushekhar out of beady black eyes and winked knowingly.

'*Patityodharini Gange Ma go*!' Ardhendu sang.

'*Ma go Ma go*,' the man took up the refrain in a voice surprisingly deep and musical.

'Who are you?' Ardhendu asked curiously. 'Another bit of discarded material from the acting profession?'

'*Byomkali Kalkatta wali*!' the man called out in a booming
voice. Ardhendu Shekhar had realized, by now, that the man was
a lunatic. He had always had a soft corner for those who lived at
the periphery and his heart went out to this one. 'Sing with me,' he
commanded. 'Let me see how good you are.' Then, kneeling on
the ground, a hand at one ear like a professional baiji, he burst
into song:
'*Hum bara saab hai duniya mé*
None can be compared hamara saat
Mr Mustafi name hamara
Chaatgaon hamara acché Bilaat
Rom—ti—tom—ti—tom . . .'
The lunatic stared at him for a few moments his little eyes
winking and blinking, all on their own, like black jewels. Then,
without a word, he ran to the river's edge and plunged into the
roaring waves. Ardhendu took out a charred stump of a cigar
from his pocket and lit it. Taking a puff he gazed out on the river
which, though it was so early in the day, was already teeming
with bathers. The black head of the madman bobbed up and
down, up and down, like a cork. He wondered a bit. He had
thought lunatics were afraid of water. Presently the man
clambered up the bank and stood before him. 'Give,' he
commanded, putting out a dripping hand.
'Give what?' Ardhendu asked belligerently.
'Anything.'
'I've nothing to give. Get lost.' He added, muttering, to
himself, 'I'm a beggar myself. What can I give another?' The
lunatic stood where he was, his neck twisted sideways, holding
Ardhendu's eyes with his own tiny, sparkling ones. A wicked
smile lifted the corners of his mouth. 'I've acted a lunatic time
after time,' Ardhendu thought suddenly. 'Why didn't I act like
this man? I should study his mannerisms and tuck them away in
my head for future use.' It didn't occur to him that there would be
no future use. Two pairs of eyes held each other—observing,
scrutinizing. Then Ardhendu rose and, putting an arm around the
other's shoulder, he said 'Come, *dost*!. Let's have some hot *jilipi*. I
have a couple of annas in my pocket.'
Ardhendu Shekhar returned to the same spot the next day to
see the lunatic rolling in the dust, whining and sobbing like a

child. But he hauled himself into a sitting position the moment he beheld his friend of the day before, and reached for the cone of *sal* leaves he held in his hand. Digging into it he brought out a *radha ballavi*. Then, jabbing his forefinger into its crisp, puffed up crust, he blew kisses at it and murmured as coyly as if he was addressing his sweetheart. 'May I nibble you just a teeny, weeny bit?' Ardhendu Shekhar watched him fascinated. He spent the next four days with the man studying him closely, storing away every detail in his memory—the expression of the eyes, the twist of the limbs. He felt he was learning acting for the first time.

On the fifth day the lunatic was gone. Ardhendu hung about the bank for a few hours waiting for him, then sauntered over to a sadhu's akhara in the burning ghat a few hundred yards away. The man was a dangerous criminal, a drug addict and a fugitive from justice masquerading as a holy man. Ardhendushekhar knew that but he hung around him nevertheless. He had played the role of a charlatan sadhu once or twice and might play it again in future. The world was full of men of different kinds and callings and the theatre reflected them all.

In order to reach the Ganga Ardhendu Shekhar had to cross the red light area of Rambagan. The place slept under the sun all day and came awake at night to the moon and stars, with music, laughter and drunken brawls. One evening, as he shuffled idly along, he was startled by the sound of loud voices flowing out from one of the houses. A male voice, slurred with alcohol, was abusing and threatening while a woman's, shrill and piteous, wept and pleaded. A crowd of onlookers hung outside the door pushing and jostling one another in order to get a better view of whatever was going on within. Ardhendu Shekhar was thoroughly alarmed. Even though a scene of this kind was not uncommon in that particular neighbourhood, he couldn't suppress his agitation. Anything might happen any moment now. The drunken monster might hurl a bottle at the woman's head injuring her badly—even killing her. He made his way to the crowd and, raising himself on tiptoe, peered into the room. O Hari! It wasn't a real quarrel. It was a scene from a play being rehearsed by a group of amateurs. He listened, ears cocked, for a few moments and recognized it. It was Deenabandhu Mitra's *Neel Darpan*.

The scene was being enacted at the centre of a long hall spread with cotton mats. Ten or twelve men and women sat in chairs scattered about the room waiting for their cues. Ardhendushekhar identified the director instantly from the open book in his hand as well as the way he fluttered about like a distracted hen and called 'Silence! Silence!' when the public outside became too noisy. Ardhendushekhar got so caught up by what he was seeing that he abandoned his plan of walking to the river. In fact, it seemed to him, that he had no will or volition of his own in the matter. His feet were rooted to the ground and would not move.

The cast was a half-baked one with no training whatsoever. The director seemed to be little better. The voices were either dim and vapid or unnecessarily loud with no modulations or nuances. One of the actors had a speech defect and he stammered and stuttered all the way through his part. And a number of the cast hadn't memorized their lines. Watching the rehearsal, that jewel in the crown of the Bengali theatre—Ardhendushekhar Mustafi, could hold himself in no longer. '*Chup!*' the rich, musical voice, teeming with inflections, hit the ears of everyone present like a roll of thunder, '*Tum shala na layak achhé!*' Every head turned around, the voice still booming in their breasts. Who had spoken those words? They were part of the Englishman's dialogue. But whose voice? The director threw a burning glance at the crowd outside and said threateningly, 'If there's any more disturbance I'll shut the door.'

The rehearsal recommenced. Ardhendushekhar inched his way to the front, slipping and sliding like a snake through the mass of bodies. His lips moved silently, formulating the words that were being spoken within. He knew *Neel Darpan* by heart—all the lines of all the characters and he murmured them in rapt enjoyment. Suddenly he forgot himself again and roared out the line: '*Hami tumar baap keno habo; hami tumar chheliyar baap hoite chai.*' The voice was slurred with liquor yet it conveyed every inflection of the arrogance and contempt with which the British planter habitually addressed his ryots. This time Ardhendushekhar was caught. The man who had been playing the role of the Englishman in a squeaking voice and pidgin English, came rushing up and took him by the throat. '*Shala!*' he screamed shaking him violently with both hands, 'You dare make fun of me! You'll get such a kick on your behind that—'

'Forgive me sir,' Ardhendu pleaded meekly. 'I didn't mean to make fun of you. It was a mistake.'

'Mistake! What mistake? What club are you from?'

'I don't belong to any club. I've made a mistake. I'm sorry.'

But even such abject humility failed to satisfy the man. He raised his hand to cuff Ardhendu Shekhar on the ear, the others shouting encouragement, 'Give him a sound beating and throw him out.' But the director had stood still, all this while, staring at Ardhendu Shekhar as if he had seen a ghost. '*Ei!*' he roared suddenly at the man who still held Ardhendu by the throat, 'Don't touch him. Bring him over to me.' As Ardhendu was dragged, protesting, over to the director, the latter fixed his eyes with a penetrating gaze on his face, taking in every detail—the tired eyes, the chin that hadn't seen a razor for five days and the soiled *uduni*. 'Who are you?' he asked gently, almost humbly.

'I'm no one. No one of any consequence, that is. I was walking down the street when I . . . I've seen *Neel Darpan* twice or thrice and remember some of the dialogue. It just slipped out. I'm sorry.'

'My name is Chhoné Mittir,' the director said. 'And I've haunted the theatre since I was a boy. If I don't recognize you by your voice I don't deserve to direct even an amateur production such as this one. You say you are no one of consequence. But I know better. You are Saheb Mustafi.'

At these words a ripple of excitement ran through the cast and through the spectators who stood outside—their eyes big with wonder. 'Of course! Of course!' Four or five voices cried out together. 'It is Mustafi Moshai! Why didn't we recognize him?' Ardhendu Shekhar stood where he was not knowing what to do. Now Chhoné Mittir knelt before him and folded his hands. 'You're Dronacharya,' he said. 'I'm Ekalavya. I've seen you from a distance all these years and marvelled at your genius. Today you stand under my roof. What a blessed day it is for me!' As if these words were their cue the actors and actresses all came forward and knelt beside their director forming a circle around Ardhendu Shekhar. The man who had laid hands on him flung himself at his feet and cried, 'Forgive me for not recognizing you Gurudev! Punish me in whatever way you wish. But give me your blessing.'

Ardhendu Shekhar's chest swelled with triumph. Flattery,

520

however base and motivated, fed a man's ego and restored his self esteem. He hadn't felt so good in many months. Applause was like food to the artist's soul. Without it he sickened and fell into a decline. Ardhendushekhar felt as though he had just woken up from a long, long sleep.

Chhoné Mitter rose to his feet and put the book, reverently, into Ardhendu Shekhar's hands. 'Guru,' he said in a voice so emotional that Ardhendu Shekhar was afraid he would burst into tears any moment. 'We are your worthless brothers—not fit even to take the dust of your feet. Break us and mould us anew. Teach us the true art.' The man who was acting Tohrab said, 'I've seen so many of your plays—*Mukul Manjura*, *Abu Hossain*, *Pratapaditya*, *Pandav Nirbasan* and so many others. Yet I failed to recognize you. I deserve to rot in hell for it. I'll rub my nose on the streets of Calcutta for a whole mile. I'll fast for seven days. I'll—'

Ardhendu Shekhar put a hand on his shoulder and smiled, 'You don't have to do any of those things,' he said comfortably. 'You're not responsible for what you don't remember. But when you speak the line *Shalar kaan ami kamre kete diyecchi go*—do it like this.' Ardhendu walked to the centre of the ring. Then, fumbling in his pocket, he brought out a piece of paper and, holding it before his audience, he looked out of burning eyes and said in the harsh, grating voice of the Muslim rustic '*Halar kaan ér khanikda chhire niyechhi . . .*'

Chhoné Mittir's amateur group, which went by the grand name of Victoria Dramatic Club, put up four to five shows each year. Unable to compete with the professional theatres of Calcutta, these plays were performed mostly in the mofussils where they were quite popular. Barring a couple of actresses no one was paid a salary. From Chhoné Mittir down to the lowest technician, everyone's contribution was a labour of love. Ardhendu Shekhar agreed to take on the responsibility of training the cast on the condition of complete anonymity. Chhoné Mittir would continue as director and his name would appear in the handbills. Ardhendu would take no money either. But Chhoné could make him a present of three bottles of whisky a day, if he so wished. Chhoné Mittir hastened to agree.

Within days of Ardhendu Shekhar's joining the club the venue for the rehearsals was shifted. This time Chhoné found a place where the public could be sealed off completely. The rehearsals commenced with renewed enthusiasm. Ardhendu Shekhar sat in a large chair in the centre of the room, the pipe of an *albola* at his lips. In one hand he held a glass of whisky. He drank all day—from the moment he opened his eyes in the morning till he shut them finally at night. In consequence he never got drunk. His brain was clear and so was his speech. Between sips from his glass and puffs from his albola he trained the actors and actresses in the art of modulating their voices and articulating their lines. From time to time he rose from his chair and demonstrated the correct gestures of eyes and hands; the tilt of the neck and the set of the shoulders till it seemed as though he was determined to produce star quality theatre from this bunch of callow youngsters.

One day Chhoné Mitter said to him, 'I wish to ask you a question Gurudev. But only if you promise not to take offence.'

'You want me to sign on a blank sheet? Very well. Go ahead with your question.'

'There's a girl called Haridasi—an actress. I sleep with her some nights—'

'What's wrong with that? Married men should sleep with other women from time to time. It improves the circulation and relaxes the mind and body. You're not asking for my permission, surely.'

'Oh no. It's like this. Haridasi lives next door to Gangamoni. Gangamoni was a reputed actress at one time and—'

'I know that. Gangamoni is an old friend of mine and I visited her often in the old days. She was better known by her nickname Hadu.'

'Gangamoni has a tenant called Nayanmoni.'

'I know. I know. It was I who gave her the name. Her real name is quite a mouthful. Bhumi—something or the other. Most unsuitable for a heroine.'

'Some people say she's your natural daughter.'

'Nonsense. I picked her off the streets and turned her into a fine actress. I've done that for many of the wenches. Hasn't Binodini been trained by me? Hasn't Kusum Kumari? Kshetramoni? Bonobiharini? Are they all my natural daughters?'

'Nayanmoni respects you as her own father.'

522

'That's her business. I haven't asked her to.'

'But she's in a difficult situation. And it's owing to you.'

Now Ardhendushekhar's brows came together. 'What do you mean by that young man?' he asked sternly.

'Haridasi tells me that Nayanmoni is bound by oath to work only under your direction. She was with Emerald and—'

'The company passed into another's hands. The members of the cast lost their jobs. Is that my fault? Does she expect me to find her work? That, I'm afraid, is not possible.'

'No sir. She doesn't need anyone's help in finding work. All the theatre companies of Calcutta are begging her to join them. Minerva sent for her. Amar Datta of Classic went personally to her. But she sent him away.'

'Well, if she doesn't want to work anymore—it's her business. What can I do about it? If she has lost interest in the stage let her catch a rich Babu and live happily ever after.'

'The girl, from what I hear, is a different type altogether. She'd rather go to Kashi and beg for a living than take a Babu. She loves the stage but, determined to honour her oath, she won't join another board until you give her your permission.'

Ardhendushekhar burst out laughing. 'Ah yes—the oath!' he said, 'I'd forgotten. The girl's a fool. Doesn't she know that in the theatre business every word that is uttered is a lie? Our tears are false and so are our smiles. Deceiving is our profession. Tell her from me that the oath she took isn't worth a horse's egg!' He laughed merrily for a few moments then, sobering down, added gravely, 'She's not only foolish and whimsical—she's an arrogant wench and I scarcely know what to make of her. Do you know she had the temerity to turn down a maharaja, a real maharaja, who wanted to hear her sing?'

'She may be foolish and arrogant but she's a superb actress and ought to join Classic. Not only for her own good but for the good of the profession. If you would only go to her and release her from her oath—'

'What!' Ardhendushekhar thundered 'I'm to go to her house! How dare you make such a suggestion? I lost my Emerald to that upstart of the Dattas. And you're advising me to help him get the actress I moulded for my own use! The girl can go to Kashi or to hell. It's all the same to me.'

523

SUNIL GANGOPADHYAY

Ardhendushekhar couldn't sleep a wink that night. He rarely lost his temper but, when he did, his brain got so heated that he couldn't think of anything other than that which had provoked him. He tossed and turned all night between snatches of fitful sleep in which he saw strange, frightening dreams. Nayanmoni's face kept appearing in them—now blurred and distant, now close, very close, and clear as glass. Thoughts, loose and disjointed, chased one another like leaves in a storm. And a savage pain tore at his vitals. He had created Nayanmoni! He had taken a lump of clay and wrought it lovingly till it took shape and contour. It was his hands that had formed the turn of her neck, the swing of her arms and the proud poise of the head on her shoulders. It was he who had taught her to smile and weep and walk with grace and dignity. But her eyes were her own. He had never seen eyes like hers. They could express the most superb range of emotions. In them he had seen the shy beauty of a wild doe; the serene tranquillity of a river under a cloudless sky; the fiery lava of an erupting volcano. Which is why he had named her Nayanmoni! She had taken an oath—Chhoné said. But when? He didn't remember. Who cared about oaths anyway? *I love you. I'll never leave you, no—not to my dying day.* People said those words and forgot them the very next minute. Was the girl mad? . . . Classic! Classic! He was sick of the name. Amar Datta had taken his Emerald and made it his own. Everyone said he was heralding a new age. It was easy for him. He had money. He was the son of Dwarkanath Datta—the wealthy agent of Ralli Brothers and Company. His brother Hitendra was a renowned Sanskrit scholar and philosopher . . .

It wasn't uncommon for scions of wealthy families to open theatre companies. They did so at the instigation of their toadies and packed up within a few months after losing a lot of money. But Amar Datta was different. He was applying himself to the theatre business very seriously. He was an extremely handsome man—tall, fair and well formed with a broad chest, powerful shoulders and a deep, manly voice. And he had acting ability. Consequently, he could play the male lead without any competition from others. He was a good director as well and had a discerning eye for props, costumes and hall decor. After acquiring Emerald he had renovated it completely, turning it into

524

the most beautiful and luxurious playhouse in Calcutta. From the lights in the ceiling to the carpets on the floor—he had changed them all. He paid his cast better salaries and got better work out of them. He had also started a theatre magazine.

All this was very well and Ardhendushekhar had nothing against it. An old theatre hand, he welcomed improvement wherever he saw it. But Amar Datta had made certain statements that set his blood on fire every time he remembered them. 'We must clear the theatre of old fossils like Ghosh and Mustafi,' he had declared. 'Their style is out. Realistic acting is the order of the day.' Realistic acting indeed! It was true that Amar Datta cut a fine figure in the role of a prince or nawab in historical plays. But could he do a Muslim peasant? A wily shopkeeper? A vagrant? Could he speak in three or four different voices in the time span of a single play as Ardhendushekhar could?

Ardhendushekhar woke up the next morning with a pounding head and aching limbs. To relieve himself of the fatigue of a sleepless night he rubbed his limbs with oil and had an early bath. Then, sitting on the veranda, he puffed at his *albola* thoughtfully. Around ten o' clock he rose and got ready to go out. After many months he took pains with his appearance. He shaved carefully and donned a finely puckered dhuti and silk banian. Then, swinging his stick jauntily, he walked out of his house and came to Gangamoni's. Ganga came running out of her room, on hearing of his arrival, and greeted him with a radiant smile. Kneeling on the ground she lowered her head to his feet then, rising, she said with a roguish twinkle in her eye, '*Ki go* Saheb Debata! What brings you to this hapless woman's door after all these days?' Ardhendushekhar chucked her under the chin and grinned, 'I missed you sorely Hadu. I've been yearning for a glimpse of your moon-like face for s-o-o long.' Gangamoni's eyes flashed the way they used to, twenty years ago, when she was slim and pretty and did romantic parts. She laid a finger on the dimple that still flickered in her fat chin and tossed her head coquettishly. 'What a slick liar you are! Yearning for a glimpse of a hippopotamus like me indeed! On the contrary, Moshai, I've sent for you at least four or five times. You're never at home. Where do you hang around all day?'

'In the samsan ghat.'

'What!' Gangamoni was startled, 'Whatever for?'

'Well, I'll have to go there sooner or later. I thought I would start acclimatizing myself.'

'Everyone has to go there at one time or another. But people wait till the call comes. You were always a strange one . . .'

'Don't scold Hadu. Say something sweet like you used to when your lips were as full and red as bimba berries and honey dripped from them.'

'Don't forget what you were like then. As handsome and foppish as a newly wrought Kartik! Not the scarecrow you are now.'

'Why did you send for me? Is the old love welling up again in your bosom?'

'Of course. Not only welling up. It's hissing and foaming like boiling milk. Now answer my question, Saheb Babu. What sort of a man are you? Why did you make our Nayan sign a bond saying she won't join any other board? Amar Datta of Classic came to see her. Ah! What a fine figure of a man he is! As handsome as a prince and so polished and charming of manner! The silly girl refused even to meet him.'

'Send for her. I wish to have a word with Nayan.'

'Look Saheb Babu. I have no idea of the figure mentioned in the bond. But whatever it is, I'll make a shift to pay it. I love the girl and won't see her ruined.'

'Death be on you woman!' Ardhendu Shekhar snapped. 'Can't you stop wagging your tongue for a moment and go call the wench? I said I wanted to see her.'

At this Gangamoni huffed and puffed her way to Nayanmoni's room and gave her the news. Nayanmoni was sitting on the floor facing her Krishna. But she rose instantly and plucking a bundle off the top shelf of her cupboard she ran down the stairs and stood before her old mentor. Ardhendu Shekhar's eyes ran up and down her form appraisingly. She was twenty-seven years old and a radiant beauty.

'How are you Nayan?' Ardhendushekhar said.

'I am well.'

'What is this I hear about an oath you took?' Ardhendu Shekhar came straight to the point, 'I remember nothing about it.'

Nayanmoni looked down at her feet. 'It happened long ago,'

she said. 'You were training me for a dance sequence when you said, "I'm taking such pains with you Nayan. But you'll leave me and go away the moment someone offers you more money." I touched your feet, then, and swore never to leave you.'

'I must have been drunk when I spoke those words. You shouldn't have taken them seriously.'

'I always take everything seriously.'

Ardhendu Shekhar looked down on the bowed head for a long moment. 'I release you from your oath,' he said at last. 'Go wherever you wish and be happy.' Then, sighing a little, he added, 'If I ever get the chance to scrape a troupe together again, I'll send for you. Come back to me then.'

Nayanmoni nodded. Then, kneeling on the ground, she placed the bundle she had brought at his feet. 'What's this?' Ardhendu Shekhar stepped back in alarm. 'It's the money you gave me,' Nayanmoni said softly. 'I've spent very little. My needs are few.'

'No! No,' Ardhendushekhar nearly screamed the words, 'Ardhendu Shekhar Mustafi may have sunk low. But not so low that he'll take back the wages he paid an employee. Have no fears for me Nayan. People say I'm old but I'm not that old. There's magic in my bones yet. I'll spring back—never fear. And then—you'll get the surprise of your life.' Ardhendu Shekhar turned his face away. His eyes, to his own surprise, had filled with tears.

Chapter XIX

Vivekananda returned to India four years after he had left it. He had been a wandering sadhu, obscure and penniless, when he first set his sights on the West. Hardly anyone noted his absence from the country or bothered to keep track of what he was doing out of it. But when he returned he was showered with all the glory of a conquering hero.

Stepping ashore at Colombo, he got his first shock being totally unprepared for the welcome that awaited him. A sea of heads stretched as far as the eye could see and thousands of voices shouted slogans in his name. From the capital he travelled to other places on the island—to Anuradhapur, Kandy and Jaffna. And wherever he went, his reception was overwhelming. He looked superbly handsome and triumphant in his orange robe and turban and his voice, when he addressed the crowds that flocked to see him, had the depth and passion of a lion's. But, within himself, he felt his strength ebbing. He was tired, horribly tired. And there was something else; some sickness he could not identify. His breath was coming in gasps, after a little exertion, and his limbs trembled with exhaustion. Mr and Mrs Sevier, who had accompanied him on his voyage to India, were alarmed. At this rate, they felt, Swamiji would have a breakdown any moment. So, they hired a ship and slipped him quietly out of Ceylon and away from the teeming multitudes. The Indian coastline lay within fifty miles of Jaffna. It was a matter of a few hours.

Swami Vivekananda's next halt was the small port town of Pamban. But even here he got little respite. The King of Ramnad was at the harbour with his retinue, awaiting the man who had returned to his native shores after conquering the West. To Vivekananda's embarrassment, the king led him to a carriage pulled by four horses while he, himself, walked alongside it. A vast crowd followed shouting 'Jai Vivekananda! Jai Swamiji!' After a while the raja felt that even this did not express the reverence he felt for the great swami sufficiently. Ordering the horses to be unhitched he commenced pulling the carriage himself. Others joined him and, for the first time in his life, Vivekananda was drawn by humans instead of animals. Vivekananda hated exhibitionism of this kind and tried to protest but his voice was drowned in the waves of frenzy and adulation that filled the air.

Entering the temple of Shiva in Rameswar he remembered the last time he was here. No one knew him then. No one had deigned to cast a glance at the weary, travel-stained sanyasi who had sat for hours on the steps of this very temple. That had been only four years ago. Now crowds were following him everywhere and people were shoving and pushing each other only for a glimpse of him.

Addressing the congregation in the temple courtyard Vivekananda's message to the people of India was startling. No Indian ascetic had ever spoken such words before. True religion, he said, could not be contained in ritual and idol worship. True religion was the religion of Man and lay in selfless service to the poor, the weak, the sick and the downtrodden. He who beheld Shiva in the hungry and the naked was the true worshipper of Shiva—not he who sat before a stone image chanting mantras.

From Rameswar to Madurai; from Trichinopoly to Kumbhakonam—everywhere he went he preached the doctrine of service to one's fellow men. But the innumerable meetings and irregular hours started taking their toll of him. Added to these was the inclement weather, the polluted air and fetid water of the south. He contracted a severe cold and cough and various ailments of the stomach. He felt sick and worn out but he wouldn't admit it and continued with his hectic schedule. And, more and more, his discourses were turning away from religion and focussing on other issues. 'Let us put an end to all rituals sanctified by tradition,' he cried, addressing a congregation in Madras. 'Let our next fifty years be dedicated to the worship of our great Mother India. The lesser gods can wait for the present. They are sleeping, now, in any case. Our countrymen are our waking gods.'

From Madras Vivekananda boarded a ship and travelled to Calcutta. Stepping into it Mrs Sevier was amazed to find the deck

piled with green coconuts so high that it appeared to be a
mountain. She wondered if the ship was carrying cargo as well as
passengers. Then someone told her that they had been left by the
people of the city. Word had spread that Swamiji had been
advised by the doctors to drink coconut water in place of
ordinary water—the water of tender coconuts being good for the
stomach. Four days later the ship docked at Khidirpur. A special
reception committee, set up by the Maharaja of Dwarbhanga,
met him and escorted him by train to Sealdah the next day. As the
train chugged its way slowly into the station the air rang with a
tremendous cry and the platform shook under the feet of
thousands of people pushing, jostling and treading on one
another's toes in order to catch a glimpse of the man who had left
the country as ordinary Naren Datta and returned as the
internationally acclaimed Swami Vivekananda. Not all the
people in the crowd had come in a spirit of respect. Many were
only curious onlookers and still others had come only to carp and
criticize. 'Look how low our countrymen have sunk,' one
whispered to another, his lips curled in contempt. 'They are
grovelling at this man's feet simply because a few sahebs and
mems have lionized him. Who had ever heard his name before he
left the country?'

'I've heard he's from a Kayastha family of Shimle,' the other
said, turning up his nose disdainfully, 'Since when have
Kayasthas been allowed to don the robes of a swami? Hai! Hai!
We're tolling the death knell of Hinduism.'

'The man is not a Hindu anymore,' the other commented. 'He
has crossed the black water and set foot on foreign soil. And he's
eaten forbidden flesh and slept with firinghee women. *Chhi*!
Chhi! *Chhi*! What is the world coming to?'

But the supporters of Vivekananda outnumbered his
detractors by far. Here, as in Pamban, the young men unhitched
the horses from the carriage in which he was to travel and
proceeded to pull it themselves. An English band marched ahead
of the carriage, playing lively Scottish tunes while a party of
Kirtaniyas, singing to the clash of cymbals, brought up the rear.
The road over which the procession went was decorated, every
few yards, with colourful gates hung with garlands of roses and
marigolds. The carriage first stopped outside Ripon College

where a great crowd had assembled to welcome the returning hero, then went on to Pasupati Basu's house in Bagbazar where an afternoon meal awaited him. Despite his exhaustion Vivekananda did not stop to rest after the meal. He went straight on to Alambazar, to the math where his co-disciples of the old days resided.

But the reunion, after four years of separation, was not as warm and affectionate as it might have been—at first. They had all been Ramkrishna's disciples. They had all left their homes in answer to their guru's call. They had banded together in the face of criticism from friends and families and suffered untold deprivations. They had all remained exactly where they were. Except one—he had crossed over to the other half of the sphere and won fame, acclaim and thousands of followers. Most of Vivekananda's brothers in religion felt awkward and alienated from him. Some couldn't suppress a twinge of envy; others were indignant on their guru's behalf. Naren, from what they had heard, had projected only himself during his sojourn in the West. He hadn't spoken a word about Ramkrishna.

Vivekananda looked at his erstwhile companions, standing stiff and silent and unsure of how to react, and decided to take the initiative. 'Why are you huddling together in a knot as if you're afraid of me?' he asked smiling. 'Have I changed in any way? Am I wearing a coat and hat and talking in English? Oré I'm still one of you. I'm your old Naren.' Then, thumping Latu Maharaj on the back, he cried, 'Kiré Leto! Why is your face all crumpled up like a fried brinjal? The rest of you is nice and plump.' At this Latu put out a hand and stroked Vivekananda's back and chest lovingly. 'You haven't changed at all Naren,' he said. 'Yet we hear such reports of you. You travel from place to place in Bilet and America and knock the sahebs and mems over with your lectures. So many people come to hear you that the audience spills out into the streets. "Who but Naren could achieve such distinction?" I tell everybody. "He's the one Thakur picked out from among us for his special blessing."'

At these words the tears rose in Vivekananda's eyes. 'Leto,' he said softly, 'Your hand on my breast makes me feel whole again. I've missed you all so much . . . so much.' His voice trailed away. Then, dashing the tears away, he became his old cocky self.

531

'Won't you offer me a hookah?' he exclaimed. 'I'm sick to death of cigars.' Someone hurried forward with a hookah. Now Vivekananda seated himself crosslegged on the floor exactly the way he used to, his back resting against the wall, and took a deep pull. 'Ahh!' he breathed in satisfaction as the smoke curled into his lungs. 'There's nothing like sitting with old friends. I haven't felt so good in years.' Now his co-disciples came forward and sat around him in a circle. 'Naren,' Shibananda asked, 'I hear you've established many centres in America for disseminating the message of the Vedantas. Is that true?'

'I'll tell you about that later. Let's talk about old times. *Ha re* Tarak! Do you still feed the jackals? I remember how you used stand at a window in the house in Barahnagar and call out into the night, "Bhonda! Bhonda!" A baby jackal used to come slinking through the woods crying "Ghon! Ghon!' and you used to throw him pieces of ruti.' Vivekananda's imitation of both Tarak and the jackal was so life-like that everybody burst out laughing. The stiffness went out of Vivekananda's old friends and they started warming towards him. No one slept that night. They huddled together as they used to in the past, exchanging news and reminiscing till dawn.

A few days later Vivekananda was invited to the royal palace of Shobhabazar by Raja Radhakanta Deb. Here, under a vast structure set up in the palace *chatal,* five thousand people were gathered to felicitate him—many important personages of the city among them. No one had heard Vivekananda speak before but they had all received glowing reports of the power and passion of his rhetoric and were eager to hear him. But he began on the mildest of notes: 'I stand before you today—not as a sanyasi or a religious preacher. Look on me as one of your own boys who was born and spent his life in this great city. *Janani janma bhumischa swargadapi gariashi.* Who can forget these words?' This was the first of many meetings and many addresses the delivering of which became more and more strenuous everyday.

But, despite the hectic pace of his life, Vivekananda's dream of establishing a mission which would be engaged in selfless service, did not fade. The country was in a worse state now than ever before. He realized that on his return. Famine after famine were ravaging the land and people were dying like flies. Added to that was the plague which, originating in Surat, was spreading on a killer wave across the land. Any moment, now, and it would engulf the whole country. There was work to be done; a great deal of work. But before plunging in he had to find workers, sensitize them and band them together.

One day Girish Ghosh came to see him. Vivekananda rose and embraced his old friend tenderly. 'On which board are you working GC?' he asked, 'You move so fast that it is difficult to keep track.'

'I stick with those who can hold me,' Girish Ghosh replied with a smile. 'I'm back with Star at present. But let's not talk about me. Tell me about your exploits in the land of the sahebs. I hear you've even changed your name. But I'll tell you straight away that I refuse to call you Vivekananda. It sounds too distant and formal. I shall continue to call you Naren.'

'Certainly. Call me whatever you wish. What are you writing these days? I'll never forget your *Bilwamangal*. Is it running anywhere? I should like to see it again.'

'That can be arranged. But you don't look well at all Naren. You're only thirty-four and there are white streaks in your hair and rings under your eyes. You were such a handsome man only four years ago.'

'People talk of my fame and success abroad. They don't realize how hard I had to work. I drove myself so relentlessly that at times I felt the blood bursting out of my veins into my head and heart!'

'Hmph! I can see that well enough.'

'You're just the same as ever. Plump and comfortable like a well-fed hen. Are you still chasing the wenches? Or have you grown too old for that? And what about Ma Kali's prasad? How many glasses do you put away each night?' Vivekananda dug an elbow in his friend's ribs, then called out to the servant, 'Oré! Bring in a hookah.'

'You haven't given up your hookah I see. And you speak the same language.'

'I am the same person. I have to be flippant at times or I'll die of boredom.'

Now Girish hemmed and hawed a little. Then, taking a

desperate plunge, he said, 'I wish to ask you a question Naren. The other day, at Raja Radhakanta Deb's meeting, you spoke for quite a long time about our guru Sri Ramkrishna. Yet, in England and America, you didn't even mention his name. He's the avatar of the present age. But no one has heard of him except here in Bengal.'

Vivekananda was silent for a while. Then he said somewhat ruefully. 'It isn't true that I didn't mention him at all in my lectures abroad. I have talked about him in small groups and to my special friends. My disciples have all been initiated in the name of Sri Ramkrishna Paramhansa Deb. But I avoided extolling him as an avatar in the larger gatherings. That, I felt, would have an adverse effect. The people of the West don't want a new religion or a new avatar. Their own Christ is avatar enough for them. They live in an age of science and can respond only to the logical and rational. And that's what I did. I appealed to their reason and logic and won them over.'

'I really don't see how. Why were they willing to listen to you? They are rich and prosperous and believe in enjoying themselves.'

'That's just it. The more the physical enrichment the greater the poverty of the spirit. Most Americans sense a vacuum in their lives and hanker for some spiritual solace. I went to them with a bargain. "You give us technical and scientific knowledge," I said, "and we'll give you a philosophy that will pour the balm of peace on your tortured souls." He stopped short for a moment as if contemplating what to say next. 'You may have heard that I plan to open a mission in Thakur's name—'

'A mission!' Girish exclaimed. 'Like the Christians? I've heard that missionaries travel to the most inaccessible parts of the world and distribute bread and biscuits among the naked aborigines. Is that what you're going to do next?'

'I'm not joking GC,' Vivekananda said solemnly. 'I intend to get together a band of *brahmacharis* and *brahmacharinis* who will dedicate themselves to self service. They'll go from village to village educating the masses. And by education I don't mean literacy. That too, but more important even than teaching people to read and write is to inculcate in them a sense of self respect and self worth. The country must awake from her deathlike stupour and—'

'*Bhai ré*!' Girish cried out in a tormented voice. 'You've been away from the country for so long—you know nothing about the condition it is in. Men are not men anymore. Sickness and starvation have dehumanized them so greatly that husbands are pushing their wives into the river and grabbing their share of food. Sons are murdering their fathers. Mothers are selling their children. The list is endless. Reports come in, every day, of corpses rotting in their beds. Their near and dear ones, on the verge of death themselves, have neither the means nor the strength to burn or bury them. Jackals slink into the huts of peasants in broad daylight and feed on human flesh—both living and dead. It's a dark tunnel we're passing through; an endless one with not the faintest sign of light.' Vivekananda tried to speak but no words came. His lips trembled and tears ran down his cheeks. He rose and left the room.

After the meeting with Girish, Vivekananda turned all his energies into establishing the mission of his dreams. The first area that needed tackling, he decided, was that of women's education. Ignorant mothers bred ignorant children. He needed teachers for the work and funds—of course. The latter was being arranged through the efforts of Olé Bull, Joe Macleod and Mr Sturdy. But what about teachers? Women, in this conservative society, would refuse to be taught by males. But only ten to twelve per cent of Indian women were literate out of which only one per cent had the ability to teach others. He considered sending for Margaret Noble. Margaret had expressed a desire to come to India and work for his mission. But would she be able to adjust to the alien environment and culture? She didn't know the language and had no idea of the heat and humidity; the filth and pollution of India. What was more important—would his countrywomen accept a foreigner as their teacher?

Famous and busy though he was, Vivekananda thought of his days in America with nostalgia. Of Joe and Margaret and Mrs Hale. Sometimes, in his dreams, he saw himself addressing a large gathering in Detroit, of striding down the streets of Chicago, of strolling gently up and down the beach of Thousand Islands. Then, when he awoke, he wondered if the reality had been a dream after all. Had he really travelled to the other side of the world, to a continent discovered just a few centuries ago, thousands and thousand of miles away?

One day Vivekananda was invited to a midday meal at Priyanath Mukherjee's house in Bagbazar along with several other eminent men of Calcutta. As they sat chatting of this and that a servant stepped into the room with the news that a man stood outside waiting to see Swamiji. He had been told that a meeting was impossible, at this hour, but he wouldn't take no for an answer. Vivekananda came out and was surprised to see that the man was an ascetic. He wore a soiled saffron robe and turban and carried a bundle slung across one shoulder. As soon as he saw Vivekananda the man put his hand in his bundle and, taking out a picture, handed it over. Vivekananda looked down to find that it was the picture of a plump, well-fed cow. He looked up enquiringly. The sanyasi explained that he was a member of a sabha that worked for the protection of the cow and that he had come to Swamiji for assistance.

'What exactly do you do?' Vivekananda asked.

'We're against cow slaughter. We're trying to save our Cow Mother from the hands of the butchers.'

'But when a cow grows old and her master has no use for her—what happens then?'

'We are planning to build asylums, all over the country, where aged and sick cows will be looked after.'

'Very good,' Vivekananda said. 'But I'm sure you've heard that there's a famine raging in the country. The newspapers report that nine lakhs of men, women and children have died of starvation. And these are figures released by the Government. The reality is far grimmer. More are dying everyday. What is your sabha doing for the famine stricken?'

'That's not our concern. Our work is to save the Cow Mother. It she is allowed to suffer our great Hindu religion will fall into a decline and—'

'I understand that. But human beings are important too, aren't they? Don't you think you should put aside the interests of the Cow Mother for the present and work to save the people of your country?'

'Put aside the interests of the Cow Mother!' The man echoed, staring at Vivekananda as if at a madman. 'Moshai! The famine is God's curse on men and women. They have sinned and are paying

the penalty. *As you sow, so shall you reap.* It's their Karma. Who
are we to interfere?'

At this Vivekananda lost his temper completely. 'I have no
sympathy with your cause,' he shouted. 'You direct all your
energies towards the welfare of beasts and are totally impervious
to the sufferings of your fellow men. Karma indeed!'

'Don't you believe in Karma?'

'If the sufferings of a man is attributed to his Karma why not
that of a cow? Perhaps it's the cow's Karma that led her to the
abattoir.'

'The Shastras say the cow is our Mother.' The man looked at
Vivekananda in bewilderment.

'I've no doubt she is. From which other womb could worthy
sons like you emerge to see the light of the world?'

Vivekananda's irony was lost on the man. 'I came to you with
a lot of hope,' he said sadly. 'We're badly in need of funds.'

Vivekananda burst out laughing. 'You've come to the wrong
place. I'm a sanyasi. A fakir. I'm begging from door to door trying
to find money for my own work. I have nothing to give you,
friend.' Then, sobering down, he added, 'I believe in the cause of
humans before animals. I believe in feeding the hungry first, then
educating the illiterate. Religion is last on my list.'

Chapter XX

Amarendranath Datta's passion for the theatre went as far back as he could remember. He had spent the long summer afternoons of his boyhood banding his siblings and cousins into a drama troupe and putting up plays on a makeshift stage set up in the drawing room of his father's house. In his teens he had haunted the playhouses of Calcutta seeing every play that was being performed including the English ones. He had roamed the streets of Sahebpara collecting magazines and books on the subject. He had no interest in his father's business. From the age of seventeen he had decided that he was an artist and would express himself on the public stage—not only as an actor but as manager and director. Now, in his early manhood, he was able to realize his dream. His father was dead and the property divided. He was rich and independent. After Ardhendushekhar's exit from Emerald it had changed hands a couple of times and now lay idle and ownerless. Amarendra's first step was to lease Emerald and renovate it thoroughly. Side by side he launched on the process of theatre making. Everyone thought it to be an idle whim and predicted that he would go the way of all the other pampered darlings of wealthy houses who had preceded him in the theatre business. But Amarendra was made of different mettle. 'I was born on the first of April,' he told those who thought fit to express their concern. 'I intend to make April fools of everyone of you.'

Amarendra knew everything there was to know about the theatre companies of Calcutta. Slowly but ruthlessly and systematically he started drawing out the best actors and actresses, dance and music masters, set and costume designers, technicians and general workers from the other companies and making them his own with the offer of better salaries and perquisites. They were all, without exception, young, energetic and talented. He avoided the elderly. They were set in their ways and wouldn't obey him.

Taking their places in the hall, for the first time, the playgoers were astonished at the transformation. The old Emerald, with its bug-lined wooden seats and mice scampering down the aisle, was metamorphosed into an enchanted palace. The audience gazed awe-struck at the crystal lamps blazing with light, the pile carpet so deep and soft that the feet sank into it, the rich velvet of the chairs and the magnificient brocade curtain. And when it went up for the first scene a gasp of wonder rose from the hall at the beauty of the set. It was a lavishly appointed drawing room with real sofas and elaborately carved chairs, carpets on the floor and paintings and mirrors on the walls. There were flowers in vases and a cockatoo in a dangling cage. And for the next scene the entire set was wheeled away and another took its place in the twinkling of an eye. This was a trick Amarendra had picked up from the English theatre magazines he had read. Backdrops and wings, even furniture would have wheels fixed under them to make movement swift and silent. Everyone watching the play was forced to admit that the young man had ushered in a new age in the history of the theatre.

Amarendra had started rehearsing several plays at the same time. But being a perfectionist he was not ready to perform till they met his exacting standards. His plan was to stage a Bengali adaptation of *Hamlet* as his debut. Girish Ghosh had tried his hand at Shakespeare before him but he had merely translated the play retaining the time and place in all its authenticity. The backdrop had shown the hills of Scotland and the cast had been dressed like Englishmen and women. Amarendra laughed snidely remembering Girish Ghosh as Macbeth. The man was old and fat and looked ridiculous in his soldier's garb. And, despite the fact that he had played the lead role, his play had been a flop. The public hadn't taken to it. The treatment of *Hamlet* was quite different. Amarendra had lifted the narrative and transported it to another time and place. *Hariraj*, for that was the name of the hero and the play, was set in an ancient kingdom of east India. The characters wore Indian costume and spoke Bengali with the hint of a dialect.

Two or three months went by, but though Amarendra had a full cast, he felt restless and dissatisfied. The actresses, particularly the heroine, were not up to the mark. Women from the upper classes had a certain innocence about them. Their eyes

shone out upon the world with confidence and trust. The women
he was working with were prostitutes whose lives had recorded a
painful, sordid struggle. This struggle was reflected in the sly,
scheming hardness of their eyes. Yet they were being made to play
queens and princesses! Amarendra shook his head sadly. There
was one, only one, who had the look he sought. Long, liquid eyes
fringed with dewy lashes, had held the audience in thrall play
after play. They had the innocence of a stricken doe. He could
never forget those eyes. He wanted her. He had to have her. He
had been rejected once but he would try again. He sighed at the
thought that there were so many would-be actresses crowding at
the door that the darwan was having a hard time fending them
off. Yet the one he sought had no use for him.

Two days later, the man deputed to keep track of Nayanmoni
came bursting into the room. 'It's done sir,' he exclaimed. 'The
girl has been released. I don't know how much she paid Saheb
Mustafi but he's let her off. She's free to join any board she
pleases. I got the news from Gangamoni herself.'

'Why doesn't she come to me then?'

'There's a snag,' the man pulled a face.

'Another snag? What is it now? More money?'

'No, no. She doesn't care about money. She wants you to
request her personally.'

'Let's go.' Amarendranath rose to his feet instantly. 'I'm
running a theatre. I cannot afford the luxury of playing tit for tat.
I'll convince myself that Irving is on his way to meet Ellen Terry.'

As the carriage rolled up to the gate of Gangamoni's house,
curious passersby stopped in their tracks to catch a glimpse of the
man who had revolutionized the world of the theatre. 'Amar
Datta! Amar Datta!' they whispered excitedly to one another,
'Ah! What a handsome man. Just like a prince!' Amarendra
brushed past the crowd milling around his carriage and walked
into the house. Word had already reached Gangamoni and she
came puffing and panting down the stairs to receive her
illustrious visitor. So did Nayanmoni—not in haste but with
slow, measured steps. Gangamoni stooped low and touched his
feet. He was the master of the company and deserved all the
respect he could get particularly after the way Nayanmoni had
treated him. But Nayanmoni herself only brought her palms

together in a namaskar. He was younger than her. She wouldn't touch his feet.

Amarendra gazed in wonder at the vision of loveliness that stood before him. She wore a simple cotton sari of a deep orange hue. Her hair was open and her neck and ams were bare. Yet she looked as regal as a princess. Amarendra turned to his secretary Ashutosh Babu with a meaningful glance whereupon he cleared his throat and began: 'We have heard that you've been released from your bond. Is that true?'

'Quite true.'

'That means you're free to join Classic?'

'I am—if you want me to.'

'Have the papers been destroyed? We don't want any legal tangles.'

'There were no papers. The bond was made purely on trust.'

'Very good. We are prepared to pay you one hundred and fifty rupees a month. A carriage will pick you up and bring you back. You'll have to obey Amarendra Babu's orders to the letter. Rehearsals will go on for as long as he thinks fit—the whole night if necessary. Do you accept these conditions?'

'I do.'

Now Amarendra Datta addressed her directly. 'Why did you force me to come here?' he asked sternly. 'You should have come to me yourself. Don't you think my time is more valuable than yours?' Nayanmoni blushed. 'I was ashamed,' she said softly, 'I sent you away once. I didn't know how to face you again.'

'Hmph! How old are you?'

'Twenty-seven.'

'No, no,' Gangamoni hastened to correct her. 'She's twenty-three. She doesn't know her right age.' Nayanmoni bit her lip trying not to smile. 'You're twenty-one,' Amarendra said firmly. 'My heroine cannot be older than me. I'll raise my age to twenty-four and you must lower yours to at least three years less than mine. The handbills will describe you as a sixteen-year-old beauty. Is that clear?' Nayanmoni burst out laughing. 'How can a woman of twenty-seven pass for sixteen? I'm afraid I'm not the heroine for you.'

'Of course you are,' Gangamoni cried excitedly. 'You can easily pass for sixteen with proper make-up on. Leave that to me.'

541

'That's settled then.' Amarendra now turned to Gangamoni. 'Aren't you going to offer me some refreshment?' he asked her smiling. 'I've come to your house for the second time. A guest is never sent hungry away from a Hindu household.' Gangamoni touched her ears and bit her tongue. 'You're such a great man Babu!' she said humbly. 'Your family is one of the noblest and most illustrious in the land. If I even dreamed that you would touch a drop of water in my house I would have—'

'Why? What's wrong with your water?'

'High-caste Hindus like you spurn us as the lowest of worms. They consider our touch polluting.' Amarendra took her hand in his and said gently, 'I've touched you. Am I changed in any way? Will the sandesh and rosogolla you serve me taste different because you handled them? We're all members of the same profession. We share a common caste.' Then, laughing at her bewilderment, he added, 'However, you needn't trouble yourself sending out for sweets this very instant. I detest sweets. I'll come another day and eat a meal you've cooked.'

'I'm not such a good cook Babu. That's our Nayanmoni. She's excellent. She prepares a special dish of *koi* fish with one side of the fish curried hot with chillies and mustard and the other tart and sweet.'

Amarendra Datta rose from his chair without comment. Walking over to a portrait on the wall he scrutinized it carefully. Two young women stood holding hands.

'Who are they?' he asked Gangamoni.

'This one is me,' Gangamoni answered with a wry smile. 'I was young and slim then.'

'And the other?'

'Binodini.'

'Ah! I've heard of Binodini but I've never seen her. She left the stage quite suddenly I hear. Why was that?'

'She had a skin disease that disfigured her face. It might have been leucoderma. Or even leprosy. She's become a recluse.'

'What sort of an actress was she?'

'Well Babu, I have to admit that she was a born actress. Very forceful. She could rain fire from her eyes one moment and tears the next.'

One morning as Amarendra sat in his private office sipping tea he heard the carriage that conveyed the four main actresses to and from the theatre roll in through the gate. Glancing idly out of the window he was shocked to see the shutters wide open and the girls spilling out with great clamour and laughter. Amarendra's brows came together in annoyance. He had made it quite clear to his female cast that he expected them to conduct themselves with due decorum; to keep the shutters of the carriage closed and to step in and out of it in dignified silence. He didn't want the public to recognize them or call out to them. Sending for the coachman Rahmat Ali he said sternly, 'You'll have to pay a heavy penalty for disobeying my orders. Half your monthly wages.' Rahmat burst into tears. 'It wasn't my fault huzoor!' he cried. 'I kept telling them to keep the shutters closed but they wouldn't listen. One Didi insisted on getting off at a bangle shop in Kolutola. The others followed.'

'Which one was it?'

'The Didi who plays Morjina in *Ali Baba*. Nayanmoni Didi. She cried "Stop! Stop!" How could I disobey her?'

Amarendra dismissed Rahmat and began pacing up and down the room wondering what to do. His rules were strict but everyone obeyed them to the letter. Everyone—with the exception of Nayanmoni. She made light of them with such feckless charm that he felt powerless before her. And he couldn't take any punitive action against her either. She didn't care for money and even the prospect of losing her job didn't frighten her. It was he who couldn't afford to lose her. Yet he had to find some way of controlling her or else the others would follow her example and pandemonium would set in.

Amarendra called out to a servant and bade him fetch Nayanmoni, Kusum Kumari and Sarojini. Then, when they entered the room, he fixed a penetrating glance on each one's face, turn by turn, and questioned sternly: 'Why did you stop the carriage and get down at Kolutola?' Kusum Kumari and Sarojini quailed before that glance and nudged Nayanmoni who answered calmly, 'There's a trinket shop in Kolutola with the loveliest of stuff. We stopped to buy some bangles. They'll go well with the costumes in *Ali Baba*.'

'If you needed bangles why didn't you tell Baral Babu? He's in

543

charge of the costumes.'

'Baral Babu has no taste. He chooses the most lurid colours.'

'You claim to know better than the dresser? I've told you several times that you're not to stop the carriage and show yourselves to the public. You even kept the windows open. Why?'

'It was very hot and stuffy in the carriage. We were feeling suffocated.'

'How many minutes does it take to get to the theatre? Don't you have a bit of endurance? Anyway, take care to keep the windows closed in future and—'

'Why?' Nayanmoni interrupted sharply. 'Are we in purdah?' Then, breaking into a fit of giggles, she added, 'We're not daughters-in-law of a *Bene* household that we must keep our faces hidden from the sun and the moon.'

'Stop laughing,' Amarendra ordered sternly. 'Take care to obey my rules in future.'

'These rules were not included in the contract.'

'What of it? Everything cannot be put down in black and white. What I'm doing is for the good of the theatre and—'

'How can it harm the theatre if you allow a little fresh air to blow on our faces?'

'The public sees you on the stage in gorgeous costumes and make-up. The glamour will wear off if you appear before them as you really are. "She's no prettier than our wives and sisters," the men will tell themselves. The awe will go out of their eyes and the theatre will lose its appeal.'

'Do people come to see us only for our looks? Don't they come to see our acting? You play the hero's role. But you move about freely in the streets without make-up.'

'It's different for men. I don't want any more argument Nayan. You'll have to travel with the shutters closed and the door shut. That's final.'

Nayanmoni turned to the others. 'Do you find such a rule acceptable?' Sarojini and Kusum Kumari looked down at their feet not daring to reply. Nayanmoni drew herself to her full height. Looking Amarendra Datta straight in the eyes, she said, 'I can't travel in a closed carriage. I feel choked. From tomorrow I shall hire a carriage for myself.' Amarendra was so taken aback at this flagrant breach of discipline that he opened his mouth to speak but no words came. 'People don't recognize us without our make-up,' Nayanmoni went on blandly. 'No one bothers to cast a glance on us.' Amarendra Datta was too shocked to reply.

A couple of days later Nayanmoni arrived around eleven o' clock in the morning to find the stage set for a special rehearsal. All the lights were burning and on a special chair, in one corner, a gentleman sat obviously waiting to see it. Nayanmoni stared at the stranger unable to tear her eyes from his face. She had never seen a handsomer man or one more stately. The heroes with whom she worked were as nothing compared to him. He was a man in his prime, about thirty-six or thirty-seven years of age, tall and well-built with a broad chest and strong muscular limbs. Thick silky black hair fell in wavy locks to his shoulders and covered his cheeks and chin. His eyes were large and lustrous and his fingers long and slender like on artist's. He wore a finely puckered dhuti and an immaculately white muslin kurta as soft as down. His feet in black velvet slippers seemed carved out of ivory. From the way Amar Datta hovered around him Nayanmoni realized that he was a very important person.

'Who's he?' Nayanmoni whispered to Kusum Kumari.

'He's the writer of the play we're rehearsing today. He has come to see the rehearsal.'

The information startled Nayanmoni. Girish Ghosh was the acknowledged master playwright of Calcutta. The other, lesser, ones hovered in his shadow. No one bothered about them. Who was this man and why was he getting so much importance? Then one of the actors whispered in her ear that the man was not only a playwright and a talented actor and singer, he was also a renowned poet and a scion of the Thakurs of Jorasanko. His name was Rabindranath. He had written the play *Raja o Rani* and had come to see the rehearsal prior to giving his consent to its performance. On hearing that the man was an actor Nayanmoni was seized with a strange longing. She wished she could act opposite him even if it was only once in her whole life.

The rehearsal commenced. Rabindranath sat in silence, his dark clear gaze fixed on the actors and actresses. He didn't interrupt even once though the cast was making more mistakes than usual. It was part of the family etiquette of the Thakurs to speak only when spoken to. Amar Datta waited in vain, for some response. Then, fidgeting a little, he asked nervously, 'What do you think of it Rabindra Babu?' Now Rabindra moved slightly in his chair. 'The prose lines are being rendered very well. But the poetry—' He cleared his throat and added somewhat hesitantly, 'The emphasis is in the wrong place, at times.'

'I know,' Amarendra hastened to agree. 'The trouble is that the cast is used to the blank verse of Michael and the *Bhanga Payar* of Girish Ghosh. The metrical system you use is new to them.'

'It isn't difficult to pick up. Take these lines for instance. You spoke them like this:

'*Eshechho pashani?*
Daya hoyechhe ki moné?

'Now if you were to intone them like this—
'*Eshechho pashani?*
Daya—
Hoyechhe ki moné?

'The emphasis should fall on the word *daya*. There should be a gap of six syllables after that and the rhyme scheme will be maintained.' Then, rising from his chair, he addressed Nayanmoni: 'Rani Sumitra! Do this scene with me. Let's begin from *Aramé royéchhé tara.*'

Nayanmoni's desire to act with Rabindranath was partially fulfilled. It was only for a few moments but the impact on her was profound. His voice, deep and resonant, rang in her ears for hours afterwards. The touch of his hand on her shoulder made the blood pound in her breast and set her senses quivering every time she remembered it. It was as though she had felt a man's touch for the first time in her life.

'You are quite good,' Rabindra told her at the end of the scene. 'Your pronunciation is perfect.' Nayanmoni stooped to touch his feet. Taking her chin he raised her face gently to his and asked, 'Have I seen you before? Your face is familiar.' Nayanmoni shook her head. A puzzled frown appeared on the poet's face. 'Why is it that I feel I've seen you? Not once . . . several times . . . something to do with a play. Ah yes! It was in Cuttack. Have you ever acted in one of my plays? In Cuttack?' Nayanmoni shook her head again. 'It was someone else then,' Rabindra murmured almost to himself. 'A group of amateurs put up my

Balmiki Pratibha some years ago in Cuttack. There was a girl in
the cast called Mohilamoni. Very bright and talented. She looked
a lot like you. Her profile in particular. Do you have a sister in
Cuttack? Or a cousin?'

'No.' Nayanmoni found her voice at last. 'I have no family in
Cuttack.' Then, lowering her head, she murmured to herself
much as Rabindranath had done a few moments ago. 'I have no
one—anywhere. I am alone. Quite alone.'

Chapter XXI

Sarala needed no one's permission to leave the house these days. She had a carriage and coachman of her own and was free to come and go as she chose. The members of her family, including the maternal branch at Jorasanko, had resigned themselves to the idea that she would live life on her own terms. Never had such a dynamic, fiercely independent young woman been seen in their family or, indeed, in any of the families known to them. At the time, high-caste Hindu women still kept themselves discreetly within the confines of the house. They didn't wear burqas like their Muslim counterparts but covered their faces with the ends of their saris at the sight of males other than fathers and brothers. Brahmo women enjoyed more freedom but still couldn't dream of leaving the house without a male escort. Sarala's mother was a Brahmo; her father a Hindu. She had inherited the enlightened, liberal outlook of her mother's family but there was a great deal in the Hindu religion that met with her approval. She knew many eminent Hindus. Bankimchandra and Balgangadhar Tilak were her father's friends. And she, herself, took quite a lively interest in the teachings of Swami Vivekananda.

Sarala was twenty-five and still unwed. Her parents had searched high and low for a suitable son-in-law and brought scores of proposals. But Sarala rejected each one of them on one pretext or the other. Yet she had no intention of remaining a spinster. She made this announcement openly and quite often. She would marry but only the man who was worthy of her. But where was such a man? Exhausted with their efforts her parents gave up their search. Now it was up to her to find a husband for herself.

But Sarala was not in a hurry to find a husband. She found a job instead. Taking up the post of Assistant Superintendent of Maharani Girl's College, she travelled to distant Mysore, alone and unescorted—an unheard of thing in those days. She was charmed with her quarters, a small two-storeyed bungalow with wide verandas, standing in a neat garden stocked with flowers and some fine old fruit trees. Inside, the house was papered and furnished with elegance and taste. A cook, an ayah and a servant together with two sepoys at the gate made up the domestic staff.

It hadn't taken long for Sarala to settle down. She liked the work. The climate was excellent and she had made several good friends. Yet she had to return to Calcutta before the year was out. Here, as in Calcutta, young aspirants for her hand started buzzing around her like bees in a hive. Sarala was used to that and knew how to fend them off. But one night she had a frightening experience.

It was the middle of summer and terribly hot. The ayah, who usually slept on the floor of Sarala's bedroom, had moved her bedding to the stair landing in the hope of catching some cooler air. It was well after midnight and everyone was fast asleep. Even the sepoys at the gate had dozed off, their heads lolling on their breasts. Suddenly the ayah let out a bloodcurdling yell. Everyone came rushing to the scene including the sepoys who jumped up from their stools and bustled in with a great clatter of weapons. It took a few minutes to calm the woman down to the point when she could speak coherently. A man had come up the stairs, she said, and unable to see her in the dark, had stepped on her arm. She had woken up and screamed whereupon he had run and hidden himself in Sarala's dressing room. While the sepoys looked at one another fearfully it was Sarala who acted. Quick as a flash she rushed to the door of the dressing room and bolted it from outside. The man, desperate at being trapped thus, smashed the glass panes of a window and leaped down to the garden below. But he couldn't escape. He had injured himself in the fall and was easily captured. When the light was shone into his face it was discovered that he was no ordinary thief. He was the spoiled offspring of a very rich contractor and one of Sarala's suitors. This incident shook Sarala out of her complacence. She had prided herself on her ability to keep her suitors at bay by laughing their proposals away. But what could she do if one of them was desperate enough to try to take her by force?

Next day the news was splashed in all the local newspapers and within a day or two it had spread all over the country. Sarala had expected a sympathetic reaction from the journalists of

Calcutta but didn't get it. 'What can you expect,' the editor of
Bangabasi wrote, 'when a high-born young maiden is allowed to
run wild? Where was the need for her to take up a job? That too
so far away from her family and friends? It is nothing but a foolish
aping of European ways for which she has been justifiably
punished.'

Sarala was incensed at this but also acutely embarrassed. Not
only for herself but for her family. On hindsight she realized that
she had acted in haste without considering the pros and cons. She
didn't need the money. Her father made her a generous
allowance. She had a happy comfortable home and more freedom
than any other girl of her age and situation. She had, really, no
reason for taking up a job in the distant south. Now she had made
a fool of herself and was the laughing stock of everyone who
knew her. Left with no option but to return to Calcutta she began
packing her bags. But her heart sank every time she thought of the
snide remarks awaiting her. 'Back so soon Sarala?' She almost
heard her friends and relations cry out in feigned surprise, 'What
happened?'

But the train journey to Calcutta opened her eyes to several
facts about her native Bengal that set her planning her future
course of action. The programme she chalked out and
implemented, on her arrival, was so strenuous and demanding
that the unfortunate episode in Mysore soon became a distant
memory. Observing the strong virile bodies of the Marathas and
Rajputs, their powerful voices and hard facial contours, she
couldn't help comparing them to the malnourished Bengalis with
their drooping eyes, emaciated limbs and bellies swollen with
enlarged spleens. Even the peasants of the United Provinces and
Bihar were sturdily built and capable of hard physical work. The
Bengalis ate a poor diet, took little exercise and preferred to
cultivate their brains rather than their bodies. In consequence
they were weak and cowardly. But could the situation not be
changed? Couldn't Bengalis be taught the art of body building?
Couldn't they be encouraged to be fierce and warrior-like in
temperament?

As soon as Sarala reached Calcutta she took on the editorship
of *Bharati* and set about renovating the journal with her usual
dynamism. She solicited articles from renowned writers and

contributed a fair number of her own. One of them was titled 'The foreign sock versus the native knock'. In this article Sarala called upon the public to report instances in which they had seen their countrymen protesting against injustice and humiliation. 'The British, soldiers and civilians alike,' Sarala wrote, 'insult and knock us about in trains and steamers, on the streets and in public places. And they molest our women in the presence of fathers, brothers and husbands. Our men swallow the insults and go home, fuming, to take it out on their wives. At most they lodge a complaint in the Kotwali. Can they not protest there and then?' Sarala's plea did not go unheeded. Reports started coming in of stray incidents in which natives had shot back. In Calcutta, a young man had tied an abusive, drunken gora by the wrists and dragged him to the police station. In Barisal a ryot had beaten up an Englishman for pushing his wife into a pond and also made him serve a sentence. In Jessore a college student had snatched the raised whip from the hand of a saheb and broken it to pieces before his eyes. Sarala's heart lifted with triumph on reading these reports. Bengalis weren't all weak and cowardly. There was hope for them, yet.

Sarala realized that the need of the hour was to build up a youth force which would have the courage, strength and stamina to fight back when assaulted. This was the only way that the stigma of cowardice could be removed from the Bengali character. She decided to set up a network of akharas spanning the lanes and bylanes of Calcutta making a beginning in her own home. The Ghoshals had recently moved from Kashiabagan to a house in Circular Road which had a large tangled garden at the back with a pond in the middle. Here she set up her first akhara, employing a Muslim ustad called Murtaza to give the boys lessons in the art of attack and defence. Sarala made it a point to oversee the lessons every evening, often taking part in them herself. Her presence was like a magnet which drew hundreds of young men to her. Some, of course, had little interest in body building and came for other reasons. Sarala discovered, to her horror, that many of the young men who flocked to her house each evening lived in worlds of their own and were completely oblivious of and indifferent to the needs of their country. All they wanted was to hover around her and whisper sweet nothings in her ear. But Sarala knew how to dampen their ardour and managed to bring a number of them around to a more responsible frame of mind. One of the first things she did was to hang a large map of India on one wall of the drawing room. Everyone who came in was made to stand in front of the map and fold his hands in reverence before proceeding to the back of the house. The second was to tie red bands on the wrists of the young men and make them swear an oath: 'I solemnly pledge,' she made them repeat after her, 'that from this day onwards I shall serve my country with my heart and soul and body. I shall overcome all the hazards that lie in the path of preserving and cherishing the honour of my motherland. With this rakhi I seal my oath.' Thus she inculcated a feeling of respect for the country in the group she had formed around her and which was rapidly gaining in numbers.

One day a young man called Monilal Gangopadhyay came to her with a proposal. He belonged to a literary society which was to celebrate its Annual Day in a week or so. The members, it seemed, were keen on having Sarala as the chief guest. Sarala was surprised. A young woman presiding over a function that highlighted the activities of an all male club was an aberration. Besides, her contribution to literature was nothing compared to that of many others in the city. If at all they wanted a woman—wouldn't her mother be a better candidate? But Monilal wouldn't listen to a word of what she said. The members of his club wanted her and only her. And then, suddenly, an idea came to her head. She could use the forum to flag off a scheme she had been toying with for some months now. And that was to identify and launch a regional hero.

Balgangadhar Tilak had been immensely successful in Maharashtra both with his popularization of Ganesh Puja and his launching of Shivaji Maharaj as an icon for Maratha youth. Needless to say, the rest of India did not share these sentiments. English historians had no opinion of Shivaji. They called him 'the mountain rat', and denounced his perfidious killing of Afzal Khan. Indian intellectuals, from Bengal in particular, tended to agree with the British. But Tilak's defence of Shivaji was readily accepted by his own people and, to tell the truth, even by Sarala. Yet Sarala wanted an icon from her own region. After a good deal of deliberation she hit upon Pratapaditya. 'I'm willing to preside over your meeting,' she told Monilal, 'but upon one condition. You must help me organize a Pratapaditya Utsav. He was crowned king on the first of Vaisakh. Let us mark that day by honouring him. Start by collecting all the material you can find about his life and reign, then get one of your members to prepare a citation. Remember to give his courage and valour the utmost prominence. We will honour his memory—not with readings from literary texts but with demonstrations of physical prowess. Scour the streets of Calcutta and get together the best sword fencers, lathiyals and wrestlers. I shall present gold medals inscribed with the message *Deva durbalghataka* to the best performers.'

The first of Vaisakh arrived. Sarala stepped on to the dais dressed in a white silk sari with a veil partially covering her head. Her neck and arms were like moulded marble—stark and bare of adornment. Taking up a garland of blood-red hibiscus she hung it on the full-size oil painting of Pratapaditya that stood on one side. Then she took her seat without a word. The events commenced. Never had these obscure club premises of Bhabanipur witnessed so many people together. Crowds milled around the combats spilling out into the streets. People climbed trees and rooftops and peered through the windows of neighbouring houses. It was a historic moment! Bengalis, contemptuously dismissed by the other races of India as 'rice eating cowards', were wielding weapons and a beautiful young girl from one of the highest families in the land was standing on the dais calling out encouragement.

Next day the newspapers were full of praise for the occasion. Even a staid, conservative paper like the *Bangabashi* gushed admiration: 'Ah me!' the column read, 'What a sight these eyes beheld! What a gathering! No speeches, no readings, no thumping of tables. A great son of Bengal was honoured by demonstrations of unparalleled skill and valour! A high-born Brahmin maiden, tenderly reared, bestowed prizes of honour to the strongest and the bravest with her own delicate hands. It seemed as though the ten-armed goddess had stepped down from Heaven and taken refuge in her person.'

After this the Pratapaditya Utsav gained in popularity and

553

was celebrated in several other neighbourhoods of Calcutta. Enthused, Sarala began delving into the history of Bengal and discovering new heroes. One of them was Pratapaditya's son Udayaditya. No one had heard of Udyaditya for history held no glory for him. He had lost his kingdom to the Mughals. But what impressed Sarala was the fact that he had faced the vast army pitted against his own feeble one and fought alongside his soldiers to the death. Was not fighting and dying for one's country an act of valour? The time had come for the young men of India to emulate his example. Sarala set a date and started making arrangements for holding a meeting in honour of Udayaditya.

The venue chosen for the occasion was the celebrated Albert Hall on College Street and the eloquent speaker Kshirod Prasad Vidyavinod was invited to preside and address the audience. Despite a good deal of search no portrait of the dead hero could be procured. Sarala decided to set up a sword, instead, to which everyone who came would pay floral tribute. It was an antique sword, very valuable, with emeralds and diamonds studded around the hilt. Sarala had borrowed it from the family of a wealthy zamindar of Calcutta.

The meeting was to commence at four in the evening. However, a few minutes after noon, Shreesh Sen came running to Sarala with the news that the trustee of Albert Hall, Naren Sen, had locked them out. He had heard that the boys were going to worship a sword and, since natives weren't allowed to carry weapons, it might be considered a treasonable offence by the rulers. 'There's no way out,' Shreesh told Sarala. 'We'll have to cancel the meeting.'

'There *is* a way out,' Sarala answered, her face flaming. She swept inside the house and came out, a few seconds later. Thrusting a fistful of money into the hands of the gaping Shreesh she commanded him to go book another hall as close to Albert's as possible. 'We'll hold the meeting exactly as planned,' she cried. 'No one can stop us. The newspapers have carried the news. Hundreds of handbills have been distributed. How could Naren Babu do this to us? It's insufferable!'

Sarala dashed off a letter to Naren Sen that instant. Her sense of outrage was so great that her pen raced over the paper: 'If you try to stop the meeting,' she wrote, 'You'll have a whole nation against you. All the newspapers will carry the report that you, an elderly Hindu and an acknowledged leader of Bengal, lost your courage and tried to prevent the young men of the country from performing a symbolic worship of strength.'

Naren Sen's face clouded as he read these words. He had heard of Sarala Ghoshal's popularity and power over the younger generation. On the other hand, a worship of arms was a traitorous act and the rulers could come down heavily on him. Memories of the Sepoy Mutiny were still fresh in his mind. He sat, in glum silence, for a long time trying to make up his mind. Then, taking the key out of his pocket, he sent it along with a note to Sarala. She could hold the meeting if she wished, he wrote, but if there was trouble she would be held solely responsible.

In the few hours between this exchange of letters Shreesh Sen had booked Alfred Theatre on Harrison Road. It was very close to the Albert Hall and now Sarala had two options in place of none at all. Which one was it to be? Everyone would come to the latter for that was the venue publicized in the handbills. On the other hand it was important, Sarala felt, to expose Naren Sen for the cowardly retrograde that he was. Sarala decided to hold the meeting in Alfred Theatre. A group of volunteers were stationed outside Albert Hall to lead the people to the new venue.

Sarala didn't attend the meeting. While it went on she stood before the map of India in her mother's drawing room, her eyes closed in reverence. A wave of patriotic feeling swept over her. What a vast, what a great country was hers! Composed of so many races and cultures! So many religions! Hindus, Muslims, Sikhs, Christians and Buddhists had all found a place here! How blue the sky was here; how bright the sun! Yet it was being held in bondage by a small knot of men from a damp, fog-ridden island thousands of miles away. Her hands clenched and unclenched themselves with a passion she couldn't explain even to herself. Something must happen soon! She willed it with all her being. A wild tornado must come bursting from all directions shattering this structure of false governance and set her country free. Tears poured down her cheeks but they were tears of joy. Her lips parted and she sang softly:

'*Namah—Hindustan*
Har har har—Jai Hindustan

SUNIL GANGOPADHYAY

Sat sri Akaal—Hindustan
Allah ho Akhbar—Hindustan
Namah—Hindustan'

Chapter XXII

Dwarika and Basantamanjari descended from the train at Mughulsarai to encounter the noise and bustle of milling crowds. It was the evening before the Purna Kumbha when men and women from all parts of the country congregated at Prayag to bathe in the holy waters of the confluence of the Ganga, Jamuna and Saraswati. Legend had it that Jayanta, son of Indra, had stolen the kumbha or pot of *amrita* from the demons and was carrying it to heaven when his hand had trembled and a few drops had fallen into the water. It had taken him twelve days to reach his destination. A day's journey for a god being equivalent to a year's journey for a man, the sages declared that every twelve years amrita, which is inexhaustible and ever renewable, appears in the waters of the confluence. And he that drinks of it and bathes in it is blessed.

Dwarika was dressed in an impeccable English suit complete with bowler hat. An expensive jamawar shawl was draped over Basantamanjari's head and shoulders, the embroidered end of which was pulled low over her face. Holding her by the hand Dwarika pushed his way through the massed bodies his eyes darting here and there. He was looking for Ratikanta the official of his estate whom he had sent on in advance to make arrangements for their stay. Ratikanta was on the look-out too and a few minutes later all three were sitting in a buggy on their way to Allahabad.

Dwarika had prevailed on Basantamanjari and obtained her consent to the marriage. But it couldn't take place before the year of mourning his mother's death was over. Basantamanjari had insisted on it. He had suffered a number of other disappointments as well. He had wanted a solemn ceremony in accordance with Hindu rites. But not a single priest was ready to conduct it. Basantamanjari was not only a widow—she was a prostitute and, as such, an outcaste from Hindu society. An outraged Dwarika had decided to thumb his nose at the clergy and diehards by going through a civil ceremony and holding a grand reception afterwards which all the enlightened elite of the city would attend. But, to his shock and horror, only sixty-five guests turned up at a reception organized for fifteen hundred. Dwarika had ordered the rarest of delicacies for the occasion and he had to suffer the humiliation of seeing them thrown out on the street in heaps. So great was the quantity left over that enough beggars could not be found to consume it all. The people who had been most voluble in their encouragement of his venture had stayed away from the feast. It was this fact that had hit Dwarika the hardest. In his disgust he decided to leave the city. Now he wandered from one pilgrim spot to another as and when the whim took him.

'Uncover your face Basi,' Dwarika said to his wife as the horses broke into a canter. 'See how blue the sky is. And how the wings of the cranes shine like silver against it.' Basantamanjari pushed the shawl away and lifted her face to the sky. Her lips smiled but her eyes were moist with the tears she had shed in secret. 'You've been weeping again,' Dwarika admonished her tenderly.

'I keep wondering—'

'What?'

'My life was like a slender stream without ebb or flow. Then it swelled into a mighty river with many currents. I felt as though I was being sucked in. I wonder where the tide is taking me now.'

'Again!' Dwarika said with a touch of impatience. 'Again you start your foolish prattle about streams and rivers. There are many rivers in the world. We've seen some and we'll see more. We may even go to Puri and see the sea. But they have nothing to do with your life.'

'Beyond the sea lies the ocean,' Basantamanjari murmured dreamily. 'Rivers pour their waters into the sea which, in turn, merges with the ocean. Shall we see the ocean?'

'Yes—if we go to Kanyakumari. Would you like that?'

'Yes. But what if the ocean swallows me up? What if I'm borne away on its waves?'

'What nonsense you talk! So many people visit Kanyakumari and return safe and sound. Why should you be borne away?'

'I don't know. But I seem to see something like that happening to me. I see myself being lost in a great expanse of turbulent water . . .'

'We won't bathe in the sea,' Dwarika said hastily. 'We'll sprinkle some water on our heads and—' Basantamanjari smiled at the look on Dwarika's face. 'I can swim,' she said pressing his hand in reassurance.

They reached Allahabad after midnight. The house Ratikanta had rented for them in Nurganj was neat and comfortable and Dwarika was pleased with the arrangements. After washing away the grime and fatigue of the journey Dwarika had a lavish meal and came and stood on a veranda overlooking the river. It was nearly two o'clock but the scene outside was alive with noise and movement. People walked up and down, the lanterns in their hands dotting the dark like glow worms. In between the specks of swinging light Dwarika's eyes discerned dim, dark shapes lying on the bank. They were evidently sleepers wrapped in blankets. 'Basi!' he called out to his wife who stood before a mirror inside the room combing her long black hair, 'Come here and stand beside me.' Basantamanjari hesitated. She had taken off her jacket and chemise and her neck and one shoulder were bare. Dwarika took off his shawl and wrapped it around her. 'The night is dark,' he whispered as he took her hand and led her to the veranda, 'No one will see us.'

'There are so many people down there,' Basantamanjari said in a wondering voice. 'Do you think any of them know us?'

'It's not likely. Bengalis prefer to go to Gangasagar which is nearer home. However, some do come to Prayag.'

'I thought I saw someone just now. Someone we know.'

'Nonsense! It's as dark as pitch out there. You couldn't possibly have seen anyone's face.'

'I didn't see his face. I recognized his walk. I don't know who he is. But I'm sure I've seen that walk before.'

'You're crazy!' Dwarika's tone was indulgent but he sounded a little worried.

'Let's go to the Triveni,' Basantamanjari's voice came suddenly out of the dark, eager and expectant as if hanging on his reply.

'At this time of the night? Nonsense! Besides I've already dismissed the carriage.'

'We'll walk. After all we have the whole night before us. We'll stroll along the river as slowly as we please. Won't it be fun?'

'No it won't. Don't you feel the chill rising from the water? I'm frozen. Let's go in.'

Placing a hand on Basantamanjari's shoulder he consoled her with the promise, 'We'll go tomorrow at break of dawn. We'll watch the sun rise over the confluence.'

'Let's stay awake till then,' Basantamanjari begged. 'There are only a few hours left. I don't feel like wasting them in sleep.'

'Yes—if you promise to sing to me all night.'

Putting his arm around her Dwarika led her in. Then he stretched himself out on the bed his head in her lap. 'I'm so happy,' Basantamanjari murmured running her fingers through his hair, 'So happy! If we could only sit like this under a tree—its branches waving and its leaves shimmering above our heads.' Dwarika, exhausted by the rigours of the journey and lulled by the warm comfort of his beloved's lap, muttered sleepily, 'In spring . . . on the way to Brindavan . . . Sing to me Basi,' before floating away on the wings of slumber. Basantamanjari laid his head down gently on the pillow.

Basantamanjari woke Dwarika up at cock crow. But Dwarika only snuggled deeper into the warm cocoon of his satin quilt and murmured indistinctly, 'We'll go another day.'

'No,' Basantamanjari said firmly. 'We'll go today. You promised me.' Dwarika sat up with a groan. Then, splashing some water on his burning eyes and struggling into his clothes, he ordered the carriage. In a few minutes the two were on their way to Prayag.

They reached the confluence to find a huge hibiscus-coloured sun already risen over the edge of the river its red gold reflection trembling on the still dark water. Thousands of pilgrims thronged the waterfront and innumerable heads could be seen bobbing up and down in the river. No separate ghat was assigned for women. They bathed within inches of strange men, then rose and walked away oblivious of the glances that followed their dripping forms. Dwarika turned to the veiled figure by his side and said, 'Women don't observe purdah on this day Basi. How can you see anything if you keep your face covered?' At his words Basantamanjari pushed her veil aside and looked around, her eyes wide with curiosity. 'I recognize this place,' she said after a while, 'I think I've come here before.'

'You've heard about it. That's why it seems familiar.'

'Let's go there,' Basantamanjari pointed a finger to her right.

'Why?' Dwarika asked, surprised. 'The left side is much better. It's quieter and cleaner.'

'No, no. We must go right. We must.'

'Silly girl,' Dwarika laughed indulgently. 'You're behaving as though you really know the place. Very well then. Let's go.'

Basantamanjari walked rapidly ahead, Dwarika following her. There was a great press of people but she avoided them by moving from this path to that till she came to a row of shops. Dwarika sniffed at the delicious odours that hung in the air and realized that he was prodigiously hungry. Dwarika liked his comforts and Basantamanjari pampered him outrageously. 'So this is why she insisted on coming this way,' he thought. 'She wanted to give me my breakfast. But how did she know the shops were here?'

Standing before one of them Dwarika surveyed the scene with interest. Rich milk frothed and bubbled in an enormous wok over a charcoal fire sending out clouds of fragrant steam. In another, huge saffron-scented jalebis were curling and twisting in sizzling fat—each gold ring the thickness of a man's finger, hollow from within and bursting with syrup. In the next shop kachauris were being sold on lotus leaves, four to a portion, with a mound of halwa glistening with sugar and ghee and liberally sprinkled with nuts and raisins. Saliva squirted into Dwarika's mouth in anticipation. Standing outside the shop he ate his fill of the rich viands passing his tongue over his lips to catch the crumbs. He offered some to Basantamanjari but she shook her head. She wouldn't eat anything before her bath. Satiated at last, Dwarika threw the leaves away and ordered a large pot of milk. He loved hot milk and this was as thick and sweet as kheer.

'Ogo!' Basantamanjari plucked urgently at the sleeve of his kurta, 'Come this way. There's someone there . . . you remember I saw someone we knew last night.'

'Where?' Dwarika raised his face from the pot. The foam from the milk clung to his whiskers. Basantamanjari did not answer. She tripped on ahead of him her footsteps as sure and

swift as a doe's and he was obliged to follow. After a while they
came upon a sadhu in saffron sitting on a rock. He wore a soiled
and tattered dhuti and his hair and beard were matted with weeks
of dirt. A lathi with a bundle tied to one end rested at his feet. He
looked weary to the bone. Basantamanjari stopped and pointed a
triumphant finger. 'There!' she exclaimed. Dwarika stared at her
in dismay. The man was a total stranger.

'Who is he?' he asked curiously.

'Don't you recognize him?'

'I haven't seen him in my life.'

Basantamanjari laughed a tinkling little laugh whereupon the
sadhu raised a tired head and looked straight into Dwarika's face.
Two pairs of eyes held each other for a long moment. Suddenly a
shiver ran through Dwarika's frame. He had recognized the man.
It was Bharat. A wave of emotion passed over him but he didn't
know what it was. Was it joy on seeing his friend, lost to him for
so long? Or was it fear—of the woman he had married? How had
she known Bharat was sitting here? From where did she get these
strange powers?

Dwarika stood dumbfounded for a while. Then, walking up
to Bharat, he placed a hand on his shoulder. 'Bharat!' he said, his
voice breaking with the power of his feelings. Bharat kept staring
at him but wouldn't speak. 'It's me, Dwarika! Don't you
recognize me?'

'Dwarika,' Bharat echoed as though in wonder.

'Yes. And this is Basi—my wife. You remember
Basantamanjari? I took you to see her once. I married her and . . .
why don't you speak? Is anything wrong? Are you hiding from
someone? When did you come here?'

'Last night.' Bharat spoke at last but his voice was flat and
toneless.

'Have you become a sadhu?'

'No.'

'Then why are you dressed like one?'

'It makes life easier—somehow.'

'Where are you staying?'

'Nowhere.'

'Come with me then. I'll take you home and—'

'I'm quite comfortable sitting here.'

'Nonsense! How long can you stay sitting on a rock? You must come home with me. I insist.' Dwarika took hold of Bharat's hand and pulled him to his feet. 'I've rented a house in Nurganj,' he went on. 'It's a big house with many rooms. You'll be quite comfortable. We've met after so many years. Do you think I'll let go of you that easily?' He dragged Bharat along as he spoke and Bharat followed without offering any further resistance. Basantamanjari had stood silent all this while. Now she brought her lips to Dwarika's ear and whispered, 'He's hungry. He hasn't eaten in a long time. Why don't you buy him something to eat first?'

'You're right,' Dwarika replied. Leading Bharat to a sweet shop he bought him a pot of milk and a lotus leaf piled with hot jalebis. Bharat ate and drank mechanically, his eyes blank. Dwarika tried to enthuse him with reminiscences of their college days. 'Do you remember the confectioner in Maniktala? He made wonderful jilipis! Much smaller than the jalebis here of course. But very crisp and crunchy. How we loved them! But we had so little money then—we could never eat our fill.' Bharat threw the empty leaf and pot away and said, 'I think I'll go now.'

'Go where? You're coming home with me. Why do you hesitate? Is there anyone else with you?' Bharat shook his head. 'That's settled then,' Dwarika said happily. 'We arrived last night too and mean to stay a month. We'll see the sights together . . . Akbar's fort and Bharadwaj Muni's ashram.' In his happiness at seeing his old friend, in a place so far from his native land, Dwarika did not notice that Bharat was not responding to his overtures. He was going along with him but mindlessly like an automaton.

Reaching the house Dwarika ordered a servant to fetch hot water and fresh towels for his guest. Then, giving him a set of his own clothes, he made him bathe and change. The two friends had their midday meal together, with Basantamanjari in attendance waving away flies with a palm leaf fan. The hot bath had relaxed Bharat's tensed muscles and now, with the good food, warm in his belly, he had difficulty in keeping his eyes open. 'Go to your room and rest for a while,' Dwarika said, 'We'll talk in the evening.' Then, returning to his own room, he helped himself to a paan from Basantamanjari's silver box and took up his *albola*.

563

'You're amazing Basi!' he exclaimed when she came in an hour later. 'He's my friend but I didn't recognize him. And you—'

'He's very unhappy,' Basantamanjari interrupted abruptly.

'He's always been like that. Ever since I've known him at least. He lost his parents as a child. And, as far as I know, he has no relations at all. What he needs is a wife. We must find one for him and—'

'I have a feeling he's lost his wife. Quite recently—'

'What did you say?' Dwarika sat up with a jerk. 'Lost his wife? But he isn't even married!' Then, glancing sharply into her face, he asked, 'How do you know he has lost his wife?'

'I . . . I don't know anything,' Basantamanjari stammered. Dwarika's furrowed brow and stern glance quelled her. 'I get the feeling he's passing though a bad phase. Some private grief . . . like the death of a wife—'

'You and your feelings!' Dwarika exploded angrily, 'I'm tired of them! I want an ordinary woman—not a sorceress. Wait—' He stood up. 'I'll go and ask Bharat this very minute.'

'No, no. Please don't,' Basantamanjari begged. 'Not now when he's resting. And I may be wrong. Quite wrong.'

But Dwarika had walked out of the door. Stomping up the stairs he came to Bharat's room. It was empty. The bed was neat and smooth and folded upon it in a tidy pile were the clothes Dwarika had lent him. Dwarika rushed out to the gate where the darwan informed him that the Babu had left about an hour ago, adding, 'He had his lathi and his saffron bundle with him.'

564

Chapter XXIII

Leaving Allahabad behind Bharat joined a group of pilgrims who were walking to Vindhyachal. Three days later, weary and footsore, he sat outside the temple of Vindhyavasini and tried to take stock of his situation. But his mind felt empty and wouldn't take hold of a single thought. His eyes wandered here and there and finally rested on a group of men sitting in a circle within the precincts of the temple. Their lips were moving together and he realized that they were singing. Straining his ears to hear them above the din made by the crowds milling around him, he heard words that sounded like Bengali but uttered with a strange inflection. It wasn't Oriya. He was sure of that. Presently one of the men rose from the circle and came and sat beside him. He was small and fair with a shaven head out of which a shikha sprang, thick and strong and waving like a flag. He wore no upper garment though it was the middle of winter and bitterly cold.

'What district of Bengal do you come from?' Bharat enquired politely by way of opening the conversation. But, for some reason, his question infuriated the man. 'You Bengalis think everyone comes from your part of the world!' he cried indignantly. 'Is there no other region in this country? No other language? We come from Assam. Our language is Assamese.' Bharat shrank a little from the man's wrath. Then he remembered that his mother had been an Assamese. Somehow the thought made him feel quite kindly towards the stranger. 'I liked the song you were singing,' he said smiling. The man threw a sharp glance at Bharat's face and, seeing nothing there but a shy innocence, he responded in a considerably softened tone, 'I'm glad of it.' Then, pausing a little, he added, 'We've been travelling for over a year. We've seen Prayag, Mathura, Brindavan and all the Peethasthans where Sati's limbs lie scattered. The only one left was Vindhyachal, where the toe of her left foot fell, and we are here now. Where do you come from?'

'Puri.'

'Ah! Jagannath dham. A great pilgrimage! I've been there twice. Then you are not a Bengali. Yet you speak the language.'

'I've had to learn it to converse with my clients.'

The man's face darkened at these words. 'We have to learn it too,' he said after a glum silence. 'It's a compulsory subject in our schools. Our women are discarding the *mekhala* and have taken to wearing saris and our boys trim their hair in the Bengali fashion. I can't stand this aping of another culture.'

'I would like to go to Assam,' Bharat said quickly in an effort to steer the man away from the controversial subject. 'I've heard that the scenery is very beautiful.'

'That's no problem,' the man cried enthusiastically. 'Why don't you come with us? My name is Lakshminath Phukan but I'm better known as "the fiddler of Shivsagar".' I can easily put you up in my house. Do you have money for the fare?' Bharat nodded. The man plucked at a pouch tucked into his waist and took out a green betelnut. 'Have some *gua*,' he said offering it to Bharat. Bharat knew that, in Assam, offering betelnut was a symbol of friendship. He took it from Lakshminath and put it in his mouth.

Bharat had been wandering aimlessly ever since Mohilamoni's death a year ago. He had given up his job, sold everything he possessed and, leaving his son with the child's grandparents, had set himself adrift on the sea of humanity to be cast from this shore to that at its will. His wife's death had had a strange effect on him. His heart hadn't burned with anger at the unfairness of life or been crushed by sorrow at losing her. A strange lassitude had taken possession of him. He seemed to accept the fact that happiness was not for him. Death had stalked him all his life and was still stalking him. There was no sense in fighting it. In any case he had no fight left in him. There was only one thing that frightened him and shook him out of the stupour into which he had fallen. He had observed that whenever he was alone by himself and looking into the eyes of a deity in a temple, his lips started moving of their own volition. He strained his ears to identify the sounds that came out of his own mouth and found that he was whispering, 'Birds, birds, birds', repeating the word over and over again till his eyes rolled and his lips frothed with the effort. At such times his head would move forward and backward and he got an uncanny feeling that the rest of his body was immobile as though planted firmly in the earth. Only his head was moving, being pulled to and fro by a string. People would stare at him when he was afflicted thus. Some would run away in fear. Others, wiser and more considerate, would try to shake him out of his frenzy. Coming to, all of a sudden, he would find his face streaming with sweat and his limbs shivering like leaves in spring. Then he would run like one possessed, his mind shrieking out the question: 'Am I going mad? Is the blood of my forefathers rising up in me, corroding my brain and poisoning my very existence?' In his desperation he would jump into a nearby stream or pond and dip his burning head in the water over and over again. 'I'm Bharat Singha,' he would tell himself, 'I'm well educated. I've studied English and Logic and Mathematics.' Then, when his head and body had cooled, he would seek out an inn, eat a good meal and sleep for a long time . . .

Bharat joined Phukan's group but abandoned it the night before it reached Varanasi. 'Why am I going to Assam?' The thought came to him suddenly, 'Because my mother was born there? Does that make it my motherland? Is there anyone waiting there for me with open arms?' In a flash he came to a decision. He would walk away in the opposite direction. He had enough money to keep himself going for two years. He would wander about as the whim took him.

One day Bharat stumbled over a jagged stone and got a nasty cut in his big toe. He ignored it and continued to walk though the pain increased steadily and the toe began to fester. Finally, when he could walk no more, he started travelling by train, hobbling his way between stations. He took care not to go east. He didn't want to see Calcutta or Cuttack ever again.

At Nagpur station he decided that he needed a few days of rest. Hiring a tonga he came to a dharmashala which took in travellers on the payment of eight annas a day. He was shown into a large room when ten or eleven people were already accommodated. There was no furniture in the room. Those who wished to, could hire a mat, a pillow and a blanket on the payment of another four annas. Bharat handed over the money and, seeking out a corner, spread his bedding on the floor. Then he lay himself down and slept, at a stretch, for the next twenty hours.

Waking up the next day he found that his foot was swollen to twice its size and his head and limbs were burning with fever. Sitting up with difficulty he brought his foot to his mouth and started blowing on it. The man who lay next to him, a plump youth also in saffron with a growth of matted hair covering his cheeks and chin, looked curiously on. After a while he mumbled a question which Bharat didn't understand. The language sounded quite alien to his ears. Shaking his head Bharat stood up. He hadn't eaten for two whole days and was ravenously hungry. Limping his way painfully down the stairs he came out into the street. Fortunately, he didn't have to go far to look for food. There was a shop right opposite selling kachauris and laddus. Bharat bought some and ate his fill. While he ate he looked at his swollen foot and thought, 'I suppose I should see a doctor. But what if I don't? Gangrene will set in and the toe will fall off. The leg might have to come off too! But what of it? There are so many cripples in the world. I can be one of them. Does it really matter? The pain is excruciating of course but I've lived with it for so long—I'm loath to let go of it . . . People who have a purpose in life need all their limbs. I have no purpose. I can do without . . .'

Upon this thought he hobbled back to his place in the dharmashala. The young man lying next to him raised his head at his entry and said something. Again Bharat didn't understand. But this time he responded to his fellow traveller's attempt at friendship. He had bought more food than he could eat and some kachauris and laddus were left in the *sal* leaves he held in his hand. Passing the bundle to the young man Bharat smiled kindly at him whereupon the former sat up and started cramming the food into his mouth as fiercely and ravenously as though he hadn't eaten in days.

Coming from the east Bharat had no idea that the place of his sojourn was at the centre of a storm. About a month ago, the chief officer of the Plague Commission, an Englishman called WC Rand, had let loose a reign of terror on Maharashtra—the province being badly affected by the plague. In the name of plague control, armed soldiers had stormed into people's houses knocking over furniture and kitchen utensils, molesting the women and beating up the men if they dared to protest. If anyone showed symptoms of any illness, be it a stomach infection or a common cold, he was bundled off to the camp, his agonized cries falling on deaf ears. There, more often than not, he caught the contagion and died. This dehumanizing treatment of his fellow human beings had enraged Tilak and he had written several burning articles in *Maratha* and *Kesri*.

Fired by Tilak's courage in denouncing the rulers, five young men decided to take the law into their own hands and exterminate the hated Rand. A carefully laid out plan was put into execution. On the night of the Diamond Jubilee of Queen Victoria's coronation, three brothers—Damodar, Balkrishna and Vasudev Chapekar—together with their two friends, Sathe and Ranade, took up strategic positions outside the Governor's residence where a grand dinner and dance was in progress. The plan was to shoot Rand as soon as his carriage rolled out of the gate. But Balkrishna, who was to give the signal, mistook the carriage of another guest, a young army officer called Lieutenant Ayerst, for the Plague Commissioner's. In consequence Ayerst was shot at and killed. In a few seconds the boys realized that they had made a mistake for Mr Rand's carriage came to the gate even as Ayerste's coachman whipped up his horses and galloped away with a screaming Mrs Ayerst. The next minute Rand fell under the bullets of the assassins. Thus two Englishmen lost their lives at the hands of natives. The five young men escaped and could not be tracked down despite all the efforts of the police.

Fuming with resentment, the authorities ordered the arrest of Bal Gangadhar Tilak averring that it was he who had incited a group of well-born, well-educated boys and turned them into terrorists and traitors. Denied bail, Tilak was thrown into prison like a common felon. Some days later he was brought from Poona to Bombay where a hearing was scheduled in the High Court. But no counsel agreed to appear on his behalf. In desperation, Tilak wrote to his friends Sisir Kumar and Motilal Ghosh and requested them to help him out.

The news came as a shock to the educated elite of Calcutta. A meeting was held at the office of the *Amrita Bazar Patrika* and was attended by Ashutosh Chowdhury, Janakinath Ghoshal, Anandamohan Bosu, Rabindranath Thakur and Umeshchandra Banerji among others. It was decided that two senior barristers would be sent from Calcutta to appear for Tilak and that the expenses would be met from contributions from all the gentlemen present.

In the meantime, the hunt for the five absconding youths was on with the police raiding every house in the Marathi mohallas and turning the lives of all Marathi boys above a certain age into a living hell. The air was thick with rumours. One day Damodar and Balkrishna had been seen in Aurangabad; the next day in Kolhapur . . .

Bharat knew nothing of all this. And so he hadn't the faintest idea that his young roommate was the absconding Ranade. After the assassination the five friends had decided to go their separate ways assuming, quite correctly, that the police would find it difficult to track them down individually. Starved and exhausted, his limbs burning with fever, Ranade had been on the run for weeks. With the police on his heels like a pack of baying hounds, he had fled like a pursued animal from place to place to avoid capture and sure death.

That night Bharat was rudely wakened from sleep by a tremendous blow on his back. Opening his eyes he saw a huge figure towering over him, a burning mashaal in his hand. His heavily booted foot was raised for another kick but before he could direct it Bharat sat up, straight as an arrow, and cried out angrily in English, 'How dare you touch me?' The man sprang on him and, clutching him by the hair, forced him into a standing position. Now Bharat saw that there were five of them in the room and that they were policemen. One, a white-skinned Anglo-Indian, came forward at hearing a native speak his tongue and asked roughly, 'Who is this bastard?' Then, taking Bharat by the throat he raised his fist. But, before he could strike, Bharat hit him full on the mouth his bony fingers leaving their mark on his cheek and chin. Then, all five fell on him and beat and cuffed and kicked him till he lay on the ground half dead. The informer, who had brought them to the dharmashala, now pointed a finger at Ranade, whereupon they yanked him out from under his blanket where he lay shivering with fever and fear. They fitted shackles not only on him but on all the other inmates of the room and dragged them off to the Kotwali. Even then Bharat had no idea why all this was happening to him or what wrong he had done.

Chapter XXIV

The first glimmer of grey had started paling the inky darkness of a winter night when a great ship inched its way into the estuary, the strong beams of its searchlight cutting a path over the black water. The passengers were in their bunks, fast asleep. Only one young woman stood on the deck gripping the rail with both hands. It was the end of January. The fog lay thick over the Ganga and the air, though not as cold as in her native habitat, had a decided nip in it. She shivered under her shawl, not so much with cold as with apprehension. She had severed all her links with England and come out to India. But would her new country accept her?

After Swamiji's return to India, he had written to Margaret from time to time giving her his news. She had learned, from those short dry missives, that the Ramkrishna Mission had been established and that work was in progress. But, to her bitter disappointment, Swamiji had dissuaded her from coming to Calcutta in every letter. She was to stay in England, he wrote, and try to raise funds for the Mission. Margaret had felt let down, more so because he had allowed the two Americans, Olé Bull and Joe Macleod to join him. They had donated a lot of money and were keen to see how it was being spent. But whereas their intention was to spend only some months in the mysterious country they had heard so much of, Margaret wanted to pass the rest of her life in it. 'Why can't I go out to India?' she thought resentfully. 'With him by my side I could do anything I could achieve the impossible. Without him everything seems so meaningless.' She conveyed her feelings to Mr Sturdy who wrote to Vivekananda that he was making arrangements for Margaret's journey out to India since she had resolved not to stay in England any longer. Now Swamiji softened his stand and wrote her a letter:

My dear Miss Noble,

A letter from Sturdy reached me yesterday, informing me that you are determined to come to India . . .

Let me tell you frankly that I am now convinced that you have a great future in the work for India. What was wanted was not a man, but a woman; a real lioness, to work for the Indians, women specially.

India cannot yet produce great women, she must borrow them from other nations . . .

Yet the difficulties are many. You cannot form any idea of the misery, the superstition, and the slavery that are here. You will be in the midst of a mass of half-naked men and women with quaint ideas of caste and isolation, shunning the white skin through fear or hatred and hated by them intensely. On the other hand, you will be looked upon by the white as a crank, and every one of your movements will be watched with suspicion.

Then the climate is fearfully hot; our winter in most places being like your summer . . . Not one European comfort is to be had in places out of the cities.

You must think well before you plunge in, and after work, if you fail in this or get disgusted, on my part I promise you, I will stand by you unto death whether you work for India or not, whether you give up Vedanta or remain in it. 'The tusks of the elephant come out, but never go back;' so are the words of a man never retracted . . .

I will stand by you unto death. Whenever she thought of that sentence a tremor of ecstasy passed over her frame. What more could she want? Now, with doubt and fear gnawing at her, she took hold of those words, repeating them over and over again like a mantra.

The ship glided into the harbour even as dawn broke over the horizon casting a dim orange glow over the rows of faces on the bank. Margaret scanned them eagerly. Would she find the one she sought? Surely he wouldn't come for her himself! He would send one of his disciples . . . Suddenly a thought occurred to her making her heart leap with joy. 'But no one else knows me! He'll come. He'll have to.' Her eyes darted from this face to that as she pushed her way through the crowd. Then she heard a soft, deep voice call from behind her, 'Margot!' Margaret spun around and got a shock. It was Vivekananda, but how he had changed! No wonder her eyes had passed over him and moved on. A saffron dhuti, folded in two, was wrapped around his middle like a lungi. The upper part of his body was bare. Only a thick wrapper covered his back and chest. His head was shaved and the shock of hair covering his cheeks and chin was flecked with gray. Margaret bent down to touch his feet but he moved back quickly. 'Come,' he said gravely, 'The carriage is waiting.' Margaret felt a cold chill around her heart. He was seeing her after such a long time. And he hadn't even a smile for her.

Sitting in the carriage by his side she threw a surreptitious glance at his face. He was looking so old and ill! How old was he? She made a quick calculation. He was three years older than her. That made him thirty-four . . . . But he looked close to fifty! 'I've aged, haven't I?' Vivekananda asked her as though he could read her thoughts. A smile flickered over his mouth but did not touch his large, sombre eyes. 'Don't you like my beard?' he continued cheerfully, 'I started growing it last year when I went to Darjeeling.' Margaret shook her head. Her lips quivered and she felt close to tears.

Some months after Vivekananda had returned to India the doctors told him that he was suffering from diabetes. A strict regimen was prescribed. He was to give up rice and potatoes, eat a lot of meat, drink very little water and keep his mind cool and undisturbed. Since this last was not possible in Calcutta, with the work of the Mission swelling day by day and more and more people coming to see him, he had taken the advice of friends and moved to Darjeeling. The solitude and cool mountain air had revived him somewhat and he had felt much better. But the moment he came back to Calcutta the symptoms returned. This time he shrugged them off. How long could he sit among the mountains twiddling his thumbs. He had work to do.

Passing the maidan, the carriage clattered down the Esplanade and stopped outside an English hotel. 'I've made arrangements for your stay here for the present,' Vivekananda told Margaret. 'You'll have to adapt to the real India sooner or later but it needn't be from today. In the meantime, start learning Bengali. A tutor will come to you from tomorrow.' Leaving her at the entrance of the hotel he stepped into the carriage and drove away.

Margaret bathed, ate and slept for most of the day. Then,

towards evening, she walked out of the hotel and stood outside it surveying the scene before her. She was surprised at what she saw. She had expected heat, dust, black faces and filthy smells. But the streets here were wide and clean with tall trees on either side. The people walking in them and passing by in carriages were mostly white like herself. There were a few natives but they weren't dark and ugly. Their skins glowed a rich golden brown and they were elegantly attired in silks and velvets. The city, she thought, was exactly like London. A little distance away, between Fort William and a row of splendid mansions, she could see the great maidan of Calcutta which, with its shady trees, stretches of water and winding walks, reminded her of Hyde Park.

Several days passed. There was no sign of Vivekananda or even a word from him. Margaret's heart swelled with rebellious feelings. Had she come out to India to spend all her time mooning about in an English hotel. She was learning Bengali, it was true, but that didn't satisfy her. She wanted to be near Swamiji and help him in his work.

After the math in Alambazar had been destroyed by an earthquake, Vivekananda had decided to establish a new one in Belur. Taking a house on rent for the present, he was looking around for suitable land in the area. Living so far away from Calcutta, he had no opportunity of keeping in touch with Margaret. However, one day, on a visit to Balaram Bosu of Bagbazar, he sent for her. That day Margaret saw, for the first time, how the common folk lived. There was no sign of planning anywhere. Dark, ill-ventilated houses, some with mud walls and tin roofs, stood higgledy piggledy in a network of narrow lanes and alleys. Oxen roamed about freely rubbing shoulders with humans and pi-dogs fought and snarled over the garbage that rose in foul smelling heaps in street corners. Margaret's heart sank at the sight but she pulled herself, firmly, together. She had come out to India to serve; to improve the quality of the lives of the people. And she had come prepared . . .

Entering Balaram Bosu's house she saw Vivekananda lying on a wooden bedstead in the middle of the room smoking tobacco from a long pipe. Raising his eyes at her entry, he pointed to a chair and said gravely, 'Sit down.' He puffed at his pipe for a few minutes without speaking. Margaret could hold herself in no longer. 'When shall I begin teaching school?'—the question burst out of her. Swamiji laid aside his *albola* and turned to look at her. He saw a tall, trim, erect figure with gold brown hair and deep blue eyes wearing a neatly cut cream silk suit and sturdy English shoes. She looked so alien, so out of place in her present environment that he found it difficult to talk to her.

'In due course of time,' he said at last. 'Where's the hurry?'

Margaret felt deeply hurt. He was so cold and detached! So different from the handsome, brilliant, high-spirited young man she had idolized so much! Her eyes clouded and her palms turned cold with apprehension. Had she made a mistake in leaving everything and everyone she knew and coming out to this strange country? Was she chasing a mirage? She knew that men and women did not interact freely with each other in this country. Besides she was a foreigner and he a Hindu ascetic. Why, then, had he written the words *I will stand by you unto death*? What did they mean?

Joe Macleod and Olé Bull arrived a few days later. Turning down Vivekananda's offer of putting them up in an European hotel, flatly and firmly, the doughty Americans drove straight from the harbour to the house that Vivekananda had rented in Belur. They were charmed with the place. Set among green lawns and flowering trees, the house was large and airy with many windows out of which the Ganga could be seen in all its majesty. It was the month of February and the breeze that blew from the river was soft and mellow. 'I must show you the land that I have chosen for the math,' Swamiji said that evening as the three sat in the garden sipping their tea. 'What land?' Joe cried, astonished. 'We don't need more land. This is a lovely bit of property. Why don't we build the math here?' Vivekananda shook his head. 'I like to think big Joe,' he said quietly. 'The math I envisage will be large enough to accommodate up to a hundred disciples and keep them in comfort. And on feast days, such as the birth anniversary of my guru, thousands of men, women and children will attend the celebrations and partake of prasad. *Belur Math*! The name will be on everyone's lips. People will flock to it as to a place of pilgrimage. I see all this in my mind's eye Joe.'

The tide being out, it was not possible to go by boat so the party had to walk half a mile through tall grass and thorn bushes.

The women stepped gingerly forward, fearful not only of the burrs that scratched their arms and stuck to their skirts but of the snakes that might be lurking underfoot. Presently they came to a wooden bridge spanning a canal. Actually, it was hardly a bridge. It was only the stout trunk of a palm tree flung carelessly across from this bank to that. 'Tck! Tck!' Swamiji clicked his tongue in helplessness. 'Can you two ladies walk across it?' he asked anxiously.

'Why not?' Joe answered, putting a neatly shod foot on the tottering trunk. It was coated with mud and slime and was quite slippery in places but Joe stretched out her arms like a professional rope walker and negotiated it with short quick steps. Olé Bull was obliged to follow and she did so, her feet not as swift and sure as Joe's but steady. Vivekananda burst out laughing, well pleased with his protegees. 'You Americans are indomitable!' he said. 'You don't give up.'

But even Vivekananda hadn't a clue to how indomitable American women could be once they had made up their minds.

In the middle of the land that Vivekananda had chosen for the math was a small tumbledown house with a leaking roof, broken windows and dust lying thick on everything. There was a garden around it but it had been neglected for years and was wild and tangled. 'Mrs Bull and I could stay here,' Joe exclaimed as soon as they reached their destination. 'Are you mad?' Vivekananda laughed away her suggestion. 'It has been abandoned for years and it is falling to pieces.'

'We could repair it.' Joe glanced at Olé as she said these words and the older woman nodded her head in affirmation. Vivekananda stared at them in dismay. He had seen their homes in Boston and New York and knew how they lived. 'It's easier said than done,' he thought.

But the two women proved him wrong. They fell to with a vengeance from the very next day. An army of workmen took over the house and, under their guidance, stripped the roof of its rotten tiles and tore down termite-ridden woodwork putting up fresh material in their places. They replaced the glass in the windows, painted and papered the walls and polished the wooden floor. The palm trunk across the canal was thrown away and a strong, stout wooden bridge was put up in its place. Next the ladies took on the garden. They hired a couple of gardeners and, with their help the grass was cut, the trees trimmed and pruned and flower beds dug and planted. Then, after all the workmen had left, Joe and Olé did up the inside with stuff they had bought from the Calcutta bazars—mahogany furniture, curtains, carpets, pictures, plate and silver. And, under their skillful hands, the dilapidated tenement in an obscure village of Bengal became a neat and charming cottage that could have stood in Dorset or Kent.

'I can see that you have fallen in love with Bengal,' Vivekananda said to the two women on the day of the house warming. 'So I've decided to give you Bengali names. Joe is full of life and vitality. So I shall name her Jaya. And you—,' he said turning to Ole, 'You remind me of my mother. She is like you, calm and patient and loving. I'll call you Dheeramata.' A couple of days later, when the ladies had settled down in their new home, Vivekananda asked them if they would allow another young woman to live with them. 'She's an Irish girl,' he told them, 'much younger than you. But she has insisted on coming out here to help me in my work.' Joe and Olé assented readily. Now Vivekananda sent for Margaret and gave her the news. 'You'll like it there Margot,' he told her, 'Mrs Bull is a good and kind woman who spreads love wherever she goes. You'll come under it too—you'll see.' Margaret heaved a sigh of relief. She felt she had come home at last.

Margaret fell in love with Belur right from the first day. The air was pure and fresh and the surroundings green as rain-washed emerald. Birds of different hues flocked and twittered in the branches of the many trees in the garden. From the back of the house a flight of steps led straight to the river. Often, when she had nothing to do, she would sit on the steps watching the boats pass up and down. Sometimes she could hear snatches of song in an eerie alien tongue.

But best of all was the fact that here she saw Swamiji everyday. He came in the morning before sunrise and shook them all awake. Then they had breakfast together under a huge mango tree, laden with blossom, that stood in the middle of the garden. They laughed and chatted and teased each other just like the old days. Sometimes he would give them lessons in Indian history.

577

SUNIL GANGOPADHYAY

Sometimes he regaled them with tales from the Ramayan and
Mahabharat. One day, in the middle of one such story, he fixed
his dark, unflinching eyes on Margaret's clear, blue ones and said,
'I wish to give you a Bengali name Margot. From this day I shall
call you Nivedita. Do you know what that means? It means *one
who has dedicated herself.*'

578

Chapter XXV

Radha's eyes have lost their light
Her heart is wrung with pain
Lonesome is the path she treads
Through storm and pelting rain . . .

Every time she saw Nayanmoni these days Kusumkumari sang
these lines smiling and dimpling wickedly. The other girls
laughed. Everyone had noticed a change in her. She was not the
old Nayanmoni any more. She mooned about like a lovesick
maiden. But no one had a clue to the object of her affections.

After her separation with Bharat, Bhumisuta, or Nayanmoni,
had turned her back on the other sex. Like Meera Bai of ancient
legend she had taken a vow. She would devote herself to Sri
Krishna and he would be the only man in her life. Whenever she
felt disturbed or unhappy she would stand before the image of
Krishna, in her room, and pour out her woes to him in song and
dance.

But, of late, a strange thing was happening. When she sat, eyes
closed, before her Krishna she saw—not his dark, smiling,
child-like face but that of a man in his prime; a face so brilliantly
beautiful that it could evoke a god's envy. She gazed upon that
face as if a trance. It was as perfect as an image carved in ivory.
Masses of silky black hair waved down to the smooth column of
his neck and covered his cheeks and chin. Deep, dark eyes looked
into hers holding them with penetrating power. Then, before her
swimming senses, the vision faded and changed. It became the full
figure of a man, dressed like a prince, in a gold-embroidered
achkan. His frame was tall and powerful but his hands were like a
woman's—long and sensitive with tapering fingers. And his
voice, when he called her by her name, was as deep and sweet as
the chords of a veena. He was a man among men!

It didn't take Nayanmoni a split second to identify him. He
was the poet Rabindranath. She had seen him, first, at a rehearsal

579

of *Raja o Rani* at Classic Theatre and been thrilled by his touch. After that she had seen him twice—once at another rehearsal and once among the audience. There was nothing unusual about remembering a famous personality. Then why did Nayanmoni feel as though her world had come crashing down? Strange new sensations were overwhelming her; sensations she had never experienced before. In fact, she didn't even know they existed. Her Krishna was receding into the shadows and someone else, a man she barely knew, was taking hold of her mind and senses. Nayanmoni trembled with an unknown fear. Why was this happening to her?

A feverish yearning to see him and be with him possessed Nayanmoni. But he lived in a world so far removed from hers that even to think of it was absurd. She knew that well enough. She did the next best thing. She tried to reach out to him through his books. She bought up as many titles as she could find and started reading till late into the night. She enjoyed the stories and some of the novels but of the poetry she understood very little. Yet she went through them doggedly, line by line, till the sense started coming to her in flashes:

I would shatter the enclosing walls
And reveal the secret yearning of my heart
But only the words find release
The pain lies buried in bruised heaps

Why? This was exactly how she felt! How every woman felt when in the throes of a hopeless love! How did the poet know what lay in a woman's heart? The ecstasy; the pain; the terrible desolation!

Nayanmoni felt restless and disturbed. Her mind was in a whirl. She had adjusted to her misfortunes and had accepted her new role in life. She had been willing to live it out alone with only her art to sustain her. But now, a desperate loneliness swept over her. She was young and beautiful and had so much to give! But the one she wanted to give all she had was not ready to receive her offerings. With every poem she read her blood leaped up in response. The words seemed to touch her as physically as if the poet had caressed her with his long, beautifully moulded fingers. Every time a verse moved her particularly she was overwhelmed with the same sensations she had experienced when

Rabindranath had taken her face in his hands and guided her
during the rehearsal of *Raja o Rani*. Aching with unfulfilled
desire, day after day, a strange lethargy overtook her. She lost
interest in the theatre; in the people around her and even in her
day-to-day routine. She continued with her rehearsals and
performances and carried them out commendably through sheer
force of habit. But everyone could see that her mind was
elsewhere.

One evening, on her way to a rehearsal, it seemed to her that
the carriage was taking much longer than the usual time to reach
the theatre. She pushed up the shutter and peered out of the
chinks to see how far she had reached. To her surprise she found
that the street she was passing was a strange one. She had never
seen it before. Opening the window she tried to call out to the syce
but her voice was lost in the clatter of the galloping horses. A
puzzled frown appeared on her forehead. There was no need to
panic. She knew that. The syce was old and trustworthy. But the
question remained. Where was he taking her? Had Amar Datta
fixed another venue for the rehearsal?

Half an hour later the carriage stopped outside the high iron
gates of a splendid mansion. The dance master of *Classic*, Nepa
Bose, came hurrying forward to receive her.

'Ah! Nayanmoni,' he cried, stretching out his hands in a
welcome gesture quite unusual for him. His attire was unusual
too. In place of his usual dhuti and banian he wore a bright red
shirt over yellow pyjamas. A tall fez sat atop his black curls. His
mouth was full of paan and his eyes were bright with kajal.
Nayanmoni's brows came together. Ignoring his outstretched
hand she stepped out of the carriage and asked sharply, 'What
place is this?'

'This is Maniktala. You are in Kalu Babu's garden house.'

'Aren't we rehearsing tonight?'

'Of course we are. Kalu Babu has decided to hold it here.'

'Where are the others?'

'I don't know about the others. Kalu Babu ordered me to
receive you at the gate and bring you to him.'

Nepa Bose led Nayanmoni up the gravel path that ran
through the garden to the portico of the house. As they stepped
into a wide hall blazing with lamps, the crimson velvet curtain of

581

one of the doors was pushed aside with a white hand loaded with rings, and Amar Datta stood in the room. Nayanmoni stared at him. She had never seen him in such a dishevelled state before. His satin vest was crumpled and his hair fell untidily over his face and neck. As he walked towards her she noticed that his gait was unsteady and he held a bottle in his hand.

'Who else is coming?' Nayanmoni asked sternly. 'Why have you sent for me before the others?'

'There are no others.' Amar collapsed on one of the sofas. 'Today's rehearsal is only with you.'

'What do you mean? What play—?'

'It's a dance rehearsal. We'll decide on the play later.'

'That's absurd,' Nayanmoni looked at Nepa Bose. 'I must know my character first. How will I express myself in the dance otherwise? I'm afraid it's impossible for me—'

'*Ei*!' Amar Datta shouted suddenly. Turning a pair of fiery, red eyes on her he said, 'How dare you look at him when I'm talking to you? I'm the master. I order you to dance.'

'You're not *my* master and I'm not accustomed to taking orders,' Nayanmoni's jaw hardened and she went on, 'I'm not obliged to dance for your entertainment as per the terms of my contract.'

'Why do you keep throwing your contract in my face every time I ask you to do something? Are you working for a jute mill? Don't you know that in the performing arts the director's wish is the last word? You're an impertinent wench and deserve to be punished. I've a good mind to make you dance naked.'

Nayanmoni gave a short laugh expressing her utter contempt of him and his power over her. Amar Datta was taken aback. Not knowing how else to control her, he said with a sulky edge to his voice, 'You'll have to obey me Nayan. If the others can—why can't you?'

'What others?'

'Why Kusum, Bhushan, Khemi, Bina, Rani—all the girls. They all come at my command and pleasure me.'

'You're drunk Amar Babu,' Nayanmoni said gently but firmly. 'You don't know what you're saying. I'm leaving now. I'll talk to you tomorrow.'

'Ahaha!' Nepa hurried forward in an effort to mediate.

'Where's the harm in dancing a few steps when the master . . .
er . . . Kalu Babu wishes it so much? Do the swan dance you
perform so well and—'

Nayanmoni did not condescend to answer him. Her eyes
burned into his with such a strange light that he stepped back
hastily. But those wonderfully expressive eyes failed to quell
Amar Datta. He rose from the sofa and advanced menacingly
towards her. Grabbing her by the hand he said roughly, 'I'm not
drunk and I *am* your master. You'll dance if I command you.'

'Let go of my hand Amar Babu,' Nayanmoni said coldly
without a trace of fear. 'I don't allow anyone to touch me without
permission. I've sworn an oath—'

'What oath?'

'I've sworn to kill the man who dares to do so.'

Now Amar Datta was truly flummoxed. He dropped her
hand and, turning to Nepa Bose, muttered rebelliously: 'She's
sworn to kill . . . who does she think she is? Maharani Victoria?
She's only a common slut and look at the airs she gives me! I'm the
master and she won't obey me.' Then, suddenly, something
completely unforeseen happened. Sobbing loudly he fell to his
knees and tried to clutch her feet with both hands. Nayanmoni
stepped back in surprise at which he lost his balance and fell, face
forward, to the ground. But the shock of his fall failed to sober
him. He rolled all over the floor like a spoiled child, whimpering
and crying incoherently, 'Just the swan dance . . . please Nayan . . .
I'm the master . . . no, no I'm not the master . . . how dare you
humiliate me? Just this once . . . please Nayan . . . I'll never ask you
again.' Nayanmoni burst out laughing. So did Nepa Bose. *'Ki go!'*
the latter winked at Nayanmoni. 'The man's turned lunatic—as
you can see. Will you indulge him just this once?'

Nayanmoni shook her head and walked out of the room.
Reaching home she bathed for a long time scrubbing her body
rigorously with a gamchha as though she was trying to cleanse it
of the impurities that clung to it in her encounter with Amar
Datta. Then, seating herself before the image of Krishna, she shut
her eyes and murmured—not a prayer but a verse from a poem:

I've surrendered life and soul.
And kept for myself only my shame
Guarding it in secret through night and day

From the rude glance of prying eyes

'I can't get anywhere near Rabindra Babu,' she thought suddenly. 'But I can write him a letter. Yes—that is what I'll do. I'll write to him.'

Chapter XXVI

It seemed as though Vivekananda's sojourn in the West had spoiled him for his own country. It was a strange thing but after his four years in the temperate zone his body had lost its ability to cope with the heat and humidity of tropical Bengal. He suffered from continual bouts of fever and dysentery getting a brief respite only when he escaped to the hills. But the moment he returned to Calcutta his troubles started all over again.

A few months after Margaret's arrival Vivekananda's health declined so sharply that he had to leave the city and go to Darjeeling on the advice of his doctors. He felt better in the cool mountain air but he couldn't stay there for long. On hearing the news that plague had broken out in Calcutta, Vivekananda hastened back. He felt responsible for the three women who had travelled across half the globe to come to him. He had to see that they were safe. Besides, this was the time to plunge into the work of the Mission in right earnest.

Vivekananda began organizing relief work as soon as he reached Calcutta. His disciples formed groups and moved from slum to slum nursing the sick, burning the dead and teaching the unafflicted how to protect themselves from the dreaded contagion. This was the first time that such a programme was undertaken in the city and many were puzzled by it. Hindus, though hospitable by nature, had no concept of organized service. They wouldn't turn a hungry man from their door but if they saw someone dying in the street they would pass him by without a qualm. They believed that it was his Karma that had brought him to this pass. It was no one's fault and no one's responsibility. Besides, it was but right that he atone for the sins of a previous birth. People were horrified at the sight of sadhus moving from hovel to hovel and touching low-caste men and women; even corpses. Sadhus were holy men and commanded reverence. Their only obligation to the society that nurtured them was to bless ordinary householders and propitiate the gods on

SUNIL GANGOPADHYAY

their behalf. Some of Vivekananda's brother disciples had misgivings too. As ascetics they had surrendered the lay world and embraced the spiritual. How could doctoring the sick and feeding the poor lead to the advancement of the spirit to which they were committed and which could be achieved only through prayer and meditation? Besides, wasn't it the responsibility of the Government to provide relief from natural disasters? And where would the newly founded Ramkrishna Mission find the funds? Vivekananda tried to answer these questions as patiently as he could but sometimes he lost his temper. 'Give your souls a rest for the present and look around you,' he cried in a burst of irritation. 'People are dying in thousands. As for funds, I'll sell the land in Belur if the need arises. What will I do with a math if I can't help my fellow men?'

Fortunately for him, the pestilence disappeared from the city as suddenly as it had come and he could keep the land. But the grinding work and sleepless nights took their toll of him. He became so weak that the doctors were alarmed and ordered him to leave Calcutta immediately. This time he decided to go, not to Darjeeling but to distant Almora where Mr and Mrs Sevier had taken a house. The three white women, eager to see more of India, clamoured to go with him. So did some of his disciples.

Thus it was quite a large party that set off from Calcutta to Kathgodam by train. Then, after enjoying a day's hospitality in the Raja of Khetri's mansion in Nainital, they started the climb to Almora on horseback. Vivekananda, who was feeling better already, had meant to leave early in the morning but an unseasonal shower delayed them by several hours. In consequence, they were nowhere near their destination when the sun sank behind the mountains and dusk enveloped them like a shrouding mist.

Nivedita, who was seeing the Himalayas for the first time, gazed on them entranced. She had never seen a more magnificent sight. In the falling twilight, the majestic peaks loomed before her eyes higher than any peaks she had ever seen—the snow on them rose flushed by the last traces of lingering daylight. Above their heads, out of a violet sky, two stars glimmered, soft and lustrous as wave washed pearls. Nivedita reigned in her horse and waited for Vivekananda to come up to her. The moment she saw him she

586

exclaimed joyfully, 'What great good fortune is mine that you have brought me here! I'm so happy! So happy! It seems to me as though we are travellers together on an endless path . . .'

'It seems to me,' Vivekananda cut in dryly, putting a rude end to Nivedita's romantic effusions, 'that we won't reach Almora tonight. We'd better start looking for shelter.'

'I don't mind if we don't find any. I'd like to ride among the hills all night.'

Vivekananda stared straight ahead of him and said gravely, 'You're lagging behind. Go on ahead and join the other ladies.'

'Why?' Nivedita fixed her wide innocent blue eyes on his face. 'I like being with you.'

'This is not Europe Margot. In India you must follow Indian ways.'

'I'm trying my best to do so. Surely you can see that? And why do you call me Margot? I'm Nivedita.'

Vivekananda sighed, 'You're still British at heart,' he said. 'The flag of Britain is your flag.'

Nivedita's lips parted. She was about to speak; to protest. But she controlled herself. Ever since she had come out to India she had noticed a change in Vivekananda's manner to her. She wondered why he was so tense and withdrawn with her and so free and relaxed with Joe and Olé. When they were all together he was almost the man she had known in her own country. But, when alone with her, he was curt and invariably critical of her conduct. If she went to him with a query, when he sat alone, he grew quite irritated: 'Go ask Swarupananda,' he said brusquely, '*He's* your tutor—not I.' It was obvious to Nivedita that he was avoiding her. At such times the hot tears rose to her eyes and her heart swelled with indignation. Had she come out to India only to learn Bengali? Didn't he realize that she had come out of her desperate need of him? That her heart was where he was?

One morning, as Vivekananda sat in Mrs Sevier's drawing room expounding the doctrine of Moksha to his followers, Nivedita asked in all innocence: 'Why are Hindus so keen on attaining Moksha? They practise so many austerities; spend years in meditation and worship only to escape rebirth and achieve personal release. But why? Life is so beautiful. And to live is to be useful. Isn't it better to be reborn, over and over again, and use

587

your lives to serve your fellow men?' Vivekananda turned quite livid at her audacity in questioning the worth of a Hindu spiritual concept. 'You've understood nothing of Moksha,' he burst out angrily, 'or you wouldn't have said what you did. You Europeans can only understand the linear; the progressive; the material. And your eagerness to serve humanity is aimed at feeding your own egos. Learn to conquer your base instincts first—then talk of spiritual matters.' The Americans looked at him with shocked eyes. The rebuke was so harsh and the fault such a minor one! What did he want of the girl, they wondered. Did he expect her to surrender her Western identity; wipe out the conditioning of centuries simply because she had come out to India?

That afternoon Joe Macleod found Nivedita lying on her bed sobbing bitterly. Placing her hand on her back, the older woman said gently, 'Something is making you unhappy Margaret. Would you like to tell me about it?'

'I've burnt my boats Joe!' Margaret raised a tear streaked face from her pillow. 'I have nothing to go back to.'

'Why do you have to go back?'

'Because there's nothing for me here. I left everything and came out to him. But he hates and despises me.'

'That's not true Margaret. He's your guru. He's trying to mould you into a better human being. That is why he is harsh with you at times.'

'I don't mind that. I can endure every punishment he thinks fit to heap on me. What I can't endure is being kept at a distance. His indifference is breaking my heart Joe! How can I live on, here, after you two have left?'

'We're not going. Not for a long, long time,' Joe passed her fingers tenderly through the girl's golden brown hair. 'Don't lose heart. All will be well.' Then, after a moment's silence, she added, 'Don't make the mistake of judging him as you would any other. He's no ordinary man. You must remember that.'

'I know. I know.' Margaret cried clinging to Joe. 'And I'm trying. Believe me, I truly am trying.'

That evening Joe had a private talk with Vivekananda. 'Swamiji,' she addressed him with her usual directness. 'Why are you torturing the poor girl so?' Vivekananda was startled. 'What do you mean?' he cried. 'Torturing what girl?'

'The Irish girl—Margaret.'

'She came of her own will. I had warned her that she would have to face numerous problems. In this country—'

'I'm not talking of those problems. Margaret showed me a letter you wrote to her when she was in England. There was a sentence in it: *'I will stand by you unto death whether you work for India or not, whether you give up Vedanta or remain within it.* You wrote those words didn't you?'

At this a deathly pallor spread over Vivekananda's countenance and the light went out of his eyes.

'Didn't you?' Joe prompted gently.'

'Yes,' Vivekananda answered in a hoarse whisper, 'I did.'

'Those words are her only prop. You must understand that. We are a Western people; conditioned for centuries by the material. Physical renunciation is not easy for us. You must be patient.'

That evening, when the whole party set off for a walk, Vivekananda left the others and come up to Nivedita. He walked beside her, in silence, for a few minutes. Then, turning to face her, he asked abruptly, 'What do you want of me?'

'You are my lord,' Nivedita whispered. 'My king! Don't banish me from your presence. Give me a place, a little place, at your feet.'

Vivekananda strode away from her without a word. After that no one saw him again. Night fell on the mountains and the walkers returned. But he wasn't in the house either. The ladies were frightened but Mr Sevier assured them that all was well. Swamiji had left a note saying that his mind was disturbed and he needed seclusion. He was retreating to the hills to spend a few days in prayer and meditation. He would come back when he felt whole again.

Swamiji returned after three days. Thumping a brother disciple on the back he cried heartily, 'Look at me! I haven't changed a bit. I'm the same young sadhu who walked his way all over the country eating what he could find and sleeping in fields and meadows. I was in the forest for three days and I never felt better.'

But his behaviour with Nivedita did not change. He continued to snap at her and lecture her on her shortcomings for the

589

flimsiest of reasons. And, when alone, he took to walking up and down, his steps quickening with the turmoil in his heart. Sometimes he was heard to mutter. 'I must go away again . . .'

One evening he came into the garden where the Seviers sat with Joe, Olé and Margaret watching the sunset. 'I've made a mistake. I must go away again,' he announced abruptly. Five white faces looked up in shocked concern. And they saw something that they wouldn't forget in all their lives. Swamiji stood before them, his right arm raised, forefinger pointing to the sky. And before their staring eyes his form seemed to swell and expand till, by a trick of the fading light, it hid the mountain behind him. A few seconds later everything became normal again. Swamiji stood before them just as he had always been. His face was calm and unlined and his eyes clear and bright. In the west the sun disappeared in a riot of rose, gold and pearl. And, from the east, a sickle moon slid up like a slice of silver against a sky of indigo velvet. Swamiji looked up at it for a few moments, then turning to the still staring group, he said, 'Tonight is the second night of the new moon. It's a special night for Muslims. Shall we make it special for us too? Come, let us hold hands under the moon and, like it, begin all over again!'

Although he didn't address her directly Nivedita knew that his words were meant for her.

Chapter XXVII

With the pelting rains of Sravan the Padma and Gorai rivers had swelled to twice their size. *Padma Boat,* the family bajra of the Thakurs of Jorasanko, glided lightly and swiftly over the vast expanse of turbulent water like a wondrous bird, dazzling white and incredibly beautiful. It was so large it could be manned by only half a dozen men. Inside, it was fitted up with every luxury that could be imagined—carpets, curtains, French furniture and chandeliers of Belgian glass. It had been designed and built by Dwarkanath Thakur. Debendranath had lived in it for months together whenever life in the city had palled on him. Now his son Rabindranath occupied it, not for the purpose of touring the family estates, but for enjoying a holiday with his wife and children.

It was a lovely morning, clear and bright, with a slight nip in the air. The bajra had cast anchor in Shilaidaha by the bank of the Padma. Rabindra sat in a patch of sunlight on the deck reading H. Hudson's *Green Mansions.* From time to time he looked up from his book and gazed fondly on the children as they played around him. Madhuri, Rathi, Rani, Meera and Shomi were his own. With them was his nephew Neetindra whom he had brought along. Presently Neetindra came up to him and said, 'Robi ka! I'm trying to persuade Rathi to go ashore with me in the jolly boat and look for turtle eggs. But he refuses. He's scared of the water.' Rabindra's glance rested on his eldest son. He was a boy of ten with big eyes and a shy smile. His head had been tonsured on the occasion of his *Upanayan* and was now covered with fine, black down.

'Why Rathi!' The boy's father closed his book and came up to him. 'Neetu tells me you're afraid of the water. If you know swimming you have nothing to fear. I'll tell Badan Miya to start teaching you from tomorrow.'

'I won't get into the water,' the child cried out in fear. 'The crocodiles will eat me up.'

'Silly boy! There aren't any crocodiles. And, even if there are, they won't come anywhere near you. They're afraid of humans.'

'No Baba Moshai!'

Now Rabindra did a strange thing. Picking the boy up, he flung him into the water with a swing of his powerful arms. The other children looked on with anxious eyes and little Meera burst into tears. Some of the oarsmen came running up. But Rabindra stopped them from jumping in with a gesture. He stood on the deck, arms crossed over his chest, and watched the little black head bob up and down and the frail arms and legs thresh frantically in the water. Madhurilata clutched at her father's hand. 'Rathi's drowning Baba Moshai!' she cried. 'He's going under.' Rabindra placed an affectionate hand on the girl's head. 'He won't drown,' he said smiling. 'Just wait and watch.'

'Let me go after him Robi ka,' Neetindra begged. But Rabindra wouldn't let him. After a few minutes more it seemed to him that the current was bearing Rathi away. In a split second Rabindra tossed off his banian and tucked his dhoti firmly into his waist. Diving in, he swam with powerful strokes up to the boy. He took hold of his shoulders but didn't bring him back. 'Watch me,' he said releasing his grip and setting him afloat. 'Move your legs and arms the way I'm doing. Don't be afraid. You won't drown.' Half an hour later father and son returned to the bajra. 'You've had your first lesson Rathi,' Rabindra said patting his son on the head. 'The rest will be easy.' It was true. Rathindra learned swimming in the next two days and became so fond of it that it was difficult to get him out of the water.

Rabindra believed in the direct approach—whether it was in communicating a physical skill like swimming or teaching a language or a literature. He had no opinion of the conservative British method of imparting instruction. His own school days had been far from happy and he was determined that his children should not suffer as he had done. He did not send them to school. Instead he employed two tutors—an Englishman called Mr Lawrence to teach them English and a pandit for Sanskrit. And, whenever he found the time, he gathered them around him and told them stories from the Ramayan and Mahabharat. Then, after they had gained a degree of familiarity with the ancient epics, he read out extracts from the writing of Michael

Madhusudan Datta and Bankimchandra. He knew, of course, that much of what he was reading would be quite incomprehensible to them, but he believed that the power and beauty of the language would enter their ears and, at some later date, find its way into their minds.

Rabindra had given this matter of education a great deal of thought. Some alternative method had to be found. How would it be, he thought often, if he started a school of his own? A school in which the ancient system of education, prevalent in Vedic India, could be revived. His nephew Balendra, greatly excited by the idea, was trying to persuade him to open an institution in Shantiniketan. But he wasn't ready for it just yet.

Rabindra had come to Shilaidaha with the express intention of spending time with Mrinalini and the children. But he rarely got the opportunity of being alone with them. As in Jorasanko, there was a constant stream of visitors on *Padma Boat*. Surendra and Balendra came every other week. They were so fond of their Robi ka that they couldn't be separated from him for long. But Bibi, who could easily have come with her brother, stayed away. She didn't write either. That is—not to her Robi ka. Rabindra had heard that there was a new man in her life and that her letters were addressed to him.

Jagadish Bose was another frequent visitor. Whenever he came he demanded to hear a new story. In consequence, Rabindra was writing a lot of short stories these days. The historian Akshay Maitra, the district judge of Rajshahi Loken Palit, and the Deputy Magistrate of Kushthia Dwijendralal Roy, were also to be seen quite often on *Padma Boat*. It was a happy time for Rabindranath and the days passed by as lightly as though they had wings. In the evenings the friends sat together on the deck enjoying the cool breeze that blew up from the river and the delicious snacks Mrinalini prepared in her kitchen. For, here on *Padma Boat*, as in Jorasanko, Mrinalini kept herself occupied with cooking and serving her husband, children and guests.

When alone, Rabindra made up for lost time by writing feverishly. Poems, stories and prose pieces emerged from his pen in an unending stream. The only thing he wasn't writing these days was letters. The epistolary phase with Bibi was over. Now he only answered the odd letter she wrote. Or anyone else wrote.

One day he received a strange communication.

Hé Manavshrestha, it ran, I have received you within my soul as a husband and lover. Yet I shall never expose myself before your eyes or ask anything of you. That was all. Rabindra turned it over in his hand wondering where it had come from. There was no signature and no address. He read the letter again. This time the warm blood rose up in a wave suffusing his face and neck. His lips softened in a smile. It was clear that he had a secret admirer and that it was a woman—a young woman. The thought filled him with elation. He folded the letter and put it carefully away. A similar epistle arrived the next week. And the week after. Gradually they fell into a pattern. Every three or four days a letter arrived conveying the emotions of a young woman who had surrendered her soul to this 'man among men' but asked for nothing in return.

One day Rabindra received a letter from Gyanadanandini informing him that Bibi was to be wed. The prospective groom was Jogeshchandra Chowdhury. Bibi had given her consent to the match and, if Robi had no objection, she would like to set the date as early as possible. Jogesh? Rabindra was startled. Jogesh and Pramatha Chowdhury were Pratibha's brothers-in-law and Bibi's suitors. But, from what he had heard, Bibi had set her heart on Pramatha. Of course Jogesh was the more eligible of the two. They were both barristers but Pramatha, though sensitive and articulate, was briefless whereas Jogesh had a flourishing practice. But, as he saw it, it was Bibi's choice entirely and he lost no time in conveying his approval.

But, despite prolonged negotiations, the marriage could not take place. Gyanadanandini had several conditions one of which was unacceptable to Jogesh. She wanted him to leave his family and make his home with her. This he refused outright. He had a proud, independent spirit and he would brook no interference in his personal life. With the breaking of the match a bitter feud ensued between the two families. Gyanadanandini had never been so humiliated in her life. She gave vent to her indignation constantly and freely and poor Bibi, overwhelmed with guilt at having brought her mother to this pass, shed many bitter tears in private.

One day Sarala came to see Bibi. 'What sort of a girl are you?'

she demanded in her forthright way. 'You love one brother and you agreed to marry the other! How do you think you would have felt living in the same house? Could you have looked upon Pramatha as a brother-in-law? You're lucky the proposal fell through. Now do something and do it quickly. Tell Mejo Mami the truth.'

'I can't,' Bibi faltered helplessly. 'Can a girl raise her eyes to her mother's and tell her she is in love? Has anyone ever heard of such a thing in our society?'

'There's always a first time. And a girl like you should set a precedence. If you can write twenty-page letters to a man addressing him as *Mon Ami* you can surely tell your mother you're in love.' She looked sharply into Bibi's face. The girl's cheeks were stained a rich crimson and there was a glint of tears in her fine dark eyes. 'Well,' Sarala continued in a softened tone, 'If you can't—I'll do it for you. I'll tell Mejo Mami you care for Pramatha.'

Sarala was as good as her word. Encountering her aunt she poured out the whole story. She had expected resistance; even angry denial. But, strangely enough, Gyanadanandini's response was entirely favourable. She had no objection, she said, to Bibi's marrying Pramatha. But her condition remained. She wouldn't send her only daughter to live among strangers. Her son-in-law must make his home with her.

Pramatha, whose hopes of marrying the girl of his dreams had been severely dashed by his own brother, lost no time in agreeing to Gyanadanandini's condition. But the Chowdhury family rejected the proposal outright. They had never heard anything so ridiculous in all their lives. Two brothers vying for the same girl! Why? Was there a dearth of girls in the country? Gyanadanandini was in a quandary. She had been told by Sarala that Bibi had set her heart on Pramatha and had vowed to remain a spinster all her life if she couldn't marry him.

One day Jyotirindranath came to Shilaidaha—not for any work of his own but as ambassador for his Mejo Bouthan. He was so changed that, leave alone the subjects, even the officials of the estate could not recognize him. The complexion of beaten gold that could once have invoked the envy of the gods had darkened and dulled to a tarnished copper and the flashing dark eyes had burned themselves out and were now the colour of ashes. He stooped a little and his voice, when he spoke, quavered a bit like an old man's. 'We need your help Robi,' he said to his brother. 'Mejo Bouthan will feel extremely humiliated if this marriage does not take place. Pramatha's eldest brother Ashutosh is a friend of yours. Use your influence with him.' Rabindra sat silent, for a few moments, looking down at his feet. He found it difficult to look into his Natunda's eyes. They brought back memories of Natun Bouthan and the old sense of guilt. Besides, he wasn't sure he wanted a part in what was going on. The whole thing was a mess. Mejo Bouthan was far too arrogant! As for Bibi–she should have expressed her true feelings right from the start. Had Jogesh agreed to live in the house in Baliganj she would have been married to him by now, wouldn't she? It was quite natural for the Chowdhurys to feel resentful.

Rabindra refused to go back to Calcutta and sort the problem out despite Jyotirindra's repeated requests. But he agreed to write to Ashutosh and he did so—a twenty-page letter explaining the circumstances. Jyotirindra carried the letter back with him and showed it to his Mejo Bouthan and her daughter before posting it. But Rabindra's efforts yielded no results. The Chowdhurys were determined to keep the daughter of the high-nosed Gyanada-nandini Devi out of their family. Pramatha, on the other hand, was determined to marry her. He told his prospective mother-in-law that he would do so even at the cost of breaking with them.

Which was what happened. Gyanadanandini emerged from the battle, scathed but triumphant. Her beautiful, brilliant daughter would marry the man she loved. But she wouldn't cover her head and serve her husband's family like an ordinary Hindu wife. She would have a home, near her mother's, where she would live like a queen. She would have every comfort, every luxury she was accustomed to even if her husband earned little or nothing. Her mother would look after them.

The date for the wedding was set in March. Indira would be a spring bride.

Chapter XXVIII

The shy wild flower of Nadiya, Bansantamanjari was an accomplished equestrian these days. She could be seen riding side saddle on a white mare, this cool spring morning, beside Dwarika's dappled roan. Her head was bared to the sun and wind and she sat her horse as light as a feather, unlike Dwarika whose horse panted and sweated beneath his weight. From time to time she urged the mare into a gallop and shot ahead of her husband with a laugh: 'I must have been a Rajputani in my previous birth,' she cried, 'I feel I've been riding all my life.' This, of course, was not Rajputana but the Punjab. Dwarika and Basantamanjari had come a long way.

From Rawalpindi to Muree and onwards . . . till they reached a village called Baramullah, by the bank of a river. Although Basantamanjari's enthusiasm for riding had not waned Dwarika had had enough of it and he welcomed a rest. From Baramullah they could take the water way to the valley of Kashmir. The boats here were as large as bajras and fitted with every comfort including a kitchen which served excellent food. The river was fast flowing and full of currents and the boat Dwarika had chosen skimmed lightly over the jade green water. The scenery on both sides of the river was breathtaking. They passed mountains, covered with dark virgin forests, rising into the bluest of blue skies over which flocks of white birds flew in graceful formations. There were snow peaks in the distance on which the soft orange and gold of a sunrise or sunset poured itself in a stream of unearthly light. In the deepening shadows of dusk, the sky took on the most delicate hues ranging from the palest mauve to the deepest purple. And when the moon rose in the ink-blue sky, throwing long shafts of silver on the trembling water, Basantamanjari couldn't keep her happiness to herself but had to express it in song. Sitting on the deck, in a shower of moonbeams, she sang one song after another stopping only when the moon had set and the night was over.

597

One afternoon, as the boat cut its way through the green gold
water the oars splashing softly against the silence of sky and
mountains, Basantamanjari rose suddenly from her place on the
deck and pointed a finger in the direction of the bank. 'Red hair!'
she cried in a wondering voice.

'What was that?' Dwarika asked startled. 'What did you say?'

'There's a woman there with hair the colour of hibiscus. I've
never seen anything like it before.'

Dwarika looked in the direction of the pointing finger. A large
boat had cast anchor near the bank and, on its deck, a group of
people could be seen sitting around a table sipping tea from
porcelain cups. Four of them were women—white women.
'They're foreigners,' he explained. 'They have hair of different
colours. Yellow, red, brown—even white as snow.' Then peering
closer, he added, 'There's a man with them too I see. There he
is—talking to the boatmen. Do you see him? He's wearing a
saffron robe. Since when have sahebs started dressing like
sadhus?'

'Is he a saheb too?'

'He must be. A native would hardly be travelling with white
women. And look . . . he's smoking a pipe. Chha! What an insult
to saffron!'

After spending a week in Srinagar, Dwarika took a boat to
Anantnag. Kashmir was set high on the mountains but it had
innumerable valleys through which rivers and their tributaries
ran incessantly turning the kingdom into a web of silver. From
one stretch of water to another they floated, without a care, till
they reached Pahalgaon—a tiny village by the bank of the Lider.
Though small and obscure Pahalgaon was crowded with tourists
for it was from here that the trek to Amarnath commenced.
Sravani Purnima, the night on which the Shiva linga in the cave at
Amarnath would manifest itself in all its glory, was only a few
days away. There weren't enough inns and resthouses to
accommodate the large number of pilgrims that poured in here
from the rest of India during this season, so tent owners did a
brisk business. A structure of canvas and bamboo could be hired
on a small payment and put up anywhere. By the time Dwarika
and Basantamanjari reached Pahalgaon the mountain slopes
were already dotted with tents of varying shapes and sizes.

Choosing one for himself Dwarika joined the rest of the throng. Till now he had had no plans of journeying to Amarnath. It was an arduous, dangerous climb and all Dwarika had wanted to do was to indulge his senses and enjoy himself. But the sight of so many men and women, bent on the same mission, fired him with an enthusiasm he had never felt for anything religious before. He decided to join them and see the famed Shiva linga of ice and snow with his own eyes.

As for Basantamanjari—she had never been happier in her life. That night she crept out of her tent and, running down the slope, came and stood by the river. She gazed upon the scene entranced. Never had her eyes beheld such beauty. The waxing moon was pouring a stream of liquid silver over the black water filling every nook and cranny as though the river were a granary. The soft lapping of the water over the smooth cobbles made music in her ears. And, from over the mountains, a wild sweet breeze blew over her caressing her limbs and lifting the strands of her hair. She felt her soul deepen and expand; grow rich . . .

The sound of Dwarika's footsteps walking rapidly towards her brought her back to reality. 'You must have been worried about me,' he cried then went on to explain. 'Something rather nasty has happened. A sadhu has appeared from somewhere with four white wenches in tow. He insists on taking them to Amarnath. Do you remember the women we saw on the boat? They are the ones. The man is not only no ascetic—he's a dirty scoundrel. One isn't enough for him. He must have four to warm his bed. The other sadhus here are up in arms. They have declared that they won't allow their shrine to be polluted by the presence of *mlechha* Christians. But the pipe-puffing montebank insists on having his own way.'

'Have you spoken to him?'

'No. I heard all this from our group leader Yusuf. The Naga sadhus are threatening to attack the charlatan. You know how murderous they can get. Their trishuls—'

'Ogo! Stop them. Stop them. No one must touch the young sanyasi. He's no charlatan.'

Dwarika stared at her for a few moments then asked softly, 'Do you know him?'

'No,' Basantamanjari shook her head slowly from side to side with a lingering movement. 'I know nothing of him. But, just for a second, I saw the two of you together. You stood facing each other. The sanyasis's hand was on your shoulder and you were talking . . .'

'Don't be silly. You didn't see anything. You imagined it. I don't know any sanyasi. Unless, of course, it's Bharat—'

'It isn't him.' Basantamanjari's voice was strangely insistent. She wasn't looking at Dwarika. Her face was turned away and her eyes were fixed on a spot beyond the hills as though she saw something there. 'I've seen your friend Bharat. This man is another. I've never seen him in my life.'

'You've never seen him! Yet you see him!' Dwarika broke out impatiently. 'Are you in a delirium that you talk such nonsense?'

'I don't know,' Basantamanjari turned to him waving her white hands in a helpless gesture. 'I only know that you must go to him. He needs your support. He's waiting for it. *Ogo!* Don't delay. Go quickly.' She clutched his hands as she spoke and shook them with feverish insistence. Some of her urgency communicated itself to Dwarika. He gazed wonderingly at her for a long moment. He couldn't find it in his heart to reject her appeal. Disengaging her hands, hot and dry and light as fallen leaves, he walked back the way he had come.

Pushing his way through the crowd Dwarika reached the spot the new sadhu had chosen for himself. In the light of the two mashals that were planted on the ground Dwarika saw bundles of bamboo, canvas and rope lying unopened on the ground. The men who had come to erect the tents stood helplessly by. From time to time they cast fearful glances at the group of Naga sadhus who stood a few yards away daring them to do their work. These Naga sadhus were terrifying in their nakedness and the malevolence in their fanatical eyes. But the new sanyasi and his followers didn't look perturbed in the least. The women were chatting together in low voices. A little distance away from them the sanyasi walked up and down the bank as calmly as though he was taking his usual after dinner walk. Approaching him Dwarika saw that he was quite young, fair for an Indian, and extremely handsome in his robe of orange silk and black cap. It surprised him, for some reason. He hadn't expected him to look quite like that. And even more surprising was the fact that he was singing to himself in a low voice. Dwarika recognized the song. It was a composition by the bard of Halisahar, Ram Prasad, addressed to the goddess Kali. The man was a Bengali In a flash Dwarika knew who he was. 'Naren Datta!' he exclaimed. The man stopped his singing and turned to look at him. 'My name is Dwarika Lahiri,' Dwarika said coming forward. 'You're Naren Datta of Shimlé, aren't you? I've heard you sing at the Brahmo Mandir in Calcutta. I recognized you by your voice. Don't you remember me?' Vivekananda smiled and shook his head regretfully. He didn't remember Dwarika. 'We were in Presidency College together,' Dwarika tried again, 'But only for a while. Then you left—' Vivekananda continued to smile and shake his head. 'I am sorry for what is happening here Naren,' Dwarika continued. 'But I shouldn't be calling you Naren. You're a great man; a holy man now—' Vivekananda came forward and put a hand on Dwarika's shoulder. 'Never mind that my friend,' he said. 'Call me Naren if you wish. I haven't heard anyone utter that name for so long now. It brings back memories; many memories . . .' The voice trailed away. Dwarika trembled—not at the thought that he had received the touch of the great Swami Vivekananda but at the recollection that Basantamanjari had seen this scene in her mind's eye.

Now Vivekananda led Dwarika to the place where the ladies stood together and introduced them one by one. 'Why do the sanyasis find our presence offensive?' the lady named Jaya asked him. 'Is it because we are women?'

'It isn't that,' Dwarika answered her, his face red and embarrassed. Then, leaning over, he whispered in Vivekananda's ear, 'It's because they are Christians.'

'But that's absurd!' Vivekananda dismissed his theory with a laugh. 'This place is crawling with Muslims. If a Hindu shrine isn't defiled by the presence of Muslims why should it be by Christians?'

'The Muslims are local people they have imbibed a great deal of the Hindu faith over generations. They believe in Amarnath. The ladies with you are aliens. It's not the same thing.'

'I've brought them all the way from Calcutta. I can't send them back.'

601

'What is the alternative? A confrontation with the other sadhus! Would you really like that Naren?'

'Hmph!' Vivekananda grunted and fell silent. He took up the subject again after a few moments. 'I accept the fact that they shouldn't be allowed inside a Hindu temple,' he said, 'But why are the sadhus objecting to their staying here? This place is no temple. It's an ordinary village. The kingdom of Kashmir has Hindus, Muslims, Buddhists and Zoroastrians. What's wrong with Christians?'

Even as he spoke a violent ululating was heard and a group of Naga sanyasis came striding up to where they stood. At the sight of their naked ash-smeared bodies, wild tangled hair and evil-looking tridents Dwarika's heart missed a beat. He glanced nervously at his companion. Vivekananda's face was calm and unlined. He stood with his arms crossed over his chest and waited till the leader of the group stepped forward and stood before him.

'Pranam Maharaj!' Vivekananda bowed his head over folded hands in humble greeting.

The sadhu's eyes pierced malevolently into the young man's. Then they softened. 'You're a true yogi,' he said. 'I can see the holy light shining out of your eyes. You desire to break the old and build anew. That, in itself, is a good, a worthy endeavour. But while pursuing a cause you mustn't lose respect for the sentiments of others. The sadhus here do not wish to stay in close proximity to the *mlechha* women you have brought along. Why not remove them elsewhere? You can easily put up your tents higher on the slope. There's no dearth of space.'

Vivekananda was silent for a while. 'Very well,' he said at last. 'I'll pitch my tents on the top of the mountain. But I wish to take my guests with me to Amarnath. You must allow me to do so.'

'I will. And I'll stay close to you all through the journey. Instruct these women to treat the sadhus with deference and respect. That will ease the situation.'

'I will Maharaj.'

However, on further consideration, Vivekananda decided to leave the women behind. They were very keen on going but Vivekananda pointed out the difficulties they would have to face—the long hours of rough climbing over rocks and briars, the lack of even the most basic amenities, the inclement weather and

the fear of wild animals. It wasn't like going mountaineering in
Switzerland, he explained, where all the comforts they were used
to were provided along the way. Hindus believed that the greater
one's sufferings on the path to a pilgrim spot, the sweeter the
fruits. He was able to convince the other three but Nivedita stood
firm. She would go where he was going. She had left her country,
she said, to make India her home. Why couldn't she undertake
what other Indians did? Vivekananda was in a fix. It was one
thing taking four women along with him. The other pilgrims
would look on them as a team. But travelling with one woman,
and that too a young and beautiful one, was foolish. It would give
rise to unnecessary rumour and speculation. Vivekananda knew
that the other sadhus had not forgiven him and were waiting to
catch him in a misdemeanour. But Nivedita brushed his
arguments aside and advanced some of her own. She was here to
gather experience; to merge into the mainstream of Indian life.
What better opportunity would she get than joining these
thousands of men and women, all bent on the same mission? And
who cared what people thought anyway? She didn't. Did he? At
this point Vivekananda lost his temper. 'Even if I don't,' he cried
irritably, 'It isn't the only consideration. There's a practical side
which you are overlooking. You'll have to climb fourteen to
fifteen thousand feet. Have you even seen a mountain that high?'

'There's always a first time for everything. And I've come here
ready to do what everyone else is doing.'

'Look at your shoes,' Vivekananda laughed sarcastically,
'with their tapering heels and delicate laces. Do you intend to
walk over ice and snow in them?'

'No,' Nivedita answered coolly. 'I shall walk barefoot like the
rest of you.'

Now Joe Macleod, who was in the habit of indulging every
whim of the younger girl's, came to her defence. 'Swamiji,' she
said, 'Don't forget that you were seriously ill not so long ago. If
you can undetake this arduous climb why can't Margaret? She's
young and healthy. Besides, you need someone to look after you.'

'Sanyasis don't need anyone to look after them.' Vivekananda
answered sullenly.

'Vivekananda ji.' Sheikh Shahid-ul-lah, the government
official who had been entrusted with the welfare of the pilgrims,

stepped forward. He was a young man of about thirty-four and very smart and handsome. He could speak fluent English and had become quite friendly with the ladies. 'Why are you trying to prevent the memsahib from going with us? I give you my word that she'll have no difficulty whatsoever. I'll look after her safety and comfort myself.'

'You're taking her responsibility then?'

'Of course.'

'Very well,' Vivekananda turned to Nivedita and said solemnly. 'You may come with us but don't depend on me to look after you. I shall be on my own. You'll see me rarely and, that too, for short intervals. If you need anything you must ask Shahid-ul-lah.'

Nivedita smiled. The tears brimming over from her wide blue eyes made her face look like a flower with dewdrops clinging to the petals. Joe passed her a handkerchief. 'Wipe your eyes Margaret,' she said. 'You've won.'

The party started off at dawn the following day. There were about three thousand pilgrims under the leadership of Shahid-ul-lah and his minions. A large number of porters followed bringing up the luggage. Vivekananda and Nivedita walked at the rear of the group for a while then, suddenly, Nivedita discovered that he had left her. Looking up she saw him on a mountain ledge in the centre of a group of sadhus flailing his arms in the air and crying out *Hara Hara Bom Bom*! in unison with the others. Nivedita pulled her woollen shawl closer over her slim shoulders. The air was turning chilly and a light drizzle, driven this way and that by gusts of wind, was falling. Nivedita's porter walked behind her holding an umbrella over her head. Ahead of her the other pilgrims walked on, careless of the cold and rain, skipping over puddles and laughing at each other when they slipped and fell. Nivedita craned her neck to catch a glimpse of Vivekananda. He had recently recovered from a serious illness and caught cold easily. But the throng of pilgrims had swallowed him up and he was lost to her.

The first day's walking drew to a halt at a place called Chandanbari. The rain had increased into a steady downpour and the wind was piercing. There was no sign of Vivekananda but Shahid-ul-lah came bustling over to where Nivedita stood with her porters. 'Miss Noble,' he said, leading her away higher up the slope 'You'll be more comfortable at a distance from the others. They're a noisy lot.' Then, under his expert guidance, her tents were pitched, her luggage stowed away, and all made cozy within. Nivedita shed her wet things, put on a warm dressing gown and waited. Wouldn't Swamiji come to her? Not even on this first day? Resentment rose in her gentle heart. She was being treated like an outcaste; a leper. Swamiji was avoiding her and Shahid-ul-lah had taken care to keep her separated from the rest of the pilgrims. How could she ever get to know anything about this ancient land which was to be her own if she was to be kept forever apart? She wanted to merge; to be assimilated in this vast sea of people . . .

Nivedita opened some of the bags of food they had brought along. Joe had packed immense quantities of *chiré, khoi* and molasses and every variety of fresh and dry fruit available in the bazar for them to eat on the journey. Filling a huge satchel with the best of them Nivedita handed it to a porter with instructions to carry it for her. Then, donning a mackintosh, she picked up a large brass bowl and climbed down the hill to the first tent. It was occupied by a highly revered sadhu, chief of his sect, with many disciples. Tiptoeing inside, she found him sprawled on a bed against masses of pillows. The other, lesser ones, sat around him in a ring. Two little boys in saffron crouched on their haunches on either side massaging his legs and thigh, naked to the groin, with hot oil. Another rubbed his fingertips on his damp scalp. The sadhu looked up as she entered and recoiled involuntarily. But Nivedita knelt humbly before him and touching her forehead to the ground, placed the bowl, heaped with fruit, at his feet. The old man's eyes glittered at the sight and slowly, reluctantly, he placed a hand on her head.

Nivedita went thus, from tent to tent, till she had visited a dozen holy men and received their blessings. Gradually word spread that the memsahib was no irreverent, irreligious alien. She was as devout as she was beautiful and had come on this pilgrimage to Amarnath in a spirit of true faith and respect for the Hindu dharma.

But, back in her tent, Nivedita was overwhelmed with loneliness and despair. Would he never come? It was only the first

605

day. Miles of territory lay ahead of her. Would she have to traverse them alone? Suddenlyalmost as though she had willed his presence, Vivekananda stood in the room. He had his *japmala* in his hand and his lips were moving in prayer. Calling out to one of the porters he pointed to a gap in the tent and said, 'Pull the ends together and bind them tightly. A cold wind is coming in. And don't forget to put a hot water bottle in memsahib's bed.' Then, turning to her, he said briefly, 'It's been a tiring day for you. Have something to eat and go to sleep early. We leave this place at dawn.' He hurried away as quickly as he had come.

Nivedita had hoped that Swamiji would come to her, once more, just before they left. Hence she delayed the packing up of her luggage and the pulling down of her tent till Shahid-ul-lah came striding up the mountain. 'Why Miss Noble!' he cried, surprised. 'You're not packed yet. Is anything wrong?' Nivedita turned her face away to hide her tears. 'Have you had breakfast?' Shahid-ul-lah probed. 'You won't get the time, you know, once we start moving.' Nivedita shook her head. She didn't need any breakfast. Shahid-ul-lah got everything packed in a jiffy and Nivedita took up the journey once more.

It was a lovely morning. The sky, washed clean by yesterday's rain, was a clear unflawed blue and the sun shone, dazzling bright, on the snow peaks. Along the narrow mountain path the pilgrims walked, the line winding and unwinding over slopes and valleys, like a giant snake. Nivedita walked in the rear her heart heaving and her eyes downcast. Suddenly she heard a voice call out to her, deep and resonant as a roll of thunder, 'Margot!' Startled, she looked up to find Vivekananda leaning against a boulder and smiling down on her. 'Good morning Margot,' he said pleasantly. 'Did you sleep well?'

'Yes,' Nivedita murmured softly, 'Did you?'

'I didn't sleep a wink,' Vivekananda replied. 'I am in a fever of impatience to reach Amarnath. I doubt if I shall be able to eat or sleep till I do.' Then throwing her a searching glance, he said, 'Listen Margot! I'm here for a reason. Look ahead of you—' Following the pointing finger Nivedita saw that the path was sloping down to a valley through which a river ran—now frozen over into a sheet of ice and snow. People were crossing it in twos and threes, slipping over the smooth surface, losing their balance and falling . . . Some were crawling across the surface on bare hands and knees. 'Look at that old woman Margot,' Vivekananda said, 'She's crossing over barefoot. I wish you to do the same. It will be hard for you, I know. You've never walked barefoot in your life. But I want you to rise above your Western upbringing; to do what the others are doing. Can you?' Nivedita stooped to unlace her shoes then, pulling them off her feet, she threw them down the slope. 'I'll never wear shoes again,' she said softly. 'I didn't mean that,' Vivekananda said, 'Only for this stretch . . . I want you to prove to everyone who cast aspersions on you that you can do what every Indian can.' Gesturing to a porter to pick up the discarded shoes Vivekananda walked rapidly ahead with Nivedita by his side.

Setting foot on the frozen water Nivedita's heart sang within her. She remembered her childhood when she had run and skated over ice and snow and played games with the other children. Vivekananda had a stick to support him. She had nothing. Stretching her arms out like a ballet dancer she walked gracefully, step by step, till she reached the other side. 'You were very good,' Vivekananda exclaimed in surprise, 'but your feet must be numb with cold.'

'We all walked barefoot a few centuries ago,' Nivedita answered.

At the end of the day the weary pilgrims set up their tents in Wabjan, twelve thousand feet above sea level. Exhausted to the bone though she was, Nivedita's concern was entirely for Vivekananda. The climbing had been really tough and there was a good deal more to come. Could he withstand it? Though he wouldn't admit it, he was a sick man and needed constant attendance and care. But he was giving her no opportunity of looking after him.

Vivekananda didn't come to her that night nor the next morning. Nivedita got her things together and set off with the others, her heart heavy and resentful. Why was he avoiding her? What had she done? After walking a few hundred yards she heard a commotion at the front of the line. Hurrying to the spot she found that a river, its water as pure and clear as crystal, was flowing down the side of the mountain and a number of men were bathing in it. Others were standing on the bank taking off their clothes in preparation for plunging in. Among them was Vivekananda. Nivedita ran to his side and grabbed his arm. 'What are you thinking of?' she cried. 'The water is as cold as ice. Can't you see how the people are shivering? You'll catch your death!' Vivekananda disengaged his arm from the clutching fingers and said solemnly, 'I will do what I must. Don't forget that I'm a Hindu ascetic. Now leave me and go ahead with the others.' Then, seeing her hesitate, he commanded her in a stern voice: 'Obey me Margot! Walk on with the other women. It isn't proper for you to stand here where men are bathing. Don't worry. I shan't come to any harm.'

Half an hour later a ragged little urchin came running up to Nivedita. 'A sadhuji has asked you to wait for him. He's coming up the mountain.' Nivedita leaned against a boulder and waited. What sadhuji wanted to see her? Could she dare to hope it was Vivekananda?

It was. In a few moments he came striding up, dripping from head to foot, yet smiling and swinging his lathi with jaunty movements. The upper half of his body was bare and the lower wrapped in a soaking dhuti. 'Look Margot!' he cried, 'I've bathed in the river and I'm still alive. In fact I'm feeling better than ever. What I'd really like now is a chillum of tobacco.'

'Change into dry clothes at once,' Nivedita almost screamed at him.

'All in good time,' he answered pleasantly. 'Yesterday's climb was over sharp rocks and thorny briars. And you insisted on doing it barefoot. Let me have a look at your feet. They must be badly cut . . .'

'They're alright,' Nivedita said trying to hide them. But Vivekananda wouldn't let her. He forced her to sit down, then, taking her tender white feet in his hands, he examined them closely. They were torn and bleeding. 'I'm getting a horse or *duli* for you,' he said putting them down. 'You can't walk on those feet.'

'I can,' Nivedita protested, 'They don't hurt me a bit.' But Vivekananda dismissed her plea with a wave of his hand. 'That's nonsense,' he said smiling. Then, fixing his fiery dark eyes on her dewy blue ones, he said gently, 'You don't have to do what I do Margot. I'm a sanyasi. You're not. Why do you torture yourself?'

608

Nivedita's feet were bandaged and her shoes strapped on under Vivekananda's supervision. Then a horse was procured for her which she rode for the rest of the day. It was a wonderful ride. The air was strong and bracing and as deliciously cold as among the hills of her native land. The flowers that grew in the valleys and slopes were familiar too. She saw banks of Michaelmas daisies covering the hills with their delicate purple, shell pink anemones in sheltered clefts forget-me-nots peeping out of emerald moss, dove grey columbine with silky petals, lilies of the valley and wild roses in profusion. She sniffed the scented air drawing deep breaths of ecstasy. The sense of exile that had been torturing her all these days crumbled and fell away and her heart felt as light as a feather. And every time she thought of those warm comforting hands on her cold, lacerated feet (and she thought of them often) the most wonderful sensations washed over her. She felt she had come home at last.

Towards evening the line of pilgrims drew to a weary halt and, selecting a mountain slope, transformed it into a township of tents. It was the night of Rakhi Purnima—the last night of their climb upwards. They would set off again at midnight so as to reach Amarnath at dawn. There would be little sleep for anyone tonight. Nivedita made up her mind. She wouldn't wait for Vivekananda to come to her. She would seek him out herself and they would walk this final stretch and have their first view of Amarnath together.

After a wash and meal she set out on her search—a wraith-like figure in her white gown. She peered from tent to tent till she came upon him sitting with a group of sadhus in a circle. In the centre, an elderly ascetic, with long matted hair and grizzled beard, was singing a Vedic hymn in a monotonous drone. The air was thick with smoke rising from the incense burning in a thurible. There was no way of getting to Vivekananda. The doorway of the tent was jammed with human bodies and he sat at the far end. He looked weary to the bone. His face was as white as paper and his eyes sunk in pools of shadow. Nivedita could see that, despite the haze and the distance at which she stood. But she could do nothing for him. Sighing in resignation, she came away.

There were no horses for the last lap of the journey which was such a steep climb that only human feet could negotiate it and that too after exercising the utmost caution. Nivedita's feet were still sore and hurting but she walked rapidly ahead her eyes darting this way and that for a glimpse of Vivekananda. But he wasn't at the front of the file either and Nivedita was forced to walk on keeping pace with the others.

The path wound upwards dramatically over slippery snow-covered rocks for about two thousand feet. This was the most dangerous part of the journey. It was easy to lose one's footing and be thrown down the precipice thousands of feet below. Several accidents took place each year most of them fatal.

After inching their way painfully over steep rocks and jagged cliffs for several hours the pilgrims beheld a sight that sent a shout of jubilation through their lines. Before them lay a stretch of level ground covered with a blanket of fresh fallen snow which glimmered like a ghostly sea of silver under the fading moon. On the other side the eastern sky was paling with the first grey light of dawn. Singing and ullulating the frenzied pilgrims ran across—slipping over the snow, falling and reaching out to one another. The perils of the journey lay behind them. Amarnath was less than a mile away.

Nivedita tried to stand aside and let the others pass. She wanted to wait for Vivekananda. But the crowd washed over her in joyous tumult and carried her along on its waves. On and on she went, propelled by the force of faith behind her, feet flying, her ears deafened by cries of *Hara Hara Bom Bom* till she was washed ashore at the mouth of the cave of Amarnath. Was this the merging she had envisaged and yearned for? If it was, why did it leave her so restless and dissatisfied?

Nivedita entered the cave along with the others. It was huge and filled to overflowing with men and women singing, shouting, laughing, rolling over the ground and sobbing with joy in front of the shining pillar of ice that was the phallus of Shiva. Nivedita stood on one side her back pressing against a rock. She felt a sense of anti-climax. Was this all there was to see at the end of such a long, hard perilous journey? Water dripping from a crack in the roof and solidifying into a column of ice? What was so wonderful about it? She had expected . . . she didn't know what she had expected. But the reality was far from overwhelming. She had hoped that the collective faith of the people around her would

610

touch a chord in her soul; would set it quivering with ecstasy. But nothing like that happened. Dismayed, she looked on the phenomenon with lacklustre eyes.

Vivekananda came in after a while. He had bathed in the river and his dripping body was naked except for the flimsy bit of saffron that covered his genitals. His eyes were stark and staring and his feet unsteady as he ran towards the linga. Flinging himself, face downwards, he knocked his head on the ground several times. Then, rising, he stood with his eyes closed and his head bowed over folded hands. His lips moved in a silent chant. After a few minutes, it seemed to Nivedita that his body was swaying from side to side. Afraid that he would fall, she made a rush towards him, but stopped herself just in time. She remembered that he was a Hindu and a sadhu and she a woman; a Christian woman. She couldn't pollute him with her touch in this holy place.

But Vivekananda didn't fall. He gathered himself together with a supreme effort and walked out of the tent reeling and stumbling. Nivedita followed him. 'Do you feel unwell?' she asked anxiously. 'Shall I send for Shahid-ul-lah? There might be a doctor among the pilgrims—' Vivekananda turned his large, bloodshot eyes upon her face, 'I saw Him!' he cried in a wondering voice. 'He revealed himself before me! Do you hear me Margot? The great Mahadev—first and supreme among the gods of the pantheon—stood before me in a cloud of blinding light . . .' Nivedita looked down at her feet. She was embarrassed and didn't know how to respond.

The return journey was much easier. Crossing the Hathyar lake they reached Pahalgaon on the afternoon of the following day. Joe and Olé, who had missed them sorely, were standing by the Lider waiting for them. After a wash Vivekananda and Nivedita sat down to their first hot meal after nearly a week. Tucking into freshly made chapatis and vegetables and washing them down with great gulps of smoking tea, Vivekananda gave a sigh of satisfaction. 'A cigar is all I need now to make life perfect,' he said. Lighting one, he pulled deeply on it. Joe and Olé, consumed with curiosity, pressed him for an account of all that had taken place. 'I've had the most awesome experience of my life Joe,' Vivekananda said, 'The sight of the linga set my pulses racing. My heart trembled like a leaf. I shut my eyes. The light was unbearable. Then I felt something pulling at me; pulling me out of myself. I felt as though I was floating in space. I was frightened and ran out of the cave. But in my heart I knew that the great God Shiva, Destroyer and Preserver, was drawing me to Him . . .'

After hearing Vivekananda's account Joe turned to Nivedita. 'What was your experience Margaret?' Nivedita blushed. 'To tell you the truth,' she began, throwing a nervous glance at her guru, 'I enjoyed the journey very much. The scenery is spectacular. But inside the cave, I felt nothing—nothing at all. And I saw nothing that, in my eyes, appeared to be a miracle. The famed linga was only a trick of nature. I'm sure there are dozens of such ice pillars in the caves of Europe. I couldn't see what there was in it worthy of veneration.'

'The eyes of your mind are shut like a newborn's,' Vivekananda said, 'And your soul sleeps within you. That is why you saw nothing and felt nothing.'

'I admit it,' Nivedita confessed humbly. 'I'm raw, ignorant—not ready yet for a spiritual experience. But if you had helped me just a little; if you had sent only a tiny spark of the great fire that lit your soul I could have—'

'You talk like a child Margot,' Vivekananda cut her short. Then, looking at Joe, he said, 'She understands nothing. Yet the great pilgrimage she undertook will not go waste. She'll receive its fruits when she awakens—older and wiser.'

Chapter XXIX

The incarceration of Balgangadhar Tilak sent shock waves not only through the country but across the seas to Great Britain. The killers of Rand and Ayerst had been caught and hanged. Not a shred of evidence had come to light connecting Tilak with the crime. The English intelligentsia was disturbed and angry. Why was Her Majesty's government in India following a policy of such brutal repression particularly against a highly educated, distinguished leader of the people like Tilak? What was his crime? That he had criticized the inhuman behaviour of the Plague Control officials in his newspaper? What, then, was the meaning of the term *freedom of expression?* Max Mueller, acting as their mouthpiece, appealed to Queen Victoria to give orders to release her distinguished Indian subject without delay.

With Tilak's release the others, held without evidence, in the Rand and Ayerst murder case were set free one by one. Thus, over a year after being forcefully taken from the dharmashala in Sitavaldi, Bharat found himself standing outside the prison gates. His money and belongings were returned to him and he was given, in addition, a sum of one hundred and twenty rupees as wages for his labour in the oil mills. In all these months Bharat hadn't shaved or cut his hair. It stood out from his head, now, in a vast tangled thatch and was the breeding ground of thousands of lice. Some of them had travelled south and lodged themselves in his beard. Bharat couldn't sleep at night for the constant activity in his head and face. Sometimes, finding the itching unbearable, he scratched so viciously with his broken fingernails that blood ran down his scalp and chin.

Bharat's first action, on walking out of the prison gates, was to enter a barber's shop and shave the whole mass off. His head felt light and delightfully free and, with this new-found freedom, the old compulsion to wander about as a roaming sadhu dropped from him. Looking into the barber's mirror he saw a clean shaved head, fair healthy cheeks and a neat profile. He decided to become a gentleman and get himself a new lease of life. But where would he go? Calcutta was barred to him. So was Puri with its unhappy memories. Here, in Poona too, he had had a bad experience. Suddenly he thought of Patna. He had been there once and had liked the city. He decided to go to Patna.

He bought himself a full suit of Western clothes and shoes to go with it. Booking himself into a hotel, he bathed, changed out of his filthy saffron and wore his new clothes. Then he ate a lavish meal, went to the station and boarded a train to Patna.

Taking his seat in a second class compartment Bharat looked curiously about him. The young man sitting in a corner by the window drew his attention. Not for his looks, that was certain. He was of medium height and his body spare and frail in its loosely fitting English suit. A scattering of pockmarks on a face without beauty or distinction rendered it plainer than ever. What compelled Bharat's attention were his strange ways. He had six or seven books open before him from which he read haphazardly between puffs from a cigarette. He smoked incessantly and was extremely clumsy in his movements. He was constantly dropping something or the other—a book, his spectacles, his cigarette. And if anyone came forward to help him pick them up, he shrank into his corner and cried 'No, No' as though in extreme distress. Bharat wondered if he was an Anglo-Indian. Whenever he spoke it was in the language of the rulers. Bharat heard him ask a peanut vendor for an anna's worth of peanuts in English.

Presently the young man rose from his seat dropping a book and a handkerchief at the same time. As he stooped to pick them up Bharat saw that his purse was halfway out of his pocket. 'Mind your purse,' he warned. The young man straightened himself and pushed the purse deeper into his pocket. 'Thanks,' he said and walked swaying down the aisle. Curious to see what he was reading Bharat moved to his corner. And then he got a shock. The book nearest to him was Bankimchandra's *Krishna Kantér Will*. He picked it up and turned it over in his hands. A wave of nostalgia swept over him. He hadn't read Bankimchandra in so many years!

The young man returned a few minutes later. He had washed his face and was wiping it with a large handkerchief. 'Can I borrow this book for a couple of hours?' Bharat asked him in

Bengali. 'What?' It seemed the young man didn't understand
Bengali. Bharat was puzzled. He was reading a Bengali book but
couldn't speak or understand the language! How was that
possible? He repeated his request in English and the young man
agreed instantly. 'Yes, of course,' he said, then went on to add,
'Going far?'

'Up to Patna.'

The young man put out his hand and shook Bharat's. 'I am A.
Ghosh. Coming from Baroda and going to Deoghar.'

'My name is Bharat Kumar Singha,' Bharat said in Bengali,
'I'm coming from Poona. You don't look a Bengali but you have
to be one with a name like Ghosh.' His travelling companion
frowned.

'Say that again,' he said. Bharat obliged, whereupon he
answered 'Yes—Bengali by birth.' Then, opening his cigarette
case, he offered Bharat its contents. Bharat helped himself and
said in English, 'You read Bengali fiction. That too
Bankimchandra. Yet you can't speak Bengali?' A. Ghosh smiled.
'I can,' he said with charming candour. 'But I make many
mistakes. And I can't understand it when spoken to, unless each
word is enunciated slowly and properly.' He, then, proceeded to
tell Bharat about himself. His full name was Aurobindo Ghosh.
He taught in a college in Baroda and was the Gaekwad's private
secretary. He was going to Deoghar to see his maternal
grandfather who was old and ailing.

'How long have you been in Baroda?'

'Seven years.'

'That's too short a time to forget your mother tongue.'

Aurobindo smiled. The story of his life, he told Bharat, was
strange; unlike anyone else's. He had never known mother's love
as a child. She was insane and had been so for as long as he could
remember. His father was a famous civil surgeon and a pukka
sahib. Aurobindo and his two elder brothers had received their
primary education from Loretto Convent in Darjeeling. Then the
whole family had moved to London where his youngest brother
Barindra was born. After some years his parents had returned to
India with the infant Barin. The others had been left behind in
England. Their father had sent them money from time to time, at
first, but soon the sums stopped coming and the boys were left to

fend for themselves. Aurobindo had spent the next fourteen years in England. His parents, it seemed, had forgotten that he existed. It was in England that Aurobindo had met the Gaekwad of Baroda. Impressed with the youth's learning, the former had offered him a job and taken him along with him to his kingdom. Through his fourteen years' sojourn in a foreign land Aurobindo had tried to cling to his memories of the Bengali alphabet, to which he had been introduced as a child, and could still recognize the letters.

'Amazing!' Bharat exclaimed.

'Bengali is our language,' Aurobindo continued, 'and its literature our pride. Where in the world can you find a writer of the quality of Bankim?'

'Have you read Robi Babu?'

'No, but I've heard of him. I must get hold of some volumes of his poetry when I'm in Calcutta. What do you do in Patna?'

'Nothing,' Bharat answered with a smile 'I'm going there to look for a means of living.'

'Is Patna a good place for that?'

'Not really. I had to go somewhere. So I thought—why not Patna?'

'Why don't you come to Baroda? English-speaking young men like you can easily find employment there. Besides, I could appeal to the Maharaja on your behalf. He'll never turn down a recommendation of mine.' Then, warming to his theme, Aurobindo continued, 'Why don't you come with me to Deoghar for the present? My grandfather would be happy to offer you his hospitality. And, then, we could go back to Baroda together.'

'But my ticket is up to Patna!'

'That can be easily remedied. We'll extend it to Joshidi by paying the difference. Meeting you was really lucky for me. I was looking for someone to help me with my Bengali.'

Bharat smiled and shook his head. 'Not this time,' he said, 'I have some personal work in Patna which needs immediate attention. But I'll keep your offer in mind and come and see you in Baroda.' He wondered how his new friend would react if he knew that Bharat had been held on the charge of a murder conspiracy and was just out of jail.

On reaching Deoghar, the first thing Aurobindo did was to

bathe and change into a dhuti and kurta of coarse cotton from the mills of Ahmedabad. Lighting a cigarette he asked the old family retainer who was hovering around, 'Where's Barin?'

'Where else?' the old man pushed his lower lip out in sullen indignation. 'That whore keeps showing up from time to time. And he runs off to her. There's no stopping him.'

Aurobindo threw his cigarette away and came to the room where his grandfather Rajnarayan Bosu lay on his bed. He was paralysed from neck downwards but he could lift his arm just a little. Looking on him, with his great thatch of snow white hair and merry black eyes, no one could guess that he was dying a slow, weary death. 'Ki ré Aura!' he exclaimed, smiling up at his grandson. 'You've grown into a really big boy. And I hear great things of you. They say you have enough learning in your head to put a dozen pandits to shame. Come, come closer.' Lifting a trembling hand the old man stroked the boy's cheeks and chin.

'How old are you Aura?'

'Twenty-seven.'

'Twenty-seven! And still unwed!' Rajnarayan Bosu gave a great cackle of laughter. 'An eligible boy like you with a job as a king's secretary! Do you mean to tell me that the girls' fathers have left you alone all these years? Very bad,' he bared his toothless gums in a grin and wagged his snowy beard, 'We must remedy the situation at once. I haven't eaten at a wedding feast for years. How I long to dip my hand, right up to the wrist, in a rich mutton curry!'

'I'm not ready for marriage yet Dada Moshai.'

Aurobindo's grandfather pretended he hadn't heard. 'I'll look around for a suitable bride,' he said. 'Brahmo girls are being well educated these days. You won't have a problem conversing with your wife. By the way, haven't the Congress netas got to you yet? From what I hear it's a den of anglophiles. They'll snap you up.'

'I have no faith in the Congress. It's completely out of touch with the needs of the people. All the leaders do is curry favour with the Government.' He rose to leave. 'You must rest now Dada Moshai. I'll see you again in the evening.'

Coming out of his grandfather's room Aurobindo lit a cigarette and waited for his brother. Barin came home towards noon. His face was flushed and his eyes secretive. Aurobindo looked on him with affection. 'Where were you?' he asked. 'I heard you left home early this morning.'

'I was with Ranga Ma,' the boy answered shuffling his feet. 'Don't you have school today?'

'Ranga Ma wouldn't let me come away without a meal.' His face started working and tears glistened in his eyes. 'Why can't I stay in her house, Sejda? No one loves me here except Dadu. If you would only tell Bara Mama—'

Aurobindo ruffled the boy's hair. This little brother of his was even more unfortunate than he was. After trying out a variety of treatments without success on his mad wife, Swarnalata, Dr Krishnadhan Ghosh had decided to keep her in a house in Rohini with his two youngest children. For himself he had taken a mistress and, moving with her to a house in Gomes Lane in Calcutta, he had proceeded, like many of his ancestors, to drown his sorrows in drink. Barin and his sister were left to grow like weeds in the fearful shadow of their violent, insane mother. She would beat them mercilessly whenever the whim took her, then cackle with laughter to see them weep. They tried to run away several times but were easily caught and brought back to be beaten black and blue. One day Krishnadhan Ghosh came to Rohini and was appalled at what he saw. The children were emaciated from lack of proper nourishment and their eyes had the furtive look of living with constant terror. He realized that if he left them where they were they would grow up as ignorant and uncouth as street children. He requested Swarnalata to let him take them away. But, though she gave up her daughter quite readily, the mad mother refused to part with her son. Separated from his sister Barin's life became harder than ever.

One evening, as Barin was playing in the garden, a big ferocious looking man walked in. Approaching Swarnalata, who sat on a bench under the bakul tree, he said, 'Would you like to buy some flowers Memsaheb?' Then, throwing the basket of flowers at her feet, he clutched Barin's hand and, pulling him along with him, ran out of the gate into the street.

Recovering from her initial shock and bewilderment in a few seconds, Swarnalata ran into the kitchen and picked up a long evil-looking knife. With this in her hand she chased the kidnapper but, her clothes restricting her movements, she wasn't able to catch up with him. Dragging the weeping, protesting boy over the rough, uneven ground his abductor took him to the station and hauled him into a train to Calcutta.

When they reached the house in Gomes Lane, the next morning, Barin's body was a mass of bruises and he had fainted from fear and exhaustion. On regaining consciousness, he felt a soft hand stroking his face and arms and a sweet voice murmuring in his ear, 'Oh! My poor baby! My lump of gold. How you have suffered!' Little Barin had never heard such words in his life, nor such a voice. From that day onwards the tall beautiful woman, who was his father's mistress, become Barin's Ranga Ma.

It was Krishnadhan's great good fortune that he had found himself a woman whose beauty of mind and soul matched that of her exquisite face and form. It was she who had insisted that he take his children away from the mad woman and give them proper care and education. While Krishnadhan lived she had been, to him, all that a wife should be. She had given him a happy home, been a mother to his children and had even, by gentle persuasion, weaned him away from his drink.

But on Krishnadhan's death, everything changed. He had made a will in which, after setting aside a sum for the maintenance of his insane wife, he had left his property to his companion and his younger children in her care. But the bigots of the Brahmo Samaj were appalled. Krishnadhan was a member of their clan. He couldn't be allowed to set up a woman of loose morals above his wife and leave his children in her care. It would reflect on them all. One of the bearded worthies of the Samaj came to visit Barin's newly widowed Ranga Ma and condole with her on her loss. Then, in a voice dripping with honey, he said, 'Can I have a look at the will Ma?' The poor girl, in all innocence, handed it over to him. He was older than her father and she felt no distrust. The old man thrust the document in the pocket of his jobba and rose from his seat. 'The will is forged,' he declared in a voice that had changed dramatically, 'And you're no better than a street whore. You have no right to Krishnadhan's property.'

On the pretext that Krishnadhan hadn't married her, the bereaved woman was deprived of everything including the care of the children she loved. Barin was sent to his grandfather's house in Deoghar. But he hated it there. He yearned for his Ranga Ma and she for him. From time to time she came to Deoghar and stayed in the dharmashala where Barin could visit her.

Aurobindo had only heard of her. He had never seen her. 'Let me take you to Ranga Ma,' Barin begged his brother. 'She'll be so happy to see you.' But Aurobindo shook his head. 'She's your Ranga Ma Barin,' he said patting his little brother on the head. 'She's nothing to me. I'm my mother's son.' Breaking into a laugh, he added, 'My lunatic mother's lunatic son.'

Chapter XXX

It was a cold frosty morning in early winter. Maharaja Radhakishor Manikya stood at the window, his eyes resting on the blue waters of the lake in which a pair of snow white swans glided about in loving dalliance. The old palace, in which his father Birchandra Manikya had lived with his many wives and concubines, had crumbled to its foundations after a severe earthquake had rocked Agartala several years ago. It had not been rebuilt. Instead, a new palace was rising at Naya Haveli. The room in which Radhakishor stood was in a much smaller, humbler abode belonging to one of his officials. This was where he resided at present while waiting for the completion of his new home.

Ever since he came to the throne Radhakishor had been beset with difficulties. There was hardly any money in the treasury. After the earthquake, his financial situation had become more critical than ever. The political front was alive with plots and conspiracies for Bara Thakur Samarendra hadn't given up his claim to the throne. The British were also putting pressure on the young king in several ways.

These nagging worries, however, failed to cast a shadow over Radhakishor's mood this bright winter morning. He had woken up, rested and refreshed, after a good night's sleep and his usually jaded appetite felt sharp in the clear frosty air. Falling on his breakfast of hot kachuris, fried eggs and halwa, he ate with relish. Then, taking up the latest issue of *Bharati*, he proceeded to go through it with calm enjoyment. As he read, a shadow fell across the door and a servant came in with the news that Mahim Thakur stood outside waiting to see him.

'Send him in,' Radhakishor commanded. Mahim was a member of the family and the king didn't stand on formality with him. Mahim came into the room in a couple of minutes. He had a large, clumsy packet wrapped in oil paper in his hands and a letter in a long slim envelope. Putting them down on the table he made

621

his obeseiance and said, 'These are from the poet Rabindranath Thakur?

'For me?' Radhakishor asked, his face glowing.

'Yes.'

'It's a strange coincidence. I was reading an article of his—'

Opening the packet the king found that it contained a length of white silk. He felt the texture with a puzzled frown. It was quite rough and coarse. He wondered why Rabindra Babu had sent him such a present. It was hardly fit for a king. 'It's not very fine silk,' Mahim explained, 'but it's valuable, nevertheless. It has been woven by the silk weavers of Rajshashi. The British wield such a tight control over the silk industry that the country's indigenous weavers are left without a means of living. Rabindra Babu feels that we should encourage them and buy their stuff even it it can't compete in texture with Lancashire silk. He has bought up vast quantities of silk and is sending lengths of it to his friends. He says it has the touch of Mother India.'

Radhakishor touched the cloth to his forehead murmuring softly, 'The more I hear about this young man the more I marvel at his qualities. Poets, I had thought, were self-centred creatures who sat writing all night, crouched over a lamp, with no thought for anyone or anything else. But Robi Babu is the greatest poet this country has ever seen and yet he has such a sweeping range of other interests! He's not only a superb singer, actor, playwright, music composer and administrator—he is also a patriot of the finest order. His love of his country defies description. It knows no borders—physical, religious or cultural. For him, the entire landmass from the towering Himalayas in the north to its southern-most tip is Bharat—the Motherland. I've heard him say so in several speeches. Write him a letter of thanks Mahim. By the way, can't we start a silk weaving industry in Tripura?'

'We certainly can Maharaj. We need to get an expert to guide us.'

'Start working on it. And send for the tailor. I wish to get a suit made out of this cloth and wear it to the Governor's durbar . . . Another thing. I'd like to invite Rabindra Babu for a visit to Tripura. What do you think?'

'It's a good idea. I could go up to Calcutta and—

'You're ever eager to rush off to Calcutta. I have a better plan.

I'll go to Calcutta myself and invite him personally. These winter months is a good time to be in the metropolis. So much goes on by way of entertainment. Jatra, theatre, circuses and magic shows. And there's something new that is the rage these days, I hear. It's called a moving picture. They say that people can be seen walking, laughing, dancing and riding in pictures—'

'It's called the bioscope Maharaj. A saheb called Stevenson has set up his instrument in Star theatre. People are flocking to it.'

'It's the strangest thing I've ever heard. How is it possible to see pictures moving?'

'It's the age of science, Maharaj. All kinds of queer things are happening. When I was in Calcutta, last August, I saw something called *Electric Light* in some of the mansions of the wealthy. There's neither oil nor gas in the dome. The light comes on at the flick of a switch and burns on and on till the same switch is flicked back. The light, Maharaj, is so bright that it puts gas lamps to shame No sputtering; no flickering. As steady as the sun. And there's no fire in the dome. I touched one and my hand wasn't burned.'

'Make arrangements for my visit at once Mahim. I wish to see all these things with my own eyes. Rabindra Babu's great friend is the scientist Jagadish Bose Maybe he could explain to me how these things work.'

Mahim nodded, then handed him some letters to sign. Picking up the first one Radhakishor frowned. 'Who drafted this letter?' he questioned angrily.

'The secretary did, Maharaj. I've read it through. There are no mistakes.'

'I'm not talking about mistakes. This letter is addressed to Anandamohan Bosu. Is he a Bengali or isn't he?'

'He's a Bengali Maharaj.'

'Then why are we writing to him in English?'

'Because English is the language of the courts. The barristers speak no other—'

'They may speak English, Persian or any other language they please. It is of no consequence to me. Our national language is Bengali and all the letters going out from our kingdom will be in it. If the great Babus of Calcutta can't read our letters let them hire people who can. Go, get the letter redrafted in Bengali.' Then just as Mahim turned to leave the room, he said: 'Wait, do you remember a man called Shashibushan Singha? He was our tutor during my father's reign. A very learned man with immense knowledge of both languages—English and Bengali. We need people like that in our kingdom.'

'I remember him Maharaj. I've met him once or twice in Calcutta.'

'Can he be persuaded to return to Tripura?'

'I doubt it. I asked him several times but he refused. He has developed a great hatred for the royals of Tripura.'

'Why? There must be some reason. Do you know what it is?'

'I do . . .' Mahim hesitated. 'It's a bit . . . a bit awkward.'

Radhakishor rose to his feet and walked towards Mahim. Then, putting a hand on his shoulder, he said, 'Don't be afraid to talk to me. I'm not averse to hearing the truth.' Still Mahim hesitated. 'Has Master Moshai accused me of anything?' Radhakishor probed gently. 'I can't think why. I've never opposed him in any matter or shown any discourtesy.'

'Shashi Babu believes that you had a hand in the killing of Bharat.'

'Who is Bharat?' The blood drained away from Radhakishor's face.

'He was a brother of yours. Your father's son by a kachhua. He was a meritorious scholar and a great favourite of Shashi Babu's.'

'Ah! Yes. I remember now. He used to live in Radharaman Babu's house. Hai! Hai! So Master Moshai believes I ordered the killing! Does he not know my nature? I faint at the sight of blood. I can't even kill a bird. Besides why would I want to kill Bharat? He posed no threat to me.'

'You may not remember,' Mahim coughed delicately. 'But, at the time we talk of, His Majesty your father, was about to marry his youngest queen. There was some talk of Bharat's over reaching himself—how I do not know. Anyway, the Maharaja found his presence offensive. It is believed that you engineered the killing to please your father.'

'That's nonsense. I was against the match myself because it gave more power to the Manipuris. Besides, I knew nothing of Bharat or of his creating difficulties for my father. I was hardly

aware of him. Tell me, Mahim. Is the Shashibushan Singha who
writes in *Bangabashi* the same person as our Master Moshai?'
'I'm quite certain it is. He often writes of Tripura.'
'A terrible thought has just occurred to me. Suppose he writes
of the incident and attributes the blame to me? My reputation will
be ruined. I'll have to seek him out and clear my name at once.'

A week later Radhakishor left for Calcutta. The first thing he
did upon his arrival, was to send a message to Jorasanko. But the
messenger returned with the news that Rabindra Babu was
enjoying a holiday with his family in Shilaidaha and no one knew
when he would return. Next Radhakishor sought out
Shashibushan Singha. Shashibushan had changed a great deal
from the slender, handsome young man who had tutored the
princes of Tripura. He had put on weight and could almost be
called portly. His hair, powdered with silver, had receded from
his noble forehead till it assumed the form of a fringe around a
shining dome. He had had a nasty fall from a train, in
Chandannagar station, a couple of years ago and had injured his
knee cap. He had walked with a limp ever since and that too with
the help of a shark-headed cane. His personality had changed,
too, with the change in his appearance. The fierce idealism and
passionate love that had characterized him were spent and there
was nothing left of him other than the prosperous gentleman and
good husband and father that he was. He thought of Bhumisuta
sometimes and was filled with wonder. What was it about her
that had driven him, as it had, to the border of insanity? And
Bharat—poor Bharat! He pitied the boy. All Bharat had ever had
in this world was Bhumisuta's love. And Shashibushan had
snatched it away. He hadn't won it for himself but he hadn't let
Bharat enjoy it either. If he had only been more patient; more
controlled, Bharat wouldn't have been lost to him. And
Bhumisuta wouldn't have drifted away; wouldn't have been
reduced to earning a living by dancing on a stage. He knew that
the actress Nayanmoni was Bhumisuta. He had seen her several
times.

When Mahim came to Chandannagar with the message that
Radhakishor wished to see him, Shashibhushan laughed and
answered, 'I was Maharaja Birchandra Manikya's servant and
would have rushed over at his command. But the present king

was my pupil. It's not possible for me to bow before him and pay homage.'

'You needn't bow before him,' Mahim said. 'Maharaja Radhakishor Manikya doesn't care for formal courtesies. He won't expect it of you.'

'He's the king and there's a certain protocol which should be maintained. In any case, what does he want of me?'

'You were in the service of the kings of Tripura. He would like to give you a pension.'

'Pensions are for those who retire from service. I resigned—voluntarily. Tell the king that I don't qualify for a pension. Besides, I'm quite contented with what I have—which isn't too little. I live quite well as you can see.'

When Mahim took this message to the king, the latter said, 'If Master Moshai won't come to me I'll go to him myself.' And he insisted on having his way despite Mahim's pointing out that kings didn't go to people's houses uninvited. However, the shrewd and intelligent Mahim managed to effect a meeting between the two without compromising the dignity of either. He knew that Shashibushan was in the habit of visiting the offices of *Bangabashi* quite regularly. One evening he accosted him in the street outside and said, 'The Maharaja is waiting for you in his carriage.' Shashibhushan was taken aback. Before he could react, he had the strange experience of beholding the king of an independent realm step down from his carriage and walk towards him. Folding his hands humbly before his erstwhile mentor Radhakishor greeted him, 'Namaskar Master Moshai!'

'Jai to the Maharaj!' Shashibhushan was forced to respond, 'I hope all goes well with you.' At this point, Mahim, who was standing close to them, suggested, 'Why don't we sit in the carriage and talk?' Shashibhushan hesitated a little before complying with the request. 'I have a train to catch,' he muttered. 'I must get back to Chandanngar.' Leading him to the royal carriage Radhakishor assured him, 'I'll take you to the station myself. We can talk on the way.'

As soon as the carriage started moving Mahim cleared his throat importantly and said, 'The Maharaja wishes to ask you a question. May I put it to you on his behalf?'

'Certainly.'

'Many years ago, when the old king was alive, you and I had a conversation regarding the disappearance of one of the king's sons—a boy named Bharat. You had said that, in your belief, the crown prince had hired assassins to murder the boy, then bury him in the jungle. What you said was in confidence and I've kept it a secret all these years. But over a week ago I told the Maharaja about it, about your suspicions I mean—'

'You must believe me Master Moshai,' Radhakishor leaned forward in earnest supplication. 'I know nothing at all of the matter. You've known me from childhood. Do you really think me capable of such an act?' Shashibhushan frowned. 'When did we have this conversation?' he asked Mahim.

'When the old Maharaja had just moved into his house in Circular Road.'

'There was a reason for what I said.' A smile flickered over Shashibhushan's ageing face. Turning to Radhakishor he said, 'I never held you guilty of the crime. You are sensitive by nature; incapable of an act of violence. As a matter of fact Bharat was not killed. He was alive and in Calcutta, under my care, when I told Mahim what I did. It was done to protect him. He was still in grave danger.'

'But why did you take the crown prince's name?' Mahim asked. 'And how would that protect Bharat?'

'I wanted you to repeat the story to everyone you met. If his enemies knew Bharat was dead they would stop looking for him. As to why I took Radhakishor's name—it was done to lend credibility to the killing. Radhakishor had control over the police. It was easiest for him.'

'Bharat is alive!' Radhakishor exclaimed.

'Yes I found him, by a miraculous chance, and brought him with me to Calcutta.'

'I'm so glad he is alive. Bharat is my brother. I'll take him back to Tripura and give him his due.'

Shashibhushan shook his head slowly from side to side. 'I've no idea where he is. You see, he disappeared from Calcutta, one night, exactly as he had from Agartala. He was hurt and offended at something I had said. I doubt if I'll ever see him again.'

627

Chapter XXXI

In England and America, Vivekananda had advocated the Vedantas as containing the true spirit of Hinduism, carefully avoiding mention of Tantric rites, idol worship and other forms of devotion also included in its vast plethora. But, over the last few years, he had become a self-confessed Shaivite and muttered the words 'Shiba! Shiba!' in moments of emotion. On his return from Amarnath, however, he changed his allegiance to Shakti—the female principle of Creation—and now he cried 'Ma! Ma!' at every step. One night, in a strange frenzy, he wrote a poem entitled 'Kali: The Mother'—a terrifying poem in which the goddess was portrayed as a ruthless killer dancing a strange dance between orgies of slaughter. This Mother Power who scattered 'plagues and sorrows' and destroyed the world 'with every shaking step' was unrecognizable from the ordinary human perception of Kali, endorsed by seers like Ramprasad and Ramkrishna, as a dark, tender mother who rained blessings on her children from eyes that held oceans of mercy; who smiled on them and drew them to her breast; shared their games and became one with them.

Soon after writing this poem Vivekananda felt a strong urge to meet his own mother. As soon as the news of his arrival reached her, the old lady came running out to meet him. Drawing him into the house she covered her famous son's face with kisses and cried, 'You don't look well at all Bilé. You work too hard and don't eat enough. I'm sure of it.'

'The doctors have advised me to control my diet Ma. I've given up salt and sugar.'

'But why?' His mother cried out in wonder. 'How can anyone live without those things? You used to love wedges of Ilish spiced with green chillies and mustard. I'll cook some, today, with my own hands and serve it to you, piping hot, with a mound of rice. You'll eat it, won't you?'

Vivekananda smiled and nodded. He didn't tell her that his

heart was badly damaged and he had to be very careful. The doctors had told him that his organs had gone into a shock the moment he had plunged his body, steaming and quivering with the rigours of the strenuous climb, into the icy waters of the river at Amarnath. His heart had stopped and he could have dropped down dead that very moment. But the body has a way of recovering itself and his heart had started beating again of its own. But not without some consequences. The muscles had slackened and it was, now, hanging an inch longer than it should. It was a very dangerous condition. There was no question of improvement. It could only deteriorate.

'Shall I tell you something Bilé?' His mother smiled up at him. 'You were only a baby then and very, very sick. I went to the temple at Kalighat and begged Ma Kali to spare your life. I swore a solemn oath. I said that, if you recovered, I would bring you to her and you would roll in the dust at her feet. You did recover but, somehow or the other, I forgot about the oath. Sometimes I think all my sufferings are owing to that sin. Your ill health too . . . Come with me to Kalighat and help me redeem my pledge. Will you?'

Vivekananda hesitated. He had no objection to gratifying his mother's desire. But would he be allowed to enter the temple at Kalighat? Dakshineshwar, where his guru had lived and preached; where his own spirit had opened its petals, grudgingly, one by one, was barred to him. His offence? That, inspite of being a sanyasi, he had crossed the black water, lived in the land of the *mlechhas* and eaten forbidden flesh. And, instead of undergoing penance on his return, he was still surrounding himself with *mlechhas* and even taking them to holy places. Such brazen, blasphemous behaviour was not to be borne! Mathur Babu's son had forbidden his entry within the temple precincts.

Though considerably apprehensive Vivekananda took a chance. He went to Kalighat with his mother and, to his surprise, was welcomed as an honoured visitor. Purifying himself by bathing in the Adi Ganga, he rolled on the floor of the *chatal* thrice and, thus, he redeemed his mother's pledge. Then, taking seven rounds of the temple, he prostrated himself before the goddess.

The pledge was redeemed but his health did not improve. He

suffered from palpitations which were so severe at times that he felt his chest would burst and his heart leap out of it. Then, when the palpitations stopped, he felt weak and lethargic and could barely move his limbs. But his will was as strong and indomitable as ever. When he strode about, supervising the multifarious activities he had set in motion, no one could guess that what he yearned for most was to lie down and sleep. Not even Nivedita.

One day Vivekananda said to her, 'I'm making all the arrangements Margot. I wish you to give a public lecture on the worship of Kali.'

'I?' Nivedita cried, taken aback. 'What do I know of Kali?'

'Read the Shastras and find out.'

'I can't read Sanskrit.'

'Saradananda will teach you. I give you a month in which to prepare yourself.'

'What can I say that the educated elite of Calcutta does not know already?'

'The lecture, though ostensibly for all, will be directed at the Brahmos and Christians. They have no knowledge of the complex philosophy behind the worship of Kali. You'll point out the significance—'

'I'm sure you or one of your brother disciples will do a much better job.'

'No. It has to come from you.'

Vivekananda smiled slyly to himself as he said this. The proselytizing Christians and high-nosed Brahmos would get the shock of their lives to hear an educated, enlightened white woman, born of the ruling race, speak in praise of Kali. It would be a slap on their faces.

Albert Hall was rented for an evening and leaflets distributed which read: 'Miss Margaret E Noble (Sister Nivedita), a lady eminently knowledgeable in Western Science and Philosophy, will speak on the subject of Kali worship. We invite the intellectual elite of the city to attend in large numbers.' Poor Nivedita was left with no choice but to prepare herself for her ordeal. She took lessons in Sanskrit and the Shastras from Saradananda and, whenever she got the opportunity, she bombarded Swamiji with questions, taking down the answers in a little notebook.

'I believe in Brahma,' Swamiji said to her one day. 'And the pantheon of gods and goddesses. It may sound paradoxical. But that's how it is.'

'Yet, at one time, you rejected Kali.'

'Yes. I hated everything and everyone associated with her. I fought her for over six years. But I lost the battle and surrendered. There was no other way for me. My guru had dedicated me to her service, you see.'

Nivedita sat silent for a few minutes. 'Swamiji,' she said at last, a flush rising in her cheeks. 'You had the great, good fortune of being guided by Ramkrishna Paramhansa. Yet you denied Kali. Why are you surprised, then, that the Brahmos do the same?'

'You are right. I shouldn't be surprised. But the truth is that I surrendered first and realized the greatness of Ramkrishna afterwards. I used to look upon him as a foolish, whimsical child. But the moment I accepted Kali my eyes were opened to the truth and his greatness was revealed.'

'I still don't understand. Why did you have to accept Her? What was it that broke your resistance?'

'I can't tell you that. It's a secret that I'll carry, till my death. Suffice it to say that it was a very difficult time for me. My father had just died. We had no money. My brothers and sisters were starving. Ma Kali saw how vulnerable I had become. "Catch the rascal now," she said to herself, "It's a good time." And, sure enough, she did. I tried to fight her but, as I said, I lost. She took me, in her triumph, and made me her slave.'

On the thirteenth of February, Albert Hall was filled to overflowing well before six o'clock—the time scheduled for Nivedita's lecture. Nivedita had sent personal notes of invitation to the eminent Brahmos of Calcutta and many of them were present. Rabindranath, having no desire to listen to an eulogy on Kali, avoided attending with a flimsy excuse. But Satyendranath was there with his niece Sarala. His daughter Indira has wanted to come, too, but she was to be wed in a few days and it wasn't proper for her to leave the house. Just before the lecture was to begin a great clattering of boots was heard and Dr Mahendralal Sarkar came pushing his way up the hall. It was packed but someone recognized him and offered him his seat. He lowered his

631

SUNIL GANGOPADHYAY

bulk into it without demur and stared belligerently at Nivedita who sat on the dais. A strange man sat beside her. He was to preside and introduce her to the audience. Swamiji was not to be seen anywhere. Nivedita looked very beautiful in a gown of milk white satin with an elaborately embroidered Kashmiri shawl across her shoulders. Her eyes were bright and eager in a face radiating with the vitality of youth. After a few preliminary remarks she began: '. . . The impact of our own religion upon a fresh consciousness is often a helpful thing to ourselves.

'. . . This causes us to examine the grounds of our own creed and the meaning of it, and its demands on us . . . The Semite, dreaming of God in the moment of highest rapture, called him "Our Father," and the European, striving to add the true complement to God as the child, saw bending over Him that Glorified Maiden whom he knew as "Our Lady".

'But in India the conception of woman is simpler, more personal, more complete. For India, there is only one relationship that makes the home—that makes sanctity—that enters into every fibre of the being, and it is not Fatherhood. What wonder, then, that in India God's tenderest name is that of Mother?

'. . . And of this symbol you have made three forms—Durga, Jagaddhatri and Kali.

'In Durga we have, indeed an element of queenhood, but it is the power of the Queen, not her privilege.

'. . . In Jagaddhatri, we have some development of the notion of protection. But it is before Kali—the terrible one, . . . Kali surrounded by forms of death and destruction that the soul hushes itself at last, and utters that one word "Mother".'

'What's all this?' An angry voice rose from the assembly. 'What's going on here? An English madam is exhorting us to worship Kali and we're listening to her like sheep! Miss Noble, I was under the impression that you were in this country to further the cause of women's education. But that seems to be far from your thoughts. We've been moving towards the light, slowly and painfully. But you seem intent on pushing us back into the dark.'

'Dr Sarkar,' Nivedita smiled benignly on the old man. 'I'm only expounding the principles behind the worship of Kali. I haven't finished yet . . .'

'Damn your principles! What do you know of Hinduism?

632

You've been here less than a year and all you've done during that time is sniff around here and there and pick up jargon. Does that make you an expert on a religion as ancient as ours? Do you have even the faintest knowledge of its history; its evolution; its vastness; its catholicity? Besides, don't you realize that your exhortations are sending the wrong signals? I don't need to tell you that the worst social offenders are found among Kali worshippers. The temples are dens of iniquity, crammed with thieves, drunks, gamblers, murderers—'

'A good thing may be put to wrong use at times. But that doesn't take away from its essential goodness. Weeds crop up more easily in a garden than flowering plants. But one doesn't destroy the garden because of them. If the essential philosophy behind Kali worship is properly understood—'

'That's rubbish! The Tantric bastards are only out for what they can get. They've set up a replica of a naked whore and they indulge in all kinds of perversities in her name. They drink and thieve and slaughter helpless animals only to gorge themselves on its flesh. Essential philosophy indeed! Hmph!'

At this point someone shouted from the back of the hall, 'Why don't you shut up you old ape? Who wants to listen to you?' A chorus of voices joined him. 'Sit down,' 'Why do you interrupt?' 'We're here to listen to Sister Nivedita. Not to you.' Mahendralal turned and glared at the assembly with fiery, red eyes. 'No,' he shouted back. 'I shan't sit down. I'll expose the hypocrisy of all the scoundrels who—'

'This is not your forum. If you won't sit down—get out.'

'Try and make me.'

'*Aré* Moshai!' A comparatively gentleman-like voice came to Mahendralal's ear, 'Why don't you keep your opinions to yourself? Don't you see you have no supporters?'

At this the wind went out of Mahendralal's sails. He looked around with dazed, hurt eyes and said in a broken voice, 'I have no supporters! Is that true? Is there no one here who thinks as I do?' There was a hushed silence. Then Satyendranath rose to his feet. 'I support you,' he said quietly. 'I believe, too, that Miss Noble's speech is sending out the wrong signals.' Following Satyendranath's admission eight or ten other men stood up. '*Oré* Behmo *ré* Behmo!' A chorus of crude voices accompanied by cackles of ugly laughter rippled through the assembly. 'They can't stand us Hindus but they can't leave us alone either. Throw them out.'

'I'm not a Brahmo!' Mahendralal Sarkar thundered. 'I'm a doctor; a scientist and I—' The same gentleman-like voice, rising above the cacophony, came to his ears once again. 'You are just a few Moshai. The rest of us wish to hear Sister Nivedita.'

'Just a few!' Mahendralal echoed. 'You're right. It is a few who are trying to take the country forward. The rest are like sheep following the herd. When Vidyasagar Moshai advocated widow remarriage the bulk of his countrymen were against him.' This last comment was like a dash of oil on a smouldering fire. Pandemonium broke lose. People shouted obscenities, knocked the chairs down and some lumpens rushed towards Mahendralal. Alarmed at what was happening Nivedita appealed to the assembly with folded hands. 'Please calm yourselves I beg of you,' she said, 'Dr Mahendralal Sarkar is an eminent physician and greatly respected in this country. He has every right to express his opinions.' Then, addressing him directly, she asked, 'May I go on with the rest of my speech Dr Sarkar?'

'You may but I shan't stay to hear it,' Mahendralal lumbered out of the hall, close to tears.

Nivedita spoke for nearly forty-five minutes more. She recited Vivekananda's 'Kali: the Mother' and some of her own translations of Ramprasad's songs. A roar of applause rose at the end of her speech and she was given a standing ovation. People cheered and rushed towards the dais to offer their congratulations.

Swamiji heard the account of the evening with satisfaction. And his triumph was complete when Nivedita was invited, by the authorities, to deliver the same speech in the *chatal* at Kalighat. Though the newspapers didn't take much note of the two lectures, the strange story of a white woman advocating the worship of Kali spread, by word of mouth, till it reached every nook and corner of the city.

Chapter XXXII

Bharat could have got his pick of jobs in Patna. He knew English and was an experienced accountant. Many banks were opening branches in the city and he could have found employment in any one of them. But he didn't want to work in a bank and be tied to a desk from morning to evening. He sought an independent livelihood. Looking around for something to do he discovered that an English education had become the fashion among the Biharis and there weren't enough schools to accommodate the aspirants. He decided to open a school. Renting a large two-storeyed house for twenty-six rupees a month, he put up a signboard outside which read *Bharat Kumar Singha BA: Presidency College*. The rooms on the ground floor were fitted up with desks and chairs and converted to classrooms. The upper floor Bharat used as his living quarters.

Bharat's school became popular quite quickly. He charged the pupils five rupees a month and kept the number down to fifty. He had no desire to work himself to the bone. Nor was he greedy for money. Even from what he received he was able to put away a tidy sum each month. The parents of his pupils were generous and supplemented the fees with quantities of presents. Baskets of bananas, pots of pedas and sacks of fine, fragrant rice arrived from time to time cutting down his expenses considerably. One of them had even placed an Akbari gold mohur at his feet once.

Bharat worked hard with his students all day and spent the evenings reading. Sometimes he got bored and sauntered over to a tea shop nearby. The tea sold here was tea as the Calcutta babus drank it—a fine golden liquid emitting a subtle but delicious aroma. What the Biharis sold as tea was a thick caramel-coloured concoction smelling of buffalo milk and sweet as syrup. The savouries here, too, were not the usual kachauris and laddus. Spicy potato cakes with crunchy crusts, banana flower cutlets delicately flavoured with cloves and cinnamon and spiked with nuts and raisins, slices of eggplant and onion rings dipped in foaming batter and fried to a golden crispness came in an unending supply, hot and fresh, from the kitchen. There were chairs and tables at which one could eat and drink in comfort. The proprietor of the shop was a young man called Barin. He kept no servants and served his customers with his own hands. His cook was an elderly lady whom he addressed as Ranga Ma. Bharat had seen her once or twice and had marvelled at her stately beauty.

Barin was a gregarious by nature and unburdened his soul to Bharat within a few days of their acquaintance. He was an orphan, he told him, devoted to his stepmother and together they had opened this shop in Patna.

'Why Patna?' Bharat had asked. 'Why not Calcutta? You would get more customers there.'

At that Barin had told him that his father hadn't married his stepmother. Consequently, she was in disgrace with his relatives who were rich and powerful. One of his brothers was Secretary to the Gaekwad of Baroda. They dared not go to Calcutta from fear of humiliating their relatives. Ranga Ma had sold her house and given him the capital for his tea shop. And she slaved in it from morn till night. But it wasn't doing too well. All the Bengalis of Patna came to it, ate their fill, appreciated Ranga Ma's cooking and ran up bills of credit which they neglected to pay. Barin had little business sense and Ranga Ma was too delicate to press anyone for payment. As a result the till was nearly empty and Barin was at his wit's end. He was seriously thinking of winding up the shop and moving to Baroda. Secretary to the Gaekwad! The designation rang a bell in Bharat's mind. Where had he heard it? And in what connection? Suddenly it came to him. The young man in the train! His name was . . . Ah! Yes—his name was Aurobindo Ghosh.

'I know your brother,' Bharat told Barin. 'We travelled together on the train to Patna. He tried to persuade me to go to Baroda.' Bharat smiled and added, 'He wanted to practise his Bengali on me.'

'Let's go together Dada!' Barin clutched Bharat's hand and begged, 'You could open a school there and Sejda could find me something to do.'

'I'd like to,' Bharat said cautiously, 'but it's not that easy. I've

636

become hopelessly involved. I can't wind up my school as easily as you can your shop. My pupils depend on me.'

But, as a matter of fact, Bharat had started wearying of his new vocation. The pupils were mostly adults and all they wanted was a smattering of business English which they needed to secure jobs. 'I am at your service. I am your most obedient servant. My whole family is at your service.' Once they had picked up a few such bits of jargon they stopped coming. Bharat found it impossible to teach them anything else and became bored and irritable in consequence.

One day an elderly man came to his school. He was a wealthy industrialist and a member of the Congress. His name, he told Bharat, was Shiupujan Sahai. He made himself comfortable within minutes of his arrival and came straight to the point. 'I hate the British,' he told Bharat, 'but I must learn their language to do business with them. I need your help in the matter. But I'll tell you frankly—I refuse to sit in a classroom with boys the age of my grandsons. We must make some other arrangement. Either I come to your house, after school hours for lessons or you come to mine.'

'What can I teach you?'

'Spoken English. You must converse with me in English all the time we are together.' He thought for a few moments then said, 'I have an idea. You are a single man and spend your evenings alone. Why don't you come to my house, every day, and have the night meal with me? I can't give you fish curry but you'll get dollops of pure ghee on your rotis and bowls of fresh malai.' He laughed merrily and added, 'By the way, have you heard that the next session of the Congress is to be held in Calcutta? We could go together.'

'I have no desire to go to Calcutta.'

'Why not? Young men like you should take an interest in politics.'

'My school—'

'All schools close down for the winter. I'll tell you what. We'll make you a delegate and I'll pay for your ticket.'

'I don't understand. Why are you so keen on taking me?'

'Because you're a Bengali. Your presence will be useful to me. I neither know the language nor the city.'

'I'm not a Bengali. I'm an Assamese.'

'I know. I've made enquiries. I also know that your knowledge of Bengali is as good as that of the native born to the soil. Interacting with you will help me learn two languages—English and Bengali.'

Bharat had no intention at all of falling in with Shiupujan's plans. But the man was relentless in his pursuit. After that evening he came to Bharat's house every day and dragged him over to his own. He gave him lavish meals and doses of wisdom over them. The influence of the Congress, he told Bharat, was spreading rapidly and soon it would become a household word. This was the time to seize the bull by the horns and exert pressure on the rulers. Young, educated men like Bharat were needed to lead the country towards freedom and light. But the idea of going to Calcutta was so distasteful to Bharat that he resisted the old man's wiles with all his strength. He even toyed with the idea of giving Shiupujan the slip by escaping to Baroda with Barin. But destiny had planned otherwise.

One night Bharat was awakened by shouts of 'Fire! Fire!' ringing in his ears. He scrambled out of bed and ran to the window to see a thick column of smoke rising from below. The fire was in his own house! He made a dash for the door and opened it. The heat hit him like a wave and smoke engulfed his head making him choke and splutter. The water poured out of his smarting eyes but, even through the haze and film of tears, he saw that the staircase was on fire. Tongues of flame darted here and there licking the woodwork. Desperate for survival he ran down the steps, braving the smoke and flame, but halfway down he stopped short. All his savings were in a tin box locked in a cupboard upstairs. He couldn't leave without them. Dashing up to his bedroom he fumbled under his pillow for the key. He found it and ran towards the cupboard. But, before he could fit it into the lock, it slipped out of his trembling hand and fell, with a tinkle, to the floor. Bharat went down on hands and knees groping for the key. But the room was dark and hazy with smoke and he couldn't even see his own hand. Yet, by an amazing chance, he found the key. His hand trembled so badly that a few precious moments were lost before it turned in the lock. By the time he emerged from the bedroom, with the tin box under his arm, he found the flames leaping over the bannisters, right up to the door. There was no way he could go down now.

Bharat had come close to death so many times in his life that every nerve and sinew of his body was attuned to fight it. Gripping the box firmly he ran to the adjoining terrace and leaped out into the dark. The men who were hanging about outside, watching the fire, saw his figure come vaulting down. They ran towards him and dragged him over to a place of safety.

Bharat's life was saved but one foot was badly injured in the fall and he was cut and bruised all over. He smiled grimly to himself. He had survived another attempt on his life but his school, with everything in it, was burned down to its foundations. He wondered if someone had set fire to the house on purpose! Who could it be? God or man? But, even if it was God who was guilty of arson, he would not be shaken by the fact. He might limp all his life but he would not cringe before Him.

*

The train hissed its way into Howrah station like an angry snake belching a column of acrid smoke. Bharat's heart thumped, heavy as lead, against his ribs. He was in Calcutta again. Who knew what would happen to him now?

Bharat had broken his heel bone in the fall and been confined to bed for two whole months. During this time Shiupujan had been more than a brother to him. He had taken him home after the fire and nursed him back to health with tender care. Consequently Bharat did not have the heart to refuse his invitation to accompany him to Calcutta. Shiupujan and Bharat were not the only delegates on the train. There were people from many parts of north India forming queues in front of the tables set up on the platform. These were manned by Congress workers. 'Where do you come? Which state?' they asked each one, before doling out information about the schedule of events and facilities provided by the party. Bharat and Shiupujan joined the line and were told that arrangements had been made for their stay in Ripon College.

Hailing a carriage Shiupujan ordered it to proceed in the direction of Sealdah. Seating himself, Bharat lifted the shutters

639

and peered curiously outside. It was ten years since he had been here. Yet Calcutta hadn't changed all that much. The streets looked much the same. So did the houses. Then, suddenly, he saw something odd. A vehicle passed down the road overtaking the carriage. It had no roof—only sides and some seats. A man sat behind a wheel. He was doing nothing but twisting the wheel this way and that and pressing what looked like a balloon from time to time. *Qoink! Qoink*! A noise like a quacking duck came every time he squeezed the balloon. The vehicle moved in spurts and trembled as it moved. But its speed was phenomenal. Shiupujan's eyes nearly started out of his head. 'What's that?' he cried out, clutching Bharat's hand. 'There are no horses or mules pulling that carriage! It's moving by itself!'

'I think this is what the sahebs call a motorcar. Sometimes it's referred to as an automobile. I've heard about this new invention but I'm seeing one for the first time.'

'*Chhi*! *Chhi*! Ram kaho!' Shiupujan bit his tongue and tweaked his ears as though he had inadvertently witnessed something unholy. But his curiosity was greater than his disgust and he asked after a while, 'How does it move? Do you have any idea Bharat Babu?'

'We came in a train pulled by a steam engine. Maybe these vehicles follow the same principle.' Shiupujan snorted. He had no opinion of these new fangled inventions. What dignity there was in a horse-driven carriage! What leisured grace! This was . . . this was obscene. He glared at the motorcar which was fast becoming a speck in the distance.

Ripon College, being closed for the winter vacation, had been converted into a guest house for the delegates. But many more had come than was anticipated. In consequence all the rooms and verandas overflowed with people cooking, eating and sleeping wherever they could find a bit of space. The floors had, presumably, been washed a little while back and were wet and muddy in consequence. Bharat and Shiupujan stared at one another in dismay. Where would they find place for themselves in this bedlam? And they had come totally unprepared. They had neither bedding nor cooking utensils with them.

But their discomforts of the night were as nothing compared to what they encountered in the morning. Awaking to nature's call, at dawn, Shiupujan descended from his corner in the attic where he had spent a restless night tossing and turning on his bug-ridden hired mattress. Coiling his sacred thread about one ear he walked towards to the row of privies that stood at one end of the immense courtyard. But before he reached within twenty yards of them a horrible stench hit his nostrils like a wave. The food he had eaten the night before, from an alley hotel, churned in his belly and rushed to his throat in a sick gurgle. The privies being too few in number to accommodate the needs of so many, people had just squatted wherever they could and eased themselves on the floor of the courtyard. There was a tremendous clamour of voices shouting. 'Volunteer! Volunteer!' 'Where are the scavengers?' 'How disgusting!' 'What kind of arrangements have these people made for us?' 'So many people and so few privies!'

Shiupujan stood watching the scene, his nostrils pinched between his thumb and forefinger. Horror and disgust were stamped on every line of his face. Suddenly a hush fell on the clamouring crowd. A young man, about thirty years old, came forward swinging a bunch of besoms in one hand. He was small and slight with a long nose and sallow complexion. He wore a simple dhuti worn high, almost to his knees, and a coarse cotton vest. 'This is a sorry state of affairs,' he said in a high, slightly sing-song voice. 'The organizing committee should have made better arrangements. However, complaining won't help matters. I just bought some besoms from Baithak Khana Bazar. Let's fall to work and clean the mess ourselves.'

The delegates stared at the strange man in horror. They couldn't believe their ears. Many of them were Brahmins and others from the highest strata of society. How dare he suggest that they clean privies as though they were scavengers? The young man smiled at the horrified faces and said pleasantly, 'Let's not forget that scavengers are human beings, too, with sensibilities just like ours. If they can clean our muck why can't we do the same for our own?' Shiupujan had been so absorbed by the scene that he hadn't noticed Bharat come down the stairs and stand next to him. The young man looked at him and said, 'Come. Join hands with me.' But Bharat stood as though rooted to the ground. The others also stood where they were without moving an inch. The young man smiled and pouring some water from a bucket that stood by one of the privies began wielding his besom and sweeping up the piles of excrement. Bharat turned to go back to his room. Suddenly something came over him. He turned and walked, step by step, slowly, falteringly, towards the young man and put out his hand for a besom. The latter handed it over with a smile. 'Come friend,' he said, 'Let's work together. I'm from Gujarat. My name is Mohandas Karamchand Gandhi. What's yours?'

Chapter XXXIII

On the concluding day of the conference the camp, set up in Ripon College, was dismantled and the delegates were left to their own devices. Some went back to their home states. Others, desirous of staying on in the capital city for a longer stretch, had to find alternative accomodation. Shiupujan and Bharat belonged to the latter group. Shiupujan had some business to conduct in the Bara Bazar area of Calcutta and Bharat was in no hurry to go back to Patna. In fact he wasn't sure he wanted to go back at all.

Booking themselves into Ajanta Hotel, situated at the crossing just off Hadh Katar Gali, the two settled down for the time being. Apart from his business interests Shiupujan was also eager to enjoy the night life of Calcutta of which he had heard a good deal. 'There's a saying in our part of the world,' he told Bharat one day, after hemming and hawing self consciously for a while, 'To see the morning—go to Munger. Come to Patna to enjoy the afternoon. The twilight of Benares will evoke your admiration. But if you wish to dazzle your eyes with the bright lights of night—there's no place like Calcutta. I've been in this city for so many days, now, but I haven't seen the lights. I've been slogging all day and going to bed at sunset. You've been here before. You know the places. Please take me around and—'

'Shiupujan ji,' Bharat mumbled, his ears red with embarrassment. 'It's true that I know Calcutta. I can take you to see the Victoria Memorial, the Botanical Gardens, the Museum and the river. But I have no experience of the night life of the city.'

'We'll get the experience—together. Do you hear the tinkling of anklets? And snatches of song? I'm sure there's a baiji singing and dancing somewhere in the neighbourhood. Can't we go there? I have plenty of money.'

'You can. Many people do. But I can't accompany you.'

'Why not? Is there anything wrong with listening to music?'

'There's nothing wrong. But I don't feel drawn to that kind of music and dance.' Then, seeing Shiupujan's face crumple with disappointment, Bharat added, 'I have an idea. Calcutta is famed for its theatre. You mustn't go back to Patna without seeing it. I'll get tickets for tomorrow night and we'll go together.'

Arriving at Bengal Theatre, renamed Aurora, the next evening, Shiupujan and Bharat found a bonus awaiting them. It being Shivratri, three plays *Nal Damayanti, Abu Hosain* and *Zenana War* were being performed for the price of one. The show would go on all night. Glancing at the handbill Bharat saw Ardhendushekhar Mustafi's name among the cast. He felt his blood leap with excitement at the prospect of seeing Ardhendushekhar again. But, when the latter made his entry, in a serio-comic role in *Abu Hosain*, a wave of depression fell on Bharat's soul. Saheb Babu looked so old! So haggard! Although he did his role with his accustomed flair and finesse, the depression persisted.

There were other changes in the theatre since Bharat had seen it last. Electrical lighting had taken the place of gas jets. The decor was better and the seats more comfortable. Another thing that Bharat observed was the increase in the number of dance sequences. In every play, be it historical, social, or religious, there were at least five to six numbers in which women swayed their buttocks and wiggled their breasts to music that became faster and more frenzied as the night wore on. Bharat got an uncomfortable feeling that these dances had been devised for the titillation of that section of the audience which couldn't afford to visit brothels. For the price of a ticket they could see a play and enjoy the sense of being in the company of low women at the same time. It was such numbers that attracted crowds to the theatre and lined the pockets of the proprietor.

After that first evening Bharat and Shiupujan saw a play every evening. One night, on returning from the theatre, the two got caught in a shower of rain and were drenched to the skin. Bharat caught a violent cold, followed by a high temperature and aching limbs, and was confined to bed. Shiupujan who had, quite miraculously, escaped any ill effects, sent for the kaviraj and proceeded to nurse his young friend back to health with regular administration of the pills and powders the kaviraj had left behind strengthened with doses of ginger, honey, pepper and betel juice. After a couple of days the fever subsided and Bharat

felt well enough to be left alone. Telling Shiupujan that there was
no need to confine himself to the sick room any longer, he insisted
that he go back to his own work. Shiupujan demurred a little,
then agreed to leave. He, too, was weary of hanging about the
house all day and longed for a change. He had made a few friends
in Calcutta and was having a good time in their company. He
didn't need Bharat anymore.

Bharat's fever had come down but the remission was not
total. His head still ached a bit and he was very weak. His mouth
felt bitter and he had lost all taste for food. After Shiupujan had
left he lay in bed, thinking, for hours. The meeting of the
Congress was over. Shiupujan had seen whatever he wanted to
see of Calcutta. Soon he would be ready to move back to Patna.
What would Bharat do then? Would he accompany Shiupujan or
would he stay on in Calcutta?

The worst phase in a bout of illness is the period of
convalescence. One is not ill enough to sleep day and night and
one is not well enough to be up and about. Bharat tossed and
turned in bed and chased his thoughts. His head felt hot—not
from fever but the tension of wondering what he would do next.
At last, unable to bear it any longer, he rose from his bed in
disgust. His head spun a little as he slipped on his shirt and
prepared to leave the house. But where would he go? To the
Ganga of course! He could cool his fevered head in the soft breeze
that blew up from the river and watch the ships coming in. So
many people came to this city. So many people of different races
and colours—white, brown, black and yellow! He walked out of
the hotel and stood on the street. The day was drawing to a close
and dusk was settling over the city. Stepping into the carriage that
stood waiting at the gate, he suddenly changed his mind. He
would go to see a play. He had heard a lot, lately, about a theatre
called Classic and its proprietor Amar Datta. The young man, it
seemed, was a marvel. As brilliant an artiste as he was a clever
manager! He wondered who this Amar Datta was. He decided to
go see for himself. It was thus that Bharat's destiny brought him
to the Classic.

By the time Bharat reached the ticket counter the first bell had
rung and there were only seven minutes left for the play to begin.
All the tickets were sold out barring two priced at the fantastic

sum of twelve rupees each. But once Bharat had made up his mind to do a thing he did not waver. He went ahead and bought a ticket. Then, moving to a corner of the lobby, he stood there waiting for the second bell. Suddenly a heavy hand fell on his shoulder and a voice boomed in his ear, '*Ki ré* Bharat! Don't you recognize me?' Bharat spun around to confront a total stranger—a big, burly maulvi in a sherwani, a sequined waistcoat and a tasseled fez. He had surma in his eyes and his beard was stained with henna. The man must have mistaken him for someone else, he thought. But he had called him by name! Suddenly he recognized the man. 'Irfan!' he exclaimed joyfully. 'You've changed so much! I wouldn't have dreamed that it was you.'

'Why? I've gained some weight. But surely that's no reason—'

'You've turned yourself into an orthodox Muslim. That's why I didn't recognize you.'

'I haven't turned myself into anything. I was a Muslim and have remained a Muslim.'

'But you were a non-practising Muslim at the time I knew you. Non-believing too. I remember a conversation we had in which you told me that Darwin's theory had successfully exploded the myth of creation. Neither God, Allah nor Bhagwan created Man—or anything else. Everything evolved as part of a natural process.'

'I did?' Irfan squinted down at his friend his mouth curling with amusement. 'One reads so many books as a student and gets carried away by so many theories. Adult life is different. You have to move with the herd or you're lost in the wilderness.'

'You don't have to become a religious bigot—'

'*Oré* bhai! You have to be something; believe in something. If you don't, if you're neither Hindu nor Muslim you'll be shunned like a leper by both communities. I was born of Muslim parents so I'm a Muslim. I read the namaaz five times a day now, and feel Allah's benediction pouring down over me. But where have you been all these years? You just vanished from the city. No one had any news of you.'

'I was in Cuttack. I got a job in a bank.'

'Good, good! When did you get back to Calcutta? Are you here on transfer?'

'I came to attend the meeting of the Congress.'

'Congress! Phoh!' Irfan spat the word out as though it tasted foul in his mouth. 'I hate the Congress. I exhort all my Muslim brothers to shun it.'

Fortunately, for Bharat, he was not called upon to make an answer for, at that precise moment, the second bell was heard and the two started making their way into the hall. But even as they went Irfan's voice hissed in Bharat's ear, 'Come to my house one day Bharat. You remember the house in which I lived? Sayyad Amir Ali's house? Well! He lost all his money and his assets were put up for sale. I got the house quite cheap—'

Sitting in one of the best seats of the theatre, Bharat was conscious of the curious glances of his fellow viewers. They were all rich, important men dressed in finely puckered dhutis and kurtas with elaborately embroidered shawls thrown across their shoulders. Bharat had risen from his sick bed and walked out of the hotel, just as he was, in a soiled dhuti and crumpled *pirohan*. Added to this was the fact that he hadn't bathed or shaved for three days and his eyes burned with fever.

Looking down at the handbill Bharat was delighted to find that the play of the evening was *Bhramar*—a dramatic adaptation of Bankimchandra's *Krishna Kantér Will*. It had Amar Datta in the male lead of Gobindalal; Teenkari Dasi in the role of Bhramar and Nayanmoni in the female lead of Rohini. The last two names were completely unfamiliar to him. He had neither heard of the two actresses nor seen them perform.

Yet, as the play progressed, he had a strange feeling that he had seen the heroine before. Had he seen her in some other play? This was his first visit to Classic. Could she be on the panel of some other board as well? He strained his memory, trying to remember, till his temples started to throb and the pain in his head became excruciating. And mixed with that pain was another—in the region of his heart. He couldn't understand it. Why was he experiencing these strange sensations merely trying to remember where he had seen a certain actress before? Why was he trying so hard anyway; as though his life depended on the answer?

Suddenly he got it. The woman looked like Mohilamoni! The resemblance was not so marked when he looked straight into her face. It was when she turned her head aside and lowered her eyes to the ground . . . He nearly stood up in his excitement. But, swift on the heels of this discovery, he remembered that Mohilamoni was dead. He had taken her to the samsan ghat himself and watched her golden body burn to ashes. Bhumisuta! That's who the girl was. The voice . . . how could he have forgotten Bhumisuta's voice? She used to sing and dance. She had offered to sing for him in return for lessons . . . Nudging his neighbour with his elbow, Bharat whispered the question. 'Who is the actress doing Rohini's role? What is her name?' 'Sh!' the man warned turning his head, 'Keep your voice down. That's Nayanmoni. Haven't you heard of Nayanmoni? You must be new to the city.' Bharat observed that the man's eyes were bright with unshed tears and his voice was husky with emotion. 'Sh! Sh!' a chorus of voices buzzed. 'Quiet Moshai! Let's hear the song in peace.' Bharat looked at the faces around him. Nayanmoni's song had moved many of them to tears.

That Nayanmoni was Bhumisuta Bharat had no doubt. His heart lifted with joy at the thought that life, with all its cruelty, hadn't beaten her. She had found a means to live and she had chosen to follow the profession that he had wanted for her. She was rich and successful and people admired her. Bharat made up his mind to seek Bhumisuta out and make his presence known to her. As the curtain fell on the last scene Bharat rose to his feet and started moving towards the stage, his brain busy formulating what he would say to her. But, before he could reach that far, he saw Nayanmoni hurrying out from a side door, a shawl wrapped around her head and shoulders. She seemed to be in a great hurry. Bharat followed her as swiftly as he could pushing his way through the press of people. But, by the time he reached the street, she was already seated in her carriage with a handsome young man beside her. Bharat ran towards her trying to call out her name but it froze on his lips and remained unuttered. For some reason, Nayanmoni turned her face towards the window. Her eyes passed over his form but Bharat wasn't sure she had seen him. She certainly gave no sign of recognition. The coachman whipped up the horses and the splendid equipage started to roll down the street nearly knocking him down. A rough hand pushed him rudely aside. 'Can't you see where you are going?' The owner of the hand barked, 'Are you trying to kill yourself?'

Hours passed. The crowd dispersed but Bharat stood where he was gazing after the departed carriage. Then, when the lights went out and an eerie silence descended on the deserted streets, Bharat came to himself and started limping his way, painfully, in the direction of the Ajanta.

Chapter XXXIV

No living creature can go on working indefinitely. He needs a rest, from time to time, following which he is infused with new strength and energy. Could this be true of inanimate objects as well? Jagadishchandra Bose had thrown all his energies into establishing, as scientific truth, this fantastic, monstrously incredible theory.

The idea had come to him while working in his laboratory one night. He had made an instrument which consisted of a receiver poised over a plate of steel, its fine needle-like point almost touching the polished metal. When electric currents were passed through it the receiver vibrated. After working with the instrument for several hours he noticed that the vibrations were losing their intensity. Leaving it alone for some time he tried again. The vibrations had regained their strength. His brow furrowed in thought. Could it be possible that the instrument had become weary and had needed a rest? Jagadish conducted the test several times and came up with the same result. That which is proven becomes an established truth. Jagadish set about proving his theory with the help of graphs and sketches.

Jagadish Bose's article was published in the prestigious journal *The Englishman* and the discovery hailed as a watershed event in the history of physics. The reactions of the scientists were mixed as was to be expected. There were some who claimed that the Bose Effect ranked next in importance to Farraday's discovery and predicted that it would have far reaching consequences in the world of trade and industry. Others dismissed it as the pretensions of a quack and declared that it didn't fall within the purview of physics at all.

But the carping of the critics notwithstanding, Jagadish Bose was invited to pursue his research in the famous Davy Farraday Laboratory of the Royal Institution in London. Jagadish jumped at the offer and, taking a couple of years leave from his post in the Department of Education, boarded the ship to England spending

650

all his savings on the ticket. He had no fears for the future for his friends had assured him that they would raise a sum of two lakhs of rupees from the rich elite of Calcutta and send it out to him. But after he had left the country their resolution melted away. No one seemed ready to take the initiative and start the collection. Jagadish was a very worried man. Where would he find funds to pursue his research? He had been carried away by false promises. Even Swami Vivekananda, one of those who had expressed their admiration and pride in his achievement, hadn't given a thought to his practical difficulties.

Jagadish could have found himself a job in England quite easily. He received several excellent offers. But if he joined an institution as a paid employee he would have to surrender his rights to independent research. On the other hand, how long would he be able to keep himself together in this cold, alien country? He told himself that he would have to succumb sooner or later so it might as well be sooner. But his great friend, the poet Rabindranath, urged him not to lose heart. 'Don't take a job,' he begged in every letter. 'I'm trying to raise money for your research.'

Though scion of a wealthy family Rabindra had little money of his own. He knew many rich people but the only man he could think of approaching for his friend's support was Radhakishor Manikya of Tripura. He had taken Radhakishor to Presidency College to hear Jagadish speak about his new discovery and the former had been extremely impressed. Now, hearing about Jagadishchandra's financial difficulties from Rabindranath, Radhakishor gave him a sum of ten thousand rupees to send to his friend. But his own financial situation was precarious. The new palace at Naya Haveli had cost so much money that his treasury was nearly empty. In addition, his eldest son was to be wed shortly and his ministers were at their wits end trying to scrape together a sum sufficient to meet the expenses. They expressed their disapproval, quite audibly, in the king's presence. 'Robi Babu is a rich man,' they grumbled. 'The Thakurs have vast estates. Why doesn't he finance his friend's research himself? Why should the wealth of Tripura go out of the country?' Radhakishor smiled and told them that, if they were short of money, they should cut down on the number of ornaments that were to be given to the new princess. 'If Jagadishchandra can achieve what he has set out to do,' he said, 'he will bring back a jewel for Mother India which we can all wear proudly on our bosoms.'

The barbed remarks of the Tripura officials reached Rabindra's ears, as they were meant to, and saddened him. It was true that his father was a man of wealth but he, himself, was only a paid employee of the estate. He received three hundred rupees a month on which he had to support himself, his wife and five children. He had tried to improve his financial position by starting an independent business. But it had been a disastrous failure and he was, even now, repaying the loan of forty thousand rupees he had taken from a Marwari moneylender with interest. Though under severe financial stress himself, he had never asked Radhakishor for a paisa.

Rabindra had taken on another responsibility that was draining him financially and emotionally. He had opened a school in Shantiniketan; a *brahmacharyashram* for boys on the lines of the educational ideals of Vedic India. It had been his nephew Balendra's idea and had been put into execution under his active supervision. After Balendra's tragic and untimely death some years ago, the work had come to a standstill. But a few months back Rabindra had taken up the project once again and had thrown himself heart and soul into it as was his nature. One part of him, the practical part, questioned the wisdom of undertaking this venture. 'You're a poet,' it said, 'Writing poetry is your vocation—one you enjoy and are good at. Why do you meddle with something you know nothing about? Leave educating the younger generation to the educationists.'

'I would be happy to do so,' the poet in him answered firmly, 'if I had faith in their methods. But, as I see it, the educationists are producing a nation of clerks with the mentality of slaves. If I don't step in, the ancient wisdom of our forefathers will die out and be lost to us.'

'This is a vast country,' the invisible questioner probed, 'with millions of people. In how many can you infuse the old ideals?'

'In as many as I can, with my limited means,' the other part replied promptly. 'I have twelve students at present. I can bring the number up to twenty at the most.'

Debendranath Thakur, now eighty-five years old, heard of his youngest son's resolve and endorsed it wholeheartedly. He even offered to lend his support by sanctioning two hundred rupees a month from the estate and drew up a deed to the effect. But the expenses far exceeded that amount. It being a residential school, Rabindra had to make living arrangements for both tutors and pupils. He had to pay the former salaries which, though meagre when compared to those paid in the schools of Calcutta, were a constant worry, for the school had no income. No fees were charged from the boys—not even for board and lodging.

The boys had to follow a strict routine. Rising at a quarter past five their first task was to make their own beds and sweep the floors of their rooms. Then, after easing themselves in the fields, they bathed in the Bhubandanga canal and came back to the ashram where they gathered around a tree and recited Sanskrit shlokas. Upasana over, they were given a breakfast of halwa following which they were made to dig the land for half an hour. Lessons began after another round of Upasana with teachers and students praying together. The morning lessons ended at ten o'clock leaving the boys free to pursue their own interests till the noon meal. It was not a time to laze or play games, however. Some practised on the harmonium and sang. Others read books or painted pictures. The noon meal was a simple one—rice, a bowl of dal and a mound of stewed vegetables. That was all. Caste distinctions were observed strictly during the meal—the Brahmin boys sitting apart from the others. After they had eaten the boys had to wash their own utensils and wipe down the floor. Lessons recommenced at half past twelve and went on till four with a fifteen minutes recess at three. The boys played games till sundown after which they were given a light supper and sent to bed.

The school started off well enough but it didn't take Rabindra long to realize that he had bitten off more than he could chew. With Debendranath's two hundred rupees he was just about able to pay the salaries of the teachers. But there were so many other expenses. He was building a new house—the old one, built by Balendra, being too small to accommodate them all. He had been reduced to selling some of his wife's jewellery and felt reluctant to ask her for more. But the bill for the wooden frames and tiles of the new house was awaiting payment. Where would he find the money? Mrinalini sensed her husband's predicament and asked him what the matter was, over and over again. Rabindra evaded her questions for as long as he could, then answered with a kind of desperation, 'The wooden frames and tiles for the new house are ready. But they won't make the delivery till I've paid the bill.' Mrinalini said nothing. Putting down the bowl of barley water she held in her hands she proceeded to pull off the solid shark-headed gold bangles she wore on her wrists. 'No, no!' Rabindra protested. 'Not those. They were my mother's. You should keep them for your eldest daughter-in-law.'

'Rathi's wife will have jewellery enough if Fate wills it,' Mrinalini answered calmly putting the gold in his hands. 'Sell them and settle your bills.'

'But you have no more bangles. Your wrists are bare.'

'I saw some very pretty glass bangles at the fair yesterday. I'll buy a dozen and adorn my wrists.'

'I'm truly grateful to you,' Rabindra said humbly. 'Everyone calls me an impractical fool. But you, you've given me your support in every way. I'll never ask for your jewellery again. I promise you that. It's for the last time.'

Mrinalini turned her face aside to hide a smile. Her famous husband was so caught up in his big schemes that he spared no time or thought for his own family. There were so many expenses and so little money. Being an excellent housewife she managed to keep the household going on whatever little he gave her. But there were times . . . Mrinalini sighed. This was not the first time she was parting with her jewellery and it wouldn't be the last.

It was a charmed night with a full moon enveloping the ashram in a web of beams as soft and clinging as a piece of muslin. The inmates of the house were fast asleep. Only Rabindra sat writing far into the night. He had promised Sarala an article on ancient Indian literature and was working on it with complete absorption. Suddenly, on an impulse, he rose and walked out to the veranda. Breathing in great gulps of the warm, sweet air laden with the scent of *juin*, he was struck by a sudden thought. He hadn't written a love poem in years! Ever since Bibi's wedding. . . He wondered why. Had love forsaken him? He tried to recall Natun Bouthan's face but the image that came before his eyes was dim and blurred as though floating under ripples of green water. He broke into a sweat at the thought that he was losing her. 'No, no!' his mind shrieked out in panic. 'I can't let that happen to me. I must write of love. Love is the only thing worth living for. Whatever else I do—that must come first.' He went back to the room and sat down at the table with fresh resolve. Before taking up the pen, he drew his watch out of his pocket to check the time. It was a gold watch gifted to him by one of his relations when he married Mrinalini. He pressed a little button at the side and the lid sprang up revealing the letter engraved on the inside. Gazing on that first letter of his name he forgot to look at the time. He forgot that he had sat down to write a love poem. Other thoughts crowded into his mind. Mrinalini was ill. He was sure of it. He had seen her lying down at the oddest of hours. But when he asked her what was wrong she said she felt perfectly well . . . The salaries of the teachers were due. He would have to pay them soon or lose his credibility. He hadn't been able to raise the money yet. He wouldn't, he couldn't ask Mrinalini for any more jewels. He would sell his watch instead.

Chapter XXXV

It was the month of Chaitra and a storm was imminent. The sky loomed, dark and menacing, over the Padma which stretched out like a sea on either side of the steamer that floated slowly on its surface. Swami Vivekananda stood on the deck gazing on the vast body of water. He had never seen such a magnificient sight in his life. It was his first visit to East Bengal and he was entranced by the beauty of her rivers.

The sheet of shining water was dotted with fishing boats a few of which flitted, lightly as moths, around the steamer. It was the season of Ilish—the fish dear to the Bengali heart and palate; for Ilish not only made several delectable dishes—it was a thing of beauty. Swami Vivekananda looked on interestedly as the fishermen dragged in their nets heavy with the leaping, struggling fish. 'They are the river's jewels,' he thought whimsically, 'They shine against the dark water like pieces of silver.' Calling out to one of the disciples he said, 'Go buy some Ilish from the fishermen, Kanai. We'll have a nice spicy *jhol* with our rice tonight. And some wedges fried crisp in their own fat.'

'But . . . but,' the boy hesitated. 'Ilish is very oily. It will make you ill.'

'It won't. Besides, that's my concern—not yours. You go to Sareng Saheb and ask him to buy a basketful. They'll fleece us if we go to them ourselves.'

Kanai did as he was told then came back and reported, 'They've agreed to give us the fish at an anna a piece. Each one is between one and a half and two seers. I think three or four should be enough for us.' But Vivekananda shook his head. 'Buy a whole rupee's worth. We'll invite the sareng and the mallas. After all, we're on this boat together.' While the fish was being dressed in the ship's kitchen, Vivekananda had another idea. 'Look for some *puin* greens,' he commanded Kanai. 'They make a wonderful *chacchari* with Ilish heads. Tell the sareng to stop the boat at one of the villages by the bank.'

An hour later Vivekananda sat puffing thoughtfully at his
albola when Kanai appeared before him. Behind him stood a man
with an enormous basket piled high with *puin*—the leaves and
stems thick and glossy and swollen with rain. He had also
procured some excellent rice—long grained and fragrant.
Vivekananda nodded to show his approval. There would be a
good meal that night on the boat and he would serve everyone
with his own hands.

Reaching Narayanganj the party stepped into the train that
was to take them to Dhaka. Swamiji's visit to East Bengal had
been undertaken with a purpose. His mother had expressed a
desire to visit Langalbandha on the bank of the Brahmaputra and
had urged him to take her there. Unlike other sanyasis
Vivekananda had not broken his links with his family. He
supported his mother and a widowed sister out of the fifty dollars
sent to him, every month, by Joe Macleod. Though not well at all
he had come all the way from Calcutta at her wish. His mother
was old and this was the first request she had ever made to him.
Langalbandha was a great pilgrimage! It was said that Parasuram
had bathed at Langalbandha on Budhashtami and cleansed
himself of the sin of matricide. It was a strange coincidence that a
grihi mother had expressed a desire to take a dip in the same spot
with her sanyasi son.

Stepping down from the carriage, at the *deuri* of the mansion
where he was to stay with his party, the first question he asked
was, 'Has my mother arrived?'

'She'll be arriving the day after tomorrow,' he was told.
'Brahmananda is bringing her.' Vivekananda was relieved.
Brahmananda was the Chairman of the Board of Trustees of the
Ramkrishna Mission and a reliable worker.

Brahmananda brought the old lady, her daughter and a few
other women on the day scheduled, after which Vivekananda
hired a boat large enough to accommodate them all and started
on his journey. East Bengal had a maze of rivers melting into one
another. The party sailed down the Burhi Ganga which joined the
Sheetalaksha at Narayanganj, then down the Sheetalaksha to the
Dhaleswari river whose waters flowed into the Brahmaputra.
Water! Sheets of golden water dotted with tiny islands of the
purest emerald! Vivekananda's sick, weary heart felt soothed at

the sight and his eyes closed in ecstasy. But on reaching Langalbandha on Budhashtami he got a rude shock. The place was crawling with pilgrims cooking, eating, quarelling with one another, urinating and defecating. A sea of heads bobbed up and down in the water which had been churned into a sickly, lurid yellow. Ashes from the cooking fires, leftover food, faeces and vomit were littered so thickly on the bank that it was difficult to find a place to put down one's foot. Vivekananda was horrified. Cholera would break out here any moment. Calling the members of his entourage together he cautioned them against drinking the river water which, being holy, was being drunk freely and carried away in pots and bottles by the pilgrims. 'There's a tubewell there,' he said, pointing a finger, 'Pump up some water when you're thirsty. And try to get to the middle of the river before you take a dip. The water is cleaner there.'

'Oré Bilé!' his mother cried out in fear. 'I don't know how to swim. I'll drown.'

'I'll take you with me. I'm a strong swimmer. Don't you recall my swimming days at Hedo Lake?'

Holding his mother by the hand Vivekananda led her gently onwards. Suddenly the old lady burst into tears. 'Why Ma!' Vivekananda exclaimed. 'What is the matter? Have you stepped on a thorn?'

'No Baba! I weep from happiness. I never thought you would hold my hand again. I thought you were lost to me.'

'But why? I've left your house but I haven't let go of you. No, not for a moment.'

Vivekananda led his mother to a patch of clean water and, holding her gently by the shoulders, helped her to take a few dips. Then, equally carefully, he led her back to the bank. Returning to the middle of the river he swam for a while. But he couldn't carry on the exercise for long. He tired easily these days. His breath was hard and short and his limbs felt as heavy as lead.

Vivekananda had made another trip to America mainly to collect money for the Mission but also to try and cure his ailments. But both efforts had drawn a blank. Josephine had done all she could. She had called in the famous specialist Dr Hellmann and Vivekananda had been treated by him for several months. Dr Hellmann had told him that his heart and kidneys were

658

considerably damaged but had held out hopes of a cure. But, after all those months of treatment, Vivekananda was not feeling any better. In fact his condition was worsening day by day.

The party did not tarry at the place of pilgrimage but set out on the return journey as soon as the bathing was over. 'Tell me the truth,' Swamiji asked sternly as soon as they had taken their places in the boat, 'Have any of you drunk the river water?' All of them shook their heads and hastened to assure him that they hadn't. Swamiji turned his face away and smiled. 'I took a few sips when none of you were looking,' he said sheepishly. 'People say it's holy water and cures all diseases. I drank some in the hope that it would cure my asthma.'

There's a saying that a husking pedal will hull rice even in heaven. Though on a holiday Swami Vivekananda was being forced to give discourses, meet streams of people and answer their queries even here in Dhaka. Sometimes he was so weary of it all that he was tempted to go back to Belur. One afternoon, after a prolonged discourse and question answer session, Vivekananda came into the inner apartments for a bath and meal. Feeling warm and sticky he decided to stand on the balcony for a few minutes and let some fresh air play over his body. A phaeton stood in the street below with a crowd of people around it. Some of his disciples could be spotted among them and some of the servants of the house. They were talking in agitated voices and one of them was waving a stick. Curious to find out what the matter was, Vivekananda sent for Kanai. 'What's going on there Kanai?'

'Nothing,' Kanai answered shortly. Vivekananda saw that his ears were red with embarrassment.

'Has someone come to see me?'

'It's of no consequence. You go back to your room.'

At that moment a face appeared at the window of the phaeton. Vivekananda could see it clearly. It was a girl's face, very pretty but heavily painted with rouge on the cheeks, surma in the eyes and brows darkened with kajal. It didn't take Vivekananda a second to identify her profession. She was a nautch girl. He understood, too, the reason for the commotion outside and Kanai's embarrassment. 'Send her in to me,' Vivekananda commanded and turned to go into the house.

A few minutes later two women entered the room. One was

middle-aged and stout with a face darkened and coarsened by the ravages of time. The other was the young woman whose face he had seen at the window of the phaeton. Now, as she stood before him, he saw that she was very young, about seventeen, and a ravishing beauty. Even though it was mid afternoon she was dressed as though for a mujra in a blue spangled sari, sequined jacket and heavy ornaments set with pearls and diamonds. They touched their foreheads to the ground at Vivekananda's feet, then the older woman took up her tale. 'Sadhu Maharaj,' she said. 'We are poor, defenceless women in need of your help. This is my daughter. Though no one would realize it, looking at her, she's very, very sick. She suffers from acute asthmatic attacks and is in such agony at times that she rolls on the ground and weeps. Save her Maharaj. We have come to you from very far with a lot of hope.' Vivekananda burst out laughing. 'You've come to me!' he exclaimed. 'But I'm the wrong person. I attempt, not very successfully, to cure the ills of the mind. But of those of the body I know nothing. I'm not a doctor.'

'Everyone says you're the greatest sadhu living,' the woman persisted. 'Read a mantra over my child's head and release her from her agony.'

'If there was such a mantra I would read it for myself. I'm a victim to asthma too and, like your daughter, suffer agonies when the attack comes.'

Now the woman burst out weeping—harsh, racking sobs rasping their way out of a chest congealed with years of repressed grief. 'You're testing me, my Lord!' she cried knocking her head at Vivekananda's feet. 'But I'm unworthy of it. I'm a lowly woman led astray in my youth by the wiles of a man and abandoned thereafter—'

'I'm not testing you Ma. Sadhus are humans just like the rest of you. If they had the power of bestowing life and health they would be immortal themselves, wouldn't they?'

But the woman continued to weep and plead then, seeing that Vivekananda only shook his head sorrowfully, she said, 'Touch my daughter and give her your blessing. That will be mantra enough for her.' Suddenly the girl rose to her feet and pulled her mother up by the hand. 'Come away Ma,' she said. 'We're wasting his time. We are fallen women—despised by all who see

660

us. He won't touch me.' Vivekananda smiled. Stretching out his hand he placed it on the girl's head. 'If, by blessing you, I can soothe your pain away I do so with all my heart. Now you must do something for me. If you find a doctor or a sadhu or anybody who can cure your asthma be sure to let me know. I suffer such terrible agonies! I would be grateful for some relief.'

661

Chapter XXXVI

Swami Vivekananda had sent Nivedita on a tour of Europe and America, ostensibly to disseminate the message of the Vedantas but really to collect money for the Mission. Away from the country Nivedita saw the true India for the first time. Never in her actual sojourn in the country had she empathized, the way she now did, with the millions of human beings who lived lives of poverty, ignorance and subservience under an alien rule. She saw, clearer than ever before, that her work could not remain confined to doling out lessons to fifteen or twenty girls in a schoolroom situated in a bylane of Calcutta. The first task before anyone who loved the country and was witness to her humiliation, was to rid her of the foreign yoke. But how was it to be done? As far as she could see there was only one man in India who had the ability to draw the masses together and enthuse them to fight for freedom. And that was Swami Vivekananda. He knew the country as no one else did. The native rajas were his friends and wouldn't hesitate to take up arms against the rulers at his bidding. One of Nivedita's favourite fantasies was the sight of her beloved Swamiji standing in the midst of a mammoth congregation shouting slogans of freedom. And, drawn by the power of his tremendous personality, men, women and children were rushing towards him like clouds of moths flying straight towards a flame; like giant waves rolling and crashing in a mad race towards the shore.

But that, as Nivedita knew very well, was not to be. Her guru was an ascetic who had given up the world in an effort to enrich his soul and reach the Divine. He would not take on the job of rousing the rabble. And he would not enter into any confrontation with anybody no matter how noble the cause.

While in America Nivedita had heard of Okakura—the great academician and philosopher of Japan. Joe Macleod had told her that Okakura cherished a dream of drawing all the peoples of Asia together under one banner and creating a vast Asian race

662

that could overpower the European. As soon as India launched on her struggle for freedom Japan, Korea and some other countries would join her and help her win her independence from the British. Okakura was already in India on his mission. He was meeting people and pledging support on behalf of his own and several other countries of the East—not moral support alone but military and financial as well. Nivedita was overjoyed on hearing the news and decided to hurry back to India and throw herself into the struggle.

Okakura was to meet the important people of Calcutta at a great reception thrown for him by Olé Bull. Among the guests were Ashutosh Chowdhury, Pramatha Mitra, Bipin Pal, Chittaranjan Das, Sakharam Ganesh Deoskar, Subodh Mullick and Rabindranath Thakur. Okakura, as befitted his status as chief guest, sat in the centre of the gathering with Olé Bull on one side and Nivedita on the other. He wore a black silk kimono, embroidered with the five petalled flower which was his family crest, thin stockings of Japanese cloth and grass slippers on his feet. His complexion was unusually florid for a Japanese and the lids fell, heavy and languid, over his eyes. He had a small moustache. It being a warm evening, he fanned himself constantly with a fan painted in shades of red and yellow. Okakura sat leaning back on his chair—his attitude one of complete ease. Nivedita, who had taken upon herself the task of introducing him to the assembly, was doing most of the talking. She was telling the guests about Okakura's book *Ideals of the East* the manuscript of which she was editing; of the extent of the research the writer had done on the cultural traditions of the various Asian countries and of the similarities that he had found. The congregation noted, not without surprise, that Nivedita was not even touching on the subject of the spiritual. She was spending hour after hour singing the Japanese gentleman's praises.

Sitting in his room in Belur, Swami Vivekananda heard about Nivedita's latest craze and felt disturbed and angry. Independence! He snorted in disgust. Was it a piece of candy in a child's hand that could be snatched away upon a moment's whim? Who didn't know or admit that living under a foreign rule was humiliating? Hadn't he, Vivekananda himself, spoken against it? Hadn't he exhorted the youth of India to strike back? To sacrifice their lives for the sake of the country? Freedom was desirable and the nation should start preparing for a struggle even unto death. But was the leadership for it to come from a Japanese gentleman and an Irish lady? Vivekananda had no opinion of Okakura. The man had immersed himself in the pleasures of the flesh. And, according to Vivekananda, no great goal could possibly be reached without abstinence and sacrifice.

About a month and a half ago Nivedita had come to see him. She wanted his permission to visit the ashram at Mayawati with Okakura. 'You've just returned from a long trip abroad,' Swamiji said with a calmness that belied his true feelings, 'You haven't even settled down yet. Your school needs your attention. This is hardly the time to go off again.'

'We need a place where we can be alone,' Nivedita replied. 'We have a lot to discuss. The work we have undertaken—'

'I have heard of it. But let me tell you Margot—you're chasing a mirage. Educating the women of this land is far more real. And that is what you should be doing.'

Nivedita was peeved by the tone of his voice. But she neither contradicted him nor expressed her resentment. Lowering her eyes to the floor she murmured, 'The most important task before me now is to launch a movement for the independence of the country.'

'No one denies the value of independence. But, before stirring up the masses, it is important to educate them first. The people of this country are still living in the dark ages. They are ignorant and backward and teeming with superstitions. They're not ready for independence.'

'Thoughts of this kind only weaken the resolve. This is the time to strike. To fell the English with a tremendous blow.'

'You talk like a child Margot. Put an end to all this nonsense and get back to your work. And stop associating with Okakura. The man's worthless.'

Nivedita was speechless with shock. How could Swamiji have used such a term of abuse for a great man like Okakura? And why? Was it . . . could it . . . be envy? But how was that possible? Her guru was the greatest of all living men! Such base emotions couldn't come anywhere near him. Yet . . . Nivedita suddenly remembered that he had spoken in similarly derogatory tones about Jagadishchandra Bose. Nivedita had been eulogizing the scientist and outlining his achievements when Swamiji had shut her up with the words, 'The man is a *grihi*! Bound by earthly temptations and desires! Tell him, since he is so close to you, that in order to attain greatness he must learn the value of abstinence and austerity. You needn't concern yourself with Jagadish any further.'

Now, seeing her standing silent but implacable, Swamiji went on, 'You say you wish to initiate a struggle for freedom. How easy do you think it is going to be? The British are the most powerful race on the earth today. With what will you vanquish them? Do you have bombs? Cannon? Money?'

'Japan will give them to us. Korea is willing to help. And many other countries of Asia! All we need to do is unify the people and enthuse them.'

'Is this a dream?' Swamiji burst into a peal of mocking laughter. 'A vision or a fantasy?'

'Nogu has assured me—' There was pain in Nivedita's voice. Pain and bewilderment.

'Nogu!' Vivekananda's brows came together. 'Who is Nogu?'

'Count Okakura is called Nogu by his family and friends.'

Now Vivekananda could hold himself in no longer. 'You go too far Margot,' he thundered, his face flaming. 'I've heard you call Jagadish Bose Khoka to his face. *Khoka!*' he mimicked her accent cruelly. 'Do you know what that means. It means *baby boy*. Is he a baby boy? It is typical of the contempt with which the white-skinned Westerner treats the Oriental! Would you have dared to address the great men of your land by their pet names—Harry, Larry or Gary?'

Nivedita's face took on a deathly pallor. Swamiji was accusing her of holding the people she loved in contempt; of riding roughshod on their sentiments. What could be further from the truth? 'You call me a white-skinned Westerner,' she said after a while, desperately trying to control the quivering of her lips, 'Who knows, better than you, that I'm a daughter of India? You have dedicated me to her service. That is why I am Nivedita.'

'No. I haven't dedicated you to the service of any country. You're a disciple of my guru Sri Ramkrishna Paramhansa; a daughter of Sri Sri Ma. I brought you here to serve humanity; to follow in the footsteps of the great Gautam Buddha.'

'I haven't strayed from the path of service. Is not freeing the enslaved service to humanity?'

'Listen Margot. It is time you got a few things clear. We are ascetics committed to serve God and man. Politics is not for us. If one of us gets involved in any activity banned by law the whole Mission will be threatened. You have two options before you. To stay with the order and obey its rules, or leave it and follow your own inclinations.'

Nivedita remained standing in silence, her eyes on her feet. 'You must sever your connections with the math,' Vivekananda went on inexorably. 'We don't want the eyes of the police on us.' Now the still, bowed figure stirred into life. Nivedita stooped and, touching her mentor's feet, walked out of the math. Then, a few days later, she left for Mayawati accompanied by Okakura.

Vivekananda was shocked on hearing the news. He hadn't expected it. But, strangely enough, this act of blatant disobedience on the part of his favourite disciple did not anger him. What he felt was a sense of loss. Nivedita had left him. She wouldn't come back. Not because she didn't want to but because he had forbidden her. He felt somewhat ashamed of himself. He had been too harsh with the girl. Harsh and intolerant! He thought of going to see her in her house in Bagbazar. But he felt too weak; too tired. The thought of crossing the Ganga frightened him. He rarely moved from his room these days. The effort of negotiating the stairs left him breathless and exhausted.

Yet, one morning, on seeing his disciple Sarat preparing to leave for Calcutta in the boat that belonged to the math he called out from his window, 'Wait Sarat! I'm coming with you.' Then, wrapping a shawl around his bare back and chest he came striding down the stairs, out of the math and stepped inside the boat. Sarat stared at him in astonishment. 'You're not well at all,' he cried. 'Tell me what there is to do and I'll—' But Swamiji had already ensconced himself comfortably on one of the planks. 'Don't worry about me,' he said smiling. 'Just take me to the ghat at Bagbazar and drop me off.' Then, reaching his destination, Vivekananda leaped out of the boat waving Sarat back into his seat with an imperious hand. 'You don't have to come with me,' he said before striding off in the direction of Bose Para Lane.

Nivedita had just taken a bath and was standing before a mirror combing her hair when she heard a rustle at the door and turned around startled. Seeing her mentor in the doorway she stood transfixed her hand lifted halfway to her head. 'There was no one downstairs,' Vivekananda said casually. 'So I came up.' Nivedita came slowly out of her trance.

'My Lord!' she murmured.

'How are you Margot?'

Nivedita pushed a chair towards him. 'Please sit,' she said softly. 'I will,' he replied. 'But not for long. I have to get back to the math.' Vivekananda did not sit for more than a few minutes. The effort had been too much for him and he could feel the spasms coming. Soon he would be too breathless to speak and that would alarm Nivedita. 'Come to the math,' he said, rising to his feet adding with a kind of desperate urgency, 'As soon as you can.'

One morning, a few days later, Nivedita came to Belur. She looked very beautiful in a flowing dress of white silk and rudraksha beads around her neck. Prostrating herself on the ground she touched her head to Vivekananda's feet. 'You came only because I asked you,' Vivekananda said with a twinkle in his eye. 'Not because you wanted to.'

'Why do you say that? I would have come immediately on my return from Mayawati. But you were away.'

'That is true. I went to Bara Jagulia for a week. My disciple Mrinalini Bosu had been urging me to come to her for a long time. I thought the change would do me good. But I came back feeling worse than ever.' Then, as if suddenly remembering his obligations as a host, he rose to his feet. 'You've come a long way,' he said. 'You must be hungry. Just sit quietly in this chair like a good girl while I cook you some breakfast.' He bustled off in the direction of the kitchen and returned, half an hour later, with a smoking thala in one hand. In the other he held a stone tumbler of iced milk. Nivedita saw that the thala contained a mound of rice, some boiled potatoes and a small heap of jackfruit seeds—steamed, peeled and sprinkled with salt and mustard oil.

'Won't you eat with me?' she asked timidly.

'Today is Ekadasi. A fast day for me—as you know.'

After Nivedita had eaten he insisted on washing her hands and wiping them. He did it meticulously drawing the clean, white towel lovingly over each finger. Nivedita blushed with embarrassment. 'What are you doing?' she cried, trying to pull back her hand. 'It is I who should be serving you.' Swamiji had been laughing and singing snatches of song all this while. But, on hearing these words, his face turned grave and sombre. 'Jesus washed the feet of his disciples,' he almost murmured the words. His eyes, looking into hers, had a strange expression—one she couldn't fathom. 'That was on his last day on this earth,' she thought to herself and her heart sank at the thought. 'Swamiji!' she asked brightly, struggling to push back the tears that pricked her eyelids. 'You remember what Joe Macleod said to you when you told her you wouldn't live beyond forty? She said you were created in the image of Gautam Buddha and that his best work was done between forty and eighty. You have a long way to go yet.'

'No Margot,' Vivekananda shook his head. 'I've given . . . whatever I had to give. I have nothing left. It's time I went.'

'You have a great deal more to give!' Nivedita cried passionately. 'Who else but you—?' Her voice choked on a sob and tears poured down her face.

'Sometimes it becomes necessary to cut down a large tree to enable the smaller ones to grow.' Swamiji smiled at her. 'I have to make room for you.'

Swamiji woke up the next morning feeling as though he had never been ill in his life. Swinging his legs down the side of his bed he was surprised to find that the swelling had disappeared. He walked over to the window and felt no pain. And, strangest of all, it seemed to him that his vision had improved. Everything looked brighter and clearer. He washed and changed, then, proceeding to the puja room, he sat down to his *jap* and meditation. Three hours passed. Then a sensation, long forgotten, stirred in his belly. He realized he was hungry; prodigiously hungry. 'I haven't eaten well in months,' he thought, 'That's why I feel so weak and tired.' He made up his mind. He would eat a good meal that day. All the things he loved. *Ilish*! His soul craved the delicate fish. He could see it in his mind's eye—thick, rich wedges nestling in oil and spices. Rising, he went to the door. 'Byaja! *Oré o* Byaja!' he called. A young disciple named Brajen came running up the stairs. 'Tell them in the kitchen to send for some Ilish. I've a mind to eat some today—in a rich *jhal*. I'd like some fried too and some in a sweet and sour sauce.

Vivekananda fell hungrily on the food as soon as it was served. Pouring the fried fish along with its oil on the smoking rice on his thala he looked around. 'Get me some green chillies,' he ordered. When they arrived he crushed a couple between his fingers and, mixing them with the rice, ate big handfuls with noises of relish. When the last course, the sweet and sour fish was served he licked his fingers over it and remarked, 'Yesterday's fast has left me terribly hungry. I've never enjoyed a meal so much.'

After he had eaten he sat for a while talking to some visitors who had come to the math. Then, it being the hour for meditation and prayer, he decided to go back to his room. 'I feel very well to day Byaja!' he told the boy as he helped him up the stairs. 'There's hardly any pain and my limbs feel wonderfully light.' But, on reaching his room, he exclaimed, 'Why is it so hot in here? And so stuffy! Is there a storm brewing outside?'

'No, Swamiji. The sky is clear without a trace of cloud.'

'But I feel very hot and stifled.' Looking at Swamiji, Brajen was alarmed. His face was beaded over with sweat and he was breathing with difficulty. 'Open all the windows,' Vivekananda commanded collapsing on the bed, 'And fan me for a while.' Brajen hastened to obey. But, despite the strong breeze that blew in from the window, Vivekananda cried, 'This heat is killing me! Fan me harder Byaja. I'm sizzling all over.' He turned over on his side. His hands trembled a little and a cry escaped his lips—a cry like that of a child in his sleep. His head slid from the pillow and fell on the edge of the bed. Brajen leaned over his guru in alarm. Was anything wrong? Was Swamiji trying to say something? Was he hungry? There was some cold milk in the room. Should he give him a few sips? 'Swamiji!' he called out frightened. Now Vivekananda turned over and lay on his back. A deep sigh escaped him, then all was still.

Brajen kept calling him, over and over again, for the next two minutes. Then, bringing the lantern close to his face he got a shock. Swamiji's eyes were open but the pupils had moved to the extreme ends and stood transfixed at the bridge of his nose.

Brajen peered hard but could detect no rise and fall of the chest or abdomen. Running out of the room, like one possessed, he howled out his news to the inmates of the math. Now everyone came crowding into the room and leaned anxiously over the still figure. The older disciples exchanged glances. Was it a *bhav samadhi*? Or a *maha samadhi*? Some of the younger ones burst into tears. Others, more in control, bustled about making the necessary arrangements. The doctor was sent for from Barahnagar and a messenger was despatched to Balaram Bosu's house in Bagbazar where Brahmananda was spending the night. Nivedita lived only a few houses away but no one thought of informing her.

The news reached her the following morning. Snatching up a shawl she ran out of the house, just as she was, hailed a carriage and came to Belur. Swamiji's room was crammed with people weeping, chanting the name of Ramkrishna, and talking in agitated whispers. They made way for her as she walked in softly, on bare feet, and came to where her guru lay. Kneeling on the floor by the side of his bed she gazed, dry eyed, into his face. It looked just as she had seen it the day before. Only the eyes were as red as hibiscus and runnels of blood had run down the nose and mouth. Calling for some cottonwool she wiped the blood tenderly away.

Around two o'clock in the afternoon someone said to her, 'You must rise now. It is time . . .' Nivedita moved away without a word. It was a hot day but she felt the bitter chill of desolation. Fingers of ice seemed to clutch at her heart, rendering it numb, as she watched the disciples bathe Swamiji in gangajal and put new saffron robes on him. Then they carried him, laden with garlands, to a sandalwood pyre set up under a huge bel tree in front of the math. Nivedita looked on as the sanyasis chanted mantras and placed their guru's belongings, one by one, on the pyre. Among them was the shawl he had worn on the day he had come to see her. 'Can I have that?' she asked Saradananda on an impulse. Then, seeing his surprised look, she added, 'As a keepsake, I mean.'

'Well,' Saradananda dithered a little. 'As a rule everything a sanyasi has used in his earthly life is supposed to burn with him. But if you're very keen—'

'No. No.' Nivedita interrupted hastily. 'There's no need to break the rule.'

The pyre was lit and the flames, fed by streams of pure ghee, rose to the sky. Nivedita had never seen a cremation before. Now she sat, hour after hour, watching the man she loved burn to ashes. The cold feeling around her heart intensified. She noticed that no one was talking to ber. No one had offered her any consolation. She was an outsider already . . .

The hours went by. The sun changed from a white hot blur to a ball of fire that matched the colour of the flames that were still licking the body. Suddenly Nivedita felt something touch her hand. Startled, she glanced down at it. A piece of the shawl she had wanted as a keepsake had come flying from the pyre towards her.

Chapter XXXVII

Rabindra was hard at work on his novel *Chokhér Bali* fifty-three chapters of which had already appeared in serial form. It had an unusual plot; a strange love triangle with two men, one married one single, both in love with a mysterious widow called Binodini. The novel had proved quite popular. Rabindra received letters, after every instalment, from readers anxious to find out how it was going to end. Rabindra wasn't sure of what he wanted to do. Should he kill off Binodini? That was the simplest, neatest resolution. Mahendra could go back to his gentle, lovely wife Asha. And Bihari! Rabindra's hackles rose at the thought. Why should the poor girl die? She was a widow and she wanted love and physical fulfillment. Was that a crime? Widow remarriage was prevalent in many parts of the world. Even here, in India, Vidyasagar Moshai had had a law passed . . .

A servant entered the room and placed three letters on the table. Rabindra turned them over in his hands. One was from Shilaidaha, one from England and one, addressed in Rathi's handwriting, from Shantiniketan. He slit open the envelope with the foreign markings first. It was, as he had guessed, from his son-in-law Satyen. He had married his second daughter Renuka to the young man and sent him to America to study homeopathy, buying his ticket and undertaking to meet all his expenses till such time as he was able to earn his own living. Rabindranth had a high opinion of homeopathy as a form of treatment and it was gaining quite a measure of popularity in the elitist circles of Calcutta. But Satyen had disappointed him sorely. He had not even reached America. He had broken journey in England en route, and had been living in London for the past year studying homeopathy—or so he said. And now he was writing to his father-in-law for money to buy a ticket back to India. He couldn't abide England anymore, he wrote. He hated the climate and the people were too cold and formal. His studies, too, had ceased to interest him. He was desperately homesick for his own country and wanted to return immediately. Rabindra's heart sank as he read the letter. He had been sending Satyen ten pounds every month for the past year plus something extra, now and then, for clothes, sightseeing and entertaining his friends. All that money was wasted! A ticket from London to Calcutta cost seventy-five pounds. From where, in his present financial state, would he find the money? Anger and resentment stirred within him. But he quelled them with his usual self-control. He wouldn't do anything that might hurt his daughter. Renu was only eleven years old and very sickly. She had been suffering from a slow fever and fits of coughing for several months now...

He sighed and opened the letter from Shilaidaha. Bad news again. Nayeb Moshai had written that the estates were in a bad way. Virtually no rent was coming in. His presence was urgently required. But the third letter took Rabindra's breath away. His face turned pale with shock. Whatever he had anticipated, it hadn't been this. Mrinalini was ill; very ill. He couldn't understand it. She was a strong healthy woman and had never been ill in her life. She was pregnant, of course. But that, surely, was a natural condition. She had given birth to five children without turning a hair...

Next day a man arrived from Shantiniketan and gave him the details. A few days ago a Munsef Babu of Bolpur had invited Mrinalini and her children over for a meal. It had been raining heavily and a lot of mud and slush had collected outside the house. Stepping out, on her way back, Mrinalini had slipped and fallen and was suffering from severe stomach cramps ever since. Her condition was so bad that she couldn't move from her bed. Another cause for worry was that she was eating virtually nothing. She had no appetite and felt nauseous all the time. Rabindra was extremely distressed by the news. But he had so much work in Calcutta that it it was impossible for him to rush to his wife's bedside. He did the next best thing. He sent a message along with some medicines, through the man, to Mrinalini.

But Mrinalini's condition did not improve. She lay on her bed, day after day, not murmuring a word of complaint for the simple reason that there was no one in the house to hear her. An old aunt of hers had taken charge of the kitchen and, thanks to her, the children were getting their meals on time. But she was too old and

673

feeble to nurse the patient as well. Reports kept coming in of Mrinalini's deteriorating condition owing, as Rabindanath realized well enough, to the lack of adequate treatment and care. He decided to bring her back to Calcutta and see that she received proper medical attention. But who would go for her? He was up to his neck in work. An anthology of his complete poems was coming out, volume by volume. Though Mohitchandra Sen was the official editor Rabindranath had insisted on arranging the order of the poems himself and writing the introduction. At length, unable to go himself, he asked Mrinalini's brother Nagen to bring his sister over to Calcutta. Rathi was to come too.

But Mrinalini was not at all happy at the though of leaving Shantiniketan. Humble, though it was, her home here was the only one she had ever known. Jorasanko, with its size and splendour, awed and intimidated her. Besides, there were too many people there with too many demands and expectations. Here she was her own mistress and could run her household and look after her children in her own way. But, broken in health as she now was, she didn't have the strength to protest. Tears of weakness poured down her face as she was carried into the train and laid down on her berth.

Lying in her compartment Mrinalini saw the world, familiar to her from her childhood, rush past. Fields of golden stubble; orchards of mango and jackfruit; swaying palms and bamboo clumps; children playing and old men peacefully smoking their hookahs in tiny villages...Suddenly Rathi cried out excitedly, 'Ma! Ma! Look at all the lotus. *Ogo* Ma! There are thousands!' Mrinalini raised herself on an elbow. A small pond, in the middle of a deserted meadow, had turned into a sheet of green and gold—the yellow buds and blooms pushing their delicate heads proudly out of a nest of leaves. Her wan lips smiled and her eyes, dimmed with tears and sunk in their sockets, gazed with eager longing. Somehow she knew it was for the last time. She would never see the scenes of her childhood again.

Rabindra was not in the house when the party arrived at Jorasanko. He was out attending an important meeting with his publisher. But he came into his wife's room the moment he returned in the evening, hot and exhausted with the efforts of the day. His heart thumped heavily as he looked on her face. All the

674

blood had drained away and death stared at him out of her eyes.

Mrinalini smiled up at her husband. 'You're soaked through with perspiration,' she said. 'Go change into something else.' But Rabindra didn't move from her side. Picking up the fan that lay by his wife's pillow he started waving it over her wasted form. 'It's been very hot in Calcutta for the last two days,' he said. 'Is it as bad as this in Shantiniketan?'

'One doesn't feel the heat so much there,' Mrinalini answered. 'Besides the evenings are always pleasant with cool breezes blowing. I hear Satyen is returning. Is that true?'

'Yes. I've sent him the money for the ticket. He should be arriving soon.'

'That's good news. It's time we arranged their *Phool Sajya* ceremony. Renu is almost eleven and a half.'

Rabindra nodded, though his mind was troubled. Renu had attained puberty a few months ago and was ready, according to the elders, for cohabitation with her husband. But she was so frail and weak! Besides, the ceremony would cost money.

'Send for Beli and Sarat from Mungher,' Mrinalini begged. 'I haven't seen them for so long.' A joyful note crept into her voice. 'The whole family will be together again.'

'Everything you wish for will be done.'

Rabindra made all the arrangements for the *Phool Sajya* ceremony but couldn't stay for it. The Raja of Nator was going to Shantiniketan and Rabindra had to accompany him. The Raja was a family friend and had helped Rabindra out, in many ways, in the past. Mrinalini was loath to let him go. She wanted her family together, she cried repeatedly, but Rabindra was not in a position to humour her. He went to Shantiniketan and stayed on there even after the Raja's return. There was so much to do; so many problems to attend to. Besides, the thought of returning to a house full of relatives was an uninspiring one. He didn't worry about Mrinalini. Beli had arrived. She would look after her mother.

Mrinalini's condition worsened every day. Her square, sturdy healthy body wasted away till it was reduced to a handful of bones. She suffered from incessant pain in the lower abdomen and no doctor could diagnose what was happening within her. The pain was so sharp, at times, that it woke her from her sleep.

She would sit up shuddering—runnels of sweat streaming down her face and neck.

Satyen had returned from England and was living in Jorasanko. Rabindra had never seen anyone as selfish and self-centered as his second son-in-law. Not sparing a thought for his ailing wife and dying mother-in-law he spent all his time devising new pleasures for himself. Not content with the hundred and fifty rupees a month his father-in-law was giving him, he constantly demanded more and sulked if he didn't get it instantly. Of late he had started pestering Rabindranath for two thousand rupees to open a dispensary. Rabindra realized that he had made a mistake in his choice of a son-in-law. He couldn't bear to look on his daughter's face. She was only a child. But her husband's harassment of her father did not escape her notice. His helplessness and humiliation burned in her heart. In her misery she turned away from everyone. She lay in bed, her face to the wall, coughing incessantly. Of late, bits of blood had started appearing in her sputum.

Her husband came nowhere near her but her father did—often. And, at such times, though her face was turned away she recognized the touch of his hand on her head and burst into a fit of sobbing—her little bird body quivering on the sheets. Rabindra's heart was wrenched with pain. What could he say to her? What consolation could he give? She was his flesh and blood. And she was suffering! Though only a child she was enduring the pain and humiliation of being a woman. And he, her father, sat watching helplessly. It was too, too cruel!

But, despite the fact that there were two serious patients in the house, Rabindra was away from it most of the time. Jagadish Bose had returned from England and was being feted and lionized Felicitations were showered on him and parties given in his honour. And everywhere he went Rabindra was invited too. Rabindra found himself in a quandary. His best friend insisted on his presence by his side in this most glorious phase of his life. But Rabindra had so many problems. His wife and daughter were critically ill. His eldest daughter, his only support, had gone back to her husband's home. Rathi, just coming into manhood, had taken to wandering all over the city. He needed a pair of sharp eyes watching him and a strong guiding hand. The younger boy

Shomi was a total contrast to his brother—quiet and introverted to the point of being a recluse. He moped about in dark corners of the stairs and attics reading one book after another. Reading was a good habit but moping wasn't. He needed to be brought out of himself... And the baby Meera! His heart turned over in pity every time he thought of Meera. She was at an age when she desperately needed a mother's love. But her mother didn't even look up when she came into the room. Rabindra had seen the child standing at the door for hours together gazing longingly at her sick mother, then walking softly away.

One evening Rabindra came into his wife's room. 'Why do you keep your eyes open all the time?' he asked, taking her hand in his warm, strong clasp. 'If you kept them shut you might be able to sleep.' Mrinalini raised her eyes to her husband's face. Tears gathered in them and rolled slowly down her cheeks. 'Why did you send Shomi to Shantiniketan?' she asked in a broken whisper as her husband wiped her tears tenderly away. 'You never even told me.'

'He was lonely here. He needed the company of children his own age.'

'He has never stayed away from me. Who'll look after him there?'

'He'll stay in the ashram with the other boys. He'll eat, sleep and study as they do—'

'I'm going away. I'll never see Shomi again.'

'You mustn't say such things. You'll get well soon. Try and get some sleep.'

Mrinalini turned over on the other side and Rabindranath left the room. He returned at nine o'clock and came to her again. Mrinalini lay exactly as he had left her, lying on her side, her eyes open and staring. The nurse he had engaged for her sat on a stool by the side of her bed fanning her with a palm leaf fan. Rabindra took it from her and gestured to her to leave the room. 'It's very hot isn't it?' he asked his wife brightly. 'Unusual for November! Do you suppose we'll have no winter at all this year?' There was no reply. Once again the tears oozed out, slowly and painfully, out of her eyes. 'Have you had anything to eat?' he probed. 'Would you like some hot milk?' Mrinalini fixed her eyes, sunk in deep pools of shadow, on her husband's bright, dark ones but did not speak. 'She's hurt because I sent Shomi away without telling her,' Rabindra thought. 'I'll send for Shomi,' he said in an attempt to mollify her. 'It is you who are pining away for him. He isn't homesick at all. Besides children have to grow up and leave their parents some day or the other. We must stop clinging to them.' He waited, eagerly, for some response but none came. Rabindra was puzzled. Perhaps her hurt and anger was deeper than he had assumed. '*Ogo!*' he abandoned his superior tone and spoke in a chastened voice. 'I know you have several grievances against me and I don't blame you. I have many faults. I haven't been a good husband to you. I haven't given you the time and attention you deserved. But things will be different from now I promise. Only get well soon and I'll never leave your side again.' But Mrinalini neither moved nor spoke. Only the tears fell, thick and fast, on her pillow. Now Rabindranath was truly alarmed. 'Rathi!' he cried out in panic. 'Come and sit with your mother.' Rathi came running in. 'Ma! Ma!' he called out to her again and again. But Mrinalini didn't respond to even her son's call. Now everyone knew the truth. Mrinalini had lost her speech.

Rabindranath hastened to send for the doctor but it was too late. Mrinalini lay, just as she was, her eyes fixed and staring. Rabindranath sat by her side all night looking into the eyes that lacerated his soul. Towards dawn he saw them widen as though in wonder. Then, as he leaned anxiously over her, a mist fell over them. Suddenly her head dropped off the pillow. A shudder passed over her frame and she was dead.

Chapter XXXVIII

Nivedita did not allow herself the luxury of grieving over her loss. Swamiji had loved this country with a rare passion and commitment and had worked himself to death trying to better the conditions of her people. Who would take over from where he left off? The question plagued her constantly. His disciples in Belur seemed content to pass their days in weeping and chanting prayers in his memory. Nivedita had visited the math a number of times after Swamiji's death and tried to enthuse the inmates into carrying their guru's work forward. But their behaviour towards her had been cool and evasive. Once she had taken Okakura with her but they had ignored his presence completely. Nivedita and Okakura had sat for a while under the bel tree at the spot where Swamiji had been cremated, and then come away. The next day she had gone alone and taken her place beside Saradananda. She had always got on well with him. Saradananda knew English and they had often had long discussions on various subjects. 'Don't you think it is time we stopped mourning and started working?' she asked him directly. 'So much is about to happen in this country! Shouldn't our math play a part in it?' Saradananda sighed. 'I've been thinking about it,' he muttered avoiding her eyes. 'I've even had discussions with Brahmananda. Our beloved friend and guru Naren has left us. Things have changed considerably. So many decisions need to be made. Why don't you speak to Brahmananda?'

Brahmananda was sitting in the veranda adjoining Swamiji's room when Nivedita came to him. The door was ajar and she could see Swamiji's bed and the window at which he had stood, looking out on the Ganga, when walking down the stairs had become too painful for him. It was raining and the river was shrouded in a fine mist. Nivedita waited for Brahmananda to speak. Then, nothing forthcoming, she murmured gently, 'Don't you have anything to say to me?'

'Sister!' Brahmananda cleared his throat pompously and

679

returned question for question, 'Do you love our math? Does the welfare of the Ramkrishna Mission mean anything to you?' Nivedita's blue eyes widened in shock. What sort of a question was this? The Mission was Swamiji's ideal; his dream. Hadn't she worked by his side and helped to build it up? Had she not given it all she had? Her country? Her own people and culture? Her personal life? 'I'm sorry to be the one to tell you this Nivedita,' Brahmananda continued. 'Your association with the math and Mission must end. Your presence here is a threat to us.'

'A threat!' Nivedita echoed. 'What kind of threat?'

'You've changed your ideals. You've entered politics. We can't afford to have anything to do with you anymore. However,' and now he cleared his throat and spoke quickly, almost as though he had rehearsed the lines so often that he had them by heart, 'The money you have raised for the Mission by your personal efforts is legitimately ours. Cheques and drafts are still coming in. You have no right to them. You must deposit them here, as and when they come, without delay. And you must make an announcement in the newspapers to the effect that you have severed all your connections with Belur Math.'

A wave of anger and self-pity swept over Nivedita. 'No!' she wanted to cry out, 'I'll do no such thing. I have as much right to be here as you. I've lost him whom I adored and revered. I feel his presence here. How can you deprive me of that comfort?' But she said nothing. Brahmananda glanced at her out of the corner of his eye. Her face was as white as a sheet and her eyes glittered like blue ice. Brahmananda felt uneasy, even a little guilty. He tried to soften the blow. 'Our personal relations,' he said, 'will remain the same of course.' Nivedita rose and ran down the stairs and out of the house regardless of the driving rain in her face and the mud and slush under her bare feet.

Cut off from the math Nivedita was faced with a real problem. How could she live on in this country? She had enjoyed a certain position as Swamiji's disciple. People had come forward to help her and she had never had to worry about where she would live and where her next meal was to come from. But now she was truly destitute. She considered going back to England and rejected the idea instantly. By doing so she would be admitting defeat. She would live on here. She would find a means of doing so.

One morning, a few days later, a young man came to see her. He was an Englishman, very tall and thin, and in his face Nivedita detected a curious blend of intelligence and humility. Nivedita hadn't seen such a face in many years. 'My name is Samuel K. Ratcliffe,' he said, with a disarming smile. 'I arrived from London a few days ago.'

'I'm just about to have my breakfast,' Nivedita said. 'Why don't you join me? We'll talk as we eat.'

Over breakfast Ratcliffe told her that he was a journalist by profession and had come out to India as Associate Editor of *The Statesman*. He had heard her speak at a tea party and been impressed not only by her knowledge of the country but by her attitude to Indians. His fellow Englishmen, he told her, never wearied of pointing out the shortcomings of the natives. If they were to be believed, all Indians were liars and cheats, oppressive to their women and their religion was an abomination. 'But in your speech,' his face lit up at the memory, 'you spoke of a glorious past and a wonderful heritage. I felt as though another world had revealed itself before my eyes. I decided, then, that I would request you to write for my newspaper. Will you do so?'

'I? Write in your paper?' Nivedita stared in disbelief.

'Yes. We need insights such as yours Besides your language has force. I've read some of your articles.'

The offer came as a windfall for Nivedita. A column in a prestigious paper like *The Statesman* would bring in a regular income and solve the problem of her livelihood. Besides she would enjoy the experience of sharing her thoughts with thousands of readers. She smiled into the eager face opposite hers. She liked the young man very much.

Her immediate worries taken care of, Nivedita turned all her energies into her chosen task—that of preparing the ground for the independence of the country. Taking Okakura with her she went from forum to forum trying to enthuse the public into accepting his proposals. Calcutta was full of secret societies and Nivedita was in touch with them all. The members of Pramath Mitra's Anushilan Samiti were an enthusiastic lot and ready to jump into the fray. Jatin Bandopadhyay's boys, charged with Nivedita's speeches, were prepared to lay down their lives for the country. Nivedita had heard that these societies were being

681

financed by rich and important men who preferred to remain incognito. One had even offered a reward of a thousand rupees to every young man who was successful in killing a British officer. But one person she felt unsure of was Sarala Ghoshal. Her aakhra was the first one to be established in Calcutta. The boys were taught bodybuilding, fencing with lathis and sword fighting. But to what purpose? It seemed to Nivedita that they did not have a goal in sight. Or, if they did, it was blurred and indistinct.

Another factor that disturbed Nivedita was Okakura's own attitude. He had proceeded on a tour of the other states of India and returned a changed man. He wasn't open with her anymore. Nivedita got a distinct feeling that he was keeping a great deal back from her. Whenever she asked him what preparations for revolution were going on in the other states he had the same answer, every time. 'There are piles of dry tinder lying everywhere. The country will go up in flames the moment the fire is kindled. But Bengal must provide the spark.' Nivedita couldn't help feeling that these were just words; fine words without meaning or substance. She, herself, was so eager; so keen. She had given a thousand rupees, out of her meagre savings, to Okakura just before he had proceeded on the tour. And she was working so hard—she was wearing herself to the bone! But he seemed content to drink his brandy, smoke his expensive cigars and discuss Art with Gaganendra and Abanindra while waiting for the spark that would set the country ablaze.

Nivedita noticed another thing about him. He was too partial to the society of women. He visited Sarala Ghoshal's house often and, once there, refused to budge for hours. Sarala's house was always full of guests with many beautiful women among them. Okakura had an obvious fascination for a friend of Sarala's called Priyamvada. But, of late, Nivedita had seen him throwing wistful glances at another visitor—an actress called Nayanmoni.

One evening Nivedita came to Okakura's house in Chowringhee to work on the manuscript of *Ideals of the East*. It was a large and well appointed one for Okakura had expensive habits and liked to live in style. Nivedita found him reclining in an easy chair sipping brandy. Between his fingers was a glowing cigar. He motioned her into a chair opposite him. Then, as she read out her corrections, he listened to her, nodding solemnly from time to time. Presently he put down his cigar and rose from his chair. Coming up to her he put his hands on her shoulders and tried to draw her towards him. Nivedita sprang to her feet and wrenched herself free. 'What is the meaning of this?' she cried.

'I . . . I . . .' Okakura stammered, taken aback by her vehemence. 'My intentions are honourable.'

'You touched me!' Nivedita asked in a wondering voice, moving further away from him. 'How did you dare to do such a thing?'

'You . . . you looked so beautiful with the evening light falling on your face. As pure and serene as a goddess. Will you marry me Miss Noble?' he sank to his knees before her and added, 'I beg your hand in all humility.'

Nivedita's eyes blazed with fury. What was the man saying? Didn't he know who she was? She was Vivekananda's Nivedita! How could he imagine that she, who had known a man of Vivekananda's stature, could ever turn to another? Scenes from the past flashed before her eyes. She had been so young and Swamiji so brilliant and handsome! She had loved him with all the power and passion and irrationality of youth. She had wanted him not only as guru and mentor but as a woman wanted the man she loved! 'Can we not live as man and woman?' she had asked him once pushing aside all shame and modesty in her desperation. *Living with a woman did not stand in the way of Sri Ramkrishna's search for the divine.* The words had welled up in her heart but not reached her lips. Swamiji had gazed on her face for a long while. Then, as though he had heard the words, unspoken though they were, he had held her eyes with his own dark sombre ones and said, 'I cannot do what my guru did Margot. I am not Ramkishna.'

Nivedita had tried to argue the point but Vivekananda had stood firm. 'Our people won't understand it Margot. Such a thing is not possible here.' He had looked away as he spoke and the colour had flooded and receded, by turns, in his face and neck. It was after this exchange that Swamiji had initiated her and made her take the vows of chastity. She was a *brahmacharini* now.

Nivedita looked at Okakura with hatred in her eyes. 'You wish to marry me?' she asked. 'How many wives do you mean to collect in this country? Do you suppose I haven't noticed the fond

683

glances you bestow on Priyamvada and the actress Nayanmoni? I also happen to know that you proposed marriage to Sarala Ghoshal and that she turned you down. Are you here, in this country, to help spark off a revolution? Or are you here to make love?' Okakura took a step towards her and tried to speak but she waved her hand at him in dismissal and continued. 'Your promises of Japan and Korea coming to our aid were false, were they not Mr Okakura? You came to this poor country and enjoyed her hospitality. You were feted and lionized. And all the time . . . all the time—,' Nivedita's voice choked on a sob and she fought for control. 'Even your grand design of unification of the Asian nations! What will it lead to, if achieved? To the supremacy of Japan, is it not? I see everything so clearly now. I've been blind...blind.' Nivedita rushed out of the room pausing only once to turn and say, over her shoulder, 'You'll never see me again.'

Her words were prophetic. A few days later Okakura abandoned all his efforts in India and went back to his own country.

Chapter XXXIX

Aurobindo Ghosh sat every morning poring over his books. The object of his study was his mother tongue and he pursued it with such a degree of fastidiousness and asked so many questions that his tutor Dinendra Kumar Roy felt ready to scream with exasperation at times. Reading aloud from Deenabandhu Mitra's *Lilavati*, that morning, Aurobindo raised his eyes to his tutor's. 'What is *piriti*?' he asked. Dinendranath had anticipated the question. 'It is an emotion,' he explained, 'that has to be experienced to be understood. You'll know what it is when it hits you.'

'Hits me!' Aurobindo echoed, 'What do you mean?'

'Get yourself a wife and you'll know what I mean'.

'Not a bad idea.' Aurobindo answered calmly, considering the suggestion. It didn't even occur to him to blush from outraged modesty or wax indignant at Dinendranath Kumar's impertinence. Barin, who sat in a corner of the veranda a little distance away from them, burst out laughing. Putting down the book he had been reading, he rose from his chair and walked up to his brother. 'I know just the girl for you Sejda,' he said conversationally. 'She's the daughter of one of Baba's friends. A beautiful girl and very well educated. And coming from a Brahmo family she's very smart and free. She can—'

'Chho!' Aurobindo dismissed his brother's proposal contemptuously. 'I can't stand Brahmo girls. All the ones I've seen wear shoes and stockings, play the piano out of tune and speak of love in affected voices.'

'But...but,' Barin was taken aback. 'We're Brahmos.'

'Baba was a Brahmo but I'm not,' Aurobindo announced firmly. 'I don't want an English-speaking or piano-playing bride. What I would really like is a traditional Hindu girl—the kind one finds in Bankimchandra's novels. Hindu women are soft, gentle and kind. They love their husbands with an unswerving loyalty and devotion.' Barin and Dinendra burst out laughing at

685

Aurobindo's naiveté. 'Those are imaginary women,' Dinendra pointed out, 'characters from books.'

'Do you mean to tell me that such women don't exist?'

'Even if they do they're not for you,' Barin enlightened his brother. 'No traditional Hindu will accept you as a son-in-law. You're born of a Brahmo family, for one thing, and you've lived in England for years and years, for another. You're a *mlechha* in the eyes of the ordinary Hindu.'

'I can do penance and return to the fold—can't I Rai Moshai?'

'It is possible,' Dinendra returned guardedly. 'But the process is long and difficult. It will mean partaking of cowdung.'

'So what? I'll eat cowdung if I have to and become a Hindu. And I'll find myself a wife like Bhramar.'

The talk veered around the subject of marriage for a while. Presently a stranger walked in unannounced. The three men looked on curiously. No one was surprised at this intrusion for Aurobindo kept open house and friends and neighbours walked in and out as they pleased. The man, they noted, was tall and burly and bursting with muscles. 'I've come to you with a lot of hope,' the stranger began, addressing Aurobindo directly, 'I need your help.'

'Who are you? Where do you come from?' Dinendra asked.

'My name is Jatindranath Bandopadhyay and I come from an obscure village in Bengal. I have wanted to be a soldier from early childhood. I have travelled all over the country in search of a job—without success. Do you know why? Because I'm a Bengali. The sahebs distrust Bengalis. So do the native rajas.'

'That's common knowledge and doesn't surprise us. What does is your aspiration. You are the first Bengali I have met who has cherished a lifelong desire to become a soldier. Why is it so?'

'I'm a strong lathyal and can take on ten men at a time. I can fence swords and wrestle with champions.' He whipped off his shirt in a flash and revealed a deep wound on the chest. 'This was made by a tiger. I encountered him in the jungles of Ayodhya and fought him with my bare hands. But he couldn't get the better of me and had to run away.'

Aurobindo looked at him appraisingly. 'I didn't know Bengal could produce men like you,' he said. 'I'm truly glad to meet you and I shall recommend you to Madhav Rao. In the meantime—'

686

he coughed delicately, 'Do you have a place to stay?'

'I eat here and there and sleep under the stars.'

'Stay here,' Aurobindo said impulsively. Then raising his voice he called out to the servant. '*Oré*! Give the Babu some oil and a gamchha.' Turning to his guest he said, 'The midday meal is ready. We'll eat as soon as you've had your bath.'

The evenings were very quiet in Aurobindo's house because that was the time he devoted to his writing. While in England he wrote poetry and, like other English poets, he frequented pubs, wore his hair long and discussed art and literature in coffee houses. But over the years he realized that, no matter how well he wrote, he would never be one of them. 'What do you know of such things?' the eyes of his contemporaries told him. 'The intellectual must be free and you belong to a subject race. You haven't known freedom in hundreds of years.' The Irish were under British domination too but they commanded respect. They were fighting for their independence. Indians hadn't shown a trace of resistance. It seemed as though they were perfectly content to remain a nation of slaves.

That evening Aurobindo came home from college, had a wash and a cup of tea and sat down to his writing as usual. But, for some reason, he couldn't concentrate. Scenes from the past kept flashing before his eyes. His mind was distracted and restless and he sat for hours the pen idle in his hands. Presently he rose and came to the room where Dinendra, Barin and Jatin were playing cards and talking in hushed voices from fear of disturbing him. 'Barin,' he said sternly. 'Do you mean to spend the rest of your life idling your time away in gossip and cards?' All three looked up startled. Aurobindo had never spoken to Barin in that tone before. 'No...no' Barin stammered in reply. 'I had a tea shop in Patna. I can open another if I get some money.'

'Well I shan't give you any. Not for a tea shop—I mean. I don't want my brother to be a shopkeeper all his life.'

'What else can I do?' Barin scratched his head in embarrassment. 'I haven't received much education and—'

'You can work for the country.'

'You mean open a Swadeshi shop?' Barin's face brightened.

'No, I didn't mean that. Can't you think of anything other than shops? Working for the country means ridding her of the

687

foreigner.'

'How can I do that?' Barin stared at his brother in dismay.

'Are you ready to go to Calcutta Barin?'

'Of course. But what am I to do there?'

'Scout around and get a band of boys together. Strong, healthy, well-educated boys from good families. Then arrange to train them in the martial arts. Be sure to preserve the utmost secrecy. Societies of this kind are found in the north and south of India. Shall Bengal lag behind?'

'Collecting a group of young men and training them should not be difficult,' Dinendra said. 'But to what purpose? What is your goal?'

'To free India from foreign rule.'

'Is that so easy?'

'There are thousands of sepoys in the Indian Army who are ready to fight their masters at the call of the country. There are thousands of Adivasis in the mountains and forests who are skilled fighters even if their weapons are primitive. They are like heaps of dry leaves waiting for the spark that will set off a mighty conflagration. And you'll be providing that spark.'

Jatin had been listening to Aurobindo quietly all this while. Now he stirred in his seat and said, 'I'm greatly impressed by what you're saying Aurobindo Babu. I would like to join Barin and form a society. I'll go back to Calcutta tomorrow.'

'That would be best for you. Why should you be content to serve as an ordinary soldier in a native raja's army? Use your strength, skill and experience to free your country from bondage. Work together with Barin. He will comb the streets of Calcutta and collect a band of young men. You will train them in fencing, wrestling and shooting.'

'We'll leave tomorrow,' Barin said. 'But we'll need money. Where is that to come from Sejda?'

'I'll give you some to begin with. But sooner or later you'll have to fend for yourselves.'

'We'll start a collection,' Barin cried excitedly. 'We'll go to all the rich men of Calcutta and ask them for funds.'

'You'll do nothing of the kind. Your watch word must be *secrecy*. You'll expose yourselves to danger if you forget it. Besides, a country's independence isn't such a cheap commodity that it can be bought with charity money.'

'But . . . But . . . what else can we do?' Barin stammered out the question.

'Commit burglary,' Aurobindo answered. His face was smooth and calm. Not a muscle twitched. 'Rob the rich. Kill if you have to.'

'What are you saying Moshai?' Dinendrakumar cried out startled. 'You're inciting boys from good families to rob and kill!'

'We are undertaking a struggle the like of which has never been seen in the history of the world. There can be no value judgements in a cause like ours. The end justifies the means.' Aurobindo lit a cigarette and put it to his lips. 'Don't think I'm speaking on an impulse,' he continued, 'I've thought on these lines for years . . . and now all three of you must swear a solemn oath. You won't breathe a word of what has passed between us this evening to a living soul.'

Barin and Jatin left for Calcutta the next morning. And, within a few days, Barin launched on the job of enrolling members for his secret society. As luck would have it, the first person he encountered in the streets of Calcutta was Bharat. 'Bharat Dada!' he exclaimed in surprise and delight. 'I can't believe my eyes. I've been thinking of you for the last two days!' But Bharat's response wasn't quite so effusive. He was afraid Barin would pester him again to enter into a partnership. 'What brings you here Barin?' he said a trifle guardedly. 'Have you opened a tea shop in Calcutta?'

'No, no' Barin waved his hand dismissively. 'I'm doing something quite different.' Then, bringing his mouth close to Bharat's ear, he whispered. 'I'm working for the country. We've formed a secret society and I need your help. Will you become a member Bharat Dada?'

The house in Circular Road was old and somewhat decrepit. There were two shops on the ground floor—one selling grocery, the other homeopathic medicines. The first floor was vacant. It had been occupied by the landlord but he had bought another house quite recently and moved away. A quiet, unassuming Brahmin family lived in the four rooms on the top floor. The head of the family was a tall, hefty looking man in a dhuti and banian through which his *poité* peeped out—thick and strong and white.

689

He wore a string of rudraksha breads on his neck and a dab of sandalwood paste on his brow. Looking at him no one could dream that he was the famous Jatin Bandopadhyay and that his house was the headquarters of the Secret Society.

When Bharat first came here he had marveled at the way Jatin Babu had transformed himself from an orthodox Brahmin gentleman to a fierce wrestler and lathyal. Doffing his banian and tucking his dhuti securely between his legs he had picked up a lathi and commenced spinning it round and round in strokes as sharp and incisive as lightning. The others who came to the house were Barindra Ghosh, his uncle Satyendranath, his friend Hemchandra P. Kanungo, Debabrata Bosu, Bhupendranath Datta, Rakhahari Sarkar and Amitbikram Goswami. But if the members were few in number their weapons were even more so. Two swords, ten lathis and one pistol was all they had. Bharat was appalled. How could they hope to crush the might of the British empire with such a pathetic supply? But he didn't leave or give up hope. He decided to bide his time and see what the future held.

One evening, as they sat together listening to the howling of the wind around the house and the lashing of the rain on the shutters, Amitbikram said sheepishly, 'This is just the weather for *muri* and fritters. With gulps of hot tea of course.' Barin closed the book from which he had been reading extracts to his friends, and rose to his feet. 'An excellent idea!' he said, 'The shop next to the ironmonger's sells freshly popped *muri*—warm and wonderfully crisp. As for their fritters—' he sucked the juices that trickled from his palate in anticipation. 'But you'll have to contribute two pice each.' Everyone nodded, their faces eager and ready to comply. Only Jatin brought his brows together. 'Who'll pay for the tea? I haven't opened a charity establishment.' The members looked at one another in surprise. Who had ever heard of paying a family man the price for a cup of tea? But Barin solved the problem quickly and efficiently. 'Tell them in the kitchen to start boiling the kettle,' he said. 'We won't pay you for the tea but we'll let you off the two pice.' He dashed out of the room and returned, a few minutes later, with his purchases. And almost at the same time Jatin's sister Kuhelika came into the room with a dozen cups of steaming tea set out on a thala. Kuhelika was a fine looking girl with a firm, well-knit body and a face which had more character than beauty. Her eyes flashed with intelligence and her mouth was perpetually curved in a mocking smile. At first everyone had thought her to be a spinster. Later they had discovered that she was a virgin widow. 'Why don't you join us?' Amitbikram smiled at her but Jatin quelled him with a glance. 'Go back to your work,' he told his sister severely. 'Can't she have some *muri*?' Amitbikram tried again but Kuhelika had left the room.

The reading recommenced and a discussion followed regarding the relative merits of the Shivaji Utsav started by Tilak in Maharashtra and Sarala Ghoshal's honouring of Pratapaditya and Udayaditya. Most of the members expressed the opinion that they should join Sarala and help her in her work. At this point Bharat rose and walked over to the window. His eyes were on the pouring rain but his thoughts were elsewhere. He had heard from Jadugopal that Bhumisuta had become a friend of Sarala's and could be seen at her house every evening. Sarala was teaching her some songs composed by her famous uncle Rabindranath Thakur.

Bharat spoke rarely as a rule. But now he turned to his compatriots and declared firmly. 'We mustn't think of joining Sarala Ghoshal.' The others looked on in dismay. 'Why not?' Satyendra asked a trifle impatiently. 'Because freedom will not come to us by dancing in the streets and demonstrating our skills with a couple of rusted swords,' Bharat replied. He took a deep breath and continued. 'And it won't come to us this way either. We meet every day, talk and have tea. When are we going to undertake anything real and worthwhile?'

'What can we do with one pistol and two blunt swords?' Amitbikram cried. 'The Japanese gentleman assured us that Japan and Korea would give us weapons. But nothing came of it. And now I hear he has gone back to his own country.'

'There's no dearth of weapons in the world,' Jatin said, his voice deep and solemn. 'I had a talk with a Chinaman from Pagoyapatti. He said he could get us any number of guns and cartridges from Hong Kong. But we have to give him the money. From where do we get it?'

A clamour of voices arose. Many suggestions, most of them

691

impractical, were made. The rain pounded, harder than ever, against the windows of the house as the evening wore on. Thunder rumbled and lightning streaked across the sky. Their arguments exhausted, the members of the Samiti looked on one another's face despondently. The night had turned chilly and they shivered with cold and a sense of hopelessness. Suddenly Amitbikram said, 'This is just the night to eat khichuri and omlette.' The mood of the group changed. A chorus of voices took up the cue. 'Yes of course!' 'A wonderful idea!' 'Just the night.' Jatin Bandopadhyay's glance passed over the faces, hopeful and eager. 'Very well,' he said carelessly. 'I'll give orders in the kitchen. But you'll have to contribute a rupee each.' Then, seeing the disappointment writ large on their faces, he added quickly, 'Aurobindo Babu sends me thirty rupees a month. I have to pay the rent, feed my family and carry on the work of the Samiti on that paltry sum. I'm broke all the time.'

'Jatinda,' Hemchandra spoke for the first time that evening. 'We can't even think of embarking on a revolution on thirty rupees a month. We'll need money. Big money. And the only way we can get it is by robbing the rich.'

'That's exactly what Aurobindo Babu said,' Jatin replied.

Just then a tinkle of bracelets was heard outside the door. Amitbikram threw an eager glance in its direction and putting his hand in his pocket brought out a ten-rupee note. 'There's no need to start a collection. This is on me.'

'Bravo!' Satyen Babu cried. 'Ten rupees is a lot of money. We can send out for some *Topse* and have it fried crisp with our khichuri.'

'Who'll sell you fish at this time of the night?' Jatin snapped. 'And in this weather too! There are a couple of dozen duck's eggs in the house. Content yourself with omelette for the present.'

'I can't go home tonight Jatinda,' Amitbikram threw him a pleading glance. 'Srirampur is a long way off and the rain is getting worse. I'll have to sleep here'.

'You'll do nothing of the kind,' Jatin told him sternly. 'If you can't go home—go find a place in Bharat's mess.'

Ten days later seven young men hired a boat from Chandpal Ghat. They didn't want any boatmen, they said. They would row the boat themselves and bring it back a week later. It was a bright moonlit night and the craft skimmed over the Ganga smoothly and rapidly. To all intents and purposes it appeared to be a pleasure cruise. But if one lifted the planks of the *patatan* one would find a dozen oiled lathis, a couple of swords and a pistol nestling beneath. Jatin and his group had decided to target a middle class household in a village between Hirak Bandar and Diamond Harbour. The very rich had armed guards. Some even kept dogs. Jatin had transformed himself from an orthodox Brahmin gentleman to a Muslim *majhi*. Looking at him in his checked lungi and singlet and observing the skill with which he maneuvered the boat no one could dream that he was playing a part. But the others had started getting cold feet. 'How would it be Jatinda,' Barin asked the older man, 'If I stayed on in the boat and the rest of you went ahead? I could raise an alarm if the police came after us.'

'No,' Jatin said firmly. 'We're in it together and we sink or swim together.' Amitbikram lay on his back his head against the prow. His eyes were glazed and he seemed wrapped in his own thoughts. '*Ki ré* Amit!' Jatin gave him a push. 'Are you going to lie here all night? Get ready. We're leaving in a few minutes.' At these words Amit stirred and turned his eyes towards his mentor. His voice, when he spoke, was as weak as a bird's and his lips trembled a little 'What if we get caught Jatinda? My family is a reputed one—' Now Hemchandra spoke up. 'We're not robbing to enrich ourselves,' he said firmly. 'What we are about to perform is an act of extreme valour. We're not dacoits. We're patriots.'

For some reason, these simple words fired all seven into action. They rose, as if with one will, and started preparing for their nocturnal tryst. They blackened their faces with soot and smeared their bodies with quantities of oil. Then, tucking their dhutis between their legs, they took up their weapons. Jatin held the pistol, Bharat and Hemchandra had a sword each, and the others picked up lathis. Then, upon the stroke of midnight, they crept towards the house they had identified.

The deed was accomplished so swiftly and smoothly that Jatin and company were left with a sense of anti-climax. It had been easy; too easy. They had leaped over the wall and kicked and banged at the door of the room where the inmates lay sleeping.

Within a few minutes an old woman had come out and, seeing a bunch of boys, had shouted curses at them. 'Who are you and what do you want you black-faced monkeys?' she had cried, quite unaware of the gravity of the situation. The others had been taken aback at this volley of questions but not Jatin. Firing his revolver in the air, he had called out in a terrible voice. 'Give us all the money and jewels you have! In absolute silence! Open your mouth once again and you're dead.' After that that it had been a matter of minutes. A little old man had come hobbling out of the room and, thrusting a bundle at Jatin, had said in a quavering voice. 'That's all we have *Baba sakal*. Take it and leave us to die in peace.'

Back in the boat they had opened the bundle. It contained six hundred and seventy-two rupees and about a dozen pieces of jewelry. They had stared at one another. Burgling was so easy! Why hadn't they thought of it before?

Their next target was the house of a rich moneylender of Tarakeshwar. This time they were forced into a struggle. A Bhojpuri darwan armed with an iron rod and two burly men servants appears on the scene and between the three they were an adequate match for the seven. However, Jatin's gun won the day. The moment they heard a shot being fired into the air, the three dropped their arms and allowed the assailants to ransack the house. No one was killed or injured and the burglary wasn't even reported in the newspapers.

But even though the police had no clue to these nocturnal activities the members of the other societies knew what was going on. Most of them didn't lend their support. Surendranath Banerjee, who was negotiating with the British for self rule, was appalled at these acts of terrorism. So was Sarala Ghoshal. Sarala was so disturbed at what was happening that she tried to break up Jatin Bandopadhyaya's aakhra by appealing to Tilak to make a public denunciation. But Tilak refused. By doing so, he told her, he would be betraying his own countrymen. The police would be on the alert and a bloodbath would follow.

The aakhra broke up a few mouths later but not through Sarala's efforts. The seed of disintegration lay within. Ever since its inception, Jatin and Barin had been fighting for supremacy. Now after the two burglaries, the cold war turned into an open feud—bitter and angry. Jatin felt that he was the natural leader being the strongest and most skilled in weaponry amongst them all. Barin believed that his was the right. The society was his brother's brainchild and it was his brother's money that was financing it. The first open quarrel was over who was to take charge of the money collected. Barin insisted that, as the representative of the founder, the society's funds should be vested in his care. Jatin did not agree. This initial disagreement swelled into a mighty ego clash resulting in bitter recriminations from both sides. The breaking point came when Barin accused Jatin of keeping a mistress and passing her off as his sister. 'Kuhelika!' he exclaimed with a sneer. 'Can that be anyone's real name? It's a pseudonym which betrays the truth of the situation. Jatinda is keeping the relationship hidden in a cloud of mystery.'

When this last accusation reached Jatin's ears he felt sick with shame and shock. Calling all the members together he threw the bundle of money and jewels on the floor. Then, dragging Kuhelika in by the hand, he made her raise her sari to the ankles and expose her feet. Placing his own beside hers, he said, 'Have a good look.' The boys stared in surprise. The feet were identical in shape down to the pronounced clefts in the big toes. 'Such genetic similarities are found only among blood brothers and sisters,' Jatin said. 'Does this clear my character gentleman?'

Jatin left the house the next day and went back to his village. Satyendranath, who had disliked Barin's attitude from the start, submitted his resignation. The others went out of circulation, too, one by one. Only Barin and Bharat were left. One evening Bharat arrived at the house to find a big lock hanging on the door. Barin had abandoned the aakhra.

Chapter XL

After the disintegration of the aakhra Bharat felt as though he was suspended in space. He didn't know what to do or where to go. Staying on in Calcutta indefinitely was neither possible nor safe. So when Hemchandra Kanungo invited him to accompany him to Medinipur he gave the matter serious thought. 'How long can I stay in your house as a guest, Hem?' he asked ruefully. 'You'll long to get rid of me after a while.'

'I may or may not wish to get rid of you,' Hem answered, 'But that's not the question here. *You* won't be comfortable staying as my guest for long. I have another idea. I've inherited a small farm in the outskirts of Medinipur. Why don't you go and live there? No, no! I'm not offering you charity. I suggest you buy it. I have no use for it and I hardly ever go there. I've been thinking of selling it for quite some time now.'

'I've never lived in a village Hem.' Though tempted by the offer Bharat demurred a little.

'Medinipur is hardly a village. It's a bustling town with many educated people living in it. It has a library and, what is more, a society like the one in Circular Road. You'll find plenty of people to talk to.'

'Give me a few days to think it over. I'll let you know as soon as I decide.'

Bharat left for Medinipur a couple of weeks later. Hemchandra met him at the station and said, 'Let me take you to the farm first. See if you like it.' Hiring a buggy the two friends drove to the edge of the town where a small dilapidated cottage stood on several acres of land. There was a garden around the house which had obviously been laid out with taste and care at one time, but was now reduced to a wilderness of weeds and tangled undergrowth. The pond in the middle had stone ghats around it but they were broken in many places and the water was choked with algae. Bharat could see some rice fields in the distance and orchards of mango and jackfruit. But the place was

696

completely deserted. Not a soul was to be seen.

Hemchandra shouted for the mali Siddhiram, who was also the caretaker, in vain. Then, giving up, he picked up a stone and hammered at the ancient lock till it broke and fell to the floor. The door creaked on its rusty hinges and swung open to reveal an interior that left Bharat staring with dismay. Dust lay thick on everything and cobwebs hung in festoons from the walls. The floor was pitted with holes from which mice scampered gaily in and out. 'You're disappointed, aren't you friend?' Hemchandra asked with a smile. 'Things will look quite different after a thorough cleaning and some repairs. Come home with me for the present. You can take charge of your new property when it's ready for you. By the way, I hope you're not afraid of ghosts. The house is supposed to be haunted. My grandfather kept a mistress here for many years and she died in this house. Members of my family claim that they have heard peals of laughter and the tinkling of ankle bells at the dead of night. That's why no one comes here anymore.'

'I've had close encounters with death so many times that I've ceased to be afraid of anything—natural or supernatural.'

Bharat moved in within a week and adjusted to his new life with an ease that was amazing even to him. He gave up his city clothes and wore a checked lungi and singlet. He stopped shaving and soon a thick stubble appeared on his cheeks and chin. All day he pottered about, on bare feet, watering his shrubs, planting new trees and pruning old ones. Siddhiram, Bharat discovered, was a better cook than a mali and Bharat decided to switch roles with him. So while Siddhiram cooked and cleaned Bharat tended the garden. The evenings were spent in Hem's company. The two friends sat together by the pond, now cleared of weeds and hyacinth, chatted of the past and made plans for the future.

'We swore on the Gita to dedicate our lives to the country,' Hem said one day. 'But we haven't kept our oath Bharat.'

'What can we do by ourselves Hem?' Bharat replied 'Someone must give us the direction. Aurobindo Babu's silence is uncanny. He seems to have given up hope. Shall we do the same?'

'By no means. The boys of Medinipur haven't given up the effort or the hope. Let us work with them. It may be that the lead for a great revolution will come from an obscure town like ours.'

697

A few months later Satyendranath arrived in Medinipur and took on the task of restructuring the Samiti. Bharat's house became the headquarters of the new aakhra and several boys, handpicked and initiated into the movement by Satyen, moved in with him. Here they received several kinds of instruction. Along with secret training in the martial arts they were given lessons in economics and history. Satyen explained the reasons for the country's declining economy and regaled them with stories of other great revolutions of the world. While Satyen was engaged in educating the youth of the country Hemchandra went from village to village on a rickety bicycle trying to win over the common man. He began by targeting schools and schoolmasters. He had lengthy discussions with the latter out of a conviction that, if they could be fired with a desire for freedom, they would pass it on to their pupils. Bharat accompanied him quite often and never failed to be amazed at his drive and dedication. Unlike Bharat, Hem was married and had a family. Yet he spent months away from home without a murmur. Even more surprising was the fact that he never put himself forward or claimed the right to leadership. He worked in the shadows and allowed Satyen to bask in the limelight.

One evening the whole group sat together in Bharat's house talking of this and that when one of the boys said suddenly, 'What has become of Curzon's grand plan of the Partition of Bengal Satyenda? Why is no one talking about it anymore?'

'The Bengali Babus were so fiercely opposed to it,' another replied, 'that the sahebs lost their nerve. It is possible that Curzon has changed his mind.' Everyone's face brightened at the thought. Everyone's except Hemchandra's. 'I hope he hasn't,' he muttered sullenly.

'Why do you say that?' Bharat asked curiously. 'Surely you don't endorse Partition! Don't you realize that the plan is to divide Hindus and Muslims and bring Bengal to her knees?'

'I realize that—of course,' Hemchandra replied. 'What you don't realize is that an act of this kind is needed at this juncture. It will shock the people out of their lethargy. The sleeping nation will wake up roaring for revenge. It might be a good thing in the long run.'

Even as he spoke a boy of about twelve came running into the

698

room. 'May I have a word with you Hemda?' he cried, his face flushed with agitation. Hem looked at him indulgently. He was Khudiram, a very bright lad but wild and wilful and always up to some prank or other. 'What is it Khudi?' Hem asked smiling.

'I want a pistol Hemda. Shall I go to your house?'

'A pistol!' Hemchandra exclaimed startled, 'Whatever for?'

'I want to kill an Englishman. The magistrate slapped an orderly for no fault whatsoever. How dare he? The white-skinned firinghees think they can do what they like in our country! Why should we allow it?'

'The sahebs are all powerful Khudi. If you as much as touch the hair of the magistrate the police will shoot you down like a dog.'

'I'm not afraid.'

'Don't talk nonsense Khudi!' Hemchandra said severely. 'You're too young to think of violence. Go home.'

The boy's face fell. He went away dragging his feet in disappointment. Hemchandra turned to Bharat. 'Did you see that Bharat?' he asked. 'Khudiram is only a child but his blood is boiling with a sense of injustice. With a few thousand boys like him we can launch a struggle the like of which has never been seen in this country.'

Bharat rose at dawn, the next day, and sauntered out into the garden. Plucking a twig from a neem branch he commenced brushing his teeth and examining each tree, bush and creeper running his hands lovingly over the leaves, flowers and fruits. The oleander was bending over under its wealth of blood red blooms. His heart lifted with triumph at the thought that this was his creation. The place where it now stood had been an arid patch overrun with dry scrub. He had cleared the land, dug the soil and planted the seed. He had watered it and watched it take root and grow to healthy, vigorous life. He turned his eyes to the banana clump. What a strange, wonderful green it was with the sun glinting on the leaves. Surely there wasn't such a golden green in the world!

Around eleven o' clock, when Bharat was engaged in scraping out a mound of termites from the root of a mango tree, a boy came running in with a message from Hem. It was Khudiram. 'Hemda has had an accident,' he said. 'He wants you to come to

699

the loom house at once.' The loom house was a simple shack situated at the other end of the town on one bank of the Kansai river and adjacent to the shrine of Hazrat Pir Lohani. Three handlooms had been set up here and a coarse type of cloth was woven by local weavers. Hem often held his meetings here. It was also a refuge for a number of boys who hated their homes and schools and had volunteered to work for the country.

Bharat rose from his knees and, throwing his shovel aside, had just turned to go into the house when he heard a rustle accompanied by a hissing sound. Then, as he stood rooted to the ground, a giant cobra reared its head from inside the broken mound swaying from side to side and staring at him with beady eyes. Its long greeny black body slithered out slowly and coiled itself within inches of Bharat's feet. Bharat's blood turned cold. He looked around with dazed eyes for a stick but, before he could move, Kudiram had pushed him aside with a thrust of his strong, young arm. 'Move away Dada!' he yelled. 'I'll deal with this fellow.' Picking up a handful of dust he threw it at the snake targeting the eyes. Then, like a skilled snakecharmer, he started circling round it picking up handfuls of dust and throwing them at intervals. The snake hissed louder in its fury and swayed more fiercely. But, being foolish and cowardly by nature, it couldn't take the boy's attack for long and tried to slither back into its hole head foremost. Now Khudiram sprang forward and grabbed it by its tail. Swinging it in the air with strong circular motions he dashed it against the rough mango trunk, over and over again till, its bones smashed and broken, it lay on the ground—a lifeless mass of battered flesh and bits of glistening skin.

'Why did you have to take such a risk?' Bharat scolded the boy severely. 'We could have killed it with a stick.' Then seeing the boy's face crumple with disappointment, he added, 'Let's go now. Is Hem badly hurt?'

Reaching the shack they found Hem lying on a string cot with a bloodstained bandage on his brow. One foot, swollen to the size of a pumpkin, was coated with a mixture of lime and turmeric. 'Why Hem! What happened?' Bharat asked his friend in a burst of concern. But Hem did not bother to answer his question. 'Satyenda has returned from Calcutta,' he cried. 'He has brought a number of newspapers with him. The Partition of Bengal is

700

about to become a reality. But, do you know Bharat, the Bengalis are not weeping and beating their breasts. Or begging the rulers to desist. They are holding meetings in street corners and protesting against the Bill.' Hemchandra sat up in his excitement. 'Satyenda tells me that students have joined in large numbers and are going ahead with their slogan shouting right under the bloodshot eyes of the police.'

'But how long can they do so?' Bharat asked in a bewildered voice. 'The British have weapons. We have nothing.'

'There are kinds and kinds of weapons. Ours will be boycott.'

'Boycott! What is that?'

'It means to denounce and abjure. The British are a nation of shopkeepers. The way to hit them where it hurts is to cripple their industries. Indians will take a pledge to stop using British goods. We'll give up wearing shoes and stop buying their cloth. We'll take to smoking bidis instead of cigars. And we'll use country mollasses in place of white sugar.'

'What shall we wear then? There's no such thing as Indian leather and all our cloth comes from Manchester and Lancashire.'

'We'll wear khadams or go bare foot. And we'll buy cloth from the mills of Bombay.' Hem paused to take a breath and continued, 'A huge meeting is being organized in the Town Hall of Calcutta on the seventh of August. Many eminent men are joining it. I've a mind to go. Will you come with me?'

'No,' Bharat replied after a moment's hesitation. Hemchandra frowned. Then, almost as though he was speaking to himself, he muttered, 'It's going to be a historic occasion from what I hear. We're close to something. Something really big! This is not the time to remain tucked away safely on a tiny farm. All right-thinking people should set themselves adrift on the mainstream and sink or swim with their countrymen.'

'How will you go?' Bharat asked bluntly. 'Your foot is too badly injured for you to attempt anything so foolhardy.'

'Go I shall—even if I have to crawl all the way. I'll show myself to a doctor first of course. Calcutta doctors are wizards. I'm confident I'll be able to walk in a few days.'

'I'll come with you,' Bharat said suddenly.

SUNIL GANGOPADHYAY

'You don't have to. Not for my sake at least. I don't want your charity.'

'You may not want it. But you'll have to take it all the same.'

'No!' Hemchandra shouted, his face flaming. 'You stay here with your piddling bushes and creepers. I shan't take you with me.'

'You can't prevent me from boarding the train,' Bharat laughed, 'Or from leaving it at Howrah. And there's no law that decrees that I can't walk by your side through the streets of Calcutta.'

Bharat was as good as his word. Throwing a few things together in a bag he boarded the train to Calcutta accompanied by Hem. Then arriving at Howrah Station, he hired a hackney cab and drove straight to Dr Mahendralal Sarkar's chamber in Bhabanipur. He had accompanied Shashibhushan there a number of times and knew the place. But, alighting from the cab, he looked around with a puzzled frown. The street outside had always been packed with carriages and people at this hour. But now the place looked quite deserted. Only two carriages stood waiting, a little distance away from the gate. Walking in they were informed that Dr Sarkar was examining a patient and would send for them in a few minutes. They would have to wait, till then, in the reception room.

After half an hour or so the man returned and ushered them into the doctor's chamber. Walking in first, with Hem hobbling behind, Bharat got a shock. A life-sized portrait of Dr Mahendralal Sarkar hung on the wall facing the door and in the vast leather chair, on whose seat Mahendralal's enormous bulk had rested in the past, a stranger sat—a small midget of a man with a weaselly face, a toothbrush moustache and a pair of hornrimmed spectacles.

'D-doctor Mahendralal Sarkar!' Bharat stammered. 'Is he...is he...?'

'You must be new to the city.' The man took off his spectacles and started polishing them with a handkerchief. 'Dr Sarkar died several years ago. I was his assistant.'

'But your man said—'

'I'm Dr Sarkar too. Come, let me have a look at the foot. Tck! Tck! It's a bad sprain but nothing that a week's rest will not cure.'

702

Applying some ointment he bandaged it neatly and said, 'No moving about. And no climbing stairs. Stay indoors as far as possible.'

Leaving the doctor's chamber Bharat took the same cab and drove down to his old lodgings. By a stroke of good luck he was able to secure a room on the ground floor. Forcing Hem to lie down he sat in a chair beside him and ordered some tea. The mess lounge, in which the inmates relaxed in the evenings, was also on the ground floor and snatches of their conversation came floating in through the open door. Although Bharat had never associated with them, in the past, he knew the kind of talk the Babus indulged in. It was office talk mostly, spiced with juicy gossip about sexual exploits in the brothels of Rambagan and Hadh Katar Gali. But, this evening, he was surprised to hear them discussing the impending partition in voices seething with resentment and making plans to join the procession that would march to Town Hall. From their excited, agitated voices it was obvious that they were all raring to go.

Bharat wondered how the change had come about. Bengalis were a peaceloving people, lazy and tolerant, and they loved status quo. They respected the British for bringing law and order to the country and upheld their right to rule. Many had wept inconsolably at Queen Victoria's passing away. What had happened to them now? Why did the partition of their province, designed by their masters in the interest of better administration, incense them so?

Next morning, to everyone's surprise, news came that all the shops of the city were closed for the day. No call had been given for a hartal. The shopkeepers had taken their own decision. As the morning wore on the streets started filling with people and cries of *Bande Mataram* could be heard. Bharat was familiar with the song. The words had been penned by Bankimchandra and set to music by Rabindranath Thakur. But the crowds in the streets were not singing. They were repeating the first two words in a kind of shout. Bharat had never heard slogan-shouting in his life and he listened to it with wonder and a strange sense of exhilaration. 'Send for a carriage Bharat,' Hem ordered, 'We must go to College Square and join the procession marching to Town Hall.'

703

SUNIL GANGOPADHYAY

'But the doctor has forbidden you to move!'

Hem dismissed the doctor's orders with an impatient gesture. Looking grimly into Bharat's face he said, 'If you don't do as I tell you I shall hobble out of that door and join the crowds. No one can stop me.' Bharat sighed and went out into the street. Dodging the masses that kept pouring in from all sides he secured a carriage with great difficulty. The two friends got in and the horses inched their way slowly towards their destination.

'Who got all these people here Hem?' Bharat broke a long silence. 'Someone must have organized all this.'

'No one organized anything. The National Congress could have given a call but it didn't. People are coming on their own.'

'Most of them seem to be students. And see—they are the ones who are trying to maintain order.'

'Students are the lifeblood of a nation; its real strength. Do you know why, Bharat? The ordinary adult has responsibilities and they weaken his resolve. It is not so with the young. Youth is indomitable.' Looking sadly down at his bandaged foot Hem sighed and continued, 'To my dying day I shan't cease to regret the fact that I couldn't participate in this historic procession in the true sense of the word; that I couldn't march shoulder to shoulder with thousands of my countrymen. Couldn't I have chosen another time to take a toss from my bicycle?' Bharat burst out laughing at this infusion of the comic in Hem's lament. But Hem didn't laugh. 'Your legs are whole brother,' he said to Bharat. 'Why are you sitting in the carriage? Get down and walk with the rest. You can brag about it to your grandchildren in the years to come.'

Bharat sprang out of the carriage. He was glad of it because now he got a better view of what was going on. There were people from every walk of life. Students and teachers, clerks and barristers, rich Babus and middle-class householders, Hindus and Muslims were walking side by side with not a thought for caste and class. The last were few in number but a tall, bearded Muslim cleric dominated the scene. Standing in the centre of the procession he was shouting *Bande Mataram* with great force and energy. On enquiring about the man's identity from the people around him Bharat was told that he was the famous Maulvi Liaquat Hossain.

704

As the procession approached Town Hall several others, longer and weightier, began converging from the lanes and bylanes and, within seconds, the place turned into a sea of people. The elders put their heads together and decided that, in view of the unprecedented numbers, three meetings with a common agenda would be held instead of one. A resolution would be passed and sent to the Viceroy demanding withdrawal of the irrational and infamous Partition of Bengal. And the populace would take a pledge to boycott all British goods till their demand was met. The crowds cheered and clapped at this announcement. 'Take off your shoes brother,' Hem hissed in Bharat's ear. 'Spark off the boycott.' Bharat leaped to the roof of the carriage at these words. 'Friends!' he shouted in a voice that sounded strange even to his own ears. 'From this moment onwards I boycott everything British. I begin with my shoes.' Stooping, he pulled off his leather pumps and swung them in the air. Then he flung them upwards as high as he could. This set off a frenzied flinging about of boots and pumps. Some took off their coats; some even their shirts Some dashed into the godown opposite and, carrying back armfuls of straw and jute stalks, proceeded to build an enormous effigy of Lord Curzon and set fire to it. And all the while cries of *Bande Mataram* filled the air as deep and terrifying as the roar of ocean waves.

Sitting in the Viceroy's office Lord Curzon heard the shouts. But his face was calm and placid without a trace of fear or anxiety. He knew what was going on. Every ten minutes his private sleuths were reporting developments. Now his lip curved in a smile as an adult's does at a child's threat. He knew the Bengali race. They were lazy and weak and incapable of sustaining any effort for long. This was a temporary excitement and would fizzle out in a few hours. Turning to the Police Commissioner Andrew Frazer, Lord Curzon said, 'Conceive the howls! They will almost slay me in Bengal.'

Chapter XLI

Contrary to everyone's expectations Rabindranath Thakur displayed no reaction whatsoever to the proposed Partition of Bengal. He neither lent his voice at the rallies and meetings, nor did he take up his pen in protest. People were surprised at his attitude and speculations were rife. Was he under the impression that it was an empty threat? A bogey to frighten the natives with? Or was his faith in British justice and fair rule so great that it swamped his patriotic considerations? In all probability, his indifference stemmed from the fact that he was overwhelmed, at the time, by domestic upheavals. The grand patriarch of Jorasanko, Debendranath Thakur, had passed away peacefully in his bed at the ripe old age of eighty-seven leaving the whole of Bengal mourning as at the loss of a father. Passing over his elder sons he had appointed his youngest as chief trustee and executor of his last will and testament. In consequence Rabindranath found himself so deeply embroiled in mundane tasks that he rarely found the time to even pick up a pen. Besides, his own health was troubling him. He was suffering from piles and the pain was so excruciating that, stoic though he was, he found it unendurable at times.

But the moment he realized that the British had every intention of implementing their plan and that it was soon to become a reality, he shook himself out of his personal troubles. His faith in their governance suffered a rude shock. They claimed that, the Bengal Presidency being too large and unwieldy, they were dividing it in two in the interest of better administration. Their argument was tenable but only up to a point. Rabindranath could see the sense of carving a separate state out of Bihar and Orissa. But why divide up the Bengali-speaking zillas and graft some of them on to Assam? The reason was obvious. The Bengalis were slowly awakening to a sense of nation and country. And this was being achieved through their language. The intention behind the partition of the province was to strike a blow

706

which would stem the spread and development of the Bengali language. This was gross injustice. Even Sir Henry Cotton, erstwhile administrator of British India, had admitted the fact.

Rabindranath was primarily a poet and composer and his protest came in the form of songs. *Amaar sonaar bangla ami tomai bhalobashi* he wrote on a still, lonely night in Shantiniketan and set it to the tune of a song he had heard the runner Gagan Harkara sing in Shilaidaha many years ago—*Ami kothai pabo taaré amaar monér manush jé ré.* This song caught the public fancy to such an extent that it was now being sung at all the meetings. This was followed by a host of songs in praise of the motherland—*O amaar déshér mati; Jadi tor daak shuné keu na aashé; Saarthak janam amaar; Ami bhay karbo na bhay karbo na,* among others. Apart from writing songs Rabindranath was attending meetings these days and speaking at them. He had also lent open support to the boycott movement.

Tossing aside the resolution passed at the meeting in the Town Hall as carelessly as though it was a scrap of waste paper, Lord Curzon set a date for the dreaded event. On the sixteenth of October 1905 Bengal would be split in two! The nation was appalled. How could the rulers be so insensitive; so indifferent to the wishes of the people? Sitting in the train on his way to Calcutta from Giridi on the night of the ninth, a week before the impending disaster, Rabindranath composed a song that reflected his shock and anger:

The tighter they tie our limbs,
The sooner our bonds will break.
The harsher the glare of their bloodshot eyes
The better our eyes shall see.

Now is the hour for ceaseless work;
no time for empty dreams.
The louder they roar, the sooner oh! Brothers
our slumber shall shattered be

The harder they try to break with force
The stronger shall they build.
The more they strike with frenzied hate,
wave upon wave will spring.

Lose not hope you suffering souls.
The Lord of the Earth still wakes.
If they trample the truth beneath their heels
Their flag will be dragged in the dust;
Their proud flag will be dragged in the dust.

A call for total hartal was issued by the leaders. On the sixteenth of October Bengalis from all sections of society, high and low, rich and poor, Hindu and Muslim would tie rakhis on each other's wrists and take the pledge of brotherhood. On that day, a day of national mourning, all hearths would be cold. No fires would be lit and no food cooked. The British wanted to divide Bengal. But they would do so only on their maps. In their hearts the Bengalis would remain undivided.

The historic day dawned. The sky was a clear, flawless blue with soft, white clouds massing near the horizon. The air had a nip in it as though it held the promise of approaching winter. Rabindra loved this season and had expressed this love in many of his songs. But, perfect autumn day though it was, Rabindra's heart did not lift up in ecstasy. It beat, slow and heavy, with fear. Would the masses respond to the call? Would Hindus and Muslims come together in a spirit of brotherhood? What if a clash took place and riots followed?

But if Rabindra had any fears about the success of the call, the other members of the Thakur family didn't. Preparations had started weeks ago. Thousands of rakhis had been bought and were being sent out by post to friends and relatives living outside the city. The western veranda of the mansion of Joransanko had been transformed into a centre of frenzied activity. Mounds of rakhis lay on one side beside piles of envelopes. The members of the family, men and women alike, were working furiously—writing addresses, pasting stamps, sealing envelopes and carrying them to the post office. Some of the women were even engaged in making rakhis. Only one member of the family took no part in all this. And that was Jyotirindranath. News of the boycott had reached his ears but it failed to enthuse his spirit. He spent his day, as usual, reading and staring out of the window. But a slow anger burned in his breast. His had been the first attempt to strike a blow at British industry. But his countrymen hadn't lent him their support. They were boycotting British goods now and making a great virtue of it. Why hadn't they thought of it a decade and a half ago? Why hadn't they boycotted British ships and saved his company? The country's history would have been quite different if they had. But they had abandoned him. They had ignored his pleas and sold their souls to the ruling race.

That day Rabindra rose at dawn and shook the sleepers awake. They were to go first to the Ganga and bathe and purify themselves before joining the pledge-taking utsav. Rabindra wore a simple dhuti with no shirt. A muga shawl was flung carelessly around his shoulders and his feet were bare. Looking up and down at Abanindranath he said pleasantly, 'Take off your shoes Aban. We shall walk barefoot to the river.' Walk! Abanindranath was alarmed. He was a fastidious young man and a dandy. He seldom walked anywhere and wore slippers even within the house.

'But...but,' he stammered. 'The road to the river is full of stones and nails and pieces of glass!'

'We shall walk barefoot nevertheless,' his uncle announced inexorably, 'like the rest of our countrymen.' Leaving the great gates of his ancestral mansion behind, he walked rapidly to the waiting crowds and became one with them. *Banglar mati banglar jal, banglar bayu banglar phal* he sang as he walked and thousands of voices took up the refrain. And thus they came to the river.

At first Rabindranath couldn't see the water for the sea of human heads that bobbed up and down. There were thousands of people on the bank too—laughing, singing, shouting *Bhai bhai ek thain, bhed nai bhed nai* before tying rakhis on one another's wrists. Rabindranath took a few dips then, changing into a dry dhuti, joined the utsav. Abanindranath stared at his uncle in bewilderment. Robi ka seemed to have undergone a metamorphosis. He, who was so aloof and withdrawn by nature, so polished in his manners that they bordered on the artificial, was tying rakhis and embracing everyone, indiscriminately, not caring if the man was a Brahmin or an untouchable. Aban even heard him saying to a sepoy, 'Come brother. You're Bengali too.' But the man put his hands behind his back and said ruefully, 'Forgive me huzoor. I'm a Muslim.' Rabindra's face fell. He had heard that a large section of Muslims favoured partition and had

709

welcomed the move of the rulers. Reports were coming in of communal tension in several zillas of East Bengal. 'As you wish,' he said gently and turned away. But another man came forward his arm outstretched. 'I'm a Muslim too,' he said, 'and I would be proud to wear your rakhi.' After that it seemed to Aban that his Robi ka was in imminent danger of being suffocated to death by the press of people who wanted to wear his rakhi. Brahmins with poités gleaming against bare brown chests, firinghee priests in robes and rosaries, Muslim clerics with hennaed beards, aristocrats and scavengers, clerks and barristers, watchmen and watermen clamoured and pushed one another to get close to him.

On the way back to Jorasanko Aban declared, 'You're twice your weight Robi ka.' Rabindra laughed, looking down at his arms. They were covered with rakhis, one on top of another, from the wrists up to the shoulders. 'Let's go to Nakhuda Masjid Aban,' he said, 'and tie rakhis on our Muslim brothers.' Abanindra was terrified at the suggestion. 'Don't attempt anything so dangerous Robi ka,' he said. 'Do you want to start a riot?'

'Why do you say that?' Rabindra asked surprised. 'We'll go to the mosque and take permission from the Imam. It he refuses we'll come back home.'

'Do as you wish, 'Aban replied. 'Count me out.'

Abanindranath walked rapidly away. Rabindra stood watching his retreating back for a while. His lips curled in a smile. Then, turning to the others, he said, 'Let's go.'

A few minutes after his arrival at the mosque Rabindra was ushered into a small room where the Imam sat talking to some of the maulvis. He was very fair with hawk-like features and looked quite regal in his velvet robe with his snowy hair and beard. His eyes were bright and surprisingly young in a face as old and wrinkled as a piece of parchment. He looked up as Rabindra walked in through the door and a look of respect came into his eyes. It was obvious that he who stood before him was no ordinary man. 'As you know,' Rabindra began, after touching his right hand to his forehead in the customary Muslim greeting, 'our rulers have passed a bill dividing our province. But we Bengalis must remain undivided in spirit. We must remain brothers as we have for centuries—Hindus and Muslims together. In this dark hour, when we are being tested, let us take a pledge of everlasting brotherhood. Let me tie a rakhi on your wrist as a token of that pledge'.

The Imam turned his eyes on the faces of his companions, turn by turn, as if seeking support. But no one spoke. A grim silence prevailed. The Imam smiled—a wide beautiful smile that lit up his eyes and filled every nook and cranny of that ancient, noble face. 'Come my son,' he said, stretching out his arm.

Chapter XLII

On her way to the theatre Nayanmoni often took a detour. 'Go through Chitpur Road Rahmat Miyan,' she would call out to the coachman. But in what hope? Did she really believe that Rabindranath would come walking out of Jarasanko Gali, one day, and she would see him in person? She was spending all her free evenings in Sarala Ghoshal's house these days learning his songs. They, of course, were not meant for the theatre. She sang them to herself at home, her eyes closing in ecstasy. Then the face she thought of during all her waking hours came before her eyes. Had the memory of Bharat dimmed with the passing years? No. Bharat was vivid and alive in her heart and there was no place for another. Why this yearning for Rabindranath then? Nayanmoni thought about it a great deal and came to a certain conclusion. Bharat was the man in her life. He was the only husband she would have—if any. But a woman needed a god. Sri Krishna had been her god once. She had offered him her devotion in song and dance and shared all her joys and sorrows with him. But the image had changed. It was Rabindra's face and form that came before her eyes now—not Krishna's.

Her life at the theatre had also undergone a change. Classic had fallen into a decline and the blame for it was Amar Datta's—entirely. Puffed up with the successes of the past few years he had bought up the crumbling Minerva and, having renovated it at great expense, had proceeded to run the two theatres together. Since he could be physically present in only one place he left the running of the latter to his employees whereupon Minerva suffered loss upon loss—the men in charge bleeding her systematically. Amar Datta was forced to plough in some of his profits from Classic into the sick Minerva but still the theatre wouldn't pick up. Any other man in his place would have written it off as a bad investment but not Amar Datta. His ego couldn't allow him to accept defeat. But all his efforts notwithstanding, Minerva crashed threatening to bring down Classic along with it as well. Now he, who had had so much money only a few years ago that he didn't know what to do with it, was reduced to borrowing from friends, relatives and even moneylenders. His stars were against him perhaps. For, added to his money troubles, came another blow. His audience started dwindling—why no one could tell. His plays lost their appeal and no matter what he tried to do; wherever he tried to turn, he met with loss and failure. In his frustration he took to drinking and, doing so, he lost whatever little grip he had on himself and on his cast.

Around this time, when Amar Datta was changing plays every other night in an effort to woo back his fast disappearing audience, Nayanmoni suggested that they put up a dramatized version of *Chokhér Bali*. It was her favourite novel and she empathized with the situation in a strange kind of way. In Bihari and Mahendra she caught glimpses of Bharat and Shashibushan. Did she see herself as Binodini then? No. She had never met anyone like Binodini in her life.

'*Chokhér Bali!*' Amar repeated thoughtfully after her. 'Well—if you say so. But it had better perk up the box office. We're in a bad way.' He threw her an affectionate glance as he spoke. He hadn't paid her salary for four months now but she hadn't complained even once. And she hadn't responded to overtures from other companies.

But even *Chokhér Bali* failed to revive the declining fortunes of Classic. One night, immediately after a performance, Amar Datta sent for Nayanmoni. Walking into his office she saw him sitting at his ease, his feet propped up on the table. He had already drunk more than was good for him and he was pouring yet another glassful from the whisky decanter by his side. Nayanmoni stood waiting for him to speak. She hadn't had time to remove her make-up and she was still wearing the white *than* which was her costume. 'You've failed me Nayan,' his mouth twisted bitterly. 'I staged *Chokhér Bali* on your recommendation. But it's faring even worse than the others. Do you know what our earnings are for today? One hundred and eighty-seven rupees.'

'You can't blame the play for that.' Nayanmoni said quietly. 'The fault lies in our acting. We're not good enough.'

'Nonsense!' Amar Datta banged his fist on the table. Then, bringing his face close to hers in a drunken leer, he said, 'The

713

play's as dull as ditch water. We need to pack in some explosive stuff. Start preparing two dance sequences and—'

'You're drunk,' Nayanmoni said coolly. 'You wouldn't be making such an absurd suggestion otherwise. Binodini is a high-caste Hindu widow. And you want to make her dance! The audience will throw rotten eggs at you.'

'*Chup*!' Amar Datta roared like a bull. 'How dare you use that tone of voice with me? I *am* drunk and I intend to get drunker. But I'm the master here and you're only a paid employee. You'll do as you're told.'

'I can't obey you in this.' Nayanmoni looked straight into his eyes as she said so. Her checks were flushed and her nostrils flared with distaste. Inflexibility and determination were stamped on every line of her face and form. Amar Datta couldn't bear her insolence. Springing from his chair he made a lunge at her and slapped her full on the cheek. 'Get out of my theatre,' he shouted, the words slurred and indistinct. 'Get out this very minute.' Nayanmoni's face turned white. Her eyes blazed and her cheek stung where he had hit her. But she said nothing. Pulling the edge of her *than* around her shoulder she said softly, 'I'll be glad to do so. In fact I've wanted to leave for quite some time now. But I didn't. Do you know why? Because I didn't want to be the rat that deserts a sinking ship. But, by dismissing me yourself, you've set me free. I'm going. You'll never see me again.'

Amar Datta was too outraged to speak. He opened his mouth but no words came. He kept sitting, sunk in his chair, and watched her slender form walk out of his door and out of his life.

In the theatre world nothing remains hidden for long. Word spread, within a few hours, that Nayanmoni had left Classic, and messengers from other companies started coming to her door with offers. But Nayanmoni had the same answer for everyone. Folding her hands humbly before them she said, 'I have no desire to act anymore. In Classic —or on any other board.' She did not move a hair's breadth from her stance despite all the pleas, arguments, flattery, promises of excellent terms and emotional blackmail that were showered on her. But, in her heart, she knew that if one person came to her she couldn't refuse him. Rumours were floating about that Ardhendushekhar was trying to get a cast together. But, fortunately for Nayanmoni, it didn't materialize and she was not called upon to redeem her promise.

Nayanmoni felt wonderfully relaxed and happy these days. For the first time in her life she could live exactly as she pleased. The days passed one by one, long and languorous and she savoured every moment of her new-found freedom. One day she suddenly thought of Sarala Ghoshal. She hadn't been to see Sarala for a long time and, now that she thought of it, she hadn't even heard of her lately. The city was agog with excitement over the Partition of Bengal and processions and meetings were being held at every street corner. Why was Sarala's name never being taken? She was hardly the type to sit quietly at home when so much was going on. Nayanmoni decided to go that very evening and find out.

Standing outside the door of Sarala's house in Baliganj Nayanmoni looked around in surprise. The house and grounds had always been full of people at this hour. But now they were deserted. Not a soul could be seen. After knocking for a long time a maid opened the door and asked her to come in. Then she gave her some news that stunned Nayanmoni. Sarala was not in Calcutta. She was nowhere in Bengal. Where was she then? In Punjab with her husband. Husband! Nayanmoni stared at the woman as though she had gone mad. Sarala had gone to Mayawati—an ashram in the mountains. That much she knew. But what was this talk of a husband in Punjab?

The truth of the matter was that, while in Mayawati, Sarala had received an urgent summons from her parents in Deoghar and had hurried there to be confronted with strange tidings. Her marriage had been fixed and the arrangements made, down to the last detail. There was no way she could get out of it now. Sarala stared in dismay, first at one face then the other. Janakinath did not speak a word but his eyes were grim and his jaw firm with determination. It was Swarnakumari who spoke. 'Sarala,' she began in her strident tones. 'Upto this day we have allowed you the kind of freedom that girls of your age and status can only dream of. But you've proved yourself unworthy of it. I pass over your activities, which though difficult to reconcile to at times, may be deemed worthy as service to the country. I speak of something far more serious. You told your father and me that you wished to remain a spinster. That you weren't interested in any man. Yet you allow your name to be linked with some man's or another's every single day! Gossip and slander follow you wherever you go. How do you think we feel? Is there no limit to our endurance? It is time you thought of your family—' Then, in short, cryptic sentences, she told Sarala that a husband had been chosen for her. He was a Punjabi landowner, a wealthy widower named Chaudhary Rambhaj Datta. Their choice had fallen on him out of a special consideration. Swarnakumari and Janakinath wanted their daughter out of Bengal so that her innumerable suitors would cease to pester her. Out of sight; out of mind. Sarala would go away with her husband and make her home in a haveli in distant Punjab. And, in due course of time, her disgrace would be forgotten.

Brave Sarala! Bold, rebellious Sarala! She who had broken so many conventions and lived life on her own terms, stood before her parents her eyes downcast not daring to object. She, who could have chosen a husband from dozens of handsome young bucks from the first families of Calcutta, was forced into marrying a man she had never seen in her life—a man much older than herself and one whose language and culture were totally alien to hers...

Nayanmoni returned home with a heavy heart. She had welcomed her freedom from the theatre in the hope that she could work with Sarala; could help her in her innumerable causes and learn her uncle's songs. But that hope was gone. Nayanmoni sighed. Destiny was never tired of playing tricks with her. But she wouldn't give up. She would find her own way out of the mess her life had become. She would find her own self. And...and she wouldn't call herself Nayanmoni anymore. As of today she was Bhumisuta.

Chapter XLIII

Following the Partition of Bengal a struggle ensued, between ruler and ruled, the like of which had not been seen in anyone's living memory. The Boycott Movement, launched in a spirit of idealism and sacrifice, took an ugly turn. Students abandoned their education in vast numbers and streamed into the political arena. Picketing, looting and burning became the order of the day. Now the British government was forced to sit up and take notice. Arresting a couple of leaders, from time to time, was easy. But what control could possibly be exercised on a whole generation of youth ready to embrace death in a bid to free their country from foreign domination? How many could be arrested? How many hanged? Retaliation was swift and brutal but the stream did not recede. It grew fuller and more turbulent with each passing day.

With the Boycott Movement in full swing some members of Jatin Banerjee's aakhra got together once again and started a newspaper called *Jugantar*. It was openly anti-establishment and contained scathing criticism of the British and their policies in its columns. Being able to hit out at the rulers with impunity was a heady experience for the young men and they savoured the feeling for a while. But soon they got restive. The rulers didn't seem to be taking any notice of what was being printed. What was the use of lashing out at them when they shrugged it off as the feeble kicking of infants? Action was the need of the hour, they decided. Planned action.

One evening Barin called the members to a secret meeting. 'You all know what's happening in East Bengal,' he said. 'The police have let loose a reign of terror and our boys are dying in hundreds. The man behind these killings is the Governor of the new province—the infamous Bamfield Fuller. He is not only killing Bengalis, he is dividing the Hindus and Muslims. "Divide and rule" is his policy. He must be punished for his crimes. Today, at this meeting, we must pronounce him guilty of genocide and pass the order of his execution.'

'We may pass the order,' Satyen murmured thoughtfully. 'But who will carry it out?'

'One of us,' Barin replied coldly. 'We'll identify the executioner through a draw of lots.'

But the draw of lots turned out to be unnecessary. Hem offered to take on the task and, after a little hesitation, the others agreed. The deed, it was decided, would be carried out in Shillong where Bamfield Fuller was taking a holiday. Barin would go there first and, keeping himself in the shadows, observe the Governor's habits and movements. Some days later, Hem would proceed to Shillong and get a proper briefing. Then, carefully choosing the time and place, he would swing into action. For this purpose he would be given two pistols and a couple of crude country-made bombs. But Hem, for all his insistence, could not undertake the hazardous enterprise alone. Bharat insisted on accompanying him.

The tracking down of Fuller turned out to be a wild goose chase. As soon as Hem and Bharat reached Shillong they got the news that the Governor's holiday was over and that he was now in Gauhati. The three friends followed him to Gauhati to be informed that he had left for Barisal that very day and no one knew when he would return. Onward then to Barisal! But even here disappointment awaited them. On their arrival at Barisal they discovered that the bird had flown—back to Gauhati. Having come this far no one was in the mood for giving up. But destiny had decided to play a cruel trick on them over and over again. Back in Gauhati they were told that Fuller was in Rangpur.

Chalo Rangpur! The indefatigable Barin raised the slogan and the two others followed. But, arriving at Rangpur, the three boys found themselves in dire straits. The money they had brought along was almost gone. In addition, their advent in Rangpur was looked upon with great suspicion by a group of would-be revolutionaries of the town. These young men did not belong to any structured group. Nor did they have a leader. They were keen to participate in the struggle they had heard of but didn't know how. They had offered to start a society in Rangpur and had asked for financial support from some reputed leaders of Calcutta. But their appeal hadn't even been considered. Stung and humiliated at this treatment they were in no mood to befriend the three strangers from the capital city. They submitted Barin and the others to a stiff cross examination and demanded to see their weapons. This Barin refused to do. He would show what he had, he said, but not publicly. They could select one from amongst themselves who would visit him in secret and see what he had in his possession.

That evening Barin's group waited in a little clearing in the woods at the edge of the town when a man came striding up to them swinging a lathi. His appearance was far from prepossessing. He had a short, squat body, packed with power like a goonda's, and his hair was cropped close to a round hard skull. But his eyes were merry and his voice pleasant. 'My name is Jogendramohan Das,' he said introducing himself. 'I've been sent by the boys to inspect your weapons.' Then, picking up a bomb from inside the cloth bundle that rested at their feet, he asked, 'Have you tested this? Will it work?'

'It will,' Barin replied curtly.

'I doubt it. What will you do if it fails? In my opinion this is not a bomb at all. It is an ordinary cracker.'

'We have a second line of action ready,' Barin told him. 'If the bombs fail we'll fire revolvers at point blank range.'

'You'll have to get very close to the Governor to do that. He keeps several bodyguards around him. They'll blow the skull off your shoulders.'

'We're prepared for that. My friends here have dedicated their lives for the cause.'

Jogendra looked Hem and Bharat up and down. 'Ready to die even before the event!' he exclaimed. 'What kind of revolutionaries are you? And why do you propose to sacrifice two lives for one?'

'Their deaths will inspire others and—'

'But isn't it far better to devise a plan of action that is fool proof? Have you gentlemen heard of the dynamite bomb? It is the invention of a famous scientist of Sweden—Sir Alfred Nobel. Dynamite can be sparked off from a considerable distance. And it is so powerful that a mountain can be reduced to rubble in a single blast. If you can get hold of such a bomb you will achieve your end and save your lives at the same time.'

719

'From where can we get such a bomb?'

'We can make it ourselves if the materials are available. But we'll need money. A great deal of money.'

Barin left for Calcutta the very next day to raise money for the new action plan. Hem and Bharat stayed on in Rangpur in a tumbledown house at the edge of the town which Jogendramohan had procured for them. A week went by, slow and monotonous, the boys passing their time in cooking, eating and reading novels of which they found a goodly store in one of the cupboards. There was no sign of Barin and not even a message. Hem and Bharat's finances had sunk so low that they were eating boiled rice and *jhingé* curry every day. *Jhingé* grew wild in the jungles and Bharat picked a basketful, every morning, choosing the greenest and the tenderest. Then the day came when the last handful of rice had been eaten and starvation stared them in the face. The boys bathed as usual and lay down, with a book each, prepared to fast till Barin returned. Around eleven o'clock Jogendra came to see them. 'You haven't lit a fire today!' he observed, poking his head into the kitchen. 'Aren't you going to cook?'

'No,' Bharat replied promptly. 'There were a lot of leftovers from last night's dinner. We had a late breakfast—a very heavy one.'

'What leftovers?'

'Well,' Bharat enumerated slowly. 'Pulao and mutton curry. Mutton tastes even better when left overnight. We had lobsters in coconut cream too and a sweet and tart sauce made with sorrel and raisins.'

'Why didn't you buy some sweet curd?' Jogendra's eyes crinkled in a benevolent smile. 'And some of Rangpur's famous *Pat kheer*?' Then, still smiling, he continued. 'I came to take you to my house for a midday meal. Of course I can't offer you the delicacies you seem to have eaten already. Only *dal bhaat*—'

The two friends looked at one another and burst out laughing. Jogendra joined in. 'I saw you cooking a mess of *jhingé* last night,' he told Bharat. 'I was amazed to hear it had turned to lobster and mutton curry by the morning.'

'Give me a bidi Jaguda,' Hem begged. 'And a cup of tea as soon as we reach your house.'

Barin returned the next day. His mission had been unsuccessful. He had managed to collect only twenty-five rupees. But he had brought a message from his brother. 'Rob the rich,' Aurobindo had commanded as in the past. 'Use arms if necessary.' But, though Hem and Barin were ready to obey, Bharat was not. He couldn't rob and kill his own countrymen. It was immoral, for one thing. For another—it would tarnish their image. 'We won't kill anyone,' Barin said hastily. 'We'll only scare them by firing in the air. And if they press too close we'll maim them by firing at their ankles. We're not doing this for ourselves Bharat da. We're doing it for our country. Why do you forget that?'

After some persuasion Bharat was won over. Two other young men of Rangpur were also drawn into the plot and a house identified with their help. It belonged to a Brahmin moneylender of Nabagram—a mean, miserly old man who drove his creditors hard and had amassed a great deal of wealth in consequence. It was no crime, the boys told Bharat, to take the man's ill-gotten gains away from him. And the job would be easy. The Brahmin kept all his money and gold in a pillow and slept with his head on it at night. A namasudra servant slept outside the door but all he had was a lathi. Entry into the house wouldn't be difficult. There was a *chalta* tree, growing by the cowshed that adjoined the house—it's branches almost grazing the roof. One of them (here Hem offered himself) would clamber up the tree, crawl down the roof and jump into the courtyard. He would open the front door for his accomplices who would spring on the sleeping guard and overcome him. Then they would break down the door of the room in which the Brahmin lay sleeping and snatch the pillow away from him.

But the plan, laid down so carefully, misfired even before it was put into action. On the night of the proposed robbery Barin, Hem and Bharat waited in the shadows of the trees surrounding the Brahmin's house, with one of the Rangpur boys. It was past midnight but there was no sign of the other one. The night was hot and close and the neighbourhood dark and silent. Not a sound could be heard except the drone of the mosquitoes that swarmed around them and bit viciously into their arms and necks. The minutes passed slowly; wearily. Then a full moon rose

721

in the sky illuminating every line of the house and trees and flooding all the dark corners with a haze of silver light. The boys stared at one another in dismay. They had set the date and time without caring to ensure that it was a moonless night! How could they have been so foolish? And why was the second boy so late in coming? Had he lost his nerve at the last moment? Or had some harm come to him? The boys had a quick consultation. Should they abandon their mission for now and come back another day? Or should they go ahead? Bharat was in favour of the former but Barin, with his accustomed bullishness, managed to persuade the others to leap into action without further delay.

The boys watched with baited breath as Hem inched his way up a swaying branch of the *chalta* tree. They could see his figure clearly in the moonlight as, reaching the roof of the cowshed, he gave a spring then slid rapidly down it clutching at the straw with both hands as he went. The instant he disappeared from sight the boys stood up gripping their weapons, ready to rush forward. But the minutes passed and Hem didn't open the door. Suddenly a clamour, as of many voices shouting together, came to their ears. The words were muffled and indistinct and seemed to come from a great way off. Then, as they stood staring in horror, they understood what was happening. A great band of men were coming towards them. The mashals in their hands looked like points of flickering light from the distance and the words they were shouting, though still blurred and faint, could be identified. 'Dacoits! Dacoits! Grab the *salas*! Kill them!'

'Run!' Barin yelled, taking to his heels. 'We've been betrayed by that son of a bitch,' the Rangpur boy shouted as he followed. 'What about Hem?' Bharat cried after them. 'He's still in the house.' Not caring to answer the two ran into the belt of trees in front of them and were out of sight in the twinkling of an eye. Bharat rushed towards the door and banged on it shouting, 'Come out Hem. We've been caught.' There was no reply. But Bharat would not give up. He continued battering at the door screaming out Hem's name, over and over again, till he was hoarse.

'Here's one of the rascals,' a voice came to his ears startling him and he whirled around. As he did so, a spear came hurtling through the air and pierced him in the lower abdomen. A runnel

722

of fire shot through his frame but he didn't even cry out. Whipping out his revolver he fired two shots in the air. His assailant, though unhurt, fell to the ground in fear and rolled away from him. Now Bharat ran as fast as he could in the direction Barin had taken, the spear sticking out of his belly. He tried to pull it out as he ran but it snapped in two. Bharat stared at the butt in his hands in horror. And then his eyes fell on the blade planted in his stomach. After that first fiery rip he had felt nothing. He still felt nothing. Only a strange emptiness as he saw the bloody pool around his crotch grow larger and larger . . .

Hem! He tried to think of Hem. What had happened to him? If he had had the sense to run back to the tree and hide in its spreading branches no one would find him. But what about himself? Would he be saved? The crowd was pursuing him. He could hear their cries in the distance. His heart thumped as loud and violent as a drum. His limbs shook with exhaustion. He could feel the warm blood ooze out of his belly and run down his thighs and legs in sticky streams. The stench was overpowering. Bharat retched violently and vomited but didn't dare stop running. Coming to a river meandering between the trees he plunged in. The water came up to his knees and he splashed his way across it quite easily. Then, clambering over the other bank, he came to a clearing in the forest. A tiny temple, abandoned years ago, stood within it—its mossed walls glimmering eerily in the moonlight. He could hear his pursuers baying after him. Was it real? Or was he imagining it? He ran towards the temple. His foot struck a stone step and he fell. Picking himself up in a flash he darted up the steps and through the door. He looked wildly around for a place in which to hide. But the place was flooded with moonlight and every corner was visible. He tried to close the door but it swung back on its hinges groaning noisily. Suddenly Bharat fell—his head hitting the stone floor. After that—oblivion.

723

Chapter XLIV

Basantamanjari rose before dawn and came and stood on the deck of the bajra. Around her the vast waters stretched, lusty and turbulent, and as boundless as the sea. Facing east she sank to her knees. Every morning she kneeled thus waiting for the sun to rise above the Brahmaputra. Then, when her eyes beheld the wonder of the great crimson globe leap up from the dark swirling water, she brought her palms together in a pranam. Closing her eyes she strained her senses as though, by doing so, she would be enabled to hear the music of the spheres. Sometimes she hummed a few strains that sounded like muffled weeping. She sang rarely these days and, even then, only to herself.

Basantamanjari had everything a women could want—a splendid home with many servants, pretty clothes and jewels and a husband who loved her to distraction and indulged her every whim. God had even blessed her with a son. He was six years old now, a beautiful child and very intelligent. But none of her good fortune seemed to touch her. It looked as though she belonged to another world and had strayed into this one by mistake. Her body was here but her soul was somewhere else. She spent hours gazing at the moon, the rising sun, a stretch of water, even a clump of trees—her eyes steadfast, her lips moving soundlessly.

This morning, as Basantamanjari waited for the day to break, a strange agitation came over her. Her eyelids fluttered, her heart beat fast and drops of dew appeared on her brow. She rose and ran down the steps to Dwarika's chamber. Dwarika lay sprawled on satin sheets in the middle of a vast carved bedstead. He looked every inch a zamindar with his fair complexion, ample paunch and salt and pepper whiskers. He had bought an estate in Jangipur, in the new province of East Bengal and Assam, and was enjoying a pleasure cruise in the waters surrounding it. '*Ogo!*' Basantamanjari tried to shake her husband out of his slumbers, 'Give orders to the boatmen to set sail. We've been anchored here for three days—'

724

'What . . . what?' Dwarika started up in the middle of a snore.
'We've been here for three days and I want to move on.'
'Yes . . . yes—in the afternoon,' Dwarika mumbled indistinctly. Then, turning over to the other side, he started snoring once
again. 'No!' Basantamanjari cried, beside herself in her
desperation. 'We must move on now. This very instant.' She
pushed him with all the strength in her delicate arms till he was
forced to open his eyes. 'It's barely dawn, ' he said helplessly,
trying to dissuade her, 'The boatmen are fast asleep.'
'They'll wake up at your command. Even if we could go in a
small boat—'
'Go where?'
'To a place . . . I don't know quite where. But come with me
please. I've a great longing—'
Dwarika sat up with a groan. No matter how hard he tried to
resist her strange fancies he always had to give in at some point or
the other. His little wife held him securely in her clutches. He rose
and dressed quickly then, waking up one of the men, took his
place in the boat with Basantamanjari at his side. The tiny craft
skimmed over the dark water under a sky heavy with cloud. 'It's
not going to rain, is it?' Dwarika asked fearfully. 'I don't want to
get drenched.'
'A few drops of water won't harm the great zamindar babu!'
Basantamanjari laughed merrily throwing her head back and
making her long diamond earrings flash and sparkle against her
arched neck. Dwarika gazed at her, his eyes glowing with
admiration. What a beauty she was! The years hadn't touched
her. She was slim and graceful like a young girl and her skin was
as smooth and unflawed as a rose-flushed marble.
Presently they came to the mouth of a river meandering away
from the Brahmaputra. It was so slender, one could even call it a
stream. 'Shall we go back Basi?' Dwarika looked up hopefully,
'We've been sailing for over an hour. Chhotku must be awake by
now.' The truth was that he had started feeling hungry. Dwarika,
though not born a zamindar, loved to indulge himself like one. He
glanced at his wife as he spoke and was faintly alarmed. She sat so
still, she scarcely breathed, her large dark eyes fixed on the
stream.
'Can we sail down that for a while?' she pointed a finger

without turning her head.

'There's nothing to see there Ma Thakrun,' the boatman answered for Dwarika. 'That is the Dharala river. It gets so shallow after a while and so choked with trees that the boat can't move.'

'I love trees,' Basantamanjari murmured.

'Just for a few minutes then,' Dwarika conceded. 'Then we'll go back. I'm dying for a cup of tea.'

After a quarter of an hour's sailing the oars started making a scraping sound as though touching the pebbles on the river bed. 'The water is only knee deep here,' the boatman announced and, almost at the same time Basantamanjari cried out, 'Stop! Stop!'

'Why?' Dwarika exclaimed, alarmed. 'The forests here are infested with wild animals. Do you want to become food for one?' Basantamanjari pointed to a small stone structure, almost buried in trees, on the farther bank. 'That's a temple,' she announced omnisciently. 'Let's go and see it.'

'How do you know it's a temple?' Dwarika asked, his eyes following the direction of the pointing finger. Then, as if trying to reason with a child, he said, 'Even if is, it must have been abandoned years ago. There's nothing to see—.'

'There is! There is!' Basantamanjari cried with a strange insistence. Then, when the boat came to a halt, its keel grazing the tree roots that lay submerged in the water, she leaped out and ran towards the broken steps. Dwarika followed her as best as he could. Suddenly she stopped and whirled around. 'There's something there,' she told Dwarika her eyes burning into his.

'Then we shan't go in,' Dwarika's voice sounded relieved. 'Let's start on our way back home. It's late enough as it is.' But Basantamanjari shook her head. Her eyes filled with tears. 'You go in and look,' she begged him in a choking voice. 'Why should I?' Dwarika cried impatiently. 'It was not my idea. And anyway—' Before he could finish his sentence Basantamanjari sank to her knees and started knocking her head at his feet. 'Go,' she cried, bursting into tears and repeating over and over again, 'You must. Or it will be too late. Too late.' Dwarika sighed. Everyone who knew her, including her own father, believed she was imbalanced. Only he, Dwarika, had always insisted that she was different, perhaps, from other women but not abnormal. But now even he had to admit that her brain was unhinged. And her condition was getting worse day by day. He decided to take her to see a specialist the moment they reached Calcutta. For the time being, of course, he had no option but to obey her. Lifting his dhuti fastidiously with one hand, Dwarika picked his way gingerly towards the ruined shrine his shining pumps squelching noisily over wet earth and rotting leaves. Negotiating the moss-covered crumbling steps with difficulty he stepped through the open door into the inner sanctum and peered cautiously around. At first he could see nothing. Then, his eyes getting accustomed to the dark, he discerned a broken clay image of Kali standing in a niche against a wall. The head, its fiery red tongue sticking out fearfully, had rolled away and was resting in a corner. One arm was gone. The Shiva at her feet, however, was surprisingly large and whole. But what was that dark red patch just below its navel and on the ground where it lay. Dwarika went a few steps forward then recoiled in shock and horror. For what he saw was not a clay image but a man in his prime. The dark patch was blood, thick clotted blood that stood out in great globs around the blade of a spear that was planted in his belly. And the face—the face was that of his friend Bharat.

A murderous rage came over Dwarika. The blood rushed to his head and the blue veins throbbed in his throat and temples. Rushing out of the shrine he came to the place where Basantamanjari still knelt in the mud and slush. Seizing her by the hair he screamed in an unnatural, high-pitched voice, 'What are you? An enchantress? A witch? Answer me. Or I'll . . . I'll—'

'I don't know,' Basantamanjari, who hadn't stopped weeping, broke into loud piteous sobs. 'Believe me I don't know. I'm your wife. My only wish is to serve you.'

'You dragged me out of bed! You brought me here. Why? Why?' His voice broke. Tears ran down his cheeks and he babbled incoherently. 'My friend . . . my poor friend! Such a violent death! Why did I have to see him? Why do you make me suffer so?'

Now Basantamanjari wiped her tears and asked gently, 'Is he dead?'

'He must be. There's so much blood . . . so much—' His teeth clenched as he spoke and the muscles at one side of his mouth

727

SUNIL GANGOPADHYAY

twisted as though he was having a fit. Yanking her to her feet he
dragged her towards the shrine. 'Haramzadi!' he cried grinding
his teeth. 'Who is he to you? Why do you bring him into our lives
over and over again? I must have an answer or, by God, this day
will be your last.'

'He's nothing to me.' Basantamanjari shook her head. Her
eyes had an odd glazed look. 'I've never even exchanged a word
with him. I didn't know he was in there, believe me. Only
something; someone seemed to pull at me so hard . . . I tried to
resist . . . but I couldn't. I was dragged to this place. I didn't come
here on my own.'

They had entered the temple as she spoke. Suddenly she
wrenched herself free from Dwarika's grasp with surprising
strength and, rushing up to Bharat, sank to the floor and took his
head in her lap. Then, muttering something to herself, she tried to
prise his eyelids open. 'What are you doing?' Dwarika snarled at
her. 'Performing Tantric rites?'

'No,' Basantamanjari's voice, though soft, was firm and
compelling. 'I know neither tantra nor mantra. But I think he's
still alive. Go and fetch some water.'

Dwarika picked up a clay pot, cracked at the rim but whole,
lying on the floor and dashed out of the room. He returned a few
minutes later and handed it, brimming over with water, to her.
Basantamanjari took up a palmful and threw it with great force
aiming at Bharat's eyes. Then another and another, on and on,
her strokes getting harder and more frenzied with the passing
minutes. It seemed as though she was willing him back to life with
all her soul and all her strength. Dwarika felt uneasy. It was
obvious that Bharat was dead. Why didn't Basantamanjari accept
the fact? And what was that strange expression on her face? He
couldn't fathom it. Then, just when he was about to command
her to stop, Bharat's eyelids flickered and sprang open. A tremor
ran through his frame. 'Ma,' he murmured looking straight into
Basantamanjari's eyes. 'Ma,' he repeated. Bharat hadn't seen his
mother in his life. But, traversing the twilight zone that lay
between death and life, it was to her that he spoke.

A couple of weeks later two gentlemen came to Classic theatre
and asked to see Amarendranath Datta. It was just after curtain
call and Amar Datta was in his green room removing his make-up

and taking swigs from a flask of whiskey. Convinced that they were creditors he snapped at the servant boy who had brought up the message. 'I can't see anyone just now. Tell them to get lost.' But the boy hesitated. 'One of them is a barrister,' he said. 'He says he knows you.' Amar Datta's brow furrowed in thought. What barrister had come to see him? And why? He wasn't involved in any law suit! 'Ask them to come in,' he said after a while, 'and bring a couple of chairs.' Then, seating himself, he fortified himself with another draught from his flask.

He recognized Jadugopal instantly, rose to his feet and greeted him with folded hands. His companion, Amar observed, was tall, fair and portly with flecks of grey in his whiskers. He was dressed very nattily in a gold-bordered dhuti and silk baniyan, wore several rings and carried a silver-headed cane. It was easy to see that he was a gentleman of leisure. 'We've come to see one of your actresses Amar Babu,' the stranger began, 'A girl called Bhumisuta.'

'Bhumisuta!' Amar Datta echoed frowning. 'There's no such person here. In fact I haven't heard such an outlandish name in all my life.'

'*Ohé* Dwarika,' Jadugopal smiled at his friend. 'Perhaps you do not know that Bhumisuta's stage name is Nayanmoni.' Then, turning to Amar Datta, he added, 'Nayanmoni is on your board isn't she?'

Amar Datta's handsome features twisted in a grimace. 'She was,' he answered, 'but not anymore. She left Classic some months ago. She's an arrogant wench with no respect for her betters. I vowed to teach her a lesson. "Get out of my theatre," I told her. "I can collect sluts like you in dozens with a sweep of my foot." Tell me gentlemen—what call has a woman, who dances on the stage for a living, to act so prim and proper? Too pure and chaste to sleep with me! I threw her out and I swear—'

'I've no desire to hear what passed between you,' Dwarika interrupted his host's drunken babble with a gesture of dismissal. 'I need to see the young woman urgently. Perhaps you would give me her address.'

'Are you gentlemen planning to open a theatre? Well, let me warn you. She'll be a lot more trouble than good. And if you're aiming to keep her as a mistress you may as well know—'

729

'We're interested in neither of those things,' Dwarika broke in impatiently. 'Now if you could just give us—'

Suddenly Amar Datta burst into tears. Dropping his head into his hands he tore at his hair and cried frantically, 'I've lost her. I've lost my Nayanmoni. She's left me desolate. What shall I do? How shall I live? No one wants to see my plays anymore. My creditors bay at my heels, from dawn to dusk, like a pack of wolves. I'm doomed! All I can do is drown my sorrows in drink!' Amar Datta's voice had started slurring. His body shook with drunken sobs. Realizing that nothing more could be obtained from him, the two men rose to their feet. 'We'll come back another day Amar Babu,' Jadugopal said and walked out of the room.

The next evening the two friends went to see Girish Ghosh's *Siraj-ud-doulah* at the Minerva. Girish, Dwarika thought, had the proverbial nine lives of the cat. He went on and on. Old age and sickness, reversal of fortune, deaths in the family—so much had happened in his long eventful life but he had withstood it all. Just when he seemed to be utterly down and under, he resurfaced to the top, roaring like a lion, in superb triumph. Of late be had come into his own again. His *Balidaan* had acted as a powerful shot in the arm for the dying Minerva. Now with *Siraj-ud-doulah* the house was full again. The play was doubly popular because it had appeared at a peculiar juncture in the history of the nation. By dividing Bengal the rulers had attempted to drive a wedge between the two communities. All right-thinking Bengalis, Hindu and Muslim, had seen through the ploy and were resisting it as best as they could. By depicting Siraj-ud-doulah, the last independent Nawab of Bengal, as a heroic figure who sacrificed his life for the independence of his country, Girish had touched the hearts of both Hindus and Muslims. Siraj-ud-doulah's many vices—his vicious temper, his lack of foresight, his debauchery and arrogance—were conveniently forgotten. Only his extreme youth and his vulnerability remained. In Girish Ghosh's play he emerged as a tragic protagonist—a victim of his age and time.

Dwarika and Jadugopal were very impressed with the play. The stage sets and costumes were brilliant. Girish Ghosh's son Dani, in the role of Siraj, gave a fine performance. But the two truly outstanding ones came from Ardhendushekhar Mustafi as

Danasa Fakir and Girish Ghosh, himself, as Karim Chacha.

At curtain call the two friends decided to go backstage and congratulate the playwright. They found him lying back in an easy chair, looking thoroughly spent. He was, indeed, too old and too afflicted with rheumatism to prance around on the stage. But once on it, he forgot everything—his age, his painful joints, his diseased liver—and internalized the character he was portraying with a rare fidelity. Now he listened, smiling, at Dwarika and Jadugopal's extravagant compliments and remarked, 'You are educated men. It is to be expected that you understand the subtle nuances of the play. But what about the common man? Do you think he'll be able to appreciate its spirit?'

The talk veered away from the play to politics and from thence to the subject of Nayanmoni's whereabouts. 'Yes of course I know Nayanmoni,' Girish replied to their question. 'She's a handsome girl and very talented. But I hear she's left the theatre. As far as I know she's not on any board. As to where she lives—I haven't the slightest idea. You'll agree that I'm too old now to run after pretty women. I sleep best in my own bed and my bolster is all the companion I need.' He laughed at his own joke and added. 'Perhaps Saheb has some idea. Let me send for him.'

When Ardhendushekhar came into the room, a few minutes later, Girish looked at him with an amused smile. 'These gentlemen have come here looking for Nayanmoni. You were the one who brought her to the theatre. You must have some idea of where she is.'

'She used to room with Gangamoni,' Ardhendushekhar said slowly. 'Gangamoni loved her as her own daughter and left her the house with everything in it when she died. But Nayanmoni didn't stay there after her death. She sold up everything and went to live in a rented house—no one knows where. One of our actresses—a girl called Tagar—claims that she has seen her, several times, bathing in the Ganga at Kashi Mittir's Ghat.'

Around seven o'clock the next morning Dwarika and Jadugopal arrived at Kashi Mittir's Ghat and took up their positions, under a tree, a little distance away from the area demarcated for women. The bathers would have to pass them on their way out and, if Tagar wasn't a lying minx, they would catch Bhumisuta sooner or later. This third attempt proved lucky for

731

them. After about half an hour's waiting they noticed a ripple of excitement pass over the crowd of beggars hanging about the women's ghat. It was obvious that someone was distributing alms on her way out. In a few minutes the crowd thinned, scattered and disappeared and the woman came up the steps. It was Bhumisuta.

'Bhumi!' Jadugopal called out excitedly. Bhumisuta looked up. Her face was serene and bore no sign of surprise. 'What are you doing here Jadugopal Babu?' she asked pleasantly. 'We've been looking for you for several days now,' Jadugopal replied. Then, pointing to Dwarika, he said, 'Dwarika has news for you. You remember Dwarika? You saw him once many years ago—' Nayanmoni shook her head. She didn't remember him. Now Dwarika came forward and said, 'Our friend Bharat is ill; grievously ill—practically swaying between life and death. If you wish to see him for the last time—I mean . . . there's no time to lose. The doctors have given up hope.' Nayanmoni betrayed no agitation at the news. Fixing her beautiful compelling eyes on Dwarika's face she asked quietly. 'Has he sent for me?'

'No. Not quite in the way you mean. He is very, very ill! Beyond sending for anyone. He lies in a coma all the time with rare intervals of consciousness. And then he tosses and turns and talks gibberish to himself in a high delirium. Sometimes he mutters "Bird, bird, bird" over and over again. At others—words and phrases that make no sense at all. One day my wife caught him knocking his head on the pillow and murmuring "Bhumi! Bhumi! Bhumi!" and asked me what it meant. I understood at once that it was you he wanted. I went to Jadu and—'

'I'm an actress,' Bhumisuta said, cutting him short. 'We're looked down upon by decent people. Will you allow me to enter your house?'

Dwarika smiled ruefully. 'You don't know to whom you speak. My wife—' Then, leaving his sentence in mid air, he added, 'Come quickly. There's precious little time to lose . . .'

When they arrived at Dwarika's mansion, Basantamanjari came forward and took Bhumisuta's hand. 'I have seen you on the stage,' she began with a smile. But, at the sight of the look on the girl's face, her smile froze and her words faded on the air. Bhumisuta's great dark eyes were stark and dry. Her lips were as white as chalk. Her voice, when she spoke, was totally without expression. 'Where is he?' she asked.

'I'll take you to him,' Basantamanjari said softly, 'but you must prepare yourself for a shock. He looks like a corpse already though he still breathes. The doctors have given up hope. But you can save him. I feel it in my bones. Hold on to the man you love, sister. Bring him back as Behulah brought Lakhindar . . . '

Bhumisuta walked with slow, hesitant steps into the room. Basantamanjari hadn't exaggerated. The tall manly figure that Bhumi had loved so dearly had shrunk to the size of a sickly child's. Bharat lay in the middle of a vast bedstead, a small crumpled mass of skin and bones, sunk in the sleep of death. His colour was waxen white; his limbs emaciated and skeletal. He looked, indeed, like a corpse except for the faint rise and fall of his chest. Bhumisuta stood gazing at his face. How long was it since she had seen him last? It seemed to her that aeons had passed since the night Shashibhushan Singha had brought her to him and he had spurned her. What if he did the same now? What if he opened his eyes and said, 'Why are you here Bhumisuta? I have no need of you.' A shudder passed over Bhumisuta's frame. Her heart beat, dull and heavy. Pulling herself together with a tremendous effort, she put out her hand and placed it slowly, gingerly, on Bharat's forehead. It was the first time she had touched a man of her own volition. But though the man was almost dead her pulses leaped up at the touch—as though an electric current had passed from his body into hers . . .

Bhumisuta nursed the patient all day, sponging his limbs, placing cool compresses on his head and feeding him with spoonfuls of thin mutton soup and fruit juice. At night she slept in his room on a mat on the floor. The days passed one by one. Bharat breathed on but his condition remained static. Some days the fever rose from afternoon onwards and he was delirious by the evening. On others he lay in a coma for hours at a stretch, immobile—not uttering a sound. At such times Bhumisuta was filled with dread. Would he slip away as he slept?

On the night of the eleventh day of Bhumisuta's arrival, Bharat turned over on his side and exclaimed, 'Oof! Ma go!' then sighing deeply, he muttered, 'Water! Water!' The voice was strong and compelling, the words clearly formed. Bhumisuta broke out in a sweat. He was coming around. There was no doubt of it. But what if he opened his eyes and recognized her? What if he still hated her? Should she call Basantamanjari? Then, dismissing the idea as absurd, she walked with slow, resolute steps to the crystal decanter of water that stood on a table in a corner. Her hands trembled as she filled a glass but she didn't hesitate. Lifting Bharat's head to her breast, she held the glass to his lips. And, for the first time, he drank as though he knew he did, thirstily, in great gulps. Then, turning over on his side, he fell asleep.

Bhumisuta kept vigil beside Bharat's sleeping form all night. Taking the emaciated hand she pressed it to her breast murmuring, 'I won't let you go. I won't! I won't! You abandoned me once. I won't let you do it again,' with a strange insistence as though by articulating those words she would imbibe the power to hold him. Basantamanjari had told her that true love was like incense smoke that rose from the heart and enveloped the loved one in an invincible cloud. The hours passed slowly. Then, as dawn broke, suffusing the room with the first faint pearly light of day, Bharat opened his eyes and looked straight into hers.

'Who are you? he asked in a wondering voice.

'I'm Bhumisuta,' she answered simply.

'Bhumisuta! You've travelled a great distance to come to me. How battered you must be! How weary!' Then, turning his eyes this way and that, he muttered, 'What place is this?'

'This is your friend Dwarika's house. In Calcutta.'

'Calcutta!' Bharat's brows came together. 'But I didn't go to Calcutta. Ma go! How hot it is!' Bhumisuta saw that his face was beaded over with sweat. It was a good sign. The fever was breaking. She wiped it away with a cool cloth and, picking up a fan, began waving it over him. Bharat drifted away again but woke a few hours later.

'Who are you?' he asked again.

'I'm Bhumisuta.'

'Do you live in this temple Bhumisuta? Kapal Kundala had hair flowing down to her feet just like yours. I didn't touch her. Believe me. She was broken when I found her. Her head had rolled away . . . Will she punish me for what I did? She tried to kill me many times. Many, many times! I fought her with all my strength. But I have no strength left. She'll kill me!' Suddenly he screamed like a frightened child. Clinging to Bhumisuta he cried, 'Save me Bhumi. Save me!'

734

Meera had been a child when her mother, Mrinalini, died. Now she was thirteen and her father was looking for a husband for her. Word had spread among the young men of Calcutta that marrying a daughter of the Thakurs was as good as getting a beautiful princess and half a kingdom. In the present context, of course, the half kingdom was equal to being sent to England to study at the Bar. But his experience with his second son-in-law had left Rabindranath determined not to get into any financial involvement of the sort again. Renuka had died of consumption, after prolonged mental and physical agony, but he was not rid of her husband. Satyendra continued to make demands on him.

One day a young man came to him carrying a letter from his father Bamandas Ganguly of Barisal. Rabindranath looked at him appraisingly. He felt himself drawn to him in a manner he hadn't felt for any of Meera's would-be suitors so far. The boy was seventeen or eighteen years old, tall and fair with well-cut features and a superb physique. His bright dark eyes looked confidently into the older man's. Rabindranath was even more impressed when he heard him speak. Nagen, for that was the boy's name, had a pleasant voice, spoke briefly and to the point articulating his words with ease. Altogether, there was something about him that drew Rabindranath like a magnet. This was the husband for Meera. He felt convinced of it.

In his reply to Bamandas Ganguly's letter Rabindranath added a proposal of marriage between their children. The response, though prompt, was disappointing. An alliance with the great house of Jorasanko would be an honour for him, Bamandas wrote, but, unfortunately, his son was not ready to marry just yet. He was too busy with his work for the Sadharan Brahmo Samaj. Besides, he wished to complete his education. Rabindranath wrote back suggesting that both aspirations, though worthy, were not incompatible with the married state. Immediately on the heels of this missive word came from

Bamandas that Nagen wished to go to America to pursue higher studies. If his prospective father-in-law could make the arrangements the wedding could take place at once. Rabindranath sighed, his eyes thoughtful. The expenses for study in America were higher than those in England. So was the fare. Yet . . . he had set his heart on the boy and was loath to let go of him. He thought for a day or two and made up his mind. Nagen was a different type altogether, he decided. He wouldn't behave like Satyendra. Besides, poor little motherless Meera deserved the best. How could he, her own father, deny it to her?

His reasoning was completely erroneous as subsequent events showed. What he had assumed to be confidence and strength of character was actually an obdurate pride and a complete absence of sensitivity. Nagen was self-centered and self-opinionated with a total lack of consideration for others. He was also aggressively opportunistic and a fanatical Brahmo of the new school. His scorn of the followers of the Adi Brahmo Samaj was practically on par with his hatred of the Hindus.

From the morning of the wedding day itself Nagen started showing his true colours. Word was brought to Rabindranath that the bridegroom had objected to the wearing of sindoor and *alta* by the women and had declared his intention of refusing to participate in the turmeric ceremony—it being a Hindu rite. The poet's lips curled in an amused smile. Brahmo boys were too finicky these days, he thought, too fearful of anything Hindu. He decided to send for Nagen and explain to him that sindoor and *alta* were cosmetics and had nothing to do with any religion. As for the turmeric ceremony—it was part of the *Stree Achar;* one of the many peripherals of a Bengali wedding.

These being minor objections, however, they could be ignored or circumvented. Matters threatened to reach an impasse just before the rites were to start. As per the traditions of the Adi Brahmo Samaj, set by Debendranath Thakur himself, Brahmins were required to wear the sacred thread during the nuptial ceremony. Seeing that the prospective bridegroom wasn't wearing one, the purohit proceeded to hang a length of white thread, wound nine times to the accompaniment of the Gayatri mantra, on his chest, as was the custom in such cases. But Nagen lowered his brows and twisted his neck like an obstinate bull. 'I

736

won't wear a *poité*,' he grunted. The purohit found himself in a quandary. He was an old man and had been conducting all the ceremonies in the Thakur household from the Maharshi's time. Never had be been caught in such a situation. 'Why Babajibon?' he said, forcing a smile on his lips, 'You're a Brahmin are you not? You must wear a *poité* or the marriage vows will lose their sanctity.' Nagen snatched the thread from the old man's hands and flung it away. Then, rising from the bridal plank, he said in a cold, harsh voice, 'If there's a way of taking the marriage vows without that garbage—I'm ready. If not . . .' Rabindranath, who stood a few yards away from the scene, froze at these words. It seemed as though he had stopped breathing. The expression on Nagen's face and the roughness of his manner horrified him. He couldn't believe that what he had witnessed just now was real. He glanced towards the boy's father and uncles. But, instead of pulling him up sharply for his indecent behaviour, they were smiling encouragement. What kind of people were these? How would they treat his little girl? His eyes turned to his own relations No one spoke a word. For, like the Hindus, the followers of the Adi Brahmo Samaj believed that the bridegroom's party was sacrosanct. They could misbehave as they pleased in the bride's father's house. They could hector and bully and make crude jokes. No one would dare voice a protest. They were empowered by society. If they left without completing the marriage rites the girl was ruined for life. No one would marry her.

Rabindranath stood undecided. Which was preferable? That his daughter spend a lifetime with the brute he had picked out for her? Or remain a spinster to the end of her days? He yearned to hold on to her, to keep this youngest child of his with him forever. But only for a moment. Meeting the eyes of the purohit who sat helplessly, not knowing what to do, he nodded twice. It was a gesture of affirmation; of allowing Nagen to take the vows without pledging the sacred thread. But, unable to bear the gloating triumph in his son-in-law's face, he walked quietly away from the scene.

The house in Shantiniketan was packed with guests for, this being Rabindranath's daughter's marriage, he had organized a big celebration. But now the lights and the crowds oppressed his

737

spirit. Leaving them behind he came and stood in the garden at the back of the house. It was a hot moonless night of early June and thousands of stars hung like bright lamps out of a clear cloudless sky. Rabindranath raised his head and gazed upon the firmament. How vast it was! What eternity lay in its depths! Man's little joys and sorrows were so insignificant in the context of this colossal whole. He remained like that for a long time. Lines of poetry flitted and flickered in his brain:

I shall exist in the Universe
in simple faith

I shall take the air from the sky
for my own breath

The earth below my feet
shall rise in love
Sanctifying these limbs . . .

Gradually the cold grey skeins of pain and guilt that had bound his heart so tightly that they seemed to choke the very passage of his lifeblood, broke and fell away leaving it light and free.

'Baba!' A shriek reached his ears. It was a girl's voice, loud and piercing. Why, that was Meera! Rabindranath stood rooted to the ground for a moment. He felt as though his soul was being shaken to its foundations. Then, wrenching himself free of the paralyzed terror that gripped his limbs, he ran in the direction of the sound thinking furiously all the while. What had happened? Had the poor child in her agony . . . ? He remembered how her frail body had trembled under the heavily brocaded sari and bridal veil at the sound of Nagen's loud domineering voice? She was only a child but she had sensed her father's humiliation. Had she done something to herself? Had she, in her desperation, taken her own life?

Entering the house he found a number of men and women crowding at the door of the bathing room. Meera stood just within it shaking from head to foot. At the sight of her, untouched by fire, rope or blade, he felt the relief washing over him in streams of sweat that poured down his trembling limbs. He saw the snake a few moments later. It was a giant cobra and it lay

738

coiled on the threshold, its fanned out hood swaying a little, its beady black eyes blinking at the terrified girl. Some of the men had sticks in their hands but hung back, hesitating, afraid to strike. It was impossible to kill a cobra at one stroke and the wounded reptile would be sure to lash back in revenge. But the poet, who had never killed a fly in his life, took a stick from one of the men and advanced resolutely. The snake, presumably, was destined to live a few years longer. So were father and daughter. Suddenly it changed its mind. Lowering its head it slithered away, like a streak of lightning, and disappeared into a hole in the ground.

'Baba!' Meera ran, weeping, to her father and flung herself on his chest. Holding the trembling girl in a fierce embrace Rabindranath took a vow. He would shield this last youngest child of his from all pain and suffering. Ignoring social disapproval, he would protect her from her husband and his people. He would be there for her whenever she wanted him. Nothing would stand in the way of Meera's happiness. No—not as long as he lived.

Chapter XLVI

Bharat's waking and sleeping hours hadn't fallen, as yet, into a pattern. Some days he stayed awake half the night and dozed off at dawn to the chirping of sparrows. On others, he had difficulty keeping his eyes open after sunset. The wound in his abdomen had healed and his skin was cool again. His appetite had returned and he was eating as he had never eaten in his life. He was reading too. Dwarika made sure that a pile of books and newspapers were kept on a small table beside his bed.

That evening he fell asleep over the pages of Chandrashekhar Mukhopadhyay's *Udbhranta Prem* and awoke three hours later. The room was pitch dark and so silent—one could hear a pin drop. His brain was still fuddled with sleep and he wondered where he was. He was confused, too, about the time. Was it the twilight hour or very early in the morning? 'Bhumi!' he called softly but there was no response. Bharat was puzzled. Bhumisuta always knew when he needed her. She had a sixth sense about it. 'Bhumi!' he called again, a little louder. This time a door opened and a woman came into the room. She was tall and gaunt and had a mannish air. 'Are you hungry?' she asked. 'Shall I bring up your meal?'

'Who are you?' Bharat crinkled his eyes to see her better.

'My name is Annakali. I'm the nurse.'

'Where is Bhumisuta?'

'I've just arrived in this house. I don't know anything about anyone. The mistress told me to serve your meal as soon as you woke up. I'll go fetch it.'

Bharat rose from his bed the moment Annakali's back was turned and slipped his feet into his slippers. The doctor had told him to walk a few paces in his own chamber. But now he strode out of the room, down the imposing flight of marble stairs, and came to Dwarika's private sitting room. Dwarika spent his evenings here drinking with his friends. Tonight, however, he was alone. 'Why Bharat!' he exclaimed at the sight of his friend. 'You look wonderful. As though you've never had a day's illness. Come, let's celebrate your recovery with a drink.' Picking up the crystal decanter he poured a small brandy for Bharat.

'Where's Bhumisuta?' Bharat asked abruptly pushing the glass away.

'She's gone back home.'

'Why?'

Dwarika put the glass in Bharat's hand. 'Drink it up,' he commanded. 'It will do you good.' Then, fixing his large sombre eyes on Bharat's face, he said, 'You ask me why? Are you really such a complete fool? The girl came to a house where she didn't know a soul the moment she heard you were ill. She stayed here for days nursing you back to health. She threw herself, heart and soul, into your service. Why did she do so? Have you ever asked yourself this question?' Bharat sat, glum and silent, staring down at his feet. 'She gave you your life Bharat,' Dwarika went on relentlessly, 'What have you given her in return?' A spasm passed over Bharat's face. 'What do I have to give?' he murmured softly.

'Idiot!' Dwarika burst out angrily. 'What does a man give a woman who loves him? He gives her a future. Are you such a numskull that you don't know?'

'What future do I have myself Dwarika? I've pledged myself, by fire and sword, to work for the country. I can't go back on that pledge. That would amount to treason.'

'A mole ja!' Dwarika cried out in exasperation. 'Who is stopping you from working for the country? Are you the only one who has taken such a pledge? What about the others? Aren't they marrying and raising families? What about your precious leaders—Suren Banerjee, Bipin Pal, Aurobindo Ghosh—don't they have wives and children? Even your friend Hem . . . Look Bharat. You're not a boy anymore. You're a man in your prime. It's time you settled down. Bhumisuta has waited for you all these years. She has kept herself pure and chaste only for your sake. And, being an actress, it wasn't easy as you well know. Does that mean nothing to you?'

Bharat sighed. Dwarika had no idea of how much it meant to him; of how much he loved and needed Bhumisuta. But how could he ask her to join her life to his? She was so beautiful and talented. So many men, much worthier than himself, wanted her.

741

He was nothing and could give her nothing. Taking a few sips of
the brandy Bharat pleaded a headache, rose and came to his own
room. He sat on the bed sunk in thought. He was as well now, he
decided, as he would ever be. It was not fair to impose on
Dwarika's generosity any longer. He would leave in a day or two
and make his own way in the world. But where could he go? He
knew no one in Calcutta except Barin and his cronies. But his
gorge rose at the thought of going back to Barin. Every time he
remembered the way Barin had run off, leaving Hem trapped in
the Brahmin's house, his flesh crawled with disgust and the blood
pulsed and pounded in his head till he felt physically ill. Hem, he
had come to know later, had saved himself by climbing up the
chalta tree. He had remained under cover till the men had left,
then made his way back to the house in Rangpur. Hem had visited
him several times during his illness. Now he was back in
Medinipur.

The trouble was that Bharat had no money. When Dwarika
discovered him in the Kali temple he had found a gun and sixteen
rupees splattered with clotted blood in his pockets. The gun he
had returned to Barin. Now the sixteen rupees were all that he
had. Even the clothes he wore were Dwarika's.

Bharat racked his brains for the next two days. Should he go
back to Medinipur? But that would be exchanging one life of
charity for another. He would have to depend on Hem for the
farm had gone out of his hands. Just before embarking on his
pursuit of Fuller he had mortgaged it, for five hundred rupees, to
a man called Neelmadhav Chakravarty. There was no way, now,
for him to redeem it. While he thought of the various possibilities
or rather, their lack, a letter arrived from Hem. It read:

Brother Bharat,
I'm off. You won't see me again for a long time. I'm sick of
the child's play that is going on in the name of revolution.
We have no money, no weapons and no leadership. No
one has the slightest notion of how to form a secret society
or wield weapons. We are being exploited and fed on lies. I
can't take it anymore.
I'm making one last effort. I'm going abroad to Russia and
America with the intention of learning the latest methods
of secret warfare. I might even visit Paris which, from

what I hear, is full of secret societies. You'll be wondering where the money is coming from. I've sold everything I possessed and sent my wife and children to my father-in-law's house. I'm free at last. Free to do what I've always wanted.

Don't think I'm running away. I'll come back but only when I'm ready. Look after yourself and wait for my return.

Yours

Hem

P.S. Tear this letter as soon as you've read it.

Bharat read Hem's note three times in succession then, tearing it into fragments, flung them out of the window.

Dwarika came into Bharat's room, the next evening, and insisted on taking him to his private den and giving him a drink. He was convinced that the cobwebs in Bharat's brain could only be dispelled with some fumes of brandy. After downing a couple of pegs Dwarika brought up the subject of Bhumisuta once more. 'Why don't you go and see her?' he asked irritably. 'That's the least you can do.'

'I don't know where she lives.'

'Why don't you ask? Really Bharat—'

'Do you know her house?'

'Of course I do. I went there with Jadu and brought her here, didn't I?' Dwarika rose to his feet. He had drunk more then usual and was excitable in consequence. 'Let's go to her this minute,' he cried. 'No, no. I won't take a refusal. You must thank her for all she's done And so must I.' Sweeping Bharat's feeble protests aside he called for his carriage and set off with Bharat in tow.

But on reaching Bhumisuta's house the two men found the gates locked against them. The Nepali darwan salaamed politely but wouldn't let them enter. The mistress wasn't in, he told them. In fact she wasn't in Calcutta at all. She was in Kashi.

'Kashi!' Dwarika exclaimed. 'When did she leave?'

'Two days ago.'

'When will she be back?'

The darwan shrugged. He hadn't the slightest idea. Asked if he knew her address in Kashi, he shook his head. The mistress had

743

told him nothing. Only that he was to continue guarding her house and that his salary would be paid to him at the end of the month as always.

Taking their seats in the carriage, on their way back home, Dwarika put his arm around Bharat's shoulders. 'I have an idea Bharat,' he said. 'You've just recovered from a serious illness. And you're still as weak as a kitten. This is just the time for a change of air. Why don't you go to Kashi? The climate is cool and dry and you'll recover fast. Besides the food is excellent. You've never seen finer fruits and vegetables. And the milk is so pure—you can eat all the *rabri* and *malai* you want and suffer no ill effects. I have a house on the river near Dasashwamedh Ghat. It is fully furnished and there are two servants who will look after you. You'll be quite comfortable.'

The matter was settled over the next half hour and Bharat left for Varanasi the following day. Basantamanjari packed a hamper of food for the journey and Dwarika tucked a hundred rupee note into Bharat's pocket. Dwarika couldn't see Bharat off at the station because he had to attend a court hearing but he promised to visit him in Kashi as soon as he could. Bharat looked up regretfully at Basantamanjari's window on his way to the carriage. She had done so much for him and he hadn't even thanked her! Basantamanjari never came into his presence. And his bashful nature would have prevented him from speaking to her even if he had had the opportunity. His eyes shone with tears as he grasped Dwarika's hand and said, 'I don't know how I'll repay you for all you've done Dwarika. I'll be indebted to you and your wife all my life.' But Dwarika dismissed this with a shout of laughter. 'Repayment!' he clapped Bharat heartily on the shoulder. 'Don't even think of it brother! Continue to be in our debt for all your lives to come.'

Dwarika's house on Dasashwamedh Ghat was small but neat and comfortable. The ground floor, somewhat dark and damp, was the servants' domain. But the upper storey, where Bharat was lodged, was bright with sunshine. And, being right on the river, cool breezes blew constantly through the many windows keeping the rooms fresh and airy.

Varanasi was a famous pilgrim spot and a city of revels at the same time. Consequently it was packed with people at all times of the year. Many rajas and zamindars had houses here and spent months at a stretch with their favourite mistresses. Every evening the street of the courtesans in Dal Mandi reverberated to the sweet, slightly nasal, singing of thumris and kajris and the tinkling of ankle bells. And when dusk fell over the Ganga, boats and bajras descended on her breast like a flight of stately swans. Within, each boat was alive with light, sound and movement. Mashals blazed; lamps twinkled. The raja sat, wine glass in hand, reclining on satin cushions and surrounded by his courtiers. In front of him a dancing girl contorted her body lasciviously taking care to reveal her legs and thighs with every pirouette. 'Wah! Wah!' the toadies cried and threw coins and flowers.

But no matter how crowded the city, it was never difficult to find the person one sought in Kashi. For everyone came to Dasashwamedh and Manikarnika some time or the other during the course of the day. Bharat saw Bhumisuta, for the first time, bathing in the river close to the ghat at Manikarnika with two other women. Presently all three rose from the water and walked away their dripping saris clinging to their bodies, outlining every curve. Bharat averted his eyes delicately, hesitating to call out to Bhumisuta in her state of dishabille. In actual fact it was quite common for women in Kashi to walk about the streets, visit temples and make purchases from vendors after a dip in the Ganga. No one thought anything of it. The same evening he saw her sitting in the middle of a group of women listening to the Kathak Thakur at Dasashwamedh Ghat. He took up his position, under a tree, a little distance away and waited for the assembly to break. But when it did it was quite dark and Bhumisuta was, presumably, in a hurry. She walked away quickly and Bharat missed his chance of speaking to her.

There were many places of interest in and around Kashi and Vishnupada, the cook, had been urging Bharat to visit some of them, from the day of his arrival. Next morning, over a breakfast of luchi and pumpkin curry, Bharat declared his intention of going to Sarnath. He chose Sarnath not so much for its historical significance. He had heard that a group of archaeologists had identified a tell and were excavating it with excellent results. A row of Buddhist monasteries had been discovered. Besides, Sarnath was not too far away. He could return the same day, in time for the Kathak Thakur's discourse. He was determined to speak to Bhumisuta that evening.

Reaching Sarnath he wandered around the tell for a couple of hours watching the rising walls with interest. The sun was hot and the sahebs supervising the digging wore solar hats. Bharat wished he had one too. His head had started aching and his feet were weary. He tired easily these days. Seeing a huge pipal tree, a little distance away, he walked over to it and sat down to rest himself. It was cool in the shade and a sweet breeze passed over his hot sweaty limbs. 'Ahh!' he breathed a sigh of contentment. Sleep dragged at his eyelids and numbed his senses. He fought against it for a while then, surrendering, he stretched himself on the ground and drifted away on its wings. Clouds gathered in the sky and a light rain fell, pattering through the leaves, on to his limbs. But he slept through it all. When he awoke he found the day gone. Dusk was falling and the place was deserted. Bharat sat up his heart thumping with anxiety. How would he get back? Ekkas and tongas waited only when there were people to hire them. They must have gone away for not a soul was in sight. He was also prodigiously hungry. He had had nothing to eat since the luchi and pumpkin curry. But his worst fear was that of missing Bhumisuta. He could walk all the way back to Kashi but he wouldn't reach in time. The assembly at Dasashwamadh Ghat would be over and she would have gone home.

Kashi was eight or ten miles away and he was still quite weak. Yet he started walking hoping to catch a passing carriage. But within an hour or so Bharat was thoroughly exhausted. He had covered only a couple of miles on the road that wound in and out through rocks and mounds of earth. He decided to rest for a while. After a few minutes a humming sound came to his ears, low and indistinct at first, but growing louder and clearer every second. It was a motorcar coming, not from Sarnath but from the direction of Kashi. Bharat stood up in his excitement and ran towards it waving his hands. But in a few seconds he realized his folly. This was no ordinary tourist vehicle. It was a killer car and the intended victim was Bharat himself.

Bharat stared in horror as it came towards him at a maniacal speed lurching from side to side like a drunk. The headlights gleamed evilly like the eyes of a demon. A sixth sense, one that he

746

had developed through his many encounters with death, made him leap back in a flash. Flattening his body against a wall of rock he waited, his heart beating wildly against his ribs.

By a miraculous chance Bharat was saved. The car shot past, nearly grazing his shoulder, crashed against a tree a few yards away and turned over. Bharat's first impulse was to run in the opposite direction and let the victims of the crash fend for themselves. He stood undecided for a few moments then, a faint groan coming to his ears, he ran to the overturned car and wrenched the door open. There were two men inside. One lay huddled over the steering wheel. He was probably dead from a wound in the chest for his satin vast was soaked with blood. A glance at him was sufficient to tell Bharat that he was a member of the nobility. Three strings of pearls hung from his neck and the hands on the steering wheel were loaded with rings. The other was obviously an employee. He was unhurt but had fainted from the shock. Bharat pulled him out first and laid him on the ground then turned his attention to the other. The body was wedged between the seat and the wheel and it took Bharat some time to extricate it. To his relief, he discovered that the man was not dead but had fainted from loss of blood. He was small and slight and Bharat picked him up quite easily. As he did so the man's head fell back and his face came clearly into view. In the light of a rising moon Bharat saw that it was the face of Radhakishor Manikya.

Radhakishor was trying to kill him! Why? Why? The question tortured him, searing his soul, as it had done so many times in the past. He felt overwhelmed with conflicting emotions—fear, nostalgia, a strange elation; murderous rage. This was the moment to take revenge for all his past wrongs, he thought suddenly. He could put his hands around Radhakishor's throat and strangle him to death. Then, he could walk away from the scene without anyone being the wiser. However, what Bharat thought and what he did were totally different from one another. Placing his burden on the ground, he ran to a pond near by and, whipping off his shirt, brought it back soaking wet to where the men lay. The other one, he saw, had regained consciousness and was trying to sit up. 'What's the matter?' he asked, his eyes dazed and anxious. 'Has there been an accident? Is Raja Moshai . . . dead?'

'No,' Bharat answered, 'He's seriously injured but alive.' He had recognized the man by now. It was Mahim Thakur. Mahim clutched Bharat's hands and exclaimed, 'We must save him. He's no ordinary man Moshai. He's the Maharaja of Tripura.'

'I know,' Bharat said quietly. Then, on an impulse, he spat out the question, 'Why were you trying to kill me?'

'Kill you?' Mahim's eyes nearly started out of his head. 'Why should we try to kill you? The car went out of control and nearly ran you down. But it wasn't deliberate.' Then, frowning a little he peered into Bharat's face and added. 'You said you knew he was the Maharaja. Have you seen him before?'

'Not really. I guessed he was a Maharaja from the way he was dressed. But we'd better get him out of here as soon as we can. He needs a doctor.' Leaving Mahim Thakur sitting beside the still unconscious Radhakishor, Bharat went in search of a tonga and, by an amazing stroke of luck, he found one. It was coming from Sarnath and had one passenger in it. 'It's a matter of life and death Sethji,' he begged. 'If you don't give us a lift to Kashi a man will die.'

As the tonga rattled along on the road to Kashi Mahim Thakur, who had been glancing at him curiously from time to time, said suddenly, 'Your face is familiar. What is your name brother?'

'I'm Bharat Mahim Dada. Am I so changed that you don't recognize me?'

'Bharat! Which Bharat?' Mahim frowned. Then, suddenly, his brow cleared. 'Of course I recognize you. I was wondering why your face looked so familiar. Your eyes and brow bear a striking resemblance to the old Maharaja's. You're Prince Bharat—the King's son.'

'I'm no prince. I'm a kachhua's child.'

'You are a prince nevertheless. The blood of the king and his forefathers flows in your veins. Isn't it an amazing coincidence? That out of all the people in the world, you should be the one to save your brother's life?'

An hour or so later, the tonga clattered through the *deuri* of the Maharaja's palace in Kashi and drew to a halt at the porch. Within seconds, news of the accident had travelled over all the wings and everyone came running out. Arrangements were swift and efficient. Radhakishor was carried up to his bedroom and two eminent physicians of Varanasi called in. Examining the patient they found several ribs fractured and a great gaping wound on his chest. Recommending instant surgery they suggested that he be removed to the hospital. But the royal priest of Tripura who had been standing by the king's side all through the examination was horrified at the suggestion. There was only one hospital in Kashi and that was a charitable institution. There could be no question of sending the reigning king of independent Tripura to such a place. He dismissed the suggestion scornfully and was supported in this by the king's wives and mothers. It was decided that Radhakishor would be treated in his own apartments with full dignity as befitted his status and all the facilities the hospital could provide would be arranged here. The king was young and healthy and would recover.

It was past midnight by the time the wound was washed and bandaged and the preliminary treatment given. Through it all the king lay in a death-like stupor. Bharat felt dizzy with exhaustion. He had just recovered from a mortal wound and severe loss of blood and was still very weak. His muscles felt heavy and were aching. The rims of his eyeballs burned with the effort of struggling against the fumes of sleep. And now he sensed a familiar tug in his bowels which reminded him that he hadn't eaten for seventeen hours. 'I'd like to go home Mahim Dada,' he said. 'Send for me whenever you need me.' Mahim was loath to let him go at first but Bharat looked so dishevelled and distraught that he was forced to change his mind. 'You do look exhausted,' he admitted, 'And your clothes are coated with dust and streaked with sweat and blood. But you shan't go alone.' Calling for one of the carriages he sent Bharat home with a footman in attendance.

Next day, in the late afternoon, Bharat received a summons from Mahim Thakur. He was to come immediately. 'The king is either dead or dying,' Bharat thought all the way to the palace. But his mind and senses were numb. He felt nothing—neither relief nor regret. The moment he entered the palace, however, he realized that this was not a house of death. Hope and joy were stamped on every face he saw, from the darwan's at the gate to Mahim's as he ran towards Bharat and gripped his arm. 'Raja Moshai is conscious and is asking for you,' he said, guiding him

749

towards the king's chamber, 'I've told him everything.'

Entering the room Bharat saw that it was full of women. He presumed that they were the king's wives, mother and stepmothers and wondered if Monomohini was among them. The thought made him blush and set his ears ringing with embarrassment. 'This is Kumar Bharatchandra, Maharaj,' Mahim said leading him to the centre of the room where the king lay. 'Brother,' Radhakishor lifted a feeble arm. 'You saved my life. Shashi Master told me you believe I sent you to your death. That's a lie. A lie! I can swear by the Gita.' He tried to sit up as he spoke. His eyes glittered with tears and the blue veins stood out on his chalk white brow. 'Take care Maharaj!' Several voices cried out at once. 'Don't excite yourself.' Mahim hurried to his side and laid his head back, gently, on the pillow saying, 'The Kumar knows you Maharaj. He does not doubt your word.' Then, turning to Bharat, he added, 'Our Maharaja made several enquiries regarding your disappearance after he ascended the throne. But the results were unsatisfactory. The terrible deed remains shrouded in mystery to this day.'

Bharat's gaze rested on the sick man's face. It was beaded over with sweat and drops were gliding down his cheeks and chin and falling on his breast. His eyes looked unnaturally large and bright. Mahim and the others thought he was better and would live. But Bharat knew otherwise. 'He's dying,' he murmured to himself and his heart missed a beat. Radhakishor took Bharat's hand in his fevered ones and said, panting with the effort, 'You're my brother—a prince of the royal dynasty of Tripura. You've been denied your lawful rights all these years. But no more of that. You shall have your title, your own rooms in the royal palace and a monthly allowance of three hundred rupees. You must go back to Tripura. Promise me you will.' Looking on that dying face Bharat could not refuse. He nodded in obedience to his ruler's command but in his heart he knew he would never go back to Tripura or claim his inheritance.

After a while, when everyone's attention was on the king, Bharat slipped quietly out of the room. His heart felt light and free, as though it had been imprisoned within stone walls for centuries and only just been released. Every nerve and sinew of his being quivered with relief. And, with this new-found freedom, the doubts and fears that had nagged him all these years blew away like dead leaves in a storm. Walking out of the *deuri* he found that the day was spent. The sun had set and faint streaks of rose and orange clung to the sky over the Ganga. He quickened his steps. He had to reach Dasashwamedh Ghat in time to catch Bhumisuta.

This time he did not hesitate. As soon as the assembly broke he pushed his way purposefully through the crowd and came to her. 'I have something to say to you,' he said simply, 'Will you spare some time for me Bhumisuta?' Bhumisuta threw a quick glance at him, her eyes searching his face. She stood uncertain for a few moments then, turning to her companion, she said. 'Can you go home alone Charu? Hire an ekka if you're afraid to walk. Here, take some money.' Unfastening a knot at the end of her sari she took out a few coins and handed them to the girl.

The crowd dispersed and a deep silence fell on the ghat. The shadows of dusk gathered around them as Bharat and Bhumisuta made their way down the steps and came to the edge of the river. They sat, not side by side but on different levels looking out on the boats that glided over the water like moving lamps. Slowly the stars came out, one by one, and a full moon trembled in the water at their feet. Bhumisuta broke the silence. 'Are you completely recovered?' she asked softly. 'Yes . . .' Bharat murmured, 'yes . . .' Then suddenly he cried with a vehemence he hadn't known he was capable of. 'Why did you come away to Kashi? Why? Why?' Bhumisuta was taken aback at the passion in his voice. 'Because . . .' she stammered in reply, 'Because I've never come to Kashi. I thought I would offer prayers in your name.'

'Offer prayers? For me? But I don't deserve your prayers Bhumisuta. You nursed me back to health. You gave me my life. What have I given you in return?'

'You've given me everything.' Bhumisuta said so softly that her voice was almost lost in the sound of the water.

'Why do you say that?' he cried out in an agonized voice. 'Tell me! You must tell me! What have you received from me except pain and humiliation? I don't deserve your prayers Bhumi. Nor your love. I'm weak and worthless. I'm empty . . . empty. I can't tell you how I—'

'Do you remember the night you took me away from the

house in Bhabanipur? The night of the riot? I was sitting, lost and frightened, on the steps of a house. You came looking for me. I saw the expression on your face when you found me. You held my hand and said, "I'll never leave you again." I've carried that memory through all my struggles and sorrows.'

'But I didn't keep my promise. Like a fool I thought Master Moshai was more deserving of you. My eyes and brain were clouded. I didn't look into your heart. I didn't sense your humiliation. I've made many mistakes in my life Bhumi, but I've regretted them and suffered for them. I've spent years looking for you. I went to Orissa thinking that you'd gone back from where you came. I lay, sick and destitute, among the beggars outside the temple of Jagannath in the hope that you would come. I lost heart over and over again but did not give up for a long, long time. Then—' Bharat's voice changed. It became solemn and charged with meaning. 'My circumstances changed. I found a job, status, friends. I married an Oriya girl and had a son. She resembled you greatly and I was happy. But I wasn't born for happiness. She died and everything I had built up died with her—'

'The child?' Bhumisuta asked gently.

'I couldn't bear to look on his face after she went. I left him with his grandparents. I haven't seen him since.'

'That's unworthy of you. Why should you deprive an innocent child of his father's love? Take him back into your life.'

'Yes I will. I can—now.'

Silence fell between them. Then Bharat asked, hesitating but curious, 'What about you Bhumi? Have you never been drawn to another? Were you not tempted—ever?'

'I gave myself to you the day you took my hand. My heart and body I've kept untouched—for you. But I've loved another man with my mind—as one loves a god.'

'Who is he?'

'The poet Rabindranath Thakur.'

Bharat nodded gently. 'That is possible. Yes, quite possible.' Silence fell between them once again. It lay unbroken for a long time. Bharat raised his eyes to the sky out of which the stars hung like clusters of jewels. The moon swam in and out of clouds in a haze of opalescent light. Bharat murmured some lines from a verse of Rabindranath's poetry:

You and I have floated here on the stream that brings from the fount
At the heart of time love of one for another.
We have played alongside millions of lovers, shared in the same
Shy sweetness of meeting, the same distressful tears of farewell—
Old love, but in shapes that renew and renew forever.
Looking up, he saw Bhumisuta's eyes swimming in tears.
'Why do you weep Bhumi?' he asked tenderly.
'Tears are welling up in my eyes. But I do not weep.'
'So much has gone . . .' Bharat murmured, 'So many days, months and years. A vast expanse of space and time lies between us. Can we ever come together Bhumi? You seem . . . you seem so far away.'
'Why, here I am sitting by your side!'
'That night . . . the night you spoke of, when I found you sitting on the steps of a house in Kolutola . . . I took your hand in mine. If I ask for it tonight . . . will you give it?'
Bhumisuta's lips quivered. She turned her face away to hide her emotion. In the same instant the moon slipped from behind some clouds and rained its beams on her. Bharat stared at her profile, bathed in moonlight, eyes lowered, long lashes resting against one cheek. His heart missed a beat. A flood of old memories welled up within him and merged with the present. The moments passed. Bhumisuta turned to him and placed her soft damp palm on his.
They sat, hand in hand, looking out on the river, a sky full of stars above their heads—a vast sheet of water at their feet. Words were redundant between them now. They conversed in the language of silence. They sat as though frozen in time; as though they had been together from the beginning of life itself and would be together for aeons and aeons to come.